FOREWORD

LIVING ABROAD IN CHINA and Buenos Aires as a young girl—always a stranger in a strange land—I found books to be crucially important companions. I began reading at four and have never stopped. Very early in kindergarten, I was writing plays and illustrating them. I do believe lots of writers sketch—we literally see stories first of all visually, almost like running movies in our heads. Most storytellers gather images (scraps); then we weave blindly, unsure of final shapes or outcomes. But the power of this imagery lights the way, and ultimately we SEE the story as translated into words on a page—often a clumsy reincarnation. Then our job is to enable the reader to see as well, because storytelling is a *participatory* art—successful fiction sets off powerful reverberations in the reader. Happy result? A magical fusion takes place: The writer provides the raw materials, always careful to leave room for the reader's own idiosyncratic memories, imagination, dreams, emotions to conjoin with the author's. The reader is very much part of the creative equation. Good fiction is not a solo. Good fiction is a duet! And together we create imaginary worlds. No author ever writes the heart of the matter, the only one who can do that is the reader.

Much of my material comes from dreams. Eight stories in this collection are fantasies, drawn straight from dreaming. Often I write them first as poems, then re-calibrate as stories. Whatever form these dreams may take, disentangling the hidden conflicts of the heart remains the core enigma in my "real" and imaginary life. As E.M. Forster puts it: "Fiction reveals the hidden life at its source. It makes the invisible secrets of life as it is lived *visible*."—this is the writer's primary task. Equally important to me is to make sure *emotional truth* under-girds the content of each individual story. It constitutes my own personal and professional goal in writing fiction.

My deepest thanks to Townley Budde and Melanie Owens for their extraordinary help in bringing this book to fruition.

HOUSEBROKEN

"These stories in *Housebroken* have a cumulative effect of reinforcing both each other and the underlying themes that connect them, very much like a pond with many unique water lilies that all spring from a single underwater stem."

—C.D. Hopkins, author of *Captain Nitwit*
& *Trading Husbands*

HOUSEBROKEN

Barbara Leith

iUniverse, Inc.
New York   Bloomington

These stories originally appeared in the following publications: "Housebroken" in Other Voices; "Pieta" in Hawaii Review; "Surface Tension" in Carolina Quarterly; "Bobby Shaftoe" in Kansas Quarterly; "Free Fall" in The Southern Review; "Down Under" in West Branch; "Killing the Steel" in Per Se; "Double Printing" in Nebraska Review; "Morning Ablutions" in MacGuffin; "Boxes" in West Branch; "Riding the Wheel" in Sepia; "Down by the Pool" in Pikestaff Forum; "Please Wait" in Turnstyle; "A Plate of Peas" in Nebraska Review; "After the Ceremony" in Other Voices

iUniverse books may be ordered through booksellers or by contacting:

iUniverse
1663 Liberty Drive
Bloomington, IN 47403
www.iuniverse.com
1-800-Authors (1-800-288-4677)

ISBN: 978-1-4401-6634-1 (sc)
ISBN: 978-1-4401-6635-8 (ebook)

Printed in the United States of America

iUniverse rev. date: 09/28/09

For dear Christopher, David and Diane

Through desert to oasis, you walked with me

TABLE OF CONTENTS

HOUSEBROKEN

THEY GOT THE KITTEN because Molly hated coming home from the office to empty rooms. Hated the long nights alone when Hank was off studying at the law library. She wanted a dog, but dogs weren't allowed in the apartment building. Neither were cats, but who was to know?

Actually she disliked cats. Hank was the cat lover; his mother bred Burmese and showed them as well. Bench shows, they were called. Life in a cage. This seemed to Molly the most unnatural existence imaginable for a pet and added to her grudging dislike of Hank's mother in particular, and by association, of cats in general. Secretive creatures, cool and unapproachable.

Hank disagreed. He argued their inapproachability was a virtue, a clear sign of their superiority to dogs. "Self-respect," he told her. "You'll never catch a cat fawning on you like a pooch does. Totally self-reliant, cats are. I admire them."

The day they brought the kitten home, he told Molly he was allergic to cats. They gave him asthma.

"*Now* you tell me," she said. She was layering a carton with old towels. The carton was the last of the wedding gift boxes and still had the frilly white excelsior packing—perfect for a mattress, she had exclaimed, feeling very domestic. But he said to put toweling on top or else the kitten would mistake it for kitty litter.

He sat on the floor cradling the kitten against his chest. It was a tabby, a tawny gray and gold—seven weeks old and full of spunk, a girl kitty, he announced. Now he looked at Molly and smiled. "It's ok though. My asthma days are long gone."

"How do you know?"

"Haven't had an attack since you and I met, have I now?"

"No."

"Well, then?" He had his lawyer Q.E.D. look on his face, impatiently expectant, leaning forward with a hard little glitter in his eyes.

"But we haven't had a cat, either. Until now," she said, not sure what he was driving at here. These Socratic question and answer games irritated her. Granted, she wasn't logical. Inductive, deductive reasoning, who cares? She

1

had told him this on their first date nine months ago. And he said he adored her for her illogic, that he had a lot to learn and she could teach *him*. But three months into the marriage, and he was still as rational as ever. More so, if anything. And she felt backed into corners when they discussed things, even something as simple as this asthma business. So, now she decided to ask what he meant. Trying to second-guess him was where she usually got into trouble.

"What do you mean exactly, Hank?" And with a little private thrill of entitlement—of having turned the tables on him—she reached to take the kitten away from him, place it in its snowy featherbed.

The kitten mewed. Molly picked up the old alarm clock and wound it, then nestled it down under the towels. The ticking was supposed to simulate the mother's heartbeat. Stave off loneliness. Time would tell, she thought, maybe even literally do the trick. She wished she could purr.

He was explaining now, "Psychosomatic in origin, childhood asthma," he was saying. "Tensions at home, that type thing."

She thought about that a moment. "You mean leaving home cured you?" she asked. And wondered if she were leaving herself wide open.

But he said with a laugh, "Leaving home and meeting you." He looked at her. "What you want to hear, correct?"

She laughed too, and they left the kitten in its box and went into the bedroom and made love, but the whole time they lay there, what she really wanted to have him say over and over again was: I love you, I love you, I love you.

They had big arguments about this. At first he would simply observe, mugging a little, "I married you, didn't I?"

"But I want to hear you say the words," she told him.

"The evidence isn't in the words, silly. It's easy enough to mouth off, it's harder to show it. The way we treat each other. In our behavior, our actions."

"Please don't stand there and give me lectures."

He always looked surprised when she got annoyed that way. "But I'm not lecturing you, I'm telling you what I think," he said slowly.

"And I'm telling you what I *need*. I need to *hear* it, darn it all."

"You can't demand love," he'd answer. And then he'd look sad. His mouth would tighten and she could see what he was going to be as an old man, the sharpness of the nose, the stubborn knob of the chin. The clean lines of his bones became harsh; the firm expression hardening into the smug obstinacy of the self-righteous—a hard-featured stranger, in fact. "Cotton Mather," she told him once. He stared at her. His eyes were so cold she almost shivered.

One night he told her, "Stop beating on me, for God's sake!" She threw off the bedcovers and went into the living room. Then she groped her way back along the walls until she reached the linen closet. She got out a brand new blanket, a wedding present so new it was still in the original plastic. Ripping the plastic open sounded very loud in the dark.

She rolled herself up in the blanket and lay down on the couch. It was the first night they had spent apart. The kitten jumped up on the sofa. It wanted to play. It put its cold paw on her cheek, then scooted down under the blanket. She lay very still. It jumped down on the floor, started batting the ping pong ball, its favorite toy. The ball skittered across the kitchen floor.

More scrabbling noises. Out in the bathroom, in the litter box. Then silence.

She pressed her nose into the scratchy tweed of the couch. Should she go back and get a pillow? Then she heard Hank say, "God**damn** it, cat!" The light came on. He was standing there in the doorway. He was holding the kitten who had its spiky wild-eyed look which meant they were in for a long night. "Please, Molly," he said. "Come back to bed." He put the cat down on the rug, turned off the hall light.

She said nothing, just curved herself deeper into the sofa cushion. In the dark she could hear the sound of his breathing, a harsh sound as if he'd been running. Or making love.

Then he was touching her. But she stiffened, pulled away from his hand. "Leave me alone," she told him, and she felt excited inside, scared that he'd go, but at the same time triumphant that she had managed again to turn the thing around so that he was the one who was begging *her* for a change. His voice cracked. He started telling her she must not to do this, not to rupture the thing, the thing was too precious, couldn't she see how precious? "Please don't do this, don't, Molly," he was saying at the end, and he sounded in the darkness as if he were almost crying, his voice choked and thick.

"Go away," she told him, and, finally, after a long while, he did. They never discussed this night. But she could tell something had been damaged. Forever. He had seen for the first time that she wanted to hurt him. From this they both learned to put their love at one remove. She never asked him any more if he loved her.

Sometimes though when they were going somewhere or doing something fun, playing chess, playing with the kitten—she forgot. "I can't help it, I love you," she would tell him. He'd nod, pull her close to him. Once in a while he'd say, "Hey, Moll, we got a good thing going."

But did they? How could it be a good "thing" if the relationship itself was off limits as far as discussion went? "Talk's cheap," he told her more than once. She didn't know how to respond when he said things like that. "But *I'm* not?" Or: "Love's expensive?" What the hell? When she lost her temper or did something that annoyed him, or hurt him, she would sit on the edge of the sofa armrest, run her fingers up the back of his neck to where the soft hairs grew, then under his ear, back along the jawbone to his mouth. "I'm sorry," she'd say. "Please, Hank. Really. Forgive me."

But he didn't seem to understand the concept of forgiveness. He nodded absently, changed the subject. He took her hand and held it still against his chest. He smiled at her. But the words of forgiveness he couldn't say any more than he could say "I love you." They sat quietly and watched the kitten scoot along the floor. He called it a "cat-ten" now, six months old, long and rangy. Its coat was thick, silky to the touch. When it dozed on the windowsill in the late afternoon sun, the black stripes of its face looked like worry lines leading straight up from the ridge above the eyes, disappearing over the top of the head. They had named the cat Scooter.

They took her everywhere. She loved riding in the car, in the very back, down in the deep well between the back seat and rear window. It made a perfect cave. As soon as they got in the car, Scooter jumped down into her cave and went to sleep. Even on long trips. Even when they went camping, they took Scooter along. Or just for a walk in the city park. She trotted behind them like a dog. The same thing in the apartment. When they moved from one room to another, she was right behind them, trying to pounce on the heels of their shoes. This is how they got the idea for playing hide and go seek. She held the cat. He hid in the bedroom closet. He called, "Scooter, *come* kitty!" The cat leaped off Molly's lap, flashed to the hall, pausing for a micro-second at the bathroom door, then disappeared into the bedroom. Meanwhile, Molly hid somewhere, usually behind the drapes in the living room. Then she heard glad cries from the bedroom and Hank and Scooter came racing out to the living room.

"Go find her!" he said. Silence. Molly could hear him panting—and she could sense Scooter was getting close, but who can hear a cat padding on a carpet? And then she felt the prick of claws through the nubbly fabric of the drapes. She swept them aside, swooped the cat up in her arms.

Sometimes when the cat slept on the windowsill, they both tiptoed out of the room, hid in the tub, behind the shower curtain. Molly tried not to giggle; he put his hand over her mouth. She licked at his palm. The cat sensed their absence almost immediately. Not more than a couple of minutes went by. They huddled in the tub, and sure enough, the shower curtain started to twitch, and then the long front leg was snaking around the curtain, and they started laughing, and the cat sat on the edge of the tub, licked its paws carefully, gold eyes regarding them with polite disdain. Then they ran—all three—out to the kitchen.

June came. Hank graduated with high honors, and more to the point, a job waiting for him in San Francisco. They had a month of freedom, so decided to drive back east, spend a week at the beach, then up to her parents for a short visit. Her roommate was getting married in August, so she would fly to join Hank after the wedding. Her husband, the lawyer!

The day they moved out of the apartment, the Wilsons from downstairs came out to the driveway to say goodbye. They were a middle-aged couple who pretty much kept to themselves except for friendly nods at the mailboxes or cheerful comments on the weather on the way out to work in the mornings.

Mrs. Wilson smiled as Hank fastened the last box on top of the car. Mr. Wilson cleared his throat. "Been nice having you folks on board," he said.

His wife laughed. "Honeymooners and all, we didn't quite know what to expect."

He finished it for her. "Wild parties and what have you."

"But you all were so quiet, we hardly knew the place was occupied," the woman added, still smiling.

Mr. Wilson grinned, nudged his wife in the elbow. "Got a chuckle though," he said. "Hearing you play those games up there last couple a months. Chasing each other, I said to the wife. A good sign."

They all shook hands, and as they drove away, Molly said to him, "Oughtn't we have told them? It was Scooter?"

He shook his head, chuckling. "Hell, no. Give them a kick, hey, hon—remember those crazy honeymooners we had back then. Can't you just hear 'em?"

She wanted to add—make it a joke actually—that it was pretty weird it took a cat to get him into the chase mood. But she knew that wouldn't go over, so she held still. He didn't like talking in the car much; it was fine if she talked, just chattering on. But mainly he liked to concentrate on the road, staring straight ahead, hands light on the steering wheel. The silence felt like criticism to her. She knew this was dumb when they started on the trip. But by the time they got to the ocean a week later, she wasn't so sure. His profile against the window looked angry. When she wanted to stop at stores or historical sites, or even a decent restaurant, his mouth went tight. "We got a month's vacation here, you want to fritter it away on junk like that?" he kept saying.

Finally, she simply said nothing. She watched the telephone poles and the road ahead, and how the white line got swallowed by the blue hood of the car, a long white tapeworm that occasionally broke into segments but mainly stretched unbroken down the monotone gray of the road surface. And she understood why the cat always slept in the car, what else was there to do, caged and muzzled this way?

She climbed into the back seat, curled up into the shape of a pretzel

and slept. Something warm was settling under her chin; it was Scooter, also
pretzel-shaped. Molly dozed, lulled by the smooth hum of the car and the
purring of the cat, a sound as comforting to nuzzle against as listening to
the sound of rain falling outside, a cozy sound, a reassuring murmur of
contentment—that's all she wanted from him. Would he label purring as
cheap talk? No, he'd say it was natural vocalization, and she could come right
back, hunch her shoulders forward, and bark out in appropriate prosecutor
style, "Precisely! and your behavior appears as *unnatural* to the defendant
here, you stinker, say you love her, love her, luvver, luvver..."

"Hey, lover, we're here!"

She jumped. They were on the island. There were no other cars around,
the causeway behind them totally empty. They passed abandoned house lots,
the foundations showing, the streets laid out and even brave street signs—
Ocean Drive, Beach Haven Road—but the sand drifted over concrete pilings
and it was clear this was a beach development that wasn't going to happen.

"Why?" she asked him. She had her chin on the back of the front seat,
her left elbow poking into his shoulder. "It's a ghost town."

"Ran out of money, maybe?" he said. They stopped the car about four
miles down, when the paved road gave over to hard-packed beach grass and
not much else. They set up the tent at the foot of the bluff, in a little hollow
protected from the wind. He enjoyed putting up the tent, securing the stakes,
making the whole thing shipshape. He sent her to gather driftwood for the
fire. The cat stayed in the car until they began cooking dinner. Then she
tiptoed out onto the sand, lifting one fastidious paw at a time, giving it a
little shake with each step.

He laughed. "She thinks it's the world's biggest litter box."

Molly flipped the hot dogs over in the skillet. "Hadn't thought of that.
Hope she uses discretion."

"Discretion? You bet," he said fondly. "You gotta remember this is the
Queen of the Cats we got ourselves."

The cat hunched in close to Molly's thigh. Hank reached over, stroked
Scooter's back. Her pupils narrowed as she studied the flames; she began
meowing. He cut off small chunks of raw hot dog, put it on a paper plate.
Scooter ate quickly, crouched over the plate as if the wind might snatch her
dinner away, her tail lashing back and forth. While they finished eating, she
groomed herself. But not as thoroughly as she did inside the house...or the
car. He commented on this. They decided it was her version of roughing it.
He smiled. "We're anthropomorphizing like crazy, you realize."

"So?" she said. "Isn't that what pets are for? To get all sentimental over?"

He didn't answer. He took handfuls of sand and put out the fire.

"Why can't we let it just die down, be so pretty to watch," she argued.

She was already in the sleeping bag and in a mood to watch embers glow, watch the first stars come out, listen to the moan of the surf.

"Sack time," he said. "Always put your fires out at sack time. S.O.P. Standard operating procedure."

He closed the flaps of the tent. The cat had followed him inside and crawled into the very bottom of the sleeping bag. Molly touched her; the fur was soft and warm against bare toes.

Hank was taking off his jeans, his sneakers. She could sense the shape of his body against orange tent walls gone totally black now, sense it more than actually see it. A black shadow in a black shadow-box sealed up tight. Airtight, you might say.

"Know what? I've just about had it with S.O.P.," she said, teasing him, but she was tired of the drill instructor quality to his commands; camping across the country with him made her feel like a rookie recruit. It was just that Hank was so damn capable at everything. Even his patience when she did something dumb, inept, felt like a rebuke, as if he were dealing with a slightly retarded person. His good will when she was clumsy. The little aphorisms: "Better safe than sorry." Or: "No point in crying over spilt milk." "Once burned, twice shy." Or this latest quote and she wondered how after ten months of marriage, he had become a stranger, more strange to her now, more alien in his maleness, his resolve, his withdrawals into pained silence, than anything she could have dreamed of a year ago. S.O.P. my foot, she thought; SOB's more like it, and she let the tears slide out of the corner of her eye and then, as he wriggled in beside her, more tears came, and she could feel him stiffen, roll away from her, turn his back. And she started crying harder so that the sleeping bag jiggled around her shoulders, and after a while he said, "Shit, I don't need this," and got dressed and went outside.

In the morning they drank their coffee in silence. The sun came up at 5:30; they could hear gulls crying. The wind had shifted, an on-shore breeze now. Scooter was chasing fiddler crabs down to the lower part of the beach. Then she raced back to the tent to make sure they still sat there. Back down, this time to stalk a small bird, a sandpiper with bright yellow leggings. They watched the cat. She neutralized their hostility; it was safe watching her play. After a while she stopped, sat back on her haunches, and began to scratch, moving her head back and forth with quick jerks. Then she jumped up, flinched, and came streaking back up the dunes. She was meowing. And then they saw the flies. They were all over her, a cloud of them. There were places on her face and ears they could see blood. Big green horseflies. Hank got out the repellent, began spraying it over the cat, on them, on the walls of the tent. They dripped 6-12 all over their jeans; so much, the fabric was soaked. Scooter disappeared inside the tent, into the sleeping bag. But the flies bit so hard, they decided to escape into the ocean, not the tent—saltwater seemed the only place left to hide.

They flung towels over themselves, ran fast down to the surf, through the breakwater, and dived deep into the water. They swam out to where it was over their heads. Looked back. It looked so peaceful back there, the tent up on the slope of the hill. Nothing but sand and sky and their car a blue dot way up by the beach grass on the crest of the big dune.

"Why?" she asked him. "Where on earth did they come from?"

"From the wild horses. Over on Chincoteague."

"Will they go back?"

"If the wind changes."

"Look, Hank!" She pointed toward the shore. "I can't believe it," she said. Scooter was standing at the water's edge, her mouth opened, and they could almost imagine they could hear her crying. She sat down, stared at them—in one smooth motion, she rose and started walking right into the surf.

Molly grabbed him by the arm. "Cats can't swim, can they?"

"This one sure can, by God. "

"She'll tire, she's only a kitten, she'll drown!"

But by then Scooter was well launched, and swimming towards them, her head disappearing under a wave, then bobbing back up. They started towards her, she looked like a drowned rat at this point, her eyes bulging out of the wedge-shaped face, her mouth drawn back to show the sharp canines as she gulped for air. The ears pricked forward like triangular black sails in distress, poor darling kitty.

They reached her, but he said, "Hold it…she'll scratch." He picked her up by the neck and she hung from his hand like something paralyzed. When they waded into shore, he put her down on the beach and she shook herself but then she began to wind in and around their feet, and they could hear her purring even over the noise of the breakers.

They shut her up in the car, un-pegged the tent, rolled up all the gear. They worked fast. The horseflies got in their hair, they stung everywhere, and by the time they drove away, they had so much blood running down their arms and legs, she had to take a damp beach towel and blot it all off. First him, then her.

"What a disaster," she said finally. He wouldn't talk; it was because, she knew, he was disappointed. And he was angry. Whether at her or not, it didn't matter any more. They drove straight through to her family's house. The trip took eleven hours, and the whole time they hardly said more than a dozen sentences to each other. He was polite to her parents. He laughed at her father's jokes. He complimented her mother on the fried chicken, the coffee mousse. He teased her mother, he talked politics with her and baseball with her dad. He really enjoyed them, she could tell; he let his guard down with them. They made no demands was why; they required nothing of him emotionally.

In bed, they slept far apart, and the cat had to go from one side of the bed to the other, alternating warm nests every couple hours. Hank stayed three days, then left for the new job while she stayed on for her college roommate's wedding—ostensibly to join him later. She didn't want to think about what might happen after next week; it was still too raw, the separation that existed now and turned them into smiling strangers, careful not to touch.

He took the cat with him. He wanted companionship driving across the country. And anyhow, her mother hated cats and made no bones about it. Losing Scooter was what really hurt; learning how to love her, learning now to let her go. This was what growing up was all about, what was meant by maturity, and she wanted none of it. She wanted to go hide in the dark somewhere and cry forever. Instead, she had to dodge her mother's questions: "When will you be joining him?" "Where will you all be living in San Francisco?"

The real questions she tried to blank out, the unspoken ones alternating with her mother's voice, the ones like: How do you get a divorce? What do I tell everybody? Where should I work, here or go back to Denver? Or what?

She didn't let him into her mind. She blanked him out; a black shadow against the black tent, that was the way she pictured him.

One night very late the phone rang. She answered it before it could wake her parents. It was Hank. He was calling from somewhere in Arizona, collect from a pay phone.

He asked how she was, how her folks were. How the roommate's wedding was shaping up. Then there was nothing but the hum of telephone wires. When he spoke again, his voice sounded cracked and at first she thought it was a bad connection. He sounded as if he had bruised his windpipe.

"I lost her, Molly," he said.

"Who?"

"Scooter." And then he began to make awful noises—as if something were clawing out of his throat, painful and raw. He said they had been camping in the desert, way north of Tucson somewhere. And Scooter loved the desert, loved scampering out of the car to stalk sand lizards. He spread the sleeping bag out on a ground tarp in the sand; she curled up at the bottom as usual. In the morning she was gone. He spent five hours driving up along the buttes, climbing down in the arroyos calling her. But he never found her. She was gone.

Finally she said in a low voice, "Do you think she ran away or what?"

"I don't know, honey. I tried. I mean she loved the desert the way she got used to the beach that time, she was happy."

"Did something get her, eat her, I mean?"

He didn't answer for a minute. "No," he said finally. "We've got to think she's just fine out there somewhere, hightailing over the dunes after some critter, some juicy lizard she just can't turn down."

Then she began crying. "The worst part's...." she said, "I mean...I can't bear to think of her missing us. Of her trying to find us."

He began talking right through that last part, "I know, I know ," he said as if he couldn't bear hearing her say what he felt. "I know you loved her, Moll—I loved her, too, I couldn't say it, I should've said it, I love you, Molly, I need you here, I love you, God, what was my problem anyhow? You—."

She listened to him say the words. She cupped the phone close under her chin as if it were a face caressing hers, and she wondered as he kept on talking if love always came sheathed in pain, in loss, and how many times would this lesson have to be learned? Or maybe it was never learned? Maybe just glimpsed sideways, the same way you see a gray-gold paw come sliding around a curtain. And retracted claws start to hook out from feathery toes and what was seconds ago all velvet softness now cuts as swift and sharp as a razor blade.

But what's remembered is the feel of soft velvet. Or a cat poised at the water's edge. But now was not the time to tell him. He knew it anyhow. He knew it long before she did.

So she simply sat there, cradling the phone—and listened to him talk—and to the way his voice sounded. The words, she realized, didn't really matter.

Pietà

—

If.
If not.
If she escaped.
If they had met.
If no message is sent.
If you have a true vocation.
If you'll agree, Señor.
If only.
If.

If—small sturdy word—Vargas smiles, so small it surely staggers beneath its twin saddlebags of what might have been…and what may be. *Thou mirror of righteousness, thou cause of joy, thou excellent vessel of devotion, thou morning star, thou healer of the sick.*

The priests come and go. They are all old here. Like Vargas, this is their final home.

The smells from the kitchen spill out into the refectory. The fathers who are too sick to dine communally have their trays sent upstairs to their rooms.

Vargas wheels the cart to the elevator. He pushes the button to the 3rd floor, the infirmary floor. If he is late, one of the nursing sisters is always standing by the elevator door, tapping her foot impatiently. She never speaks except to mention the hour, the minutes past the hour that he has squandered.

He tried once to explain how the cooks downstairs were running behind because of the extra meals, the retreats when hard-eyed businessmen from Miami come for weekends. Or laughing strangers who stop to see the chapel on their way to Disney World.

"Thirty…thirty…" was all he could think to say. So he let the words die on his lips, stillborn the way they are so often these days when he looks into eyes that do not care, that shift beyond him to the metal cart and the plates stacked neatly with their shining metal hats pierced by small holes to put

11

your finger in and lift them up and see the pale yellow of custard and soft scrambled eggs, no butter on the dry wheat toast.

"Never butter, never jam, Juan!" Elena scolds. Elena is the newest cook. "They are all on the bland diet, those fathers," she says. She waggles her finger at him. "You must never add anything to the trays, do you understand?" She speaks rapidly in broken Spanish, a bastard Miami-street tongue. She has a fat woman's jolly smile. Her dark eyes glow when she talks, voice soft as the kindness that he knows is in her, no matter how sharp the words.

"I understand, Señora," he answers and waits for her to pat him gently on the shoulder because she is aware that beasts of burden still respond to voice and touch, and he will carry as much as she asks of him, no matter how laden the trays, how heavy the garbage pails, the cartons of institutional brand tomatoes, mayonnaise, green beans in their twenty pound cans, the slatted boxes of lettuce from the loading dock.

He spends much time back here on the loading dock, making sure that the crates are piled neatly. He checks to see that the lids of the garbage pails are clamped on tight so that no reek of rotting food will drift in to the kitchen where Elena works with the old one who drinks and the young gringo on leave from the university who leers at Elena in a way that is not honorable.

The rubbish goes to the dumpster. But the garbage must wait on the platform until the white truck appears. He is afraid of the smells and he is afraid of the rats. But the rats do not come because he sweeps carefully around the whole platform, around the pavement below where the delivery trucks roll up and their black oil dribbles on to the gravel, coating the sharp bristles of his push broom, and then he must pour kerosene on a cloth and wipe the bristles so that they stand up as shining clean as pine needles.

The push broom has broad shoulders and a sturdy straight handle made of varnished white pine which feels glassy smooth in his hands. It pleases him to see how wide a path it makes in the dirt, this broom. From studying the gardener out there now on the tractor-mower, he learned long ago to move the broom in the shape of a giant square, working into a series of smaller and smaller squares, tighter and tighter, smaller, smaller so that finally in the end he has come back to the beginning, back to when Anna used to stand on the grandmother's back stoop, shaking the mop, the mop with the long tangled ringlets which he helps Anna braid sometimes when the grandmother goes to the market to sell the eggs and bargain for fresh tripe. Their mother does not wish them to visit the grandmother, who is poor. But their father insists on these visits so that they may know what it is like to run barefooted in the soft dirt and play tag with the goats as Papa had once done as a boy.

"Is she not beautiful?" asks Anna. The mop is a lonely princess waiting for her rescuer to gallop up the dusty pathway to the back porch where the mangle stands, steam from freshly washed clothes rising like mist around the princess who leans over the wooden railing, shading her eyes against the bright sun to see the figure capering below on his silver stallion, the handlebars decked with small red banners that flutter in the breeze when the horse gallops fast.

"I am coming, mi corazon!" calls the princess, pale ringlets cascading over her shoulders. But just as she turns to creep down the staircase, her jailer discovers her. He grabs her long hair. "No!" she screams. But he is strong. His beard is bushy with tight black curls, so coarse these curls, as to be obscene.

"Your lover should not send messages to the castle. My spies are paid well," he leers. He smells of garlic; a bandolier is slung across his chest. Then, with a cruel smile, he shouts down to the horseman below, "Here she is, Don Vargas! She is...indeed coming to you!" and casts her over the railing, falling, falling, her ringlets catching on the bougainvillea bushes. Chickens scratching in the dusty yard squawk with alarm, then scatter back into the safe darkness of the henhouse. A feather floats in the air, a sunbeam of iridescent color, coppery brown and gold.

"Is that a feather, Juan?"

Elena stands beside him. She has taken off the big apron she wears when she cooks. She lights a cigarette; she has pretty hands with small wrist bones. The skin on the knuckles is stained a deep yellow. This is because after every meal Elena selects a fresh orange from the bowl of fruit she keeps in the center of the soapstone table, peels it, then takes the inside of the peel and rubs it slowly over the backs of her hands. He likes to watch her do this. He knows her skin smells fragrant and feels as finely grained as a linen altar cloth. *Thou mirror of righteousness, thou tower of ivory, thou rose...*

"Si," he says, and blows at the feather. "A chicken feather, I think. "

She shakes her head, smiling. "No chickens here, Juan. It must be from a robin. " She looks around the clean flooring of the platform, the neat piles of boxes. "You are very good at your job, amigo. I have never worked in a place so clean as this before. Immaculate!" *...by God's most singular grace, preserved free from all stain, most blessed virgin, Mother of divine grace, thou purest Mother...thou most chaste Mother...*

He ducks his head, grips hard the broom.

"Father Xavier himself mentioned this to me. Our hardest worker, Vargas, he said." She drags deep on her cigarette. "Hot today," she adds. "I will go for a swim when I get home."

He says nothing. He can see her diving into blue water and the white columns of her legs flash like the fins of a bonita, the fish the rich Yanquis hunt for in their swift boats, the little chairs in the stern twirling like circular thrones. On the docks, the men stand to have their pictures taken; the bonita shimmers in the sunlight. A few drops of blood spill from the hook in its mouth.

"Do you live far from here, Juan?" she is asking him now.

"Mi casa," he says proudly. He waves his arm at the gardens, the stone buildings, the glistening dome of the chapel.

She looks surprised. She runs her tongue along her bottom lip, a lip as full and wet as a peeled plum. She takes one finger and removes a fleck of tobacco, then glances at him.

"You studied once to be a priest, the Reverend Father told me," she says in a low voice, but she is not looking at him any longer. They both watch the gardener who is mowing the side garden now where the Jesuits are buried. The huge square grows smaller, pale green stubble pressing in on all four sides, pressing into the dark green of the unmown grass...*thou gate of heaven, thou morning star, pray for us.*

"In Havana," he says and starts to add "at the seminary," but then stops. The picture is gone, those dark cloisters so cool at any time of day, the white marble slick underfoot but the footsteps fade even as he reaches for the words.

"And then," Elena continues, "the fathers smuggled you out. And you came here to Miami. To study at the university." She is speaking very softly now, even sadly. But there is a question in her voice.

It is the same question in his mind. Coming from the Commons with his letter in his hands, the red stamp slashing across his own neat script: RETURN TO SENDER: ADDRESS UNKNOWN. And then the yellow bricks of the Administration Buildings—the red tiles of the roof, the pain of the sun blinding his eyes. The faces of the gringo students turning toward him as he fell—pale white balloons floating higher in the white sunlight—while he points to the bell tower visible between the royal palms, the campanile striding tall and white across the campus lawn to where he slumps, watching it come closer, the tall white warrior chiming the lament for the dead and dying while Anna waves from the truck, "We shall meet in Miami, my bother!"

"Me, I was born right here. Here in Miami," Elena is saying to him. "But my great aunt Martina was from Cuba. She got out before you did, before the bad times. The purges. They lived in the mountains, Sierra Maestre. It was from her I learned to cook. Roast pork and sweet yams, cheese soup, black beans and rice. So delicious...but not," here she laughs, "not food for the fathers, verdad?" She pauses, smiles fondly. "Martina made this most wonderful dessert, soft cream cheese she let me whip and whip, then she would fold in puree of mangoes. Such a pretty yellow color. We only had this on feast day, and when I made my holy communion."

He studies her. She is his age, a middle-aged woman with lines in her face but he can see the little girl she must have been, the delicate wrist on that forearm before it turned to fat, the great hollows of the eyes as she gazed up at the priest and opened her mouth to receive the host.

"I was there too," she says.

He stares at her. Her lips are the full lips of that young girl in white but the teeth are stained from much tobacco. But it is still a lovely smile, no? still youthful in the round face with the full brow that is the same polished ivory as the meat of a coconut, waxy smooth.

"Si," she goes on, "back in 1960. I was working in the University cafeteria then. Is that not the year you came to study here in Miami?"

He shakes his head. "Si, perhaps. " He smiles, holds his hands up to show they are as empty as the mouth that will not form the words aloud, too many butting each other out of line, scattering around in his head like balky goats.

She touches her hair. It is pulled back tightly in a round bun, straight back from the high temples. The bun reminds him of a large black donut. Her ears lie flat to the head. She is wearing bright red earrings, a cluster of little red plastic flowers. He wonders if it hurts to wear these earrings, to pierce the pale skin so that blossoms may grow there, scarlet stigmata against the fleshy lobes.

"Ah, Juan. " She is laughing, eyes merry. "We probably saw each other many times. I may have handed you your Jello and punched your meal ticket. Not so?" She grins at him again, then stubs out her cigarette with the heel of her white sandal.

"Perhaps," he repeats and rubs his chin, the stubble harsh against his thumb. He sees that his bluejeans are very stained and that two buttons are missing from his shirt. He cannot remember when he took a shower. It must have been the night before, he thinks, but the nights are as interchangeable as rosary beads and only the clicking of his feet on the marble transept is real....

"Pray for me, father," he says. She looks at him quickly. Then she leans over and touches his bare forearm.

He shuts his eyes; the iron shutters close inside the window. The room is dim; in the clothes cupboard hangs the black cassock of the seminarian, black as the wrought iron balcony outside the window, black as the shrinking silhouette of El Morro Castle as the ship disappears behind the lighthouse. The lighthouse blinks à Dios while the boat leaves the harbor. In the breeze he can smell the stink of rotten sewage floating in the oily water, and over the rotten smell, the sweet musk of black orchids blooming around the stucco walls of his father's house. At the end of the long driveway stand two small trees with bright green leaves and clusters of red flowers at the tips of the branches. The flowers shine glossy red in the sea of leaves and long sharp spines. He has asked his father the name of these strange trees.

His father hugged him. He smelled of cigars & mojitos, the rum cocktail he drinks out on the patio. "Crown of thorns, my son," his father had said. "To look at, Juanito—not to touch. "

Elena turns to go back into the kitchen. She gives him a smile and a quick wave. He watches her open the screen door. For a heavy woman, she has a light step, and the back of her legs curves so sweetly down the full calves to thin ankles which carry uncomplainingly the weight and bulk of her—fragile white bones which will not stagger no matter how heavy the burden.

He says softly, "If you need…." But she has passed inside the dark doorway, her cheap white sandals slapping on the stone floor.

He strokes the broom, then jabs the tip of the handle hard against his forehead, so hard there are white lights inside his eyes but they will not last, they never do. They flick by as quickly as the fairy hummingbird he and Elena…no, Anna!… it was Anna, Anna beside him, chasing through the oleander bushes, seeking to put salt on its whirring tail.

He rubs his forehead. The old pain is starting again.

Beyond, in the garden, the mower drones where sleeping priests wrestle with their carnal dreams. Small flat stones mark the head of each grave. No names. No dates. Only the white stone and the shrouded figure of the mother weeping at the far end of the garden, weeping for each son she has lost and will lose, over and over again.

"If…" he says again, then shrugs.

This too is a conversation he has never been able to continue. So he places the push broom up on the rack over the garbage pails, hanging it on the small dowel he's made to help prop up the broad shoulders in a straight line. He checks to make sure all is tidy, then goes inside, careful not to let the screen door slam.

The door of the utility closet is locked; he has the only key. It is a walk-in storeroom where he keeps all his cleaning supplies. There is in here always a strong odor of ammonia.

He does not turn on the light; there is no need. His foot brushes against a bucket which clanks its usual greeting. He can hear the clatter of dishes from the kitchen down the long hallway, and farther away the chant of evensong.

He waits; lets his eyes grow accustomed to the darkness.

She waits also, waiting for him there in the niche between the shelves and plumber's helper. Her hair falls in long pale ringlets. Her face is in shadow but he knows that she is smiling, her patient smile which is here for him each time as both welcome and benediction.

He drops to his knees, bows his head. He can smell the stink of his shirt, of his unwashed armpits, but he takes out the rosary from the hip pocket of his jeans. The beads slip through his fingers; still he does not lift his head because he and she are joined together in lamentation, and there is much pain which they might glimpse in each other's eyes, so he simply murmurs in a low voice the words that never desert him, the familiar words he must address her by: *Hail Mary full of grace, blessed is the fruit of thy womb Jesus, pray for us....*

SURFACE TENSION

THERE IS A MAN who watches me. I pretend not to notice. He stands below me, way down on the far side of the hill. Stands there, hands in his pockets, his face a blur, looking upwards. He's framed by a peculiar kind of fuzzy light that blots out everything else—the sky, the road, the brown fields beyond him. Strange. He's nobody we know; he's not from this part of the world, that's for certain.

First time I saw him was three weeks ago. I was picking blueberries, and I knocked over the bucket. The blueberries rolled all over the grass like fragile purple marbles, hundreds of them, skittering beyond my fingers.

"Oh, shoot!" I go. It's the kind of thing that upsets Alvaro, me too for that matter. HAND-PICKED MAINE BLUES, the sign reads. Alvaro claims folk always stop when they read those words HAND-PICKED. "Sign that reads FRESH BERRIES won't do it, sis," Al tells me each year come picking season. "FRESH might mean yesterday-fresh."

Business is best come mid-August. That's when our tomatoes are finally their juiciest, the cukes—good and hard. The squash is starting to blaze out back in the garden—fiery orange and yellow splashing through the broad leaves, leaves so broad they make me think of wild things that grow in jungles, those Amazon pictures we look at in the old *Geographics* I keep stored out in the parlor. Before the electric came few years back, that's how Al and me got to see the world out there. Not now. Now all we do is turn on the knob of the big Philco Al bought me—last Christmas it was. Myself, I'd still rather study those pretty *Geographic* photographs on that glossy paper so smooth to the touch.

Not Al though. First thing in the morning, he heads for the television, flicks it on. "Weather reports," he says. "Crop prices."

I mean we're sure not big crop farmers—not by a long shot. It's the berries and the apples that keep us going. That's what tourists are looking for—plump Maine blues and early Macs, nice and tart. We hire out for apple pickers. The blueberries Alvaro and I can pretty much handle ourselves. Al's fast but I'm thorough.

Al was up to the house when the berries spilled. Even so, I looked back to make sure he wasn't checking on me through the window. The white curtains billowed, no sign of Alvaro. Good; makes me nervous, him fussing so.

So I inched along in the high grass, trying hard to find those rascals. A couple squished beneath my elbows. What a mess. Al won't notice, he never does. I always come home with blue stains all over my dress, my knees and elbows. He don't say a word. He just carries me to the bathroom, runs a whole tub of hot water, then helps ease me down. "Call when you're ready," he tells me, staring at the clawed feet of the tub. Al's the kind of man who looks down a fair amount. I figure it's because he's used to studying the soil underfoot, checking for cinch bug and all those pesky things he's fighting from seedtime right through to the first early frost. Running a truck garden's not an easy proposition, but we get by.

"Sure beats fishing," Al claims. Al used to fish for herring years ago, but after the third cannery closed down, so many folks out of work, he chucked it.

"Live off the land," he told me. "Old terra firma you can depend on pretty much. She won't stab you in the back way the durn sea does." And he'd give me a fierce kind of smile, clump off to the shed in back, his work boots loud on the wood flooring. I wish we had ourselves some fancy linoleum, leastways in the kitchen. I like to look at those pretty colors they show in *Sears Catalog*, the way those floors shine waxy bright as a ripe Mac Intosh. But Alvaro, he says, "This here's a working farm, Christina—not some fancy folks' dollhouse. Grow up, girl."

I'm still baby sister in Al's mind. I mean it's kind of sad in a way, here we be, both in our thirties, and me as helpless as one of the new tabby kittens out there in the barn. Not that I'm fretting. I understand Alvaro, he's an Olson through and through. He's taken good care of me, my whole life. He carries me around, helps me into my chair, fusses over me, bathes me like a baby. And he never complains. He's got a soft spot in him, Al does, beneath his gruff way of talking, his silences sharp as flint.

He promised Mama he'd always care for me, and he's kept that promise. Still, he gets ornery sometimes, cranky. Like spilling the berries, the clumsy things I do. Clumsy not because of the polio, mind you, but because, as he says, I'm forever woolgathering.

That's how come when I knocked over the bucket that afternoon, I got so cross. Pure and simple woolgathering was the cause. Comes from being too close to the ground maybe, so many things to look at. I had three quarters of the pail filled, but then I saw this wonderful critter crawling along the lowest branch of the berry bush. He was some kind of caterpillar, never saw the likes of him before.

That caterpillar was so beautiful, it seemed to me a shame he'd have to go through the hard business of breaking through the cocoon. "Why bother?" I told him, right out loud.

He was a pale silvery color with narrow bands of black outlining each section of his body. Two feathery stalks—like the tall plumes that horses wear in the picture books—waved from both his head and his tail. The plumes were transparent, soft and gauzy as thistledown. There was this black central cord they seemed to spring from, finer than silk thread. He had a black face as well, shiny black like a coat button. I couldn't see his eyes, but it sure looked like he was smiling at me. He had at least five pair of feet. They reminded me of tiny galoshes. They started moving in the very back, and then the wave of movement traveled in a ripple to the next pair, and the next. He really scooted, all five sections of him, right onto the palm of my hand. When I looked down at him, his body was so transparent I could see the pale pinkness of my own skin clear through the silver fuzz of his.

I reached out to pick a leaf for him to nibble on—that's when the pail went flying.

"Shoot!" I go. The caterpillar went very still, I placed him back on his bush. And then's when I felt certain that somebody was staring at me, staring at me hard. I looked again up across the field at the house.

But the curtains still blew across empty windows. Beyond the house, stood the barn, and beyond the barn, the pale gray curve of the sea. Fog was coming in, and I could hear the first low moans from the lighthouse way past the cove.

I turned my head then and looked down the hill. There was someone standing there, a man. His arms were folded, and he was watching me. I couldn't see a car, I couldn't see his face. But he was a stranger, that much I could tell.

I stared back. Why wasn't I scared? I don't hold with strangers much, none of us do around here. I mean we're civil, tell them how to get back to the Interstate, agree that Maine is tough to live through in the long winters. But we draw the line at chit chat. You have to with a roadside operation like ours. As Alvaro says, "Chewing the fat any doggone fool can do. Putting bread on the table is what counts." Work is the way of life up here, work to make things grow, to dig them up, to pay off the second mortgage, to put a little aside for the new roof the barn needs. "Making do," Al calls it.

The stranger turned, and began walking away, farther and farther away until his dark shape had become a blur, and my eyes hurt from straining to see.

Oh, Al's right, I know he's right. But sometimes I wonder what goes on beyond these brown hills, down the Interstate, the black ribbon of road snaking by the shoreline, past the rocks, the cliffs where shearwaters nest and once Al brought me an egg, freckled just like his nose used to be back then.

I still keep that egg on the bureau in my room beside Mama's picture, all faded brown now but her smile still gleams out of the shadows, her big eyes glow back at the photographer. She was young and a bride back then; she sits stiffly in the high-backed chair beside a tall potted palm. Her black hair is cut short, bobbed I think they called it those days. Mama was Portuguese and she gave me and Alvaro not only her dark coloring but also the names of her own brother and sister. She met my father when he fished off the banks of Provincetown, and he brought her up to Maine, brought her to bleak hillsides and rocky beaches and the sound of the wind so lonely at night, sweeping in from the ocean.

She brought him laughter, and a way of tossing her head, black eyes snapping, and she would tease him, saying, "You big Swedes! All you Olsons know is tides and the herring. There's more to life, querido mio." She died with that last baby of hers, our baby brother we never saw. My father was lost at sea up near the banks of Newfoundland, but I think he had already lost all he really loved long before.

I keep my treasures in Mama's sewing box beside my chair in the kitchen. My good garnet brooch, my gold crucifix. Her silver thimble. Her ribbons she tied her hair back with. The miniature scissors given to her by a favorite aunt—these lie side by side with all the pretty shells I collect when Alvaro takes me to the beach. And the ticket stubs from our favorite movies Al takes me to see, the people all staring as he carries me down the aisle. And a small colored picture of Mary cuddling the baby, her head tipped forward so that their haloes interlock, and something about the way she smiles at him reminds me of Mama. On the back of the picture these words printed from St. Augustine: "We never lose those we give to God."

Or to the sea, I would like to add.

Alvaro doesn't hold with the church, just like our Papa. He's an Olson all right. "A whole peck of trouble worrying about this world," he grumbles. 'Got no time for cogitating about the next." He looks down at his plate of food when I say grace; the lamp shines on the little bald spot that's starting to show on the top of his head.

Those pretty black curls, they're receding faster than the tide these days. And they'll never come back. Makes me sad. He's still a fine figure of a man. I watch the tourist women in their bright shorts and striped tops looking at him sideways. They like the heft of his shoulders underneath his blue work shirt, his brown arms with the corded muscles rippling as he loads a bushel of apples into the backs of fancy station wagons. He never looks up once. When they pay, he ducks his head, rubs his chin, then hitches at his overalls.

"Talk your ear off, don't they now?" he says to me when the people drive away. I nod, keep on polishing apples. I want to tell him about the stranger. He's come back every day. Even from the kitchen window where I sit until it's time to mind the vegetable stand, I can see him down there, looking up the hillside.

He shades his eyes, peers hard like he's lost his way, trying to get his bearings. But he's not in a car, there's no bicycle around. No busses come out this far. Where can he come from? I want to ask Alvaro, but Al's got no patience with trespassers.

Once—couple of years ago it was—some kids came to the orchard, spread a blanket under the trees. They were having a picnic, our home grown apples for dessert. They were laughing and the laughter mixed real nice with the music that blared good and loud from the radio of the old Studebaker parked close by.

Alvaro didn't say a word. He got down his rifle, the one he uses when he and Jake Coggins from down the road go deer hunting. He walked out to the edge of the field next to the apple trees and fired three shots. Some crows flew up out of the grass, squawking and flapping their wings. It was quite a sight watching how fast those youngsters scrambled out of there. They left the blanket behind; Alvaro uses it now for bedding down the barn cats when they have a new litter.

If I were to tell him about this stranger lurking, he'd most likely blast him right off the property.

I wish I could see the man's face. I know he's trying to see mine.

Three days ago, there was another man watching. He marched up and down past the barn. Alvaro had taken the pick-up truck, gone into town for a new oil filter for the tractor. I was sitting by the window like before, and at first I thought it was the same stranger. But this man was dressed like a police officer, except he was real old, too old to be a regular patrolman. Still, he was wearing a badge; it glinted in the sun. He was dressed in some kind of guard uniform, dark blue. He carried a holster, but he moved real slow. He didn't look up at the house once. Fact is he looked kind of bored, like he could hardly wait for time to pass.

He was gone by the time Al got back from town. I was so nervous by then, I dropped the sewing basket. Al didn't say a word, just picked up all the spools one by one, the packet of new needles, Mama's scissors, my shells, and the jewelry. He fingered the crucifix for a moment, then put it back in the box with the other things and placed the box in my lap. He looked tired, kind of whipped.

"Alvaro," I said, and touched his arm. Something about my voice made him look at me, really stare at my face, eye to eye.

"What's wrong?" he said quickly. He worries about leaving me alone when he drives into town. He worries about me, period.

I smiled, pointing at the sewing basket. "Thanks" was all I said. It's hard talking to a man like Alvaro, it's like we've both gone kind of rusty. Probably a real good thing we got Cable.

The next day, there was the same guard in the uniform. Then when he left, pretty near lunchtime it was, I saw another come round the side of the house. He wasn't old, this one but he was fat, very fat, so I knew for sure these couldn't be regular police. Old and fat, who in their right mind would hire them? Not even in our little town where all they do is drive round nights and shoo off youngsters necking down by the pier.

But these guards—what is it they're doing here? Alvaro—he will chase them away, I just know he will.

They pace by the house. They look at their watches.

I look at mine. It's almost high noon, and Al will be coming in from the garden soon. Sure enough, I see him starting into the pasture, he's carrying two big crates. He stoops forward from the weight of the things, eyes on the ground as usual.

I sit up very straight and still. I can hear a murmuring somewhere, like the sea when a storm's kicking up. But the sea is flat today, flat and calm as a pewter platter, winking in the hot sunshine.

Alvaro disappears for a moment behind the shed. There he is. He's walking straight toward the guard. The guard lounges against the old weather-beaten wagon Al keeps meaning to chop up for firewood but he never will—reminds him of the old days when we still had the mules is why.

He passes right by the guard. Neither one of them bats an eyelash. What is this? Has he paid these men to watch over me? Is he that scared something will happen?

I am.

My hands are shaking so, I can hardly hold the paring knife. Alvaro likes big slabs of tomato with his dinner at noon. But I can no more slice into that red pulp than cut my own flesh, what's wrong here?

Al's working the old pump outside the kitchen door, getting the worst of the dirt off his hands and arms. The murmuring sounds have gotten louder; it's almost like the way people sound in church, right after Mass, quiet talk but lots of it. A bell's ringing, the red pulp is floating up towards my face, the seeds so close I can plainly see the slimy envelope that houses each one, and then there's the thump of his boots, kicking off the sods of earth against the iron door scraper, yes, and the tomato is cool and wet against my cheeks....

He put me straight to bed, made me promise to sleep or he was going to call Doc Haskins. I tried to tell him it was the heat, women pass out in the heat all the time, so do grown men, soldiers—but that made me think of the guards in their blue uniforms, so I held still, let him fuss over me.

The next day it was so hot in the house.

"Indian summer early this year," Alvaro commented briefly,

He brought me a soft boiled egg and my tea on the big enameled tray we never use except for company now and then. It has large red flowers painted on it. I guess they're enameled but they look so real, a person wants to reach right out and pick them off, smell deep inside the scarlet throat of the flower, so deeply that pollen dusts the tip of your nose.

I told Alvaro I wanted him to take me outside. "So I can pick the last of the berries," I added.

"You're not picking squat for a while, missy. You're taking it easy," he said. He looked very grim. He folded his arms across his chest the same way the guards had done. All he needed was the holster, I thought, and I grinned up at him. But his face was very serious.

So then I said, "I promise not to pick," making my face as innocent as a child's, "But it's hot. So hot up here. No breeze," We both glanced over at the window. The curtains hung straight and limp; the sun streamed through the lace, they looked so filmy, like dandelion puffs, like the shimmer of the caterpillar I found the day that the stranger first came.

He carried me down the hill, Alvaro did. He carried an old quilt as well, the one he always puts beneath me, though my legs can feel neither heat nor cold, wet nor dry.

"Not today," I told him, "It looks so hot, the quilt, The grass is dry anyhow."

He stood above me, and he smiled, "You just bask here a spell," he said. "No picking, no preserving, nothing but you and old man sunshine."

And the man down the hill, I wanted to add.

But I never looked around until Alvaro started back across the fields. Then I turned. This time the man was standing so close, I could see his face. He was squinting at me, but that could have been because he was facing into the light

I nodded. He kept on staring. He had a good face, not stern like Alvaro's but with strong bones, kind mouth. It was his eyes that I liked the most. They were deep set, blue like my papa's, and they were searching me out, studying me like a book, and seeing me as I'd never been seen before, looking at me not as Alvaro's poor gimp of a sister but something beautiful sprawled out in that high grass, the feathery stalks tickling my arms, the earth so solid beneath my rump.

"Who are you?" those eyes asked.

I reached one arm out. "Take me with you," I said. But he couldn't hear me. I could see that he hadn't heard, his eyes still asked the same question. Maybe the murmuring drowned out my voice.

So I held out both arms. There was something hard right in front of me. I groped, trying to find a break in the slick surface, but it was solid as a shield all in front of me. My fingers kept sliding down the smoothness marred by bumps here and there—bumps like roughened skin, like goose bumps,

But I've got strong arms to make up for my foolish legs. I pushed, fingernails scratching then slipping against the canvas, no use—it was very rigid so I took my fists and I clenched them the way boxers will do on the television and I punched hard again, so hard I fell forward, and just as the canvas started to rip, jagged edges scratching my arms, I saw a large white room with a red velvet rope and over there by a shadowed archway, the startled face of the fat guard, hand on his holster; and then, flecks of paint started sprinkling like black sand all down my white dress, in my hair, and I could see in the stranger's wide blue eyes so close to my own that I had made a mistake, that I was not supposed to be in his world, but rather, he—in mine.

BOBBY SHAFTOE'S GONE TO SEA

THE NO VACANCY SIGN out in the parking lot is blinking. The light is a harsh ochre color. It shines right in the window, right into Clare's eyes, flashing on the wall next to the bed. It pulses, she's decided, like staccato sunbursts. A Morse code in neon, sending secret messages.

"Hey, doll, what's the big hurry?" he's saying to her. His breath is hot, slightly sour. She shifts, turns her head towards the wall.

She tries to count the slow beats, the pauses between blinks. **Ta** dum/ **ta** dum and pause. A boring rhythm, but now she can begin to make out patterns on the wallpaper where the light hits it, the actual shapes of what she first took to be only random splotches.

Patterns. Patterns of flowers growing across the wall in orderly rows. Daisies. And some kind of bell-shaped flower? Daffodils, probably. Or maybe bluebells? Bluebells and cockleshells—no, *silver* bells and cockleshells/and Johnny shall have a new master. Wrong rhyme, who cares? The last lines she can remember exactly. Johnny must have but a penny a day/because he can't work any faster, and this john's like all the rest, so why kid herself?

She wonders again what secret code is spoken in nursery rhymes. She shifts her hips. He's heavy on top of her. She traces the outlines of a daffodil across his back, the cool vertical stalk, the graceful up-swelling curve of the yellow throat, quick scalloped edges of the fluted petals...six-petaled, a monocot.

"Relax," he tells her. She's already forgotten his name.

Her neck's stiff, so she turns her head away from the wall, stares straight up at the ceiling, his cheek rough against hers.

Headlights sweep across the bed, slant up the wall, then jackknife across the ceiling. A car door slams. Low voices then the tinkle of glass breaking. Someone says "Shit!" Footsteps go past their window, a girl giggles. The footsteps fade away.

She presses both palms flat against the sloping mound of his buttocks.

"You're so smooth," she says, and she watches daffodils massed on a hillside...Jack and Jill...go up the hill...to fetch a pail of water.

Thousands of daffodils, growing wild above the creek, dancing all across

26

the field, but they hadn't noticed at first. They had run screeching up the hill pretending they were Irish thoroughbreds galloping in the Grand National, leaping Beecher's Brook, hooves flying off the ground, clods of dirt trailing like a black comet behind them, the brook a muddy slash beneath. They were out of breath panting hard, flanks glistening, their necks covered with lather, white lather slick as soapsuds, blood pumping, pumping so hard that the heart will spatter right out of the great barrel chest which strains against the martingale, strains to reach the last crest of the hill...

"...and Jill came tumbling after," she says, voice thick.

But he doesn't answer; he's panting, and pretty soon, he rolls over, one arm flung across her breast. He snores.

She can hear Lynn calling, calling "WAIT, Clare!", and she can remember what they said that afternoon more distinctly than anything he's said to her all evening, either in the bar or afterwards.

And she had waited, snorting a little, pawing the ground with her left sneaker, then whinnying as Lynn stumbled up beside her.

"Can't we just stop a minute?" Lynn had said, and then flopped down on the ground. Her face was bright red. "See, my Keds are completely soaked." She hitched at her shorts, white an hour ago.

Clare squatted down beside her. She picked a blade of grass to chew on, sucking at the sweetness. She tried to spit out the sodden pulp the way men did it.

"Here," said Lynn, and demonstrated. "Sideways. Like this." She spat, a perfect arching loop of green from the corner of her mouth. Then she lay back on the grass, arms pillowed beneath her head. "Why," she asked, "do we always have to be horses? It's boring."

"Because," was all Clare said. Lynn never asked this question except when she was losing. "It's how you play the game, ladies," Mrs. Wickes always told them. Mrs. Wickes taught them botany and field hockey. She was British and terribly strict about good stick-work and good sportsmanship both. And memorizing parts of the flower—stamens and pistils—they had giggled over the sex stuff. Monocots like daffodils bore only one seed leaf.

She smiles; she still remembers her botany. Still remembers how Lynn kept staring up at the sky, and how finally she'd poked Lynn's arm, and Lynn, eyes closed now, murmured a drowsy, "What?"

"Look. It's all flowers here. Thousands of them. Growing wild." Lynn sat up. Daffodils bloomed all around them, cool and elegant among the tall grasses. Lynn reached out, touched a stalk. "Pretty," she said, with a dreamy smile.

Lynn should know; she was the prettiest girl in the Lower School—grave gray eyes and the skinniest wrists and ankles Clare had ever seen. Lynn was going to be May Queen, and get to sit on a throne—actually just the

Headmistress' big chair covered in purple velvet—while the rest of the sixth grade did the Maypole Dance which Miss Hunt was teaching them every afternoon this whole month.

Clare stood up. "I've got an idea," she told Lynn and started picking daffodils left and right.

"Now what?" Lynn sounded bored, and did another sideways spit.

"Let's pick this whole giant bouquet. And then we can take it. You know, take it over to Miss Hunt." She waited for Lynn to laugh, or worse, get that teasing half smile at the corner of her mouth, but Lynn only looked wide-eyed at her.

They both had a crush on Miss Hunt; they had for a month now. Every day after school they talked on the phone about her. What she had said. What she'd worn. They tried to suck in their cheeks to look hollowed like hers. They both cut their hair short and Clare asked to have a permanent wave—Lynn didn't need one—to match Miss Hunt's wild black curls. They took to wearing dirndl skirts; their mothers claimed they looked incredibly tacky, like a pair of gypsies.

That sounded wonderful to both of them. They were sick with love for her, sick in the pit of the stomach, little flutterings of fear in the throat when they asked Miss Hunt a question. She was clothed in splendor; she was the white center of the flame. She burned so brightly they felt radiant inside and out—and in fact, each time she spoke to them in her husky voice, they both went beet-red.

Just as Lynn was doing now. "You mean, actually go to her *house?*" she said, with this funny little croaking sound.

"Sure."

"But we don't know where she lives."

"I do. I looked it up." And she smiled at Lynn in triumph.

"In the phone book?"

"Yes, silly. Come on. We can drop them off on the way home. She lives only three blocks from the school over on Ardmore."

They picked in silence for a while. The daffodils were still wet from the dew, cool and smooth to the touch, like touching the inside of your own lips. The stalks made a nice crunching noise when they snapped, she can hear it now, clear over his snoring and the traffic noises outside, and she watches how Lynn worked in careful circles around the flattened place in the grass where she'd been lying, but she herself struck out in all directions, zigzagging up and down the hill. And how they made that big pile, a huge pile with the blossoms all facing one way, up the hill. The pile kept growing larger; they must have had at least a hundred daffodils, two hundred?

Lynn finally stopped. She pushed her hair out of her eyes. "Isn't that enough?" she asked. But what she was really saying was "That *is* enough," in the firm tone she used—her grown-up voice was the way Clare thought of it—the voice she used mainly to boss her younger brothers when they got to acting like brats. Which was most of the time, Clare had to admit.

She nodded at Lynn, picked three more stalks. Her fingers were sore, and the sun felt hot on the back of her neck, the backs of her legs. She held the flowers straight out in front of her. They were so gorgeous. They smelled fresh and faintly sweet, and then she noticed how the silky hairs on her forearm gleamed gold in the sunlight, her arm, *her* arm, and for a moment, a brief moment all trembling and gold at the same time, she thought to herself, "I am alive, I am someone. Here, right here. This is *me*," and she wanted to tell Lynn this amazing thing and yet she didn't, she couldn't, it was too big a secret and too silly, and she didn't have the words to say it aloud, but she knew it was important, it had to do with these daffodils and this love she felt inside her hot as sunshine, this moment of discovery that by loving someone else she had found out...what?...what was it? It was already slipping away from her, but she would get back to it later, get back to this moment of the sun burning hot on her skin in the stillness of a spring morning, and Lynn saying in a slightly cross voice, "Let's get out of here, Clare."

So she placed the last three stalks on the top of the pile, placed them gently so as not to crush the fragile long throats which made her think of Miss Hunt's long neck, the skin the color of palest ochre...

"That's pronounced *oaker*, girls. Spelled *o-c-h-r-e*," Miss Hunt had told them. "Light playing on skin tones, gives it a yellowish value, not boring pink. Use your eyes!"

She was their art teacher, and she taught them folk dancing as well. She rushed around the school, looking grim, preoccupied. She mocked their work in the studio. She made fun of their neatness. "Don't be so cautious!" she kept scolding. "Be bold. Paint how it feels to you, not just how it looks. Don't copy everything. Experiment, let yourselves go."

Clare had hated her back in fifth grade. But this year when she was in Studio Class, Miss Hunt sometimes would stop in front of Clare's easel, cock her head. "Ahh," *ye...ess*" she'd say in a low voice, drawing the *yes* out so that it sounded almost like two or three words, not just one, then she'd drift on with quick light steps to the next easel.

It was lovely how Miss Hunt walked, a floating sort of walk, a skimming movement that water spiders have as they stalk among the lily pads, the water trembling with the faintest single ripple. And indeed, much as Clare would rather have seen her as a thoroughbred, there was a spidery look to Miss Hunt's body, the long narrow waist, pale white arms, big head on that wobbly neck, those popping blue eyes that stared into Clare's so fiercely that Clare always had to glance away in the end, glance back at the easel, seeing the painting now as Miss Hunt saw it, colors muddy, composition all lopsided, and the careful drawing beneath the paint not beautiful at all but simply a lifeless copy. The worse an artist she knew herself to be, the more Miss Hunt murmured that long delicious "Ye...ess," each time she paused at Clare's side.

Once—it was a month ago—she had put her bony hand on Clare's shoulder while she lectured on and on about tonal values and freer brushwork. Clare tried not to let her shoulder muscle quiver beneath the light pressure of that hand. Instead, she stared straight ahead to where Lynn was standing over by the stone sink, washing out paint jars, and smiling right back at Clare, the mirrored shadow smile of the best friend who has guessed the secret and wants to be included.

That had been the best part, when Lynn guessed. That...and picking the daffodils. Clare smiles again, up at the ceiling.

His arm is heavy across her chest. She tries to edge away, but the arm presses down, and he moans in his sleep. She stares hard, sees them gathering up the bunches of flowers, cross back down over the creek. But then what? There's only a blank space, she can't remember anything more until Lynn was pressing the buzzer. And they looked at each other. Lynn's gray eyes were shining. Her shorts were all stained green in places, and both of them had grubby knees, muddy sneakers—then the door opened.

What had she said? She'd stood there in the doorway, Miss Hunt, wearing a white bathrobe, chenille like a bedspread, not gypsyish at all but more what someone's mother would wear, and her face was puffy with sleep.

She smiled down at them, blue eyes bulging big as usual. And then she glanced down at the daffodils bunched in their arms, and her smile changed from surprise to something different, something between laughing and crying, although Clare couldn't see what in the world there was to cry about.

They held the flowers out to her.

"For me?" she asked, and gathered the bouquets in close to her chest. She looked first at Lynn, then Clare. Her mouth was pressed in a still straight line now, very serious. And Clare could almost feel the quivering of that thin bottom lip, the embarrassing blood pounding through the web of veins that pulsed in ugly knots along the temples of Miss Hunt's head which now dipped forward as she nuzzled the daffodils, and they could plainly see a row of gray hairs all along the center part of her head, a spiky trail of gray against the jet black.

"We have to go now," Clare said fast just as Miss Hunt was asking, "But won't you come in?"

And they had turned and run down the porch steps while she called after them, but they couldn't hear her.

They didn't say a word until they got around the corner. Finally Clare whispered, looking back over her shoulder, half hoping Miss Hunt might be running after them so they could out-gallop her, "She almost cried, you know."

"She **dyes** her hair," was all Lynn said.

And the next week Lynn made her call up Adam Phelps, the tall boy who always waited by the stone steps after school, talking easily to Lynn but looking all the time at Clare with the slightly crusted eyes of a sick spaniel. Fickle, God how fickle they'd been, the two of them, a couple of bored hummingbirds skimming from one person to the next.

Miss Hunt faded back into just another teacher, scurrying around the studio, scowling at their pictures, in the afternoons showing them how to weave the Maypole ribbons into a brightly colored braid, up...and over... and down, backwards and forwards. A braided pattern of yellow and green ribbons that formed and reformed around the circle of sixth graders in their white dresses and pale yellow sashes, faces so solemn, feet slipping on the slick grass of the hockey field, a garland of dancers quite as beautiful in memory, now, as any wilted bouquet of daffodils.

And yet it's the daffodils she remembers. How it felt to be raw in love. To reach out and touch the swell of the corona, a candled yellow-white, flaring like a trumpet from the six drooping lobes of the petals. What it was to breathe deep into the mouth of the flower where the pistil rises on its slender filament, towering above the stamens that flank it in a circle. The stamens form a tight cluster around the filament in the same way sturdy sentinels must stand guard around a secret tower, but the secret should be left unspoken, the shame lies in the reality.

Her left leg's got a cramp in it, calf muscles bunched and tight. She tries to lift up his arm so she can roll over on her stomach. But his hand cups her breast, and he shifts his head deeper into the hollow of her neck. Automatically, she shifts with him.

He murmurs something. She listens.

But it's only gibberish. She looks over at the wallpaper again. In the slow pulse of the neon light, the wall almost seems to be breathing. **Ta**-dum/ **ta**-dum...someone-someone's gone to sea/silver buckles on his knee.

She stops, squints into the darkness. Yes...silver buckles on his knee/he'll come back and marry me...

Pretty Bobby Shaftoe.

FREE FALL

WHY IT WAS SHE happened to be sitting alone at that particular moment she could not afterwards remember, and the reason hardly mattered except that if the others had still been with her she would not have been looking straight ahead, gazing idly down the long aisle of the ferry cabin, wishing she had a seat next to the ocean instead of being wedged here on one side by the children's sweaters, *Mom, it's summer!* piled on top of Harry's briefcase, *Guess I better look over those actuarial tables,* and on the other side by the uncomfortable solidity of the bulkhead which partitioned the passenger cabin from the tiered vault where cars waited to disembark down the gangway to the island still two hours away, and she glanced at her wristwatch again, impatient for the end of this journey, this tiresome preliminary to a month of freedom then realized in the same way a wild creature will freeze by the water's edge that she was being scrutinized, but whether from behind or by someone across the aisle she couldn't determine; and she thought ruefully how civilization has dulled our basic survival skills, the primitive instinct for fight or flight still functioning but those fine discriminations we need to help pinpoint the precise source of danger, blurred if not atrophied by our millennia-long ascent from coral cave to condominium. We lie exposed.

She sat very still.

She could feel the ship engines throbbing below deck. They matched the throbbing in her eardrums, the surge of blood pounding up from her throat, leaving a hot stain across her cheekbones.

Where were the children? She wanted to get away. She wanted to spring from her seat and go find them. Warn them not to get too near the deck railings. Or go find Harry. He understood how she felt about the perimeter of things.

"Don't get too close to the edge!" she was always saying. The edge of the sidewalk. Or steep staircases. Or the water. Ocean, pool—it didn't matter which. Boundaries were necessary.

Timid as she was about herself, she was even more so with the children. They felt like floating extensions of her own body, projecting wildly in all directions, constantly testing the limits both geographical and parental while she hovered and dithered and shrank as they hurled themselves forward. She, Nell Warren, that girl who once flung herself along seaside cliffs in exactly the same joyful way her kids did now.

That same Nell who crouched so long ago on the narrow ledge of the railroad trestle and waited for the 4:17 to roar beneath her and for the hot steam to curl upward and kiss her face. Who braced her hands against the cold steel bar while the roller coaster teetered at the very top, poised on the perfect vertex of ascent and descent, then tipped ever so gently forward in a free fall through screaming space while down below the toy buildings of the amusement park flew upward with an acceleration of speed and size terrifying to watch, swelling bigger and bigger and rocketing towards her in a collision course so certain, so inevitable, that in the end each time she covered her eyes to shut out the moment of impact.

With a shudder, she sat up straight on the hard wooden bench, orienting herself by the reassuring thrum of sober machinery grinding away beneath her, and to her right, by the slow swell of the gray ocean, lifting and falling beyond the porthole splashed with spray.

What made her turn her head to examine that empty seat across the aisle? She couldn't explain it. The act was involuntary as if an invisible bridle controlled her range of motion. Indeed, she felt guided to the right by a series of firm tugs so that even in the act of glancing sideways, she was puzzled by this unwilled movement when what she really wanted to do was to hold still—not move at all, not turn her head sharply to look backward, past the rows of seats to the EXIT sign at the far end of the cabin, then up the aisle again, one seat at a time, slowly scanning the faces one by one until finally she found those eyes that had been staring so long at the back of her head that she was sure her neck must be branded the same fiery red as her cheek had to appear to him now that he could see her face. And she was staring directly into his eyes, a reckless stare, remembering too late the complex hazards of glancing back.

His forehead was too big. It spoke of intelligence and pain.

Swollen was how she'd thought of it that first time she ever saw him watching her at a dance long forgotten except for that initial glimpse and those few words they'd spoken when introduced:

"Nell, as in *Wait Till the Sun Shines, Nellie?*"

And she had said, "Gus? As in Augustus Caesar, to match that imperial brow, I suppose."

And then she had danced away from him, spinning out of reach as quickly as the circumstances of their brief meeting were erased. Try as she might later on, she was never able to remember where the dance had been held, or who had been with him, those precise details of place and time obscured like a window streaked by the rain. But not his forehead. That she had not forgotten. Not the painful swelling of the temples, the skin pulled so tight it had the shiny look of new scar tissue.

No, that image had been seared into her memory even though his name itself got misplaced, shuffled, discarded, and lost in the course of a protracted love affair which brought her no joy. Only a glittering diamond. She wore it for five months, then returned it, conscious only of relief and a brimming gratitude to her father who traveled down by train to speak on behalf of the whole family, telling her shyly that a broken engagement was far less damaging than a loveless marriage—advice so totally unexpected from this mildest of men that she listened and was empowered by his stumbling words to break free of a relationship she found to be more constricting than the ring cutting deep into her flesh. When the ring came off, her finger throbbed. She wasn't sure which pain hurt most—the constriction of wearing it, or afterwards, when the blood was finally permitted to move freely. Moving free. That's what she had chosen. A whole glorious year of it. She moved from man to man. The best part was when she would call it quits. Something about the comical change in their expressions—the shock instantly replaced by anger—something in this pleased her although the pleasure was one she could take no pride in.

She knew she ought to feel guilty, or at the very least some vestigial form of compunction. Instead she was buoyed along by a kind of joy, skimming close to the surface of danger but seldom touching it.

Or touching it but then withdrawing so fast that the ripples had stopped in the time it took to glance backward, the water quite sealed over and glassy smooth. Names, faces—they sank and were gone. All she knew in the mornings was that she was still free to do and love as she pleased. Knew as well that quick jab of peculiar happiness which came from breaking the rules and conquering the impulse which in the past had required she always put herself second, the other person first. Always careful of others—careless of self—these divergent pulls were now brought into tandem, and crippled no longer by scruples she flew fast along a shoreline littered with the fragile skeletons of the timid and the conscientious. Until she saw him once again. Discretion, other loyalties, she had moved beyond them by then. What she wanted, she took.

She saw him many places, always with the same blonde.

At a concert.

At the university library.

Working out at the gym.

He was never alone. And then finally one night at a big party given by one of his medical school classmates. He was again with that irritating woman, shrill, blonde, and proprietary. But Nell never looked once in their direction the whole evening long until she spoke to him in the pantry where he had gone for more ice and she had gone to find him, to stand in front of him, smiling and saying lightly, "You won't remember, but we met four years ago."

And he had put his hand to his forehead, rubbed it slowly, and in the short silence before he spoke, she had known that particular gesture was not accidental but linked to her earlier joke about his Augustan brow, so she looked full into his face with the calm assurance that he had not forgotten hers. Then he had answered, "You're Nell Warren and you've been dodging me all night."

She had waited a moment, watching him, memorizing the texture of the pale skin, the unexpected fullness of that grave bottom lip. Then she had said with a shrug, "I'm not exactly used to tracking people down."

"No," he said. "I imagine you're not. Never the hunter, always the quarry, correct?"

"Something like that."

"And no longer engaged, someone told me."

"It wasn't…." She stopped, stared down into her wineglass. Had she drunk too much? She felt dizzy. But not from the wine. No, it was him. She was disconcerted by his directness, unsure of her ground now where she had been so sure just a second ago. She held the glass up against her cheek to feel its coolness, then whispered, "It didn't work out." Even now, on the ferry, she can still hear his answer:

"You broke it off is what I heard."

"Yes."

"Not ready?"

"Yes again."

"We seem…" he was picking his words carefully, "…to have this small problem with timing, you and I."

"We do?"

"Over there." He looked past her. Out in the dining room, the voices rose and fell with the pulsating shrillness of seabirds feasting at the water's edge. And then he was staring back at her again. "She," he said, cocking his head toward the voices, "she thinks we're headed toward something permanent."

"Oh? And you, what do you think?" Had she really asked him that, in that way?

"Me? Good God, I don't know. I mean, I'm not sure. Third year of med school, it would be rough. On both of us. Plus I haven't got a dime, although she says her salary will carry us through, no problem there." And at that point, he had smiled at her, a quizzical smile, teasing her, daring her to go on.

"An excellent rationale for marriage." The words slipped out of her mouth automatically, as if they had known each other for years, not minutes, but still the contempt in her own voice, the hard edge surprised her.

"Point taken," he was saying. "I'm not proud of it. But these last couple of years I've been drifting, you might say." He paused, then added, "Emotionally, you understand. Not professionally."

"Not any longer," she told him. She glanced up so he could read in her eyes this secret they shared. The secret that danced before him. She watched him study her. He was trying to understand, she could tell, what manner of person she was, and the reasons for this complicity of looks and words that passed between them, had in fact passed from the very beginning and made of two strangers, intimates.

It puzzled him. It gnawed at him. Months later he referred to it explicitly. "Not intimates," he said. "Collaborators." But not a collaboration he understood. He looked unhappy, fine-drawn, his eyes dark and troubled. "Nell," he said, "I'm afraid."

A flutter of guilt passed through her. The fluttering started deep in her diaphragm. For a minute she couldn't speak. She noted the guilt with a sense of relief, with the sense she was safely grounded again. To look at him and see the fear, to listen to his questions, spoken and unspoken, and want to answer them honestly, kindly—there was a solid comfort here. The comfort of no longer being airborne. Although when she was with him, each time she looked at him, he made her lightheaded, made her lurch inside, staggered by what she felt for him. Yesterday, tomorrow, they didn't exist any longer. Only the present. Only him sitting across from her, frowning. He worried about things that didn't matter, he was frightened of things that didn't even make sense. Afraid? What was there to be afraid of?

She tried to explain this to him. She tried to couch the explanation in a way that would make him feel secure. She told him then how she'd schemed to meet him again, to be at places they were bound to run into each other. To make him fall in love with her. But not by running away as she had done for too long, but by turning and seeking him out, face to face.

"...that was the secret," she concluded. He was smiling. She must have touched him at some level. But something still troubled him, shadowing his eyes despite the smile. Some doubt which still distanced him from her, which in a disturbing way appeared to haunt him.

So she tried again to meet him halfway, adding, "And the fact is you knew it too. Right from the start. At the dance, remember?"

"I remember all right."

"*So,* doesn't that explain it? What you call this collaboration, not a word I like particularly. Empathy's better. Empathy of spirit."

He was leaning forward, almost eagerly, as if she were handing him a gift. Which she was, in a sense. She was providing him with the key to what had passed between them.

But now he frowned. "Empathy of spirit? You're playing word games, Nell. Say it in plain English, you're the English teacher."

"Then listen to me. We knew, we both knew from the very beginning what was going on. Not the possibility, the *certainty.* You understand? But not for then. For later...later...we *knew* it."

He got up, brushing past her with impatience. He stood with his back to her, looking out the window at the rain. He spoke in a voice that might have held a note of mockery, she couldn't be sure.

"Later? Sure, later, you were engaged to what's-his-name. You weren't even..."

"...even available?" She had finished it for him. "So? Neither were you three months ago. I mean what difference does that make? It wasn't the others that held us back. It was...oh...the potential of the thing. Like, you know, like something held in reserve. That had to happen at a different point in our lives." She stopped. "Look," she told him, "would you please turn around? I can't keep on talking to your back."

And he had turned around. He had come over and she can still see him sitting down beside her on the green couch, very close as if in apology. And he had said to her, "All just words, Nell. Beautiful talk. But what does it mean?"

"It means I don't like your saying we're collaborators—I mean we're doing nothing wrong, Gus."

"Ok, ok, big deal, so I'm out of line."

"All I'm trying to say is...you know...why can't you think of us as allies? Working towards something *together.* Like collaborators on a book."

"Yeah, you're right, I don't know what's bothering me." He had shifted his legs. His movement had triggered her own, like watching someone yawn. She stretched her legs as well.

Then she said, "Stop gnawing at it. You'll understand all this sometime, I know you will. We both will, you'll see." She was laughing, she remembered that distinctly. But then she had touched his temple, so fragile and round it reminded her both then and now of an egg, what was called a "starter" egg made of glistening porcelain, lying just beneath the shiny envelope of skin. "Does this hurt?" she whispered.

"No. Does this?" And he had kissed her so hard there was only one breath between them, shared textures of mouth, skin, and tongue.

The taste of him, that much she never forgot. The rest was all hazy, a soft golden blur. As if their whole relationship could be sifted down to a few gritty scenes. The first meeting. That rainy night they had argued about the collaborator issue. And that last night of all when he announced he was quitting medical school.

"My life's coming apart," he told her. But he was smiling so broadly, it took her a minute to separate his words from his expression. "You're all I've got right now, Nellie."

"That's not so," she said quickly. She reminded him he was doing well, he loved medicine—his brother a surgeon, his father a cardiologist.

"Precisely. Following in their footsteps, it's pathetic."

"It's not!"

He got up and began pacing back and forth across the room, his chin buried in his chest. And she could picture him so clearly gesturing in a toga, she could see him as Napoleon rallying his soldiers limping in the snow. He was talking very calmly about how his whole life had been pre-programmed. He didn't know what he wanted to do. Or who he really was, what he wanted from the future. Maybe he should go be a beachcomber, maybe go sign up for a hitch with the Airborne, surely he'd qualify as paratrooper medic.

"Why are you telling me this?" she said quietly when he finally fell silent. He was staring angrily down at his shoes as if they were to blame for pointing him in the wrong direction, this bizarre road he wanted to follow.

He raised his eyes, and then he said very simply with only the ghost of his earlier smile, "So you'll talk me out of it."

"NO!" she cried. "That's not fair."

"Nell, listen, I can't think straight anymore. It's true. We're on clinical rotation this month, and today I walked into the ward, and I'm standing there, gawking at a routine IV procedure. I couldn't remember how to set it up, so the chief resident—"

"Gus," she interrupted, laying her hand over his. "You're overtired is all. You—".

"Listen to me, will you? Watch my lips," and he had moved his mouth like a fish gulping for air, and she had wanted to slap him then and there.

"I am listening to you, Gus, you're obviously exhausted, ok? Maybe even mildly depressed, you need to—".

"What I *need* is no more amateur psychologizing. What I need is you, Nell. Which come to think of it is fairly dumb. You're the one that sees me as unhappy, all this pain business you've been feeding me since day one. Depressed? Listen, I didn't know what the word meant until I ran into you. You live in a fucking fairy tale, Nellie, you made me part of it."

She had gotten angry then. Scared as well. She didn't even want to look at him, to meet his eyes, to see the pain, the real pain, that showed on his face. He looked deformed. Ugly, he looked ugly. He looked the way she felt inside, and so she told him, "It's your decision. Go ahead, go be a nothing."

"I'm hurting here, Nell, really hurting. Is that really all you can say? Face you with something real for a change and you run screaming into the night?"

"That's not fair, you're twisting everything, I haven't gone anywhere."

"But you will. You'll go find yourself another pretty toy to play with. The safe kind, guaranteed not to break. Or fall off the shelf."

"Why are you blaming me? What have I done?"

"Nothing," he said wearily. "That's precisely the point. I should have known. I did know...at some level."

"Some soldier you'd make, you're weak, I need someone strong, somebody I can lean on." An expression had come over his face then that had made her stop, her words dangling in mid-sentence, hovering on the edge of a high place she was too frightened to look over. The infection had begun, right there.

And then into the silence that followed, he had observed with a sleepy smile, "After the mating, the meal. Correct? Then she eats him, the black widow, not so?"

"What *are* you talking about?"

"I'm talking about what's-his-name. The fiancé. And all the others."

"Damn you," she said to him. "What's that got to do with this?"

"Everything and nothing." He reached up and rubbed his eyelids so hard she wanted to snatch at his fingers. "Damn me is right," he agreed. His voice sounded muffled. She wondered if he were crying, he *was* crying, she had never seen a man cry, she wanted to jump up and run home, lie down on her own narrow bed, lie flat on the mattress where nothing swooped and swerved the way being with him had from the first.

Grounded, yes. He had grounded her all right. But too close to where the waves broke, the water a cold icy band circling her ankles, and all she could see as she was sucked down was not the ocean, only spray.

The spray. It splashed like teardrops against the porthole above his head still sharply turned in her direction. A foghorn sounded, moaning over the thrum of the ferry engines.

She jerked her head, her neck was stiff, she must look away now, it was time. It was time and it was the only kindness left that she might render him.

She was blushing again. But now it didn't matter, he couldn't see her face any longer, she was staring straight ahead. Why had she looked back? From this minute on he would always be this unremarkable balding man with a lumpy forehead and the accusing stare of the betrayed conspirator.

A stare that made her flinch like a thief.

After all, wasn't that the message he'd been sending her, their glances meeting with the pure sharp ring of crystal touching crystal while she read in his eyes a toast to this ending she had led him to from the beginning.

A toast to their mutual fragility.

Today, he robbed her of the past.

Back then, she robbed him of the future. She never suspected what he had known instinctively. And had tried to tell her, to warn her that time like gravity has its own laws, immutable, inescapable. And that the present is like some great barrier reef sunk deep in yesterday—its pale coral branches a ghost forest growing up out of limestone skeletons so far down no drill can reach the bedrock that anchors them.

Down under

In the winter the southeast trade winds blow the swells north towards Queensland, and the beaches are almost deserted. The waves break evenly, rising and falling in long curving arcs along the shoreline—fifteen miles of open beach from south of Brunswick Heads clear down to Byron Bay.

"Too bloody cold to swim in August, mates," (except he pronounced it *mites*), the shopkeeper told them. Then with a cocky smile, soft eyes amused at Dru's alarm, Simon's quick frown, the man added, "But you Yanks don't seem to mind. Goo'dye to you then. And mind the rip tides out past the point."

So, all week long she and Simon went body-surfing. Riding those waves was like sliding down rolled satin. She couldn't seem to get enough of it, flu or no flu. Neither of them could. Only two days left now...then goodbye, Byron Bay.

The hot sun baked the nape of her neck and the tender spot along the tips of her shoulders. But the rest of her felt numb—the submerged half—those wavering pale appendages which gleamed beneath the surface at a double remove, bisected by the water's refraction so that above, she was still a woman, while below she'd become a fish...a dolphin...a brown seal.

A stranger from the waist down; on fire above, burning like dry ice.

They had been in the ocean most of the morning. Three hours? She was long past feeling that first dull ache in the groin when the cold water lapped up over her thighs. Or the pain of bunched muscles coiled up hard along her calves and shoulders, the almost sweet sickness in the small of her back.

Sunlight quivered on water the color of rippled turquoise. Everywhere she looked, the tiny prisms of light danced in the spray—iridescent, shimmering so bright they made her squint. When she shut her eyes, the rainbow arcs of pure light burned red and orange against her eyelids.

She stood beside Simon in the deep water, waiting for the next set of rollers. The waves came in families, five or six beauties in a row, then a long pause in between—sometimes as long as five minutes—as if the sea rested, catching its breath before the next foaling.

Simon nudged her. The skin on her forearm burned so hot, she noted with surprise the stippling of goose bumps. "Out there," he said. He jerked his chin.

They watched the horizon, waiting for the next group, studying each swell for size and speed and conformation so they could make the split-second decision: catch it? or let it go.

"**Here** comes one!" she yelled.

He shook his head. "Nope, too small."

"Oh, honey, this one's perfect!" They both surged forward to meet it, turning sideways trying to judge the pull of the current against their legs, but the wave easily outran them.

"Whoops," he laughed. "Too late."

"Here's one," she said. "Take it!"

"You too, " he called, getting ready, spreading his arms in a wide embrace, welcoming the wave.

"Too big," she told him, but now he couldn't hear her.

"EEE HAW!" he yelled, plunged, and was gone.

Then a smaller wave, three feet high, more sedate, more her speed, came billowing towards her.

"Wait!" she told it and began paddling fast to gain speed before it passed her by. The wave was swelling beneath her. She stroked fast, keeping slightly ahead of the roll. Faster, faster, yes...and now she took a deep breath, poised her body taut as a bowstring, yes! and then she became the arrow twanging free, shooting down the long roaring slide, planing across and over and down the broad hump, over the edge and down the face of the wave rolling down down suspended for a second in mid-air as she fell, a ripple of fear flashing by as fast as her own white body falling—too big? misjudged the drop?— and then the answering comfort of the glassy green tunnel, the silken chute skimming her along at a million miles an hour, cradling her forward and home to foamy water while the sandy bottom reached up and scraped her hands, her elbows, and she was beached again.

Beside her, Simon raised his head. He shouted something. But the pounding of the surf was too loud in her eardrums. She nodded, let her body be tossed by the churning backwater. She flipped over on her back, wind-milling her arms to keep afloat. For about the third time in an hour, the straps on her suit slipped off her shoulders. The top floated down around her waist. She lay there letting the foam kiss her nipples. The suit ballooned up, the bra cups engorged with water.

Laughing, she closed her eyes as another wavelet from the backwash flooded over her face, lifted her gently and began pulling her out to sea. She went limp. Take me. Take me.

"Take it off!" Simon was crouching beside her. He wasn't grinning any more, he wanted to be part of this whole thing, he didn't want her to experience it alone. Each time they went bodysurfing he seemed to forget that ultimately riding the waves was a solitary act. He's jealous, she thought happily, and smiled up at him.

He braced one hand under her back; the other cupped her breast. The nipple was hard as a rivet. "What if someone comes?" she said.

Now he was smiling, his special fooling-around leer she loved. "They should be so lucky," he said. He began pulling the suit down her thighs, and off.

"Simon," she murmured. But he just laughed again. He got up and splashed back up to shore where they had spread their towels. He waved the red bathing suit like a scarlet banner over his head.

She rolled back on her belly, put her face down into the water. Intermission time. The water was so transparent she could see the scalloped white sand as clearly as if she wore a diving mask. She tip-toed her fingers along the scalloped ridges. The sand was packed hard and firm, had to be the whitest finest sand in the whole world, no question. Under her fingertips the delicate ridges rose and fell, miniature mountain ranges darkening as her body came between them and the sun. The current went still for a minute then sucked towards a new wave. She looked around. Simon was coming back in. He sloshed through the surf, grinning like an ape. She jackknifed into the next wave, started swimming fast out to the big rollers, alternating the crawl with dolphin flips beneath the surface, savoring the sound of her arms slapping against the water in clear hard strokes cut short as Simon caught her by the wrist. "Gotcha!" he said.

She twisted and rolled over on her back. He dragged her along by both arms, tugboating her out to the deep place beyond the breakers. The water felt so smooth against her skin, swirling between her thighs, washing over her belly, pooling between her breasts. Lovely liquid caresses; she shut her eyes against the burning glare of the sun. Even shut, her eyes stung.

"Ride's over," he said. He let go of her arms.

"Never want to wear a bathing suit again," she said. She kept on floating, locked her legs against his middle. He was looking back to shore. "Take off yours," she told him.

He slid his hand along the inside of her thighs, then stopped. "Hell," he said, "some dame just came down with her kids. Looks like what's-her-name you were talking with yesterday."

"Vanessa."

"Well, Vanessa's just plunked herself down beside our towels. And the kids are headed for the water. Terrific." He glanced down, smiling, brown eyes so much bigger without his glasses. Or was it that the lenses distorted their depth? At night in the moonlight when he lay sleeping, the eyes were sunk so deep he might as well have been a stranger or the carved effigy of a medieval saint. It made her nervous. She would trace a smile around his lips with her finger. Instantly the stone became flesh, and he was Simon again. "Fun's over," she said.

"For now, anyways. Come on. We're missing some beauties." He unwound her legs, pulled her upright. She slid in close, touching his cold skin.

"I can't ride in like this," she told him. "What about my suit?"

They stood swaying together in the water. He put one marble foot over hers. She slid her hand inside his trunks. "Jesus," he sighed.

"I'll have to stay out here till she leaves."

"Aussies swim naked all the time. Remember those two chicks down by the point yesterday?"

"I remember all right," she said dryly.

"Well?"

"Ok, I'll ride a couple more. But then you bring my suit before we get out for good. I'm sure not chatting up Vanessa bollicky naked."

He nuzzled her neck. "What salty ears you got, grandma."

They rode in three more big ones, then Simon retrieved her suit and they finally came out of the ocean. At the water's edge, Vanessa's children were building a magnificent sandcastle with turrets and crenellated battlements. The boy, the one with the limp, wouldn't look as they walked by. But the girl gave a shy smile. "Super castle," Simon told her. She ducked her small dark head, and murmured, "Thank you."

The sand crunched hot and dry underfoot. Vanessa glanced up from her book and greeted them. Her hair was curly, dark like her daughter's but she wore it drawn back from her face in a complex chignon. She wore no makeup, not even lipstick; her fine skin was very pale.

"You two must be bloody exhausted," she laughed, taking off her dark glasses. Her eyes were gray, a beautiful clear gray with long, oddly pale lashes.

"Only when we get out of the water," Dru told her.

Vanessa shaded her eyes, looking up at them. Dru moved a bit to block that pale face from the sun. "Weren't you freezing out there?" Vanessa asked.

Simon chuckled. "We're from New England. That's the warmest water we've ever set foot in, it's all relative you see." He flopped down on the towel. "I'm bushed. What time is it?"

"Almost noon," said Vanessa. "What time did you go in? Dawn?"

Dru giggled. "Quarter to nine," she answered, and lay down flat on her stomach, letting the sun cook sore muscles, cook the damn flu right out of her.

"Remarkable," observed Vanessa and took up her book again.

Sun. Hot sand. The sound of the surf booming. "Boomers" is what the Aussies called the big waves. Booming like a giant clock all up and down the long sweep of beach, tolling in the tides. After a while, Simon got up and said he was going back to the room, "Have a little lie-down, think with my eyes shut."

Vanessa watched him head back up the dunes. "First morning you chaps were surfing, my son said straight off you were Americans."

Dru sat up. "How on earth did he know that?"

"I dare say because only Yanks go swimming in August. But then too, the way you look, the way you act together."

Dru studied her feet; the tops were getting pinker. She scrunched the toes under the sand, digging deep. "Very observant, your son," she said.

"He's a good kid, Robbie is," said Vanessa, proud, unequivocal about her pride.

"The limp, Vanessa. Did he break his leg?"

Vanessa watched the children playing tag with the little waves. The boy ran fast, the gimpy leg extended forward stiffly, compensating with a quick hop on the good leg, moving with a kind of erratic grace. "Actually," she answered, "actually his hip was smashed. When he was just a tyke. A lorry smashed into the car."

"Oh God."

"My husband was killed instantly."

"Oh, Vanessa." There was a short silence. Then Vanessa smiled, her lips in a controlled thin line. "It was awful. The first year was the worst. But he jolly well taught me to be a survivor, Robert did. He was English, you see. I met him at university in London. Then he came back to Sydney. He was in the rag trade, sports clothes." She stopped, lit a cigarette, her hand shaking only a little. "Care for a smoke?" she asked Dru.

They sat there smoking, looking out to sea. After a bit, Vanessa continued. "He took care of me, my Robert. Left me a beautiful home in Paddington. Heaps of money." She pulled hard on the cigarette. "So, I can afford to kick up my heels. Travel a bit with the kiddies. Back to England. To the continent. He left me free to come and go as I please." She glanced at Dru, gray eyes mischievous. "So you see, I'm that rare bird in Australia. An independent woman."

Dru stubbed her cigarette into the sand then covered the butt quickly. "But what about the feminists, the women's movement?"

Vanessa hooted. "I don't want to disillusion you, but your average Australian bloke ranks feminists one notch below the Abos."

"Abos?"

"The Aborigines."

"But the people we've met, I mean in Sydney, they seem so with it. So modern."

Vanessa studied her, then shook her head slowly. "Listen, Dru, we're at least fifty, sixty years behind the times here. And the sods are not about to—"

"Mummy! Mummy!" The children came running up, chattering, begging for lunch.

Dru stood up, yawned. "Simon's got the right idea. Time for a nap." She rolled up her towel, grabbed the beach bag, smiled at the kids wolfing what they called their "tucker."

"My flat at seven, then?" Vanessa said.

"Tie for Simon?"

Vanessa gave a casual wave. "Simon may go tieless. Ta."

And tieless he went. They both slept all afternoon. When Dru finally woke up her back throbbed, her head. She could feel the pulse racing fast in her throat.

Simon looked worried. "You shouldn't have gone surfing, not today, darling. You look feverish."

"Fiddlesticks," she said. "The ocean's the only place where I really feel good," and stared at herself in the mirror. Her cheeks were flame red, her body looked a healthy bronze against the white dress. The sun had bleached her hair with copper streaks. She looked anything but sick. A little wild-eyed maybe, but not sick. Unfair in a way.

Simon stood beside, staring at her mirrored face. "You look as if you just swam over from Tahiti," he told her.

"Don't I wish I had. This country. I don't know. Makes me feel so...oh, primitive or something. God, it hurts to talk. Shall we go?"

When Vanessa opened the door, Dru almost didn't recognize her. She looked like a professional actress, a film star expertly made up, the long lashes dark and lustrous now, eyebrows defined and arched, the full mouth glossy, painted a deep shade of coral. She was teetering in shiny high-heeled boots and wearing gaucho pants of brown velvet, an expensive vest over a yellow silk blouse. The sleeves billowed as she drew Simon and Dru inside.

Dru glanced around the room. The men were dressed simply, cotton sports shirts open at their tanned throats, jeans or chinos. But the women! Elaborately decked out plus they all seemed to have the same kind of hairdos, aureoles of curls fanning out in kinky circles around their narrow rouged faces. Lots of hand-tooled jewelry, silver mostly, swinging from their ears, clanking against their wrists as they gestured to each other with sharp birdlike movements that perfectly matched their chirruping voices.

Like a bloody aviary in here—Dru blinked. She could talk to the men with her eyes. But the women? They seemed scared of silence.

Someone murmured something at her elbow. "Pardon?" she croaked.

Two of the women were speaking to her, their heads cocked as they checked out her plain white dress. "You a chum of Nessa's?" the taller one was saying.

"Actually we just met. A week ago. On the beach."

The women glanced at each other. "Oh, our Nessa's a comber all right," the short one, a blonde, trilled.

"I beg your pardon?"

"A beachcomber. On the prowl, you might say. For something special," she added. And tittered.

The tall woman smiled. "Dear Nessa, we really adore her! But she's very much into doing her own thing, as you Americans put it."

"Lucky Nessa," said Dru, trying to edge away.

The blonde stepped closer, shaking tight curls. "Unlucky, actually. She needs a man to stand by her. A solid father-type to give those kids a real home."

Dru tried to smile. The women went on chattering: Vanessa. The barbecue at Ian's tonight. Were Dru and Simon going? Ever seen a rainforest? How long would she and Simon be in Byron Bay?

The noise in the room spiraled around her. It was hard to breathe. The room was so hot. Her neck throbbed. A cool hand touched her arm. Vanessa was handing her some white wine, drawing her toward the group of men by the window, introducing her to a dizzying circle of faces that smiled and nodded, mouths opened wide, gentle eyes smiling in lazy amusement.

Simon stood guard right beside her now, fielding their saucy questions, charming them all with his chitchat, his enthusiasm for Byron Bay.

"Speaking of fun, there should be loads tonight, at Ian's," said Nessa.

"Will you be joining us?" one of the men (nice gray eyes) was asking Simon.

"Well," Simon paused, and the man added, "Smashing parties Ian gives."

"Is it far?"

"Just twenty miles actually. Bit south of Murwillumbah," Vanessa chimed in. "Where you had dinner that first night, remember?"

"Oh yes," Dru said. The croak had faded to a whisper. "Losing my voice," she explained, smiling up at the gray-eyed man—men. Did everyone have gray eyes in this country? She and Simon had a nickname for the men. the *soft eyes* they called them.

Vanessa tucked her arm through Dru's. Everyone was talking fast, Simon was signalling with his eyebrows: want to go?

"Yes," she whispered again, and the group began surging towards the open door, the shrill laughter of the women floating out into the night.

Vanessa drove the way she dressed—flashy and fast—with great style. The caravan of cars followed behind them, a necklace of headlights gleaming at regular spaced intervals.

They were driving through virgin rainforest. The road snaked up and up, hairpin turns doubling back and around with sudden lurches.

The trees whipped by them, ghostly white in the headlights, pale branches arching over the road. Tangled vines twisted around the trunks. The smell of eucalyptus filled the car, sharp, medicinal. And another smell underneath—very sweet. Vanessa said they were wild orchids.

The rainforest seemed to press against the road as if it might swallow the car.

They veered sharply to the left, rounded a curve, and then the trees were gone. They had reached the top of the mountain. Open space. Open sky.

A couple of small outbuildings stood on the left, backlit by the flames of a huge barbecue pit. Perched above them on top of a steep rise was the main house. It was a low square structure. A full veranda ran around all four sides. They could hear rock music playing, lazy laughter. A couple of Japanese lanterns hung on stakes that were jammed into the rock garden, lit the steps leading up to the house.

Vanessa jumped out of the car and stretched. "Isn't this bloody marvelous?" she cried, and started running up the steps. "Mind you don't stumble," she called over her shoulder.

There were fifty-six steps in all, zigzagging back and forth. By the time they reached the last one, Dru felt as dizzy as she had back in the car. They were up so high! The Southern Cross shimmered in the unfamiliar sky. A bigger sky than back home—immense—a blue-black canopy which all of a sudden she wanted to dive into or was it soar up to?

But instead she was led inside, led into a very big oblong room built of mahogany logs. An enormous stone fireplace ran across one side of the room. The other three sides were mostly glass doors opening onto the veranda, except for one corner of floor-to-ceiling bookcases. A house to match the sky and the land. Bloody marvelous indeed.

More smiling faces, introductions, laughter. More wine, hands clapping her on the shoulder, Simon really relaxing now, telling dirty jokes, Vanessa reciting a mock bitter explanation for the second-class citizenship of Australian women.

"...all dates back to the convict settlements," she was saying. "Women could be bought then as wives. For seven years at a stretch." She glanced around at the sleepy smiles of the men, who grinned, chuckled, enjoying the show. The rest of the women had moved off to the fireplace. Occasionally one would look over at Vanessa, Dru and the men.

"But surely times have changed, Nessa," Simon interjected.

Vanessa smiled. "No," she replied evenly, her voice calm but something else rippling beneath. Anger? Contempt maybe. Or only wry amusement, Dru couldn't tell. "No, we're still quite rooted in the Victorian era," Vanessa went on. "Neither sex ever managed to recover from the originally stained arrangement struck at Botany Bay." She glanced across at the women by the fireplace. "The problem is, we serve the men gladly. We're afraid not to."

"Ah, Ness, luv." Their host, Ian Curley, golden-bearded, slim-hipped, put his arm around Vanessa's waist. "But you lasses serve such enchantment, how can we ever change? Don't be a wowser, dear. You'll frighten our new chums." He ran a finger intimately along her jaw and up across her lips. She smiled, cool, detached.

The men laughed. A few waved their beer cans high. Somebody whistled. Ian added, "Let's go tuck into those steaks, shall we? should be about ripe now."

People broke up into pairs, moving slowly towards the veranda. Ian looped his free arm around Dru's waist, his other still twined around Vanessa. Dru glanced back at Simon; Simon winked.

"Two beauties for the price of one. The royal prerogative of the host," said Ian, nuzzling them both. The soft brush of his golden beard tickled Dru's cheek.

Then for an instant, Dru heard an extraordinary laugh, braying and raucous, ringing loud and with total abandon. It sounded like somebody drunk, totally out of control. Scary. "What on earth?" she whispered.

"That, luv, is my kookaburra," said Ian proudly. "He's practically tame. Marvelous bird. Lives out in the bottlebrush tree."

"What a wild sound," Dru said.

Ian nodded. "Isn't it though. His name means laughing jackass. You can hear the bloke a half mile away. I say," he stopped, studied her face. "Would you like to feed him?"

Dru stared back. "Feed him? Feed him what?" Simon stood beside her again.

"Raw lamb steak. Adores raw meat, especially when fed to him by beautiful women. Right, Nessa?"

Vanessa threw a warning glance at Dru, then Simon. "He's quite tame. But he might peck you."

"Will it hurt?" asked Dru, and Simon murmured into her ear, "You don't have to do it, honey."

"Not if you keep quite still," said Ian. "Right then! Do come outside, Dru." And he drew her away from Simon. "Nessa, be a doll, would you," he said. "Go fetch my Polaroid from the bedroom. Must record this for the Yanks to show back home."

Smiling, he guided Dru past the sliding doors onto the wide veranda. Below she could see smoke rising from the barbecue. A couple of men stood by the grille, laughing, flipping steaks with long pointed forks. There must have been three whole lambs butchered for this meal; she'd never seen so much meat cooking at once.

"Here you are then. A big chunk." Ian handed her a piece of raw lamb, thick and bloody. "Now, mind you hold out your arm very straight. Don't move a muscle when he takes it, just stand still as a statue. I'll whistle him up," and he put two fingers to his mouth and blew a couple of loud blasts. The candle inside the Japanese lantern on the railing flickered.

She stood there. She held the meat gingerly between thumb and index finger. Gray puffs of smoke slithered up between the railings. The air smelled rich and strange—of roasting meat and charcoal, of eucalyptus and the damp mold from the rainforest below them, massed and dark.

She didn't dare look down again. She felt dizzy from the wine. She stared straight out in the black velvety night. She was totally alone. She must make herself hard, unyielding.

Hard, the way Simon got when he went off to work in the mornings, what he called his "go fight the tigers" mode, something so implacable about men and work. They shut down, shut off tenderness like shutting off a spigot, and what was eating Simon when she walked out here, his face darkening when she brushed past him? Jealous again? Of the attention from Ian? No, more like with the bodysurfing—jealous of a solitary experience he couldn't be a part of—men were so very strange. But he'd get over it quickly, he always did.

She waited. Her arm was getting tired, it felt heavy as stone, this was ridiculous, maybe the whole thing was a joke, a practical joke, maybe she should go back inside to Simon, and just as she started to turn away from the railing she heard a great beating of wings and the kookaburra flapped down to her hand and gripped her wrist, his black eyebrows a dark mask against the startling whiteness of his face.

One mad eye gleamed out at her as he cocked his head, snatched at the meat—missed and his sharp beak dug into the fleshy pad of her thumb like a knife cut, a swift deep pain—but she held steady and he pecked again and the meat disappeared and so did the kookaburra, grazing her hand with his talons as he flew away in a great flurry of flapping wings and an explosion of bright light.

People were clapping, Simon was frowning.

"Look, your thumb's bleeding," he said, but not gently, so curt the words sounded like an accusation. But she looked past him, ignoring him because now they were all cheering, the men's deep voices booming below the light splash of the women's. And Vanessa was tearing off the print from the camera and giving it to Simon, who shook his head, and stepped back, away from the circle.

Ian was smiling, his gray eyes brilliant in the light from the lantern. "Well done, lass," he told her. "You didn't flinch for a second. Most women yank their hands back when he swoops down at them."

Dru wanted to explain that the bird was as scared as she was, neither of them sure who was prey, who predator. But now her voice had gone completely. So she pantomimed: his talons grappling her wrist, their eyes both rolling in fright, the bird flying off into the darkness.

The circle of faces was glowing with laughter, laughing with her, not at her, she knew. And so she spread her arms wide to show how much she loved their cocky kindness, their challenging soft-eyes, and the wild gentleness of their ocean—their breakers that hadn't broken her. And yes, even their strange primitive bird who laughed like a woman cresting to climax, greedy and free, and clearly—for one splendid moment—gone quite mad.

CRANKED UP

READING PERIOD BEFORE FINALS—WE get the week off—so I'm thumbing home from the drug store. Or where the drug store used to be. They razed it since I was home last.

Nothing there but a bunch of dirt. The other stores teeter on the edge of the vacant lot. A new bank's going up soon, at least that's what the sign promises. The owner of the old drug store, Mr. Pritchard—he told me he was fixing to retire anyhow. "Along comes the bank," he winked, "makes me an offer I can't refuse."

If Mr. Pritchard's still in town, must be tough to drive by and see this big hole in the ground. I bet he's taken the money and run. Run to wherever retired pharmacists go. Which I sure—like—hope is warm, warmer than spring in New England. I mean around here not even the crocuses get their act together till May. My last semester, and then—see ya! I'm outta here.

Been walking into this bitchin' cold wind a good half hour. I mean I stood on the corner next to the bus depot wearing out the old thumb, but no dice. It's take-a-hike time, so I start down Route 27 past the state park, crossing over the interstate, through the woods skirting the new cemetery, the road finally narrowing down to the four-way intersection where the drug store stands.

Correction: Used to stand.

Just as I reach the traffic lights, a Z 28 red Camaro, smoked glass windows, gleaming alloy racing wheels, comes gliding up beside me. The dude's got the thing gunning full throttle. Guy leans over, opens the door.

"Where you headed, son?"

"Ten miles south of town, near the reservoir," I tell him.

The guy waves me in. He's got his sports shirt open the first three buttons, and the chest hair is gray and curly. He's wearing a gold link choker. It figures.

"No problemmo," he shouts over the music, and varoom! we shoot the yellow and it's a good thing the local black and white's not parked there in the driveway of the Greek church, hiding behind the big forsythia bush. They nab lots of speeders coming off the Interstate that way. Folks here in town know they're stashed there during rush hours, so everyone pretty much cools it along this stretch.

Not this dude. He's an old guy, maybe 45, 50-ish. Big shaggy head, lots of curly black hair, beefy face, big red hands—really massive. He's got one of those leather-covered steering wheels, the kind with bumps underneath to separate the fingers, help with the grip. Cool.

The bucket seats feel plush, covered in "Genuine Australian lamb's wool," he tells me. All very jazzy—in some circles. Take my kid brother, it would definitely—like—blow his mind. "Dynamite car," I say to the guy, just to be polite.

He nods. He's miles away. He's got Bruce cranking from the front and back stereos. His big hands—humongus class-ring, nails cut short, thick knuckles—beat against the steering wheel, taking turns, first, the heel of the right hand comes down real soft in time with the guitar chords. Then the left hand starts in. Now it jackhammers in tandem with the drums while the sax soars high and lonely around the rasp of the voice sawing away at the wound. A voice which you might say is both wound and the wound's bandage, the gauze real tender but adhesive pulling at the small hairs.

I speak loud enough to be heard over the stereo—thing must have run him couple of K at least. "Oh yeah, man. Just what I needed. Some Springsteen, excellent."

He glances over. Our eyes connect for the first time. And here comes a big smile splitting the face, eyes slit almost shut by overlapping wrinkles. My mom calls them laugh lines. "Not wrinkles, Brad!" she goes. "Cut me some slack, honey."

No kidding!" the guy's saying. "Everybody on the planet loves the Boss. Saw him last month, down in Providence. UN-be-liev-a-ble." He sing-songs the syllables, making it a word rich enough to carry the wonder, the magic of the thing, of the small figure standing out there on the giant stage, a tiny black silhouette kissing off despair, giving the finger to everything that's crumbling, rusting away to nothing while the voice soars *"No retreat, baby. No surrender."*

We swap stories about the Providence concert and the Centrum last winter. The big one in Saratoga last July, 34,000 standing there moaning "Bruuuuuuuce" as we waited in the mud. The rain had stopped a couple of minutes before Hank and the E Street Band came out on stage. The crowd swayed in the dark like this one giant organism—all of us fused together by the fire in the gut lit by that voice, by that burning hope of hanging in there no matter how much grief you gotta take or how often you may mess up and just want to walk away, walk into the room—shut the door.

"You make the Providence scene?" he's asking me now.

I laugh, shrug. "Came this close, this close, " I tell him. "Ad in the college rag for his Thursday night gig: 2 TICKETS, BEST OFFER? I call, ask what it would take to nail them. Guy tells me someone offered $130, "Make it 140," he goes, "you got yourself a deal." I figured he was lying, told him that was pretty steep, I'd check with my buddy, get back to him. So I get this chick to call with a pitch for a hundred. Guy say he's waiting for a call-back. That's me, see. I call, say I can't swing it, forget it. So then I give the chick the hundred bucks, she hotfoots it over to where the guy lives. No dice. Someone squeezes us out, offers 120 bucks. That close, that close." I shake my head, laughing again.

The man grins. "You missed a good one. Darn small place, you could really eyeball him. See the sweat flying."

We listen to the music. We're cruising past the center of town, past the conservation fields, approaching the old cemetery where all the patriots are buried—no room for yuppies, sorry, son. The guy fiddles with the volume control. Bruce is cranked up full decibel now, and suddenly the guy's reaching out fast towards the glove compartment, then jerks his hand back like he's stung or something. He clears his throat, gives me a big shit-eating grin, and ends up with this—like —formal head-bob of apology.

"Hey, mind if I smoke?" he's asking.

He breaks me up, I mean here it is his car and all, but with a straight face I tell him, "Sure, go ahead." So he grabs a pack of Marlboros (what else?) from the glove compartment, pushes in the lighter, fumbles with the pack. He lights up, sighs, "Get so much static at home, car's the only place I can smoke anymore." He looks out the window at the gravestones whipping by in pale neat rows. A yellow truck is parked along one of the winding cemetery roads. Two men are off-loading some heavy duty tractor mowers.

"Coffin nails," he says. "That's what we used to call them. The wife gets all over my case. So do the kids. Even my girlfriend's gotten into the act. "You gotta **quit**, Wayne! Please!" He stares straight ahead, takes a long drag, watches the smoke curl up above his head and twist out the side window. "Giving me grief. The whole pack of them. Who needs it? Day and night. Me, I just go out and tool around for an hour or so. Listen to Bruce, open this baby up. Corners real good, she got herself a fantastic suspension. See this little sucker here?"

"That switch thing, you mean?"

"Correct. What you have here is a three-way adjustable suspension. Old lady wants to mosey down to the market? All you do is set it on SOFT. Then one more twist and she's ready for hard cornering. You want to really line out? Like now? You set this gizmo for STIFF FRONT/SOFT REAR, and she spreads her wings like an eagle. She eats up highways, this baby. Cruises like a dream come true."

He leans back against the lamb's wool, his shoulders not hunched for a moment. He's relaxed. He stubs out the coffin nail, wipes away a little mound of ash into the ashtray, taps it shut with an efficient click.

We're tooling down the long stretch of road that runs by the golf course, I mean we're really flying now. The greens look to be in fine shape, shaved velvet, a deep emerald color. The speedometer reads almost ninety, but the road's clear of traffic, nice and dry, swept clean of the winter's gravel pretty much. Up there on the crest of the hill just past the pond, four golfers are standing at the edge of the fairway.

"You do any golfing, son?" he's asking.

So I tell him how I'm trying to organize a foursome from college, a little graduation expedition down to Hilton Head Island after school's over, stay with some buddies who work as greens-keepers.

"Oh, jeez!" he says. "Hilton Head. I played them all, all sixteen courses down there. UN-be-liev-a-ble area. Best golf in the country." He starts decelerating, we're coming up to the big curve by the reservoir. "Getting close?" he asks me.

I nod. "Around this curve, about three quarters of a mile on the right. Big brown house. With a barn."

"Check," he says and goes on, "Oh yeah, man! In the old days, like I was down to Hilton Head—say five, six times a year. No solo stuff, not anymore, not when you got yourself family obligations. Kids all yammering for Disneyland. Wife wants Vegas. Girlfriend wants a piece of the Big Apple. Whatcha gonna do?"

Bruce is winding up the last couple bars to *My Hometown*. The man taps the wheel softly. "No foolin'," he's saying. "That is definitely one beeyootiful island." He shakes his head real slow, looks over at me and smiles. His eyes are tired; under the heavy chin the skin is starting to sag, plumping over the tight gold choker around his neck. "Beeyootiful," he murmurs again. He pulls the car up smoothly to the driveway beside my house. Bruce is finished now, and for the first time the thrum of the engine can be clearly heard, and the throaty burbling of the mufflers.

"She idles rough," he explains. "Got a three quarter cam on her."

"Wild set of wheels, pal. I mean really awesome," I tell him as I climb out, reaching for my duffle bag stashed in the rear. "Hey man, thanks for the lift. Later."

The guy leans way over the passenger seat. He smiles again, the same leathery smile as before except there's something sort of homesick-looking around the eyes, in the droop of the mouth.

"Knock em dead in Carolina, you hear? Beeyootiful!" and as he reaches to close the door, he adds—shaking that massive head. "I was your age, kid, I'd be thumbing my way down tomorrow."

And he gives me a high five. The door closes with a heavy thunk, and then the Camaro slides back onto the pavement, mufflers exploding like bogus thunder in the silence of the empty road.

"**GO** for it!" I say. To no one in particular.

TOUGH APPLES

MY CRADLE LANGUAGE, MY safe cocoon these silken sounds they sing to us, to every American baby they sing their lapping lullabies, our gentle Spanish nursemaids who croon of rice with milk, of dappled criollos galloping across the pampas, hoof beats slowly fading into silence while we were rocked to sleep.

Their words too have faded into silence, not even an echo.

Oh where—*where* did I put them? Why can't I hear them as clearly as I see Sara over there by the pantry door? See her coming towards me with a silver tray of hors d'oeuvres to pass among the guests at my parents' asada out here on the patio. And trotting after Sara is Teresa, our silly parlor maid giggling as usual. Beyond them in the kitchen leaning against the slate sink, Antonio with his mustache blacker than his shiny boots still argues with Consuelo, the cook. She is slicing plump tomatoes grown next door by the Sullivan's head gardener, Manuel. I turn away and there's dear Manuel himself, standing on his tall ladder propped against the wall between our two houses, and now he shyly waves his clippers through the eucalyptus leaves while I edge around the fringes of this party, smell the bifes spattering on hot charcoal, and listen to the grown-ups whisper as I glide by.

"You know..." significant pause, "Molly's an only child," but I pretend I haven't heard, that I'm not ashamed although the way they say *only child*, I know it isn't good, and my mother's best friend adds with a loud sniff, "They've really spoiled her rotten." Quickly I mutter "Tough apples!" then toss my braids, shrugging past that awful lady which only confirms her poor opinion of me.

"Spoiled rotten" I hear her hiss down through the years.

Spoiled rotten. Only child. These are the words I do remember. And I remember how the next morning after the asada, I began telling myself that Patrick and Brian Sullivan were not just my best friends but actually my very own brothers—no more only child for me! And how every evening while it was still light, I used to kneel on the window-seat in my bedroom and stare across the driveway at their house gleaming through the ghost-gray screen of eucalyptus and make believe that I too was a Sullivan boy just for today, just for tomorrow, just for a little while.

Next to Sara, Patrick was my favorite person in the whole world. I loved Patrick Sullivan. His hair was bright as straw and his whole face splattered with freckles, hundreds of them. Freckles looked so American. I never got a single one on my face, only a couple on my shoulders where it didn't count.

Brian's hair was black and his eyes a fierce sparkling blue fringed with thick black double lashes like a doll's. Sometimes Brian got a crazy expression in his eyes so we had to look away, shy of the danger in him but drawn to it at the same time. All Brian cared about was the war and fighting the Nazis. He taught us all the words to *Coming in on a Wing and a Prayer* and *Don't Sit Under the Apple Tree*, and I was so proud when I could announce that my uncle back home in Tampa had just joined the infantry, shipping out next month. It proved my patriotism, like my hoard of old ration books.

But Brian wasn't impressed. "No kidding," he said in a flat voice, then added, "our cousin Eddie, he's a turret gunner. On a B 29," and he scowled.

Then Patrick began telling me in a kind voice how Eddie had already gotten a purple heart and two ribbons. I knew Patrick was also bragging but in a nice way, an explaining sort of way so that I wouldn't feel like a dope.

That spring Eddie's plane was shot down over Germany. Then came the news that Eddie was dead.

The boys showed me the newspaper clipping. They took turns carrying it in their wallets until the page got so creased the print looked blurred as if it had been soaked in water and then dried out. But that didn't matter because we had memorized all three paragraphs. There wasn't any picture of Eddie which was a shame since Patrick and Brian hadn't seen him for a long time, way back before the war broke out when it was still easy to visit the States.

We didn't mind. We knew what Eddie Sullivan looked like. He was beautiful and he was brave. When something seemed too scary or too difficult, we would yell to each other, "*Do it for Eddie!*"

The Sullivan boys were fraternal twins, "Hatched from different eggs," explained Patrick, winking at me. They had this younger sister, Virginia, ten years old like me. Virginia was fat and not much fun. She was blonde, same as Patrick, with damp doughy hands I hated touching. But she was my passport to the twins.

Naturally I saw the twins every day at school. They were in the eighth grade, and we passed each other like strangers down the long mustard-colored hallways—fifth graders by definition being invisible. But I didn't care. At home they belonged to me. Right after school, Virginia's maid would call Sara on the telephone. I suppose Mrs. Sullivan had to clear the invitation first. I hardly ever saw their mother. Or mine either, for that matter.

High brick walls shielded the grounds of the Sullivan estate with its big gardens that stretched like a park for three acres or more. My father told me that they were one of the richest American families in Buenos Aires. "Real big shots," said my father. My father's world was measured by big shots and small potatoes.

Beside the wall between our two houses ran the long straight row of eucalyptus, and all day long eucalyptus seeds, their capsules shaped like tiny cups, spilled over the wall into our driveway, crunching under our feet. The seeds had the same sharp herbal smell as the stuff Sara rubbed on my chest when I got a bad cold. Actually they smelled like home, that is to say, my Argentina home but I never realized this until we moved back to the States. It always made me homesick later on, the smell of eucalyptus. Or Vicks Vapo-Rub.

Because Mrs. Sullivan didn't want us making a commotion in the house, most days we played in their park, ramming our bikes down over the terraced lawns, pretending to be LSDs on the beaches at Anzio. But some of the time we got to play gaucho. Actually, the twins were the gauchos, and I got to be the wild black stallion they chased across the pampas, my long mane rippling as we careened down the green velvet slope of the lawn, bucking up our bicycles when we got to the flat part of the grass.

"Whoa!" yelled Patrick, and I would nicker deep in my throat, whipping my braids back and forth. The boys had made lassos by cutting off the wooden handles from a couple of Virginia's jump ropes. Usually the lassos would get tangled up in the spokes of the bike wheels, and then the twins would start in cussing. I loved it when they got mad like that, the dangerous grim look of their chapped lips and the little drops of sweat creeping up their temples and making their hair damp and curly as if they'd just had a bath.

"Shit-fire!" Brian would growl.

These words fell on my ears like music and I practiced this new expression at home, teaching it to Sara who then innocently used it in front of my mother. Who of course bawled Sara out. But she didn't rat on me—my darling Sara never told. And she never carried a grudge. "Bueno, no more sheet-fires" was all she said on the subject. I picked three pale purple orchids from Sullivan's garden and presented them to her. She had spared me a spanking. My mother was the one who administered spankings, telling me once how her own daddy, my grandfather, made her go cut a switch from the bushes outside. "And," she frowned, "I can assure you switches hurt a hell of a lot more than the back of my hand."

"How does Mummy know that?" I asked Sara.

"Hush, little one," Sara answered. "And how are you knowing I love orchids?"

I explained I knew she loved beautiful things. And then she bent down and she kissed my forehead. From then on every time Brian said evil words, I remembered first, never to pass them on to Sara. And second, I never forgot how she protected me. Always.

Patrick's repertoire was not as rich as Brian's so he had to resort to makeshift embellishments such as "Double shit fire", dear Patrick. And then the two of them would begin wrestling each other like puppies tumbling over and over on the grass, the harder the body contact, the more they liked it. I used to crouch beside them and try and tickle their bare stomachs under their shirts, or tie the laces of their Keds together. And then they grabbed me, and Brian held my ankles while Patrick tickled me so hard I couldn't laugh but began choking.

Virginia, the world's biggest sissy, was terrified her brothers might hurt each other—or worse yet, hurt me. She sat huddled in her mother's lounge chair up on the patio, shrieking every two minutes, "Careful, boys!"

Usually about then—me choking, Virginia shrieking louder and louder—Manuel would happen to shuffle by with his rakes and clippers, tipping his straw hat in greeting. As long as we didn't trample his flowers, he didn't mind our games. But I noticed that Brian and Patrick invariably got tired along about the time Manuel showed up.

"Have fun, niños," he always told us.

Manuel was our friend. Once when we asked him if we could use one of his flower beds to plant a Victory garden, he agreed, then rubbed his chin for a minute and added, "Get permission first from the Señora, por favor," nodding his head towards the terrace where our parents were sitting, drinking cocktails.

No dice.

Everyone smiled vaguely, then waved us off to play. Away we slouched. Behind us, grown-up laughter drifted over the clink of highball glasses.

But Manuel was different. Like Sara, he listened to us. While the twins fiddled with their bikes, I wandered over to where Manuel knelt by a freshly turned flower bed.

He didn't speak for a while, which was nice. I stood there and watched how his hands moved with quick fluid motions, how the trowel flashed in the sunshine and then a scoop of dirt appeared in a neat cone-shaped mound, and how the seed nurslings nestled down in their circular beds, pat, pat, pat as the earth was tucked around them again.

My mother had often told me that my hands were what she called "utterly useless." Manuel's hands had ropy blue veins which swelled when he dug up the dirt. His fingers tiptoed gently around the seedlings. To my eyes they looked graceful, those magical hands, despite the thickened joints and the brown skin of the knuckles so cracked it belonged on an iguana, not a man. Even a very old man like Manuel, although Sara had told me he was only thirty-five. "Pero," she had gone on, "you must understand, Miss Molly, that people who work with their hands as does Manuel—they age very quickly."

Worried, I asked Sara if hers would get old and leathery like his.

She studied me, then smiled. "No, querida. I am a lucky person. I work inside taking care of you."

"Goody!" I squealed and gave her a kiss. Later I decided that Mother was only pretending to scorn my hands and didn't want them to look old like those of Manuel who was now sitting back on his haunches and fanning himself with his straw hat. He asked me how school was going, and I told him very well, except for music class.

He smiled up at me. "You dislike the music, niña?"

I scuffed wavy lines in the dirt with the toe of my sneaker. "It's not fair we have to sing," I muttered.

"Why not, Miss Molly?"

"Because some people simply—simply cannot!" I replied. "My music teacher, she hates me. And my voice," I added. Miss Sewell was tall and fat and looked as if she might be jolly. But she was not. She acted stern and angry, and she accused me of not trying. "You are alto, Molly, you are also very lazy. Not only do you not try, you make too many excuses. You disappoint me very much."

Manuel tugged one of my braids gently. "You like better playing with the boys? Riding your make-believe horse?"

"I'm not riding the horse, I *am* the horse!" And I snorted and pawed at the ground with my left hoof.

He chuckled, bent down with his trowel again, pat, pat. "A very wild horse, I am thinking. Verdad?"

"The fastest and wildest in all of Argentina!" I whinnied, and Manuel laughed. "I have to go now. Adios, Manuel." And I ran off to find the boys.

They were sprawled by the driveway, their bikes next to them, the shiny chrome handlebars twisted at an unnatural angle like horses with broken necks—horrible! I knelt down and straightened them, poor things. Boys could be such jerks sometimes.

"Let's go ride around the block," said Patrick.

"No, let's play prisoner," and Brian sat up, eyes glittering.

"Not now, Brian Sullivan, it's too hot!" Virginia's voice sounded shrill. Not that I could blame her. Brian always made sure she was chosen prisoner of war which meant being tied up with the jump rope and left in the potting shed.

"Hey, Brian, we better wait till Manuel goes home," Patrick said.

Virginia was calling me so I went up the hill to the patio where she sat hunched over something in her lap, stringy blonde hair falling in her eyes.

She was holding a black lacquer box. "Guess what?" she said.

"What?"

"Look," and slowly she began lifting the lid. "Look what my aunt sent me all the way from the States. *Gone with the Wind* paper dolls, and they're real too!"

"You lucky! Let me see."

"Only if you play with me."

"I *am* playing with you, Virginia, don't be a sap."

She put the lacquer box down on the end of the chaise lounge and carefully lifted them out, one by one, Scarlett, Rhett Butler, Melanie, Ashley—they were all there, smiling up at us. My hands trembled as I spread them out across the glass patio table.

One of the twins was yelling for me, but I ignored him. They were bored and mainly they didn't want me ditching them and playing with Virginia. Tough apples, it served them right. Too wild for their own good, my mother claimed, and sometimes I used to wonder if being a twin (even one from a different egg) meant you got a double dose of energy, instead of the single dose the rest of us had. Or the half dose Virginia ended up with.

I told the boys to scram. When they saw they couldn't get a rise out of us, they swung up on their bikes, and the last we saw of them they were heading out the big iron gate, yelling cat calls the whole way.

For the rest of the afternoon we danced at the ball, burned Atlanta, delivered Melanie's baby, shot the Yankee deserter, and hardly argued at all.

After the maid brought out lemonade and hot scones, I asked Virginia if she'd trade me the paper dolls. I tried to sound casual, but she wasn't fooled.

"For what?" She eyed me suspiciously and slathered on more butter and guava jelly all over her scone. The jelly dribbled down her chin while she chewed.

"For whatever."

She didn't answer for a few minutes. Then, little eyes squinting in triumph, she said finally, "Okey dokey...for your Princess doll."

"Gee..." I hesitated.

She began to put all the paper dolls back in the lacquer box, humming a little tune as she placed their clothes first, smoothing out the tabs at the top. Next she laid the minor characters four across in layers. Scarlett's sisters looked like saps to me; they stared blankly up at the sky. Then came the final layer, Melanie and Ashley, Scarlett—the lid began to close, so I said quickly, "Ok. It's a deal."

The lid flew back open, thin metal hinges squeaking.

"Plus all her dresses," Virginia added. She had me hooked, and she knew it. I sighed. "Right."

We studied each other in silence. The Princess was a gift from some big shot my father knew who came from Switzerland. And the doll he gave to me was clearly not American. She was three feet tall and wore a peasant costume with embroidered smocking. She had sad eyes and her very own hope chest. But I left her the way she came. She was a person, too dignified to be dressed and undressed all the time. She smiled sadly at me from the big chair in my bedroom, a foreigner now, just like me. But at least she had grown up in her native land. She had roots, she understood who she was.

Still, I knew she was homesick. And now here I was trading her for some silly paper dolls. The thing was, they were *American.*

Virginia and I stared at the lacquer box. "What will your mother say?" she asked finally. What she meant was: Will your mother find out and tell mine?

"She only comes in to my room to kiss me goodnight, she's no problem."

We shook hands on the deal, but I knew with a lurch in my stomach who was going to be the real problem.

Sure enough the next morning Sara was making my bed and glanced over at the empty chair by the window. When she asked where the Princess was, I told her. And I showed her the new paper dolls. I talked real fast and smiled a lot.

She listened to the whole story, then folded her thin arms across her chest. Uh oh. Her eyes got very wide. The lids were faintly lavender, pansy eyes I had said once. "No, no, orchids!" she had laughed.

"You make a stupid bargain," she was saying now, her voice soft as usual, slipping over the pretty Spanish vowels.

I shrugged. My cheeks felt very hot.

"Your parents, did you tell them?"

"No, Sara."

"Madrecita del Dios! You play with fire, little idiot, then pretend nothing is burning." She was speaking very fast, tapping at the silver cross which lay in the hollow of her neck. In her black uniform, she looked like a nun, I thought. A pretty young nun. Virginia had told me they were called postulants, but then she added, "Sara's much too old to be a postulant, Moll. She's *twenty-four!*"

"Don't you dare tell them either," I ordered Sara.

She motioned me to the dressing table. "Hurry," she said. "You will be late for school. Antonio is waiting already with the car."

I sat facing the double mirror. Sara unfastened my pigtails, and began brushing my hair with short jabs.

"Ouch!"

"Be silent."

"You are hurting me!"

"You are a baby."

"On purpose too! Ow, Sara!" My scalp burned and tears smarted up in my eyes.

We glared at each other in the mirror. Sara was not much taller than I was, and we both had black hair except hers was short and curly and hugged her delicate head like a glossy black satin cap. I liked to pretend she was my pretty godmother who had leaned over my cradle when I was born and made three good wishes. I kept trying to get her to marry Antonio, but they both hated each other, and much as I begged, Sara would have nothing to do with him.

"He gambles," she would say, her pale lips thin with disapproval.

Antonio lived in the servants quarters over the garage. But Sara had her very own little whitewashed room beyond the pantry. She even had her own radio. We would sit in there together drinking maté and listening to Spanish love songs. She liked to play the radio very loud, the music pounding.

My head throbbed. Now she was braiding my hair. She separated each strand with a quick jerk upward. Even though my eyes were watering, I smiled into the mirror at her.

"I wish I looked just like you, Sara," I said.

"You are a very foolish little girl." She frowned.

"But I want to be beautiful. Like you."

She said nothing, pressed her lips tight.

Silence.

"You love me, Sara?"

"Hold still, little one." Her hands stopped their jerking, and she smoothed the top of my head.

"Know what? You look just like Scarlett O'Hara," I said.

"Basta with this Scarlett. All day long you jabber Scarlett nonsense. And that is the reason we are in this ridiculous business with the Sullivan girl. She's a cow, that one. And greedy as well."

"But you loved the movie! You cried more than me, each time we saw it."

The horn was honking outside.

"Caramba! That idiot, always in such a hurry." She murmured wicked things under her breath.

"Cursing is a sin, Sara." I practiced fluttering my lashes like Scarlett peeping up at Ashley Wilkes.

"Stop making cow eyes," she told me. She was tying bright green ribbons on each braid, and her hands moved in nice swoops. Efficient hands. Loving hands, most of the time.

"I do *not* want those ribbons, they look ridiculous."

"You are the ridiculous one. You are a young lady. Not a crazy boy. Not a wild horse on the pampas." She studied me in the mirror, stepping back to check her work. "Basta," she said.

"But I hate being a young lady, it's so *DUMB*."

"Do not say hate. Hate is not a word used by people of gentle breeding. Hurry now. Antonio's probably getting cross and smoking too many cigarettes."

I jumped off the stool, grabbed my brown book satchel from the desk, then glanced at the empty chair. "Promise not to tell about Princess, por favor?"

She shook her head. "Have I ever told?" she sighed, rolling her eyes.

Now I ran over and hugged her tight, her narrow shoulders felt as delicately boned as a bird's wing and her skin smelled like nutmeg.

The horn tooted once more, very loud this time. Antonio would be grinding his last cigarette under the heel of his shiny black boot, nervously fingering his mustache, glancing first down at his new wristwatch and then up at my bedroom window.

"Off with you and your promises!" Sara scolded, flapping her arms at me as if she were brushing crumbs from her black uniform.

I ran out the door laughing. On the way downstairs, I whistled a few bars of *Arroz Con Leche*, the song Sara sang when she was happy. Sara's voice was light and true, but singing was my downfall so Brian and Patrick taught me how to whistle like a boy, with my tongue flat up against the roof of my mouth.

That afternoon after school we were playing Tarzan, and the boys coaxed me up to a branch that hung high over the garden wall, the highest we had ever climbed. We sat hidden in the feathery leaves, spying on people out for a stroll along Avenida Forest. Nobody glanced up, not once.

We could see right down into Dick Trumbull's garden, and we watched the chauffeur polishing their black Buick. Dick was seventeen and didn't know I lived on the same planet, much less the same street. He was the champion diver at the country club, and when he stood there gleaming at the end of the diving board, then silently sliced through the green water below, I tried to think of many ways to drown and how Dick Trumbull would rescue me.

Brian started chanting, "Molly loves the Dicky-Bird!" over and over again. Brian knew where all the tender places were so I tried to sock him, but he scrambled up to the next branch and when I began to follow, swinging my leg up, I slipped and my hands began sliding down the bark, the tree seemed to tilt, and now I was looking right down at the gravel driveway and into Virginia's open mouth, red and glistening. She held Princess under one arm and Princess too hung upside down, her long flaxen ringlets trailing on the gravel and snagging on the pebbles.

"Be careful!" Virginia was shrieking. "You'll break your neck, Molly Stafford!"

I pulled myself back up straight and hugged the trunk tightly and my forehead pressed so hard against the bark that its jaggedy ridges dug like fingernails into the tender skin on the tip of my nose.

"Hang on, Molly!" yelled Patrick.

I could hear him racketing down the other side of the tree. A small branch whipped my face as he went by. Brian followed him, but more slowly.

I said nothing, just shut my eyes so the tree wouldn't tilt again.

From below Patrick was calling, "I'll go get Manuel, you be brave, Moll! Remember, do it for Eddie!"

"Maybe she's dead!" wailed Virginia.

"Nobody dies sitting up, you jackass," Brian told her. Virginia started bellowing, and Brian launched into a steady stream of *shit-fires*. I almost smiled.

When Manuel finally got the ladder up to me, he was very gentle.

"You're supposed to be a wild criollo stallion out there on the pampas, Miss Molly," he said in his nice kidding voice. "Not a monkey in a tree."

He told me to open my eyes and look upwards at the sky, and his hands braced my shoulders as I stepped backwards and down, my left foot dangling for a second in mid-air until it found the rung. After that it was easy.

When we reached the ground, Manuel patted me again on the cheek, gentle hands, kind hands, and then he went away carrying his ladder. I wanted to hug him.

The boys said nothing, but Virginia sniffed. "You three are nuts and Mummy says you are nothing but a real tomboy and a spoiled brat, Molly Stafford!"

Patrick, my good-natured Patrick, grabbed her arm. "You squeal, you're a dead man, I mean it."

Virginia wrenched away. "Stinker!" she told Patrick, then went flouncing down the driveway with Princess in her arms, patting her on the back like she was burping a baby. Over Virginia's lumpy shoulder, Princess looked straight into my eyes.

That was the beginning of the bad stuff that spring. I put the paper dolls away inside my Mary Jane shoe boxes in the closet. Dolls were dumb. I spent more and more time with the twins. Sometimes I wondered if the Princess sat gazing out the window from Virginia's bedroom, her sad eyes staring at my house through the eucalyptus trees.

Sara kept fussing at me that I looked too thin and I was wearing myself out keeping up with the boys. "Tough apples" I'd answer. We started riding our bikes outside the gates, whizzing three abreast down the sidewalks. Hibiscus bloomed over the tops of the garden walls and little stalks would catch at our hair as we rode by.

One Saturday morning we went clear around the block. The street sloped down a very steep hill, and I was out in front but Patrick was catching up, he was almost neck and neck so I peddled faster and the stallion gathered his haunches for one last surge of power, and then where there had been dappled sunlight filtering down through the palm trees across the bumpy bricks, there was now a huge black wall sliding slowly in front of me, barring the way.

I hit it and flew clear over the hood of the black sedan that was inching out of the hidden driveway.

My elbows were scratched, but I was ok because I had landed on the soft dirt next to a big palm. Shaking but ok.

Not Patrick.

He had slammed right into the side of the car, and his right shoulder was hunched at a strange angle, the arm hanging lopsided like a broken wing. His face looked green. I took his good wrist and sat down beside him, and felt his forehead, and even though it was clammy and cold, his skin felt as sweetly familiar to me as my own.

The driver of the car looked green too. "Broken his arm, the poor little one!" he was shouting, and he kept pounding one fist on top of the other like he was counting one potato, two potato.

Lots of people started jabbering around us. Someone flung a blanket over Patrick, and then after a long while, the ambulance came and took Patrick away.

The tall policeman in the white uniform gave me and Brian a ride home. We left the two bikes, all smashed and crooked, behind on the sidewalk.

When we got back, the policeman talked to Sara at the front door. She kept hugging me and kissing me on the top of my head the whole time she was answering the policeman's questions, her thin arms around my shoulders, shielding me. That's when I knew Sara really loved me. "Probrecita," she kept murmuring.

My parents got very upset, so did Mr. and Mrs. Sullivan. There was this big squabble. I was forbidden to play with the twins, even with Virginia. In fact, I was never ever invited there again.

One night I waited up until my parents had finished dinner and were having their brandy and usually in a pretty good mood. I made my pitch, not beating around the bush.

"Riding lessons?" my father repeated, "but what—"

Mother's voice sliced through the rest of his question. She was sitting over by the Victrola. There were no lights on in that part of the drawing room. She was smoking. I could see the red glow of her cigarette dilate and then contract. Her face was in shadow.

"Don't be an ass, Howard," she was saying. "It makes perfect sense. The kid wants to be a horse. Failing that, let her learn to ride the damn things."

"But she's only ten, it's dangerous."

Mother sighed. "And what..." she drawled, "could be more dangerous than running around unsupervised over at Sullivan's? Cocky little bastards, those twins. They take after their charming father, a real horse's ass."

I glared at the cigarette. It kept blinking at me like the small red eye of a dragon. "I love the Sullivan boys," I told her, my voice shaking. "And I hate you for taking them away from me."

Then my mother's voice shot back across the darkened room—half bitter, half amused, "To borrow a phrase you seem to dote on, sugar—tough apples."

* * *

So THEY SENT ME to a riding academy run by a Viennese riding master. The lessons were held in a huge white building shaped like a hexagon.

Herr Schneider stood in the middle of the ring, tapping his boots with a riding crop made from the hide of a wart hog. The handle was ivory, "The tusk of a wild boar, Fraulein," he told me, and then smiled.

He lunged me on a white mare. Slap-slap went the whip against his boots when he got impatient. Both the mare and I knew the sound well.

"Balance, Fraulein! You are not a sack of potatoes up there!"

"Heels down!" he would thunder. And a moment later, "You are not driving a locomotive! That mouth is soft as velvet, treat it tenderly like your own."

"Gentle hands, Fraulein! I *beg* of you."

My lunging lessons finally ended. I said goodbye to the white mare, and graduated to Caballero, an enormous bay gelding who knew, as did the mare, when inexperienced riders were put on his back. He soon became my best friend, he filled the empty place of losing the twins, and although he couldn't speak, we understood each other because in the silence of a horse there is room for deep understanding. Caballero was a Portugese Lusitano. Herr Schneider told me I should be honored to mount such an animal. He explained how long ago Lusitanos were bred to be warhorses because of their courage, then later used for mounted bullfighting—they were a breed famous for their extraordinary gentleness. And Caballero *was* a gentle giant—he stood well over sixteen & a half hands. Facing him head on was like looking way, way up at this huge brown mountain with two kindly eyes glowing back at me. I used to stroke his satiny neck and then we would nuzzle each other. He smelled of sweet clover and sun-dried prairie grass. I'd pat his velvety nose, and he'd go chuff-chuff, and then his muzzle touched my mouth, and he inhaled deeply—his way of knowing me, breathing me down into those great lungs of his. Up there on his broad back felt to me as if I were being rocked in a cradle, so comfortable, so steady. But then one morning when our class were going around the ring at a very fast gallop, I slid off dear Caballero. I lay in the tanbark and stared up at the hooves sidestepping my face. Herr Schneider had solemnly promised no horse would ever willingly trample anyone. "They will not harm you," he told us. Certainly my Caballero never would. This I knew.

I lay very still and watched the huge dark shapes float over me, kicking up little spirals of shavings as their hooves hit the ground. I wished the Sullivans could see how brave I was, how I didn't even flinch.

"*Do it for Eddie!*"

And I did.

A year later my father got transferred back to the States. For my farewell present, Sara gave me two beautiful books, one about a dog, one about horses. On the flyleaf of the horse book she had written in the scrawling loops of a schoolgirl: "Para querida Molly, this heart of mine gallops wherever you may go, little one."

At my new American school the principal announced I was from Argentina. The next day they asked me to get up and sing something in Spanish in front of the whole assembly. I sang *Arroz Con Leche*, Sara's song when she was happy. The rows and rows of faces in the big auditorium looked like smooth white eggs with no features. I sang as loud as I could, my voice cracking in the high places.

My music teacher in Buenos Aires had fussed at me so many times, "No, Molly! You are alto! Never sing soprano, your voice—it will not go this high."

Stony calm, I stared out at the rows of eggs watching me blankly, and I reached for the high C at the end of the song. Then I turned away and took my seat with the other students. I smiled at the tame American girls in their pale fuzzy-pink sweaters. Their eyes, I could see now, flicked sideways, lizard eyes half shut but watching lazily, constantly checking, constantly studying each other.

The boys I ignored completely.

I never spoke Spanish again. Not to anyone. I put the childhood words away in a safe place where they could never get spoiled, and then, after a long while, I forgot how to play with them. Or even what they meant.

KILLING THE STEEL

HE DROVE ALL NIGHT. He drove straight through, all the way from Boston straight down to Ravensport, West Virginia. He was on the road an hour after she called him.

The car radio played country, mournful ballads of hard luck, cheating lovers, and honor reclaimed in fly-specked bars. Her turf, not his.

Six hundred miles, give or take, the miles flicking by as fast as the songs. West along the Mass Pike, dropping off on 84 through Hartford. Ugly city. Monolithic insurance towers patrolled the highway, glass-sheathed facades reflecting back the late afternoon sun.

The rest of Connecticut. Rolling hills. The old state penitentiary, Victorian brick, marching across the horizon to his left. To his right the new prison nestled in a hollow almost out of sight except for the two feet of barbed wire cartwheeling across the top of the electric fence.

Across the Tappan Zee bridge. Darkness as he crawled through traffic around the Poconos, past the neon lights of the new gambling casinos set so close to the road, they blocked the view of the river. Built without windows. But the tourists didn't care. Scenery was not what they came for. Not any more.

Then west through the long oblong of Pennsylvania, winding gradually south on Interstate 70, and across the state line, and pretty soon, another river fading slowly from black to gray to brown as he dropped south.

Every half hour the soft drawl of the d.j. slid in between the sets.

"Morning, folks," the voice on the radio was murmuring. "1330 on your dial, this is Wheeling, West Virginia bringing you Country Countdown, and here's...."

His shirt stuck to the back of the seat. There hadn't even been time to change. She called him at the office right after his 4 o'clock seminar, Florentine Painting in the Quattrocento. He went straight home to the apartment which meant skipping the Friday faculty meeting. The hell with the new tenure policy. But she had already gone.

"Number 27 this week, *Homesick Blues*." Twanging chords, slow thumping rhythms. It had been the southern lilt to her that he loved. The

71

rising inflection that made every statement a half question, bubbling up beneath that lazy voice, thick as honey.

"Honey, I just got a call," she had said. "I got to leave. Yes. Today. No... no, Max, *please*! It's my only chance, I have to." And then just before she hung up on him, "You take care, darling, you hear?"

And click, she was gone.

Leaving nothing behind except for those dark crimson guitar picks on the end table and a big bunch of freshly picked daisies placed square in the middle of their bed. She had wrapped them in foil. When he took off the foil, he found layers of wet paper towels wound carefully around the stems. And drops of water like late falling tears still on the petals.

Late falling tears, Jesus, this stuff was insidious. Give him a good harmonica and watch out, Nashville! He smiled. Nashville, her Mecca, her promised land. "Just got a call" she had said. Would she head there direct? No, she'd drop home first, home to Ravensport. Then head on to Nashville. And the big time. All year long she kept hoping, "Just one good demo record, honey, and the sky's the limit."

He cranked the window down. The air smelled of burning gases and molten metals. Of oxides and sulfides. Of red hot coke and white hot steel.

"Hot-metal" they called the liquid pig iron when they tapped the blast furnace after the smelting. "And we're talking *hot*," she used to tell him. "2000 degrees Fahrenheit." The molten iron was funneled into hot-metal cars on tracks that run directly to the open hearth furnace. There, the pig iron gets cooked into steel.

Oh, he knew the whole damn process from soup to nuts, she sure talked about it enough, her cheeks flushed just remembering. Her brothers worked in the steel mills back in the old days. The whole family had for three generations.

Fuel gas and oxygen get piped in at one end, then you add the molten pig iron to a soup of scrap metal, limestone and iron ore. The meltdown begins. The limestone, now changed into lime, rises slowly to the surface, combining with the impurities to form slag. The liquid slag floats on top, cherry red and bubbling like lava. "Like looking into hell, honey," she said, laughing. "But so beautiful."

Then the alloys are added. "Same as adding spices to a batter," she explained. "See, the secret of good steel," she said, almost chanting, "I mean we're talking good steel, strong steel here, what really counts is the reaction between it and the slag." He never had understood chemistry but she made the process sound as straightforward as a recipe, little smidgen of this, little smidgen of that, tap the furnace to check the batter.

The next to last step is to take the dissolved oxygen out of the finished melt so it won't react with carbon to form carbon monoxide. What you do is add aluminum just before the melt's poured. Then she told him how fully deoxidized steel is called "killed" steel because it lies so still. No bubbles. Finally, the molten steel is poured from the ladle into ingots, ingots as perfectly shaped, as precisely molded as new loaves of bread straight from some giant oven.

She said all she ever wanted to do was go work at the mill as a hot-work laborer.

"My best friend wanted to be a ballerina," she told him, wrinkling her nose. "I thought that was sissy stuff. Everyone else, all they dreamed of was getting hitched and have dozens of kids. They wanted something safe. Not me." She had glanced at him for a moment, half teasing, half in apology. Then she blew at the dark strand of hair straggling across her forehead. She wore her hair pulled back severely, but it suited her. That face. A late Renaissance madonna, del Sarto, maybe. The perfect oval, the clearly defined hairline framing the oval like the outline of a heart. "My widow's peak," she called it. Framing the dead white skin, the perfect half circles of the black eyebrows, the fine steel gray eyes. She never seemed to blink. She peered out at the world without flinching.

"Only because I'm half blind," she used to laugh. And then start to fish around for her contact lenses which she was always losing. They slipped from her hands faster than tadpoles flicking through pond water and she was always scrambling down on her hands and knees, groping along the floor, giggling that she saw better with her hands than with her poor old eyes.

And, in fact, he liked her better without the contacts. She stared at him unblinking, staring at him and through him and beyond to something shimmering out there. It made him want to turn his head and see it too, savor it with her, taste what she tasted, hear what she heard, mourn what she mourned.

"Coming up on two minutes before six o'clock in the morning, folks," the d.j. was saying now. "Eighty degrees out there, going to be hazy, hot and humid. Chance of thundershowers..."

The thumping chords began again. And then the chorus: "Someone's going to pay for the things you do..."

He rolled up the window, switched off the radio, switched on the air conditioning. The river wound below to his right, coiled beside the highway like some great brown water snake sliding between the West Virginia hills. He could see the steel mills ranged along the banks of the river, the latticed girders going up the sides of the blast furnaces, carrying the skip cars loaded with coke and iron ore. Thick black smokestacks stood tall as ship masts above the sheds. They shimmered in the heat.

He took the next ramp off the highway. RAVENSPORT the sign read. FASTEST GROWING...but the legend had rusted and he couldn't make out the rest.

The town was spread over a series of steep hills overlooking the river, but it was getting too hazy to see much. The buildings were mostly brick, set close to the street. Lots of pool parlors and bars. Not a motel in sight. A lovely square building stood next to the police station. Big veranda, bright green rocking chairs, and flower boxes with petunias cascading down. This must be the old hotel, the Ravensport Arms, where she got her first waitress job back in high school. He pulled the car over, parked. No meters in Ravensport. Nice touch. Southern hospitality for you.

Inside, the lobby was cool and dark. A big fan whirred slowly from the ceiling, making a quiet lapping sound that seemed to fit the tempo of the place perfectly.

"Morning!" chirped the young guy at the desk. He smiled at Max, pushed over the registration book. He was wearing a bow tie he kept fingering. The tie moved up and down with his Adam's apple. Friendly looking kid, doing everything but wagging his tail.

"Say, where can I get some breakfast around here?"

"Came to the right place, sir. Coffee shop's just opened. Best home fries in the county." The clerk glanced down at the register. "'You sure a *long*, long way from home! Welcome to Ravensport, Mr. Farrar." The bow tie gave a big bobble.

"I'm looking for a rooming house. On Gardenia Street. In the 300 block."

"That's easy. Gardenia's only the one block long." And the boy gave him directions. Then he added, "you lose your bearings, ask anyone. Folks here real friendly. I just got here myself. Where I come from, people don't cotton much to strangers," and he swallowed hard, Adam's apple bobbing like a ping pong ball.

"Right." Jesus, just his luck, draw some homesick hillbilly. "So, chances are you wouldn't know any of the waitresses who worked here. Like four, five years ago?"

The boy shook his head, then brightened. "Got it!" he said and leaned over the counter, man to man, jerking his thumb towards the dining room. "Betty Lou Haskins can help you. Talk your ear off, but she's been here long as the hotel. Old as God. Nobody Betty Lou don't know." And with a little flourish, the desk clerk reached out and rang for the bellhop. "Front!" he said, and winked.

The home fries he had to admit were as good as the kid had promised. So were the sausages, "made from our own hawgs, fresh killed and cured at the Farmer's Market, out past River Street," Betty Lou Haskins told him.

Kid was right about her too. She talked straight through the orange juice to the end of the meal. She smiled down at him, face serene, skin as unlined, as smoothly rounded as a young girl's. Folding her arms, she watched Max mop up the last of the egg with the last of the biscuits. Then she asked her first question. "Good to see a new face in town. You planning to be with us for a spell?"

"Just a day or so," he answered. "Nice town, Ravensport."

"Seen better days," she said. "Little more coffee, sir?" she asked, and bent down and poured, so close to him he could smell the fresh scent of Mennen's Baby Powder. Clean lady. Nice lady. Kind.

"That was absolutely first rate," he told her.

She beamed. "Best cooking in Marshall County," she said. "I've been waitressing for almost forty years in this very dining room."

"Forty years!" Max repeated, and stirred his coffee. He glanced up at her. "Then you must have known a good friend of mine. Worked here about five years ago. Brenda Carls was her name."

She looked down at him, eyes wide. Startled? or simply puzzled, he couldn't tell. "Carls?" she was saying. "Doesn't ring a bell."

"Tall, black hair. Very attractive?"

She frowned. "Only Brenda I knew worked here was Brenda Lee Carlucci."

He leaned forward. "Was she pretty?"

He watched her. She didn't answer but instead started to brush crumbs off the tablecloth, then fiddled with the silk rose stuck in a blue ceramic jug between the salt and pepper shakers. She tried to smile, picked up his plate, glanced over towards the door leading to the kitchen.

"My goodness," she said. "I'd best get back to my station, our rush hour's going to start up. But you just take your time, you hear?" and she patted him on the arm. And left him, walking quickly, past the other tables, past the swinging doors into the kitchen even as he was calling out after her, "But Carls, that must be short for Carlucci!"

A group of men sauntered into the dining room, sat down over by the window. They were dressed in light blue denim shirts and wash pants. When Betty Lou came out of the kitchen with a fresh pot of coffee, they started in joking and laughing with her. Locals. Probably guys from the mill, just off the late shift.

Then a sleepy young couple came in, followed by a family with three hungry-looking kids, and he could see that Betty Lou Haskins was lost to him for the rest of the morning. She never looked once in his direction, so he finished his coffee and left a three dollar tip.

He hadn't meant to frighten her. But frightened was what she'd been.

* * *

THREE HUNDRED EIGHT GARDENIA Street was not what he expected. Not a rooming house but expensive condominiums. What Brenda would have called swanky. But she never had this kind of money, what in hell was going on here anyhow? MODEL CONDO: INQUIRE WITHIN. When he rang the bell, the door was opened immediately by a heavy-set man, dressed in a business suit but his bulky shoulders seemed to resent the pull of the expensive material. He was holding papers in one hand, a cigar in the other. "Howdy," the man said, still studying the papers. They looked like contracts or leases.

"Sorry to bother you. I'm trying to track down an old friend. Used to live here about a year ago, before she moved to Boston?"

The man shuffled the papers, glanced up briefly. Hard eyes, revealing nothing. In neutral. "Name?" he said, and took a puff on the cigar.

"My name's Farrar. Max Farrar."

"No. Friend's name."

"Oh. Sorry. Her name's Brenda. Brenda Lee Carlucci."

The man's eyes shifted, looking out beyond the door, out into the dark hallway. "You best step in, Mr. Farrar. Hang on, I'll go get the wife. She handles the tenants." And he turned and disappeared beyond the office door. He had recognized Brenda's name all right, no question.

The carpeting was so thick, Max felt he was sinking into soft sand. He waited. The model condo was all glass and white plastic and chrome fittings. Very modern, very shiny, very ugly. Not her type place. Jesus, Brenda. You said plastic has no soul. No passion, not like steel.

The office door clicked shut again. He looked up. A tired looking woman was walking across the rug noiselessly, smiling at him with a soft, nervous smile.

"Can I help you, sir?" she asked. Her voice was husky.

"Thanks, I hope so. I'm trying to locate Brenda Carlucci. She used to live here. She's been up in Boston for a while. Until yesterday actually."

She studied him, smiled softly again, her hand fluttering up to her throat. "Won't you sit down for a spell?" she said. "Rest your bones. So hot today, air conditioner's not working in here like it should," and she motioned him to one of the chrome and leather chairs.

They sat down, and she chatted about the weather, and the possibility of rain later on—my, how the gardens needed it—and had he ever been to Ravensport before?

"No," he answered. "My first visit. Beautiful country. I hadn't realized it was so hilly here in West Virginia." This was going to have to proceed at her pace, at country rhythms he wasn't used to, by elaborate indirection and friendly smiles and coming at things on a tangent.

"Well, now," she said finally. "Don't expect we can be of much help to you. We hated to see Brenda go. Sweet girl. She didn't leave no forwarding address."

"But what about her mail?"

She looked at him kindly. "Well, honey, guess she handled all that down to the Post Office."

"How about roommates? People that knew her?" He was getting tired of quizzes.

She stared at him, and then looked carefully down at the rug. "Brenda Lee—" She paused, then went on fast. "Brenda Lee didn't have a roommate."

"Friends?" he shot back.

She answered quickly, eyes flickering towards the office door. "Oh, we don't—uhm—get involved with our tenants' personal lives, not ever."

"What about her job with the band? Where she worked? Maybe someone there could help me. She can't have just disappeared into thin air. I talked to her yesterday afternoon."

The woman shifted in her chair. The worn hand crept up to her neck again, fingers softly pattering around the collar bone. "I'm not sure," she said.

"Not sure? You mean where she worked?"

"No sir, we knew where Brenda Lee worked all right. But that place closed down about six months ago. After she quit, of course." She looked at him steadily, the pulse going fast now in her throat. "Thing is, son," she smiled in apology, "the law had to close it down."

"*What?*"

"Well, it wasn't that bad, honey. I mean it was one of Vince Stella's roadhouses, you know. He got himself least seven or eight in the state."

"And?"

"I reckon things got out of hand. The gambling and all. And the sheriff got fed up and came in and closed it right down. Falling out amongst thieves, you might say," and she laughed, a rusty laugh which made the cords on her throat bulge out, and the hand crept back up to cover them.

He sat back, staring first at her, then down at the white rug. Sheriffs, yet; in-fucking-credible. Bring on the spittoons. "So," he said, "a dead end, you're suggesting. How about colleagues? She played with a group, didn't she?" He tugged at his collar; it was *hot* in here.

She nodded. "Brenda Lee played the git-tar, yes, indeed. She played real pretty. We'd be sitting out yonder in the courtyard, out by the pool. And we used to hear her practicing. I said more than once to Claude, Claude—he's my husband—I told him Brenda Lee ought to hie herself down to Nashville. Clear out of Ravensport fast as she can."

He took out his address book. His hands were shaking. "How about family? Her brothers perhaps?"

She shook her head. "Brenda's kin all gone, honey. Her folks died when she was just a little biddy thing, that much I know. And she didn't see much of those two brothers of hers. Not after she started working for Vince Stella."

He hunched forward on the edge of his chair. "Where does Stella hang out?"

She gave a low cough. "Listen, son, you can't just walk up and talk to that man. Let me think here. Pam. Pam something. Her best girlfriend. Used to come over some and swim in the pool. Pam Goldthwaite. That's it. She's a dancer, teaches over at the Vendalia Studio. Up on Main. You talk to Pam. Maybe she can help you." She looked at her watch. "Almost 11. I surely hope you find her." And she smiled, a timid smile which brightened as he smiled back, them dimmed as she turned back to the office.

He thanked her and started to walk out. But she paused for a second with her hand on the office door and whispered, then ducked her head, and disappeared as quietly as she had come, the door closing with a soft click. He let himself out into the hallway. And as his steps rang out hollow against the polished red tiles leading to the foyer, he decided what she had whispered had been, "Take care, you hear?" the words floating across the room like some chorus he'd heard before. A lament, a warning? Or just Southern comfort?

* * *

SO THIS LEGGY BLONDE was Pam Goldthwaite. He could see the dark roots showing along the part in her hair which she wore in two pigtails tied with bright multi-colored yarn. She stood against the barre by the big mirror, thin shoulders drooping, sweaty, her long dancer's legs swathed in baggy leg warmers. She spoke to him over the shouts of a dozen kids doing their pliés at the far end of the room, rising stiffly, uniformly, a row of marionettes. Over by the big window, a white haired old woman played the same five measures over and over, staring out the window as if her hands were totally autonomous, sweeping slowly back and forth over the keys.

"I don't know, Mister," Pam Goldthwaite was saying. "Brenda never was much of a letter writer. She called me though off and on. Told me about you being a college teacher and all. How nice you were, how kind." She stared at him hard, then laughed. Her front tooth was a little crooked and bit charmingly into her bottom lip. Her eyes kept roaming past his, checking out the kids. "Straighten that arm, Mandy!" she yelled. "Charlene, tuck in your gut, you look pregnant!"

She looked back at him suddenly. "Hey, buddy, she's gone. Let it be, ok? Best thing ever happened to Brenda, when she got out of this town. Leave it alone." She reached for the towel hanging over the barre and wiped her forehead, her neck. "Sweat like a pig in this racket. Might as well be stoking the hot stuff down to the mill." Her mouth twisted into a mock bitter grin. "Brenda ever tell you about wanting to work at Steel?"

He nodded.

She sighed. "Darn girl never did get over not being born a boy. She wanted to be out there courting danger every inch of the way. Well, she got it ok, a belly-full. From the first minute she ever laid eyes on Vince Stella."

"Listen, Pam. Level with me. Just who *is* this Stella character?"

She shrugged, swung the towel over her shoulder, did a deep knee bend. "You ever heard of a company town?"

"Sure."

"Well, Ravensport's a company town. Only the company's not Bethlehem Steel, it's Vince Stella and Co."

"You make this all sound fairly melodramatic."

She shrugged again. "Listen, friend, you're not going to find her. And if she's lucky, Vince won't either. He tracked her to Boston, meaning now she's on the run again. So if you really care about her, I mean the way the rest of us do, darn it!" and the tooth bit into the lip so hard the flesh turned white, "just pack up and head on back to Boston. Go back to your Yankee college and your seminars. Forget Brenda was ever up there. Or you down here. And you better do…it…fast."

She hung the towel over the barre, clapped her hands, and called to the dancers. "All right, kids! Fourth position. Places, everyone, quickly!" She cocked an eyebrow at him, and studying his expression, she said, "Look, Mr. Max Farrar, I loved her too," and ran to the center of the studio, her body moving with the fluid grace of a big jungle cat, the muscles along the thighs bunching and unbunching like smooth coils of rope.

Look, I loved her too. Famous last lines of Western Literature. He turned and walked out, slamming the door but the wood was so swollen from the humidity that the damn thing stuck halfway.

He walked on down Main Street. A fat woman in purple slacks waddled ahead of him. She was holding a toddler by the arm, so tightly the kid was whining, trying to wriggle free. Only time Brenda ever cried. Hurt puppies or hurt children.

The air felt heavy, and the sun was burning hot and sullen on the brick sidewalks of Ravensport, West Virginia, Fastest Growing Steel Town in the U.S. of A. "Hard times, honey," she told him one night, shaking her head slowly, the loosened black hair shadowing her face.

He was passing an old fashioned red, white and blue barber pole. He stopped, looked inside. All three chairs empty. Why not? Then go tackle Stella, face to face. Too many hysterical women in this town. Brenda would laugh.

A bell jingled as he opened the screen door. He walked in. Behind him, the screen door shut slowly with a long drawn out twanging.

Inside, it was cool and smelled of old leather and after-shave lotion. He sank down into one of the chairs. A radio was playing 1330 Country. A voice croaked out into the empty room: "*You got to know when to hold them/know when to fold them/know when to walk away/know when to run.*" Just then the barber came out of the back room and turned off the radio. He smiled, a little guy with bright dark eyes, a thin face, and gentle hands that flicked the scissors expertly and fast. Almost as fast as he talked. Talked about the mill and the lay-offs, about union troubles, no future in farming, kids all pack up and leave, soil's too rocky anyhow. "Shave?" he was asking. He took the soft brush and dusted off the neck hairs, then powdered quickly with a big puff.

Max smiled, leaned back against the soft leather. "Sure, why not?" he answered. "I drove all night. I could use one." He shut his eyes, shut out her face.

The barber was brushing on a good rich lather, brushing it on really thick. It felt cool, so cool. Max opened his eyes, watched him take the old single edge razor and scrape carefully along Max's cheeks.

"One thing we got lots of is salt in this state. Rock salt all up and down the river. Used to make table salt back in the old days. Big industry for West Virginia. Gone bust now. Still use salt for these new chemical plants, so maybe we break even. Almost. But nothing can make up for the layoffs. At Steel."

"I imagine you've seen plenty of changes over the years."

"Sonny, you wouldn't believe what I seen in my time. And I won't plug up your poor old ears with it, neither."

Silence. He was working the razor up under Max's chin now, over the Adam's apple.

Max talked through his teeth, trying to keep his head still. "Listen, you ever heard of Vince Stella?"

The barber put the razor down. "Son, not while I'm shaving you, *please.*

It's your throat, not mine." He shook his head. "Sweet Jesus," he sighed. "How you hear tell of Vince?"

"Oh, a buddy told me. Told me this was a company town."

The barber smiled. "Oh, I get it. Want to put a little money down?"

"Maybe."

"Got some nice action going in the 5th. Odds real good." The razor slid smoothly. The barber began whistling.

"Sounds great," said Max.

Still whistling, the barber took a clean hot towel and began wiping the little bits of lather still left. "Oh yeah," he chuckled. "We got plenty of action in Ravensport all right. Lots of cash floating round these old steel towns. Funny, hard times but people still want to bet."

Max cleared his throat. "I gather Vince controls the action here."

"Last ten years it's been Stella, sure. Before that it was the Lombardi brothers. And before them," he cackled, "before them it was old man Gardenia."

"You mean Gardenia Street was named for him? A hood?"

"Son," the barber looked at him. "Son," he said slowly, "you don't know *nothin'*. Old man Gardenia did good things for this town. Sports scholarships, building fund for the new library, you name it."

The barber wiped his hands, then held up the hand mirror to show off the perfect trim at the back of Max's neck. "Tell you the truth, guess I got a soft spot for him. Gardenia's the one who broke me in. Long time ago, forty years maybe?"

He was washing the razor in hot sudsy water. He kept glancing in the mirror while he talked, bright eyes sparkling as he remembered. "Yeah, Gardenia was one sweet guy. Took care of his people. I started out as barber's assistant in his old shop. Down the other end of town, close to the river." He watched Max's face in the mirror. "You seen the river?"

"Yes." Looping brown coils, curving through the hills.

"Pretty, hunh?"

"Very pretty," Max answered, and tapped his foot against the metal footrest.

"Anyhow, each week I paid my fifty cents—for protection, see—to Gardenia. One day at the pool hall this guy stopped me, offered me a job. Wanted me to run a little numbers game at one of his joints. He heard I was fast. Fast and hungry. So I told him let me think on it."

The barber laughed. He picked up another towel, began drying the razor, polishing the steel until it sparkled. "So, what do I do? Me, I hotfoot it back to Gardenia, Gardenia controlled all the rackets in town, he did the hiring and firing. He wasn't too happy. Can you guess what happened next?" The barber stared hard at Max.

"No."

"Week later, this guy who tried to steal me away from Gardenia? They fish him out of the river, dead as a mackerel."

"Christ!" Max could feel his stomach knotting up. Hard cold knots. *Like looking into hell, sugar.* And she had laughed.

"Hey," the barber shrugged. "That's the way it goes, sonny, in a company town. Kept my nose clean ever since." He snapped the towel so it made a loud smacking noise. Max jumped. "That'll be six bucks, Mister." He took the money but he wasn't looking at Max any more.

Now the cash register was ringing followed by the jingle of the screen door. Max turned to see. A tall guy in a red baseball hat clumped in, wearing heavy work boots and faded jeans. He rubbed his hands together. "Howdy, Jake."

The little barber looked up, face creased in a wide smile. "How do, Earl. How's it going, big fella?"

The big man hunched his shoulders. "Could be worse, Jake. Could be worse." He glanced over and right through Max. "Ok, old timer," he said to the barber. "What's the action today?"

Jake began to whistle again. He stopped, grinned. "Depends on the color of your money, good buddy." He winked.

And then the two of them began laughing, hard laughs like dogs barking, barely looking up as Max crossed the room and walked out. *Know when to walk away, know when to run.* Max didn't look back. Behind him, the little bell ran once more, and the screen door was swinging shut, very slowly, with that long lonesome twang of a country song, winding down.

Her turf. Not his.

DOUBLE PRINTING

SHE TOLD HIM IT was over. He didn't believe her, that much she could see. She told him she was going back to Stewart. "Lindsay—" he began.

"Wait," she said. "Hear me out. Please, Luke." He listened. She kept on talking. She talked in spurts with long silences in between, staring past his head and out the window. November already.

The trees were bare—angry black spikes nailed to a slate gray sky. Overcast today, no good cloud formations. Not in November. Luke had taught her how you could add clouds to a clear sky by using two separate negatives. It was called double printing. A complicated technique, it meant keeping a stock of cloud negatives, then matching for subject and light with the picture negative—the cloudless one.

"So why bother?" she had asked him that first time he took her through the procedure. He smiled then. And stroked his beard. In the red light of the darkroom the beard looked like pinkish spun glass—what the children used to call angel's hair, draping it gently over the Christmas tree, occasionally nicking their fingers.

"Technical enhancement," he shrugged. "Smarter, actually..." he paused, raised the enlarger, "...to wait for a cloudy day. No point in rushing things, not in this racket." They had been working side by side at the two enlargers. He kept cautioning her to go slow.

And now hearing her voice rushing the sentences, she almost smiled. She stopped, tried to breathe deep. "The trick is in the timing," he was always telling her. "Control the pace, and you control the game."

She looked over at him. He was waiting, not sure she had finished. She said nothing. He turned abruptly and walked out the door, down the hall past the darkroom.

His footsteps sounded loud. He refused to put carpeting down, he didn't like rugs or curtains. "Why cover up good hardwood? Or shut out good light?" he said.

But the living room looked so barren, she brought the rug from the other house, the old Chinese rug that had been in the children's room. Stewart hadn't even noticed it was gone; the design was called the Tree of Life. When

83

they were small, the kids used to crawl across and point to the monkeys, giraffes and unicorns climbing up and down the trellis of blue and red flowers that ran along the borders. She would take their hands and let them trace each animal. The embossed design was made of a slightly coarser knotted wool.

"Bumpy," they'd tell her.

"No," she always answered. "Soft. Soft "

She could hear him in the bedroom, pacing back and forth. Then it was quiet.

In a little while he came back. He stood leaning against the door jamb. He was wearing his old sheepskin jacket, the one he wore that first afternoon when she looked up from the card catalogue and he was asking where they kept their back issues of *Popular Photography*.

He wasn't big like Stewart. But he seemed tall in the same way a dancer looks elongated from the stage, larger than life, brilliantly lit by the footlights. He had none of the strutting bravado of short men, nor—luckily—their stumpy legs. His were long-shanked and gold-sheathed with soft blonde fur; in bed they felt like warm logs stacked beside hers. In college he had been a soccer player. "You can always tell by the thigh muscles," he told her. She patted one thigh, solid as the swollen haunch of a horse. "Practically deformed-looking," he added. "No," she whispered. "Lovely. Lovely."

"...what you're doing?" he was asking. "Do you? really know why?"

She shook her head. All the carefully rehearsed reasons, they were flying right out of her mind, reduced to muted mumbles. Just as a year ago, all sensible advice seemed to be sounds at one remove, as faint to the ear as the rustle of newspapers out in the Main Reading Room.

Her friends, smiling nervously, "You'll only be hurt, Lindsay. This isn't like you!"

Stewart hunched in the booth at Friendly's, jaw line lumpy with anger. "You're a fool, Linny, a damn fool."

Her family wailing all the way from Pennsylvania to California, "But dear, what about the kids?"

What about the kids was their remarkable resilience. As if they had been waterproofed against disaster. Busy with Graduate Record Exams, they barely seemed to register the fact that Mom had run off with a 35-year-old photographer, free-lance yet.

Had she been the same way at their age? Had Luke? She could believe it only of Stewart. The man should have been born a duck, emotionally impermeable to sorrow

At Christmas the kids went off to Aspen; it was a relief to everybody. In January, she moved in with Luke. In March, Stewart began divorce proceedings, but then a month later, stopped. In April naturally; the cruelest month. Stewart was nothing if not a traditionalist. Somewhere along the line that winter and spring he ran out of steam. And anger as well.

Poor Stewart. He took to calling her at the library during her lunch hour. He would talk, and she would stand there in the cataloguer's empty office, listening to him, idly touching the piles of new acquisitions, the shiny new dust jackets unmarked as yet by call numbers. And her fingers slithered back and forth across the smooth bright paper while Stewart progressed over the months from indignation through hectoring to stern lectures on responsibility. From sarcasm through bitterness and finally, last week, to begging.

"Lindsay." She looked up. Luke was putting on his gray work gloves. "What?" she asked.

"I'm going out back. Chop some wood." She glanced at the woodpile outside, stacked neatly next to the gate. "We've got plenty," she said. "You got way ahead last…"

"Give it a rest, Lin," and he opened the front door, walked around to the back of the house out of sight.

She shivered, stood up, took a bottle of Windex down from the cupboard and started shining up the windows with newspaper rolled into a loose ball. The newsprint left a hard finish on the glass. It was one of the few household tricks Stewart had taught her. A handyman, Stewart was not. Clumsy, actually. With tools. With family.

"Come back, Linny," he said. And then, she couldn't believe it—as she stood there stacking new books, automatically alphabetizing by author—his voice broke. For the first time in all their twenty-five years together, he began sobbing. He hung up on her so quickly she thought maybe she'd imagined those strangled noises. She jerked her hand. The book tower toppled and crashed onto the floor, their spines splayed out, pages creased, bright dust jackets humped high like circus tents.

"How could you?" Stewart kept asking.

But she couldn't answer that question. There were the obvious reasons. Luke was beautiful. Luke was ten years younger. Luke was suffering, he needed her. And then that secret reason she could see reflected in the faces of people when they came up to the circulation desk. How their eyes went wide as they took another glance at her.

"You look wonderful, Mrs. Randall," they chanted. "Cut your hair?"

"Gone on a diet? a cruise?"

She watched them fumble for their library cards. She smiled back. She knew her eyes sparkled, her skin was glowing, and that her hair looked glossy again, shiny and dark in a soft new cut—no more dead ends just like the ads promised. But not from a plastic bottle of shampoo. No, from a sweet-faced man who loves me, Lindsay Randall, forty-five going on fifteen.

Luke made her beautiful. Stewart simply made her lists, each word in caps to signify importance. THINGS TO DO THIS WEEKEND: TO FILE WITH TAX STUFF. TO INVITE NEXT MONTH, carefully subdivided into: A) PERSONAL B) PROFESSIONAL.

Dear Stewart. So organized which was the skill he admired most in her as well. "You're the librarian, aren't you? My making-order-outta-chaos Gal Friday, right?" he said at least once a month, when the bills rolled around. If she got a tension headache, he'd come over to the desk and knead her neck. "We're a team, aren't we, Linny?" he'd say. "Where would I be without you?"

The answer to that she had known for years. Exactly the same place, no doubt. Stewart—the showcase academic—so distinguished, so successful. He looked the part of a dean. The silvery gray crest of hair above the Roman senator forehead. Those heavy-lidded eyes. The slow precision in the way he talked. His colleagues stood in awe of him; the students idolized him. Except these days he only taught one course, a high level seminar for Economics majors only.

He missed the teaching, he said. "Miss the kids," he complained.

He meant it. She knew he meant it. He was good at missing kids. His own as well. They had grown up almost unnoticed by him. "Good job," he murmured absently when they brought him their trophies, their honors. "Haven't got time," he told them. "Too many irons in the fire," he growled in that rich deep voice which always reminded her of a wind instrument of some kind—a bassoon, perhaps? "Can't seem to say no," was the inevitable coda.

Except to his own children, she suggested. "Think I'm killing myself for the sheer fun of it?" he'd snap back. "Can't you see this is all for you and the kids? Get off my back, Linny," and stamp off to his study.

The children went off to college. She went back to work full-time at the university library. And Stewart? Stewart went on trips. The chancellor tapped him more and more often to wine and dine prospective donors, rich alums, private corporations hungry for tax write-offs. Last fall he started asking her to come with him. But she told him she couldn't leave the library.

"Take your vacation time piecemeal," he suggested. She shook her head. "Can't. They need me."

He frowned. "The budget crunch," she added quickly. "We had to drop two part-time people this summer."

The frown disappeared. His face smoothed out into its noble Augustan mode.

Money problems he could accept, he could grapple with. Nothing pleased Stewart more than to roll up his sleeves and plunge in with his projections, graphs, flow charts, punching in the figures at the computer terminal, the screen a shifting mass of numbers forming and reforming in phalanxes of squared-off digits, vast columns of numbers marching smartly to his commands, glowing a pale evil green against the black screen.

TAP TAP TAP went his fingers against the gray keys. A quiet alien kind of humming those keys made. A series of muted clicks, they bore witness to the smooth running of a machine that could think like a man, typed by a man who thought like a machine.

It frightened her. She started working extra weekend duty. The house felt so empty. When Stewart was away, she closed the door of his study. She draped an old plaid blanket over the terminal. The first time he saw it, he laughed. "Hey, it's not a canary" he said. But she tried to explain how the black screen made her nervous. "Thing looks like a corpse. With its eyes open."

And he said, "You premenstrual or what?" Later, when she told him about Luke, all he could come up with was, "Menopausal. Forty's fidgets."

"That's a cliché," she said quietly.

"No. You're the cliché," he replied, and picked up his briefcase and left for the airport. That was the weekend she moved in with Luke.

She took very little. The Chinese rug. Her winter clothes. Pictures of the kids. Her favorite books, about six cartons worth.

She left him a note. And lists, of course. She left him the name of her lawyer, which bills had to be paid, the engagements she had canceled, the laundry stubs for his shirts, the telephone number of the cleaning lady.

She drove the yellow Subaru. When she got to Luke's, he was back in the darkroom and yelled he couldn't come out until he finished up the last batch of enlargements.

All the way over in the car she had pictured his face when she walked in. He had been begging her for three months to leave Stewart. He looked haggard. He lost weight. His jeans hung on him, flapping around his waist. His face got thinner, the fine eyes meant for laughing gone all hollowed. She told him he looked like the people he photographed. His new book was called *The Homeless*. He had already sold it to a good house in New York, the same publishers who had commissioned his first on Vietnam. Which was still selling nicely, ten years later. He didn't claim to be a writer, just a photojournalist, "emphasis on the photo," he smiled. "My camera does my talking."

Right after she first met him, she checked his book out and that whole week, she was haunted by those faces. The men he had met those two years over in Nam. The suffering of the people who lived there as well as the soldiers who fought there. And all of them trapped in a war nobody believed in.

"A nightmare, Lin," he said. "And we couldn't seem to wake up from it."

"Your book woke up some people," she reminded him. His hand lay across hers, a small narrow hand. The skin always felt hot.

That was what she noticed that first day he came into the library. He looked like someone running a high fever. First she saw the golden beard above the dirty white curls of the sheepskin collar. Then the smiling eyes, the ruddy color of fine-grained skin stretched taut over high cheekbones. His face flamed out of the shadowy silence around the circulation desk. And she had stood there staring at the bronze glow of his cheeks, the rosy curve of the bottom lip half hidden by gold brown hairs. It was all she could do not to reach out to touch him, to warm her fingers against the flushed skin.

"You've gotten cold feet." She jumped.

He had come back. He was standing by the door, arms folded, one shoulder against the frame. His left eyebrow was cocked in a circumflex, mocking her. His face seemed fuller, older, a triangle of hard intersecting planes.

She put down the bottle of Windex. She sat down at the table, moving like an old woman, exaggerating the slowness.

He was waiting. So, in her crisp librarian voice, she said, "Hardly call it cold feet at this juncture."

He kept quiet. She added, more gently this time, "Be fair, Luke."

He took a toothpick from his jacket pocket, reamed it between his front teeth with quick jabs. She could feel the prick against her own gum. "Look," she said, "it's simply too late in the game, you and me."

He stepped forward so fast she flinched. He was talking fast, too, all she could catch was the tag end, "...we've gone through too much."

"We?"

"Yeah, in this together; remember?" He flung out his arm. He pointed at the bookshelves built for her, at the walls covered with pictures he had taken of her. Blow-ups. Color prints on the new matte paper. Black and white contacts. Experimental shots using bounce lighting with electronic flash. With regular flash bulbs. With available light.

His favorites he had dry-mounted. In the beginning she was embarrassed to see her own face smiling, frowning, laughing from every wall. But after a month she got used to it. She was able to discuss density ranges and exposure latitudes with him, oblivious that it was her image they were talking about, her own eyes smiling back at the two of them. Following them as they walked out to the darkroom to fiddle with the enlargers, stir the prints in the stop-bath, check the wash water or pressure between the drum and the cloth belt of the print dryer. She loved the fact he treated her as a bona fide apprentice into the mysteries of the art—not just a flunky doing his scut work.

"Together, damn it all," he repeated. He nodded now at the desk where the galleys of the new book lay neatly piled. They had been proofing them for the last two weeks, working late into the night after she got home from the library. Now the galley proofs were ready to Fed Ex tomorrow. All morning long, he had been on the phone with his agent, making plans for the publicity tour, sixteen cities in twelve days.

He rocked back on his heels. He was still feeling cocky, she could tell. Savoring what lay ahead, tasting the success, warmed by the white hot glare of the publicity machine revving up to peddle his vision of the country's homeless. The vision he'd sweated over, that she had helped him complete. He wanted only to have people see, really see the faces, "maybe touch their consciences for a sec," he said. All those haunted faces. The street people, the bag ladies. The Chicanos picking apples in Michigan. The Cuban exiles in Miami. The Nicaraguans in hiding. All the rootless people.

He was blowing on his hands. "Colder in here," he was saying, "than it is outside. This is dumb, I'm turning up the thermostat. Aren't you cold?"

"Like you said...only my feet."

"Lindsay. Don't do this, just don't, ok?" He sat down beside her at the table. His knee touched hers.

"I have to, Luke," and her words came out very softly—not what she intended at all. "He needs me."

His cheek went red—as if she had slapped him. But she kept on talking. She patted his thigh muscles, she could feel the quadriceps flex under her hand. "...taking a medical leave of absence," she continued. "Acute anxiety crisis, his doctor said."

He stared at her hard. So she added quickly, "He's all alone, Luke. He's going through hell."

"No kidding. And you didn't go through hell to come to me?"

"Same kind of hell, going back," she reminded him. She looked out the window.

As if he needed a reminder. As if he hadn't taught her how to make herself intact again in the eyes of the college community. To hold her head high, disregard the gossip, the careful politeness of colleagues who pretended they didn't know what nice Linny Randall had gone and done. To ignore the speculative looks of the men as they checked out their two-week reserves.

At the end of each day she went home to him. He took her in his arms and same thing every afternoon—his blue work shirt smelling of hypo and developer—he'd say, "Who gives a sweet damn what they think? It's you and me, Lin."

Him and her. She edged away, folded her arms on top of the table. She touched the smooth place on her ring finger—the skin white and shiny. "Right partnership," she said. "Wrong timing."

"What's that supposed to mean?"

"Listen, Luke, it's all downhill for him from now on. I've messed up the past. And I'm killing what's left ahead. What he was working for. Can't you see? He's coming apart!" She hated the sound of her voice, rising up into a wail this way. Breathe deep, breathe from the diaphragm. Control the contractions, control the pace and you control the game.

All she could see of him now was a blur of golden beard. "He's suffering," she said.

He sat so still. His shoulders hunched forward, head ducked down into the fur collar. She added, "I just can't bear it, Luke, watching somebody suffer."

He jumped up and walked over to the desk where the galley proofs lay stacked. He picked them up, held them high over his head, waving them like a banner, then dropped the whole stack.

The pages fluttered down across the rug—the Tree of Life, the monkeys—hidden by the white paper. "Suffering," he repeated. "What in hell do you think this is about? And the Nam book?"

And me, I've suffered, Luke, she wanted to say. Instead she asked him, "Then why can't you show a little compassion? Stewart—"

"I don't give a tinker's damn about Stewart."

"Ironic, isn't it? You of all people, I mean. The connoisseur of suffering, as you bill yourself."

"Stop twisting my words."

As if he hadn't spoken she said, "You were hurting, Luke. That's why I came to you. To take away the pain."

He was looking at her as if she had just dropped in from Mars. "That's sick, Lin. That's not the way it was."

"It's not sick," she answered. She paused, searching for the right word—the one that would begin the whole process. Then she said slowly, "Don't you understand anything? It's the weakness in men that women love."

"I don't have to listen to this."

"No, because you're scared of the truth."

"Get serious, Lindsay."

"Grow up, Luke." He flinched. She felt something tearing loose inside. She went on fast. "Go find someone else, someone your own age. Not just another nice mummy."

Silence. A kind she recognized, the kind that fell so often between her and Stewart. A familiar enemy, this hush in which the after-echo of the words sounds louder than the voices that have spoken them. But the curious thing was, she knew, that only one side of the dialogue gets played back. He could hear only the words she had said, and she, his.

So, when he began speaking again, she blocked the sound. She concentrated on his face instead. The blur was gone now. His face was changing as he spoke. Shifting. Sliding. The angle of the jaw. The planes of the cheekbones forming and reforming into alien shapes, alien textures.

And yes, what she had been waiting for all this time was seeping now into his eyes, settling now into the fix of his mouth beneath the soft gold beard.

She turned. She walked away from him, fueled by the contempt which she'd finally been able to read in his expression.

She went into the hall, heading towards the bedroom. As she walked past the darkroom—he'd forgotten to close the door again—she got a sharp whiff of acetic acid. The whole hallway smelled of Kodak Ektaflow.

She sniffed. Her nose prickled as if it wanted to sneeze—but couldn't. The stuff smelled strong, but she didn't mind.

It reminded her of the pure sharp fragrance of cider after it's turned.

Morning ablutions

IN THE NIGHT WHEN you were young came the questions. In the night when you are old come the questioners.

"Do you understand?"

I understand nothing. But these words he does not utter, he only thinks them—his head sunk down on his chest—staring at the floor.

"I repeat, do you understand?"

I understand the wicked flee...when no man pursueth. He smiles, but still he is mute. He is an old man, and this, a familiar dream.

"You do not answer my questions."

And you shall not question my answers. This response pleases him, both in its formulation and the fact that it too is stillborn.

"You will be left now to consider. We will be back."

I was only a child! What do you want from me? But his silent shout is muffled.

And then the light goes on. The interrogations take place only at night, in the middle of the night when—bedclothes warm, his limbs heavy and prickling with sleep—he opens his eyes and sees that he is being observed.

For long minutes nothing is said. He sits up, swings his legs over the side of the bed. He stares at the floor, at the boots of the men who sit opposite. They sit very erect. The man who never speaks sits in the chair by the table. The other sits on the table and swings his leg back and forth, a slow pendulum of movement. The tip of the boot mirrors the light, a gleam of polished black leather.

He does not let himself look up at their faces. Enough to hear the voice with its clipped consonants. He does not want to see the eyes, he does not want this voice to be humanized. No smiles, no frowns—only the familiar cadences, the timbre, the phrasing.

"We are not speaking of betrayal. We are speaking only of details here, precise details. Who forged your identity card? How was this done, please?"

The room is so quiet that he can almost believe he hears the nervous ticking of the interrogator's watch. But this of course is impossible. It is his

own pulse he hears, the thrumming tick-tick-tick so loud in his eardrums it
blots out the questions he knows by heart.

"Who bribed the conductor?"

"Was it the peasant woman—your mother's neighbor—who found the
safe-house in Bretagne?"

"At the station, what did she say to you, votre mère? Did she say
goodbye?"

"What did you reply? *Do not make me go? Come with me, Maman?*"

The boot stops its swinging movement. There is complete stillness in
the room. He waits for the next sentence. It is always the same. It is not a
question, it is a simple statement of fact. The voice has gone flat, the flat
drone of the interrogator, sure of his evidence now, reciting the established
charges, covering the known ground, the pocked moonscape of common
knowledge, disputed by neither of them.

"You got on the train. Alone. You left them behind, skulking away in the
dark, the night scavenger, saving his own skin. Do you understand?"

He understands only one thing. He understands that he is guilty but that
this is not an admission he will ever make aloud, no matter how many nights
the interrogator may address him, black boot swinging beside the silent figure
who says nothing, who holds a spiral notebook and sits there, pencil poised,
forever waiting for the confession that will not come—the atonement that is
not permitted.

* * *

EACH MORNING HE LOOKS in the mirror. Each morning he lathers gaunt
cheeks with magic foam that transforms the harsh oblong of the jaw into the
avuncular curves of a white-bearded patriarch whose staring eyes he is careful
not to meet. A patriarch of almost sixty years cannot be responsible for the
silent panic of his youth. In the gray-vaulted dimness of the Gare du Nord,
his mother had pressed the ticket into his hand. Trembling, he had taken
it—what other choice was there? "Your Breton cousins," she murmured. "They
are your cousins, if anyone asks. You will be working for your Tante Elise at
the factory—cutting patterns, tu comprends?" And he had nodded yes, smiled
at the conductor, climbed aboard the train—afraid to wave, afraid to speak.

She had drilled and drilled him in the accent, the Breton accent of those
strangers who would shelter him. Each night after his sisters had fallen asleep,
he sat up with her while she coached him in pronunciation, in the vernacular
expressions he must use as automatically as the Parisian street argot which

she hated to catch him teaching Felicité and Marie Yvonne. Eyes blazing, she would snap, "If your Papa could hear such gutter talk!"

And ashamed, he fell silent, sick in his gut at the corruption of the streets which infected him, and in turn, his family. He felt rancid each time he returned to the apartment, more rancid than the packets of black market butter he smuggled past the concierge whose bead-black eyes followed him up the stairs just as they had watched the day his papa was taken down those same steps—head bowed—then turning for one quick glance up the stairwell at the family grouped beside the banister, at his son straining to follow while Maman grabbed at his sleeve and hissed, "Tais-tois, mon fils," and then more gently, "You must be the man now, he depends on you." And the sleeve had torn, but by then the shadowy face below was gone, the front door slammed, and the concierge stood where his father had stood, peering up at them, her eyes the same bottle-black color as those polished leather boots thumping down the staircase while outside klaxons wailed their obscene farewells.

He shaves very carefully, watching islands of skin surfacing through the lather with each stroke of the razor which he shakes into the sink jerking his wrist the way you might shrug off a fly—except this foam is flecked with tiny dots much smaller than a fly—tiny specks of human hair peppering the whiteness exactly as soot will speckle city snow, so that in the end, what was once a pure and fluffy white has become a dirty gray, "All cats are gray in the dark, n'est-ce pas, mon petit?" the concierge whispered when she caught him one night tiptoeing past her door, holding out in front of him his normally flat book satchel that bulged with tins of powdered eggs and a precious sack of white flour, bartered booty in exchange for Papa's imported cigars, the last box empty now, but Maman hugged him before he left the house, "We shall manage, mon cher, I have a plan, dépêche-toi," she whispered and ruffled his hair, oily from too many weeks without soap. Oddly enough, that was the worst, the film of dirt that grew like gray scabs over the apartment, the tabletops, the sink, even the dishes, all the things his mother used to scrub, and shine; and now all her days were spent in whispered consultation with the peasant woman from Saint Brieuc who lived next door with her idiot son, in endless conversations on the phone with someone named Elise—his mother's hand shielding the mouthpiece as if the very wires themselves might eavesdrop, gesturing with her free hand "Study! Study!!" when he looked up from his books to watch the way her mouth formed words that seemed sour to the lips and those hollow triangles beneath the cheekbones where once his father pinched rosy flesh, "Plump as apples," he would laugh, "and just as tart," and she would pretend to cuff him away but smile as she made the gesture, that radiant smile that had gone down the dim staircase with Papa, never to return again. The smile since then was a stretching of lips across teeth too big for the mouth which he had never really noticed before, and made him think of a dog he'd seen once at his grandparents, a female baring sharp yellow fangs when Marie Yvonne tried to lift up a new puppy whose eyes were still sealed shut in that first most dreamless sleep of all.

He turns on the tap. He watches the water swirl away with the foam, then rubs his palm across his chin, his cheeks, smooth again, and he splashes after-shave lotion across his face. It stings in a pleasurable way. It even manages to bring a faint tinge of color to sallow skin, to pores all tightly closed. Yet even now—as his fingertips caress the smoothness—begins the slow progression of hair follicles pushing up...and up...to emerge as the prickly shoots of late afternoon, the midnight ripening into coarse stubble, and then the morning harvest as dawn breaks and he reaches for his razor once more. Why not grow a full beard? he wonders silently, but the answer is always the same. It would be his father's face he must watch in this mirror, even though his own beard would be streaked now with gray while Papa's was a lustrous black. But the high-bridged nose is the same, the disdainful nostrils and the eyes he cannot face are Papa's eyes, the mouth is Papa's mouth, and now he wants to leave, it is time, it is late. He wipes the razor. He puts it away on the shelf, and the brush and the shaving cup, and he wipes his hands on the towel and turns to go, but the eyes command him to look into the mirror, so he stares first at the shiny chrome of the faucet, then slowly up the yellow tiles of the wall to the metal rim that brackets the glass.

And now the eyes are gazing at him. But they are kindly. They are not angry at all nor the least bit sad, no—they smile back at him with that familiar wink which meant they shared a secret—this father, this son—they are the night hunters who must each evening go out and forage for the maman and the cubs back in the cave, and they must catch the young gazelle by her beautiful fawn-colored throat of such exquisite suppleness and sweetness, then drag her back to the lair all glistening with blood and tenderly drop the body, "Faute de mieux, mon brave, now you must be the man of the house, you must be their fierce protector," the smiling eyes are reminding him as they do each morning of his life.

Yes, each morning: the sink, the mirror, the eyes, and now the time has come to address the mirror in the sharp clipped consonants of the interrogating officer whose midnight voice he knows so well. But the words are not his. The words are the ones his mother spoke when they passed the closed green door of the concierge, and he can still see his mother avert her face as if they are passing a public urinal, sniff sharply, then mutter under her breath but he can read her lips, "Putain, sale boche!" and hurry them out to the vestibule.

But what he repeats each morning are not these exclamations but rather the very last thing she said as they walked slowly down the stone steps of the apartment building, and the shock of seeing Maman spit at their concierge cowering below them at the coal-cellar door is still fresh as the first morning she did it, spit precisely like a man, right over the iron balustrade, and then she spoke the way he speaks now in his cold interrogator-voice—not hers, no—but the scorn is the same, and beyond that note of scorn, his own unique contribution—his alone—that special loathing of the self-accused:

"Jackal," he says. "Do you understand?"

I understand nothing.

SPANISH MOSS

AND THEY TAKE ME to the house—no, not the house itself but where it used to be on this street which back then was called a plain old avenue but now is gussied up to boulevard, see the sign? Branch Blvd. it reads—and nodding, they tell me, *yes, yes, look, Lillianbelle! Down there, the grove was right down there, this whole block all grapefruit trees, remember?*

But I don't know why they're excited, these cousins I mean, sure, this may be the street but it's not the street I want to remember and these fancy estates with their spiky St. Augustine grass and their swimming pools, they screen that house I'm looking for, they obscure the memory and yet for my cousins they constitute proof, concrete evidence of something gone, vanished from everywhere except a couple of old albums, the snapshots brown and curled at the edges.

Proof, however—that's not really what I'm after, is it? No, what I want is the essence of that place and time, and now I realize I must do what my Creole grandmother called *meubler* and furnish each room: the cracked yellow oilcloth on the kitchen table, the old mangle crouched out on the back porch. No, it's harder than that, I've got to close my eyes and build the whole house plank by plank—what's the word here? *échafauder*, yes, erect the scaffolding bit by bit and then maybe I can see those people inside who taught me one summer about love and treachery and how the two are rooted together, bound as tightly as the Virginia creeper vine that climbs round and round the tall New England pine outside my door.

First there is the gate. It's a dark green iron gate, rusted in the hinges. The squeak when the gate swings open sounds painful, a sharp creak of protest. But to my ears, it sounds a cry of rusty welcome.

Up the sandy path to the front steps. The house has squat dingy gray pillars across the front, the sides of the house are stucco, a bungalow type of construction popular all over Tampa back in the thirties and forties.

On the front porch nodding gently back and forth is an old rocking chair. The bright peacock blue paint has flaked off the armrests, exposing the bare wood. This is my grandmother's rocker, except my cousin Timmy and I didn't call her Grandma, we called her Mama, the same as her daughters did.

97

Mama took us in one whole summer while my own mother went to nurse
Timmy's in Boston. Both our daddies were overseas fighting the war. I don't
believe Timmy could even remember his father, maybe that's why we spoiled
him so.

Once we dragged Mama's rocker out in the front yard. She sat down,
uneasy with having her hands idle, with being stiffly posed while somebody
takes her picture. She smiles at the camera, a shy mysterious smile, face half
averted, dark eyes glowing. Behind her, the moss hangs heavy off the trees
like a swag of drapery in a photographer's studio, dulled by the late afternoon
sun to a monochrome of soft gray halftones. I remember the feel of Spanish
moss, thickly textured and very dense with tight curls peculiar to the touch
as if they should be coarse like wiry hair but instead are soft—soft enough
to stuff into a pillow—and spongy light. And I can still see the color, that
strange bleached out gray under-coated with the palest green of very old jade.
This must be what gives moss hanging on trees that ghostly look, as if the
green has been frightened off in the same way that blood drains from a face
in shock or pain, and all that's left is a shutterclick of rose beneath chalky
white skin.

So Mama sits there in her rocking chair. They had me stand behind her,
one hand on her bony shoulder. We are all dressed up. Maybe it was her
birthday. She is wearing her good black shoes, and she will take them off the
minute the box camera has been put away and we troop back into the cool
house for lemonade. The shoes hurt her bunions. Most of the time she wears
old canvas sneakers with holes cut on either side so the bunions, she explains,
"can breathe easier."

I stand gawky tall and proud behind her rocker. I'm wearing my best
jersey jumper but I'm not wearing a blouse underneath because it's so
hot outside. Mama must have just done up my braids because they look
uncharacteristically neat tied with two plaid ribbons on the ends.

My cousin Timothy is posed right in front of Mama. He too is dressed up
in his best Eton jacket and short pants. His fluffy blonde hair gleams in the
sunlight. He doesn't rest against Mama's knees. He doesn't touch her at all.
He smiles that slightly false smile of a child used to being photographed. He
had been such a beautiful baby, and at four, he's an extraordinarily handsome
little boy with the unassailable composure of those blessed with physical
perfection. Timmy was accustomed to being smiled at, but just as when you
bend down to examine the perfection of an orchid and draw back in surprise
because there is no scent, so it was with Timmy. The trusting smile began
and ended with those exquisitely curved lips, with the frank clarity of shining
blue eyes which gave back nothing. Because there was nothing to give. Mama

used to say in her gentle voice, "Timmy's not a hugging child," and leave it at that.

We spoiled him, we catered to him, our only reward that manly little smile. He hardly spoke a word. He hardly needed to. He was Mama's very first grandson. I was her first granddaughter, six years older than Timmy, but along with the other two females in the household that summer my job was to take care of the "little man" as we called him. Later on he would have kid brothers and those brothers would be like my very own and bring me here to see where the old house used to be but not until long, long afterwards, and that summer Timothy was my only cousin—and *only* my cousin while I wanted him so much to be my brother, my playmate, my best friend.

Mama's youngest daughter, Esther Mae, still lived at home then as well. Esther Mae was actually my aunt, but I liked to pretend she was my older sister. She was seventeen and really boy-crazy. She used to give me and Timmy rides on her bike. With him, she only poked around in front for a while, but she took me off on real excursions. At first I sat in back but it was uncomfortable and I was afraid my legs would get caught in the spokes. So Esther told me to perch on the front handlebars, which meant steering wasn't easy.

But she knew the road to the drugstore, "So well," she said, "I could ride you there with my eyes closed." And I believed her since that's what she was practically doing already. Sitting on those handlebars was like being in the very first car of a roller coaster. She took short cuts through old vacant lots and then down the railroad embankment.

"Hang on, Belle!" she shouted. The weeds flew up at me, so did my stomach, and I shut my eyes and was sure the tires had left the ground and we were flying. But then the thud, the crazy swoops as Esther Mae swerved to keep us on course, keep us from tipping over—and I knew that we were still earthbound—and I, disappointed.

At Liggetts Drugs & Sundries, we always sat at the same little table with wrought iron legs painted white like fancy patio furniture in the movies. Esther kept staring at the new soda jerk. His name was Lester Lee Wilcox, and although he was only a ninth grader, he was—like me—very tall for his age. And so good looking—I mean really handsome, and he slicked his curly black hair down with Vitalis which put me in mind of an adorable but rather wet cocker spaniel.

"Isn't he cute?" Esther kept saying. "Oh shoot, guess I'm robbing the cradle but that boy's downright cuddly!" She sipped the last of her ice cream soda so hard the straw made the same embarrassing sucking noises bath water makes gurgling down the drain.

Lester knew she was giving him the eye. His big ears went beet red. He turned his back to us and started messing with the jug of Coca Cola syrup.

"How about a Coke, honey?" Esther was asking me.

I shook my head. "I'm full," I told her as well as being a little nervous, not to mention mortified, but that part I kept to myself. Esther didn't hold with criticism. My granddaddy claimed she was born bull-headed, and just as ornery as any bull calf he'd ever dealt with.

She poked her straw around the bottom of the glass, skimming up foam. The straw was bent, flattened at the end with pink lipstick smudges smeared all over. "Mama," she said, "keeps harping how I shouldn't eat chocolate, claims if I leave off eating the stuff, my skin would perk up in no time."

Esther had a pretty face with dark glowing eyes like Mama, but her skin was red and angry, inflamed with acne. Made me want to wince looking at it head on. But she had nice teeth, a gleaming white Ipana smile which she kept in reserve strictly for boys and folks outside the family. She may have inherited her mother's prettiness, but she had her daddy's mean temper.

"A matched pair, the two of them," Mama said. "Got that Shannon mean streak, you just can't fool with it," and shook her head slow but with that sweet sad smile of hers that made us all love her so. Mama never raised her voice. She let Daddy, my grandfather, take care of that department. He worked as a brakeman for the railroad, and he wasn't around much, he was always stalking off to union meetings. "The Brotherhood," he called it. Since I understood perfectly how important brothers were, it seemed to me altogether sensible my grandfather set such store by his.

He was a tall skinny man and sort of flapped when he walked, stooping over a bit. Mama told us proudly he'd been movie star handsome as a young man, but all I remember is this beautiful thin nose, curved like the beak of an eagle. And an eagle's hooded eyes which would blink shut all of a sudden, then glare out at a person, blazing, and make you want to disappear fast.

Esther wasn't scared of him though. He kept threatening to whip her when she came in late at night. Next morning he'd be stomping outdoors and cutting a switch from the camellia bushes beside the front gate. But he never used the switch on her, just slapped it against his coveralls while the two of them commenced to hollering at each other. Then at a certain loud stage of the game, Esther Mae went running up to her bedroom, threw herself down on her stuffed panda, and howled up a storm.

Daddy would clump out to the back porch and sit on the top step, pitching corn at the chickens—white leghorns proud as peacocks—and puff fast on his cigar. He always smelled of cigar smoke, it seemed steeped into his hide not just his clothes. Sometimes he swooped down and gave me a bear hug. It frightened me, the smoky smell of him. Smoke means fire.

When these squabbles went on which they did regularly because Granddaddy was trying to tame my aunt Esther—'beat the tar out of her" was what he said although he never got to the tar, it lay there hot and smoldering beneath the pitted skin—anyhow when these fights erupted, Mama used to invite me and Timothy out for a stroll in the side yard where the grove of grapefruit stood. Wandering along under the trees, we each took hold of one of Mama's soft hands, pausing a second or so while Mama held Timmy up high to grab us a grapefruit. He tossed it down to me. The skin felt smooth and warm from the sun. Then we ambled back to the front porch, Mama easing down in her blue rocker.

"Belle, honey, could you kindly fetch the salt cellar?" she asked. Mama never gave a direct order, but instead transmuted all her requests into questions which in turn made compliance twice as easy for the person asked. That question mark at the end helped you feel free, not boxed in, the door always ajar, an invitation as opposed to a command.

When I got back with the salt shaker, Mama had already peeled away the thin rind of the grapefruit, and we three sat there eating one section at a time, dosing each piece with salt to bring out the sweetness.

"Only way to eat grapefruit," said Mama.

"You mean with salt?" I asked.

"That too, honey. But right off the tree's what I meant."

"Those dumb Yankees, they don't know what they're missing," I added even though geographically speaking I suppose I was a Yankee, but like my grandfather always told us, what counts is blood, not where you happen to live.

Now Mama smiled, patting me on the cheek. Timmy didn't say a word, he just tucked all the grapefruit seeds carefully in his pockets. Later he and I would put them in his toy dump truck. They made terrific mortar shells.

Mama stood up and wiped her hands on her apron. "You all run want to run along now, maybe go play out front for a spell? Keep a close eye on him, you hear, Belle?" and she went back into the house, shutting the screen door softly behind her. Mama never slammed a door, no more than she ever raised her voice.

By then the sobs from Esther Mae's room had stopped. And the radio was turned on. Either Daddy was listening to H. V. Kaltenborn, or Esther had switched on *Stella Dallas, Backstage Wife*, I really couldn't tell, all I could hear was steady murmuring interrupted by static. But whatever the program, the radio being on signaled a ceasefire was taking place, for the time being anyhow.

Playing out front along the sandy road, those were the best times Timmy and I had together. He owned a whole fleet of cars and tanks. He loaned me his tractor made of heavy metal painted bright red. It had fat wheels, real rubber he told me. Their treadmarks left crisscross designs in the sand.

"Rurr-rurr" I went. I was plowing fields, cotton fields with long curving furrows—my, how they pleased me—those lovely tractor-tire zigzags spaced as evenly as fishbones. Timmy, on the other hand, was playing war.

"Aaaaaak-aaaaaak" he'd reply. After a while I let his tank shoot the tractor which rolled over and over in the sand, finally coming to rest upside down, one huge tractor wheel spinning slowly round and round. Then we'd start up the war from the beginning again. He won the battle each and every time, but it altogether tickled me to see at the end of each skirmish how many furrows curved beside the road before the mortar shells killed my tractor. At least, I thought, the land's still safe, the land survives.

Sometimes Timmy took big hunks of moss off the trees to camouflage his squadron. He liked making surprise strikes, and even though I knew what was coming (I could plainly see the clumps of moss nested along the perimeter of my plowed fields), it was frightening in that drowsy silence when the machine guns began to fire and the moss lumped itself up and began moving straight at me, a miniature hedge on wheels rolling slowly towards the tractor, the whine of bullets and heavy mortar fire so loud and all. The moss bore down steadily, the turret gun of the tank poking through its curly grayish green tendrils like the long trunk of some prehistoric monster, half plant, half metal. Terrifying! We played this game over and over until Mama's voice floated out from the house, "Time for supper, you children good and hungry?"

I liked going inside to wash up, this being one of the times Granddaddy didn't scare me, not a bit. He would stand Timmy on a little blue stepstool to reach the sink, and soap first his hands then his face. And sometimes just for fun, he washed my hands too, even though he growled, "You a mighty big sprout now, sugar." His fingers were hard with calluses and stained yellow from nicotine. But when he grabbed that bar of Lifebuoy soap and slid it over my hand, working up a good rich lather, it felt so nice and set me to thinking of my own father fighting the enemy far across the sea. I think Granddaddy knew it made me both happy and homesick at the same time.

Once he said, "Used to do this for your mama too, when she was just a tadpole your age." His voice was gruff. At the sink his cigar smell didn't bother me but seemed nice, cozy in a funny way. Standing close to him reminded me of Mama explaining how in the eye of a hurricane everything goes still and the wind just plain can't get you. Same thing when I climbed up on Granddaddy's lap after supper and snuggled against his red suspenders while he read me the funny papers. Then it was safe, and even when Esther Mae came in the living room to dicker for the loan of his old Model A, he never got grumpy. We had plenty of gas rationing coupons because he always walked to work, and also because railroad employees got an extra allotment since they were important workers in the war effort (which made me right proud of Granddaddy).

All he said to Esther was "Nobody in the rumble seat" but he never even glanced up when he handed her the keys. "Home by ten or you're in hot water, I guarantee you, sister," he added. Esther giggled and flew out the door.

She had gotten her driver's license a week earlier. That was the end of our bike rides to the drug store. But she was swell, she let me borrow her bike and Mama trusted me to go all by myself to the A & P for some oleo or a loaf of bread. Afterwards I was allowed to stop by Liggetts for a soda. I sat right up at the counter on a slippery black leather stool, but my legs were long enough to brace against the footrails so I didn't slide off. I hunched over the newest copy of *True Detectives* while Lester tended to the other customers. Then at last, he started mopping the marble counter and talking to me. He told how he was going to enlist in two years if the war kept up. I didn't let on I was only ten years old. He talked to me like an equal, and his ears were such a nice shell pink I understood why Esther Mae gave him the glad eye. I made my lips purse up pretty sipping my chocolate soda, but I drew the line at sucking noises.

Then one evening while it was still light out and Timmy was in his pajamas listening to *Mr. Keen, Tracer of Lost Persons* and Esther was at the movies, everything changed. Forever. Mama and I were sitting out on the front porch, shelling peas. They made a loud clatter dropping into the big white enameled saucepan. It was quiet outdoors, the birds had gone to bed by then, and the air felt cool for a change.

"Fixing to rain tomorrow," said Mama.

"How you know that, Mama?"

"Bunions cut up fierce just before rainfall, honey."

I was just going to ask her when could I go to the movies with Esther when we heard somebody whistling out by the front gate. The hinges squeaked, and then in through the gate walked Lester, his ears a bright watermelon red. He was carrying a carton of ice cream, hand-packed.

"My, my!" whispered Mama. "Looks like we got ourselves a gentleman caller." Lester didn't hear her, he was trying to click the gate shut, but I didn't care, I only wanted to clear out of there fast, and I did, skeedaddling through the screen door before he wheeled around.

From my bedroom window I could hear his voice hitting highs and lows over and under Mama's, and the slow thumping of her rocking chair. Mumble, mumble for a good ten minutes or so. Finally the front gate creaked shut again. Then Mama's footsteps past the parlor into the kitchen followed by the clunk of the Kelvinator being closed, she was putting away the ice cream. Then silence, and after a while a tap at the bedroom door. She came in, sat on the edge of my bed.

"He's a right sweet youngster," she said. "You taken a shine to him, honey?"

I buried my face deep in the pillow, I couldn't look at her.

"It's ok, baby ," she said gently. "It's just fine to like boys, trouble is Lester Lee's a little too old for you. You see, honey, he didn't realize you were only ten, you being so tall. He apologized right away for the mistake."

Her voice was so reasonable and matter of fact calm that it made me cry. She patted my shoulder, murmuring "There, there, sugar. Time enough for all that," and then began telling me how in couple years those age differences wouldn't matter. Then she slid into the Creole French of her Louisiana childhood: "Tais-toi, mon petit chou."

But I cried into the pillow, not sure which was worse: leading on Lester, getting caught at it, or the fact this was the end of black and white sodas for the rest of a terribly long summer.

When Esther heard about this (I figured Timmy must have told her), she didn't tease me, she didn't even get mad. She winked and looked like the cat who swallowed the canary. She got chummy with me, telling me all about her new boyfriend. I decided I had finally graduated to being her sister, not just her bratty Yankee niece.

One Saturday morning she invited me to go swimming with her over at Silver Springs. Timmy couldn't go—he was too young. He couldn't swim a stroke yet, but I could, and all morning long I swam closer and closer to the springs in the middle of the lake. The water felt really ice cold there. Huge signs posted along the banks warned bathers not to swim directly over the springs because of the whirlpool.

DANGEROUS: FOR EXPERT SWIMMERS ONLY! the sign read.

Esther was sprawled under a catalpa tree talking fast to her sailor friend when I finally swam straight across the springs. I could feel the water pulling at me from below, and I flutter-kicked fast over the cold spot, convinced the whirlpool would suck me down. But it didn't, and Esther waved at me from the catalpa tree. After a spell, she and the sailor whose name was "Hobbes, Franklin Hobbes, Miss" throwing in a quick salute—anyhow they went up to the bathhouses to change. Then they came running hand in hand down the hill and jumped in the water, splashing each other like a couple of fifth graders. The rest of that day Hobbes taught Esther and me how to do backward somersaults underwater.

When we got home, Mama was just putting the fried chicken on the table. She smiled when we walked in the door. Timmy wanted to know all about the whirlpool so we took turns describing how dangerous it had been, and how maybe next summer he would be ready to learn the crawl.

My grandfather didn't say much. He was busy working on his fried chicken , making more smacking sounds than Timmy ever did. I think Daddy must have had false teeth because of the little click-clicking noises when he chewed, even soft foods like grits and cornbread. He told Esther Mae and me we looked like a pair of drowned rats, and pretty much left it at that.

For dessert we had peach pie, Timmy's favorite. He waved his fork when Mama brought the pie still steaming hot from the oven. "Me first!" he announced. About the only time Timmy ever did speak was at meals, propped up to table level on a stack of Sears & Roebuck catalogs. "Yummy!" he exclaimed, eyes gleaming.

We all fell to eating fast. Being the men of the family, Tim and Daddy got seconds. Daddy finished his piece off with three huge clicks, then with a polite belch reached for his cigar. He leaned back, asked if I had learned any new strokes that day. He was so proud we knew how to swim. Neither he nor Mama ever went swimming. "Too scared of the gators," he would tell us, and lunge at us open-jawed, eyes rolling.

"I mostly did the Australian crawl," I told him.

"Plus you learned the backward somersault," Esther reminded me between mouthfuls. She looked good that night. When she got a nice tan, nice honey-gold color, her acne almost disappeared and you couldn't help thinking she was a pretty girl after all. It was a relief not to have to slide your eyes away from that angry skin.

"Oh boy! Hobbes, he made it look so easy, me and Esther caught on fast!" I said, and grinned at her. But her eyes narrowed, the lids came down half-mast and she had that hungry eagle look of Grandaddy's like she was fixing to peck your poor old eyeballs right out of their sockets.

A foot kicked my shin hard under the table. I stared down at the pie, pushed my fork into the sticky part of the crust where the brown sugar hardened into a glaze pretty much the consistency of black tar.

"Hobbes?" repeated Daddy. "Who Hobbes?"

Nobody said a word.

Daddy put down his cigar. Bad sign. "Esther Mae," he said quietly, the calm before the storm, "be much obliged if you'd give me a straight answer."

"Just an old friend, Daddy," she answered and tried to dazzle him with that white-gleaming smile of hers. But her eyes were angry, they didn't match her mouth. And my grandfather knew she was fibbing. He could read her easy as an open book, he claimed. I believed him, and I think Esther did too, them being as alike as two peas in a pod, according to Mama.

"Some no account trash you picked up," Daddy went on and started puffing again on his cigar, blowing angry smoke rings up at the kitchen light overhead. The flypaper rippled.

Esther leaned forward, she was breathing hard too. "He's *not* trash, I'll have you know, he's nineteen years old and in the United States Navy and he's home on leave. What's more he's very much in love with me."

Daddy's face went pale. His hand holding the cigar trembled. Mama leaned over to pat his shoulder but he shook off her hand the way stock animals do a horsefly, a sort of quiver and shudder at the same time.

"You're grounded, missy," he announced. "No more car and that's a promise. I will not have me a deceiver for a daughter." He glanced over at me and added, "Who drags a young'un along as alibi. Now you hie yourself off to your room, you hear?" And he slammed his fist so hard on the table, a plate slithered across the yellow oilcloth and hit the floor with a crash.

Timmy looked down at the broken plate, up at my grandfather's face, then over at mine, and commenced to bawl. Another crash as Esther Mae stood up, knocking over her chair. She was so furious her lips went ropy white. The only person she glared at was me as she turned away from the table. "Judas!" she hissed and was gone.

She never spoke another word to me the whole rest of that summer. She looked right through me. Daddy made her get a job at the Nedick's orange juice stand, so she wasn't home very often. And when she was, she would sit in her room and read movie magazines. Mama was very patient with her. "Don't you fret," Mama told me. "These black spells, they have a way of blowing over. Like a summer squall. Pay her no mind."

I was now the one who took Timmy for bike rides. We swooped down the railroad embankments going lickety split. Once I took him over to the sand hills by the quarry. The tires bogged down and we both flew off the bike. But it was soft sand. Timmy didn't say a word, just picked himself up. When he got back on the bike, he held me tight around the waist and kept whispering in my ear, "Faster, Belle, *faster!*" I knew I was taking chances (Mama trusted me to use good judgement) but sharing the danger was a present I could give him. I liked seeing his eyes shine. We still played out by the front gate some, but not as much. The fun had gone out of our war games. Pretend-danger wasn't enough any longer. Going fast and folks heaving plates at each other seemed much more exciting than playing war.

I decided I might have struck out being a kid sister but at least I still had a younger brother. The trouble was Timmy never gave much back, just smiled with those ghost blue eyes of his. I was hungry for talk, even those loud summer squalls of Esther Mae's. With her gone so much, Mama used me more and more for chores. Timmy was my assistant. Early each morning we had to gather pullet eggs, and I taught him how to reach in ever so gentle and lift the warm egg out of the straw, cradling it with both hands because his palm was too small to cup the egg. He only broke a couple the first few times. I was proud of him. We also got to help Mama with the laundry. On wash days I was allowed to turn the mangle although my arms felt like jelly squeezing the big sheets. I was good at the pillow cases though.

Our best chore was going out by the woodpile at the far end of the property past the grapefruit trees, to gather kindling for the stove. Timmy was supposed to stand at the edge of the woodpile and pitch the sticks I found into the red wagon. We were not supposed to climb on top of the woodpile. "Too rickety," Mama told us. "Too many snakes."

But it was too tempting. I liked to work my way up to the very center of the pile, then jump from one stack to the next pretending I was actually a mountain goat, the kind with the curly horns. One morning Timmy followed me up. I looked around and there he was, teetering right behind me. He was grinning, his cheeks pink.

"You get yourself right back down, buster," I said real quick and glanced over towards the back porch to make sure Mama hadn't seen us.

"You not the boss of me," he answered and hopped along a narrow plank that bridged the two piles.

"I most certainly am," I said. But he looked so happy, I shut up. It was plain to see he had much better balance than I did. He scrambled ahead, he was actually squealing with excitement, Timmy, my silent man.

"I'm a Flying Fortress!" he yelled. And he was. He flew up and down that woodpile so fast it made me plain dizzy watching him. Dizzy, also jealous of how surefooted he was, and how behind him I moved as slow and cautious as an old lady. I had to stop for a second, I had a stitch in my side. I jumped down on the ground, and then as I looked up I saw something wriggling close to Timmy's blue Keds, diamond shapes on its back, a rattler for sure.

But I couldn't get a word out. I pointed. And he looked first at my face then down at his sneaker. The snake slithered beside his toe for an instant and then it was gone and then Timmy lost his balance—and he started to fall.

I can still see him falling towards me, floating down, down, although of course it happened much faster, but there he is, eyes huge, his mouth a big O shape, and I'm reaching out to catch him but he falls to the right of me, on top of an old board.

And then the screams begin.

It was his leg, he'd fallen on a rusty nail. No blood, only a deep puncture mark in his calf, and then this long purplish furrow. He screamed so loud I thought my heart would explode. I grabbed him, but he pulled away, hitting at me, his little face all screwed up in the effort of screaming.

And then Granddaddy was running towards us through the weeds and Mama came flying down the porch steps, her face a blur, all I could see were her great dark eyes like two black holes.

Daddy scooped up Timmy, swung him up light as a pullet feather, the whole time making clucking noises and shaking his head.

When Mama reached us, Timmy stopped crying. He pointed at his leg. I felt as if I had driven in the nail myself, I couldn't speak a word while they kept on asking, "What happened, baby?"

But Timmy found the words for both of us. He glanced up at Mama who kept fanning her apron like a fluttering wing over his leg, then at Granddaddy. And then finally he stared at me, and he pointed right at me, the faithless Judas goat who led him straight into danger, he was right—I mean I know he was right—and in this tiny angel voice but so clear in the silence after all the screaming, he said, "She pushed me."

BOXES

—

BOXES. BOXES OF GROCERIES in the kitchen, the pantry—bags of sugar hard as concrete. Boxes everywhere. Shoved under the beds. On top of the bureaus. Wedged into closets.

The house was swollen with junk piled so high she and Hank couldn't even get into the room they had left for last, his mother's bedroom.

The door was jammed shut. So while his father watched them gravely from the flagstone walk, Hank jimmied open the screen and helped Molly climb through the window. She scraped her knee on the sill.

"You ok?" he asked and steadied her under the elbow, voice kind but not his eyes. He was angry—not at her, of course. Angry at the mess, at his mother's death, and trying hard not to show it. But it washed over them both, his anger, scaring them both as well. He was, in fact, behaving like his mother. They both knew it. The room smelled of old pills.

"I'm fine," she said, "It *reeks* in here," and she grabbed a bottle of cologne from the vanity table and sprayed the stuff all around. But the sharp smell wouldn't go away. It was as if it had soaked into the bones of the house.

Boxes. Boxes of patent medicines. Of white kid gloves; of old hats and new sweaters never worn. Boxes of dress fabrics, the patterns cut and pinned but left unfinished, the pins beginning to rust. Boxes of wedding presents never sent, the silver tarnished, the gift cards yellowed with age. Boxes of recipes—many the same ones she had copied out for Molly. Recipes and toilet training—the only topics they had ever talked about together comfortably. Cartons and cartons of old newspapers and magazines and pamphlets on *How to Lose Fifty Pounds in 10 Weeks*. Directories for the Siamese Cat Association of America, the Chess Club, and all the other organizations the woman had belonged to for over sixty years right up to last spring and the stroke—and the long summer's dying.

The first couple of days after the funeral they had tackled the kitchen. The freezer was jammed with homegrown berries and Blue Lake string beans frozen as far back as five years ago, their dates still printed with a bright red magic marker across the plastic lids. The vegetable bin in the refrigerator was covered with brown slime, enough rotting food to fill all three big garbage pails out on the kitchen stoop. It irritated Molly that her father-in-law hadn't even tried to clean out the fridge but stayed outside burning trash all day long. He was still reluctant, she knew, to come near the sanctuary of the kitchen.

The kitchen had always been off limits to everybody, even the grandchildren. "She's mean," they used to say. And Hank would tell them patiently, "She's just tired, kids. She wasn't always like this."

"Out!" she would say with a sharp sniff, her face flushed and angry. "I don't *want* help." She drove them all away, disdaining offers to set the table, ignoring family jokes before mealtimes, glaring at the old man who never once looked in her direction.

Two strangers co-existing, so sad. But which had come first, Molly wondered, the old man's aloofness? Or the wife's hot disdain? Had they ever stood side by side watching the chickadees at the feeder outside the kitchen window, her washing the dishes, him drying?

It was the same with her clothes. The old man wouldn't come near them, wouldn't touch anything of hers. He would only help with loading the station wagon, then stand in the driveway and wave them off. He looked so fragile to Molly, his shoulders too narrow for the old plaid shirt, but he still stood erect, silver hair glinting in the October sun, standing tall—almost as tall as his lanky son—waving at Hank and Molly with a slow courtly gesture. A man of great reserve and a remote kind of sweetness, and still at eighty-six the handsomest man Molly had ever met. "He's only forty years older," she told Hank. "Too bad I didn't meet him first."

"I got lucky," Hank would say, grinning.

The second week they started on the newspaper and magazines. They took them to the scrap paper place across the bridge in the old section of town out near the steel foundries.

The routine became a ritual. Hank would back the wagon close to the loading dock. Drop the tailgate. Grab a carton, pull, and swing it up on the platform. Grab, pull, swing. She got into the rhythm of it after a while. But she still couldn't do it as fast as Hank. She kept reminding herself they were a team. Why then did she want to win? To match his grimness, his resolve? Something infectious about the house that pulled people apart, was that it? A house in which love had curdled long ago, long before she married Hank.

The Willy brothers watched them from the loading dock. There were three Willys—men of about sixty or so, she judged—very fit, their blue shirt sleeves rolled up, sinewy arms swooping up the boxes to weigh them on the big scale. Silent men. Very polite but taking it all in, shrewd eyes darting from the newspapers down to the Connecticut license plate, then back to Molly and Hank standing beside the station wagon, heaving cartons.

On the fourth day, first the cats had to be left off at the Humane Society so they got there late. But the Willys were waiting as usual. The oldest Willy—he seemed to be the official spokesman—took out a pencil stub, licked the point then began jotting down figures on a small pad of paper. "Been doing some reading, I see," he said. He had a strong Pennsylvania Dutch accent, dropping his consonants in a guttural sing-song.

Hank smiled. "Twenty year's worth, you might say."

The oldest Willy glanced down at his pad of paper, and grinned. He had bad teeth but a good face, alert, not missing a trick. "Three and a half ton so far," he announced.

Beside him, the tall brother, the one with a butterfly tattooed on his left arm, patted the bales of paper. The bales rose in stacks clear up to the rafters, heavy wire bound tightly around each bale, so that in the gloom of the big shed they glimmered like pale towers bunched so tightly together they formed a solid canyon of paper which dwarfed the three men standing in front.

The tall brother coughed. Right on cue, the oldest Willy cleared his throat. "My brothers and me..." he stared straight down at Hank, "...we know who you are."

Hank shifted for a moment, then looked up, waiting. Molly could tell he was braced for something bad. She took his hand, squeezed it.

The old guy was squatting down now on the platform. He stuck the pencil stub behind his left ear and rubbed his hands. "*You* used to come here with your mama!" he said triumphantly.

And then the three Willys were laughing, and Hank was laughing too. "You're right," he said. He looked happy, really happy for the first time in months. Molly wanted to jump up on the platform and hug all three Willys at once. They had given him back to her, intact again.

"Ja. We remember you. Little fella, you and your two sisters. Your mama used to bring you. Spring and fall. Like clockwork."

The tall Willy spoke for the first and only time. "You was only this big," and he held his tattooed arm out waist-high.

"Ja," the other brother—the bald one—nodded.

"I remember," said Hank. "And you let us climb up on the loading platform. We jumped on the scales. God..." and he glanced over at Molly, "so long ago!" his eyes soft now, the hard glaze gone at last.

The tall brother coughed once more. The senior Willy nodded again. "Strong lady, your mama," he said. "Ja, fierce! She picked them boxes up like they made of feathers. Used to baling hay, she said. Back in the old days, when she was young girl."

"Right, right. What a memory."

"Me and my brothers, we never forget a face."

Hank shook his head. His grin was lopsided, half amused, half amazed.

"Ja...in the old days. Let's see. Montana? Your mama was born in Montana somewhere, wasn't she?" The old Willy's face creased up in a snaggle-tooth smile. He was showing off, Molly realized. For her, for Hank. But just as he was adding, "She was a schoolteacher, right?" a blue panel truck began backing up beside their station wagon.

End of performance; end of show.

So Hank shut the tailgate. They both climbed in the car, the Willys all waved goodbye, and he and Molly drove back to his mother's house.

Because even though his father was waiting for them by the back door, it was still the mother's house.

Always had been, always would be.

The only place the old man had carved free for himself was the green chair by the bookcase in the living room. That and his spartan bedroom upstairs with its narrow cot, his desk, his files with the gold plaque the library gave him when he retired, and his tweed hat placed squarely on the maple chest of drawers. His overcoat hung on a hook on the back of the door. A room of clean smooth surfaces, no clutter. Not even a rug on the hardwood floor.

The room suited him. Every time Molly peeked in, she wanted to cry. Or scream. That he had been shunted aside and forced to camp out like a stranger in his own home. Was that it though? Or had he simply withdrawn? He seemed so indifferent, always greeting them with that remote smile when they returned from the trips to the dump and Goodwill and the Willys, and thank God, the Humane Society today with the damn cats. The four cats he had penned out on the back porch. All he would do was feed them. Otherwise he ignored them, left them leaping like wild things from one carton to the next, clawing at the screens, waiting for someone to speak to them, fondle them. To set them free.

"Yo ho," her father-in-law was saying. His face looked less gaunt this afternoon. He had even shaved. He seemed to Molly like a man waking up from a bad dream; he was beginning to lose that haunted look. Maybe Hank was right. Maybe it was getting the cats disposed of—the last link.

After dinner he even began joking around a little.

It was getting dark outside. Hank turned on the lamp by the bookcase and the one beside the sofa where she was sitting. She was sorting through more boxes, flipping through magazines mixed up with old letters and moldy clippings. The papers smelled. She hated even touching them. Beside her on the couch was a pile of studio photographs. The mother at sixty. At forty. As a young bride. The face receding in time, smoothing out, the mean lines around the mouth disappearing—the mouth itself becoming fuller and softer, the hard glitter in the eyes changing to wry amusement, the pale gold of the hair growing longer and fluffier. She looked mischievous and full of fun. Like her son, in fact; not a resemblance Molly had ever seen before.

Hank was sprawled out on the floor. He was trying to organize the bills. "Got the checkbook handy, Pop?" he said.

His dad sat in his green chair by the bookcase. A lapboard lay across the armrests. He had his yellow legal pad in front of him, with the little square boxes he drew beside each job still left to do. He kept lists. Lists of chores. Lists of things he said he simply couldn't remember any longer.

"Checkbook," he repeated. He shook his head. His eyes twinkled, fine dark eyes, his legacy to son and grandchildren. Deep-set, steady. Beautiful. "Got to check my books to answer that one, my boy," he said, and chuckled.

Molly held up an old clipping. "Listen to this!" she told them. She read a long account of how Hank's mother had been voted the "most talented and popular coed on campus, Queen of the May Court..." She stopped. Nobody said a word. So then she added, "Is that when you met each other, at college?"

Her father-in-law fiddled with his row of paper clips lined serially before him on the lap board. He shook his head, didn't answer.

Hank glanced up at her, so she changed the subject. "Tell your dad about the Willy brothers."

Hank looked around the living room, out into the dark hallway where more boxes were stacked. He stretched, "You'll love this, Pop."

Then they began taking turns telling the old man how the Willys all remembered Hank, and watching his dad's expression, Hank embroidered the story. He started getting hammy. She loved it when he got like that, clowning, acting out the gestures, catching the precise Pennsylvania Dutch inflection of the voices. "Throw the cow over the fence some hay," he ended up. His father chuckled.

"Molly and I, we decided those three got a good thing going," Hank went on. "It's like they share a collective intelligence. The oldest one does all the talking. But the other two are right in there, giving him the cues. Amazing,"

"Used to know three kids like that myself, once upon a time," said his father. "Been my observation it only works when you got yourself a strong ringleader," he added. "Someone assertive, in fact."

Molly laughed. "You tell him, Pop."

"Hey, no fair ganging up, you two,"

"Your father and I simply have to keep you in line," and she picked up an old report card, "Hank *must* restrain his tendency to be bossy. I love it! They had your number, right there in the third grade."

"Back in those days," her father-in-law was smiling, "we used to tell his sisters, he's not bossy, girls. He's just a take-charge kind of person."

"Ah hah," said Hank, "Vindicated!" He moved up against the sofa, his back nice and warm against her bare legs. She gave him a slow nudge with her knee. He pressed his elbow into the soft part of her calf. Connected, she thought, we're connected again.

"And a good thing too," his father observed in a quiet voice. The sisters had flown in for the funeral. For three days they darted around the house like magpies, placing red dots on things they wanted, green dots on the stuff they didn't, chattering in their high voices, teasing Hank, trying to comfort their father. But he only got quieter and more remote. When they finally left, twittering good-byes from the taxi, the house felt comfortably silent once more.

Except for the cats. Yowling out on the back porch.

And now the cats too were gone. And it was just the three of them, cozy in the yellow pool of light from the lamp on the bookcase.

The books were all gone as well. The empty shelves looked naked beside the old man. Every so often he would reach over towards a shelf, then check himself, sigh, probably remembering, Molly supposed, that they were all boxed out in the garage, ready for their new Connecticut home. She thought she had finished mothering chores when their last child graduated from college. But it wasn't to be. At least he wouldn't play hard rock.

"Back home when I was a boy," her father-in-law began. And told them a long story of a summer out under the wide Montana sky, working as a cook for a geodetic survey of the Sweet Grass hills, just him, his best friend, the pack horses and a geology professor. "Learned a fair amount about surveying that summer," he was saying. "But never did graduate much beyond beans and bacon in the cooking department." He straightened his yellow pad, stared steadily at the dark window and beyond.

Molly arched her foot. Hank shifted, letting her stretch out her leg. They waited.

"You asked when I met her, Molly," the old man continued, and he folded his hands together on top of the legal pad. He had Hank's hands, elegant long fingers with the kind of polished fine-grained skin that looks and feels like old Chinese silk. So smooth. So cool. She knew this although she had never once touched those hands except for brief handshakes. This was not a touching family except for Hank. Hank had escaped early.

"Early that fall," his father was saying. "Let's see. Must have been 1928. I was working as Chief Cataloguer then. Over at the Main Library, remember, son? Down the block from the old house on Whittier? I took you and the girls to see it later on. Torn down now, of course."

"I remember," Hank answered, and put his hand around her left ankle and held it tightly.

"Your mother had finished up normal school by then. Only place she could find a job was down in Billings. Teaching arithmetic at the grammar school on Meadowlark Avenue." He took out his heavy silver pocket watch, checked it against the big clock on the wall. "Right on the button," he said, and clicked the lid of the watch shut.

"...several friends in common," he was saying, smiling out at the black window, his hands folded and still again on the lap board. "Cousin of hers was a colleague of mine, assistant reference librarian. Young Horatio Sanders. And Horatio told me..." He glanced over at them, then slowly shook his head. "Oh, doesn't matter. Point is I'd heard about her from a whole mess of folks in our crowd. But 'cept for Horatio, I hadn't paid that much attention."

He smiled again. Then for a brief instant, so quickly Molly wasn't sure it hadn't been a trick of the soft lamplight, his chin quivered. Just for an instant.

"Anyhow," his voice got very low, almost reedy-sounding, and Molly leaned forward and put her hands on Hank's shoulders, "one Saturday morning in October, I was coming down the main staircase. And I stopped on the landing. Looked down at the vestibule, saw Horatio Sanders talking to somebody, a young woman, heads real close together, and there...the sun and all coming in cross those marble floors..." and now the voice was ringing out strong, vibrant, startling in the quiet room, "and there," he finished up, "stood this beautiful blonde."

WASTED

——

DEVON ABSOLUTELY AGREED THE devil's in the details—best quote ever—somebody really nailed it. The coolest!

But while Devon's a stickler for details, Dan was not. A great follower, sure—but details? They bored him. Dan Wallace was Mr. Action Man. He never tired. He took orders well. But Dan was a wuss—always whining to Devon about the long waits between gigs—for a dude like Danny, systematic planning didn't compute. Still, he was useful on maneuvers, really strong, built along the lines of a heavy duty Humvee—total opposite of Devon who's built small like his creepy dad. And if that's not bad enough, with the face of a wimpy girl, "*heart-shaped to match your sweet, trusting heart*" his mother used to tell him, baptizing him with sloppy-wet gin & tonic kisses. His hair still fell in curls over his temples—no way could he plaster it down—all this plus being cursed with long lashes, like his sister Lavinia for God's sake. They used to razz him at school. Up until junior high, the kids even *called* him Sister. She was a year ahead of him, and Devon knew they looked almost like twins. He actually used to think of himself that way. Not as Devon—but as Lavinia's Brother. Lavinia inhaled all the oxygen at home, all the air fit to breathe—which wasn't much.

Not any longer, no more Lavinia bullshit. Not since he went to high school, and decided that from now on the name Devon was going to intimidate people. Now he had a small group of guys who think he's so weird and wild they beg to be included in his projects. Because he always plans ahead, they've never been caught. He chooses only one person at a time for his missions. Danny he likes the best. Dan follows him around like a trained seal these days, occasionally barking. "Why all this surveillance crap?" So lame to listen to but Devon would simply snarl, "Put a cork in it, Dan," and keep on watching. And waiting, watching the house—their biggest op yet—this whole friggin summer, checking the layout and the times when nobody on the crew showed up. Sundays seemed like the best bet. Even the boss took off Sundays.

So Sunday it was.

The contractors had left most of their junk behind. The six-month remodeling project finally finished and all that remained were the last minute jobs: hooking up the electricity, laying the wall-to-wall carpeting in the upstairs bedrooms, a final check by the zoning inspector—diddly squat stuff.

And now the big house sat there, shadowy and waiting for them at the end of the long curved driveway, tucked behind a mess of pine trees which screened the place from the street. But he and Danny ignored the driveway, crossing instead along the perimeters of the big old field in back where the brown weeds of summer grew tall in what last year had been a leafy green vegetable garden. From the back the house had a naked look. The shutters had all been removed for the new paint job, and the house looked like this blank face with its eyebrows shaved off. Looks, he thought, like the perfect victim.

It was a cinch breaking in. They simply smashed the small window in the utility room, using the crowbar Devon carried in his knapsack. They hadn't been sure exactly which tools had been left behind by the workmen, so they lugged along a small arsenal: hammers, the crowbar of course, screwdrivers, a funnel, flour scoops, and two pairs of lined cotton work gloves. The garbage bag they left outside by the patio door.

Inside it smelled like fresh paint and brand new nylon carpeting, really sharp and yukky smelling, and so strong they both began to sneeze. The dust didn't help either.

Danny rubbed his nose, shook his head. "Gas masks, that's what we forgot."

But Devon just began methodically unpacking his knapsack, laying out each tool carefully on top of the washing machine. "We'll get used to it," he replied. "Come on, we got three hours max, let's move it." Some days Dan got on his nerves big time.

"Roger that, Sarge," Danny answered. He wiped his nose thoughtfully with the cuff of his sleeve. "You really got this thing taped, man."

Devon nodded. "Recon is everything—*the* bottom line in hit & run strikes. Scout your enemy, then come prepared. Ok, buddy—battle stations ready?"

"Lead the way, sir," and Danny gave a smart salute.

The utility room opened up at one end of the garage. The other doors led to the small bathroom and then the kitchen. Out in the garage they found plenty of latex wall paint and turpentine. Devon had checked out the paint situation the day before, peering through the garage window, spitting on the pollen-dusted glass, then polishing it with his fist so he could see more clearly. Yeah, the crew had left everything, an absolute goldmine—assholes.

They grabbed two small quart cans of the white latex and the big old gallon can of turpentine. Then they walked through the kitchen, their footsteps ringing loud and hollow on the red tiles, but cutting off suddenly when they reached the carpeted hall and stairs. Up in the bedroom they pried off lids with the screwdrivers, then poured the latex with long sweeping motions across the freshly sanded hardwood floors. He could see Danny doing the bedrooms, splashing the paint faster and faster. But in the master bedroom, Devon took his time, beginning in the middle of the room with a bunch of squiggly lines all bunched up like the curled up bud of a flower, and then carefully working out to the baseboards in a series of spirals so that in the end the floor had turned into this painted nebula whirling in space and he almost felt dizzy when he finally crossed to the door, leaned against the jamb as he studied the pattern.

Dan poked him on the shoulder. "You done?" he asked.

"Yeah."

Danny looked down at the floor. He gave a low whistle. "Intense!" he said.

"Yeah, they oughta frame it and pay me a commission."

They both laughed and went downstairs, tracking white footprints down the blue plush carpet on the steps. They went back into the kitchen, unscrewed the top of the turpentine can, and carefully funneled the stuff down inside the brand new stove which stood uncrated and unconnected in the middle of the kitchen floor. Back out in the garage they found an open bag of Portland cement, powdery gray like old winter snow. They filled up an empty paint bucket, came back into the kitchen, and real, real easy-like, sprinkled the cement inside each of the four burners of the gas stove and inside the oven, mixing it into a rich gray sludge in the pools of turpentine. They did the same thing with the inside of the dishwasher. The last of the cement they poured down the drains in the kitchen sink, washing it all down with more turpentine.

Then they marched back to the garage and jacked open the dozen or so wooden crates lined up against one wall. Bull's eye with the first two! A new TV and an old fashioned stereo system, the kind that played ancient L.P.s like the ones his mother still kept stored in three moldy old cartons down in the cellar. The concrete dust they sifted through the vents on the back of the television. But with the stereo, something more primitive was required. So they took the feather light tone-arm and wrenched the obnoxious thing up and backwards. When it flopped back on to the turntable, the wires had popped out of the socket, spilling over the side of the stereo like black and red intestines. Awesome!

The rest of the crates held only boring household junk, except for the fancy china service and crystal glasses. Folded up in one corner of the garage was this huge, paint-spattered dropcloth which they spread out flat. Then they both took turns dropping plates and cups onto the concrete floor. It worked better when they climbed up the stepladder and dropped them from higher up. "Sweet!" Danny kept saying. The crystal was the most fun, they shattered it with hammers. Devon always made them wear the work gloves to protect their hands and eliminate fingerprints—he wished somebody'd give him a medal.

After a half hour, they picked up each end of the dropcloth and carried it tenderly, like a wounded comrade in arms, upstairs to the master bath. This room too's been remodeled, its major feature a giant sunken bathtub complete with whirlpool. They upended the dropcloth, and the broken chips of china and glass flowed down over the smooth white porcelain, making a gritty bed for somebody's fat rear end. Dev felt like jumping up and down this mission was going so slick, but as patrol leader he had to stay cool and in command, not act like a dork.

Back downstairs, he opened the patio door, collected the heavy dark green plastic bag, then snagged the two flour scoops which they'd left on the dryer out in the utility room. The room felt a hell of a lot more comfortable than the rest of the house. Cool air blew in from the broken window. It was very quiet. Way off in the distance the nice Sunday drone of a lawnmower could be heard. He dragged the plastic bag into the kitchen, untwirled the tie at the throat, then opened the refrigerator door. He shoved the bag over at Danny. "Hold it up straight," he ordered.

"Yuk!" Danny said. "This stinks to heaven."

"That's the point, careful now." Using the two flour scoops, they filled each shelf of the fridge, shoveling in piles of the rotting meat, eggshells, orange rinds, old cigarette butts, and slimy brown masses of rotten food.

"Don't forget the freezer compartment."

"Plus the vegetable bin and cheese dealies," Danny added.

"Roger that."

"Done?"

"Yeah, now shut the door. Here's the padlock."

"From your own bike?"

"Naw, some kid's down the street."

"No clues?" Danny winked.

"No clues." They shook hands, thumbs hooked in the secret handshake.

"Can we take a break?" Danny asked, rubbing behind his neck.

"Sure, we're right on schedule so far." They hoisted themselves up on the kitchen counters. Devon unhooked his canteen from his Army belt, handed it to Dan. "Here," he said, "have a slug, cure what ails you."

"Thanks, good buddy. Does this slide down easy or what?" Danny was sweating like a pig. "Hey," he said, "it's like a fucking oven in here. Let's bust open couple more windows."

"Too noisy."

"Nobody's gonna hear, whole neighborhood's up the street, that big bash at Kiley's, probably everybody sloshing it up big time." Dan stopped, wiped his forehead, stared at his friend. "Say," he asked, almost embarrassed, "your folks there?"

"Sure, they're probably totally wasted by now."

"Your mom—she kind of, like, hits the bottle, right?" Danny said in admiration.

"She goes through a quart a day, wine until four o'clock, then gin & tonics, or just gin and gin. My old man though, he keeps up with her pretty good but doesn't shout as much."

"The judge can really hold his liquor, hunhh?" Dan asked, taking another long swig from the canteen, letting the beer dribble over his chin.

"Like a real man," Devon smiled, enjoying the lie.

Today he and Danny were both rigged out in beat-up Army fatigues. Blazoned across their khaki shirts ran the legend *Special Forces Never Die... They Just Go To Hell to Regroup.* Danny really looked the part, tall with beefy biceps, massive thigh muscles. Danny's a jock. Correction, he used to be a jock. But the junior varsity coach had bounced him off the squad last spring when he got caught smoking in the field house—regular cigarettes, no biggee. So these days Danny mostly just hangs out. With Devon. Because Lavinia's been home all summer long, the two of them have been rolling around in reefer heaven. They steal the stuff from the secret cache in her underwear drawer. Anyhow Lavinia knows the score. She never tells. Who'd she tell anyhow?

Dan was getting restless, he looked spooked. "We better split pretty soon," he said.

"Look, give it a rest, this is our biggest job yet—we gotta pull it off right."

"Yeah." Dan rubbed his biceps, flexing the muscles so they swelled up hard and powerful under his tan. "Oh, yeah," he said again proudly. "Worked harder today than I have since pre-season."

"That's great. And we're almost finished here."

"All I'm saying is we better bag it before we get caught, man. They'll fry our asses for this stunt."

"So chill, no clues, remember?" Devon held out his hand, thumb crooked. But Danny frowned, turned away. "Let's bolt," he muttered.

"Not yet. Go get those big brushes. And more paint."

"Where from?"

"Where else? Out by that other junk in the garage, behind the ladder."

"What color you want?"

"Anything dark, the brown stuff they used for the outside of the house maybe."

"Check." And Danny slouched off through the utility room, shoulders hunched. The back of his khaki shirt was splotched with dark stains.

Hot in here. Devon went into the bathroom, splashed his face with cold water, then washed his hands with a sliver of crusty yellow soap, scrubbing hard.

He checks out the mirror, stares directly into eyes staring back at him, cold, unblinking, watching him with the impersonal glittering stare of a snake. And he hears a familiar voice stumbling over her words the faster she spits them out, throat muscles bunched and tight, heart-shaped face bloated, knocking stuff off the counter first by accident, then for real—Jesus, the noise! And Lavinia who's never learned to go underground like he has, shouting back, "You're not my mom, my shrink's the only mother I've ever had!" Now the heart-shaped face crumples up, and she says real soft-like with that smile which always makes him want to cry, "Not mad at you, darling Devon-boy, not you, it's the two of them." Then Lavinia sobs, "Fuck it, you're sick!" and starts walking through the swinging louvered doors to the dining room while the screeches get louder, the sound so high and jarring it makes his teeth hurt, "You stole him, squirming around in your little seersucker sundresses, tuck me in daddy, hug me daddy, kiss me please, now touch me daddy, ooh touch me right here—it feels so good, ooh." Out in the living room, sober as the judge he really is, the father pretends not to hear but when the shrieking gets too loud, he always slinks upstairs to his study, then after a while Lavinia follows him. In the mornings Lavinia's brother would find their mother passed out on the sofa, but even as she lay there snoring, smelling of sour wine, curly hair so like his own, matted and damp across her forehead, he could see still curved around her lips that sweet half smile of his long-ago, once-upon-a-time playmate who tried so hard but never could make up for a lost sister.

"Mission accomplished." Danny was loaded like a big old pack horse with brushes and paint cans.

"What took you so long?"

Danny glanced back over his shoulder. "I was watching out the garage window," he said, wiping little drops of sweat off his upper lip—he'd just started to shave this summer.

"Watching what?"

"This scumbag pulled in the driveway, came all the way up to the garage. I like to shit a brick. He just sat there in the car for a minute. Then he took out a map, guess he was lost or something. He didn't even look up at the house."

"He leave?"

"Yeah, no problem. Can we finish now? This joint bums me out."

Devon nodded, grunted "Sure." Even pack animals had their limits.

They were walking into the living room. The buckets were heavy and sloshed with a nice *klock klock* sound in the silence of the empty house.

"You know the family who lived here before?" Danny sounded super casual.

"Nope. No kids."

"So, like, what's your beef?"

Devon kept his head down as he pried open the lids. They came off suddenly with big sucking noises.

"What beef is that, Dan?"

"All this trashing the house."

"Come off it. You *know* this is our biggest raid of all."

"Cut the commando crap," Danny snapped, then looked sort of embarrassed. "Hey, good buddy," he grinned. "I mean I'm doing this like for fun. But you? the thing is…" he stops, swallows, "Well, the thing is I just don't get it."

Lavinia's brother dipped his brush, watching the rich brown paint drip back into the can in a thick solid stream at first, then slower, then stop. A couple of huge bubbles formed, arched with quivering delicacy over the paint, surface tension it was called. He poked the brush into the bubbles and popped them. Then he smiled up at Danny, his sweetest smile, his trusting smile, like Lavinia's. "Guess you might say I'm doing it for Lavinia. Sort of a present—from a secret admirer."

Danny stared. He shook his head, shrugged.

The two of them worked in silence. They coated their broad brushes with the brown paint. Great drops splattered down on the new rug. Against the pale blue, the spots looked like rusty blood. Then, painting quickly—two hours gone already, almost chowtime—across the virginal white walls they scrawled their candid messages of welcome.

CLOSE TO THE SEED

EMMA HATES BOYS. THEY scare her. They swagger by, fingers hooked in their jeans, calling out to each other in hoarse voices.

"Hey, dude."

"How they hangin'?"

"Luvvin' it!"

They lounge against their lockers, snickering. Their eyes slide away when Emma glares at them. They start crashing shut the locker doors, strutting down the long hallway. Just as they disappear around the corner, she can hear them laugh, the harsh baying of dogs on the scent, their tongues swollen and red.

Once at lunch hour some seniors, jet-setters not jocks, asked her to go for a ride in someone's car, the four of them packed into a black Trans Am, what the guys call a "macho set of wheels." Emma had to sit in back with a tall silent boy named Neal. Neal grinned the whole time, mumbling and grunting when she tried to talk to him.

They drove fast through the Pennsylvania countryside, they must have hit 90 on the clear stretches. The blonde girl in front looked back at Emma. She kept on squealing, "Isn't this far out?" Emma couldn't see the face of the boy who was driving except for his dark eyes in the rearview mirror, measuring her discomfort.

Afterwards the blonde came up to Emma in the Commons and said Neal really liked her. "Wants to take you to the prom," she told Emma. "He thinks you're a real fox."

But Emma nipped that one right in the bud. "I don't date seniors," she said. Or anyone else, but she hadn't added that part.

At school Emma goes her own way. She runs around with three girls who also don't date. One's too smart, that's Elizabeth. The boys seem nervous around Liz, alarmed by her sharp comments in class, her dark frowns. One's a cute redhead named Gwen. Gwen gets kidded a lot by the guys, but like Emma she's too shy to kid back. The third friend is Naza Vita.

"What kind of a weirdo name is Naza Vita?" a boy whispered the first day in homeroom.

"Castilian," Emma hissed back. "And you're ignorant."

But Naza Vita hadn't noticed. She never does. Almost beautiful, Naza Vita's problem is that she simply stands out too much. Just a smidgeon under six feet, she's taller than anybody else in the 9th grade except for the guys on the J.V. basketball squad. She has dead white skin and the mysterious smile of someone sleeping.

She also has her own horse, a big chestnut gelding named Cricket. Emma envies Naza Vita whose father is very rich. Naza Vita's trained Cricket since he was a yearling. She boards him at the stables where the other girls take riding lessons. She loves horses the way Emma does. Gwen and Liz ride because their folks have decided it's part of the game plan, something they have to suffer through like taking piano or going to Miss Lockwood's dancing class back in Junior High. They try to be polite about horses, but it's clear they are bored.

This puzzles Emma who every year has fallen deeply in love with a different horse. This year she adores a high-strung Thoroughbred-Arabian cross named Beauty. Mrs. Van Skiver told Emma the mare needed careful handling. She was skittish, she was a head-tosser if overridden. But with the steady kindness of an experienced rider like Emma, Beauty's totally lived up to her name She's a dainty dark bay with small pricked ears set on that refined head—wedge-shaped tapering down to an exquisitely small muzzle— revealing the typical Arabian dished profile. Her eyes are huge and express everything she's feeling. Which is a *lot*—she's really sort of a drama queen, Emma's decided—and by ignoring the drama, she manages to calm the mare down. Beneath Beauty's eyes are very dark patches, looking, Emma thinks, for all the world like glamorous eye-shadow. Arabians are called Drinkers of the Wind because of their flaring nostrils and the high carriage of the head springing out of gorgeously arched necks. Emma's convinced that Beauty not only drinks but practically outruns the wind as she gallops—her silky mane fluttering, that long tail of hers held aloft like a banner. With such a smooth, fast-flowing gait, she seems to float above the ground. The most perfect ride Emma's ever had in her whole life was the first time she was allowed to gallop Beauty for three miles beyond the stables and the paddocks, nobody else along, just she and Beauty drinking the wind together, a miraculous sort of fusion which felt as if she and the horse were one creature moving through space and time like a shooting star blazing through the sky. Mrs. Van Skiver considers the mare to be the second best hunter in her stable, and this fall Emma has been chosen to ride Beauty in the White Marsh Valley Hunt—a real honor—Emma's ecstatic.

The stables are part of the Van Skiver estate. Mrs. Van Skiver teaches the advanced classes, her new assistant handles the beginning riders. The assistant has recently come over from Ireland; he's old—25—and his name's Charles McIlvaine. Emma hasn't paid much attention to him except to be pretty impressed when she hears he trained hunters for the Grand National and to note he has gentle hands. The horses calm down when he's around.

One Sunday, she passes him working with Cinammon, a new filly Mrs. Van Skiver's just bought. "Easy lass, easy lass," he keeps saying.

For a minute or so Emma watches him run his bony red hands over the withers, down the silken flanks. The filly snorts, rolls her eye wildly so that the white shows. But he holds her head steady, gently eases the curb bit into her mouth, crooning over and over again as he fastens the cheek strap, "Easy lass." Then the filly nickers back and Emma tiptoes on past the stall, not wanting to disturb the only kind of love talk she's ever respected.

She tries to describe the scene, how she felt watching it, the next day after school. The four of them are sitting out on Emma's sun porch, eating apples—Grannie Smiths, good and hard. Their homework's scattered all over the floor. On the C.D. player Bruce is whispering the last lonely lines to *Highway Patrolman*.

"You people better steer clear of McIlvaine," Liz says. She frowns; she has thick black eyebrows, so bushy she seems angry when she's not which Emma has decided must be a major handicap. "He's a real lech."

"No kidding!" says Gwen, and hugs her knees.

"Why?" asks Emma. "How do you know?"

"I have my sources," says Liz. In the late May sunlight streaming through the windows, her skin looks sallow, almost yellowish. She jabs with her hands as she talks, "...and all the older kids hang around the tack room, practically panting after him. It's revolting."

Emma glances over at Naza Vita curled up on the davenport. For a tall person, she can curl up into the smallest shapes. Emma's concluded this is not accidental. Naza Vita doesn't say anything. She never says much and Emma figures she's probably thinking about Cricket. Or Mass or something spiritual.

Gwen sighs, picks up the black and red CD. She studies Bruce's face, sighs again. "Why..." she says, "**why** do all the good ones have to be old men?"

Liz examines Gwen, then reaches over and lowers the volume. "There *are* no good men," she announces. "Men have only one thing on their minds. And it ain't Toll House cookies."

"No worse than some girls we know," observes Emma and bites hard into the Grannie Smith. She likes eating the whole thing, everything but the stem. The apple seems sweetest the closer you get to the end of it. She simply ignores the bitterness of the seeds, swallowing them quickly as if they don't exist.

"Like my sisters," Gwen says in a cheerful voice. She eats her apple in small measured nibbles. "They're always comparing notes, which guys they've French-kissed, who's good doing what. I think Janet's even on the pill now."

Emma's afraid of how Naza Vita will react to this bombshell. Naza Vita comes from a very religious family and she's always running off to confession. In the old days she would have run off to a convent. Emma likes to picture Naza Vita in a long white habit, kneeling on the rough flagstones, pale fingers slipping through the black beads of her rosary. Would she wear a hair-shirt?

But Naza Vita says nothing, keeps on munching at her apple. She's a slow eater like Gwen. But there's a difference. Gwen chews to get the job done with a careful deliberateness quite different from Naza Vita. Naza Vita's slowness makes Emma think of brood mares ambling in the pasture, grazing in lazy aimless circles, going nowhere fast and perfectly content.

Liz stares hard at Gwen. "Your mother know?"

"About?"

"About your sister being on the pill, idiot."

"Sure. I mean Mom's always leaving these little pamphlets around, S.T.D. stuff, names of clinics." Finished, Gwen wraps her apple core carefully in a paper napkin. "I mean get real, Liz. Five daughters—what would you do?"

Liz leans forward, eyes hot. She runs her tongue over lips that always look chapped, and Emma wishes Liz would relent, wear a little lip gloss and maybe some blusher on her cheeks. "Point is," she's telling them in a husky voice, "men are the pits."

Liz has been saying this for month, for years. They all have, but Liz has gotten weird on the subject. She makes Emma feel cornered by those hot eyes boring in. Emma sits up straight. "How come you're such an authority on the subject?" she asks Liz.

Gwen giggles. "You two are something else," she says. She folds her freckled arms across her chest; she's very big-breasted, another reason she's shy around boys. She says that's all they're looking at, and Emma has to agree this is probably the case. "Look," Gwen's saying kindly, "guys are on the make, sure. Let's face it. The four of us—we're in the minority."

Liz answers in a thick voice, "Sex sucks, period."

Emma glances quickly over at Naza Vita who doesn't like dirty talk. But Naza Vita's still staring out the window at the pussy willows coming into bud. Her lips are half open, and Emma knows this is exactly how St. Bernadette looked when she pushed her face through the brambles and saw the Virgin standing there in the grotto, gold roses on her feet. She wonders what it would be like to be inside Naza Vita's mind. Gold and shimmering? Or just a dark hollow. Had the brambles drawn blood? Would a saint even notice?

"I need something dressy," Naza Vita says in her sleepy voice. She uncoils from the davenport. "For the thing on Saturday." She does a slow pirouette, pale arms fluttering above her head.

"Yuk," Emma groans. This weekend they're all invited to a big lawn party, the annual reception given by Mrs. Van Skiver for her students, past and present, particularly the ones she's grooming for the Hunt Club. Other years Emma hadn't gone. But this year everyone's getting heavy duty pressure from parents to attend. Pressure from Liz as well. She's practically insisting they must go. She claims she wants them to see Chuck McIlvaine in action at a social event.

"You just watch," Liz is saying now, "how he comes on to everyone." Her eyes glitter and she keeps licking her bottom lip.

* * *

THE RECEPTION IS HELD outside on the terrace. Beyond the French doors, Emma catches a glimpse of the huge drawing room paneled in dark wood, and elegant gold-leafed chairs upholstered in wine-colored velvet. Emma feels like they're standing in a movie set, four extras without any lines to say.

Two waiters in white jackets are marching through the French doors. They step out onto the terrace. They're carrying trays of sandwiches cut into tiny circles and triangles. The waiters brush past the girls and head for the long table. At either end of the table two giant punch bowls gleam like silver moons with a constellation of glass cups twinkling around them. A small group of grown-ups clusters at the far end.

"Members of the Hunt Committee," Liz whispers. "Looking us over."

"Looking us over for *what*?" asks Emma.

"Shhh," says Gwen. "Chill out, Em."

They can hear kids screeching nearby. Emma steps closer and peers over the balustrade. Down by the rose garden next to an old stone fountain a mob of kids, younger riders, jabber and poke at each other. Chuck McIlvaine stands in the middle, waving his arms. He looks like he's trying to organize some kind of children's game.

Emma glances around; a group of college kids saunter out from the drawing room, lounge next to the French doors. They're all smoking cigarettes. They look bored.

Liz cocks an eyebrow, nudges Emma. Gwen whispers, "Who should we talk to?"

Naza Vita says with a yawn, "All we have to do is—like—put in an appearance, Daddy said. Talk to the Hunt Club people. See and be seen is what he told me."

Naza Vita's wearing high heels, and Emma decides she doesn't like the way she looks with her dangling earrings and her hair twisted up in a chignon. She looks more like a high fashion model than a nun today, right at home on this movie set, everything shot in slow motion, nothing quite real.

A waiter drifts past them. Emma reaches out and plucks a big wad of cucumber sandwiches from his tray. The waiter looks startled, floats away from them, holding the tray higher. "I could eat an ox," Emma explains, and starts doling out cuke triangles to the others.

They watch Mrs. Van Skiver circulate among her guests. She's a thin woman with sharp eyes and a stiff way of walking. Years before, she broke her back jumping; she can never ride again. But she's an excellent teacher. She has a real passion for good horseflesh. Her entire fortune, people say, has gone into her stables. It's rumored she has the finest collection of Irish hunters in all of Bucks County.

Now she's standing in front of the four of them. She's smiling, the same tight smile, Emma sees, that she uses when somebody's cantering on the wrong lead. A reined-in kind of smile. "Girls!" she says. "How lovely to see you all! Have you met everyone?"

Naza Vita answers for them. "We just arrived," she drawls. "Lovely party. Weren't you lucky to have such warm weather!"

Emma turns her head to stare at Naza Vita.

Mrs. Van Skiver murmurs something back. She's twitching at her dress. It's made of chiffon, pale green. They've never seen her dressed in anything but a tweed hacking coat and jodhpurs. She looks scrawny, incomplete in a real dress. Emma imagines the four of them must look equally strange to her. Her hands keep flicking up to adjust the chiffon folds around her thin neck—they seem lost without the crop she usually plays with as she barks commands to horses circling around her in the ring. Now she's speaking to Naza Vita again. "How's Cricket working out with that new martingale, dear?" she's asking.

"Perfect," says Naza Vita, and then she and Mrs. Van Skiver are talking shop, the new bran mash they're trying out, the cost of trailers, what about the Pelham bit—so pretty soon Emma and the other two wander back to the silver punch bowl.

"Just us poor folks," Liz says, frowning back at Naza Vita.

"Don't be mean," Gwen tells her and starts ladling out the punch. "Here."

Liz takes the punch glass and drinks the whole thing down in one gulp. "Good looks, beautiful horses, rich daddy. She's got it all."

Emma taps her forehead. "Not quite all, Liz."

They laugh. Gwen shakes her head. "Impossible, you two."

The punch tastes cool and sweet. They each have four cups. Liz peers past Emma; her eyes narrowing. "Uh oh," she says. "Watch it, gang, here comes Mr. Macho Man. Check this out."

Emma turns around. Chuck McIlvaine is walking towards them, high cheekbones a dusky red, eyes dancing. "Common-looking," Liz called him. What that meant wasn't clear to Emma; she thought he had an interesting face, long and bony, the thin bridge of the nose flaring sharply. Lean, he moves like a thoroughbred, head up, easy flowing rhythm to his long legs, loping up the stone steps, and then—he's standing there. Emma takes another quick swallow.

"Ladies," he's saying. His voice is deep, the Irish brogue lilting the words at the end, and Emma sees him stroking the filly, *easy lass, easy lass.* She tries to focus on what he's asking them. "...be helping me with the kiddies?" He smiles around at each of them; Liz stiffens. "Actually," he continues, "I'm going daft trying to organize the little buggers."

Gwen starts to giggle. "You've had too much juice," Liz tells her.

But Gwen just nods, gazing big-eyed up at Chuck like some hero-worshipping teeny bopper. "These two," she says, "drank just as much as me."

He looks amused. "'Tis the wrong punch bowl you three have dipped into, I dare say. And a fine notion, I'm thinking."

Liz draws herself up very straight. "Least we're not acting goofy."

Gwen puts her hands through both of their arms, linking them together. "Why not act goofy? Let's go boss the kids for a while."

"Where's Naza Vita?" asks Emma.

They look over at people clustered beyond the punch bowl. Naza Vita is still talking with Mrs. Van Skiver. A couple of the Hunt Committee have joined them. In her high heels and chignon, Naza Vita has slipped away from the three of them. She looks for all the world like one of the grown-ups.

"Forget her," Liz mutters. They start down the steps to the garden, Gwen and Liz leading. Chuck falls in beside Emma.

"First of these do's I've attended," he says. "Her ladyship puts on quite an elegant show."

"It's boring. Totally," Emma says staring straight ahead.

"Give it time," he says. "Slow start, fast finish. We shall be tripping the light fantastic before it's done, I fancy."

Emma thinks that one over. "There won't..." she coughs, "won't be *dancing*, will there?"

He laughs. She watches his Adam's apple jut out against the rough-looking skin of his throat. "And if there is?" he asks with a wink.

She purses her lips. "Then we're going straight home. This is supposed to be a lawn party. That's what the invitation said."

He looks down at her. He's still smiling, but all of a sudden he is really looking at her for the first time, and she feels nervous—fluttering inside exactly the same as taking Beauty over a brand new jump. "Of course," he says politely, but she sees his mouth's curled up at one side in a mocking curve, "you may stick to the kiddies' games if you wish."

She feels her face flame. "Don't be rude," she tells him, and juts out her chin for emphasis.

He laughs again. "A head-tosser, this one! A snaffle bit won't do for you."

"Meaning what?" she asks and peers all around her. They've stopped by the fountain. Where are Gwen and Liz? Oh yeah, there they are, they're both standing in the middle of a big circle of kids. Gwen is practically bouncing with excitement. She's clapping her hands. The kids are clapping too. Now Gwen hops on one foot, now she's holding her right hand to the tip of her shoulder, now she taps the very tip of her nose. Clearly, she's gone mad.

"Simon Says," he's explaining. "She's trying to calm them down with Simon Says."

"Oh, I see. Gwen's really good at calming people down."

"Is that why she's your chum?"

"Partly."

"And what might the other part be?"

"Oh," she shrugs. "We're part of a gang. The four of us."

"Indeed?" he says, looking solemn but Emma knows he's play-acting. "And what, pray, binds this gang of four together?"

She frowns at him. "We're just good friends is all."

He says nothing, just folds his arms, waiting. So she adds in spite of herself but he's asking for it, "We all **hate** boys." And she kicks at the grass.

He pulls at his long chin thoughtfully. "Liz I can understand. And Gwen's just shy, I rather fancy. Naza Vita...ah...Naza Vita's in a trance. But you, Miss Emma," and he gives her the same appraising look of a judge standing in the ring when there's a tie and it's hard to decide, "you puzzle me."

"Why?"

"Ah. I've watched you on Beauty. 'Tis pure joy watching how easily you handle a somewhat tricky mare. Many riders would be nervous."

"So?"

"There's not a horse in the stable you're afraid of."

Then she blurts out, "But it's not *horses* that scare me!"

He doesn't answer at first so she looks at him. His whole face is so long, so angular. It's all bones, hardly any flesh. The cheekbones are so pointed they look as if they can pierce the flushed skin. It's his eyes she can't look at directly.

Then he's saying quietly, the brogue more noticeable, "What I mean, brave Emma, be remembering your name—'tis Irish for strong woman, and that fear and hate—they march hand in hand, you see. But you're not like that at all. Totally fearless, I wager."

"Horses don't talk. At least not out loud. I can't talk with boys."

"No reason to be hating the poor devils, is it now?"

Emma watches Gwen and Liz. This isn't fair. They've run off and ditched her with him. Mean. Had Liz planned this whole thing? Set a trap?

He's speaking again. When he talks there's a little indentation along the side of his nose, right above the nostrils, that quivers.

"What?" she asks, feeling stupid.

"You're a far better rider than your chum Naza Vita."

"No way," she says.

"That one," he tells her, "she'll never be a champion, mind you, no matter how much bloodstock her pa buys her. 'Tis the passion that's missing in your friend." He stares past Emma, then adds slowly, "Perfect form, she has, I'll grant you. But no heart."

"That's not true," she says. "Naza Vita loves horses as much as I do."

"She rides for the love of the ribbon," he answers. "Not for love of the animal."

Emma sips at her punch. It's gone flat-tasting. He seems to be waiting for her to say something. But what? "I don't know what to say," she tells him finally. Then she adds, looking at him over the rim of the cup, "And I don't really understand what you're saying."

"It's really quite simple. What it comes down to, my lass, is simply this. Don't fear what you don't know. Give the poor lads a chance."

"Oh, yuk!" she tells him.

He throws his back again and laughs. He has strong white teeth, and she can imagine them tearing into an apple with two big bites. She shivers.

"Spoken like a passionate woman," he says and takes out a linen handkerchief and wipes at his eyes, his lips still twitching.

She looks away. She would so very much enjoy slapping his red face. She'd love to throw the wine punch straight in his watering eyes, make him choke. But this is supposed to be a lawn party and she must handle this by trying at least to behave like a grown-up. "Look here," she says, speaking quietly but surprised at how shaky her voice sounds, "I know all about you. Don't start your flirty stuff with me. It won't work. I think it's gross. And I think you're gross. You stick to petting the horses. That's what she hired you for."

He puts his handkerchief back in his hip pocket. His cheeks look almost bruised they're such a dark purplish color now. "Emma, luv," he says, mock-polite again. "When you're a wee bit older, you'll be seeing how it is. You'll be able to tell the difference."

"The difference?" she repeats.

"Between seduction…" he grins at her, "and polite conversation."

She looks at the punch cup in her hands, takes a deep breath but just as she jerks the cup upward, his fingers catch at her wrist, digging in hard against the wrist bones. With his other hand he takes the cup away from her. He sets it down on the stone lip of the fountain. He stares at her. His mouth is still curved up in a smile but his eyes aren't dancing any more. They're serious, almost stern. When he speaks his voice is gentle, no longer mocking. It's the slow easy voice he uses with the filly Cinnamon when he saddles her up. "Bonny lass," he tells Emma, "there's something important I want you to remember."

She stands there mute. She swallows. He waits. Finally she looks away from him. "What?" she asks.

He cups her chin in his hand. His fingers feel rough and very warm. She has to look right into his eyes. They are kind eyes, she sees now, brown-green with flecks of gold radiating out from the pupil. She stares into them. The gold flickers back at her.

And now he is speaking slowly, pausing after each word. "Be choosing what you hate, my dear, as carefully as what you love." And then he leaves her, walking away with that easy stride of his, walking straight towards the circle of children who prance when they see him, clapping their hands—still children all of them—Liz and Gwen as well. They've not yet tasted of the apple, she smiles, and once more hears his voice…*spoken like a passionate woman.* The words make her throb deep inside with a peculiar feeling—peculiar but God, she doesn't wants it to stop.

GAME, SET & MATCH

THE WALLS IN THE back room of the Royal Arms Pub & Brewery are painted a deep shade of peach, a strangely flushed color, Elaine decides, as if something angry lies just beneath the surface of the peeling paint. She does not, of course, mention this to Baxter. Anyhow, he's not facing the wall, she is.

It's 9 o'clock, the main lounge is crowded and very smoky. Here in back there are only four or five people, it's much quieter but just as hazy with smoke. She fishes out her Salems, places them beside her drink, waits.

"...so bullheaded about wanting your own way," Baxter continues, leaning back against his chair. He jerks down his shirt cuffs, checking to see, no doubt, if they're the regulation quarter inch, then folds his arms, watches her.

* * *

HE HAD EXTREMELY STRONG wrists and a grip like a steel vise. When they met that first summer in Chilmark, he spent hours trying to teach her a decent backhand. "Watch the wrist action," he kept saying. "Keep it supple. Long clean strokes, then a good follow-through with the racquet. Like this," and he drew his arm across his chest in a long falling diagonal, drawing it back and then forward and up in a graceful arc. In the sunlight the hairs gleamed. They made her think of gold spikes hammered in all along the outstretched forearm and down the deep grooves made by tendons taut as rope. Even when his hands were at rest there was this deep triangular indentation below the base of his thumb, the first metacarpal, he told her. Once she had taken his hand, bent down and licked this shadowy hollow. The tendons quivered beside the small sharp wrist bones that cradled the hollow place. The skin tasted salty.

* * *

SHE PULLS OUT HER cloisonné compact, fiddles with the catch, opening it finally to check out her lipstick as well as the general lay of the land, so to speak, though mainly she just wants to get away from his eyes boring into hers. She blows little specks of powder off the oval mirror. Lines around her mouth—thirty-six and counting—and she smoothes a crease with one finger. A good face, but ordinary, best features are her eyes. "Big as a seal's" he told her once. She had wanted to know if he meant the baby white seals they slaughtered off the coast of Nova Scotia. He told her she had truly bizarre responses, "a real turn-off," he added. Her nose needs powdering, which she proceeds to do with quick pats. "I wish to hell you wouldn't groom yourself in public," he says.

"And I wish you'd get off my back," she tells him. She snaps shut the lid of the compact with a sharp click, tucks it into her new purple shoulder bag bought today because it looked like spring and because purple's a color he hates. She smiles again. "Call me bullheaded—still, my dear, it's not as if," she says, "you didn't want yours."

He stares. He looks caught off balance, good, she thinks. "Mine?" he repeats.

"Your way."

He sighs. "Conversations with you are always circular, Elaine. No matter where on the circle we start out, we always end up in the same ridiculous place we began. Round and round, going nowhere."

* * *

CLUMPS OF MANZANITA CART-WHEELED across the highway right in front of the car. Ahead of them the road shimmered in the heat. Coming up on their right a big pasture, and beyond a stand of cottonwood trees—a straggly group of slender gray saplings beside a creek bed. A couple of cows had wandered down the bank and stood there, drinking, tails switching off the flies. The rest of the herd lay in the shade of the cottonwoods.

"Hold it!" she told him. He pulled the car over on the shoulder of the road, the tires spinning up dust as they coasted to a stop.

"Want to check out those cows," she announced and got out. He followed her, they stood together by the fence. There was a slight breeze. The leaves on the cottonwoods rippled from silver to pale green and back again.

She sniffed.

He chuckled. "Strong smell of cow, I'd have to agree."

"They don't look like regular cows," she said. "They look kind of washed out, all that splotchy tan and pink."

"They're Longhorns. Texas Longhorns. Considered to be show cattle, I understand."

She pulled away from him, climbed over the gate. "I want to see them stampede," she called. And she started loping through the tall grass across the pasture towards the creek.

"Get back here!" she could hear him yelling, but she pretended she hadn't heard. The cows saw her coming towards them. They lifted their great horned heads and watched her and just as she reached the spongy grass near the banks of the creek, they wheeled and trotted off. She waved her arms. "Hey, cows!" she called. They broke into a slow canter. It didn't look like they were moving fast at all in that clumsy-rocking gait, but they easily outran her. She stopped because she was laughing so hard and her shoes were a mess where she had stepped in cow patties.

When she got back to the fence, Baxter was scowling. "Jesus H. Christ," he said.

"What's wrong?"

"You want to get shot? Get us both shot? That's got to be the dumbest stunt you've pulled yet." And he walked away, climbed in the car, slamming the door. They didn't talk for three hundred miles. When they reached the motel in Tulsa that night, he went around to the front of the car, began snatching off the feathery clump of manzanita they had wired to the bumper.

"Why?" she asked him. "I wanted to take it back home. For the cottage. It's so pretty, so delicate-looking."

All he would say was that it looked tacky and when was she going to stop acting like a ten year old. "Grown woman chasing cows," he added. "Unbelievably dumb-ass stunt."

* * *

SHE LEANS FORWARD, ELBOWS on the table which feels both damp and unpleasantly sticky. She looks past him, over his shoulder and beyond to the blank peach-colored wall. But it's not blank. She can see the blurred outline of some sort of drawing painted over but still faintly visible. It appears to be a huge mural of two people facing each other on a raised dais. They're seated on massive square seats that look like thrones ornately carved with grotesque animals, griffons probably, heraldic creatures. The wings lift off the backs of the griffons and their claws interlock on the headrest of the throne.

"...try being reasonable for a change?" Baxter's saying now in his patient voice. It's the calmly controlled voice he uses with slightly senile clients who refuse to see the wisdom of tax shelters this late in the game.

He's wearing his charcoal gray suit, so dark she calls it banker's black. She had talked him into having it made the summer before the divorce. "Must you always wear *brown*?" she'd asked him. He had started in with the usual lecture on the need for a strictly conservative dress code as opposed to her flamboyant gypsy views on clothes and life in general. But she cut him short by pointing out black was good enough for nine out of ten State Street bankers.

Now he lifts one elegantly padded charcoal-gray shoulder and shrugs. The suit's the same color as his hair which springs in dark waves over his ears, ears that lie flat to the bony head, ears as softly lobed as some exquisite soft-shelled creature from the bottom of the ocean, curled tight.

"Elaine," he repeats. He's waiting for her answer, the ball in her court with the usual topspin and she lobs it back automatically.

"Reasonable," she says, "simply means agreeing with you, Baxter. So, tell me, what else is new?"

But he's always been superb at net and he comes back with a hard-hitting volley, a confusing barrage of facts and figures, the bill of sale, the equity of the cottage having tripled not to mention the value of the land itself, beach property on the Vineyard's out of sight.

* * *

WHEN THEY GOT MARRIED, he went out and bought her the most expensive Head racquet available. The racquet lay wedged between yellow oilskin slickers and Adidas sneakers in the coat closet that whole next summer. She told him she'd much rather watch him play. They went to the cottage first on their honeymoon and kept coming back for two-week vacations, summer after summer. They loved it for its location. She because it stood on a high bluff overlooking the sea and Gay Head; he, because it was right next door to a fine clay court shared by four families, all of them "simply *mad* for the game, dahling!"

After five years, Baxter finally decided to buy the place, arguing it would be a shrewd investment, plus the rental income would offset the strain of the second mortgage. "We'll get down weekends in the fall, after the crowds have gone," he promised her.

They went down four weekends in a row. He played tennis with the neighbors, she walked the beach. They cleaned and scraped and stained the shingles to make the house shipshape for the coming winter, he said. But really because the real estate agent claimed that summer rentals shouldn't look shabby. "Off-islanders won't pay top dollar for a dump," he told them.

They fixed the roof, hung new shutters, put in flower boxes around the front windows. "All we need here is Heidi in a dirndl skirt," she said to Baxter. "I miss the rundown look. I loved those weathered old shingles. They gave the place character."

He just shook his head.

He coaxed her into celebrating Thanksgiving down there every year, but she balked the fourth time around. "I'm just not cut out to be a Pilgrim," she said. "Not on this stove. I hate half raw turkey," and that was the end of that tradition.

* * *

"SO WHY SELL?" SHE asks quietly. "Why not hang on to it. Get richer doing nothing."

"Don't you ever listen, Elaine?" he answers. "We'd maximize profits selling now. In any event, you never use it any more. What's your rationale here?"

"I don't have one really."

"It figures." He cracks open a couple of peanuts, places the shells neatly in the ashtray.

"Don't mess up the ashtray, please," she says and lights another cigarette. He glares for a second, then starts picking the shells out, stacks them in a heap on his cocktail napkin. "Everybody else in the whole world throws them on the floor," she goes on. "That's the kind of place this is." She nods down at the sawdust and the hundreds of shells at their feet, then glances up at the peach wall again.

She sees that the figures in the mural are both men, the one on the right has his head sunk deeply into his chest. His right arm hands limply over the side of the throne, his left arm's not visible. And neither for that matter are his legs. Peculiar.

"Darn it, Elaine. I really hate to drag the lawyers back into this."

"I just bet you do, honey. Anyhow, it's all in the agreement. Joint tenancy, joint ownership." She pauses. "Indefinitely unless and until both parties agree to sell." She beams at him.

He takes a sip of his drink, then a long hard swallow. He signals to the bar waiter who glides over immediately. They always do for Baxter, she thinks.

"Another round," he tells the waiter.

"Doubles again for you, sir?" And Baxter nods. A woman laughs at another table, he glances over.

Elaine follows his glance. Two women have sat down at one of the corner tables, their Louis Vuitton attaché cases parked close by their chairs. They're both in their mid-twenties with the carefully groomed good looks of young professionals.

"Swinging singles," he murmurs and smiles.

"Hardly swinging, dear," she says. She stubs out her cigarette. "Look," she tells him, "I simply like knowing the cottage is there. Like money in the bank, you see." She smiles at the analogy, impossible to talk with Baxter without sounding like corporate management or a tennis nut. But she can't ever win using his idiom, and he gets annoyed using hers, and therein, she muses, lies the story of the relationship.

When the drinks come, he tells her about the promotion, the trips to Paris, the brand new corporation headquarters being built near Corpus Christi.

She raises her eyebrows. "Texas? Won't you hate Texas?" She looks down at her Old Fashioned, picks up the orange slice, nibbles it. "Won't you miss…" she looks around, at the women in the corner, at his closed face then past him at the wall with armless man slumped on his throne, and the squared off bulk of the figure on the opposite dais. "…you know," she stammers, waving her orange slice, "all this. I mean Boston. New England." She studies her glass, willing her mouth not to quiver, "The ocean," she says softly.

He smiles. "There's ocean down there, you goose," he answers, voice gentle now.

"The Gulf, you mean?"

"Right. The Gulf."

"But that's not *ocean*. Not what you're used to." Their eyes lock for a moment, and he winces for just a fraction of a second, but she doesn't want to hear the hesitation in his voice, the regret, so she starts talking about her job, assistant to the Admissions Director who'll be retiring in a couple of years, and with any luck….

* * *

THE TOASTS HAD GONE on for so long she felt woozy, and leaned against him. His totally sloshed best man rambled on and on, and she felt his hand in hers under the table. "Hang in there," he told her. "Won't be long."

Lots of lewd laughter. The candles flickering, sparkles of light on the champagne glasses. Her mother frowning at the matron of honor who had the flu and kept sneezing every few seconds. Her dad looking shy and sad, the rosy faces turning and watching as she and Baxter stood up to cut the cake, absurd little bride and groom entwined on top of mounds of icing that looked as stiff as cardboard and probably tasted like it too, and now she was bending forward, his hand on hers guiding the silver knife and her face felt so hot from the candle flame and then her mother was screaming and someone yanked at her head, slapping at her face, her hair, and tore the flaming veil off and stamped hard and hard again on the filmy net smoking on the floor, a few red sparks left, and then the loud silence in the room while Baxter had looked at her, his face set and white, his mouth trembling, and she saw that he was not frightened for her but of something else.

* * *

"...WITH ANY LUCK," HE finishes for her, "you'll be running the damn college in ten years." He rubs his chin. There's a little nick in the cleft of it and she knows he had been nervous about this meeting with her, shaving in the Executive Washroom which he always did for important clients and some not so important ones as well which was how she knew back then that first time, his face still fresh and velvety smooth when he came home at midnight. When he leaned over to kiss her, she got a strong whiff of *Wind Song*.

"Right?" he's asking.

"Right what?"

"Right I taught you everything there is to know about institutional hard-ball."

She nods. "Just about, I guess," she says. She smiles at him.

Then he swoops in, flashing the killer grin of the mixed doubles champion who's finally spotted the weak link. "Then at least, babe, think this over. Please." He holds his hands palm out, see no tricks. "That's all I'm asking. No hard decisions now. Just give it some serious thought."

He doesn't press her for an answer and she doesn't give him one, simply another conspiratorial smile as if they're partners now, working the same side of the net. As they get up to leave she looks at the wall behind him. The figure on the left has the blocky shoulders of a giant doll, a mannequin stitched together to look real but there is a strangely alien, almost android quality to it which disturbs her. She almost leans over to touch the paint, but she knows better. It would annoy him and jar the mood.

They walk out, the sawdust soft underfoot, peanut shells cracking with the same kind of popping noise small bones might make after the feast.

SALVAGE

—

NOAH WAS BACK, AND they were all gathered down by the rock pool, everybody embarked on some serious drinking.

"Jessica" was all he said to her when he arrived hours ago, and already it was late, long past nine but not yet dark, the sky washed in pale bands of gold and salmon and lavender.

He was back and he was laughing, he'd laughed the whole damn evening without once looking in her direction—now he was telling jokes and the divers around the table were shouting and their loud voices made her eardrums pound and her cheeks burned hot from the retsina, her shoulders from too much sun, but the air felt actually chilly on scorched skin because as usual the meltem was blowing steadily now from the north strong enough to raise whitecaps.

Jessica squinted. Far out to sea the whitecaps looked like pleated ruffles of lace forming and reforming, but closer in to shore the four foot rollers were running down before the wind, breaking on the rocks of Kafatasi and curling around each end of the island.

Kafatasi. The word meant skull, and it still made her shiver.

Add to this the cold ankle-kissing spray churned up by the rock pool and she was really glad for her yellow slicker, even gladder for the fuzzy vest beneath. Living on this barren island in the middle of the Aegean—godforsaken in every way—you pretty much wore whatever kept you warm. Her skin felt rough as cracked leather, and small wonder—summers on Kafatasi were always harsh, the price of admission—take it or leave it. A resting place aptly named by the earliest sponge divers for the human skulls they saw poking up out of the sand beside the broken hulks of galleons and bronze age ships foundered centuries ago on the reef out there in the channel. Dozens of boats had gone down, splintered apart like matchsticks. The ocean floor around Kafatasi was littered with broken hulls, amphorae, cannon balls, ancient coins—the debris of centuries, pay dirt for underwater archaeologists.

"We're scavenging," Noah once said, "for beauty in the mud."

And Henry had added, "Yeah, folks, one summer on this hunk of rock and we got the big money guys hooked." Hooked—sure, but it's taken four summers, Henry dearest, not one. That part he hadn't told her. Henry excelled at leaving stuff out. "The big picture, Jessie," he was always reminding her. "That's my job."

"So here's the punch line," Noah was saying now, but she couldn't hear him, the roars of laughter sealed him off.

And her job? She used to know back in the beginning when Henry needed her in the same urgent way a feverish man seeks an oasis, a calm pool to drink from. Henry infected people with his enthusiasms, he was a genius mover & shaker who made things happen—this is what she loved in him. He was mercurial, he was funny, he was exhausting. From glee through sulks to tantrums—call it being married to an infant prodigy, she thinks. Call me his umbilical chord, his lifeline.

"...call it kismet," finished Noah. The younger divers cheered, excited because Noah was back on the dig, the very last expedition member to reach the island, and finally they could all cut loose, relax, get mildly hammered.

Everyone was happy, fueled by good will and gallons of retsina. Yet still Jessica shivered, shook her head. Negative thinking—not good, the island had this effect, it worked on her in a curious fashion so she wasted too much time doing what she called skull-dreaming, asking herself barren, Hamlet-type questions more desolate than Kafatasi itself.

Henry chuckled, raised his glass, "I'll drink to that, Noah Bey." Actually Henry only allowed on-site drinking on Saturday nights when no dive was scheduled the next day. But tonight was an exception. Tonight they'd been scarfing back retsina before, during, and after dinner in Noah's honor—Noah Gibb, Henry's artist-in-residence, his oldest colleague, his anchor.

Kasim Captain himself had brought the barrel of retsina from the mainland, making such a big deal out of the presentation Jessica wanted to shout "Encore!" They all had to stand there in this huge circle and watch the usual theatrics—a blend of shrewd self-promotion laced with dramatic posturing, vintage Kasim. First, the opening overture of three deep bows followed by the usual obeisance, a rapid series of turban-touchings highlighted by a flash of sharp teeth and quick glances around the circle of divers to make sure all eyes were on him as he addressed Henry. "With permission, Effendim, a gift from myself and my crew to celebrate the return of our honorable and beloved comrade."

Jessica had winced. Noah was their comrade in ways Henry never could be—correction, never *wanted* to be. Intimate relationships basically didn't interest Henry, only raising money, institutional one-upmanship, and well preserved artifacts. Noah, on the other hand, found pure delight in tribal events, weaving his usual spell of luminous enchantment. He simply enjoyed these people, respected their codes. They had fun together, treated each other with exquisite kindness. Over the years Noah unsnarled red tape, wooed permits out of suspicious officials, and Henry used to say wistfully, "Doors open for Noah before he even knocks—I'm telling you, he's magic, Jess!"

But Jessica understood. It was the merry boy, the primitive kid in Noah that spoke directly to these people. The wild man who laughs at danger coupled with the courteous warrior-poet celebrated in the Koran. And so friendship was born, and trust—puzzling Henry who even after all these years had never been able to penetrate beyond the slightly contemptuous veneer of formal Muslim politeness. Kasim and his countrymen transacted business with Henry Bledsoe. But it was Noah Gibb they loved.

Everyone adored him, Americans, the Brits—even German tourists—but hey, loving Noah comes easy, smiles Jessica, amused to note how her hand jiggles as she raises the wine to her lips. He's back, and it's just like old times, she and Henry and Noah yokking it up with fifteen divers all seated here at this long table at the foot of the cliff next to the little rock pool where once three summers ago, Henry and Noah had speared an octopus for supper. The water had turned black from the ink, staining their hands, their white T shirts. And Noah had laughed, "Don't worry," he told Henry. "It's not permanent. Nothing ever is from the sea."

Nothing except the wind, of course. During the day the on-shore wind was constant and wearing, humming always in the background so that you were forced to speak louder than normal. In fact, Jessica had noted over the years that here on the island everything seemed exaggerated. Louder, larger, brighter. And harsher. Kafatasi changed people. Only temporarily, of course.

Across from her, Noah was smiling, his lips moving, Henry answering him, and again she tried leaning forward to hear but the wind behind them drowned their words. And so she let the conversations continue to flow around her, and sipped the wine and watched the trawler pitch and roll at its mooring. A few feet away from the table little wavelets lapped against the pebbled banks of the rock pool. She took a box of wooden matches and lit the candle stuck in an empty Coke bottle next to the bright blue crockery jug of retsina.

Now the men were starting to sing their standard litany of risqué songs. The other two women archaeologists had long since gone back to their tent, excusing themselves primly—work to do, notes to type up. They knew the routine. After the songs came the limericks, quite naughty but no explicit sexual stuff, not when Jessica was around. No, that all got saved for the men's dorm at the far end of the island. Far from her tent, hers and Henry's.

She studied Henry. He was laughing, he was happy tonight, his cheeks puffed out in tight balloons. Happy because Noah was finally on board. For two weeks he had chafed and moaned. "Not the same without Noah," he kept telling her. "Noah's our good luck talisman, our rabbit's foot, damn it. He's got the Antiquities Commissioners wrapped round his little finger. Shit, Jessie! We need the guy."

She could only say soothingly, "Yes, darling, but he's coming soon."

And this afternoon he finally arrived. A lanky figure in white climbing over the gunwales of the trawler followed first by Kasim Captain and next by sacks of provisions carefully lowered down into the brand new sailing dinghy. The mail pouch. Four huge leather bags full of fresh water. Yellow string sacks of plum tomatoes, white onions, sweet green peppers. The whole barrel of retsina. I'm going to scream if this takes any longer, she had told herself and shut her eyes and heard the dinghy scrape against the kitchen iskele, the long pier next to the cooking shack where charcoal already glowed red in two braziers set out front. Orhan and the other two cooks ran out, Orhan triumphantly waving the carcass of a freshly killed chicken, blood still dripping from the neck. "Effendim!" he called to Noah. "For your banquet tonight!"

Kasim Captain jumped out, turned and offered his hand to Noah who sketched a quick praying gesture of thanks to Orhan. After Kasim's star turn with the retsina, the expedition members all surged forward, crowding the narrow concrete iskele. And Noah had stood there, poised lightly on the balls of his feet. He was dressed in the same old green hat—his faded tan windbreaker and khakis bleached so pale they passed for white in the glare of the Aegean sun. He was grinning at Henry as they embraced.

Watching the two of them together, Jessica had almost laughed aloud. A Greek god hugging a teddy bear. Then Noah had turned to her.

She kissed him gently on the lips. He smelled the same. He smelled of turpentine and French tobacco, and his skin scratched her cheek, the stubble anticipating the annual summer beard. "Dearest Jessica," he murmured. And she drew away.

Each time she saw him again it was a surprise, a gift she hid away every year until summer came. The clean planes of the cheekbones. The puzzling expression in his eyes, the merriment covering up something she'd never been able to fathom. Pain? Something remote and inaccessible in those deep set eyes, the whites pure as those of a child, the brilliant turquoise of the iris the same clear turquoise of the Aegean—water so transparent that peering downward she always felt as if she might fall to the bottom like a stone. It made her dizzy, that water. Rapture of the Deep was the divers' name for nitrogen narcosis. Or the Martini Rule: a major buzz for every fifty feet. A hundred and fifty feet down your judgement was seriously impaired. Drunk—*in* the ocean, *by* the ocean.

"Jess," he was saying now across the table from her. "So tell me."

"Tell you?" she repeated. It was hard for her to look at him directly, the candle was between them on the table, and the wavering light picked out the gleam of his hair, but his eyes—his eyes were in deep shadow.

He grinned, allowing her to pretend. "Tell me—how it's going, the wreck? Anything special yet?"

She cleared her throat. Each summer their first conversation was always the same, he steady and kind and loving and she choking on words not said, never said, never needed to be spoken aloud because he understood. Because thou shalt not worship graven images, and never ever—especially in this part of the world—lie down with a god.

And so she answered, "Not really, the usual mess of amphorae. Two oil lamps, really exquisite. The original anchor. Lots of copper coins, the inscriptions—"

Then Henry was interrupting. "Listen, Noah, the most remarkable damn thing is the state of the hull. Look, here's where the ship foundered." And he drew a ballpoint pen from his shirt pocket and began to sketch the plans of the wreck on the rough paper toweling the cooks provided as napkins.

"No fairsies, Henry Bey," called Gary Jordan. "No shop talk, remember? Tonight we party!" A newcomer, Gary Jordan posed a major morale problem. Impatient with Henry, fed up with the slow progress they were making on the wreck, all Gary wanted was to forget precautions and run before the wind, and all he cared about were women and the great shots he was itching to take of the artifacts, his byline in the archaeology journals—maybe even the big time. *People Magazine? Vanity Fair?*

"Yeah, man—party animals," echoed Jeff. Jeff was the youngest expedition member, a second year grad student with horn-rimmed glasses and a look of permanent astonishment. But Henry liked Jeff, thought he was a hard-working kid, "Minuscule brain-pan but muscles like an ox," Henry told Jessica.

"So, Herr Professor, what's the scoop on the mainland?" asked Gary Jordan. His black hair curled wildly in the wind and with those ugly twitching nostrils, Jessica decided, he looked for all the world like a black bull. "Any good T & A in town? Juicy frauleins?" He stared hard at Noah.

Henry broke in. "Noah's not your man, Gary. Noah never tells."

"Never tells?" repeated Gary. He balled up his napkin and began juggling it back and forth while he winked at Noah. "Our Daredevil Lady-Killer/Dragon-Slayer never tells?" he drawled. "Listen up big guy, Henry Bey's been brainwashing us for weeks with the Legend of Noah Gibb, chapter and verse, decorated war hero transmogrified into scuba-diving, sky-diving scholar, I mean we're talking the Last of the Wild Men, not so?" He hunched forward, the napkin ball flying fast now.

Stan, the chief diver, spoke up. Stan was ex-Recon Marine, an old timer. "Nothing scares him, pal," he said quietly. "That's what Last of the Wild Men means. Means testing the limits, plus knowing where they are in the first place, got it?"

Gary Jordan scowled. "Got it, dude." He swiveled back to Noah. "And you do exactly what in real life, Professor? Teach Midwestern bimbos how to draw?"

Blake, their laconic engineer, glanced over at Gary, then out at the whitecaps. Blake wasn't much of a talker but now he said to Gary, "Come off it, Jordan. We're not in some kind of pissing contest here."

"This sucks," Gary muttered. "This whole expedition sucks big time."

Noah smiled, a lazy smile. He lounged back—a tawny jungle cat, unruffled but alert, thought Jessica. "Seems to me," he said in a mild voice, "you have yourself a classic case of island fever, Gary." But Gary only glared, his face splotchy.

"Island fever's right, maybe time for another Wild Rat Hunt?" Jeff asked.

"Please," said Jessica quickly. "Spare me, ok? Grown men clubbing rats with baseball bats, not again. Too much." She glanced over at Noah, pleading.

"No, friends," Noah gave his easy laugh. "What's needed tonight is some project with a touch of class. Something with a wee spark of ingenuity."

"Any bright ideas?" Gary Jordan was still surly, cheeks still mottled.

"How about Kick the Can?" Henry joked. He scratched at his sunburnt nose. It peeled all summer long no matter how much white junk he slapped on it. But Jessica knew he was really scratching at Gary Jordan.

"Or Capture the Flag?" someone yelled down at the far end of the table, she couldn't see who it was.

"Get real," said Jeff.

"Hold it," Gary said. He was gnawing his bottom lip and staring down at the iskele where Kasim Captain's new dinghy danced at anchor. He hunched forward, eyes glittering. "Ok, mates, I'm getting a heavy-duty inspiration here." He ran his hands through his curly hair, his black horns. She shifted impatiently on the hard chair. Just looking at him irritated her—forget listening to him.

"Uh oh," said Henry. "Here's trouble."

"Now listen up!" Gary was excited. "What about the dinghy? It's Kasim Captain's special baby. His new toy."

"What about it?" Stan sounded bored.

"Look, Kasim's in town tonight. And the crew's pissed off because he took the dinghy's sail and mast with him, stored it in the hold of the trawler so nobody can sail the damn thing except him. And they're majorly bullshit—claim this reflects on their honor. So here's the deal, we'll drag the frigging boat ashore and hide it, maybe in one of the tents, piece a cake, no question."

Jeff pounded the table so hard his horn rims jiggled in rhythm. "Yeah! and then when Kasim looks for it, he'll think it's slipped its moorings. Ten to one he'll go after it in the launch tomorrow. And presto! We simply lug it back and plunk it in the water while he's gone. What could be more *perfect*!"

Jessica glanced around the table at their faces. They were all grinning now. The thrill of the hunt. They never grew up. Not really.

Henry was considering. They waited for his reaction. Then he began to snicker, rubbed his nose again. "I like it. Serve the old buzzard right. He's forever accusing the crew of stealing his stuff—or his women, what have you."

"Hell on morale," Stan agreed. "Kasim doesn't trust anybody. "

"Can you blame him, they all look like a bunch of Lascars, turbans, the whole bit," Jeff pushed his glasses higher up the bridge of his nose. "Gives me the creeps—see them splicing rope, daggers in their teeth. And Kasim Captain, he's the biggest pirate of them all. Man, he's one me-een dude."

Gary Jordan leered. "The younger sailors are scared shitless of him, he's stud duck, no question. They claim he may be seventy but by Christ, guy still has two women per night!"

"I don't know," Noah said slowly. He twirled the retsina in his glass, glancing across the table at Jessica. All she could do was to say quietly, "You know it's wrong. You too, Henry."

Nodding, Noah said to Gary Jordan, "Look, these people are like children. They've got fuck-all in the way of possessions. Why spoil it for them?"

"Oh, come off it, Noah!" Henry stood up, stretched, sucking in his stomach. "Don't go virtuous on us, not now. You're the Last of the Wild Men, remember?"

"Yeah! Wild Man," somebody echoed.

"Go for it, big guy!" Stan, even old poker-faced Stan, was laughing now.

"Whoo-EE!" Jeff twirled his baseball cap.

Whistles. Cat calls. "Well," Noah hesitated, then stood up beside Henry and drained the last of the wine. He wiped his mouth with his fist, threw a sheepish half-grin at Jessica and shrugged. "What the hell, the night is young, and more to the point we're almost out of retsina. Ok, people, you're on.

Battle stations, men!" And like a single organism, the men scraped back their chairs, gave a couple of cheers, and started down the path to the iskele.

Jessica sat there, watching them lumbering toward the water, black bear-shaped silhouettes looming against the pure pale violet of the sky. Toward the north, one star hung trembling, alone, flickering like the candle. For a moment or so it would shine steadily, then start to tremble again. She thought about Kasim Captain coming up to her twice last week to inquire about her cut foot, scraped badly on a rock. "Better, much better," she had told him. And courteously, Kasim had turned to go. Then turned back to her and bowed several times. He said to her softly, "Masallah. Masallah." God keep it so.

Curious people. Primitive at one level, but chivalrous at another. Their lives were bound up with clear-cut issues: honor, manhood, fierce pride, protection of their women and children. And maybe of brand new sailing dinghies?

The sea was calm now, glassy and still. The wind had dropped and she could clearly hear the men splashing down by the dock. Loud grunting. More splashing. Snatches of talk wafted back.

"What the fuck?"

"Rocks the size of Mt. Everest out here, oh shit—my sneaker's caught."

"Easy troops, let's keep it down to a dull roar, ok?"

Above the grunts and groans she heard Noah's laughter ringing pure and clear as a young boy's.

She got up from the table. Bits of onion and pulpy tomato seed littered the oilcloth. Soon the two junior cooks would come out with a bucket of seawater and swab down first the oilcloth, then the rough planks beneath. But always they waited until everybody had gone, no matter how late. Orhan, the chief cook, had told her once with a big smile, his gold tooth shining, "One does not clean house while guests are still present."

She flicked an oily chunk of tomato into the rock pool—bull's eye! then turned and went up the cliff. At the top she turned again and looked south past the trawler straining at its mooring, past the diving barge bobbing slowly in the wine dark Aegean, south towards the Greek islands, and she thought of Leda and the swan. And the velvety softness of great beating downy wings.

* * *

THE NEXT MORNING THEY all gathered again at the long table by the sea. Orhan and team came rushing out with thick white crockery serving plates, piled high with chunks of flatbread and goat cheese, small dishes of fresh honey, and multiple cups of chai, the bitter hot tea.

Everyone kept staring at the trawler. Kasim Captain could be seen on deck, brandishing his arms above his turbaned head. The wind had picked up again so they couldn't hear what he was saying. Then he climbed down into the motor launch and slowly began to circle the island.

The men snorted, clicked their cups together. Jessica found it hard to swallow the tea, much less the bread.

Gary Jordan smirked. "Cooks said Kasim was wading all around the iskeles at daybreak. Covered the whole shoreline, invoking Allah every third word, they claim."

"Steady, guys," said Henry. "Next time he goes by, we'll make a run for it."

Silently they watched the launch pass again beyond their line of vision, beyond the diving barge anchored off the first iskele.

"On the double, mates. Just the mop-up crew, Henry. You'd better not overdo." Noah jabbed Henry's belly playfully. "You had your fun last night."

Six of the men went scrambling up the hill. Five minutes later they were back, slipping and sliding down the sandy path, half-pulling, half-pulled by the skiff.

One of the cooks popped his head out of the kitchen shack. He clapped his hands, laughing, as he watched the men lug the dinghy down to the water's edge. A second cook joined him. The six Americans worked swiftly, fastened the dinghy to its moorings, waded back out of the water.

Just as they got back to the table, the motor launch reappeared. It glided back to its anchorage. Kasim Captain must have gone below to the engine room, Jessica could only see a couple of the crew on deck. Things looked pretty calm on board. Anti-climax. She could feel her neck muscles start to relax.

Henry glanced at his watch. "Better stop screwing around and get the first divers suited up. Water looks fine today, no whitecaps. Maybe with any luck we can bring the keel up this afternoon. Okay, Stan, it's all yours." He nodded to Stan, waiting beside him with the clipboard.

Stan began reading the roster of the day's diving schedule. "First dive of the day: Oates and Franklin, 9 o'clock sharp. 9:20 we go with Gallichio and Stearns. 9:40 Henry and Noah. 10:10 myself and—."

He broke off in mid-sentence. The three cooks had burst out of the kitchen and were trotting down to the iskele. Waving their arms. Shouting "Dur! Dur!" Stop! Stop!

Jessica glanced over at Henry. His face was stony. And she realized the whole table had gone quiet.

She turned and saw the Captain standing waist high in the water beside his sailing dinghy. His blue striped turban, soaking wet, had slipped down low over his forehead. For one long minute he stood staring at the dinghy. Then he lifted both arms high and swung down the hatchet.

Three times he struck at the dinghy. The sickening crack of the wood as he stove in the bottom sounded so loud in the silence. Then he stood and watched the little boat start shipping water, sinking lazily into the ocean. Two minutes went by. Back at the table, most of the divers had gotten up. Everyone stood motionless. Jessica could smell the fear all around her.

Henry trotted forward, arms extended, calling, "Çok üzüldüm," trying to apologize, to explain. Jessica glanced at Noah, he shook his head. Too late, he was signaling.

Kasim Captain rolled up his sleeves, sinewy arm muscles bunched, and shook his fist at Henry. Then he started swimming back to the trawler, stopped for a minute, treading water. He looked back in the direction of the Americans watching him from the dining area, and slowly spat, then continued swimming. Chunks of broken wood bobbled in his wake.

Henry stood on the iskele until Kasim had reached the trawler and was climbing up the rope ladder, hatchet jammed into his waistband.

By the time Henry got back to the table, only Noah and Jessica were left. The rest of the divers were headed up the cliff path, slapping at each other's backs, braying with laughter. Swaggering, thought Jessica, like punk rockers.

Henry took off his sunglasses, rubbed the bridge of his nose. Jessica kissed him on the cheek. "Jeff agreed to be timekeeper until we go out to the barge," she told him. "Buck up, dear. This is *not* the end of the world."

Noah stood, staring past the rock pool north towards the coast, and when he spoke his voice sounded different to Jess, the tenderness was still there, but the lilt, the exuberance had seeped away. "No, not the end of the world, but the truth is we damn well blew it, Henry Bey." He paused, threw Jessica a bitter smile. "Or as Jordan would say, we blew it big time."

Henry rubbed his nose, put his sunglasses back on. "I don't know," he sighed. "Kasim was carrying on like a psycho out there."

"Kasim simply reacted like a child. We spoiled his toy for him. Made him look a fool in front of his whole crew."

Jessica added in a low voice, "Humiliated him is what you did."

"We should have known better, Henry. Too much booze, you and me." They started climbing up the steep path, Noah leading the way.

"He spoiled his own toy," muttered Henry. "I mean these damn people are so infantile. Now I suppose he'll quit on me. Then we're really up shit creek."

Noah turned, gave Jessica a hand up as they reached the lip of the cliff.

"No," he said carefully. "I think his honor—I think it's salvaged now. He's destroyed what you might say we contaminated."

Henry kicked at the scrubby brush beside the path. They walked in silence toward the diving iskele. Jessica took his hand, gave it a firm squeeze. From up here on the crest of the ridge they could see divers already suiting up out on the barge.

Henry sighed again. "Shoot, folks, I feel like a complete toad."

"That, my friend, makes two of us. We broke faith with Kasim, he trusted us."

Henry brightened. "Tell you what. We'll buy him another dinghy."

"No, just make him the offer. Give him the satisfaction of saying no."

"You think he'll say no? To a freebie?"

"Absolutely. But making the offer we will have at least..."

"...at least restored his honor," Jessica finished for Noah.

"Actually," said Noah patiently, "he's already done that. When he wasted the dinghy. No, making the offer simply means we will have formally eaten crow. You know—how's it go in the Koran? *Each soul is hostage of its own deeds, thus it was written, thus it shall be.*"

"And Kasim will have his smelly foot squarely on our necks," frowned Henry.

"Retribution, Henry—it's part of the whole deal."

Jessica could see Jeff standing on the barge with her clipboard, he was already checking out the second set of divers. "Hurry," she told Henry. "Your dive's coming up soon, and I've got to go relieve Jeff."

They walked faster but Henry was still brooding. "All these summers here, they still surprise me. I mean they're so primitive. Cruel actually."

"Not cruel," Noah corrected him. "Closer than we are to some important stuff."

"Like what?"

"Ah, Henry." Noah spoke with light irony. "They're tuned in to the wisdom of the Prophet."

"Yeah—sure, and the old eye for an eye concept of justice, terrific."

"But Henry," Jessica interrupted. "The one's the flip side of the other."

Noah smiled at her. "Precisely. Come on, Henry Bey, you know all this. Islam, the very word means submission to God's will. Submit to Allah or you're in big trouble. Shape up or ship out."

"Next thing you'll be bleating we're all God's chillum."

"But aren't we though, Henry?" Noah laughed. "Let's split." He checked his watch. "Jess is right, we're cutting it too thin."

They walked past the work building, the only permanent structure on Kafatasi. One of the sailors from the trawler was up on the roof, replacing some of the reed mats over the bright blue plastic sheeting which covered the sloping rafters.

The sailor grinned at them as they walked by. "Günaydin, effendi."

Henry waved absentmindedly. He and Jessica continued down the cliff toward the diving dock. Jessica glanced around for Noah. He had stopped to talk with the man on the roof. Their faces looked intent. The sailor shrugged. Then he laughed at something Noah was saying. Noah waved, came bounding down the hill.

He jumped in beside them. They were already seated in the sandal, the small motorboat used to ferry divers back and forth from the barge. Jessica started up the engine.

They chugged across the water. The sea was just a little choppy now and the barge rolled gently at its moorings.

"What was that all about?" asked Jessica.

"Çok fena, çok fena seems to be the consensus. Very bad."

"Shit," said Henry. "Those turncoats, they were all laughing to beat hell when we hid the thing last night. Best joke of the summer." He picked more dead skin off the bridge of his nose, then took out the white salve and smeared it all over. He worked with short jabs, his nails clawing at the tender pink new skin. Jessica reached over and took his wrist. "Easy, dear," she told him. Talk about masochism.

"It's going to work out ok," Noah said. "I explained that Henry Bey would offer restitution. That seemed to pacify him. He'll spread the word fast."

"Aren't you glad you're back, Noah? Stuck in the middle of the damn Aegean with a bunch of psycho pirates, six greenhorn divers, and us five days behind schedule?" Henry shook his head.

Noah punched him lightly on the arm. "Get a grip, Henry. You worry too much."

"That's my job. To worry."

The sandal bumped against the barge. Noah tossed up the rope to the two divers waiting to go back to the island.

Henry asked, "Anything good turn up?"

"Not much, more coins, mostly copper. Another adze."

"Compressors working all right?"

"Fine. One of the pumps got clogged but Blake fixed it up. No biggee."

They scrambled up the rubber tires hung over the side of the barge.

"See you bozos at chow time," called Noah as the two divers climbed into the sandal. They waved back at him.

Jeff briefed Jess on who was down, who was still at the first decompression stop. She took the clipboard, hung the stopwatch on its long string over her neck. "Henry! Noah!" she called. "They're leaving the bottom in five minutes, suit up *stat*."

She watched them squeeze into their black wet suits, struggle with the weight belts, then finally spit triumphantly into their masks. They took turns helping each other strap on the tanks.

"Check your regulators," she reminded them.

"Done."

She looked at her watch. "You're on, they're just leaving the bottom for the first stop."

Henry studied the sky, "God, I hope this wind dies down."

"Henry dearest, just go, will you please. Stop fussing." She grinned at them both.

Noah smiled, squeezed her forearm. "You tell him, Jess. Ready, Henry, one, two, three." Moving awkwardly—they looked for all the world like beached sea lions, she thought—the two of them waddled in their flippers to the side of the barge, gave the thumbs up sign, then jumped backwards into the water.

She watched the flurry of bubbles disappear and noted the time on the clipboard. She licked her lips, caked with salt, cracked from the sun and constant wind. Her hair was tied back today in a ponytail, tied with thin leather thongs made especially for her by the cobbler in the village on the mainland. She touched stray wisps blowing across her cheeks, her temples. They felt spiky stiff, more like coils of wire than real hair.

Two more months, then back to hot baths every single day. She thought about lying very still in a smooth marble tub full of steaming-hot fresh water and the cool smoothness of Noah's hand as he touched her forearm and tomorrow Henry was taking the trawler over to the village to pick up the new shipment of hoses and make some long distance calls. She smiled. It took at least three hours just getting a call through. "Sorry," the international operator had told them once when they tried calling from Boston. "Sorry, sir, but that country is out of order."

And Henry would come back to the island tomorrow night, exhausted and irritable. But Noah would unkink him, he always had. And she watched herself play out her ritual summer fantasy, watched herself take the hour nap after lunch and the tent flaps would open and Noah would duck his head through, come lie down beside her, touch his lips to hers, cool smiling mouth, velvety soft lips. Soft, soft and so sweet, so thirsty.

Twenty minutes gone by. They would be leaving for the first stop now. Two minutes at twenty feet to decompress, then fourteen minutes at ten feet.

The sun beat down on the barge. She stared into the water so deep and

clear she wanted to slide through it, tumble past the schools of fish suspended
in azure, their eyes fixed and staring at her, black and white stripes, flashes of
color, brilliant crimson and silver glints of movement, circling, vanishing and
reappearing. And she would feel their slippery fins against her thighs as she
sank downwards, drifting down to the pure peace of the ocean floor where
mounds of black cannonballs lay scattered on the white sand and Noah
waited lazily for her to swim into his pale arms waving, waving in that clear
green silence...

"*Hey!*"

She jumped. It was Blake, back there in the stern tending the compressors.
"What gives down there?" He pointed at the water.

She checked her watch. "Nobody's due up for seven minutes."

"Well, somebody's coming up," snapped Blake, "and coming up fast."

They ran to the side of the barge, knelt down. Bursting through to the
surface came a black head. And a long black arm making the cut across the
throat signal for distress, then sinking below again in a torrent of bubbles.

"Christ, someone's in trouble, go see!" Her voice sounded thin against
the wind, but Blake and Stan had already put on their masks and tanks and
were jumping off the side.

Thrashing. More bubbles.

She hung over the side of the barge. Took the silver whistle looped on the
same string as the stopwatch and gave three long blasts.

Back on the iskele two people jumped into the sandal. Somebody was
starting up the recompression chamber. Along the crest of the hill people
were walking towards the tents, shading their eyes as they peered out towards
the barge. At the sound of the whistle, they froze—then began scrambling
down the cliff to where the chamber squatted, a huge silver Cyclops of a
machine, twelve feet long, seven feet wide.

She grabbed the radio. "Barge to shore, we got a problem out here,
bringing in a diver, probably bent. Find the doc, *STAT!*"

In the end it all went like clockwork. The emergency drills Henry had
stubbornly insisted on paid off. Every single expedition member worked
quickly and efficiently. Doing what had to be done.

The divers hauled Noah out of the water. Henry went back to the second
stop to decompress. "You fool, we don't want you bent too," Jessica told him,
furious, and all she could think of was *not Noah! not Noah!*

Noah's face was greenish white. Foam spewed out one side of his mouth.
He was unconscious. Jessica knelt beside him, tried to feel for a pulse...
nothing. Once, two summers ago, they had caught a sick shearwater. They
were the most beautiful flyers of all the ocean birds. They made the transition
from water to air look effortless. They rested on the waves with wings

outstretched, heads under the water. The next moment without any apparent motion—no flapping, no effort, no splash—the wave would drop out from under them and they were flying. When the next wave rose, they would be in the water again.

The men dragged Noah to the sandal. Three minutes later he was in the recompression chamber. For six hours the Doc stayed with him, followed by Henry. And then, surprisingly, Gary Jordan. Noah regained consciousness in five minutes but he couldn't see very well and both legs continued to be numb, partially paralyzed. He had lost all bladder function.

They decided he must be taken to the mainland where the American neurologist agreed he'd thrown an embolism, a blood vessel blocked by air bubbles which presumably entered the bloodstream in Noah's lungs. After a week, the residual symptoms began to disappear. He continued to walk with a pronounced limp.

Three weeks later he came back to Kafatasi to tell everyone goodbye. That's what he said, but Jessica knew it was to restore morale, let everyone see him getting around on his own steam. He laughed and joked with the divers like old times. But the crew from the trawler hung back. They seemed afraid of him, two of the sailors were fingering their amulets, the blue beads protecting them from evil spirits. Jessica was not the only one on the island who couldn't meet his eyes. Kasim Captain ducked his head when Noah handed out Swiss Army knives to the cooks and all the crew members. And Jessica carefully smiled into the middle distance as Noah limped down to the kitchen iskele.

Even with the limp he seemed larger than life, silhouetted against the sky. His sleepy smile caressed them all.

"Well, good buddy," he was saying to Henry, "I'm back on the prowl again."

Henry choked up, took off his sunglasses and wiped them carefully. "Noah, what in the hell can I say?"

"Say good hunting, pal. We've already said all the rest."

"Jesus, Noah, I just wish—"

"Hey," Noah looked at him. "I got hit, sure, but doing what I love, taking risks the way I've always wanted it, Henry. On the cutting edge, you know all that. The last of the wild men, remember?"

They hugged each other. Then Noah kissed Jessica on the forehead, a chaste kiss, a benediction, and turned to give his mocking salute. And stepped into the sailing dinghy bought for Kasim by his crew and the cooks. Kasim Captain had bowed with icy formality exactly as Noah predicted, and turned down Henry's offer with a sneer.

Jessica and Henry stood on the dock and watched for the whole time it took to stow the empty water bags, the mail sack stuffed with letters home, the newest artifacts for the museum. The trawler began to move, chugging noisily away from the island until it was no more than a speck of green against a greener sea.

Little waves lapped against the kitchen iskele. As they turned to go back up the hill, Jessica noticed an oil slick had formed, crude oil from a passing tanker. The iridescent rainbow spread in greasy circles across the rock pool. By this afternoon the water would be clear again. On shore, however, the oil washed up, coating the rocks with a slick residue which the divers had nicknamed Turkish delight. It coated their hands as well. Not even soap took it off.

Henry and Jessica got letters from Noah, he telephoned them every couple of months. But he never dived again. Two, maybe three years later one rainy Christmas Eve, they had a phone call. Long distance from Iowa.

It was Noah's brother. He was calling, he said, to tell them bad news. Noah had died in the hospital that morning—yes, today—of pneumonia aggravated by some chronic pulmonary thing, a condition the X rays indicated he'd apparently had for years. But never told a soul, especially not the docs or Henry.

The brother paused. "Last thing Noah said to us yesterday—well, actually he wrote it on a pad—they had him hooked up to so many darn tubes and things he couldn't talk there in the end. Anyhow, he wanted me to send you folks this painting he did—his favorite, he said—after he came home from the accident."

"What painting?" asked Jessica, watching the rain slash at the windowpanes.

"Well, it's a non-representational study of some kind, very big, huge canvas. You see this galleon type boat, then this broken, smaller type deal— could be a dinghy, I suppose. Underneath, all along the bottom there's these big round circles, black circles edged in red, look like cannonballs. Oh, and handprints, bright blue, splashed across the whole canvas." The brother coughed apologetically. "Tell you the truth, it's fairly wild looking. But Noah said: they'll understand."

Jessica stared past Henry, past the window, tucked the receiver tighter under her chin and forced herself to ask the next question, "I wonder, by any chance do you know what Noah called the painting?"

"Gosh..." The brother sounded puzzled. "Hang on, let me ask the wife, she remembers stuff like that." Murmur of voices in the background. Then silence.

Jessica looked over at Henry. He stared back at her, their eyes met and held, intertwined like strands of a rope.

Now the brother was back on the phone. "Jessica. Say, uh, Jess? You there?"

"Yes, still here," she answered.

"My wife, she says she thinks Noah called the painting, let's see, *It Is*—" He paused. "No, sorry—the painting's called *It Was Written.*"

Gently, she put down the phone. Message received, Noah darling. I hear you. Trust is too fragile to mess with. But Kasim was right. In the end we can salvage honor. She was still facing Henry. She took a deep breath.

The rope frayed. And broke.

COLD STONE AND WATER

EVERY OTHER SATURDAY HE'D make the four hour haul from Boston to the summer resort where she worked. The weekends that he skipped always felt like a reprieve, an unofficial permission to run wild—which, ever obliging, she did.

She begged him not to come, "Too long a drive, Wendell. You know how frazzled you get."

But he insisted just as he had for the past three summers, so Saturdays after serving lunch on the terrace overlooking the lake, she would trudge back past the kitchens and the loading platforms where fresh Vermont lettuce wilted in the hot sun, past the meat locker where Gus the butcher hacked up huge sides of beef into demure filet mignon, up the steep hill leading to the honeymoon bungalows nestled across from the tennis courts, then through the dusty hedge to the staff dorm, feet throbbing, white nylon uniform spotted by sherbet and catsup and God knows what else, reeking of grease, sweat, a thousand cooking smells, and there he'd be crouched in the silver BMW, reading his Manchester Guardian, snapping the pages as he glanced up, looking around for her, then frowning back at the paper.

She knocked on the car door with a sharp rap. "Your order, sir?"

He jumped, then laughed because she had caught him off guard. Again.

"My darling," he said, (no one said darling the way the British did, the *R* so discreetly silent, the *A* tall and elegant), and he reached out to catch her at wrist but she pulled away.

"Not now, I'm all grubby."

"You're so lovely," he said, his eyes brimming up. Actual tears. His eyes were his best feature, deep set and luminous with curly lashes and brambled reddish brown eyebrows the same color as his hair. A good face head on. But the profile? Fast start, slow finish, the noble forehead and straight nose slanting down past petulant lips to a weak chin, the bold lines petering out as if—what?—as if the sculptor had run out of marble or maybe just got bored?

"Fetched you a surprise, Katy!" he called but she was already dancing up the steps of the dorm, waving back at him, and as the screen door slammed shut, his lips sucked air noiselessly like the kissing gourami he kept in this huge tank with long cylindrical lights over the top. Poor fish. Night never came for them.

"I hate fish" she told him the first time he took her to his apartment, all stark white walls and cold glass.

"You mean to eat?" he asked, puzzled.

"To eat. And also just floating. Like them," and she had pointed at the tank.

"But Kate, luv, why? They're so pretty. I like watching them flash by. They're really rather exquisite."

She had shrugged, sloshing a few drops of Chardonnay on the white carpet. "They're terminally boring, Wendell. Nothing ever happens in there. They just keep swimming around in circles."

He moved away from her and tapped the glass wall of the aquarium. His nails were short, fastidiously cared for like the rest of him. He frowned. "When I watch them," he said, "I think of you, sweetie. So quick, so graceful."

And she had simply stared at him, touched by the compliment, repelled by the comparison—more than repelled, actually. Horrified. Push, pull. That's the way it was with them, always had been even that very first time when she came downstairs and he turned away from the bell desk and stared, brilliant eyes drilling into hers.

"Susan?" he had said and held out his hand. But she had stammered and started edging back to the elevator door, trying to explain and apologize all at the same time that she was Susan's roommate. "I'm just Kate," she told him.

He took her by the arm and began speaking gently as he led her out the vestibule, down the brick steps to the oval driveway with the polite little sign that read *College Guests Parking Only.* "Ah, curious custom, blind dates, don't you agree? Such incredible suspense, quite like waiting for Father Christmas, not so? And in this case, I'm truly dazzled to get just-a-Katy, not-a-Susan." And he laughed, a kind laugh, and squeezed her arm which struck her as both surprisingly proprietary and oddly nice.

He got a Kate, all right. Just the way he'd gotten his First at Oxford, his permanent visa to the States, his junior law partnership. "Kate's Englishman," her roommates called him; they said he was a real catch. "Thirty-five years old! He's so mellow!"

He had worked hard at charming first her friends, then her mom. "He adores you, sugar," her mother confided, and she had felt her stomach cramp with love, then pity. Pity for both of them. He understood her completely. Sometimes he forgave her. He had become part of her, and it hurt.

He was too good to her, smothered her with gifts, expensive stuff, none of which she wanted. Two months ago for commencement he gave her a diamond watch. She had already (and firmly) refused a ring. "Let's wait until October," she had said carefully. "After I start working. This whole June engagement tradition—I mean, that's—like—so lame, grab the diploma *and* the ring."

"But you will be working. This summer, up at the resort. I don't understand."

She laughed. "I mean when I start my career, honey, my fab publishing career next fall. You know, when the resort closes down. Waitressing is purely for the bread. To finance me next year."

He shook his head slowly, bit his lip. She hated when he looked sad, hated being the cause of it. Then he glanced over at her and said, "But it's been three summers in a row, Kate. Why can't you find something closer?"

"Oh Wendell, please. You know why. Best tips in New England is why. And anyhow it's wicked fun up there."

"Precisely the problem, dearest girl. Plus being such a bloody long drive."

She glanced down, examined the new watch twinkling on her wrist. Shackled with diamonds, hell of a note. "Look," she said, "I've told you a zillion times, you do not have to visit so often."

And he stared back at her steadily, bright eyes as fierce as a terrier's. "Oh yes, I do, my pet." And she had looked away.

So up he came bearing gifts, two weeks ago a pair of earrings. "Jade green, to match your eyes," he told her.

"Not jade. Swamp green," she corrected him, then added, "I never wear earrings, they make me look like a tart." She fingered the stones, cool to the touch and so smooth.

"Katykins, you noodle, do stop being tiresome and put them on. They'll be simply stunning on you. Trés chic."

She did not want chic. If he loved her so much, why in God's name was he always trying to re-wire her? transform her into some facsimile fashionista to match his vision of a proper career woman, never mind trophy-wife. She loved him best when his eyes mirrored back delight. She needed him to applaud and marvel, not carp and criticize. Why must he get so seriously wigged out over her flaws, trying to make her over into the exact opposite of the person he was attracted to in the first place? As if it weren't the real Kate he wanted but this creepy computer-generated action figure he could toy with forever—changing this, switching that. A boy-toy, she thought; that's me. Or even worse, a daddy's doll, a simulated daughter. Creepy.

"You're so childish" he said. "So bloody erratic. Why can't you ever look before you leap? Just once, sweetie."

And sullen, she would say, "We're not *all* perfect, Wendell."

"Perfection's not the issue. Just hard evidence you're trying, just some proof."

"But I do try, honey. You know damn well I do."

"Not hard enough."

All their fights started that way. Her trying, him trying. Him trying to help her balance the checkbook, to understand debits and credits. He spent hours patiently teaching her contract bridge and all about fine wine, or how to follow the stock market intelligently and never ever be seduced by IPO's. He dragged her to crowded little nightclubs to listen to jazz. The tangled music made her want to scream. She wanted to love it because he did, but she couldn't. She simply could **not**, period. Because she felt guilty, because she seriously disliked the person he wanted her to be, resentment began to curdle affection. Playing Galatea to his Pygmalion seriously pissed her off. Enough already! Spurts of anger or sulking became the norm—"perfectly illustrating, my sweet," he observed, "your extraordinary incapacity for emotional compartmentalization." When she asked what in hell he meant, he tried to explain. "Guilt, rage, being sad—with you, they're all interchangeable. Fascinating balls-up, and to my mind, fucking incroyable."

Once they were sitting at a tiny table listening to his favorite jazz group play, his knees poking against hers (in bed his legs were shorter, but he was longer from the waist up so when they went anywhere they ended up being exactly the same height if she wore flats and slouched), and he was lecturing her about fiscal responsibility and not maxing out her credit cards, and there were little drops of sweat above his upper lip and the music felt like jungle vines snaking around her face, choking off the air so she couldn't breathe and she couldn't hear what he was saying anymore, just had to sit there and watch the full wet lips flap, sweat glistening in the deep cleft above his mouth so why didn't he wipe it off why didn't he take her the hell out of there or shut up or why can't that god-awful music shut up—

"Shut **up**!" she said, and reaching across the tiny square of red-checked tablecloth, she raked his left cheek with long unfiled nails ("Get thee to a manicurist, Ophelia luv"). Two lines of scarlet bubbles beaded up, oozing out of the scratches. He shook out his snowy white handkerchief, wiped his cheek and upper lip, and they both sat there in smoky silence until the end of the set.

He still had the scars, two tiny creases in his cheek which he sometimes fingered when he talked to her, touching them proudly as if they constituted a badge of honor. "My stigmata," he said. And his smile forgave her and caressed her. And when he smiled like that, she wanted to lean over and kiss him because nobody kissed like Wendell did, fusing her mouth to his so they became one in a way they simply never could in bed, never had, never would, why not? why didn't they fit? why couldn't they play at love? the tempo was wrong, the smell was wrong, the textures—oh, everything—and all night she kept on stroking his hair as he shuddered, kept on whispering, "I do love you, Wendell, I do" as they fumbled in the dry darkness, the sheets tangled around her long legs, groping for each other like courteous strangers.

She came downstairs after her shower and saw Wendell leaning against the porch railing, arms folded, head thrown back in laughter as he charmed the two new waitresses. All three glanced up smiling as she opened the screen door.

"And here she is!" he exclaimed. "Ready, luv?" and he moved towards her, nodding to the two girls as he took Kate's arm. "Your chums were just telling me it's been a full house this week, lots of big-tipping singles. Have I got it right?"

The girls grinned, nodded. The red haired one said shyly, "Yeah, they flock up here from New York, cruising for husbands."

Wendell cocked one ironic eyebrow. "And the men cruising for wives, I dare say."

"Well..." and the girl looked confused.

"Then at least for fun," he said kindly, and she dimpled, watching Kate sideways.

How many times Kate had seen that look up here on weekends, back at college, and always at the parties thrown by his senior partners, the wives in their de la Renta originals and their beautiful make-up, artful mascara giving luster to bored eyes which suddenly began to sparkle when Wendell arrived bowing gallantly left and right, full of graceful compliments which left each woman feeling just as Kate did—adored, cherished, protected. Protected from themselves as much as anything else.

The two waitresses were still standing there, waving at them from the porch as he pulled out of the driveway.

"Another conquest," she observed dryly, and squirmed. Underneath her shorts, the bathing suit felt like an itchy second skin, much too hot, much too tight.

"Wrong," he answered. "Another *two* conquests," and smiled, his smug smile with his bottom lip pooched out, repellent in its purple-veined wetness.

"Don't worry, I'm not jealous."

"Oh, yes you are, my sweet. And savoring every spicy minute of it too. You love to have a little fur flying. All the time."

She giggled. He was right. As usual.

"How about a dip in the lake, would you fancy that?" he asked, smoothly shifting gears, then running his fingers along the back of her neck, tickling the downy hairs.

"Whatever," she said, and stretched her legs. "I'm totally wiped."

"A nice cool swim is what you need," he told her, fingers tiptoeing up along her jaw, across her lips.

They went to the cove where nobody ever came. The old rowboat was still there, moored to the dock, rocking gently in the dappled brown-gold water. "Same color as your hair," he had murmured the last time. And she had said, "Yeah, pure swamp green, like my eyes," and started swimming lazy circles around him.

Sailing was his sport, in the water he was clumsy. On deck, however, he stood tall and barked Captain Bligh-type commands, and once when she pulled the wrong set of ropes—halyards? whatever the hell they were called—he began shaking his fists and thundering at her about being sloppy and not paying close attention and why was she so flighty? Finally she turned her back on him and plunged off the stern of the sailboat down into the cold ocean water and swam back to the harbor.

"Want to swim across today?" he was asking her, peering at the sandy beach on the little island where two summers ago they found the abandoned cabin and broke in through the kitchen window. He had been ridiculously nervous, "Crikey, they could haul us in for B and E!" But she kept on laughing, "Oh chill, Wendell, we're having fun, having a really truly adventure! Our very own prime time reality show."

Inside the cabin they found rows of built-in bunk beds. They spent the whole afternoon doing a Goldilocks-glide from one bed to the next. The mattresses smelled sour. She kept on shivering and afterwards he built a fire in the huge stone fireplace, and they sat there, huddled under old gray army blankets, staring into the flames.

"Cold?" he was asking now. They stood on the dock. The water lapped around the pilings. Peaceful.

"Nope"

"You're all gooseflesh, my sweet goose-girl," and he pulled her towards him and kissed her tenderly, murmuring "Better?" He knew how to heal her. Most of the time.

She nodded. "Wendell," she said, and turned and began unbuttoning her blouse, then ripped off her shorts. "Are you staying at the motel again?"

"Right-o, even have the same wretched room. I rather think the old chap in the office must have memorized my name by now."

"Let's not go there today."

"Oh?"

"Let's just stay by the lake this afternoon. Stay outside. I mean it's just so beautiful out here."

"Of course, my sweet," he said, untying the painter. "I understand," and of course he did, he always understood.

Her fears. "I'm scared," she'd whisper when they went to parties.

"They'll love you, dearest. Just be yourself."

"But they're all so grown up, so stuffy."

"Simply more experienced."

"I feel like such a wuss, standing there."

"Just smile, darling girl. They'll find you enchanting."

Her failures of will. "You can do it, sweetie. Don't give up so easily."

The weak parts of her. "I forgive you, Katykins."

Yes, he understood her the way no single other person ever had. And applauded the good. That the applause far outweighed the nitpicking she knew perfectly well, but she also was perfectly clear in her mind about the unbridgeable differences between them. While she dreamed of waterfalls, it was doubtful he ever dreamed at all because more than once he said flatly, even proudly, "I never dream, never." And even if he did, surely he would dream of fish tanks—the care and feeding thereof. Never the twirling fish, only their container. The difference between arabesques versus rectangles, it was that simple.

She swam across the lake, the water soft and warm against her legs. Each time she turned her head to breathe, she could see him watching her proudly from the rowboat, a happy little smile pursing his lips, proud of her strong stroke and her brown arms flashing in and out of the sunlight, keeping perfect time with the *SPLAT SPLAT SPLAT* of the oars as they struck the water.

That night after she got off work, they went to the Canteen and sat around with the others, drinking beer, occasionally getting up to dance to old records from the juke box the management had put in years before. It still worked fine, yellow and red lights gaily blinking. Like—what?

"Like a Christmas tree," he laughed, holding her close. He was a good dancer, she was not. She hated dancing. She hated jiggling around the room. She felt tall and clumsy and vaguely compromised.

"Have another Molson," he said. "You deserve it."

"Must we keep dancing, Wendell? It's the dancing that makes me so thirsty."

"We must, my pet."

"Why?"

"Why? Because you always end up loving it. After you stop feeling self-conscious." He hugged her. He smelled like expensive shaving lotion. "My awkward darling," he murmured into her hair.

He kept on buying her beers and after a while it got rather fun exactly as he predicted, floating across the floor in his arms, laughing at his sly imitations of the bellhops and lifeguards, college boys who beside Wendell seemed awkward—great gangling dolts, no polish, no wit—periodically erupting into loud snorts and raunchy jokes when someone started badmouthing the Red Sox.

They all sat at the big table beside the door. It was finally getting cooler, the breeze felt good. And now Wendell was telling dirty jokes, except his were more risqué than plain dirty. And much funnier.

He was reaching the climax, his eyes jumping from face to face, reeling them all in, quietly, expertly, and they all leaned forward, expectant, as he smiled, paused for the punch-line, then with perfect timing said in his crisp English accent, "But Madame, the Lord Mayor never comes on Wednesdays. Not to the Inns of Court."

Everybody roared, really breaking up, stamping their feet, and she was laughing so hard he had to prop her against the chair with one strong, steady hand. People stood up, stretched, heading to the dance floor or the restrooms. She and Wendell sat alone now, a relief this silence. Her sides still ached from laughing and a few stray giggles kept on popping out like happy burplets.

Tony, the bartender, came over with a big bottle of champagne and two glasses, plastic, but still! He set the glasses down in front of them, poured the champagne. She looked up surprised. "What's this?"

"Compliments of an admirer."

"But who?" she asked, watching Wendell's eyes flick from her to the champagne bottle, then up at Tony.

"Over there," and Tony motioned with his head, then left them.

She looked around. Across the dance floor, three of the kitchen staff, the two German chefs and the pastry cook—were grinning at her from a booth. With them was old Gus. He was big man in his mid-fifties with a big belly and lazy smiling eyes. He raised his glass and saluted them.

"Who on earth's that chap?" Wendell was asking, voice clipped.

"Just old Gus. He's the butcher at the resort. Isn't he a dear?"

"Where in hell did you dig him up?"

"Don't be a toad, Wendell. He's just being sweet. He's the kindest person in the whole kitchen. Never chews us out like the others do."

"He must be sixty-five if he's a day."

"Fifty actually."

"How do you know how old he is?"

"Oh, we kid around."

"Meaning what precisely?"

"Oh, Wendell, do stop grilling me." And she took a sip of champagne, then raised her glass and nodded back at Gus.

"I can't leave you alone for one bloody week. A butcher yet! Sweet Christ! It's jolly well hopeless, no matter how much we discuss it."

She sipped the champagne very slowly. The bubbles danced up the stem, danced down her throat burning all the way down like the little drops of acid that now filled her eyes.

"I jolly well ought never to have allowed you to come back here this summer. Knew it last year. Who was that gigolo chap? Ronnie. Ronnie, the beach boy. And the car salesman? with the mustache? Not to mention the forty-year old Irish bell-captain." She could feel the tears start to slide past her nose so she stood up, slowly unfastened the diamond watch from her wrist. "Here," she said. "Have some ice. Sluts don't deserve diamonds," and she dropped the watch right into his champagne, then turned and walked outside to the parking lot.

He got up and followed her, catching her roughly by the arm. "Katy, forgive me. I was hasty."

"Get lost, Wendell."

But he guided her back to the Beamer, arguing gently, pleading, his eyes shining with pain and love, and in the end they went back to the motel after all.

He left the next afternoon. She stood out on the road waving until the car was only a silver speck in the distance, then looked at the new watch, still ticking away by God. Already four-thirty, dining room would open in a half hour. She loped down the long hill, past the tennis courts toward the kitchens.

Gus was sitting on the steps by the back door of the meat locker, smoking one of his perennial cigars. He smiled. "Hi ya, Kate."

"Gus! Hi. Thanks for the bubbly last night."

"My pleasure, kiddo." He flicked the cigarette into the bushes, stretched, got up and walked towards her, so tall, so massive he always reminded her of a grizzly bear, slow but powerful, dangerously laid back. "Hey, doll, sure as hell didn't mean to upset your boyfriend. He got mad, you got madder— dropping the watch in the champagne, pow!"

"No big deal. Anyhow, he's finally gone." She smiled up at him and he grinned right back, lazy laughing grin, sexy eyes. "Such a sweet surprise, Gus," she said, then went on with the question she already knew the answer to, which made her voice catch a little when she spoke. "But why?"

He shrugged. "Oh you know, Kate, kind of an impulse thing. Maybe because it really tickled me, seeing you doubled up there laughing so hard."

"Is that all?" She knew very well there was more, and she loved his withholding the whole story out of politeness but equally she relished the fun of easing the truth out of him, both of them enjoying this relaxed slow bantering, this comfortable playing with each other.

He grinned, rubbed his chin. His hands were huge, but the fingers tapered, even graceful. "The thing is," he answered, eyes sleepy and soft, "we were sitting there watching you have fun. And you looked so bitchin' gorgeous, Katy, all tanned and golden, so I say to the guys, I go: 'Beauty must be served.' Cracked them up good, I kid you not." He chuckled.

"Served?" she repeated in a low voice, so low that he had to duck his head to hear and she could smell the cigar smoke on his breath and the faint aroma of male sweat and an even fainter stench of blood, a familiar smell somehow, not at all unpleasant actually.

She studied the grizzled chin tipped above her, gray stubble stippling that pale flesh, and arching her head way back, she looked into his lazy eyes, and she laughed. Then she slid her arm into his, and they started ambling down the sandy path to the kitchens, walking with the same long easy stride, her hip jutting into his long thighbone.

From below

THEY ARE MEETING NOW in the drawing room, solemnly greeting each other, bearded and grave.

I tug at my cravat—damnably itchy in this heat. Too warm in here from the press of so much flesh crowded close together. Warm as well from this excellent Madeira I sip discreetly to mask my thirst. Our foreheads glisten in the late afternoon sun shining hot through the French doors. A ginger-whiskered gentleman catches my eye, shrugs, then pulls out a snowy handkerchief and dabs at each temple. I pity him. I pity all of us. Why do we endure these rituals? Why cannot the butler fling open those doors to the terrace, permit us to wander outside, breathe deeply of fresh air, gaze across that broad expanse of formal park to the fields beyond where even now I fancy can be heard the whistle of the North Star locomotive belching and gashing its way across our demi-virginal countryside.

Ah, progress, what desecrations we commit in thy honor! I shake my head. Like some exotic hors d'oeuvre, I am passed around by my charming hostess from one group to the next. Pleasantries are exchanged.

"Have you visited the zoological museum, Professor? Our new laboratories?"

"Are you fond of hunting? Fox, stag, hare—what is your pleasure, sir?"

"Shall you be staying long?"

I make the correct rejoinders. They understand, as do I, the true subtext. The actual questions which snake below their polite enquiries.

"Who are you?"

"From whence do you come?"

"What do you bring us, what take away?"

The President of the Proteus Society is kind enough to welcome me in a formal address to the group. He mentions briefly two of my published works: my monograph on Rousseau and the goodness of natural man, and my short treatise on the worship of nature in three of our finest Romantic poets, moving from Coleridge's fascination with man's moral blindness in relation to Nature through Byron's tempestuous identification with her savage power to the luminous truth of Wordsworth when he instructs us that:

Sweet is the lore which Nature brings;
Our meddling intellect
Mis-shapes the beauteous forms of things:
We murder to dissect.

Ah, I see our President is now making graceful allusion to the contributions which he's confident I shall add to this community of scholars. "These protean minds," he pauses for the expected chuckles, then concludes with a slight bow, "gathered here in a convergence of genius more dazzling than the Crystal Palace."

An unfortunate metaphor, I decide, recalling last year's initial fury over Prince Albert's plans for the Great Exhibition, involving quite vicious attacks on the Prince Consort for attempting to introduce "foreign stuff of every description." The even greater public outrage that ensued over some trees, those great elms in Hyde Park slated to be cut down to make way for a nightmare built of glass.

I smile, amused. In the end, no elms were cut, n'est-ce pas? Indeed not. The architect kept them, green and growing, roofed inside the glass walls of the great transept, its strong ribs modeled on the structure of an exotic lily from the Guianas whose giant leaves could actually bear the weight of a small child. How patently British, I think to myself. To house those elms within a giant crystal water lily, a shining glass palace to celebrate our bizarre apotheosis of engineering, commerce and art.

The President has finished his remarks. A brief round of clapping, of *Hear! hear!*, then a pause. They are all looking towards me. Or do they look through me and beyond? What is it they see?

I raise my glass, offer a toast to the memory of Addison. Recalling his attacks on the formalists, I quote his observation that "Works of art rise in value according to the degree of their resemblance to nature."

They stare at me, puzzled. I must make the connection for them. With a shiver (why is it suddenly so cold in this overheated room?) I add, "The lesson, gentlemen, is clear. Nourish our aesthetics at the bosom of nature, or else be doomed, our theories as self-consuming as that same serpent who devouring its tail, circles endlessly, making no progress."

They are nodding now, the word *progress* makes them comfortable, this they can understand. They smile, begin to argue. I dodge and weave between their parries. These are minds trained to reduce nature to its barest bones. What they cannot see is the living totality, not even the shadowy outlines of the creature as a whole, much less the beating heart, skin, texture. What the creature feels—and why. These are the mysteries our logic shall never penetrate, nor should we even try to venture there. I want to warn them but dare not lest my voice ring out and shatter their crystal palaces: *Some places we must not go!* Let us content ourselves with our theories, with myths pagan and Christian, classical and romantic. Let us build a glass lily to house a tall tree, and leave it at that.

Voices are growing louder. The butler passes around more wine. Our President spills some on his embroidered waistcoat, the drops lost in a field of brocaded flowers, quite elegant, actually, the richness of those intricately woven garlands. A bit of a dandy, this pompous gentleman. For the first time, I smile at him with genuine warmth. His flowered waistcoat humanizes him, indeed I can picture him revolving slowly in front of the long oval mirror, muttering anxiously to his wife, "Bit showy, m'dear?"

Still smiling, I pat the smooth lapels of my own frock coat, pearl gray, quite correct. In such discreet wear I am indistinguishable from my colleagues. We sport the protective coloration crucial to the survival of the species—in a word, we are safe. Why then this feeling of profound unease?

After an hour I put down my glass, knowing only that I am tired. And afraid.

I offer our hostess the usual evasions. A long journey. A full day tomorrow. "In such distinguished company, I do assure you, madame," I tell her with mocking earnestness, "one does not want to come off a fool."

She murmurs soothing words. "My dear colleague," she says, "but of course not." She caresses me with a smile and cool white fingertips, her indulgent voice carrying that polished assurance of the consummate hostess, ever considerate, never kind.

I bow my head. She dips hers as well, glides back to the drawing room. Beyond the arched doorway, there is a rumble of deep laughter, the sort of secret laughter which makes re-entry impossible for the departed guest. He can never be sure whether they laugh because he was there. Or because he has left.

My luggage has already preceded me to my room. I follow, climbing slowly, uneasy with this manor house, with these long curving stairs branching like the great ash tree Yggdrasil from the sleeping marble below. Are those marble floors the slain giant's teeth? From his blood, I recall, came the waters, from his brains the clouds, whilst his eyebrows formed the great wall, the thatched barricade to keep out other giants. But his eyes—what I wonder became of his eyes?

The bedroom door closes behind me. It shuts noiselessly with that rich silence heard only in very old domiciles, these country mansions built to last through centuries of assaults from without—but where danger, alas, comes solely from within.

Danger. The word invites speculation. And indeed it is a dangerous enterprise to be a guest. No mere coincidence our word *travel* derives from *travail,* a labor, tribulation, or agony. The tribulations of the journey, the agonies of the destination. And thus the solitary traveler becomes at journey's end, the guest, a word whose original meaning was *enemy* or *stranger.*

Which is how I feel in this house, and how many others? Greeted as guest, treated as stranger. The distress of the isolated houseguest—am I the only one who chafes at this arrangement? To be the alien outsider, dislocated, anonymous—such isolation renders me opaque to myself, unmoored by my faceless role of bystander. Who am I? What am I? Why am I afraid?

What folly to set out on a voyage armed only with a small valise by which we seek to replicate a home away from home. Once unpacked, how meager these artifacts from another life appear. My pitiful pile of linens swallowed in the gaping drawers of that huge chiffonnier—drawers which remind me of small coffins. And over there against the wall within the open maw of the armoire, my few garments bob in a sea of shadows, lapping against the folds of my velvet smoking jacket, dimming the deep crimson into halftones.

Yes, this bedchamber is hungry. It devours my belongings. Even my dear traveling companions, these worn leather copies of Coleridge and de Sade, look unfamiliar, indeed unnatural. They have been reduced to mere props in an elaborate stage-set designed to spotlight my total insignificance.

"You," the room whispers, "are irrelevant."

A floorboard creaks behind me. With a start, I turn around. But there is nothing to be seen.

Now the room is quiet. Quiet so that I may listen. Obediently I do.

It does not tell lies, this room. And seated here on the edge of the mattress, I can almost hear the echoing dialogue of this house, this simulacrum of home. Reason tells me I am safe here, safe from external harm. But my senses tell me otherwise.

I cough, a sound at once too loud and too intimate.

Disconcerted, I cross over to the desk by the window. The heavy damask drapes have not yet been drawn. Breezy outside, I note, and although the hour is well past eight o'clock, the midsummer sun still streams in. Seated at the desk, I take out my notes for tomorrow's lecture and begin paging through them. The rustle of the manuscript pages comforts me. Outside the window, the leaves of a giant wych elm tremble against the glass, fidgeting restlessly in a mood that matches my own.

Slowly, I reach for the pen in the marble inkstand. Perhaps the distraction of jotting down a few additional ideas might prove amusing? Formulate into a rough essay these idle thoughts which keep coiling through my brain. Let me reflect—Man and Nature? Man Versus Nature? Fascinating to trace our wildly contradictory perceptions across the millennia.

Ah yes—how shall I put this? Smiling, I jot down the title, pressing so hard with my quill that the ink splatters across the page: *Nature: Predatory or Sublime?*

Capital! Chewing on the pen, I stare out at the elm tree rustling against the window pane, then quickly begin ticking off my central thesis: How curious this full circle we have traveled in our attitudes towards nature, attitudes which have metamorphosed through so many successive guises beginning with primitive terror followed by placatory worship, then on to mythmaking, demonization, indifference, sublimation, and finally to where we stand now, mid-century.

As fast as I scribble down these lines, more ideas quiver to break free. My pen is heavy, the quill dries as quickly as my thoughts escape into thin air. I must pin them down instantly. Where we stand now? Ah, to be sure—in stuffy rooms, the richness and breadth of Romantic sentiments diminished, indeed leached into a sickly pastiche of sentimentalized clichés; the concept of nature as sublime inspiration for pure feeling and pure freedom abandoned— nature in fact dethroned; the social contract rejected, the revolutions of '48 failed; a whole nation genuflecting to our new Gospel of Prosperity whose Articles of Faith embrace religious cant, social hypocrisy, laissez faire materialism, that unholy triad we venerate these days in this curiously smug, buttoned-up epoch when few voices protest the ravages of industrialization which defile and debase both city and countryside. What an extraordinary loop we've traveled, beginning in fear and ending in suspicion, with so many gods jettisoned along our journey.

I pause, thinking of the railway train which brought me here, belching its passage across the land, past hellish machinery grinding away in countless foundries and mills. I recall Wordsworth's outraged description of factory workers, especially the children, resuming their night shift duties:

Within this temple, where is offered up
To Gain, the master idol of the realm,
Perpetual sacrifice.

One might suggest the romantic credo first posited by blessed Rousseau, *sentio ergo sum*, has been exchanged for *cui bono*. Suggest further that our rapturous faith in nature as a moral force for good has yielded, alas, to those sentiments anticipated by De Sade himself when he writes "Nature...hungers at all her pores for bloodshed, yearns with all her heart for the furtherance of cruelty." If De Sade is correct, Rousseau delusional, then what weapon do we possess to combat such ferocity—how do we harness nature to serve us?

The answer is ominously clear. Our new savior is science, applied and pure, already taming nature, raping her secrets, offering mankind salvation in a godless universe, safety from the chaos of the cosmic process. While our glorious vision of Nature as Prophet fades, shall we soon be forced to look on the gorgon head of Nature *for* Profit? And if we succeed in harnessing her prodigious forces so that we may win the cruel struggle of existence, shall science become our sole remaining key for unlocking the mysteries surrounding the progress of civilization? One unknowable question remains: Progress towards what?

Even as I place the dot beneath that last question mark, I can hear something—a muffled murmuring from far away.

I put down the pen and flex my fingers, cramped from such long bondage.

Listen!

The sound is so faint at first that I am almost able to pretend I have not heard, have not been braced all this while for the cycle to begin again.

Though houses may change, the room is the same. Always.

And so is the thing that comes up from below. Still searching for me, still sighing my name.

My name. Yes, yes—at last.

By naming me, my identity is given back, I am given back to myself. But why always so hard a bargain? To know myself is to meet my fear again face to face. And this nameless fear has now its own identity as well. Naming me, it finds its shape. And so once more it comes. Comes from below. Up from the cellars and past the baize door. Up the back staircase, it knows that I hide, here in the guest chamber.

And now yet again, I must repeat the ritual, must unlatch the casement and fling the windows open wide. The breeze stirs the damask drapes.

To stand upon this window ledge is not frightening as long as I keep my eye fixed on the broad arm of the elm which beckons me, pulls me in towards its trunk, clasping me close to rough bark. A clumsy razor, the bark scrapes my jaw. I can feel wetness along the jawbone. Has it drawn blood?

Am I bleeding, or is it the tree which weeps?

And why this sense of revulsion from its rough embrace? The elm is my deliverance, is it not? And yet I know my fear has followed me, fusing me to this bark as inescapably as flesh is bonded to frigid metal. To break free seems impossible.

I stop trying, I gaze downwards. Through these leafy branches the ground below looks immeasurably distant. A thought intrudes which I must push away as quickly as the impulse to inch my way back to the window, a suspicion this fusion is not between flesh and bark but rather between flesh and fear itself.

No, this is madness, there is no time, hurry, slither down quickly, quickly, feel the earth solid beneath me, the coolness of wet grass. Ah yes, this grass is real, these tall hedges prickling against bare skin are real as well, and so is the park which lies beyond them.

A lovely park of classical design adhering strictly to principles of unity and harmony, a series of repetitions, of diverging lines radiating to far off vistas. But I must move through it with dispatch because even now my elm may be sharing its rough embrace with that which follows me. Whilst I can make good my escape, trees, alas, are hapless prisoners. Locked in place, they stand, they endure, capable neither of choosing lovers, be they birds, rain, sunshine—nor of repelling enemies, be they vine or ax, lightning or bark beetle.

I glance around, searching for a way out. Despite its spaciousness, the park seems oddly crowded. These formal gardens are alive with tall figures, they loom over me so tall that perforce only by craning backward am I able with difficulty to examine them. Some are carved from marble, some from yew and holly. Goddesses and satyrs disport next to stags and slouching lions, their shapes a bizarre mélange of myth and the natural world blurring into white stone and green leaf as I dodge and weave past them. Past them, past a fishpond whose glassy waters reflect the small pavilion modeled on a miniature Greek temple which, in odd juxtaposition, overshadows a small botanical garden for the scientific classification of plant specimens. Next, a gentle descent along grass terraces sweeping down to a wide avenue bordered by stately beeches.

The avenue terminates in front of a magnificent fountain. I gaze upward. Diana crouches at the center, her archer's arm pulled back—how exquisite the voluptuous swelling of those marble biceps as she sights her prey! The fountain itself is dry; a line of green scum rims the sides of the basin. Beyond it, the path branches around a vast parterre of dizzying complexity, rectangles subdivided by narrow walkways whose borders define a kaleidoscope of geometrical shapes radiating outward in perfect symmetry. Circles within triangles within diamond-shaped plots, the whole framed by rose bushes and low-lying ornamental shrubs.

With a shudder, I stop. This is a labyrinth, a nightmare of formal design, of nature conforming to Euclidian principles by which the eye becomes the point of origin for all lines of vision. And wearies quickly from this burden of converging perspectives.

I wish I could blink. I cannot.

The walk is paved with brick, rough beneath me. And now at last I can see the ivied walls of the park. I keep my gaze fixed on those wrought iron gates which lead to open woods. Shadowed and dark, these woods beckon me.

The park gates are not locked. I slip through them easily, and in so doing

I feel a surge of excitement, feel that I am slipping the bonds of civilization, of symmetry and order, to wander unfettered—yes, free!—half forgetting my flight has been forced upon me, half remembering both the ecstasies and terrors of this blissful surrender to pure instinct, shed finally of the strictures of reason—that transitory guestroom we all inhabit, forever ill at ease, forever afraid to face our basic natures. I am no longer fleeing from but rather moving *towards*.

O, what rapture to be fully alive with movements so supple, with throbs of pleasure over each new sight, sound, scent encountered! A jaunty cricket crunching hungrily on a green leaf stem. The rustle of grasses as those two field mice flee for cover. The pungent fragrance of a dead meadowlark whose frail rotten carcass is wedged between the roots of a pine tree. I want to stop and examine it but there's no time so instead I surge ahead to a small clearing of dappled greens and golds, the last of this day's sunlight stabbing through the dark circle of spruce.

Up a small hummock, its crest much steeper than I had guessed. At the summit it's tempting to look back, but prudence (or is it cunning?) dictates otherwise. Voluptuously I launch myself on a zigzagging glide down the banks, the pine needles a soft bed, a slippery silken bed to enfold and explore me. I shiver with ripples of delight as these needles fondle my skin, their kisses so gentle the occasional sharp prick merely heightens the enjoyment. Former irritants no longer distress, nor does the question I push down as swiftly as the impulse to linger. Only a question of fact, nothing complex, nothing metaphysical, gentlemen. Simply this: why has this body of mine stopped feeling old?

Doesn't matter, doesn't matter, speed alone is what counts. Indeed, having escaped the confines of the park, I am moving appreciably faster. 'Tis almost dusk, and the pine trees have given way to open meadowland followed by hayfields curving beside this deep rutted road I travel on. Eyes down, I follow the tracks of what appear to be wagon wheels. To my left lie rotting haystacks, the color of wet tobacco. The stench of wet hay is so strong I can taste it on my tongue.

And then—the ground trembles.

I glance up. In front of me, a long line of oxen are crossing the road, passing from the open gate in the hayfield to the pasture on my right.

The oxen turn to stare at me. 'Tis their hides I notice first, beautiful hides splotched in shades deepening from palest cinnamon to darkest sable, except for the largest animal who is black. His forehead is wrinkled with deep furrows which lend him an air of patient wisdom. All around his mouth the hairs are white. The other beasts who follow him have horns not quite as large as his. These horns spread antler-wide in graceful curves, their sharp points gleaming. At the base of each horn where it joins the broad head just above the ear, colonies of flies cluster in an obscene purple-black garland resembling ripe blackberries. I am forced to glance away, away from calm dark eyes watching me with meek curiosity.

The herd files past me so slowly that it's possible to make a closer inspection of their broad backs which seem to be burdened by some sort of... harness, is it? I stare more closely, from this angle it is difficult to tell. But this much is clear, that is no harness, nor can I name this seeping burden slick as aspic or fresh entrails, these steaming pink membranes quivering deliciously in the cool evening air whilst the oxen plod by.

Now striding directly behind them appears the drover. He prods the beasts along by raking their flanks with a long hickory staff. Embedded at the tip of the staff is a steel hook. The drover too turns to regard me. He moves forward, towering over me. His gaze burns.

He lifts his staff and waves it overhead. Then he brings it down, stabs at my side.

The pain is white hot and I jerk away, ready to strike back. The oxen, alarmed, begin lowing, then break into a trot, lumbering past us into the open fields, kicking up dust which floats in the air. But the drover pays no attention to their flight. Instead he steps towards me, crouches down, his face before me swims hazily through the dust spirals. His mouth is wet and open as he screams. I lunge forward. His raw flesh tastes good, his blood like rusty water. Again he stabs. Now he is sprawled across me, his head so near that when he blinks, I can feel the quick sweep of his lashes. How comforting to close the eyelid, to shut out this road, these pastures. How naked the lidless eye.

We lie motionless, too bloodied to hide. He starts to moan, a deep sound from some leaking wound I have inflicted but cannot see.

My coils look sleek, the scales iridescent now with splashes of crimson, and despite the throbbing, I understand that he is no different from me. Or only in ways that do not matter. Coupled by our shared predicament we are trapped in that insatiable circle familiar to all predators—the place where our journey both ends and begins. For us no escape is possible, *we are what we flee.*

The rational faculties I can still muster recognize this inarguable truth. And yet one small part of me yearns to protest, to persuade myself 'tis only safety I seek. That I am not predator, but prey.

No! Too vain, too proud now for feeble quibbling, I hiss at this admission of cowardice, a form of weakness I find repugnant, indeed loathsome. I want to shout aloud: Look at me! Behold my articulated beauty! Marvel (if you dare) at the splendor of this undulant body writhing in triumph despite mortal pain.

What terrible joy it is to wound, to kill, to savor at last in death the sweet succulence of life. With flickering tongue, I examine the drover.

He sighs. Slowly, he pulls himself up on one elbow. His cheeks, I notice, are wet. I can see only one giant eye blinking rapidly. It gazes at me in the very same way the oxen had, with curiosity.

And could it be—with pity?

THE PROPERTIES OF GLASS

WATCH THE NUMBERS, OH yes watch the numbers so Rachel watches them flick by quickly, impersonally: 6...5...4...3...zigzagging from left to right, a numerical Christmas tree blinking *Off/On/Off/On*, pulsating steadily downwards/down/down to ground zero—down to the big O and back to nothing which is precisely where she'd started from—or is it where's she's ending up, which? And now the elevator doors slide open to street level and she can see Shirley over there by the window, the only woman in the whole waiting room.

Shirley sits hunched over. She's leafing through a magazine, hands going through the motions of flipping the pages but her fine cat-shaped eyes strain, staring straight ahead, fixed on the elevator. Behind her on the wall, the clock reads 5:15. These numbers, thank God, don't move but stand fixed and still, a staunch black against the white clock face and, like Shirley, dependable.

For a second the men in the waiting room glance up as the doors wheeze shut behind Rachel then look away, wrong lamb/wrong slaughter, and Rachel is glad, she's fiercely happy Derek isn't here among them. Facing him, watching him fumble for the right expression—not bearable, it would have unmanned her, *unman*—can a woman be unmanned? and she shakes her head and leans against the wall, feeling her stomach still lurching downwards with the elevator, her knees quivering but less so, steadied now by the relief she can read in Shirley's eyes. Pure relief, clear and unclouded whereas Derek would be looking worried, nervously smiling, struggling hard to reassure— hell, prove to Rachel she's not a burden weighing him down.

My friend, thinks Rachel. My good friend, here when I needed her. Here *because* I needed her.

They meet halfway across the waiting room. Shirley hugs her hard, then draws back to study Rachel. "You all right?" she asks, smiling, that elfin smile Rachel counts on, cat eyes reflecting back the image she needs to see, the strong Rachel she wants to be again not this weak-kneed stranger, pulling away and saying with a fake laugh, "Fine! Let's just get the heck out of here."

Shirley raises a questioning eyebrow. "Up to walking a couple blocks?"

"Forget walk, let's run!" Rachel's laughing again but meaning it this time, and she pulls her velvet collar high around her neck, ties the coat belt tighter, shivers. Truly freezing in here, time to bolt.

"Look, why don't I go get the car, you wait inside the foyer."

"No, I'm coming with you, I need fresh air right this minute."

Outside, the rain had stopped and it was already dark. People are hurrying along the pavement, heads tucked against the raw wind. No eye contact, not in November.

Shirley took her by the arm. They walk slowly, the wet leaves slick underfoot. Rachel glances up at the branches creaking over their heads. The trunks of the trees wink shiny black in the headlights from the traffic. Around the base of each tree more wet leaves lie snagged in heaps between the wrought iron railings—those spiky skirts worn by city trees as chastity belts for reasons unclear, possibly decorative, yet contravened by the litter caught between the spikes along with the leaves—what Derek had dubbed your standard metropolitan detritus, the Big Mac cartons, old newspapers, all casually chucked aside as if the very act of throwing stuff away makes it invisible. Once more Rachel shudders, leaning hard against Shirl's firm shoulder.

"Talk about fresh air," Shirley mutters, bending into the wind.

Rachel nods concentrating on not slipping. Shouldn't have worn these high heels, worse than walking on stilts. And her little toe's throbbing to beat hell. "Skates, that's what we need," she tells Shirley.

"Or skis?"

"Perfect! People actually ski on pine needles, don't they?"

"I think so. Getting tired?"

"No. I just don't want to slip is all."

"Hang on tight."

"Good old Shirley."

"Any port in the storm, right?"

"Right." But it's too hard talking over the sound of the traffic. Or was it the wind snatching their words, whirling them away as fast as the leaves? Walking, in any event, is all Rachel can manage.

Once long ago she had read a story about a woman right on the brink. Or perhaps, gone over already. The woman kept peering out her living room window to talk to the fallen maple leaves lying scattered across the green October grass. The scarlet leaves had whispered and danced on the lawn, smiling at the woman, who smiled back at them automatically—at all the happy children she was convinced they must be—playing in her front yard.

When Rachel finished the story, she had gone upstairs to her room, locked the door, thrown herself across the bed, and wept. Now, looking back, she still doesn't understand why the story made her so sad.

But the grief overarched the years, making her ache all over again for that lanky kid sobbing on her narrow maple bed with its bright green bedspread of horses and huntsmen galloping across the English countryside, and for the first time she wondered if the young girl back then had been weeping for the middle-aged woman who moves so slowly down this dark city street, wet leaves sticking to her shoes like cast off snake skins.

"Only one more block," announces Shirley.

They were passing a restaurant. DINO'S: FINE SPIRITS, FINE FOODS promised the sign above the big bay window. Rosy faces beam at them through the glass. It looked so cozy inside there, and the warm yellow light spills out on the sidewalk over glistening black puddles.

"You hungry?" Shirley's asking.

"Not exactly."

Arm in arm they walk on past. No more brightly lit windows now. The rest of the block appear to be mainly office buildings and old town houses in the process of being converted into condominiums—at least according to the notices posted on the arched doorways.

"What?"

"Nothing, Shirl."

At least the buildings still look like houses, their shells the same, but who knows what's been done to the interiors? Probably as shiny and sterile as the word suggests. *Condominium.* Ugly. Ugly last two syllables, something metallic there: *aluminium, titanium, uranium,* names she could never memorize in Chemistry. So what ever happened to the four basic elements— about as far as she'd ever gotten with the physical universe—or wanted to, for that matter. Good old reliable *earth, air, fire, water?* Amen.

"Pardon?" Shirley says, tucking in close, shoulder firm against Rachel's.

"I said amen."

"As in ahhhh-**men?**"

"Precisely!" and Rachel giggles. Ahead of them she can see Shirley's Tercel, silver-dappled beneath the black trees. "How did you ever snag a parking place so close?" she asks while Shirley scratches around in her purse for the keys.

"Circling the block, how else?" Shirley holds open the passenger door.

"Circling makes me nervous, always scared I'll never be able to actually land anywhere." Rachel starts to climb inside, then she stops. "Let's go back."

"Where to?"

"To Dino's. You know, that restaurant we passed."

"So you *are* hungry!"

"Listen, what I need is a good belt, good and sweet and strong."

"Super idea!" Shirley laughs. She locks the Tercel, and wind behind them now—an ally at their backs—they retrace their steps.

Inside the restaurant it's lovely and warm, and bright, and mainly...*warm.* They're seated at a small table beside a gold-leafed antique mirror which runs the length of one whole wall at the back of the dining room. The glass looks very old, speckled and wavy, the same transparent amber as pond-water.

"Seems our table seats four, not two," observes Rachel dryly, nodding at their reflections.

Puzzled, Shirley glances up at her, then over at the mirror. "Oh, me and my shadow, you mean."

"Exactly. Plus me and mine." And the two of them (four of them?) grin at each other.

The drinks came. "Would you care to order dinner now?" the waiter murmurs. His hands are white and narrow, young smooth skin, thin fingers elegantly shaped as he proffers the menus.

"I think not, we're—" Shirley's saying, but Rachel interrupts because now she *is* hungry, so hungry she wants very much to drain the daiquiri in one long greedy swallow, and so she tells the waiter, "Yes, we will be ordering, just give us a few minutes, please." He nods and leaves them.

"Glad your appetite's all back. A good sign."

"Do me a favor, Shirl," Rachel says, speaking fast and low. "For the next thirty minutes could you please, please stop being the concerned professional, stop playing nursie? I feel fine, I *am* fine, I haven't had a thing to eat for thirty-six hours and I'm starving. I could eat a whole damn horse at this point."

Shirley's eyes narrow, but before she can open her mouth to answer, Rachel reaches over and touches her on the hand, those knobby arthritic fingers of a much older woman—not her fifty-year old friend who winces but squeezes back instantly as Rachel adds, "Oh, sorry, that came out all wrong. Really, Shirl. It's just this whole day of people hovering over me. Like vultures."

"Well..." Shirley sniffs, her mouth still tight.

"Come on, girl! It's them I'm talking about, not you. Don't be cross? Indulge me a little. Please." And then, as she stares down at the menu, the words blur and swim all together.

And now Shirley's saying, voice soft, "Oh Rachel honey, go ahead, cry. Here," whipping out a Kleenex.

"I am not going to cry, my tear ducts are simply—confused is all." Rachel blows her nose. "Charming sound. Enough already, so what looks good here?"

Shirley ordered the veal piccata, Rachel, the chicken tetrazzinni. She tries not to gulp the daiquiri. It tastes so cool and sweet on her tongue and she can feel the strength seeping back. "Know what?" she says, smacking her lips, "This hits the spot, I'm going to order seconds."

"One's my limit, designated driver, remember, but hey— you go ahead, Rache, definitely the right move, your blood sugar's probably low. Whoops!" And Shirley stops, eyes sliding sideways, mischievously. "Sorry, can't seem to drop the jargon." She giggles and holds up her glass, face happy, the tip of her nose pink.

"Toast?" asks Rachel.

"Not exactly a toast occasion, this. But for the record I'm tickled my buddy's fine and sitting here getting pie-eyed just like old times. Cheers!"

"Cheers!" In the mirror their arms bridge the table, curtsying in mid-air as both glasses clink, and then their waiter's back. Rachel orders up another daiquiri, but when he starts to walk away, she calls, "Waiter!" speaking much louder than she meant to.

"Madame?" He turns back, flicking the snowy white napkin over his arm. He smiles down at Rachel, wonderful deep-set eyes, glowingly unhappy.

"Did you know you look exactly like Charles Ryder?"

"I beg your pardon?"

"I mean the actor who plays Charles in *Brideshead Revisited.*"

He smiles again, the tragic self-preoccupied smile of the true narcissist. "Pity," he drawls. "I'd much rather be Lord Sebastian," and saunters off with another flick of the white napkin.

"Screw him," says Rachel cheerfully, and drinks another long sweet swallow of daiquiri.

"What did you expect?"

"He's so tragic looking, I thought he'd love the compliment."

"Come on, Rachel, we've been dining off this kind of romanticizing for years."

Rachel says nothing. She taps her glass with the plastic fork shaped like a trident, Neptune, Narcissus—who gives a shit? The glass makes a dull pinging sound—not crystal, not by a long shot.

"You have this face hang up—isn't so & so exquisite, or look how he's suffered, whatever."

"You make it sound like soap opera."

"The waiter's soap opera! The creep's obviously in the middle of a three-act melodrama."

"Enjoying every minute of it," Rachel grins.

"Sure, every delicious self-referred minute."

"Still," and Rachel spears the soggy orange slice at the bottom of the glass, popping it in her mouth. "Still," she mumbles, mouth full, "he is exquisite."

When the waiter comes back with their dinner, they both ignore him.

Rachel dismisses him with a cool "Thanks" and he goes stalking off, napkin flicking from his back pocket, an angry white tail.

Shirley chuckles. "See what happens when you judge a book by its cover?"

"True, but I do wish it were possible—all that beauty wasted on a preening peacock," and Rachel begins poking at her food. She tries the pasta, the tossed salad. Nothing has any taste. All she can register is the food's texture—slippery noodles, grainy tomatoes, the rubbery smoothness of the meat which almost makes her gag. She puts down her fork, lights a cigarette. In the mirror beside her, the flame of the match shimmers briefly in a ripple of burnished gold.

Shirley keeps on eating, chewing very slowly, very deliberately. Between mouthfuls, she begins telling a long involved story about a difficult patient on the locked unit last weekend, the patient released, the family furious. But it's hard to follow the exact sequence of events, so Rachel takes her cues from the rising inflections in Shirley's voice, matching her own reaction to Shirley's expressions as they mirror first the frightened patient, then the angry father, Shirley's growing doubts, and, finally the bored cold face of the shrink, annoyed at being called in for a weekend consult.

"Hardly professional, he had the nerve to tell me," and Shirley glares, eyes disappearing to slits beneath pouchy lids.

"Actually...my doctor up there today was pretty nice, kind, very kind," Rachel hears herself saying, the dreamy words floating out like soap bubbles, totally unexpected.

Shirley sits back, carefully wipes her mouth and takes out a lipstick from her purse. "Want to talk about it now?" she asks casually, making a major production out of fumbling for her compact, unscrewing the lipstick, the pinkish brown cylinder rising slowly up and up, all smooth and moist.

Rachel turns her head away. From the corner of her eye, she can see herself profiled in the mirror, ash blonde hair fanning back from a pale crescent of cheek, cigarette trembling in the hand right next to the glass, the glowing tip close enough to burn it—except glass doesn't burn, she reminds herself, that much she did recall from high school Chemistry, and how strange it was to be told by their teacher that glass was regarded as a super-cooled liquid—not a true solid. Cool, transparent, fluid—a pool, a forest pond, she thinks, and leans her head against the smooth surface for a moment, then stubs out the cigarette.

"Not much to tell," she says at last. "Lots of waiting around mainly. The worst part was..." she pauses. The woman beside her in the mirror waits too—very still.

"...was the pain?" asks Shirley, eyes a soft kitten green now.

"No, not the pain, anything that quick is bearable for heaven's sake. No, it was being stuck up there with all those kids. I felt so old. Old as God. Most of those girls could have been my daughters!"

Shirley is nodding. "I know," she murmurs.

Rachel touches the smooth steel of the knife lying unused by her plate. She picks it up, hefting it in her palm—it feels heavy, and cold. She puts it down quickly and begins pleating her napkin, folding and unfolding it, running her hands along the creases but the cloth will not lie flat and keeps bunching up. Carefully, she lays the napkin over the knife, tucking it in neatly. Hospital corners they're called, nicely triangulated.

She lights another cigarette. The smoke spirals upwards, up to the mirror, kisses the glass, and disappears.

Across the table, Shirley is waiting, very quiet, very patient. A young bus boy silently removes the dinner plates and brings them coffee. Like the smoke, Narcissus has vanished.

"Guess that's about it," Rachel says finally.

"I just hate seeing you like this."

Rachel leans forward. "Listen, Shirl, I really am all right. I mean I don't feel *any*thing at this point. Except grateful, I suppose. Lucky, actually. Think of the alternatives."

Shirley smiles, her special nursing smile, fine-tuned in compassionate understanding, all that drivel, yes, thinks Rachel, here it comes right on schedule.

"…don't have to be brave anymore. Not with me, dear heart. Perfectly normal for you to be experiencing grief, even anger, it's part of the whole process. No matter what the alternatives might have been, the loss is still there, Rache."

Rachel looks away again, watching the woman in the mirror blow smoke rings, lazy circles that waver above the pale hair in a series of expanding haloes. "Listen, you did remember to call Emily?" she asks abruptly.

Now Shirley looks uneasy, her eyes sliding past Rachel, jumping back and forth, ranging around the dining room. "Hmmmm, yes, she'll be over tomorrow after work."

"Casserole in hand, no doubt," this ironically, but still Shirley squirms in her chair, something fishy here. "Shirley, what gives?"

Shirley wipes her mouth again, polite little pats in place of apologies. She puts her napkin down, faces Rachel. "Emily's upset."

"Upset? That I didn't ask her instead of you to take me home today?"

"No, upset with Derek."

"Derek? Why Derek?"

"Because he dumped you like a sack of mail this morning. He didn't stay with you, simply left you there, abandoned you, Rachel!"

"Hold on, that was my decision. I asked him, I *told* him not to hang around. Plus he had all the regional vice presidents flying in at ten o'clock."

"I don't give a damn if the Pope himself flew in, first things first. Derek should have been with you today. Period."

Rachel laughs then. The laugh rings bitter and hollow between them. "Sounds to me Emily's not the only person ticked off at Derek."

Shirley tries to smile, but her cat eyes are narrowed, no longer a soft green but brilliant as emeralds and just as hard. "Look here, Rachel...." She pauses, breathes deeply. "The last thing in the world I want is to get caught in the middle here."

"Middle of what?"

"Between you and Emily."

"That's not what you're in the middle of now, my friend. You're stepping in between me and Derek, and quite frankly—"

"Please, honey," and Shirley reaches across the table and places her crooked old hand over Rachel's, but Rachel jerks away. "Rachel, listen, take it easy, you must realize you're in a very labile state now, you—"

"Tell me," Rachel speaks slowly; her tongue feels thick and swollen, and her voice is shaking. "Just where do you guys—my *friends*, remember—get off making judgements about Derek?"

"All we're suggesting is he has a responsibility to you."

"You're also suggesting he's flunked, correct?"

"In a sense, yes, he flunked. It's not right, leaving you alone that way. Surely you must see that."

"I see all right." Rachel stopped. Their waiter had slithered up to the table. He puts down a silver plate with the bill tucked inside a maroon leather case. On top lie two green foil packets, chocolate dinner mints. He bows toward Rachel. "Will there be anything else, Madame?"

But Shirley replies in a clipped voice. "That's it."

He whisks the tablecloth with his napkin, nods curtly, and vanishes again.

"Jerk," mutters Rachel, catches Shirley's eye, and chuckles.

Shirley begins laughing too. "They're all jerks, Rache, every single one of them. That's all we're saying. They fade out when you need them most."

Rachel clears her throat. "If I'm not pissed at Derek, you shouldn't be. The thing is I needed to be alone."

"You can't sit there and tell me you're not upset."

"But not for the reasons you think. Derek didn't flunk, I did."

"**You!**" Shirley is looking loyal and fierce. "Why you?"

"I'm not feeling this loss thing you keep insisting on. I only feel relieved, understand? I'm not being brave, I'm being selfish. Because the truth is I feel nothing, the big zero—not a damn thing except pure relief." Rachel smiles. "Shocked you, haven't I?"

"Easy, Rache. I'm not shocked." Shirley's whispering now, her eyes flickering around to the other tables.

"You think I'm fooling myself, but I'm not." Rachel slaps her hand hard against the table. "*Look* at me, damn it, while I'm sitting here spilling my guts out!"

And Shirley jerks up her head and stares straight into Rachel's eyes. "I am looking, Rachel," she answers. "I'm listening."

"Listen with your heart for a change. That's why I need you here today, not Derek. To listen in a way he simply cannot—he's not wired that way, what man *is*?"

Shirley answers, voice low but steady. "I'm trying to. Go on."

Rachel begins lighting another cigarette, but her hand's shaking so hard that Shirley has to take the box of matches, strike one, and hold the flame steady as Rachel inhales, begins to speak, the smoke sputtering out in jerky little puffs. "What happened to me today," she says, "it's not what you think. What made me grieve as you keep putting it, was seeing those young girls, kids really. Oh, I don't know, Shirley, it was like a time warp or something. All those beautiful girls. They—"

She stops, gnaws at her bottom lip. She takes the cigarette and grinds it out in the ashtray, then says curtly, "You don't even know what I'm talking about, do you?"

"I think I do, Rachel. I think I'm beginning to."

"That's what it's about, don't you see? Those youngsters, they've never even had a beginning. I'm 43 years old, I've done it, I've had my babies. So for me there's kind of a natural ending. But you see, they—"

"Now wait a minute, Rachel. It's not all over for them, you're exaggerating again. They'll have another chance, under better circumstances later on."

"Maybe."

"But what?"

"But it's been spoiled for them, Shirl. What should be beautiful—it's tarnished now. I mean such a cruel way to start off—saying goodbye."

"You know what I think?" asks Shirley, very softly.

"What?"

"I think you were saying goodbye as well."

"Maybe so. But I can't feel sorry for myself; not directly, not the grown-up Rachel anyhow. Just for those kids—16, 17 years old and scared to death. See, Shirley? See what I'm saying?"

And now Shirley's murmuring "yes" and nodding her head and there are tears in her eyes and whether the tears were meant for Rachel or for the young girls doesn't really make any difference, does it? So the two of them sit there in silence, affectionate silence—the kind that heals—finishing their coffee. After a while, Shirley tucks some money inside the leather case and hands Rachel both pieces of chocolate. "Your favorites," she says. "Ready?"

They stand up, putting on their coats. Shirley is smiling. She begins walking toward the front of the restaurant, and Rachel starts to follow her, then stops to look back at the mirror.

The dining room is crowded now, and in the mirror a blurred tapestry of faces shimmer behind the willowy figure who stands there, staring out at the room, tying her belt, fluffing pale hair out from under the black velvet collar, white skin sallow in the amber glass.

And for the first time all evening, Rachel sees her own reflection, not in profile but face to face. And she nods quietly to the young girl poised inside the wavy glass, eyes radiant, smiling with Rachel at the good years ahead, 23, 33, 43, smiling beyond to the time of hope trembling in the distance, curled in promise like the tight green buds of new leaves in April.

"I remember," whispers Rachel. And turns to go.

The crying came afterwards, long, long afterwards.

Inside out

HE CARRIED STORMS INSIDE him, this middle child.

When he was still in the crib, he would turn mottled with rage over the strangest things. If his stuffed animals weren't aligned in a certain order at the foot of the crib. If the carousel night-light hadn't been switched on, even in summertime when the sun could still be seen butter-yellow through the sheer nursery curtains. If any of the elaborate rituals of bedtime were either overlooked or performed in the wrong sequence.

Teaching him not to lash out in anger was the most difficult job she faced as a mother. When he finally learned to talk in complete sentences, he described once to her how he felt when he got angry.

"It's my black place," he said, pointing at his chest. "Right in here, Mummy."

What he told her sounded familiar, not unlike the way she thought about herself when she was a little girl. And her father would threaten to "beat the tar out of you!" although he never laid a finger on her, not once. Sometimes when she had done something monumentally wicked, he would say slowly, measuring out each word like it tasted bad in his mouth, "Sugar, I'm just going to have to skin you alive."

And she had pictured her wickedness back then as something dark just as her son did now. She saw herself skinned inside out hanging from a clothesline, the loose tarry skin bubbling hot and flapping in the wind, a sinister silhouette more alarming in retrospect than any actual spanking ever could have been. Scared me silly, she thought. Maybe that was the whole point.

Because her parents never had time for bedtime stories, she had learned to read at a very early age. At Sunday school there was much talk about angels, and these she got mixed up with a person's soul. Ever afterward she believed that souls resided in the shoulder blades where someday angel wings would sprout. And even now when her feelings were hurt or she felt deeply stirred, she'd automatically twitch her shoulders as if to make sure, yes, my soul's intact, still functioning.

So when Tyler talked about his black place, she realized that he was on

to something—a child's version of *the devil made me do it*. And her job—hers
and Roy's—boiled down to simply this: tap into Tyler's soul by providing
some sort of angelic counter-thrust. In short, get the kid to stand his ground,
tell the devil to buzz off. Curbing those black impulses without harming the
boy, this was what being a parent was all about.

"Damage control," she had told Roy more than once. "That's pretty
much all we can do."

Roy didn't take her seriously. Actually he thought she was kidding. But
she kept remembering when Tyler first learned to walk. He wanted to try
it alone. No matter how many falls resulted, he refused their outstretched
hands. He snatched his little fingers away and tried to pull himself along by
ricocheting off the furniture. He particularly liked the sofa cushions out in
the den. One morning he veered sharply and actually managed five running
steps until he stumbled, then fell against the sharp corner of a bookshelf.

There was no cut, no bleeding, but after the bruise faded she noticed a
small but deep hollow in the corner of his lower cheek, almost at the jaw-line.
What he had now was in fact a dimple—visible all the time, not just when he
smiled. She thought this a perfect metaphor for the child, something beautiful
emerging from the internal tumult which propelled this boy forward, away
from them, away from tranquility, a small reckless skiff pointed directly
towards dangerously high seas.

Every time she studied Tyler's face, the perfect smoothness of his cheeks
marred now by the hollowed dent near his jaw, she still felt guilty. Some days
she was convinced she was inadequate to the job of being a mother, what
Roy described as her "anticipating-doom" mood. But if she (or he, for that
matter) couldn't save the children, who would? The evidence of their failure,
her failure, was always going to be there, each moment Tyler faced them.

After he fell against the bookcase, she had wept that night. "It's my fault,
I should've hung *on* to him!"

Roy tried to comfort her. "No fault involved, darling," he had told her,
and drew her in close to him. "Neither his nor yours. It was an accident, pure
and simple."

"But he jerked away, he jerked away so fast!"

"Hey," he reminded her, smiling, "sometimes that happens." He was
referring to his usual standard reply to the children when they needed
reassurance. He would hold them tight, nod thoughtfully while they
described their latest calamity, then murmur in a calm voice, nodding his
head the whole time, "I know. I know. Sometimes that happens."

She was always surprised how well this worked, how the kids always
marched off feeling much better. They needed, she concluded, more than
being clucked over. They needed the acknowledgement from an adult of

the *reality* of misfortune. That it was to be expected and that this was in the natural order of things, not singling them out alone. Proportion, she was beginning to realize, was more important than pure sympathy. While she murmured endearments, the children often cried even louder. She was seeing how sympathy both aggrandizes and particularizes pain. What she and Roy had to do now was figure out coping strategies for the kids because in the long run they'd be much better off handling it themselves than running around looking for soft shoulders to cry on.

She knew all this, she had a handle on it, she really did.

Why then was it still so tough with a child like Tyler?

She lost her bearings when he acted ugly. Being patient wasn't the issue. No, the problem was hanging on to the conviction that he really was going to turn out ok, and that she and Roy could sustain their vigil against the black place, their eyes fixed steadily on the brightness of this child, the incandescent promise of his smile when he was happy, the quicksilver grace of him when he moved (and he was always in motion, she thought wryly); his extraordinary beauty. How many times had people, even perfect strangers, stopped to exclaim, "My, what a beautiful child!"

He had a perfection of line and of texture and color which dazzled and pleased the eye. His two brothers were handsome children. But she could clearly see they were not beautiful. Not like him. There was luminosity around Tyler—his skin seemed lit from within as if a lamp were glowing inside the finest porcelain. And except for his dark moods, he was a radiantly happy child. Most of the time he raced around laughing. He was very affectionate, hugging his parents constantly, climbing up on their laps long after his brothers had stopped, to mock-growl in his husky voice, "I luff you!"

She supposed that they were teaching him to love himself as well. But she had to proceed obliquely. With the other two kids, she was on solid ground. The oldest boy was headstrong and bossy. And the youngest was the family peacemaker, serene where Tyler was tempest-tossed. Mothering these two felt easy. She knew exactly when to be stern, when to be gentle. But she was unsure with Tyler even though she believed in her heart she understood him, the core of him, better than the other two. The fact remained, however, that whenever she or Roy tried to discipline him in the quietly firm way they handled his brothers, storms erupted.

His face went blank, at first. It was as though the light inside had been switched off, the radiance gone and in its place a sullen mask, chalk-colored, which truly frightened her.

"NO!" he would say then, snarling the words, his lips curled back so his teeth showed. "I won't! You can't make me." And then he'd kick things. Break toys he loved. Last April he kicked out all the screens on the porch. The previous summer he stomped and squashed every single ripe tomato growing on the vines in Roy's vegetable garden out back. Only a year ago in nursery school he went through a prolonged biting phase—going so far as to bite one of his favorite teacher-aids.

He could be implacable. This past summer he had insisted on wearing the same black swimming trunks every single day, even in the bathtub the black trunks went with him. Finally worn down by the daily tantrums, she went to Walmart to buy duplicates in order to maintain some semblance of family hygiene. Grudgingly, he would peel off the old suit and step into the freshly washed suit. By September he was ready to wear normal clothes to kindergarten.

What to do?

Pediatricians were consulted, and close friends. A child psychologist. Many childrearing manuals.

"Just a stage," was the consensus. "He'll outgrow it, perfectly normal."

She and Roy knew there was much love mixed up inside him, along with the darkness. Three things their quicksilver child adored—his cat, army anything, and being told stories at bedtime. Monica Cat, now six, the same age as Tyler, had appeared on their doorstep, a silvery gray kitten wet and hungry, the day he was born. They had been inseparable ever since. Monica Cat was the bridge by which Tyler could be reached sometimes when nothing else worked.

His army fixation they downplayed as much as possible although they recognized it satisfied his hunger for ritual, for stylized play in which the enemy got shot down, blown up, vanquished. They marveled at how he could transform the most benign Tonka truck into a tank. Or fashion M 1 rifles from the most unlikely pieces of lumber out in the garage. Even sticks became machine guns. They decided not to make an issue out of his war games, concluding that to do so would be futile—very much like allowing the dinner table to become a battleground by forcing the child to eat—not an arena where the parent could necessarily emerge victorious. Win the battle, lose the war?

So they struck an uneasy truce with Tyler. They let him play army but they didn't subsidize the toys. Mainly they encouraged his other hobbies. He loved to draw. He loved to work out in the shop with Roy. He was good at sports, particularly ice hockey where he could out-skate and out-check harder than any kid in the neighborhood. Unlike his brothers he hated baseball. "It's dumb," he told them. "Too slow." Not even pennant fever this fall interested him. When Roy managed to get tickets last week for today's doubleheader, Tyler announced he'd rather stay home than go to the game, even though everyone was spending the night at Grandpa's afterwards.

"Mummy doesn't have to go," he argued. "So why do I?"

"We'll be fine," she assured Roy. "Me and Monica Cat, we'll keep tabs on him."

So they left, the three of them. The last thing she saw was the blonde head of the youngest, peering at her through the back of the station wagon, his nose flattened as he blew wet kisses against the glass.

Tyler wasn't even around to wave them off. All morning long he had been over next door, playing with his best friend, a silent freckled child named Freddy whose ears stood out like bright red wing flaps. Freddy had been given a pretty male kitten from Monica's last litter. This kitten resembled his mother down to the little diamond-shaped spot on its chest. He was now two months old, very frisky, and the boys were teaching him tricks, they said. How to sit up and beg. How to come on command. How to play Roll Over Dead.

She went out on the porch to call Tyler home for lunch. It was pleasantly warm outdoors, a sparkling clear October afternoon. Great playoff weather, she thought. She must remember to turn on the TV, catch up on the score, they'd grill her tomorrow, inning by inning. This was her penance for not going.

People were out in their yards raking leaves, putting up storm windows. Someone was playing country music on the radio, very loudly, a couple of houses down the road. After lunch she'd get Tyler to help rake leaves from the flower beds out front. He was a systematic raker, working back and forth in orderly rows. He claimed he was drilling troops, rasping out in his Army voice the names of each squadron as he marched past well-disciplined leaf piles.

Whatever works, she thought ruefully, and just then—just as she started to call him, she heard Freddy laughing in the next yard.

She glanced over.

Freddy, the usually mute Freddy, was laughing so hard he was rolling now on the grass beneath the open bedroom window, holding his sides and then pointing between loud yelps.

Above him, leaning out the window stood her son. He was holding Freddy's kitten, his arms thrust straight out over the window sill, and then he opened his hands and down the kitten dropped without a sound, back arched, feet splayed out to cushion the fall.

Now Tyler began to laugh as well and then he disappeared from the window and a minute later there he was, laughing with Freddy, poking at the kitten, still alive and wobbling on the grass. It kept shaking its head.

The peals of laughter hurt to listen to, and she put her hands up to block out the sound. Both boys stopped laughing when they saw who was watching them. And the kitten, dazed, lurched in circles around Freddy's feet, not even mewing when Maggie ran next door, then knelt down and gently picked it up.

"How many times have you dropped this kitten?"

"Not too many, Mum."

"Why? How could you of all people hurt a tiny kitten? Why, Tyler? Answer me!"

She set the kitten down again, then began to shake Tyler by the shoulders, and she shook him so hard his teeth chattered. The louder the clacking, the angrier she got, and she saw in his eyes something that wasn't fear but something worse, almost a look of triumph but that couldn't be right, what was she doing anyhow? What kind of example was she setting? And she asked again, panting now as hard as he was, "How *could* you do this?"

"Teach him to fly, she told me."

"Who? Who told you?"

"NOBODY!" and then his face screwed up and closed off into that blankness she dreaded, and without another word he turned and ran home.

She stood stroking the kitten. Its tiny flanks were heaving so fast it was like holding a hummingbird in her hands, but still it made no sound. She told Freddy they were going inside right this minute to talk with his mother, and it was all she could do not to reach down and yank him by those jug ears, the brat should never have been allowed a pet in the first place, what were they thinking of, letting him have one of Monica's kittens? They were only trying, as usual, to please Tyler.

That night long, long after the long lecture and the punishment—to his room without supper, no playing with Freddy for two weeks—she went on upstairs. It was close to midnight, and she was praying he had fallen asleep.

The night-light was on as usual beside his bed. And there he was, wide awake, waiting for her to kiss him goodnight. Waiting for the bed-time ritual which no matter how naughty he might have been during the day, she never yet had missed.

The shade of the night-light was painted in broad red and white stripes like a carousel. Around the base of the lamp trotted the carousel animals, capering horses stalked by two orange tigers and a pair of startling black and white geese. When Tyler was very small he could often be coaxed to sleep while the carousel revolved and the shadows of the carved animals pranced in slow hypnotic circles across the polished wood of the bedside table. Oddly, it was the shadows Tyler always watched—not the animals themselves.

"Hi, Mummy," he said. Monica Cat was snuggled up next to him. He was lying rigid under the pale blue blanket, his right arm curved around the cat, the left hand picking nervously at the blue blanket fuzz.

It was hard for her to look at him directly, and when she did all she could really make out were his eyes, and the scooped-out darkness of the dimple. "Hi," she answered in a neutral voice. "You not asleep yet?"

"I'm sorry, Mummy!" he said, and he began crying.

She went over and sat on the bed, and she stroked his hot forehead, and then his hair all coppery streaks in the lamplight—my brindled boy, my brindled child, she thought. And he put his arms around her neck, pulling her down, and she held him until the sobs had stopped, and the murmuring of her voice saying *there, there, sometimes that happens* over and over again was now the only sound in the quiet room. Finally, he lay back on the pillow, only a few sobs like hiccups left, and she said, "It's very late, Tyler. We both need to go to sleep."

But he stared up at her. "Please," he whispered. Beside him the cat stretched, then lifted her head up as well, her green-gold eyes as wide and staring as Tyler's.

"Ok," his mother sighed, and took a deep breath. "Imagine..." she said, and began his favorite bedtime story about the time before he and Monica Cat came to live in this house at the end of this street, in this town, on this planet. Then he grinned, and she leaned over and plumped his pillow while the cat settled back to doze, curled in a silken circle beside him as he listened to the description of this other faraway world and how it was a silvery shining place where neither he nor his cat looked anything the way they did down on earth.

"The truth is..." and here she always dropped her voice to a conspiratorial stage whisper, glancing quickly over her shoulder as if someone might be eavesdropping. And Tyler laughed out loud at this pantomime while she continued, "...the two of you were actually brother and sister up there in that world, and you loved each other very much."

"Could Monica speak?" he asked each time when they got to this part.

"Yes, she could."

"Did I tell her secrets?"

"You did. And Monica told you hers."

"What kind of stuff?"

"Let's see. Something scared her once so she scratched and bit. She was frightened, you see. She didn't realize biting was wrong."

"Like when I bit the nice fat lady. In nursery school."

"Exactly."

He stirred impatiently, kicking the covers with his left foot. The cat stirred as well, and began to lick her paw then carefully wash her face. "What else?"

"She said she got jealous sometimes."

"She did?"

"Sure, when you got all the attention, you were her big brother, remember. And you were braver than she was. Maybe smarter too."

He thought about that, all the time scratching the cat in the downy part beneath her ears. Now Monica was purring, her eyes shut again, only a brief twitch of the long gray tail a reminder she was not asleep.

Tyler was shaking his head. "Not smarter, Mum," he corrected her. "Bigger is all I am, I'm her big bro and I protect her. But she's the smart one. Monica Cat knows **everything**!" He touched the tip of the cat's pink nose with one gentle finger, and the purrs got much louder. "Stuff like how to catch things."

"Like the time with the king, right?"

"Right!"

"And you remember how once upon a fine summer day the king of this world where you and Monica lived decided he'd give this awesome prize to the first person to catch a flying horse."

"Really hard, hunh?" He was cueing her now, afraid she would leave out the crucial parts of the story, maybe weave in too many morals? He was cagey, her brindled boy, but hey, so was she.

"Extremely hard, but Monica found out what flying horses specially liked to eat."

"Golden apples!" Tyler exclaimed.

"So off you trotted to the royal orchards where you picked the shiniest gold apple, and after that..."

"After that we went to this field and we waited." He motioned at the cat who immediately opened her eyes and watched Tyler without blinking. He was talking fast now, the words coming out in such a rush he stammered in places. "And pretty soon this big flying horse zoomed down, and trotted over to us, so I held out the apple. He started to nibble, but I held my hand out real flat so he wouldn't bite my fingers—by mistake, of course," and Tyler threw his mother a shrewd glance.

She smiled back in acknowledgement, and asked softly, "And then?"

"And then the horse took us to the castle to see the king."

"Who said you were the cleverest and bravest subjects in his whole kingdom!"

"And we won the prize!"

"And the prize was the flying horse would carry you two right through the sky and straight down to our house here."

Tyler put his head close to the cat's. Her whiskers quivered, and he grinned, but when he looked up again, his eyes were thoughtful. And he said slowly, "But there was—like—a catch."

"Yes there was, honey," she answered, and ruffled his hair again. "The catch was that if you came to this earth, you had to come as a boy, and she…"

"And she had to come as a kitty!" he finished, his cheeks flushed.

"So you both waved goodbye to the king, and the horse spread his shining golden wings as he leaped forward up and up right into the air."

"And my Army hat blew off."

"Uhmm, yes, but you hung on tight to the reins and Monica hung on tight to you. And the horse flew through the clouds."

"We weren't a bit scared."

"No. But you did get sleepy and you closed your eyes, and the next thing you knew…"

"I was right here in my room!"

"You were?"

"And I said, hey sis, we're home."

"Ok honey, home safe and sound, and now it's time to go to sleep, all set?"

He beamed up at her. She pulled the covers snug around his chin, and the cat curled up against his shoulder.

"Goodnight, dearest boy." His lips were so soft. "Sweet dreams."

He shut his eyes, smiling still, the deep well of the dimple like a dark crater in his lower cheek. She went to the door, careful to leave it ajar even though the carousel night-light would stay on all night long.

On the landing she could hear the ticking of the grandfather clock and the faint chatter of the television out in the den.

She went downstairs, turned on the dishwasher, turned off the lights in the living room, checked the locks on the front and back doors, came back to the den to turn off the TV. She stood there, looking blankly at the screen. She was half tempted to sit down, it had been a long day—interminable without Roy here to help. And this thing with Tyler this morning, it gave her a taste of what single parents must go through. Doing it alone, the love, the discipline, wondering if she had done the right thing, struck the right tone, reached him for god's sake! but tomorrow Roy would be back and they could hash it all over, he'd tell her not to brood over it. "The kid's fine," he'd say. "Stop borrowing trouble."

Now Dave Letterman was grinning straight at her, that half sleepy, half sardonic late night greeting—the show was a very old re-run. She turned him off just as he was introducing his Stupid Pet Tricks Routine. "No thanks," she said aloud. "I've had a bellyful," and went on up to bed.

Outside Tyler's room she thought she heard whispering, yes, it was Tyler, that monkey, still awake. She smiled, then tiptoed to the door careful so he wouldn't see her and start in all over again. She could only hear bits of what he was saying.

"Ok, sis…gone now…" and then his voice dropped so low there was only mumbling. Then a few words burbled up clearly, "…out the window like you told me to," enough for her to understand that he never had really believed the blackness came from the place in his chest he pointed to so long ago. He had turned it all inside out, he believed now and in fact he had always believed that it came from Monica.

"Monica knows everything!" That's what he said. That's what he thought. That's who he was protecting, and why not? Isn't that where he had been led night after night, story after story?

Now he was mumbling again, but she couldn't make it out. All she heard was this peculiar sound in the still pool of silence after he stopped speaking.

A strange sound which made her shoulder blades throb and the small neck hairs bristle while she listened. Not as mother. Not as skeptical adult. But rather as if she'd become absorbed into Tyler's very tissues and could plainly hear from beneath the bedclothes, silky fur warm against bare skin, the low deep-chested thunder of Monica growling, instructing her brother in the dark.

HOPSCOTCH

HIS NAME IS OWEN Higbee and his wife's walked out on him.

When I dream of you, Vic darling...

His name is Owen Higbee, and he keeps having nightmares ever since Fiona went away. Right before Christmas she took off, and it wasn't until late spring that he was able to do what had to be done.

July now, and the dreams seem worse every night, the hotter it gets. Not a breeze from the lake, nothing but sticky sheets on an empty bed, and the whine of the big eighteen wheelers going up the steep grade of the Interstate.

The first dreams are river dreams—the old Canoochee thirty miles southwest of Savannah where summer after summer, the family used to spend their vacations. Swimming in the Canoochee with Sister, the water thick and warm, felt like splashing through orange paint. For years he used to think all rivers were orange. It was the run-off, of course, from the trees—those big old swamp cypress heavy with Spanish moss—leaching tannic acid into the riverbank. Yet even now, he still thinks orange is the right color for rivers to be.

And he and Sister played *Sea Hunt* together, scaring themselves diving deep against the current. Actually, the Canoochee wasn't all that deep, not more than twenty feet or so right in the middle. But twenty feet down on the bottom seemed like a hundred. Really spooky in that strange darkness, and he remembers how once back home they watched an eclipse from the back stoop and how the orange lightpricks fused together hot-black against his eyelids with only this thin sliver of orange leaking through underneath, *"Don't open you eyes, don't open your eyes!"* people warned, but in the river he always opens his eyes, yet as he stares ahead there's that same hot blackness burning his eyeballs, and he pokes at the riverbottom to get his bearings.

The guck feels soft, a butterscotch pudding softness that sucks at his fingers, and he's scared to put his feet down, scared what might grab hold of his ankle bones or toes. His chest is going to explode from holding his breath, his eardrums ache, his ribcage. But still he gropes forward, hunting for a handhold, some plants or rocks to grab and help pull himself along.

And then—something bumps hard against his foot, then begins gliding real slow up his left leg.

Each time as he shoots up to the surface, he thinks it's an alligator for sure, even though he knows full well that the thing that's bumped him had to be—of course that's what it was—only Sister snaking along the bottom, searching him out, and now he sees bubbles and then Sister's right beside him. She's laughing, her hair's plastered down over her eyes like tangled seaweed, but in the dream something's wrong with her face and those skinny white arms slapping at the water, and now he can see embedded in that smooth white skin are shells, clam shells growing straight up out of the flesh. Their ridges scrape against his cheek, the arms press him down through orange paint. And the current welcomes him with wet lips, wet orange lips that suck him straight down to the waiting muck of the riverbed.

When I dream of you, Vic darling, it's not your face I see.

His name is Owen Higbee and after Fiona left him, the nightmares have never stopped. Tonight he has a new one, much worse than the river dreams. He gets up from bed, goes out to the back porch facing the lake. Music floats across the water, the juke box going strong at Jeb's place.

He doesn't put on the light. Put on the light and the cars start pulling up. Even past midnight people assume the diner's open the second they see lights of any kind. Tourists most of them, making the long run north to Atlanta.

"Coffee, make it fast," they say. "Gotta stay awake." The diner's the last place to eat before the Interstate.

LAST CHANCE DINER the neon sign blinks all day long, right up to 10 p.m. closing time.

"Idiotic name for a restaurant," Fiona said once.

"Not a restaurant, sugar," he told her. "A diner."

"Same difference," she had answered.

Those first couple of years, give her credit, she did try giving him a hand, working out back in the kitchen, chopping onions, prepping salads, dicing potatoes, filling the plastic condiment squeeze bottles with catsup and mustard. Sometimes she'd help out as waitress now and then. But she hated to cook, hated kowtowing to what she called "low-type" people. The fact was she hated the diner, period, claimed she was going soft in the brain with boredom. So she got moving—Fiona did everything fast—and in no time flat got herself licensed as a real estate broker, went to work at the agency next to the new bank, Lakeshore Realty, it was called, Victor Randall, GRI, MRA, CEO.

I see the lake refract the moonlight...

Refract...a sixty-four dollar word, the kind Fiona liked to throw around, always working the crossword puzzles, end of the pencil between those plump lips, sucking at the tip like a soda straw. Every pencil in the place carried those toothmarks of hers, pretty white teeth, small and sharp as a baby gator's.

He stares out at the lake. He can hear the peepers going strong. Way out in the middle of the lake something splashes. Probably a loon. Fiona hated the sound loons made. "Like a g.d. zoo, this dump," she said. She got so fidgety out here in the woods, so far from town.

"More to life than slinging hash," she told him. She needed to be challenged, learn something more than how to run a Fryolator. The thrill of the chase, that's what she liked about being an agent. Loved learning how to close a sale. Loved the fat commissions, the excitement of working with a hot prospect for just the right property.

First six months she took a shine to the owner's wife. Then she took a shine to the owner. He's the one she ran off with. The wife, she filed for divorce. "Kindest thing I can say on the subject," she told Owen, "is them two deserve each other," and went back to typing New Lakefront listings.

The peepers go silent for a moment.

He opens his can of Skoal, tamps it down, nice moist wad, nice minty smell. Only good part of Fiona being gone—hot damn!—is he can chew again.

In the kitchen he chaws tobacco all the time to keep from eating. It doesn't bother the two waitresses. They only complain about him looking so peaked. Goodhearted women, Flo and Ruby. They wish him no harm.

He likes having them around fussing over him, worrying about him. Sometimes at night he wakes up sweating like a pig. That's when he needs a woman the most. Someone soft to hold him, sponge off his forehead. "Hush, baby, river's not going to get you."

When he was little, his mother always promised she'd keep him safe, keep him and Sister on this side of the crossover lines, *step on a crack, break your mother's back, step on a line, break your mother's spine.* Sister always won at hopscotch, jumping like a jackrabbit, feet flashing over the orange chalk marks, she never touched once, never stepped on the lines or hit them either with that fine throwing-stone she found on the riverbottom one afternoon, disappeared under the water so long he got scared and then he saw the ripples spread around a small white fist poking up through the water except at first he thought it must be a water moccasin surfacing, or a dead fish bellying up to the surface, and then Sister was choking, and laughing and yelling, "Treasure! Treasure!" and opened her fist to show the perfect hopscotch stone, perfect oval, flat and smooth, freckled like a warbler's egg, exactly the right size to fit between thumb and forefinger.

"A skimmer?" he asked, wanting to tease her.

But Sis had frowned, "You nuts? All that water I swallowed, you think I'm wasting this on the river?"

River's not going to get you, honey. That's what he needs now, same kind of sweet talk, don't really matter if it means anything, he needs to hear a soft voice.

When I dream of you, Vic darling, it's not your face I see.
I see the lake refract the moonlight in long keyboards of light and dark,
the black and white keys rippling silently into shore.

He yanks his feet off the porch railing. Those were the words, the exact thing Fiona was saying in his dream. She had leaned forward and crooned about the moonlight, and he listened, panting hard, it was a good three mile run around the lake. Then he started in running again, the slow motion dream-running that never gets you there fast as you want. Little saplings whip across his face. His breath cuts knife-sharp in his chest. And comes out sounding wet, like someone gargling.

The dream stops. When it started up again, Fiona's speaking from somewhere close, yes! right over there, she's holding something shiny and sharp in her right hand, and she starts creeping down through the oleander bushes to the shore. The silver blade winks in the moonlight. A whisper of cattails as she stalks him along the flats.

He's running hard. He can hear her splashing in the shallows. His feet thump on the mossy ground, a hollow thumping much louder than the violin screech of her voice keening, "Victor, Victor."

And then it started all over again, an endless loop.

He stands up. The moon's coming up past the point over there. Coming up nice and slow. The lake looks silver. Silver lake, orange rivers—enough's enough plus he's so thirsty he could spit cotton.

He goes back to the bedroom, turns on the lamp beside the bed. His wash pants are buried at the very bottom of the clean pile of laundry he keeps stacked on the chair—faster, more efficient than using the bureau drawers, Fiona would have a fit. He puts on pants, clean shirt, then snugs his wallet into a hip pocket.

In the mirror over the bureau, his eyes stare back at him, red and grainy. Almost stuck together. Looks for all the world as if he's been swimming underwater. Or crying. He goes into the bathroom, presses a cold wet washcloth over his eyelids. He probably ought to use ice, but what the hay, the lights over at the roadhouse aren't known county-wide for their high wattage, a dimness which all the horny but homely broads appreciate big time.

* * *

DIM, SURE. LAYERS OF smoke banked like early morning fog coming off the lake. But it's still bright enough to make out some faces he knows. The noise is at full tilt,

1 a.m., everybody oiled up to beat hell.

A bunch of the regulars over by the jukebox. They sit there pretty near every night. He nods.

"Higbee, you old rascal!"

"Mosey on over, Hig. It's jackpot time!" But he waves, walks on to the bar. Jeb looks surprised for a split second. But being Jeb, he keeps his mouth shut, pulls two Coors Lite from the ice chest. Slides them over without a word, one eyebrow cocked in welcome.

"Jeb."

"Owen." Jeb's the only individual to call him by his given name. Even Fiona called him Hig. He hates the sound of it.

He drinks fast. No idea how thirsty he's been all this while. The nightmares seem to cook the juices right out of him. He stares at the red medallion circles reflected from the red of Jeb's jacket in dozens and dozens of highball glasses stacked, stems out, along the back wall. The medallions wink at him as Jeb moves on down the bar, wiping the counter in lazy circles.

Someone nudges his elbow, murmurs, "Owen Higbee, as I live and breathe."

He looks up. It's Harlan, Harlan Goldman, runs the hardware store over to Ellerslie. "Howdy, Harlan," he answers.

"Hig, you a sight for sore eyes, yes sirree. Make it a double, Jeb, if you please." Harlan glances at the empty Coors bottle in front of Owen. "Plus n'other couple brews for the big spender here." Harlan is heavy-set and pretty much spills over the bar stool. He's studying Owen. "Flo allows how things are going fine at the diner. Business good, she tells me."

"Can't complain."

"Darndest thing, Hig." Harlan smacks his lips, "Mmmm! that's mighty slick bourbon, slides down real nice." He takes another long swig, then rubbing his mouth with one fist, continues. "Happened the other night, Tuesday guess it was. Phone rings, pretty late, we were just fixing to go to bed. Flo answers. Couple minutes later she comes back. Said it was the wrong number. But then in bed, she tells me it sure had sounded like Fiona."

Jeb's polishing a glass. He's standing directly in front of them, but Owen stares straight through the red bar-jacket. He can see those glass medallions winking back at him, nudge-nudge, wink-wink. He takes a slow swallow. "What did Fiona have to say?" he asks, surprised how casual his voice sounds.

Harlan shakes his head. "Flo couldn't really hear her that good. Bad connection, I guess. Flo said it sounded like it was a long distance call."

"Long distance?"

"Well, you know, the kind of thing you get sometimes. Kind of echoes back and forth, real hollow sounding, like the person's telephoning halfway around the world? Then the line went dead before she could find out where Fiona was calling from."

They sit in silence for a while. He can hear Harlan breathing hard. Harlan breathes the way a heavy draft animal does, and he even smells as if he's working up a rich lather right through his blue shirt. Now he's looking sideways at Owen and asking in a worried voice, "She call you too, Hig?"

All Owen says, and he says it calmly, because it's the God's truth, is "I've heard from her, yes." He grins at Harlan, poor bastard, he means well.

Harlan goes beet red, stammers a little. "None of my business, Hig. But seems like maybe it's time to fish or cut bait. I mean why don't you just face up to her, tell her you're filing for divorce? Like Victor's wife did? Two of them disappearing like that, it stinks. You still a relatively young fellow, Lord knows your life's not over, not by a long shot."

"Can't do that, Harlan."

"Why not? She left you, pal, you got grounds."

"Nope. Can't be done." He swings off the stool, then still smiling, peels off five bucks, tucks them under Harlan's glass. "Story's not over yet, Harlan. I'm still crazy about Fiona. But you're right about one thing, I've surely got to talk with her, face to face, no question."

Harlan nods slowly, but he looks unhappy. "What if she calls again, what should we tell her?"

"Tell her...just...just keep in touch."

Harlan frowns. "Sure thing, Hig," is all he says though. And then waves as Owen scoops up the last Coors, starts to leave "Set me up another round," he's telling Jeb as Owen steps out the door.

Cooler outdoors. Cool and quiet. The parking lot's half full still, well-lit by the tall sodium vapor lights the highway boys are putting up long all the county road intersections.

He walks around back. A couple of old fashioned garbage pails stand next to the professional-looking Dumpster Jeb bought himself last year. Fiona used to say if Jeb had any sense he'd put his trash out front, face the building toward the lake. Carve some windows with a good lakefront view, and treat his clientele to something more scenic than pine-paneled wallboard. Get rid of the half-baked air conditioning unit that just rotates the smoke. Get himself a decent juke box, new songs.

He listens. The juke box is silent. But something's scrabbling behind the

Dumpster. Rats maybe. Maybe Jeb's got himself a rat problem along with his brand new Dumpster.

He looks out toward the lake. Full moon up now, round and shiny as a ripe pumpkin. Pretty over the water, that orange light.

He takes a last swig of the Coors, then chucks it into the Dumpster. The bottle clinks down there...and something else, the crunch of gravel. And somebody saying, "Victor?"

He wheels around.

"Victor, darling."

He squints. From the shadows beside the back door, another shadow is stepping forward, one white arm held out towards him, hair in mossy tangles, lumping the shape of the head. Her voice is low, the voice in his dreams, sugar sweet, Sister sweet, Fiona sweet.

"When I dream of you."

He watches the arm sway in front of him, groping for him. He turns his head. He doesn't want to see the face. He looks at the path going down to the lake. Three miles back to the house and then some.

"I see the lake..."

Under the vapor lights the path looks almost orange, a winding orange ribbon that loops and disappears into the black mass of oleander bushes. Disappearing like an orange river swallowed by the night. Or a crossover line, the chalky marks erased by time or the rain.

His name is Owen Higbee.

He starts in to running.

SUDDENLY

"WHAT'S THE WORST THAT can happen?"

"Travis, please for God's sake stop saying that."

"Answer my question."

"The worst *has* happened, ok?"

"Answer my question, Ellen," he repeated except now he sounded slightly ticked off, already slipping into his time-to-cross-examine-the-witness mode, and she wanted to tell him *save it for the courtroom* but instead replied, "I honestly don't know, your honor." She paused, better insert a little melodrama here. "We die?"

He started laughing. "You goof-ball. Now listen, they say all canceled flights will be back in business tomorrow, so I'll get home late afternoon. You and I are re-scheduled for flight to Sydney going out from Denver Wednesday, and I talked Jack into an extra three days at the other end—he's assigning couple of my briefs to the new law clerk. Fair enough?"

"Fair's fair," she answered loyally. "Still...."

"Still and all you want our vacation **now.** Right now, correct?"

"Yep."

"Hey, Ms. Instant Gratification, trip's only postponed couple days, this is *not* the end of the world as we know it. So tell, what's it like there this afternoon?"

"Gosh, it's beautiful, nice and warm, simply a lovely September day. Lots of big branches down but except for losing power, you'd hardly guess we had a storm, least not out here. They said on the radio downtown's a real mess."

"Feel bad, leaving you stuck out there in the Colorado boonies minus wheels."

"Don't feel bad, honey. Gives me a day off."

"Still, hell of a time for the Toyota to be in the shop."

"Not your fault. I mean nobody had clue one the weather was going to go totally nutzoid, strand us both, keep you up there another day. Darn storm *would* have to come and ruin everything."

"Guess the good news is the storm's history now—power's sure to be on soon. Plus you got Greta, you got cell phone, seems to me you're all set."

"Yep, safe in our bunker in the boonies."

"Hey, Ellen-melon, why not lug out the gas grille, you and Greta broil a steak tonight?"

"Howling good idea, sez Greta."

"Call you later, post-howl?"

"Super."

"Hang in there, sweetheart, pat Greta for me."

"Will do. Bye, darling."

Silence. A silence immediately noted by Greta who stood up, stretched, staring at Ellen with what Travis called the Shepherd Stare of Significance, impossible to ignore.

"Ok already—so go stretch your legs!" With a glad yippee-eye-ay series of yips, Greta was out the screen door, off the deck, plunging down the pasture path skirting the ravine, emitting sharp pleasure barks all the way to the lake below.

The winds had long since stopped and the sun was out, amazing how balmy the air felt, Indian Summer weather, the real thing. Not too many branches down, but then she noticed their huge flowering pear had actually keeled over in a cruel jackknife. She would miss its giant crown of white blossoms next spring.

She went back inside, turned on the battery-powered radio. A bored voice trying to sound concerned but missing by several yawns, was reading the latest update:

"Repairmen have been working pretty much all night long. Emergency crews from Boulder and Colorado Springs have come to assist local personnel, but it's still unclear whether power will be restored by nightfall."

Look at the bright side, she told herself. At least it's September, not the middle of winter. Nothing like their ice storm two years ago—no heat, no electricity, no hot water—53 degrees inside, Travis building fires day and night five days running. Nightmarish!

She stared out the window at the lake where a whole mile-long flotilla of white pelicans anchored, riding out the storm like the eminently reasonable birds they were. She called them her White Vicars because of their immaculate plumage, their stately demeanor. A few vicars always hung around for weeks after the rest of the pilgrimage headed south. They glided in solemn procession on the lookout always for catfish.

She grabbed her book, whistled for Greta, and walked around the house to the back patio. Peaceful out here, she smiled, and lifting her face to the sun, eased back in the lounge chair. Heavenly. From nowhere a rough tongue licked her cheek.

"Good girl. Lie down now. Settle."

They both lay there basking, listening to the bossy Carolina wren fussing up by the deck birdfeeder. The wrens patrolled the deck, they were the supervisors, they even intimidated the bulked-up old blue jays she had nicknamed the Big Bad Blues Brothers. Inevitably when the feeder was bare, she'd glance out and sure enough, a wren would be standing beside the screen door, staring through the screen with a hissy-fit glare until Ellen appeared with more seeds.

Darn bird knows how to push my buttons, she mused, everyone around here does for that matter. Still and all, so nice to relax, just me and our girl dog holding the fort. And tomorrow Trav's home and then finally vacation time! Back to Australia, to Byron Bay and their enchanted honeymoon cottage. Back to magically empty beaches and bodysurfing nirvana. She simply couldn't wait—the perfect anniversary present! Six years married to the hunkiest guy around, and it still felt like only a year. Two, max.

She grinned, wriggled deep into the cushions. The sun made her sleepy. She closed her eyes, she could feel herself letting go, slipping down, down, drifting deliciously into her ocean dream, surf crashing on the white sand, clouds of foam rising like fog above the shorebreak, big old rollers just waiting for them way out there so she and Trav start swimming out to the good stuff—out to where gigantic breakers keep on building and building, taller and taller, too huge, much too dangerous to catch and now the waves are somehow shape-shifting into towering black trees in a black forest, a place of darkness ominously quiet until her cell phone rings and it's her cousin Lucy calling in a muffled voice, "I'm lost, Ellen!"

So she heads out in the rain toward the woods trying to run fast but only able to manage a slow motion lope, floating along one of the paths where Lucy hikes every weekend, and it's getting dark but then finally she spots the yellow slicker disappearing around the bend ahead and she screams "Lucy! Wait!" And her legs are useless rubber, but now she catches up, reaches out and grabs Lucy's shoulder. And the person in the slicker slowly turns around grinning this hungry hyena grin. Not Lucy, **no**! That's when she always wakes gasping, choking—tears rolling down her face. They burn her skin like drops of acid.

Lucy's body was found tied to a tree. She was so badly battered, it took dental x-rays to confirm identity. No witnesses. No suspects. No motive. Nothing to go on. Intoxicated with the scent of dead meat, the media gleefully labeled the murderer the Walker Stalker. Five subsequent homicides appeared to be his special handiwork, all solitary hikers or runners found along nature trails within a tri-state area. All were beaten to death, severe blunt trauma wounds to the head. But not a sign of trace evidence anywhere. Which struck the investigators, not to mention the media, peculiar as hell.

Dearest Lucy's been gone for almost three years now, but Ellen's nightmare has never gone away. Of course she realizes perfectly well that she keeps on re-dreaming it because of guilt. She listened to Lucy's message but that was all. She had no idea where the call came from, which trail Lucy had followed, or what to do except first notify the police, then the family. Lucy runs no more, but Ellen runs at least once a week, waking Travis with her sobs.

Even napping I dream this, she thinks. And opens her eyes. Her cheeks still stung so she rubbed them dry with the back of her hand. Whew, actually getting hot out here.

Beside the chaise lounge, Greta yawned, rolled over luxuriously. A second later she was growling, thunderous rumbles from deep in her chest, the danger growl, scary to hear. Now she was standing up facing the ravine, hackles raised like porcupine quills all along her backbone.

"Quiet!" Ellen ordered. She listened hard. She and Trav had this axiom: Greta never lies. *Ever.* And finally she could hear what Greta heard. Oh, sweet Jesus, something down there was working its way up the ravine, getting closer and closer.

Ellen grabbed the collar. "Stay, girl!" but Greta began barking. A spasm of barks, thunderous, her whole body shuddering in waves, unstoppable.

"Quiet!" Ellen told her again.

Silence for a few seconds. Then a thudding noise, getting louder, getting much nearer. Branches snapping. Loud panting, then a muttered "Ow!" The bushes began trembling as violently as Greta trembled, it was all Ellen could do to hold on to her collar. And now the leaves parted, and there stood a young kid, yellow-haired, red-faced, probably twelve or thirteen, breathing hard, his forearms and long skinny legs deeply scratched. On his forehead streaks of blood.

"Help," he croaked and sank to his knees, but Greta immediately went over to him, tail wagging, began to lick his temple, his knees. He threw his arms around the dog, clutching at her as if he were drowning.

"Here, let me give you a hand. Easy does it."

"Gotta hide! He's looking for me!"

She helped him to his feet, he was still shaking. She took him by the hand, murmuring "We'll get you inside, hang on." Greta led their way back to the house.

Indoors she guided him over to the sofa where he collapsed, breathing hard.

"Thirsty," he said. Beside him, Greta tucked in close, her elegant head cocked to one side, forehead furrowed with concern.

"Here you go," Ellen said kindly, and handed him a cold can of Pepsi.

"Don't drink too fast or you'll choke." She smiled, but he couldn't. "Hey, my name is Ellen. What's yours?"

"Name's Kenny. Listen, will ya? He's after me!"

"What?"

"He's coming for me."

"Who's coming?"

"This dude—crazy guy. I think he killed somebody."

"Tell me. The whole thing. Go as slowly as you can, you're safe now."

So, voice cracking every so often, he began his story crisscrossing backwards and forwards in both time and place, but she listened, she led him gently through it. Occasionally he stopped, staring into the middle distance with this remote expression, blind to where he was now, remembering. And the whole time, Nurse Greta continued to lick his scratches while he rubbed her ears, massaged her neck, scratched her chest.

"I'm a runner, cross-country," he explained proudly. "Training for a slot on our track team next spring? Junior High? My sister's on the high school team. She claims my wind sprints would leave a greyhound eating dust."

He practiced after school, also weekends, taking the trails in the state park alongside the river, then crossing the bridge and over to the lake.

"Today same as always, I stopped to check my times, on my sister's stopwatch? That's when I hear this—like weird sound—like this *gurgling*? I snuck through the laurel bushes and there's this guy, he doesn't see me. He's dressed in a plastic raincoat and booties. And he's wearing the ice hockey mask from the movie, ya know?"

She nodded. "Jason Voorhees, *Friday the 13th*."

He raised his eyebrows. "Outstanding!" he nodded, and continued. "Anyhow, this weirdo's kneeling, crouched over somebody lying on the ground—that's where the gurgling was coming from."

"Good Lord!"

"And me, I'm thinking this is a slice & dicer flick and I'm frigging *in* it. I musta made a noise, because he looks over, he sees me, grabs this humongus crow bar and jumps up, coming straight at me. But my sister—she makes me carry her mace every time I run? too dangerous running alone she's always telling me—so I squirt the stuff straight at the eyeholes in his mask. I got him good. He rips off the mask, and I'm outta there. Fast. Through the brush, down along the lake path, then up the hill—tough climb with all those brambles and thorny junk."

"Kenny, this is really scary stuff. And you—you're a hero! I mean you outmaneuvered this guy big time."

"Yeah, he tried to follow. But I was too fast. Plus he couldn't see from the mace. But he knows the direction I took is the thing."

"You got a good look at him?"

"Man, not a face I *ever* want to see again. Or hear his dipshit voice either. Totally freaked me out."

"You mean he spoke to you?"

"When he was crouched over the body, he was–like—chanting in a foreign language. Sounded like he was saying shallow, shallow over and over again."

"Shallow?" she repeated.

"Naw, more like shall-ah."

"*Imsh'allah?*"

"Bingo, you got it!"

"Means *God willing* in Arabic."

"You saying he's some sort of terrorist dude?"

"Honey, I have no idea. All I do know is there's a serial killer out there nicknamed the Walker Stalker who's already murdered six hikers. Including my very own cousin. She was the first victim, she lived a little north of Colorado Springs, what? three hours away, and until now. that was the closest of these killings. But your guy down there on the lake trail—I mean he may have come here to this town, he may be the Stalker!"

"Cow! Let's call the cops!"

She nodded, fished out her cell phone. "And then your parents."

"Yeah, fine."

"We'll talk to the police, see what's what. Hey, you might want to bathe those scratches with a little warm water." She nodded over at the sink.

"Thanks," he said. He began running water, grabbed some paper towels.

She dialed 911. She explained carefully she had a witness to a possible homicide. She sketched in the details of where and when. The dispatcher asked if the boy required medical attention

"No, I don't think so. He's shaken up, but he's come through a horrifying experience with flying colors. He does, however, very much want to talk to an officer." Then she added, "I have no car today, so unfortunately we're stuck here."

"Yes ma'am, we'll send someone out there top priority. Be almost an hour, I'm afraid, getting way out there to the lake and all. We're really shorthanded after the storm, lots of emergency calls, power lines down all over the city."

"I see."

"Name?"

"Ellen Forbes, 727 Crestview Hills."

"Name of the witness?"

"Just a sec, I'll put him on."

The kid took the phone. "My name's Kenneth Mason. I live at 10 Wildwood Terrace, phone's 540-7642."

Pause. "Yeah. I'm fine. Yep, can do. Yes'm, I'm ok thanks to the lady here." He threw Ellen a big smile. He hung up. "Can we sorta wait a little while before calling my folks?" he said. He grinned sheepishly, "Can't handle calming my mom down right now, she's gonna freak."

Ellen nodded. He'd had enough high drama for the afternoon, she was reaching her quota as well. So the two of them decided to re-amp with Tollhouse cookies, potato chips (yuk!), and fresh lemonade. She wished Travis were here. He'd like this kid. Brave but not afraid to admit being scared. Trav always claimed he could size up people by how they coped in a jam—how fast they could think on their feet, if they could remain calm no matter how frightened. She knew he'd be proud of all three of them today: her, Kenny and the dog. If she did to say so herself, *excellent* coping strategies, what a trio.

Now Kenny was embarked on a lively lecture about his hobbies, one of which was sketching birds. He talked knowledgeably with Ellen about Carolina wrens, "Bossy!" he observed, and he loved her nickname for white pelicans.

"White Vicars!" he snapped his fingers. "Uber cool! I see them on the river when I'm running. Big buds."

Greta made a discreet throat-clearing noise.

"She ok to have a cookie?" he asked.

"Absolutely. I've must say you're good at reading dogs, Ken."

"Hey, we got us three black Labs for duck hunting. And a collie bitch your Greta reminds me of. A mama's girl." He patted Greta's narrow head, glanced quickly over at Ellen. "No offense."

"None taken. I always tell Travis—he's my husband—Trav, I go, Greta and I, we're soul-sisters. So of course, he goofs around, claims he's totally outnumbered."

"She's a classy dog. Well-behaved to the max, obeys you *stat*."

"Yeah, well, she's earned all sorts of awards in obedience and tracking."

"She done any, like, attack training? *Schutzhund* I guess they call it?"

"Only the basics. Makes me nervous. Plus my German's lousy." Then, as if commenting on the topic of guard dogs, Greta began barking her very fierce stranger-on-the-premises alert.

Couple of seconds later they heard a car on the gravel driveway.

"Maybe your husband?" Ken asked hopefully.

"Don't I wish! But no, I'm afraid he's out of town." She peered through the window. "That's strange. It's a squad car. I don't understand. He's gotten here so fast, the dispatcher said it would take at least an hour."

The boy jumped up, joined Ellen at the window. They watched the cop climb out of the squad car, hitch his belt. He stood there, lounging against the fender, staring up at the house.

She felt the kid stiffen. "Holy crap. It's the guy. It's him. It's **him**!"

"Impossible, Kenny. He's a police officer."

"He's come after me like I told ya. I'm outta here!"

"Quick, go hide there in the study, leave the door ajar, see if you recognize his voice."

The bell chimed. Greta exploded.

"Quiet, girl!" Ellen ordered. She went to the screen door. The cop was tall. He was wearing aviator-style sun glasses. Disconcerting not to be able to read his expression.

"Yes, officer?" she said, Greta welded to her left knee in the never-shall-we-part heel position.

"Good afternoon, Ms. Forbes." He touched his hat in greeting. "I'm Sergeant Zumbach. I've come in response to your call to our dispatcher?"

"Yes." She worked hard to keep her voice neutral.

"Like to talk with the youngster who reported an incident this afternoon down by the lake." He paused. "May I come in?"

She hesitated. She could feel Greta revving up beside her, hackles already at half mast, *not* a good sign. Clutching Greta's collar, she opened the screen door.

A moment of silence. He stood close enough for her to see her own silvered reflection in his aviator glasses, and she wished she too had a silver shield to hide behind. She could feel a panicky giggle attack bubbling up. Step right over here folks, see the Famous Dueling Sun-Glasses! Was she losing it?

Finally he spoke. "We want the boy to show us exactly where this so-called event occurred. Not too far from your house, I gather?" He smiled encouragingly.

"Straight down the ravine through the thickest, thorniest underbrush imaginable. I truly don't know how he managed the climb up here. His face and arms were bleeding, a real mess he was so badly scratched."

He got out a small notebook. "Time the kid reached your place?"

"About 4:15 or so."

"May I talk with him, please."

The abruptness of the request stopped her cold for a moment. He was calling her bluff, throwing down the gauntlet, whatever. She felt cornered. But she managed a casual shrug, and a tone of voice to match.

"I'm sorry, officer. His parents have already picked him up. They were taking him to the station, perhaps they're already there."

He stared at her. They both knew she was lying. He rubbed his chin.

All around his dark glasses, the skin looked painfully splotched, almost like a rash.

"Tell me, ma'am. Was the kid able to describe the perp?"

"He was much too frightened, Sergeant. He just cut and ran. After he squirted the mace, he simply took off like a jackrabbit. Straight up the hillside."

"I see." The officer kept on scribbling. "Anything else he told you?"

"Not that I recall. He was totally exhausted, in a state of shock."

"The dispatcher indicated that the kid…"

"His name is Kenny, officer."

"…indicated that Kenny overheard the perp say something?"

Ellen took her time answering. This was weird, he's never even mentioned the victim lying on the ground, the whole possibility of homicide. He's going off on tangents here, deliberately avoiding the body. So she simply said in response, "Oh?"

"Heard the suspect saying odd words, I gather. Talking in a foreign language?"

"Foreign language?" she repeated, still stalling for time, ears thudding, mouth gone dry.

"Foreign, possibly Arabic?" He stopped writing and studied her face intently.

He was fingering his massive black leather belt bedecked with the tools of his trade. Radio, with the speaker on his left shoulder. Cell phone. Retractable baton—fancy name for billy club, she'd been told. Huge set of jangling keys. Handcuffs. Pepper spray. Nine millimeter Glock semi-automatic. A regular damn arsenal. The goal? Instant subjugation in the hands of a trained killer who, lying, knew she lied as well.

She swallowed hard, tired of evasions *"Im'shallah,"* she said in a clear, hard voice. "It means God willing, one of the cornerstones of Islamic faith."

"Not my bag, lady. Let's cut the foreplay, where's the kid?"

Greta growled, low and deep.

"Officer Zumbach, I never mentioned to your 911 dispatcher anything about foreign words, specifically *Im'shallah*. No way on earth you'd know this unless you were actually down there, actually 'present at the scene' as you folks say. Not to mention your squad car access to 911 calls."

She hadn't finished her sentence—already he had grabbed at his belt—and just as he was scrambling for his semi-automatic, she spoke loudly in another foreign language the attack words Greta had been waiting to hear.

"Greta, *packen!*"

The big dog lunged, leaping high and slashing at the officer's upper thigh—a fairly spectacular move which produced both bellows and blood in the same split second. Man and dog crashed to the ground. Greta crouched over him, snarling, lips curled back to show gleaming white incisors, her snout pressed against his throat. The aviator glasses had been knocked off. His eyes were an angry inflamed red. They looked swollen, they looked like they hurt, and she silently saluted Kenny and his sister.

The cop twitched his fingers, and Greta immediately nipped his thumb.

In the stillness of the room, Ellen said, "I suggest, Sergeant, you not move a muscle. Do *not* go for your weapon. She'll tear your hand off, I assure you."

He eyeballed Greta looming above him. She was panting hard, but otherwise statue-still.

The boy appeared silently in the doorway of the study, his face pasty white.

"Call 911, Ken," she told him. "Tell them it's a major emergency—we may have the Walker Stalker serial killer here. And..." She leaned over, removed the gun from the holster, placed it on the mantel she was leaning against, "...we have disarmed him. Quick now!"

He disappeared, shut the door.

"Greta, *sitz. Bleib sitzen. Pas auf*!" The dog sat, never taking eyes off her quarry.

He clutched his thigh, groaned.

Ellen said, "Listen and listen carefully. Don't dick with me. Here's what I want you to do. I want you to tell me why. These murders, *why*? My cousin was your very first victim, you bastard. So explain. **Now!**"

He said nothing. His eyes said it all—red-rimmed, they burned into hers—like looking into the molten lava of hell, she thought and remembered Travis asking what's the worst that can happen. And her own glib reply.

She held steady. "Time's up, Sergeant Zumbach. Either *you* will do as I say. Or the dog will. Your choice."

"You little bitch, you can't make me talk."

"No, but *my* bitch can."

"Inadmissible evidence, forced confession."

"Pot calling the kettle black, may I remind you of all the trace evidence you've gotten rid of these past three years? Don't make me gag. Anyhow we're not in court. We're here in my house, you're flat on your back on my living room floor. And my German Shepherd is prosecutor at this particular trial."

She waited. Greta panted. Finally he started to speak, a voice slurred by both pain and fury.

"In Kabul. Developed a taste for it."

"For what?" Except she was pretty sure she knew the answer.

"For serial murder." He watched her, glanced at Greta, continued in staccato sentences punched out like bullets—no, she corrected herself, pellets, perfectly harmless verbal pellets—they can't hurt me, I won't let them.

"Worked for Blackwater for a year. A special forces operation, helping train Afghan national police."

"You volunteered?"

"Took a year's leave of absence. That was over five years ago."

"Go on."

"Listen, I went there with this heavy duty game plan of doing some good. All jack-full of patriotism and that whole sack of horseshit we've been sold as loyal God-fearing Americans. Didn't take too long to get sucked into the feeding frenzy. My buddy on patrol went missing. Two hours later we found his body—decapitated—behind the barracks. Open season over there. Civilian murders. Military slaughter. Tribal killings—every mother-fucker around us was offing anything that moved. Talk about search & destroy."

He paused, pressed his thigh again. He studied her expression. As if trying to clarify, he said, "Not so different from the storm that blew through here last night? Knocked out power, knocked the sense outta this whole righteous town. Mass hysteria. Everybody's weirded out, running around in circles. Nobody in charge. Nobody minding the store." He stopped. "Perfect cover for murder, total confusion distracts people. Nobody notices stuff, same as my uniform acts like a perfect camouflage. What you see is police officer, not serial killer." He chuckled. "Anyhow, where was I?"

"Kabul."

"Roger that. See the thing about a hellhole like Kabul? Messes with your mind, sets off some sort of trip wire in a person. For me seeing my buddy lying there headless? that was the beginning. After couple months I find out I enjoy killing, I mean it's a real turn on. What a rush—beats the hell outta amphetamines, you know? Nothing comes close to the high of playing perp and cop at the very same time. There you are, shitting in church—and it feels so *good*. And the kicker is you actually get paid for cleaning it all up!"

"You've forfeited that particular disgusting luxury forever, you sicko."

He shut his eyes, spoke through clenched teeth.

"Hey, bitch, here's the deal. You're either the butcher in charge. Or the fresh carcass. Yummy-yummy, slurp-slurp." And he grinned like a jackal, smacking his lips.

Greta gave her worst-case scenario warning.

Greta never lies, thought Ellen, just as the cop punched the dog's snout, then reaching way down to his ankle holster, yanked out a small 380 caliber pistol, firing wildly—multiple shots—at the ceiling fan. Which stopped dead.

This time Ellen skipped the German. She spoke in plain English the ultimate command, the code word never used casually, but instantly understood, "Finish, Greta. **Finish**!"

No officer ever executed a direct order more swiftly.

Command obeyed.

In a heartbeat.

RIDING THE WHEEL

"As a matter of fact, William, I married Charlotte for her brains," Ben says to me. I can barely hear him over the booming noise of the surf.

"Come off it," I answer. Foam bubbles over my bare toes, Ben's wearing sneakers. He veers off to my left up to firmer sand, mustn't get our shoes wet, Ben the good twin. I follow him so at least we don't have to shout at each other.

He's smiling. Not at me, at the sand. "Nonetheless," he says, "it's the truth."

"Come on, Ben. People don't marry people for their brains, give me a break."

"They marry for money, do they not?"

This surprises me. Charlotte's the major stockholder in her family's company. The Mustard Queen, I call her. Privately to Sue. So I answer casual-like, "Sure. But I mean being a gold-digger—that's not the same."

"No, it's worse." He glances at me, blue eyes mild. "Ethically speaking," he adds.

"Look, Ben..." I turn to him, but the words kind of peter out, he's not listening anyhow. We're walking the beach, getting away for a little exercise after too many pancakes and sweet Carolina sausage. Getting away from the women and kids is what's really going on here. Ben does what I say, I'm the oldest by five minutes and he pretty much lets me take the lead in things up to a point. The external things, me in collision with the world at large. Me the extrovert twin, the hotshot entrepreneur. And Ben—poor passive Ben— sweet on the surface, a total wimp underneath. Emotionally landlocked, you might say. He fools folks, Ben does. He sure fooled ours. Always let me take the rap at home. "Ben," they'd go, "he's the angel." My mother staring deep into my eyes, "Why can't you be sweet?" she'd ask. "Like your brother?" Not a question I could answer. Not back then. Certainly not now. You can't really level with family is what it boils down to. Not blood relatives you can't.

Wives? I'd like to think they're different. I like to think Sue really understands Ben. That she sees him clear, sees past the shy smile, sees that under the sweetness something's lying there curled up and shriveled, maybe one of those baby hamsters he works with—all pink skin and hairless, curled up and scared to death of what's going on outside the cage.

"Look at what?" Ben's asking me. Talking with Ben is like talking in slow mo.

I don't answer for a minute. I'm thinking how Sue claims Ben's scared of living. Scared of having fun, huddled up in that ivory tower of his, passing harsh judgements in that gentle voice—badmouthing his colleagues, all Republicans, the university in general, FaceBook, cell phones—you name it, Ben's down on it.

He's waiting for me to go on. I can't level with him, I don't know how, where to begin so I say, "Come on, want to show you something."

We've come about a mile and a half down the beach. I scramble over the rocks beside the jetty. The rocks are pretty slippery with seaweed, pretty rank-smelling at low tide. I jump down on the wet sand, point toward the canal.

At least I call it a canal.

Ben would call it an estuary, no doubt, pulling at his ear lobe, reviewing the dictionary definition for me: *An arm of the sea running to meet the mouth of a river; an inland waterway.*

That's about as poetic as Ben ever gets. Ben goes by the book. Always.

Actually it's only a tidal channel lazing along to a salt marsh. We haven't explored it far as the marsh yet. The kids keep begging to.

Ben follows more slowly, inching his way down the rocks. He's still as skinny as he was years ago, no muscle on him, his arms and legs all sharp bone and pale white skin. Not a person comfortable with his body, clumsy, as a matter of fact.

"You are what you are," my mother kept saying. "A leopard can't change his spots."

Hey, it wasn't that I wanted my brother to be a jock—one in the family was enough. But when I think of the hours I spent trying to coax him outside, play with me a little—no dice. He could have learned how to pitch a decent curve ball maybe or how to dribble, the fancy footwork, dancing sideways down the soccer field. No, not jocks, just horse around, have some fun. No big deal, I just wanted to do the big brother thing. Ben, however, wasn't having any.

I reach down for a flat throwing stone, nothing but shells, but still I try to skim it across the water. "Beautiful spot, isn't it?" I say.

Ben watches the shell skip a couple of feet, then sink to the bottom. He nods.

The canal's not as wide as it gets at high tide. But it's still the width of a small river. Three or four feet deep in the middle. The water's warm here, perfect place to let the kids swim—away from the swirling confusion of the breakers. It's peaceful here, a lagoon of quiet. The air is still too.

A couple of herring gulls are patrolling the canal. They swoop low cruising the flat surface of the water as if they've spotted some breakfast, although I don't imagine any self-respecting fish would be caught dead here. I mean, why give up the whole Atlantic for this? Nothing to eat, no nice kelp to hide in. Only clear water and the flat channel bottom, the rippled white sand looking the way the Sahara desert must—except these sand ripples here have been made by water, not wind.

The children love this place. They put on their goggles, glide along the shallows. They reach down and poke at the bottom. I know how it feels. They can't put it into words, but when they come tearing up the dunes to where Sue and I are reading *The Times*, I can tell by their faces they know. Their eyes shine. They have touched the earth beyond the symmetrical scalloped surface to its deep and quiet core. They have been in communion.

"Should have worn trunks," I tell Ben. "Excellent swimming here."

He gazes around. The place interests him, I can see it in the way his eyes dart back and forth the same way they do in his lab, hitching at his lab coat, checking this, checking that. He comes alive in that white coat. Our dad wanted us to be doctors, follow in his footsteps.

"Not for me," I told Ben. "Enough docs in this family."

I think Ben took this worse than anybody else. When Dad died, he left us both a bundle so it wasn't like he cut me out of his will or anything. He had been a general surgeon like his daddy before him. Our medical line stretches back a good hundred years so I figured the clan had pretty much paid their professional debt to society and all. "Time for something fun," I decided and opened up a sporting goods store with the old man's money. Now I own a whole chain. Sue's nuts about horses so we bought a couple horses, Arabians, no less, got ourselves a time-share condo out at Vail, living the good life, three cars, the whole bit. It's what Sue wanted.

Ben didn't go into medicine either for that matter. He's into genetics. He studied rats for the first six years after he got his doctorate. Now he's working on hamsters. This is a guy who knows more about the reproductive and exercise habits of hamsters than they do. It's creepy walking into his lab.

He took me there one night. That's when they run. Nocturnal runners, we're talking weird here. The place smelled gross, a combination of damp straw and natural functioning, I suppose. But it wasn't the smell so much that bothered me as watching those poor devils on their exercise wheels. Ben claims hamsters have some kind of internal timing mechanism.

"Each one starts to exercise at precisely the same time of night," he told me, proud as any poppa.

"You mean 9 p.m. *BOOM* they're off?"

"No, William." This he said gravely in his serious-scientist voice, a signal for me to go all reverent. "No, their running patterns are individually characteristic. Show me a running record and I can identify whose it is. Distinctive as fingerprints."

"No kidding. Impressive as hell." I stopped, then went on with a dumb question but I liked seeing him so enthusiastic. "So what's it got to do with genetics?"

He touched his earlobe, just a quick checking-in. "We're studying the genetic basis of behavioral patterns."

I nod. We watched the hamsters. It was the most depressing thing I've ever seen. Talk about life on the treadmill. Those poor little bastards gave it their best shot, you got to hand it to them.

"Some life, hunh?" I said finally.

"They do this voluntarily, Will," he answered. "This is normal daily activity, like your going for a walk, Sue exercising the mare." He smiled, that tender smile of his. It was directed at the cages, of course, not me. We watched them in silence, the wheels spinning like miniature ferris wheels gone haywire.

Then he said, "They cover ten/twelve kilometers a night."

"How many miles is that?"

"Ten or so."

"No shit!"

"Plenty of shit," he said, and the smile was almost a real grin. This is when I love Ben. When he breaks loose, comes out of his shell, tries a timid joke, some mild—very mild—cussing.

"But why?" I asked. "Why do they do this?"

"They're programmed, genetically programmed."

"Question is...do they enjoy it?"

"That's a separate issue," he said. His mouth went small again, he frowned. "The whole point here is to understand the environmental conditioning of genetically-determined exercise behavior."

"Theirs is not to reason why," I joked.

But I had lost him by then. He was fishing out graphs, whisking me over to the microscope to look at his latest slides. His white lab coat flapped as he darted from workbench to cages to desk. The hamsters were still running when we shut the door. The squeak of the wheels followed us down the silent hallway. Endless sort of noise, that squeak, as tiring to the ear as the sound of surf when you're trying to have a serious conversation. Not that Ben and I have ever been too good at communicating, not really. But he's trying, we both are, he's clearing his throat now as he stares across the canal.

"Probably best not to bring Charlotte down here," he says.

We're walking along the banks of the canal. Ahead of us on a chunk of driftwood, a seagull is perched. We walk toward him. We're only about twelve feet away. Still he stares, one insolent eye cocked at us. His beak is a cruel curve but beautiful—like the curve of a scimitar and I bet just as sharp.

"Why not?" I ask. "Charlotte's the big beach fan who never has time for a real vacation, she keeps telling us."

"This side of the jetty, it's all National Seashore, correct?" he says.

The gull spreads its wings now, we're practically on top of him. The wings have black tips as if he's dipped them quickly into twin inkwells. His feathers are the color of mother of pearl. With a shriek, the gull flaps away, across the channel, soaring low, hunting out of habit, I guess. "So?" I say.

"Beach erosion," he answers. "Charlotte's all steamed up about it. Her environmental group says the barrier beaches are in a mess. This kind of estuary, it's eroding the shoreline, eating away at it like a cancer." He looks back at the sea. "Might say the ocean's chasing us inland."

"Ocean, phooey, more like Charlotte chasing up some new wrongdoing, she's always pissed off at something or other." I kick some sand with my foot. "Seems to me the environmentalists would be tickled about this canal. Nesting place for wildlife, *et cetera*."

Ben simply smiles, I think of it as his St. Sebastian smile. And Charlotte—she's the biggest arrow of all, stuck into his gizzard and there's no pulling her out.

"Christ!" I go on. "How you put up with it beats me."

"Laziness," he says. "Pure inertia."

This is a major newsflash. In fact this whole discussion in atypical. I want to be tactful here, I can see my brother's hurting. But the whole subject of wives stands between me and tact at this point. Stands in fact as it always has been between me and Ben. So all I say and my voice sounds curt, not very brotherly, "Meaning what?"

"Meaning I'm too lazy to do anything about it. She goes her way, I go mine. Then there's the whole question of the children, of course."

"Charlotte doesn't give a double damn about the boys and you know it, pal. They've been packed off to boarding school and camps since day one."

Ben stops. He stands on one leg, reaches down and examines his sneaker, rubbing at the sole. "Tar," he observes. "Let's sit down."

We sit on a hummock, a small dune with stalks of beach grass that bend sideways with the wind. Up here you can hear the surf again, and the wind blows away Ben's words. He mumbles when he talks as if he's hoarding each syllable. He's always done this. He looks sideways at me, nervously, then off at the breakers, the long curving scrolls of the shoreline. The sea's choppy today, the water's gone from smiling green to a kind of frowning black and blue. But the sky is still clear, still a good beach day.

I look up at the sun, must be past eleven already. "We better head back soon. Big expedition to Kitty Hawk."

He looks surprised. "Whose idea's that?"

I throw him a sarcastic, kitty-cornered smile. "Whose do you think?"

"They'll be bored, the children, they want to go swimming," he says. "Ride the waves," he adds softly.

"So tell her *no* for once. Put the old foot down, kiddo, you're such a pushover." The words as I say them make me angry, I wasn't even aware the anger was there. It's like saying them—actually opening my mouth and hearing what comes out—creates the anger, the same way you can be scratching at the head of a match, next thing you know the flame billows out like an orange parachute enveloping your thumb. "First comment out of her mouth yesterday. Walks in the door, looks around the cottage, says to Sue: 'But what in the world do you all *do* here for a whole month?'"

We sit in silence.

"Felt like socking her, if you want to know the truth," I add.

He says nothing for a minute. Then he simply tells me, "Don't, William."

"You started it, pal."

"*Me?*" He shoots me the injured look, his specialty—that innocent "Who, me?" expression that always worked with our folks. He is an innocent, I guess. Untouched you might say, been in hiding for as long as I can remember. Whenever Dad flew off the handle (we called it "renting"—the "rent" from parent, genus pissed off) whenever Dad got into one of his cold rages over how we disappointed him, Ben never said boo. Never wanted to tangle with anybody, it drove me nuts in a way. I wanted to wrestle with him—body contact on the rug, wriggling like puppies. Wrestle with ideas, dreams, what have you.

No way, not with Ben. I gave up on that a long time back. On the wrestling part. Not on him. Still I figure, he's opened the door here, might as well give him the straight poop, so I say, "That crack about Charlotte's brain, marrying her for her smarts."

"But it's true. I told you that already, William."

"Can't you see how lame that is? Was, I mean. Come on, Ben, wise up. The woman's impossible, she's killing what little zap's left in you, makes me sick, she controls you with her anger. And the kids too. Everybody tiptoeing around. We all have to, not just you." I give him a brotherly poke, to soften my words.

But he won't look at me. His nose is covered with white stuff so it won't burn. He doesn't like the beach, he thinks sunbathing is pointless and carcinogenic. And playing in the ocean's only for kids and dolphins. I mean the guy breaks my heart, he really does, I feel what he feels. We can't talk. But we're connected.

"You have to understand." He speaks slowly, fumbling for the right word. "She's a very unhappy person. Got no friends to speak of. She alienated pretty much everyone at work. That's why she quit that last appointment, you know, at the clinic. Even her environmental buddies, they tend to avoid her." He looks over at me, his eyes are so unhappy I have to stare out at the ocean. Then he speaks again, so quietly I cock my head toward him, lean in close. "She's very much alone, you see."

"I do see, Ben. Point is she's made her own bed, know what I mean?"

"No," he says, "it's simply too late." And he stands up, reaches down and gives me a hand up. "I thought," he adds, "she'd change. With time, you see. Then I thought I would change." He shrugs, pulls down the ridiculous baseball cap one of the boys lent him so he wouldn't get his head sunburned, he's been molting since college, poor Ben. I keep trying to talk him into a brush cut, like mine.

He shakes his head, shakes the sand off his pants. He has to keep his skin covered pretty much of the time, allergic to the sun. I smile. A nocturnal runner, you might say.

"Charlotte…Charlotte was the most brilliant student of her class," he's saying now. "That's what they told me, commencement day. The dean of the med school himself: You must be proud of Charlotte, he said. We were standing under the tent drinking lemonade—it was just before we got engaged. Remarkable insight, he told me, remarkable brain."

We're walking down along the beach, heading back to the cottage. The sand sucks at my feet. The water's cold but it compensates for the sunburn I'm getting on the back of my neck. We walk in stride. If I looked back, it would be hard to tell our footprints apart. Maybe twins have identical footprints, and I start to ask him that, he's the geneticist, he must know.

But he beats me to it. "And right that minute, right there in the tent," he says, "is when I knew I wanted to marry her."

I digest this in silence. It has implications I don't really want to think about. So just to keep the conversation going, I say, "So how about it—you like my canal?"

He nods. "Very nice, Will. An inland waterway."

We're not more than a half mile from the cottage. I wish Sue were here. Her heart mostly belongs to her horses, but she does know how to handle Ben. Like a skittish horse, you got to let them know who's the boss. She works him like she does her mare, with quiet authority, slow moves all the way as she slides her hand up Nellie's satiny cheek until she finally gets to the hard outcropping of ear, then, home free, she slips down the tense neck, and the velvet nose twitches, gradually starts blowing, a nice chuff-chuff sound. In the end she throws her arms around Nellie's neck, and I get to thinking when I watch her with the mare that this is all people really want in the end, a little nuzzling, a little body contact, warmth next to warmth.

Yeah, Sue knows all about shy critters. And with her, Ben relaxes. He'll even have a drink or two. He gets pink on his nose. He drops the tight sweet smile and actually laughs. He starts telling her about his hamsters, and for a short while I feel like family in a way we never did growing up. Funny, feeling homesick for something that wasn't. And isn't.

He's thinking about those times too because now he's asking about the brook. I know the way his mind works. The canal's reminded him.

"Remember?" he says.

I remember. How a whole gang of kids from our street used to hang around down there, used to get some old tires and float them through the culvert that ran underneath the road. Once somebody grabbed my brand new $80 soccer cleats—pulled them right off my feet—tried to sail them through as well. But they never made it out the other end, water-logged, I guess. I caught hell for that. After the spanking came the usual severe lecture on personal responsibility, did I think money grew on trees, the whole bit. This from my old man. The benevolent doctor to his patients, the cold-eyed tyrant at home. Never hugged us. But never. Never played touch football, never had the time, always on call. Always worried about complications and how the ICU was a hellhole, and the chief of surgery incompetent, Jack the Ripper he called the guy. He pushed us, Dad did, no television, get the best grades, "You've got to knuckle down, you hear?"

Knuckle down, knuckle in—I tried to get Ben to mess around at the brook. But he wouldn't. He was scared of the water, the way it foamed around the rocks and disappeared with a black gurgle in the culvert. He sat on the white fence and watched. Ben—always on the sidelines.

We've almost reached the cottage. I look up the dunes. I can see the girls running around on the front porch. I can't see either Sue or Charlotte. Ben's two boys are flying kites. They stand on the dunes at the far side of the house. The kites are in the shapes of giant fish. I bought them down in the village. Charlotte fussed at me, said I threw my money around. But I said I enjoyed throwing it plus I wanted the boys to have the fun of launching brilliant purple Japanese fish into air currents blown straight from Lisbon to this Carolina coast.

Charlotte stared at me. "You're strange," she said with a sniff. "What's Lisbon got to do with it?"

"Everything," I said. And let it go at that.

We're climbing up the hill. Ben's panting. I slow down. He's out of shape, he was born out of shape.

He stops. "Out of breath," he says.

"Fine, this last slope's a killer," I agree. We both turn and look at the ocean again.

He shades his eyes, peers out to sea. Something black arches up out of the water, curves through the air in a parabola of spray, then disappears back into the water. A school of bottlenose dolphins, working their way down the coast. They come each morning, regular as clockwork. Ben watches them. He doesn't say anything, he simply studies them. Then he looks over at me, stares at me full face. He shrugs. His eyes are shy, he looks almost embarrassed.

But when he speaks, it's in an offhand voice that matches the shrug. "We should have bucked the S.O.B.," he says in a dreamy voice.

"Who?"

"Dad." He tugs at his earlobe. "All those years, all those double messages, all that shit about self-respect."

But I don't want to deal with this—we're too close to home. "Right," I tell him. "We better head on up. They're waiting for us."

"Ok," he says. "I'll go round up the boys."

"You do that," I say and start climbing. It's tough going, this last steep part of the hill. The sand is very hot and spills away from my feet. They feel heavy as lead—a lot of effort but still not getting up the slope so much as sinking down into it. I can feel my heart thumping hard in my rib cage, and what I'd really like to do is crawl on hands and knees up the last little bit, get a little leverage going here, give my feet and the old ticker a break.

I hear myself panting, but now—I've reached the crest of the hill—oh yeah, a legitimate place to stop for a sec. There's a boardwalk leading to the cottage. I unroll my trouser legs, shake the sand out of the cuffs. The boardwalk's tricky to walk on barefoot, I'm scared I'll stub my toe again between the slats.

Eyes feel scratchy from the sand and the wind. I rub them hard as I come around the side of the house, start up the cottage steps.

Sue's standing there, on the porch. She looks at me. "Ruined your good slacks," she says. "That tar won't come off. Where's Ben?"

"Rounding up the boys."

She frowns. Her skin is so red it hurts to look at it, she stayed out sunbathing way too long yesterday. "We've been waiting almost two hours," she says. "You got the car keys?"

I pat my pocket, nod. "Here," I say. "Sorry," and hand them up to her.

She shakes her head. "Charlotte and I," she says, "are going stir crazy.

And the kids say the ocean is totally yuk, creepy things swimming by, they said."

I start to answer the cottage was her idea, not mine, but she's glaring, what's the use. She turns to go inside, then looks at me again. "You and Ben," she says slowly. "Two of a kind." She shakes her head. "What do you all *do* out there for so long, what's the big attraction?" But she doesn't wait for my answer, she never does. The screen door slams.

I look back at the shoreline, at how the waves from up here look like scrollwork, an endless series of spiral loops forming and reforming. They're impatient, I've decided, coming all that way from Portugal, in a hurry all those miles, building and building, spinning faster and faster then swelling to that final crest of power and speed to spiral home and break upon the welcoming sand, just like a wheel, I think, finally coming to rest.

HE WALKS WITH ME

AT THE TRAFFIC LIGHT a red-faced man in a BMW gives Serena the finger because she's waited too long before turning left.

His angry face scares her. The car almost stalls but she stomps down hard on the gas pedal, a real effort because her right leg jiggles almost as much as her hands gripping the steering wheel.

"Don't slip! Don't slip!" she says aloud, her mantra these days. Driving on the flattest, driest suburban streets feels like falling—like sliding down an icy mountain. She shakes her head, shifts into second, and now as she turns the wheel the dog starts baying from the back seat of the Honda, loud German Shepherd barks from deep in his throat. The dog knows this road well, and same as the red-faced man, he too is impatient. But while he startles Serena, he never frightens her.

He keeps barking the whole way—the closer they get, the louder the racket from the rear. Frowning, she turns on the FM station to drown him out. He never used to act this way in the car years ago before she went back to work full time. Now she's quit the job, she's quit every single one of her volunteer activities. She is, so to speak, at his disposal.

Somewhere she's read that animals have no concept of time. One hour is the same as a month to them. Can this be so? Maybe in the dog's mind each outing they go on constitutes their very last time together—this is the last, this is the last. How is he to know she cannot leave him? That her life these days is exactly like his used to be when she and Tom went off to work and the kids went off to college. And that now she faces precisely the same thing he once did. Empty days and silence.

Until Tom gets home at 6:30—later if there's a faculty meeting—and the silence is broken by loud yelps of welcome. They remind her of how the children used to greet Tom long ago. The purest joy! She assumes Tom must make the same comparison. They do not speak of it, however. He ruffles the dog's neck, but his eyes are on her. And always his eyes ask the same question, "How was it today? You ok?" For some questions there are no answers. Tom knows this and so he does not speak the words aloud. Nor does he expect a reply. All he has exacted from her is the promise that she will take her medication and not stay cooped up in the house all day long.

And so each morning she comes here to walk her dog. He's a big animal, and even though he's nine now, he still needs the exercise. They both do. There's a very strict leash law in their town, and only here on Town Conservation land does she permit the dog to run free.

They have this set routine. In the parking lot she lets the Shepherd jump out of the back seat of the car. But she doesn't allow him off lead until she's made sure there is nobody around. No other cars. No other dogs. He's ever so gentle with people and puppies. It's other breeds he can't accept. She understands this completely. He and she have much in common.

They walk along the gravel to the dirt path running past the tennis courts. When she unsnaps his leash, the dog bounds forward off the path to her right. He starts circling under the bushes along the bank that leads down to the pond.

He's a discreet dog. He disappears for quite some time behind the screen of buckthorn and wild blueberry bushes. The leaves are almost all gone now, and she can see him—snatches of gold and tan and black between the tangle of branches. He doesn't know she can see him. For him, the suggestion of a barrier is enough. Dogs deal in symbols.

Tactfully, she turns her head and gazes in the other direction toward the hillside. It's cloudy today, looks as though it may rain later on. She feels safe here on cloudy days, safest of all when it's actually raining. On rainy mornings they're sure to meet no one except perhaps one of the fathers from the seminary up on the hill. Or once a solitary walker in a yellow mac. No dogs though, not in the rain.

She looks around. He's barking. He's standing at the base of a sugar maple, peering up the trunk. He's after gray squirrels again. She watches him watch the squirrel take a flying leap into the next tree, a big oak. Shepherd barks furiously. Squirrel chatters back. A couple of acorns rain down on the ground but the squirrel has disappeared, probably straight into a knot hole, and all that can be seen now is the faint trembling of a branch.

The dog glances over at Serena, then trots on down the path between the trees winding to the pond. He's thirsty. Who wouldn't be after telling off that cheeky chatterbox?

"Good dog!" she calls. "You showed that rascal."

She strikes off across the open field. Soon he will join her. He usually waits until she's almost reached the slope of the hill. She takes a deep breath. Her lungs seem to expand when she walks out in this field, out here in the open. She loves it here. It's the only place she doesn't feel hemmed in, where she's finally found open space.

Once at a departmental dinner party, the guests were arguing about the most beautiful natural setting they had ever seen. San Francisco was mentioned. Sydney, Istanbul. The Loire Valley. The Greek islands.

But Serena described a summer rainstorm moving in across the flat horizon, traveling towards her in slow slanted waves across a Kansas wheat field, darkening the pale gold to a sullen brown in the same way the ocean changes color when clouds cover the sun.

She had looked at the faces around the table, then stopped. There was a short silence. Then, almost in unison, two of the guests had spoken, their voices straining to be polite. "*Kansas?*" they repeated.

And she could read on their faces exactly what they were seeing. Kansas is flat. Flat, hot, and ugly.

The man beside Serena had turned to her with a cool smile. "You want space, my girl," he said, "move out to the Berkshires. And if you think Boston winters are dreary, try sampling a Midwestern one sometime."

She had wanted to point out that in Kansas the snow doesn't go dirty gray three hours after a snowstorm but lies like a soft white sheepskin over the sleeping fields. But by then the conversation around the dinner table had left Kansas far behind, and vaulted ahead to more challenging prospects, proceeding briskly from the lower foothills of hanky panky on Beacon Hill right on up to the high Himalayas of Harvard reappointments.

Leaving Serena behind as well, staring into her wine glass still brim full of Mouton Cadet 1977 and wondering again why she's never learned to hide what she loves. Or at the very least, announce what she dislikes—red wine for starters. In Serena's circle, this is the way it is done. You lovingly dissect only what you loathe. To let down your hair is to let down your guard. Among her acquaintances ironic disaffection passes as lightly as communion wafers across parted lips, and Serena has finally realized that what is relished most is the illusion of bread.

The things she feels—delight, exuberant joy, or for that matter, despair and rage—seem to be the kind of fare sampled only by eccentrics, outsiders, or kids under the age of twelve. At one time or another, she's decided she belongs in each of these groupings, and occasionally, all three at once.

It's taken a long while but she has come to accept this. She understands now that she is a natural outlander. Tom disagrees. He is worried about her. He's even frightened, and that's what she can see in his eyes. All she knows is that in her heart she has left the pack she's always traveled with—always on the fringes, lurking at the rear—the pack she's never truly belonged to. They snap and bite. They are not to be trusted.

And for this reason she comes each day to these open fields to walk with her dog. With him beside her, she is grounded in a ritual they each need and relish, a lovely litany of smells and memories, of grass and sky, a litany so familiar it moves them mysteriously backward in time with each step forward, and Serena smiles as she watches the Shepherd who is running now on a long diagonal across the field to intercept her just as she bends into the steep incline of the hillside.

He sits down directly in front of her. He's panting hard, his tongue stretched longer than usual, the great batwing ears cocked and waiting.

She reaches down and pats his head. "Good dog," she tells him again.

He watches her. His eyes are almond shaped, wide spaced, intelligent. He watches her constantly. When she speaks the words he knows, he cocks his head to one side, ears straight up, twitching to understand completely.

He talks with his ears and his eyes. she answers with hands, and voice.

"Ok," she says. "Go on, Hal. Run!"

The dog's formal name is Prince Hal. He came to her one Christmas morning, a six week old puppy with bright eyes. He came from an H litter so it was easy choosing a name from her favorite character in the history plays. Like his namesake, Hal is of noble lineage, "The only blueblood we can claim in this family," Tom used to joke. Hal's aristocratic bearing is offset by a kind of joyful gallantry which Serena admires, even envies.

Now Hal starts trotting up the slope. He always leads the way on their walks. He rides point for her, always on the lookout.

The ground here is very rough underfoot. When she was a young girl, she used to call these clumps "tufted grass." Tufted grass meant dark skies and high winds whipping over the moors, and if she squints her eyes she can still see Catherine and Heathcliff running through the heather, laughing as they stoop down to gather a few sprigs, then slowly start the long climb up the hill to where the wind sweeps in raw and cold from across the purplish moors.

Serena stumbles, falls down on one knee. But she's not hurt. She smiles. The penalties of tufted grass.

Hal stops. He's already loped clear up to the crest of the hill. Now he wheels back down to check on her.

"Ok," she says, and he kisses her with his wet nose. She braces her hand against his neck, stands up. She holds her arm straight out in the *go out* command.

Hal's tail curves up over his croup. This is his *come play!* signal.

"Run with me," the tail tells her.

"I can't," she answers. "Too steep."

He prances beside her for a few minutes, then veers off to check out the woodchuck hole. But there's nobody home today so he sniffs, crosses back up the bill and sits down waiting for her under the clump of blue spruce.

The pine needles feel like satin spread over the spongy mattress of club moss and lichen. "Better than Beautyrest," she tells Hal. He thumps his tail politely. He recognizes a joke, even a half-baked one. "Clever dog!" she adds.

Part way down the hill leading to the meadow stands a majestic sycamore. The tree snapped in the ice storm two years ago, cracked straight down the middle of the trunk in the same way as, keel split, a ship founders on a reef. Looking at it that first winter upset her But the trunk is a lovely pearl gray color now, gradually disintegrating, being reabsorbed into the earth just as year by year the shipwreck sinks deeper into the ocean floor, the sharp lines of the hull softened by concretions of mollusks and barnacles.

Hal lifts his muzzle, sniffing the air. The black nostrils dilate *Open/Shut, Open/Shut* like a bellows. She wonders what rich messages come to him on the wind. Warnings? Promises?

They sit quietly. Behind them is the seminary. She feels anchored by the knowledge that it stands guard at their backs, the great shining dome of the sanctuary a fixed sun in this landscape, no matter how gray the sky. Here, she thinks, I cannot slip. And she scratches Hal behind his ears.

The dog will sit here as long as she does. He will not leave her side except on direct command. If they sit too long he will start to whine. But he understands this is the resting place so he doesn't move, even though they both know full well that field mice run down there in the meadow grasses. He is not a hunter, however.

Once they were crossing the meadow and Hal was loping far out in front of her and to the right. To her left she saw a baby rabbit make a wild dash away from the dog, towards the woods. Hal saw it too. He cut out on a long run, bisecting the triangle to intercept the rabbit. He scooped it up in his mouth but so gently that when he stopped, a few steps away from Serena, she could see that the rabbit was perfectly unharmed.

"Drop it!" she told him.

He put the rabbit down. Its sides heaved with fear. The pink nose quivered. Then in a flash of brown and white, it hopped away into the thicket and then the dense woods. Hal watched it calmly, almost with an expression of relief. Catching prey wasn't nearly as much fun as chasing it. He is a dog bred for one purpose only: to work. Serena thinks that Hal's real beauty lies in his capacity for perfect love. He bears no grudges, no regrets. He never sulks. He's happiest, most alive when he's working, serving as guide, as guardian, and companion.

When the children were small, Hal would herd them away from the street or the railroad tracks, pushing them gently with his nose, placing his body between them and danger. At night in the dark he leads Serena up the stairs to the bedroom.

He's programmed to protect. One night when the youngest child was blowing bubbles in the bathtub, Serena heard a wild splashing. When she opened the bathroom door, she saw that Hal had grabbed the child by the hair and was lifting the wet blonde head right out of the water.

Hal hates to see faces covered, airways blocked—by anything. Pillows. Blankets. Water. When she and Tom go swimming in the pond, they always have to leave Hal at home. Each time they dive below the surface, Hal wants to save them.

Over the years Serena and Tom have thought of ways to let Hal feel that he is a contributing member of the family, working for the common good. He carries sticks of wood in for the fireplace, letters from the mailbox across the street, small sacks of groceries. He carries notes from Serena in the study to her husband outside in the vegetable garden. "Take it to Tom," she tells him.

He insists on bringing her handbag in from the car. This is a ritual he won't be denied, and when he gets indoors he trots around and around the rooms, ears sleeked back, looking cock-a-hoop, his tail in a jaunty upward curve. Tom says that Hal is smiling when the ears go flat back this way. If she stays too long on a visit somewhere, the ears flick forward and Hal picks up her purse and heads for the car. The purse means "Time to go home now."

He's a high-strung dog, restless indoors, painfully sensitive to noise. Firecrackers terrify him. He hides in the shower stall. When there's an argument, Hal crosses nervously back and forth behind Tom, begging them to stop. If the angry voices go on, he leaves the room. He slinks into the study, lies on the red rug, whimpering. Finally in desperation he will pad upstairs to the bedroom closet, select a sneaker, and bring it down to lay at Serena's feet. "Time for a walk," he's telling her.

In time of great sorrow, Hal sits beside her quietly. He will not abandon her, not even to herself. Serena has memorized a line from the German Shepherd manual: "His great heart has brought many people out of despair."

Again she smiles. Hal whines.

"Time to go," she says.

They run down the incline towards the meadow. The meadow grass is much taller and more lush than the tufted grass in the field. Down here in the summer the crickets and cicadas make a constant thrumming noise. Butterflies flirt around the clover, honeybees as well. The meadow grass is still tall but now the summer insects have gone. All that Serena can hear is the wind in the evergreens up on the hill.

She and Hal cross to the old cart path which skirts around a stand of yellow birch. The path leads to the apple orchard, what's left of it. There used to be a dozen apple trees here. Now there's only one. The rest all died. Of what though? she wonders. Of old age? To reach the tree, she must claw her way through a maze of poison ivy and very prickly underbrush which jabs at her arms. The lower half of the tree is covered with Virginia creeper, and every year the vines twine higher around the branches.

She reaches up and pulls off two apples. Their skins are wrinkled but the flesh is still hard so she tosses one to Hal, and bites into the other. She likes the sour taste. What she doesn't like are the little brown pock-marks which probably mean worms, but she goes ahead and eats the whole thing, working on the premise that what you can't see won't hurt you.

Hal has finished his too.

"All gone," she says and spreads her palms out flat to show him her hands are empty.

He inspects them, then trots off.

They cross back to the path, following it down the knoll, then cut through a break in the hedgerow to another field, bordered all along one side by the woods leading to the pond.

There used to be a post and rail jump set up in the middle of this field. The ground is level, and for years she hoped to see a horse and rider practicing jumps. But they never came so when Hal was still a young dog, she taught him to jump the fence himself. She would place him on one side, give him the *Stay* command, then walk around to the other side of the fence. "Come!" she'd call, and then as he flew towards the jump, she yelled "Hup!" He cleared the rail as gracefully as any Irish hunter.

But now the fence has collapsed. The timbers have rotted. Today Serena notices that somebody has dragged them away.

"All gone," she tells him again. This is the last. This is the last.

They are passing along the edge of the woods now, nearing the far edge of the pond.

Hal trots ahead of her. He moves with his head low and thrust forward in the long smooth gait of an arctic wolf crossing the tundra. His powerful hindquarters drive him forward. His back is completely level. He doesn't roll or pitch but moves ahead the way a surfboard planes across the waves, gathering more power and momentum so that he seems to be skimming across the ground, and now he has moved so far ahead of Serena, she can't see him past the curve of the woods. But in a moment he will notice, and come back for her.

She starts running again, eyes on the path, and then he's beside her, and they run together down to the clearing by the pond. They're making a full circle of the pond. They will end up finally back at the parking lot.

They stop at the culvert where pond water rushes over a spill dam and then out in a stream to the woods. Hal sticks his muzzle in the water, gulps deep. Serena scoops a handful to her lips. The water's icy cold. They look across the pond. The bullfrogs and dragonflies have disappeared, but there is still milkweed growing along the banks, and they can see a family of mallards still moored over by the cattails near the old shack that skaters will use, come winter.

One day while Hal was drinking here, Serena looked up and saw a red fox running silently along the trail. The fox never once glanced over in their direction. He took the fork leading to the cornfields. One minute he was there, then he was gone, a splash of crimson slipping through the break in the fence.

She didn't tell Hal. It made her feel guilty, keeping it a secret. Still, she thought, like Tom says, you don't necessarily always have to blurt out everything you know. She, Tom, and Hal—mutual guardians, each of us leading the other away from danger.

Hal guides her now to the fork which leads in one direction to the cornfield, in the other to the trail which loops around the pond. Here there is a grove of young pine trees evenly spaced, planted in two straight rows. She can look down the long green tunnel and see clear to the end. So, despite the trees being set very close together, there is the impression of great space, of deep perspectives drawing the eye both vertically up the slender black trunks rising like spires to the sky, and horizontally down the long parallel lines of the double colonnade stretching smaller and smaller to the infinity of the parking lot.

The running is easiest on this broad pine needle carpet. This is the section she and Hal love best although each time she wonders if Hal remembers this is the end, not the beginning of the walk. That what lies ahead is not unlimited freedom but rather_the opposite. Each time too she puts this thought aside because it's too painful. Perhaps this is what he does as well.

Hal leads the way. Their footsteps make no sound. The pine canopy arches over their heads, and the wind blows cold off the pond.

It's only here in the pine grove that her legs move in a completely easy rhythm. She has never been able to decide if this is because her muscles have finally limbered up by the time they reach the pine grove, or whether there is some quality in this place which frees her, some fusion of motion and emotion in which pain, fear—and yes, even despair are canceled by this full circle they're now completing.

She is no longer aware of her body but only that she and Hal are floating down a corridor of shimmering green-gold light, a silent cloister they both feel safe in, moving forward in a state of grace as luminous as it is transitory.

When they reach the parking lot, the dog stops.

He waits for her. She pulls out the leash, clips it to his choke collar. He's panting hard again. He lifts his muzzle, pokes her hand. His muzzle has gone silver, but his eyes are still the glowing bright eyes of the young puppy she cradled that first Christmas morning.

He watches her.

She gives a gentle tug on the leash.

"Heel!" she tells him.

BEYOND THE CLEARING

UP IN THE HILL country the monsoon rains have not yet come, and from the mango grove beyond the banks of the stream can be heard the call of the brain-fever bird, wounding the silence with the sobs of a lost child.

Noontime. Like a dream bracketed by darkness and a forgetting, the village lay in deepest shadow except at dawn and then again when the sun climbed high enough in the sky to straddle the tall stands of teak which circle the clearing. Then, for one brief hour, bars of bright sunlight slant down through the trees, weaving a pattern of stripes across the dust.

Then it was that the women of the village knelt by the stream at the edge of the jungle to do their washing and afterwards to spread their clean saris carefully over the bushes in a brilliant tapestry of poppy reds, of lavenders paler than wild-blooming orchids, and shades of orange bright as tiger lilies—a tapestry of colors quite as beautiful as any bouquet picked from the royal flower gardens. Above the drying clothes swarmed honeybees, mistaking color for food.

Then into the hot sunshine came as well the old men, the grandfathers, blinking rheumy eyes as they basked in the doorways and watched the children chase sand lizards or torment the mangy cats who foraged behind the compound.

"Why must they tease those poor creatures!" said the oldest grandfather, whose name was Ramananda, and he shook his turbaned head slowly.

His companion shrugged. "Old men have soft hearts," he said, adding with a sly wink, "soft brains as well."

"Better a soft heart than a cruel hand," replied Nanda.

"Cruel?" repeated his companion. "What foolishness do you speak of now?

"Cats kill vermin, so why torment them?"

"Cats do what they're born to do. And we as well."

"Does that mean we encourage the children to harden their hearts?" exclaimed Nanda. "It's wrong, I tell you!"

"No, it's destiny," replied the other and shut his eyes as if shutting a door, and the oldest grandfather knew the subject was closed. Indeed he knew better than to have brought it up, and he could still clearly hear his mother's sharp voice, "Don't touch them, Nanda! They're dirty!" And how once he had brought home a beautiful young tabby cat and the terrible scolding that followed. All these years, and it still made no sense to him. For even a tiny kitten to cross one's path was considered the very worst of bad omens. And so the men of the village spat at them, and the women shooed them off, flapping their long skirts, and the children pelted the cats with small stones.

Why not escape? mused Nanda, watching one of the boys take careful aim with his slingshot. And yet they stay here, slinking off into the underbrush whenever they hear footsteps or children shouting. Free to run away, but not very far, trapped by their own hungers the same as us, he thought. Trapped as surely by what we loathe as by what we love. And prisoners always of our own fears.

Sighing, Nanda scratched his belly. The sun felt good and soon it would be time to call the children from their play, a few minutes more to mull this over yet again, these superstitions encircling the village—every waking hour shadowed or brightened by the omen first glimpsed at dawn. As long as they did no harm he accepted these beliefs the same way he accepted the plain facts of hot sun, old bones, leathery skin—with good-humored detachment. Had he always? Long ago had he not been scared, peering nervously each morning afraid of what his eyes might first behold? A crow or a rabbit was unlucky, but a parrot preening on a tree branch meant good fortune. Such foolish distinctions, arbitrary, illogical, he never questioned back in childhood when he too had believed that to ignore a bad omen was to invite danger just as surely as the most casual remark spoken by a man with the black tongue. Beauty withered in such cases, misfortune followed. Even the youngest child in the village knew well the story of the farmer who invited an evil-tongued man to stroll through his newly planted millet fields in hopes the man would remark on the profusion of weeds. But, alas, the man exclaimed, "Your millet seedlings look so healthy!" Next morning only the weeds survived.

Each time the children heard this story they laughed at the foolish farmer. "More!" they cried. And Nanda would tell them another tale. He was the village storyteller. He was, in fact, their schoolteacher. But the children did not know they were attending school and their eyes would go round with wonder as they listened to the many stories by which the wisdom of the village was handed down from one generation to the next. The story of the handsome prince who won the hand of the rajah's daughter by painting her portrait in such a lifelike manner that all the bees in the royal gardens were drawn to the honeyed fragrance of the portrait's painted lips. This led directly to the strange tale of the wise fisherman and why the cunning of a wise man will always vanquish an enemy more swiftly than the mightiest sword.

So many stories. Why women cry to mask their anger, and men grow angry to shield their grief. How it is the fog always recedes as you advance directly into it. And why the gods ordained that man was born both good and evil because to separate the two was to give all power to the bad and death to the good.

This truth the children could not understand until Nanda had pointed up at the sky and asked, "Can you see the moon?"

"Of course not, Grandfather! The sun's too bright!"

"But tonight, can you see the moon after supper?"

And so in this fashion the children discovered for themselves the paradox of light and dark, of good and evil, and how the moon always lives in the sky with the sun, but that it is often difficult to see them both at once.

Then Nanda had leaned forward and said, "So, little ones, it is equally difficult to see into the heart of a man and know whether he has chosen to love virtue or embrace sin. Just as the sky reveals first the sun and then the moon, so too is goodness ascendant some of the time, and then evil. And to see them together, in conjunction, you might say, is truly a rare gift."

At that point the tall boy with the ugly scar on his forehead had asked a question in a clear voice which carried beyond the circle of children and seemed to float in the dusty silence of the afternoon.

"What about you?" the boy had said. "What can you see, old grandfather?"

Startled, Nanda had stammered, "You mean can I see both sun and moon?"

"No. I mean can you see into the heart of a man?"

And Nanda had gazed at the child. The boy was clever, and despite his scar, extraordinarily handsome. His disfigurement was held to be a lucky omen because it kept him from the perfect beauty which attracts the evil eye more quickly than all else. So the scar was the boy's talisman, and boldly he would challenge his teacher.

"I am still working out the puzzle," Nanda had replied.

The boy, whose name was Karli, eyed the grandfather, trying to take the measure of the word, ready to take offense if Nanda were joking. A short pause, then the boy addressed him.

"What puzzle?"

"Only this one, my son. How easy it is to look. How difficult to see."

A feeble answer. The boy had wanted proof of true wisdom, a talisman which like his own scar might brand his teacher as exceptional, a sage divinely enlightened, not a maundering old schoolteacher with stiff joints and a long memory. A sage, thought Nanda, I'm not. But I can teach him to think like a sage himself. Already he asks hard questions, now I shall do the same.

Pleased, Nanda clapped his hands three times, massaged his aching hip, then shuffled across the dusty clearing and sat down on the grass mat in the shade of a purple-leafed sal tree.

"Story-time!" cried one of the older girls, silver bangles clinking against her thin wrists. And the children stopped their playing and came to sit in a circle around the old man. A little girl reached over to tap Nanda's big toe, displacing a buzzing fly. He smiled, and the older ones giggled, and he waited until the group stopped squirming and were comfortably settled, Karli squatting in back with the big children, arms folded as if to say "Show me, old man, your whole bag of tricks!", grave eyes staring into Nanda's as if to ferret out secrets suspected but not fully understood. The plump boy beside Karli was whispering, but as usual, Karli gave the boy a hard poke, then putting his finger to his lips shushed the group into silence. All that could be heard was the faint laughter of the women down by the stream. And the steady chirruping of crickets in the tall river grass.

In a low voice, Nanda began. "This is the story," he told them, "of why our people fear all cats. Does anyone here know the reason?" He paused and studied the circle of faces. All blank.

"Have these creatures ever harmed us?" he asked softly.

"No, Grandfather!" went the chorus of voices.

"And have we ever done harm to them? Struck them with stones, teased them without mercy?" The little ones turned around to their older brothers and sisters for answers, but the big children were silent. Two girls ducked their heads. The boys all gazed past the grandfather, peering up into the leaves of the sal tree as if a most remarkable mynah bird had caught their attention. Only Karli kept looking steadily at Nanda, his cheeks a dusky red, his voice rasping with impatience.

"Any fool," Karli said, "knows that cats bring bad luck."

There was a rustle around the circle. The plump boy next to Karli hunched his shoulders and moved a few inches away. Such an impudent remark at home would merit a beating, and while Nanda had never been known to lift his hand against any living creature, still there was always a first time.

Someone coughed. The chirrup of the crickets sounded louder now, and the grandfather's voice when he spoke was difficult for the children to hear.

But Nanda wasn't angry, he even looked pleased as he told Karli, "A good answer, my young friend. Cats do bring bad luck, some believe. But again I ask, does any fool as you put it know why?"

The pretty girl with the silver bangles glared at Karli, then in a coaxing voice answered, "No, we don't, Nanda. Please will you tell us?"

A loud snort followed her remark which the grandfather ignored. Instead, he smiled even more broadly and pressed his palms together under his chin, and the children knew that now the story was really going to start at last.

A long time ago, he told them, when gods still walked the earth, there were no small cats .

"Not even one?" asked a little boy of five who still sucked his thumb.

"Not one," said Nanda. However, he continued, back in those days there stood here in this very clearing a village much like ours, and one fine summer evening a great feast was held to celebrate the birth of a son. He was a strong baby for only six days old, and his cries when they dipped his toes in the sacred stream sounded lusty to his proud young father who was the village cobbler.

But to the mother they sounded like the pitiful mewling of the tiger kittens her husband once found abandoned after a royal hunt, and so she snatched the baby from the arms of the priest. She took the hem of her crimson shawl and dried the child's toes, then mopped the tears from the baby's face splotched with anger at this cold water on new skin softer than a spotted deer's and acquainted with dark and warmer waters where light never entered, nor cold, nor harm of any sort.

"When he still lived inside his mother's belly!" cried a ten year old, which remark was greeted with fierce exclamations of "Be quiet!" and the simultaneous contortions of several boys prodding each other in the ribs.

"Even so," nodded the grandfather, and went on to describe how after the young woman had grabbed her son and was crooning to him, there fell a great quietness over the crowd. A troubled quietness. The other women nudged each other as if to say, "She's a newcomer, that one. She does not know our ways, what did you expect?"

And the faces of the men grew dark with fear.

They knew full well that the sixth night of a baby's life was dangerous, the night when newborns were most vulnerable to evil demons. And for this reason the priests came to chant their verses, and the villagers came to feast until daybreak and appease the malevolent spirits with offerings of rice and nuts and keep their vigil bright with lights and with laughter because the evil ones seldom appear except in the quiet darkness when babies are sleeping.

Seeing the expression on the faces of the other men, the young father moved closer to his wife as if to protect her from her own rashness, born out of love.

The chief priest frowned. He glanced at the child in the arms of its mother, then at the mist rising slowly over the stream.

"Torches!" he commanded. "Let the feast begin!"

The people stirred. They clapped their hands as the music began, the thin high notes of a bamboo flute and the heavy roll of two drums.

Three young girls with orchid blossoms braided through their hair passed around sweetmeats and fresh fruit gathered only that afternoon. Although pomegranates and mangoes grew even deeper in the forest, no villager was allowed to venture beyond the clearing because in those days the jungle was a royal hunting preserve. Only the prince and his court could hunt game. This was the law of the village, and indeed the law of the land.

"Wild creatures we leave in peace, and in peace they leave us," chanted the village elders.

And the people responded, "Thus it was promised, thus it shall be."

For the pact had been struck long ago: *Do no harm* was the rule which bound them together, neither harm to their two-footed brothers swinging from tree branches, nor to their striped four-footed brothers whose guttural roars silenced the jungle birds and all the creeping creatures of the night. Only the elephants went calmly about their business, trudging through the bamboo thickets quite indifferent to the tiger's warning. Each full moon the pledge was renewed between village and jungle. At dusk a white goat was slaughtered and dragged to the foot of a many-trunked banyan tree; in the morning the carcass was gone, flattened grass the sole proof a body had rested there.

"So in this manner," said the grandfather, nodding, "peace was kept between the village and the creatures of the jungle." The children nodded back, and the little girl in front edged closer to his feet.

"And this is the story of how that truce was broken," he continued, glancing swiftly at Karli's face, which remained impassive as if to say, "I'm waiting, old man, get to the point."

And so Nanda told them how after the night of feasting, the baby woke up the next morning crying hard, and his skin was hot to the touch. The cobbler summoned back the priests, and once again the evil spirits were appeased by offerings and prayers. But they did no good. The child grew sicker.

For two days the cobbler and his wife listened to the baby's cries, then the mother, impatient with priestly mumbling, again snatched her son and ran to the center of the village and held the child up into the hot sunshine and cried out: "0 great and playful god of light, dry the tears of my son and he is yours forever, and will sing you songs of praise."

The hot sunlight, however, made the baby cry even harder. His face and body glistened with sweat from the fever, and so his mother ran to the stream, knelt on the bank bathing the child as she prayed: "0 forgive me for snatching him from your sacred waters, cool his brow and his life will be consecrated to the purity of the priesthood."

But the cool water caused the baby to turn blue with cold, and terrible chills shook his small body like a leaf in a rainstorm, and so the mother brought him home.

And on the third morning, he cried no more.

The funeral rites lasted for ten days; on the eleventh day the mother crept onto her cot, and try as he might, her husband could not comfort her. And then she too fell ill with a high fever, and her cries anguished her husband for she would not permit any priest to enter their home. All night long she would moan and beg that her son be brought to her breast. Her eyes had the sly gleam of madness. Finally, the cobbler could bear her pain no longer.

That very night he went into the jungle and he dug a huge pit, and in the pit he placed sharp stakes. The next evening when he returned, the pit was empty. But the cobbler had the patience now that is born out of desperation, so again when night fell he stole a baby goat from the pen behind the temple where the sacrificial animals were kept. And he took the kid and slashed its throat, his hand trembling so hard he could barely hold the knife. Stealthily he returned to the jungle and threw the carcass into the pit. He stole back to his house, and lay awake in the dark, waiting for the sharp cry from the jungle which finally towards morning reached his ears while his wife, exhausted, slept in his arms.

"Pray," he said aloud, and in his mind he finished the sentence: Pray that I have caught a female and that her litter be not far away.

The next night close to dawn he again returned home and tenderly took the small tiger kitten from his robe and placed it down beside his wife.

The woman groaned as her fingers touched the warmth of the kitten, and she suckled it to her breast. Then for the first time in many days, her eyes looked washed clean of madness, and with a faint smile she murmured, "See how hungry he was!"

The cobbler shook with fear, not sure of which he was more frightened— wild beasts or his neighbors? Jungle retribution or denunciation by priests and friends? Yet he knew that his greatest fear and greatest love lay rooted in the well-being of his wife, and that no pact, neither earthly nor divine, would stop him from easing her pain or promoting her happiness. This fear, he realized, must now dwell side by side with guilt in a dark place she never saw. Her joy outran any risk he had taken, any laws he had broken. So be it.

And happy she was, and the tiger kitten purred with contentment and grew fat and round-bellied. Not a single visitor came to the house because the cobbler had warned she was still crazed with grief. And the priests too were nervous, and they put a mark on the door which indicated that evil spirits still lay within.

And so the family was left alone, and apart, the three of them. Father, mother, and infant. And the months went by, months of joy and laughter.

But infants grow big. And the kitten grew into a cub, a splendid cub with glossy fur and velvet stripes. His purrs seemed to shake the very walls, and then the villagers muttered that the woman's madness had worsened. But her mind was quite clear. The cub was now too big to hold comfortably in her lap, and his hunger grew daily—hungry for more than she could feed him. She had come to a decision, and once again she was acting out of love, but this time a loved tempered by grief that lay both behind her and ahead.

That evening she sat with her husband in front of the fire, the cub dozing at their feet, his coat the same burnished gold as the flames. In a soft voice, she began to speak. "My husband," she said, "you have saved me from myself and given me back not only a babe but my sanity as well. Now, for his sake, we must return him to his rightful home in the jungle where he can have plenty to eat and run with his own pack."

The cobbler stared in astonishment at his wife. "But nobody knows," he replied. "I mean everyone in the village—they're too frightened to come near us."

A coal fell out on the hearth, and quickly with the heel of her sandal the wife kicked it back into the fire. The cub stirred, then rolled over on its back while she scratched him on the stomach and then under his chin, and his purrs of contentment filled the silent room.

And she said to her husband, "We cannot hide from our own kind forever any more than he can hide from his. It's selfish. And what's more, it's wrong."

"But..." stammered the cobbler. He knew not what to say because he was ashamed. Of his fear. And of his relief.

His wife knew well the fears he harbored and hid from her so she told him firmly, "Do not worry, my dearest, I shall be fine. But he must go back. Do this, my husband, for all three of us."

And so with a show of reluctance but secretly delighted, the cobbler obeyed. He waited for three nights until the moon was full, and then he led the tiger cub deep into the jungle. They walked for many miles, farther than he had ever ventured. Moonlight silvered the bushes. Beyond the gleaming leaves he thought he could see golden eyes glowing back at him from the darkness. Monkeys chattered above their heads as they passed by. Once a lumpy black shape slithered across the path. He jumped backwards, then realized it was a hungry cobra stalking his midnight supper.

At last he came to a cave in the hillside beside a pool where the reeds grew tall and the jungle creatures were sure to drink. A good place to leave his foundling. He took from his waistband a greasy leather bag, and opening it, he said to the cub, "Eat well, remember she loved you." And he scattered the chunks of goat meat in a trail which led from the pool to the mouth of the cave. Then without a backwards glance, he stole into the shadows of the trees. The last thing he heard was the low growl of the cub as it crouched before its feast. The cobbler covered his ears with both fists and fled home.

Four years went by. The cobbler and his wife prospered and had good fortune of many kinds but never another child. The village too prospered, and the priests told the people they had won favor with the gods who were well pleased with their virtue and their obedience to the laws.

One evening at dusk, a child last seen skipping stones in the stream disappeared. The search lasted for many weeks. The child was never found. Word drifted down from their neighbors to the north that a man-eater was abroad, a silent killer who stalked the edge of the jungle and dragged his prey away so quickly no cry was ever heard. The pact had been broken. The villagers were afraid, the priests confused. What had gone wrong?

At night the shrieks of the monkeys grew louder, and often you could hear the trumpeting of elephants, the heavy drumbeat of a whole herd crashing through the underbrush. But no one heard any longer the roar of the tigers, and this made the villagers even more frightened.

The cobbler and his wife said nothing. They were waiting.

One day, the wait was over.

Noontime, the sun high in the heavens, and the women had finished spreading the clean clothes over the bushes to dry. Nobody lingered to gossip, they were all anxious to get back home. Then as they were picking up their empty baskets, one of the younger wives screamed. She dropped her basket on the grass and she pointed, open-mouthed, at the trees.

There across the stream at the edge of the clearing crouched a great tiger. He watched them in silence, his huge gold eyes burning them with a scrutiny so intent that nobody could move, the whole group frozen into a stillness as immobile as his.

Then into that stillness emerged a sound, a deep thrumming noise unfamiliar to their ears as if a thousand bees were swarming, but deeper and richer, ebbing and flowing the way a giant waterfall will sound when heard from far away. But to one person in the group the sound was very familiar. It signified pleasure and deep contentment, and so the cobbler's wife stood up from where she was kneeling beside the stream.

And she gazed at the tiger, and she held her arms open wide. Slowly she took two steps forward, and the tail of the beast began to swish gently, fanning the leaves so they trembled in the sunlight.

But the woman did not tremble.

She smiled, and the other women watched as she began to walk faster, picking up her skirts as she forded the stream. And then she was running, and now the tiger opened his great fanged mouth and growled, and the growl deepened into a full-throated roaring which filled the air, and then she was beside him, and in the blink of an eye where there had been black stripes on a rippling canopy of gold and the brilliant crimson swirl of her skirts there was now only the rustle of the bushes and a profound silence, and whether the tiger's greeting had been one of recognition and love reclaimed, or simple retribution, nobody in the village ever knew.

"Is that the end of the story?" asked the plump boy next to Karli.

"No," said Nanda. "Not the end."

The little boy in the very front row took his thumb out of his mouth and in a worried voice asked, "And did the bad tiger come back?"

"Never," answered the grandfather. "And neither did the cobbler's wife. And her husband went to the priests and confessed his guilty secret. The priests looked grave, but they said no more until the day the first small cats appeared. Now you remember, children, until then no cats had ever been seen in our village nor anywhere on earth. But now here they were, rubbing their backs against people's ankles, first purring and then meowing most piteously, and some did pity them, and fed them table scraps. But the priests told the villagers that these creatures were the ghostly offspring of that jungle cat—evil demons sent by the gods to ensure that never again would the pact be broken between wild beasts and man."

The children waited. And the grandfather waited, his heart beating fast because he wasn't sure Karli would utter the words he prayed the boy might say.

Finally, Karli spoke. "And *that's* the reason we fear the cats?"

"Yes, my son."

"But they weren't the ones—I mean the cats didn't bring misfortune to the village. It wasn't the animals, it was the people!"

"Really? Not the fault of the cats, you're saying?"

"NO!" shouted the boy. "Look, they came, I don't know why, maybe they were sent to remind us we broke all those laws. Or maybe they came because they were hungry, and they needed something."

"And what do you think they needed, Karli?"

The boy shrugged. He glanced around the circle of children who now sat very still, aware something important was happening but not sure what it was except that both Karli and Nanda wore the same expression, each one trying to coax words from the other, each stubbornly wanting the other to provide the answer.

But Nanda was patient and quite accustomed to waiting a long time. The boy was not, and at last, eyes shining, he spoke, "Needed to be loved?"

At first Nanda didn't answer but only bowed his head. Then, rubbing his chin, he said gently, "I don't know, my son. I only tell stories,"

And he leaned his head against the trunk of the sal tree, and closed his eyes, and listened to the children scatter, calling for the cats, calling to each other.

"What if they bite?"

"What if they scratch?"

And then Karli's strong voice soaring above all the rest, "And what if they purr?"

Smiling, Nanda lifted his face up to the sun to take a proper nap the way old men always have and always will, drowsing like a tawny kitten beside a golden fire, drifting in and out of comforting dreams, those sun-drenched dreams of childhood which the young can seldom remember and their grandfathers must never forget.

LANGUOR

KATE FINALLY TOOK THE copy-editing job up in Boston to get away from Wendell Steele as much as anything else. He wasn't launched on the corporate fast track for nothing, old Wendell. Even after she broke off the engagement, he kept running after her, phoned her at work, followed her home in his new Corvette he'd bought to please her because she thought Corvettes were sexy. "Making sure you're safe," he called this vigilance.

"Clucking like a mother hen" Kate called it. He was worse than her family back in Ohio who (she knew damn well) were quietly delighted the Big Apple chapter was finally concluded. She carefully didn't tell them that the Boston job offer at a small textbook publishing house was actually a comedown, both in pay and prestige.

Her friends, however, were appalled. "What about your career ladder?" they wailed. "Your future?"

Her future lay snarled in Wendells's past, she reminded them.

But, they argued, she was "over-reacting, you got to play it safe, Katy. Be cool, don't close off your options."

Options, she frowned, more like barbed wire fencing. She shook her head, she could feel sweat beading up on her forehead, Judas priest, it was hot out here! They were helping her load the car. Boxes of books, CDs, DVDs took up most of the narrow back seat, everything piled all topsy-turvy, covered by a couple of striped sheets, bold red stripes. The ones Wendell detested.

"They make me feel like a candy cane," he kept fussing. "Why not pure white?"

"You tell me," she said. Then added, "I'm considering a striped wedding gown." She thought this mildly amusing, he didn't. She told him again he was uptight. He replied she was rude and inconsiderate. She attacked his Victorian mind set. He called her irresponsible with the ethical perspectives of an alley cat.

"You don't mean that," she had said quietly.

"No," he agreed. He rubbed the bridge of his nose. "I didn't mean it."

"Then why do this to each other?" she'd cried out.

He shook his head impatiently. He looked both unhappy and cross. His right eye twitched. "Please, Katykins, please calm—"

"For the zillionth time, don't call me that. No diminutives! You're forever infantilizing me. Can't you see I need breathing room?" she told him. "You jerk me around, Wendell, you're either babying me or moralizing. I'm bloody tired of fighting back." She swallowed hard. "There's just too much scar tissue."

He had taken her hand, kissed each fingertip, the muscle in his right cheek was jumping now. "I'm here for you, darling. I always will be." And that was the whole problem. His love entangled her. He was always there for her like this huge safety net while she wanted to be in free fall. Didn't she?

She wiped her forehead. "Must be ninety degrees at least!" she said. "Thank God I'm heading north, to all that New England coolth, presumably." She glanced at the car, then at the flushed faces of her two best friends. "Cheer up," she told them. "You're not losing a roomie, guys, you're getting free digs in Boston."

They all laughed, hugged one last time. "Write us!" they called as she pulled away from the curb. "Write soon!"

And she did, once a week, faithfully—on letterhead stationery during her lunch hour, too chancy going on line with e-mails. She told them about the new job, the potential for promotion to Associate Editor after a satisfactory performance review. She wrote about the stuffy editorial offices on Beacon Hill. Her window overlooked an old cemetery wedged in between tall brick buildings, the rosy bricks smudged with soot. She described their apartment in Cambridge: one bath, two bedrooms, three mice, and a ramshackle back porch. The railings were half rotted away so she and Liz, the new roommate, painted a broad white line to remind them to stay away from the edge. Then they painted the rest of the floor a dark forest green and hung up bamboo wind chimes and macramé pots filled with grape ivy. The plants all froze when winter came. With the extra green paint (they had overestimated by four gallons) they did the inside of the apartment as well. But then the paint ran out so they left one wall the original dingy white and covered the whole thing with a pretty red heirloom quilt Liz had inherited from her grandmother. The quilt tactfully hid the cracks and proved all winter long to be perfect insulation.

"Not only a great conversation piece," she wrote, "but saves on the fuel bill. Liz is taking Beginners Quilting after work. She threatens to cover every wall with the results. Come see for yourselves! You'll simply adore Boston, so small-town. I keep running into lots of old classmates, most of them married to law or med school people, it seems. By the way, Laura's pregnant, baby and doctoral thesis both due in June."

The married friends invited her for dinner. One week she ate mushroom risotto served with arugula and dandelion salad three nights running. "The newlyweds swap the same recipes. All courtesy of the cooking channel, Rachel Ray or somebody. Oy vey."

She and Liz bought a state-of-the-art sautoir for sautéing and five French Chef knives. They switched from beer to vintage wines and treated themselves to a hanging wine cellar to decant the bottles properly. They found a Simmons hide-a-bed for the living room dirt cheap at Goodwill, a sturdy gold tweed only slightly raggedy at the armrests. The gold looked good against the dark green walls. They went to Symphony and avant-garde productions over at the Loeb, season tickets but the cheapest seats, of course. They brought home sleek Harvard Fellows and nerdy junior faculty from MIT, a matched pair of earnest Divinity students, and a raft of MBA candidates from the Business school. They sat on the floor, drinking decent Beaujolais, listening to arguments, gradually learning to swim in the somewhat shark-infested waters of intellectual one-upmanship. She and Liz were sternly advised to subscribe to the *Wall Street Journal*, and to take up jogging immediately.

"I jog occasionally," she wrote. "Liz jogs but grumbles." She stopped and thought for a moment, then continued. "The candy cane sheets still virginally packed away, you may be interested to know. Let sleeping dogs lie, woof!" and drew a smiley face. "Incidentally, Wendell still calls faithfully every damn week, still checking up on me," followed by a frown.

The front door slammed. She folded each letter, stamped the envelopes, then stood up, stretched, working the kinks out of her back muscles.

Liz clumped in. She was wearing her clogs and carrying a bunch of daffodils. "Spring has sprung, rejoice and be exceeding glad!" she announced. "We need to buy more plants for the porch." Liz was getting her master's in Landscape Design which was—she pointed out after their grape ivy froze—no guarantee of a green thumb.

Now she finished fiddling with the daffodils, stepped back and squinted. "The line here looks cluttered, should fall into a triangle. Guess I'd better sign up for Japanese flower arrangement come summer."

"But how about your Advanced Quilting course?"

Liz twitched at a stalk. "Can't quilt in Cambridge in July, too hot."

"Hey, mailman come yet?"

"Nope, I swear he sleeps late Saturday."

"What a cushy job. Civil service is the way to go. To hell with the fast track."

Liz grinned. "That or else be a toll booth collector on the Mass Pike."

"God." Kate stood, fanning herself with the envelopes. "I got cabin fever bad, Lizzy." She went out all the way through the foyer to the front door, threw it open. She stood there breathing deep. It did smell like spring outside, fresh and new. She shut the door, stuck the letters on top of the mailboxes. LATIMER & LINDQUIST she had printed carefully when they first moved in. "Sound like a law firm or what?" she told Liz back then.

Liz had scowled. "Maybe help scare away the weirdoes."

"Worst luck," she murmured, closing the door behind her.

Liz glanced up. "What's ailing you?" Now she was piling dirty laundry into her duffel bag. Saturday was Laundromat day. Liz laundered, Kate marketed. They had tried a democratic switching-off, but Kate kept losing pillow cases and Liz claimed that shopping solely for produce was a drag.

"Oh, I don't know, Lizzie. The daily grind, I guess—stuff at work's basically deadly dull. If I *never* see another politically correct history textbook, it'll be too soon. " She yawned. "The job puts me to sleep. The thing is I yearn—absolutely *crave* something non-p.c. for a change. Something totally unconventional, you know—a little wildness. a smidgin of excitement for heaven's sake!".

"We just got back three weeks ago!"

"I know, but Bermuda didn't do it. I'm still hungry for—I don't know— exotica or whatever."

"Anything on for tonight?" Liz buckled the strap on the duffel bag. She had square capable hands, hands that could arrange flowers, or chop celery as quick as a professional chef, clop clop clop like the sound of those funky shoes of hers.

"A play at the Wilbur." Kate stretched, did a couple of deep knee bends. "A revival, Oscar Wilde's *Ideal Husband*. Quite delicious."

"Who with?"

"In it, you mean?"

"No, who you seeing it with. Gary?"

"Negative. Laura and Ned Carlisle. And another couple, Reese Travers and Nicole something. I met Reese years ago, he was Ned's roomie at Harvard, a real hunk."

"And you?"

"Just going along for the ride. I ran into Laura on Boylston when she was buying the tickets. She talked me into joining them."

Liz stared thoughtfully at the duffel bag, tested the buckle with one strong finger, then glanced up at Kate. "You'll be odd man out, methinks."

"Methinks not," Kate grinned. "Where'd I leave my specs anyhow?"

* * *

SHE CARRIED HER GLASSES in the red shoulder bag, Coach, rather elegant. The bag matched her red pumps, ninety six bucks, Italian leather, soft and supple with a sling-back heel which almost felt like walking around barefooted. Big bonus was that her legs, her best feature, were still tan from the five day trip (Special Late-Winter Rates) to Bermuda—which had been beautiful but ultimately boring, full of stuffy people sporting pink shirts and discreet paunches. She told Liz they were bound to bump into Wendell any moment. "Totally Wendell-ish" was the way they ended up describing their vacation.

The Carlisles were going up the broad marble staircase ahead of her, Ned Carlisle shepherding Laura, one hand cupped firmly under her elbow—the protective father-to-be. The other couple followed behind Kate. It had been her junior year that she met Ned's roommate but clearly he didn't remember her from a hole in the wall. But she remembered him perfectly. Except for the beard, he looked the same—chestnut-colored hair all wiry curls, high forehead almost ugly it was so broad, sleepy eyes which she knew damn well were watching her red shoes, watching her legs mount the steps, high heels clicking against the marble.

When she reached the landing, she turned to smile down, not at him but his date, a perfectly gorgeous young blonde with flawless skin, a lot of it showing, acres it seemed.

"Love this theater, don't you?" she said to the blonde. "So rococo, all these gold moldings, the mirrors." She beamed at Ned Carlisle, stooped and kindly, still clutching Laura's arm. "You men ought to be decked out in white tie and tails," then turned back to the girl again. "And us all swathed in white ermine cloaks, sporting egret plumes in our hair."

The girl blinked, then laughed politely. "I—like—don't get to the theater much," she said. "I'm doing biochemistry."

Kate cocked an eyebrow. "Really! So you're an undergraduate, you mean?"

The girl nodded, looked uncertainly at Reese who grinned at Kate. He knew perfectly well what was going on. "Nicole's swamped with labs. You, I gather..." and he paused, "were not a science major."

Laura broke in, big brown eyes twice as worried-looking behind the thick lenses. "Let's find our seats, don't you think? Curtain time's in five minutes."

Their seats were excellent, right on the first row of the balcony. Kate sat between Ned and Reese. Ned handed her a program, and she took out her glasses, put them on, studied the program carefully as the lights began to dim. She noted Reese noting the glasses. He was talking to Nicole, but when she opened her purse and unsnapped the case, she saw his head turn sharply in her direction, and then back to Nicole.

The play was clever. She leaned forward, elbows cushioned by the soft velvet of the balcony railing. The audience laughed. She felt herself floating free in the velvet darkness, floating towards the stage, up there with the cast, bantering in a clipped British accent, smiling into the hot footlights, smiling up towards the balcony where Reese sat there watching her, studying her, memorizing her. And then the house lights came on. With a small jerk, she sat back in the seat. Ned stood up, stretched.

"…some champagne?" Reese was asking.

She shook her head. "Laura and I have lots of catching up to do."

Ned bent down, touched Laura's shoulder gently. "You feeling ok?"

"Fine, honey. The baby's bound to be a Wilde Childe, no question," and Laura waved him off, then looked directly at Kate, pretty eyes magnified so large she could pass for a lemur, why *doesn't* she buy contacts? Kate wondered.

Laura was speaking softly. "…giving you the eye, my friend."

"Who?"

"Come on, Kate! Behave yourself. He and Nicole are practically engaged. She wrote to him this whole past year while he was down in Brazil or whatever."

"Honestly, Laura." Kate laughed. "I haven't said word one to him. Anyhow, Nicole's a beauty." She slipped off her left shoe, flexed her toes.

Laura sighed, then dimpled, shaking her head slowly. "He'll never know what hit him. I can see it all now."

Kate sniffed. "It's your fault to begin with."

"My fault?"

"You should've given me a crack at him years ago. All those limp people you kept fixing him up with."

"Hey, back up a sec, you idiot. You were knee deep in Wendell back then."

"Precisely my point," said Kate, trying to cover resentment with a laugh. "I needed rescuing, Laura!" but then the others were back, and she put on her left shoe and her glasses, and threw a dazzling smile at Ned as he shuffled by her. "Marvelous production, Ned!" she told him, and drew her legs up so he wouldn't step on the red shoes.

Definitely not seats designed for tall people. Each time she moved around, crossing and uncrossing her legs, she could feel Reese shifting to accommodate her change in position. It was like a slow motion dance. She kept her hands folded primly in her lap, afraid if she put her arm out on the armrest between them, she might leap up from her seat screaming *FIRE!*

In the darkness she was safe to spy him out, the smell of him, Old Spice aftershave, the sound of him rattling his program, shifting those long legs, his deep laugh reminding her she must laugh too, and then once she glanced over by mistake at his profile. His head turned immediately and she looked into his smiling eyes, heavy-lidded and knowing, and was glad that the dark hid her blush, her cheeks flaming as if he'd caught her red-handed, which in fact, he had.

The Carlisles invited them all over for coffee afterwards. They sat around shooting the breeze about travel to exotic places, and Reese's thirteen month tour of South America. Nicole glanced at her watch, murmured something about a Bio final.

They stood up to go. Ned offered to give Kate a lift home but Reese said quietly, "No sense in your going out again, Ned. Ellery Street's not far from Nicole's dorm, it's right on my way, no problemmo."

In the car they laughed together, the three of them, talking fast, no telltale lulls in the conversation. Reese drove quickly through the dark streets and parked outside the dorm. Nicole slid out of the front seat, turned to wave. "Lovely meeting you, Kate."

"Same here. Good luck on your exam, Nicole." She stayed in the back seat, afraid to watch them go up the front steps, afraid to see him come springing back, open the door.

"Come climb in front," he told her. "Enough's enough."

She climbed out slowly, sat down, nervous. He was lighting a cigarette.

"I quit a long time ago but it's rude to refuse one in Brazil. They all smoke, I mean everybody, young, old, rich, poor. I was surprised." He offered her one. She fumbled as she took it out of the package. He held the lighter steady in his hand, but hers jiggled.

"That..." and she nodded at Nicole's dorm, "was definitely *not* smooth." She stopped. He hadn't made a move to start the car, just sat there, one hand on the wheel, the other tapping ashes out the window.

He glanced over at her. A car went by, the headlights sweeping across the gleaming whiteness of his forehead, the coppery glints of his beard. "You knew it was coming," he said reasonably. "I didn't hear any protests."

"What must she think? She was so gracious about the whole thing. In her shoes I would *not* have been a happy camper."

"Nicole's a good kid, we're just old friends. Her family live next door to mine, they asked me to look after her when she got accepted at Harvard." He chuckled, rubbed his chin. "Despite what Laura may have told you. At any rate, this is what you wanted, not so?"

She straightened up, ground the cigarette out in the ashtray. "What I *want* is to go home. Directly."

He laughed again. They drove back to Ellery Street in silence. He leaned over and opened the door for her, and she scrunched back into the seat, turning her head abruptly towards the window. "Thanks for the lift," she said, working hard to make her voice sound noncommittal when what she wanted actually was to spit at him, and she got out, slamming the door, then stalked up the sidewalk, her heels tapping like angry castanets.

"Love those red shoes, amiga!" he called after her. "Muy elegante!" and drove off.

He darn well kept her cooling those heels, however. No call that week or the next. Ned Carlisle called though. The baby came two weeks early. They were naming him Reese, naturally. "That's so sweet!" she managed to say. After work she went to see Laura in the hospital. The baby was a splotchy raspberry red, a dead ringer for Quasimodo, one eye all squinched. But Laura explained that was par for the course with firstborn. She talked porta-cribs, breast feeding, and fierce lactation specialists for thirty minutes non-stop, her brown eyes a normal size without the glasses. Neither of them mentioned the godfather.

Kate went straight home and called Wendell. "Just checking in," she told him.

The next morning she woke up with the flu. She stayed home from work for the rest of the week. Friday night Reese called.

Liz marched into the bedroom. "It's him," she reported. "I mean I think it's him. Very laid-back sounding."

Kate slumped against the pillow. "Liz," she whispered, "I absolutely cannot talk to him. No way. I can't talk period. Listen to my voice. Gonzo."

Liz leaned against the doorjamb, waiting.

"I'm dying here. Tell him. Please."

Liz shrugged, clumped back into the living room. She didn't return. Murmuring, then a long silence.

Kate sat up. "Lizzie? Was it him? What did he say? Liz, you're driving me up the wall!"

Liz walked back in with a glass of brownish looking juice. "Here," she said. "He gave strict instructions to feed you lemon juice mixed with boiling hot water. Lace it with Myers rum and lots of honey. Old Spanish remedy, he claims, and he'll call you back tomorrow. For a progress report over drinks at the Casablanca." Liz folded her arms. "So what shall I tell him?"

The hot drink scalded her throat but the honey tasted good, coating the rawness. The rum simply made her feel hotter and lightheaded. "Not tomorrow," she groaned. "I simply can't."

* * *

THE CASABLANCA WAS CROWDED and very warm. He did most of the talking. She managed to croak out a few sentences, but he said, "Rest your vocal chords" and ordered her another rum toddy. "Hot," he told the waiter. "Make it boiling hot." His voice was slow and easy with little pauses in between as if he were taking stock and things looked pretty darn good.

They talked about his trip. He told her Brazil was the most lushly beautiful country despite the rape of the land that was going on, unstoppable, unimaginable. The widespread deforestation near parts of the Amazon a pure horror, like a war zone, machines everywhere, devouring the trees, laying down roads, dust, noise, and ugliness.

He told her that in every place he visited he was invited to play pick-up soccer games. "The men, middle-aged guys, college kids, small boys—they all knock off any time of day or night. Always up for a game. Even in the villages. Such a comfortable way to meet folks, talk about bonding! Nothing like playing hard together, suddenly everyone's bilingual." She saw that his eyes were the same coppery brown as his hair.

He spoke some Spanish to her, lovely liquid sounds that made no sense but felt good on her ear, cool and soothing. He described the corrupt police and customs officials, and how he had to make sure they didn't slip drugs into his backpack and then bust him unless ten thousand pesos or more got anted up. "Dangerous," he said. And gave his lazy smile. "I loved it."

"You going back to law school now?" she asked.

"No. Did some heavy-duty thinking down there. No way. I've dropped out for good. Plan to bum around this country. Travel light for a while," he said, looking at her intensely, and all she wanted to do was touch his soft beard.

"What about money?" she asked. "Finding a job?"

"Poker games. Work as a bartender. Carpenter, construction jobs. Whatever."

"*Poker?*" she repeated.

He said he'd worked his way through Harvard playing poker, betting in football pools, the horses. "You name it, I bet on it," he ended up.

"Not much future in all that, is there?" she heard herself saying, hating the words, evil toads hopping out of her mouth unsummoned, unnecessary.

He looked at her steadily, heavy lids lowered. He stroked his beard, then took the rum toddy and held it to her lips. "There *is* no future, niña. Only now. Drink up." He smiled at her, long and lazy. It made her go still inside.

He was nowhere near as handsome as Wendell, but the texture of him, the slow languorous rhythm of him in bed, she just couldn't seem to get enough.

Liz disapproved of him. She kept warning he was definitely not the type to commit.

"Commit what?" Kate laughed.

Liz had shaken her head. "Make a commitment. Stick to anything. Or anyone," frowning darkly.

"I like that in him, Liz. He's calm inside. He's not all bent out of shape worrying about careers, nervous about tomorrow, about making it. Not revved up like the rest of us."

She quit jogging. Instead, Reese took her camping in the Maine woods on weekends. He took her to the races up in Saratoga Springs, and he taught her a little bit about betting and a great deal about Thoroughbreds. He liked to build models, hand-launch gliders, and when they went to the beach he taught her about slope-soaring, launching the gliders from the cliffs, watching the bright yellow wings catch the thermals as easily as seagulls, rising and falling on currents of air like a surfer riding the waves.

By slow stages he gradually moved into the apartment. Liz sulked for three weeks and finally moved out. Kate hardly missed her, hardly registered her absence. She stopped writing letters and e-mailing, gave up seeing people she knew. Only Wendell kept in touch, his weekly calls metronome-dependable—and about as exciting. At work, she sat and looked down at the burial ground, at little white scraps of old newspapers fluttering around the gravestones. The chief editor came into her office and twice found her doodling on letterhead stationery. Nothing was said but the associate editorial slot went to someone else "more highly motivated" they told her. She went back to her desk and called Wendell.

"Better play catch up ball, darling" he advised. "Pull yourself together."

But she couldn't.

Reese didn't do drugs but she might as well have. She sleepwalked her way through dreary manuscripts, through the whole long summer, waiting only to catch the T home, float up the walk and into his arms.

He fixed the back porch railings, mended the torn seams on the sofa, put new washers in the bathroom faucet and new flooring in the kitchen. He caulked the cracks in the wall where Liz had hung the quilt, then repainted the wall a soft golden green. "Like jungle sunlight," he told her. He had a painter's eye, and the hands of a craftsman. What he didn't have was ambition.

She stopped going to the Loeb or Symphony. He taught her to play the guitar and harmonica. Evenings that summer, they sat out on the porch, staring past the hanging plants at the grimy apartment houses. They played folk, English ballads, railroad chanteys, old spirituals, calypso, a little reggae, Spanish love songs. She only knew a few chords, but enough to laze along with him, very softly in case she made a mistake.

"Isn't this more fun?" he asked her once.

"More fun?" she repeated."

"Making your own concerts," he answered. And smiled at her, that drowsy smile of his that made no demands, a smile like a lullaby.

When October came, he brought the plants into the living room and hung them from brackets on the wall. He hauled out her GPS, the Rand Mc Nally Atlas, and a bunch of her Triple A Triptiks. Every night she would work at her desk, catching up on galley proofs while he played a little on the harmonica, slip-sliding up and down the notes, holding a long tremolo like some exotic wild bird floating through the jungle, looking for...for what? Then out came the maps. He had put away all his models, the thin sheets of balsa wood, the paints and brushes, his sandpaper. He boxed them carefully, set the cartons in the closet. He hunched over the maps, flattening them across the table with his fist.

"When?" she asked him.

"Soon."

"Take me with you, Reese. I've got all that money saved up."

He shook his head. "Not now, niña. Traveling light, you know that. Some day perhaps, down the road, who can tell? But not yet."

She stood up, walked over to the table. She put her hand on his forehead, flattening her palm over the smooth skin, memorizing the width and breadth, the swelling of the temporal bones, the wiry feel of the hair springing high off the temples. He placed his hands over hers, trapping it there. His fingers felt cool.

He left the first week in December. They said good-bye in the morning.

When she came home from work, she stood outside the front door, staring at the typed names on the mailbox. She had never crossed Liz out, still the same prim LATIMER & LINDQUIST, a total failure in keeping out weirdoes from Lizzie's point of view. Hadn't kept him out, she smiled, thank sweet God in heaven.

She unlocked the front door. He had left the lights on for her in the living room. He had left his guitar as well. The guitar was propped against the gold sofa cushion, the satiny wood gleaming in the yellow lamplight. Next to it, he had placed her red shoes. The whole scene looked like a still life, post-modernist maybe, the shoes a wry splash of bright color, a slightly jarring note in the formal composition. She walked over to the guitar, plucked one string. He had taken the harmonica with him. "Doesn't take up any space," he told her.

She sat down on the couch, reached for the phone, dialed Wendell's number.

His answering service came on. She waited, her hand shaking.

She put her other hand around the throat of the guitar, letting the frets dig into her palm, hard enough to hurt.

She left her message. All she said was, "It's me. It's Katykins."

DOWN BY THE POOL

HOT OUT HERE BY the pool, palmetto leaves looking kinda dusty. They could use a good soaking. The squirrels got themselves a nest over there somewhere, we can hear the babies chittering away all day long.

"Them rascals sound hungry," I say to old man Ransom.

He pats his bag of peanuts, he's holding them in his lap. Old man Ransom's easing up on ninety-two, he makes the rest of us feel mighty encouraged about the next twenty years. Still chipper. Still got a wink for the women folk.

"Don't see their mama or daddy yet none, do you, Joe?" he says to me.

"No sir, not yet."

He smiles. "Come noon, son, they'll be here, grab more loot to take home to the nest," and he leans his head back against his beach chair, time for a snooze. Tickles me he calls me son, I call him sir.

Left the windows open up in my apartment, maybe catch a little breeze. I can hear my phone ringing up there over the racket the squirrels making, most likely one of my in-laws calling. My wife Frances—she left me a whole passel of in-laws. Good people, but they sure do like to jaw on the telephone.

Told Connie a good six months ago I got a notion to get me one of those cordless jobs. "Walk over hell's half acre with them gadgets," I tell her.

"When you figuring to go?" she sasses me right back, quick as you please. Connie sits there, ramrod straight in her yellow-striped lounge chair, the backrest cocked bolt upright. Sits there every morning holding court, under the big umbrella, first one to come downstairs, every day 10 o'clock sharp, rain or shine.

"Set your watch by her," old man Ransom tells us, also rain or shine.

Rainy days, we all of us go huddle inside the Florida room. It's set right next to the fence, takes up one whole side of the courtyard, shaded by the big palms. Whole building used to be ours, one big room all glass facing the pool, and a nice little utility kitchen plus bar for when we throw our parties Saturday nights. Hell of an uproar when they decided to put that partition in a while back. "Make room for the new office," the owners tell us. Didn't even check with the Tenants Committee. What a ruckus. Connie's daughter was down visiting at the time. Two years ago it was.

We circulated petitions, Connie organized the whole thing, naturally. Her daughter Thalia talked her into it. Except for our gang, most folks here were scared to sign, scared of repercussions, they said. What they meant was scared their rent would be raised. Nothing scares Connie. She swooped through each of the four units like Sherman marching through Georgia. She wore one of those long striped caftan jobs she puts on over her bathing suit. "Hides my ugly old legs," she explains—to me, to the whole group, doesn't matter who's listening. I don't like it when Connie badmouths herself like that. For a bull-headed woman, she keeps on surprising me. Cocky about some stuff, most stuff, but down on herself. Hates getting old.

"Got no truck with getting old," she says.

But my line's always the same. "Best looking legs in the whole complex," I tell her.

Then she frowns, puffing on her cigarette like a small chimney with a mighty strong updraft. "Knock-kneed," she answers.

"You mean knuckle-headed," I tell her. But now she's standing up, collecting her beach bag. I look at my watch, 11 o'clock on the button. Woman's got an alarm clock for a brain.

She won't wear that nice little Hamilton watch I gave her last year, when she turned sixty-eight. Not down to the pool she won't—she kept forgetting and jumping in the water with the thing still on her wrist. She's taken it to Crandall's Jewelers over to the Mall at least three times. She cried that last time and told me, "I'm getting senile, Joe." I hugged her and she didn't pull away, she just crouched there for a spell.

I try and get Connie to see she just does everything too fast. Anyone make a bet with her that it's too cold to swim that day—and *bingo*! Off she goes. Jumps right into that swimming pool. Even in January, water must've been forty-two degrees.

Everyone sitting by the pool cheered, even the Bromfel twins pursed up with a big smile. Peg Gates put down that crochet stuff she works on day and night, Harold waved his cane. Wally let out a rebel yell, and old man Ransom cackled. "Can't keep a good woman down!" He surely does get a kick out of Connie. All the guys here are crazy about her, the younger fellows come over and sweet-talk her just as much as the old gomers. Makes me proud, and Connie, she loves it.

"Life of the party," I tell her. She pretends she isn't tickled, tosses her head, runs a hand through her hair, softest hair I ever touched. Color of old pewter.

"Somebody's got to jazz this place up," she says. She stares across the pool at the young radio announcer and his new girlfriend. All we can see are their bronze backs, slick with Coppertone, and two heads close together on the beach towel.

* * *

"TIME FOR THE MAIL," she's saying. "Maybe there's something from Thalia." She turns to go, I usually give her a tap on the fanny, still as tight and round under the striped caftan as a young girl's. Rest of her too pretty much, Connie's kept in shape. Still does her exercises every morning. Turns on the news and starts in. Does everything on schedule, or better yet, couple hours ahead of time.

"What's the big hurry?" I keep asking her.

"Don't like shiftless no-account people," she answers, light gone from those green eyes. I don't want to mess with her when she gets to looking like that. My job's to keep her laughing, shine her up so she keeps on sparkling. Do a pretty fair job. She told me I'm the first guy she ever took up with who can kid her right out of being cranky. And the only man she's ever known works as hard as she does. She comes over to my apartment in Building A once a week, Thursday mornings, to give me a hand with the cleaning. But I get it all shipshape before she even sets foot in there, it's like a running gag with the two of us.

"Beat me to it again, you old so and so!" she cries. And we go out on my balcony and sit there for a spell, with our second cup of coffee. Till it's time to head on down to the pool.

"Hey, Connie," I say in a low voice.

She doesn't answer. Her eyes are closed, but she stretches a little and there's a softening around her mouth.

"You looking mighty pretty this morning," I whisper.

"Oh, hush your face," she says, trying to sound cross. I watch her left hand, I know what she's going to do next. Sure enough, she's reaching down for her little flowered beach bag she totes around everywhere, she's pulling out her compact. She studies her face, puts on a little lipstick, frowns. Now she wedges the bag under her elbow.

"Elephant wrinkles," she's saying, and closes her eyes again. "Wrinkled, knock-kneed, and pop-eyed. You need glasses, Joe!" but all of a sudden, she's smiling and looking straight at me, eyes a clear young green. When Connie smiles, her eyes remind me of smooth green stones, the kind you find washed up on the beach once in a while.

I try and get Connie to drive out to the ocean now and then, walk along the sand, hunt for shells. My wife Frances used to love walking on the beach, even that last year when she was so bad, we used to drive to the jetty on Sunday evenings. Just sit there early evening, after the crowds had gone home, sit in the car and listen to the waves.

But Connie, she doesn't like the beach. "Ocean makes me sad," she says. I don't ask her why, I don't know if it reminds her of Frances or what. My land, Connie was so good to Frances back then. She was always bringing over some little old thing she cooked up, things Frances loved, like lima beans and rice or chicken à la king. Towards the end, all she brought was mocha ice cream. She and Fran were best friends, and when Frances died, Connie took it real hard. She didn't come to the pool for weeks, neither did I. I guess I have Connie's daughter to thank for the fact we got together, both widowed, both lonely. Thalia wrote her mama to ask me over for a drink, "two of you moping in your apartments, doesn't seem right." Connie showed me the letter, months later.

Connie listens to Thalia, practically the only person the fool woman does pay any attention to. Good thing, I guess. Thalia's an educated gal, college graduate. Like my Frances was. Between the two of them, they must've skimmed off more B.A.s, Ph.D.s and XYZs than a whole ladleful of alphabet soup. My wife Frances could have been a doctor, but then she met me. And her daddy wouldn't pay any more med school bills. And that was the end of that. Instead, she came to work at the Navy Base, ended up running the payroll department. Smart woman, my Frances, a real lady. "Fallen in love with a flashy uniform!" her daddy yelled at her, well, she stayed in love after the uniform came off and I opened the deli over on West Shore. Never could figure out what she saw in me, all I know for sure is she loved Connie. Me too. Sometimes I wonder if she and Connie hatched up this whole thing. Fran knew I always had an eye for a good-looking woman.

But that's not the way those two operated, strong-minded women, you bet. Bossed the hell out of me, for sure. But not slippery, not like Thalia.

Thalia flies down to Florida twice a year, it takes this place a month to recover. She ties the whole joint up in knots. I can't get a handle on how, exactly. Well, for starters she's one beautiful woman, built like her ma, small-boned, gorgeous legs, tiny waist and those fine green eyes. She's a looker all right, Thalia, hair's the color Connie's used to be before we met, and in the sunlight, stuff looks like black ink spilling over her pretty shoulders, down that strong back of hers. Thalia teaches yoga for a living these days. "Smart as a whip, that girl," Connie claims. Smart as a whip maybe, but Thalia seems to work hard at flunking what she calls "life experiences." Can't seem to hold a job worth a damn. Way it looks to me, every time that girl gets fired, she hotfoots it off and lands another fool degree or another man, usually a deadbeat.

"Thalia's into self-fulfillment, she says she's realizing her full potential," Connie tells us, waving the letter. Nobody says much. Everyone takes turns down here bragging about their kids, so the rule is just set back and listen up real good. Not our own pasts we talk about, no, it's our children's present, their future. I don't say a word, me and Fran never were able to have us any kids.

Far as I can figure it, Thalia's fulfilled herself right through two husbands, half a dozen lovers, and into some kind of mess with the IRS boys. It's fouled up to a fare-thee-well. Connie's got a lawyer, a pal of Harold's, working on it. Harold's a helluva good bird, high-type fellow. Don't talk much, but he's always got a little twinkle in his eye, even on his bad days. Harold's got angina something fierce, but he still handles a few probate cases now and then. Nothing as screwy as this IRS thing of Thalia's.

I don't say nothing, none of my business. Anyhow, no way on God's green earth would I criticize Thalia in front of Connie, she'd take my fool head off. She's still not speaking to Mrs. Barsini over in Building C. All poor Barsini did was say something like, "That cute daughter of yours, for a psychology major she sure seems to have lots of trouble with people."

Whooeee! Fur really flew then, old Connie looked mean as a cornered alley cat. "Least my daughter's not on food stamps," she said good and loud.

Then she got up out of her lounge chair and stalked across the courtyard.

No one said boo. Old man Ransom just sat there chucking peanuts to the squirrels. I kept on looking up at Con's apartment, but she didn't come out on her balcony. The bunch of us sat quiet, Mrs. Barsini wiped her eyes, Peg Gates kept on crocheting, Harold didn't look up from his book. The Bromfel twins picked up their crossword puzzles and started printing in the answers. Plain funny them two gals, remind me of a pair of matched book ends. Finally, Wally broke the silence, Wally's always half tight by 4:00. He brings his drink down to the pool in a coffee mug, he starts up at high noon. His wife Helen comes home from work at 5:00 sharp, so old Wally's got his work cut out for him.

He looks around at us in that sly, kind of round-shouldered way of his, eyes jumping like fleas from one face to the next. "Reckon it's time for another cup, folks. Anybody join me?" And he stood up, sucked in his gut. That was our signal, we all broke for cover then, scattering like a mess of pigeons to "fix supper" or "write some letters" or "go check the dryer, been in a half hour."

No sir, I wouldn't badmouth Thalia for all the tea in China. Anyhow, she's the closest I'll ever get to having my own kid, trouble or no trouble. Last time she was here for a visit, must have been back in May, Connie cooked and scrubbed that apartment of hers which never gets dirty to begin with. She must have fussed up there a good two weeks, freezing enough chow for a squadron.

Course then Thalia won't eat but a thimbleful. "Dieting, Mother. Really!" she drawls. And then turns her head real slow to look at me, sitting there scooping up clam dip by the fistful. And she smiles. When Thalia gives me one of those soul-searching, man-eating smiles, I'm here to tell you I go on red alert. Here's trouble, I'm thinking, heart's like to thump clean out of the old rib cage.

"Tell me, Joe," she says. She stops, she's got this little half smile on her lips, wettest looking lips I ever saw on any one human individual. Big full mouth always moving this way and that like she's fixing to soul kiss you any moment. Makes a man jittery as hell, every guy she talks to downstairs can't keep his eyes off that mouth. Hardly ever can hear what she's saying, confusing because she looks like she's either putting a spell on you or talking dirty talk. Probably both. Words she uses might as well be Hindustani.

"...think Mother has an oral fixation, all this smoking, emphasis on food, never went through the anal retentive stage..."

Well, shoot, it's dirty talk after all. I just nod, smile a good old boy smile, slurp down some more chips. Connie bustles over, tries to get Thalia to eat. "You're just skin and bones, sugar," she tells Thalia.

But Thalia, she lifts one dark eyebrow, stretches her legs out, does little twisty things with her ankles, back and forth, bare feet pointed out straight. She's got long thin toes that look like if they were just a mite longer, she could hang upside down from that big palm outside, just swaying—

"Joe, you fixing to go to sleep here?" Connie's asking me. "Before the party even starts? We got work to do, buster!"

I stand up, move toward the kitchen, away from Thalia's line of sight. "What else to go downstairs?" I ask.

Downstairs the lamps in the courtyard have colored paper over them so the whole place seems full of spooky shadows like some kind of jungle clearing I don't recognize anymore, and I lose my bearings as I steer around the pool toward the Florida room. Hit my knee a good one against one of those big tubs of flowers, poinsettias, blood red under the Chinese lanterns.

Connie takes my arm. "Had yourself one scotch too many up there, sugar," she says, laughing.

Thalia glides beside us. As we walk into the party, people step aside, staring at her. Most of them know her from other visits, but as always, she makes waves. Even in crowded stores over to the Mall, folks turn and watch her. Maybe it's those yoga lessons, but Thalia moves as if she's floating half off the ground, and her green eyes slide from one face to the next. When she stares straight at me, I grin, wave my glass, and glance away toward the swimming pool. The lights are on at the deep end, and I see that the water's the same color as Thalia's eyes, greener than green water, lapping against the sides of the pool like some kind of witch's brew, not just recycled chlorine.

First folks I talk to are Wally and his wife. Wally's wobbling back and forth and a little bourbon slops on his red slacks, Wally's quite a dresser. Wife Helen loves bright colors, Wally wears them without a peep. Called peace at any price. Helen's a nice woman with a big Mrs. Santa Claus smile she wears day after day though sometimes I wonder what old Wally's up against living with someone so everlovin' patient. Poor Wally, she'd drive me to the funny farm for sure.

We shoot the breeze. Helen works at the Navy Base so she always gives me the lowdown on folks my wife Frances used to know.

I decide to get a little buzz on. Connie and I usually limit ourselves to two drinks weeknights, three on weekends, but this whole arrangement gets shot to kingdom-come when Thalia visits, all bets are off then. We take our bottle down to the Florida room, and the sky's the limit. In fact, when Thalia floats in to our Saturday shindigs, everybody acts juiced up, even the Bromfel sisters and I know for a fact they never touched a drop in their whole lives. Two old maid Baptist schoolteachers like them?

I can see the two of them standing over there by the cut glass punch bowl they always bring down each Saturday, filled with some kind of cranberry juice concoction which each twin scarfs back steadily, cup by cup. They're sure giving Thalia the old fish eye, peering down at her, their eyes bright, cheeks red as crabapples. Tallest two women I ever saw, they tower over the rest of us, close to six feet. Look like a couple of herons, those two, and I'm always surprised to see 'em standing on both legs. They seem to be having themselves some kind of dust-up with Thalia who of course is doing all the talking.

When Thalia talks, she waves her arms like Connie. But she goes about it in...slow...motion, and I try real hard to avoid eyeing those long white arms looping around for all the world like they's a couple albino snakes. Instead I move in closer and watch the Bromfels. Thalia's talking in that sweet voice of hers, pitched so low it makes folks lean forward to catch the words.

"Crucial to have a heterogeneous mix," she's saying.

The twins stare down at her.

"Say what?" I put in, you can't let Thalia get away with this stuff.

She turns, smiles her full bore smile when she sees it's me. Her teeth are a beautiful white but very small, almost pointed, and I'm reminded of a baby shark I fished up once off the causeway, back in my fishing days. Threw that sucker right back I can tell ya.

"Greetings, Joe honey," she says. "I was just saying little kids really ought to be allowed in the pool. You folks need it. Give you all a different perspective."

Hilda Bromfel draws herself up. Uh oh. Then she says to Thalia, staring over Thalia's head by a good foot, "We get plenty of perspective, thank you kindly. The little monsters can swim on weekends."

Her twin puts in her two cents. "We don't like the noise. All that splashing."

"The shouting," Hilda adds.

"The horsing around."

At this point, Wally's standing at my elbow. "You got yourself a good i-dee-ah, Miss Thalia," he tells her. "All my grandchillun like to cry their eyes out they want to swim on weekdays so bad. We ought to change the rules, seems to me." He looks around, eyes glazed, spots Harold. Harold's head of the Tenants Committee. "Hey, Harold," he waves with his glass, dripping a little more bourbon, "gotta pick them legal brains of yours."

Harold comes over. So does Connie. She's got antennae about this kind of thing, not as if it hadn't gone on before. She stands beside Thalia, they link arms and wait. Harold smiles, he likes Thalia ever since she told him this idea of propping his bed up on blocks for his angina. Claims he's been sleeping better ever since. "Owe it all to your fine daughter, Con," he says at least a couple of times a week, down by the pool.

So there we are, all standing in this circle, and Wally's glaring at the Bromfel sisters, Connie's glaring at everyone in general while Harold's looking back and forth at the four of them, and Thalia's making her hetero-shmetero pitch, and pretty soon Helen trots over and then a couple of the other tenants and what we got ourselves is a situation. Connie's eyes are getting that hard look, so I keep my trap shut. No way am I taking sides in this deal.

Voices getting louder now but old man Ransom's still snoozing over by the bar. I see Peg Gates sitting beside the door, working on her crochet, but her eyes are on her Jack. Jack's joined our group, and I figure old Peg's recalling the time Thalia organized the costume party a couple of Halloweens ago. We were supposed to come as our screen heroes so Jack comes in blackface, dressed in a chauffeur's cap and shiny black boots, I guess the chauffeur guy in *Driving Miss Daisy*. Well, sure enough, Miss Thalia decided to teach Jack how to do some rap dancing, and Jack threw his back out for six weeks and there was hell to pay. Don't have us too many dances since then.

Now Thalia's got the floor again and the men all stop and listen to her, leaning forward on the balls of their feet. Connie's eyes shine, and she keeps patting Thalia on the shoulder. Outside by the pool a little breeze has come up and the Chinese lanterns rock a little, a nice cradle-type rocking. Thalia's voice goes on and on, low, sexy, sweet as ice cream. She's talking now about tenants' rights. "Find yourself a good lawyer," she ends up. "You're being exploited."

Connie's nodding proudly. "Thalia's right. It's sink or swim. Remember our petition drive?"

Hilda Bromfel sniffs. "Lot of good that did us! They raised the rent two months later."

Jack Gates sneaks a quick look at Peg over by the door, then says in a confidential voice, "Come on, Hilda! Rent's raised every six months no matter what. Where you been, gal?" And he's giving Thalia his big old salesman grin. Thalia nods and turns her highbeams on him. Jack freezes, looking foolish as a pole-axed fawn, eyes wide, almost startled.

"I'll thank you to remember my sister and I've resided here a good many more years than you, Jack Gates," Hilda tells him. Her neck sort of stretches out longer than ever, bad sign when Hilda gets swole up like that. Then she turns on me. "Joe," she starts in. I figure I know what's coming so I take a quick slug of scotch. It's like being back in the fifth grade again, the whole class waiting for me to give the answer. "Now Joe," she's saying, "Exploitation— that's Yankee talk. What in heaven's name would Frances say?"

Minute she mentions Fran's name, the whole room goes quiet. Hilda's broken the rules. I glance over at Connie, she's not looking at me, bless her heart. But Thalia starts to wade in, green eyes blazing, so I hold up my hand like a traffic cop. "Easy on," I say, and I'm talking to Thalia and Hilda both. "Frances had no truck with bullies. We do what we have to do, Fran always said. And," I add, "that's plenty good enough for me."

Nobody says a word for a minute, Connie's smiling at me, tickled, I can tell. Thalia has this funny look in her eyes, like she really notices me for the very first time, not just a guy she's got to vamp, but a *person*. And Hilda— well, Hilda has the grace to look a mite embarrassed.

Wally mumbles, "Shay, Hilda, what you need's a good belt, cure what ails you, your sister too."

Harold smiles, then everyone's smiling. Connie starts in fussing about the new manager letting the whole place go to seed. The Bromfels rear up again, but now they're switching sides, teaming up with the opposition.

"Dumpster's a disgrace."

"You ought to see the laundry room."

"Had to call the po-lice twice last week about that couple upstairs."

Their voices rise. Thalia stands watching them, and she runs her tongue over her bottom lip, something her mother does too, and I look at them standing there arm in arm, standing so straight like young ensigns, and I can see again what Connie must have looked like when she was young. And maybe it's this weird orange light, but Connie's cheeks look plumped out smooth and you can hardly see a single wrinkle except the big vertical one between her eyes. And those green eyes the two of them got, hell, they look more like sisters right now than the Bromfel twins.

So I walk over and take each one by the arm and they both give me a little welcome nudge. "Time for your beauty sleep, gals," I tell them. Thalia actually giggles.

But Wally allows how we need one more for the road, and Hilda waggles one finger, looking strict. "You can't leave now, Connie. This is important!" And then Jack Gates adds, "Stick around, toots," leering at both Connie and Thalia, so they both smile back automatically. Connie's not a bit jealous. She gets all the attention when Thalia's not around, and I reckon she figures it's all reflected glory, bouncing right back on her when all the men shine up to her daughter. If it don't bother Connie none, then it sure don't bother me.

Harold's leaning real heavy on his cane like he's plumb wore out, but he rolls his eyes at me, gives me the old boy wink. I know what he's thinking, he'll be hearing about this for weeks down by the pool, and right now all he wants is to lay himself down in that Thalia-tilted bed of his and play hide and seek with the old angina.

What with one thing and another, we don't clear out of there till almost one-thirty. Jack Gates bets Connie she won't take a midnight swim, and course Con jumps in, clothes and all. And then Wally pushes in Thalia, and the manager comes stomping out, claims folks complaining in Building C, and the Bromfel girls light into him about how this wasn't no women's dormitory. So Harold has to step right in and do some smooth talking.

Connie asks me in for a nightcap. Tomorrow Thalia's heading back to New York. We have a couple rounds of Southern Comfort, Thalia's last day, and each of us celebrating this fact for different reasons. Finally about three a.m., we all hit the sack.

The next morning Connie and I don't get back from the airport till almost ten-thirty. Everyone's already down there by the pool, heads together, talking up a storm. They're hatching an agenda, they say, and Harold's sitting at the table under the beach umbrella, cane parked by his chair, taking down every word, eyes twinkling. He don't look so tired today. Everybody starts in telling Connie what a beautiful daughter she's got herself, so intelligent, always such wonderful ideas. "She's deep, that child," Peg Gates sums it all up, real nice considering Peg's the deep one in our group. She just goes on crocheting month in, month out, and when she finally says something, we listen up good.

Connie sits there in her floppy hat, smoking and soaking up the compliments like it's warm Florida sunshine. She looks almost feverish, little spots of color on her cheeks and she never wears rouge. "Bad for old skin," she tells me.

I glance around the circle. Everybody's mighty keyed up, not like our usual Sunday hangovers. Even Harold seems real chipper, angina must not have caught him after all. The Bromfels are hunched over the Tenant contract, arguing with Wally about some of the legal lingo. Peg Gates changes crochet needles, hums a little tune as Jack paces back and forth beside the pool, shaking his head impatiently. "We gotta be up front, y'all! No pussy-footin'!" Connie's bossing everybody right and left, green eyes glittering.

So I'm thinking it's like the whole bunch of us—not just Connie—we're running a high fever. I feel sorta homesick all of a sudden, homesick for my Frances. She studied to be a doc, she would answer my question—always the same one each time Miss Thalia leaves. What exactly we dealing with here—infection? Or a transfusion? That durn girl—is she good for us? Or what? Beats me.

Hot out here by the pool, coming onto high noon. Now old man Ransom's getting out his bag of peanuts, and sure enough, here come the squirrels out from under the old gardenia bush.

He loops a couple peanuts over to them. They sit up on their hind quarters, sharp little claws tearing at the shells, beady eyes flicking back and forth. Old man Ransom's throwing another handful of nuts, he throws too hard and they land smack dab in the swimming pool. The squirrels look back at the bag he's holding, then over at the nuts floating in the water. The way they sit so still, they could be studying just how fast them ripples spread.

ONE DOWN, FOUR ACROSS

HE HAD BEEN MARRIED once before, very briefly, but we never knew a thing about the first wife.

"It didn't work out" was the way he described that first marriage—the official version, bland, non-informative. The same version given by his business colleagues. Or by people who had known him back in Kansas in the old days. Like any good philanthropist, Donald recognizes the value of good P.R. And why not? He can afford the best. Donald Dalrymple plays to win.

Whatever the marriage had or had not been, however, the imprint of that first wife is still faintly visible, smoothed over by time and the tides of good fortune that have befallen him. But still there, still a hollowed indentation, an irregularity in the smooth shoreline of his life—and Julia's—that now and then Rick and I wonder about in a casual kind of way. I do anyhow. Rick moreorless buys the company version. But then Rick's a company man. He belongs to Donald.

Just as I belong to Donald's wife. His second wife. Julia is my best friend. She's also a Midwesterner, from Iowa. And like Donald she never dwells on the past. Today is the very first time she's ever even referred to that earlier marriage. And the way it comes up is almost by accident, a casual remark she simply lets slip, probably sorry the moment she said it. After all, she knows me very well. We've been sitting here on the couch—raw silk, pure white, very expensive—thinking hard, trying to work out the name of the poet who wrote the lines *liquefaction of her clothes*. Thirteen spaces and we're both stumped. Momentarily.

"Of course!" I say. "It's that Herrick thing, how's it go? *Upon Julia's clothes*, I think, something like that. You know, Robert Herrick's '*Whereas in silks my Julia goes/* Then something/something *how sweetly flowes/That liquefaction of her clothes.*' Lovely, actually."

Julia writes it down. "It fits," she says triumphantly. Then out of the blue she tells me—with a quick laugh—that Donald's first wife had also been named Julia.

"She was? How totally weird," I say. And wonder why she's never told me this before. We're waiting for the men to come back from the country club. They play doubles every weekend together, starting promptly at noon Fridays. "One of the perks," Donald told Rick when he hired him twenty-five years ago, "of being my senior partner."

So, just as regularly every Friday afternoon, Julia and I get together to plan the weekend round of beach parties. Or maybe a barbecue by the pool before the club dance. The guys will be home from the tournament soon, bursting in, eager as teenagers to tell us who won, and to hear what we've cooked up in the way of weekend fun and games. They call us their Management Consultants, sometimes even their CEOs. We know full well that we're only their social directors. Still it's nice, having an impressive title.

"Weird," I repeat. But Julia ignores this and tells me to wait, she's almost done. When Julia does the crossword puzzle, she's like a woman possessed. There's no stopping her despite the fact she's just dropped a bombshell in my lap. After all these years, I know the routine. Long ago when the kids were little, we used to go watch the daddies play, all of us there to cheer them on. But now come August, when the air gets so still, the sun a sullen disk in the sky, we prefer staying home, a wine cooler in one hand and a ballpoint in the other as we work the crossword from last week's Sunday *Times*. This is the ritual. Julia does not want me asking questions, deflecting us from the job at hand. I understand this perfectly.

Now she says lightly, "Not weird, simply a coincidence." She frowns and holds the paper up close. "Ok, a nine-letter word meaning *formerly.*"

Julia's always in charge of the puzzle, she always gets to hold it. I sprawl out on the sofa, careful to kick off my sandals—Julia's house-proud that way—and I try to visualize the empty squares. Except when there's a long quote and then sometimes I ask for a quick look. Too many blank spaces, I go blank as well. Julia's much better at puzzles than I am. I claim it's because she gets to look at the whole thing. But even when I actually hold the paper in my hands, she can still pluck words right out of nowhere, while I fumble, groping for the precise meaning. She calmly insists this is bad strategy.

"Wing it! Don't be so literal," she's always telling me.

In her quiet way, Julia likes to win just as much as her husband does. The big picture. That's what winners can see. No fussy details. No aimless sidetracking or useless speculation. Their vision is bold, clear, single-minded. They can visualize the whole thing, and I do envy them. My problem is I'm always searching for the small perfect stone and missing out on the mosaic's grand design. I guess I'm a miniaturist. Julia says I'm a nitpicker.

And this nit about the first wife, it's a juicy one, I just know it. So I persist. "You've got to admit it is sort of strange. I mean how'd you find out? About you both having the same first name?"

She's chewing on the ballpoint pen. She prefers pens to pencils. This is another source of mild disagreement between us. But I always give in. After all, she's the crossword champion, not me.

"It was hardly a secret, Alison," she says dryly. She stares at me over her glasses. There's amusement in her eyes. But also a warning.

But I choose to ignore it and go on questioning her because I'm intrigued. This same-name business sheds a whole new light on Donald. It opens up a rich vein of romanticism that I never suspected was there. He's a very good-looking guy, Donald, but his eyes are colder than black ice. He's charming in a predatory way, smooth, dangerous. The trouble is Donald doesn't really enjoy women, no matter how beautiful, how intelligent. The adoration he really covets is from men, other successful men—ambitious powerbrokers like he is, committed to winning. He has a way of going blank when a woman speaks to him. His mouth goes still and straight. He jiggles his foot. His eyes wander around the room. Usually he'll toss off some quick rejoinder, then uncross his long legs—black-fleeced—get up and stroll off for another drink, join the men talking about the dual currency bond issues around the wet bar. After all this time I still find Donald intimidating. And yet like a killer shark, so sleek, so supple, he fascinates me.

Julia's gone totally vague. She keeps murmuring, "Hmmmn, I can't remember." Now she's asking, "Who wrote '*Our birth is but a sleep and a forgetting*? Shakespeare?"

I take a long sip of wine cooler. "So what was she like?" I say. "Did Donald ever talk about her? I mean when you two first met?"

"Hang on, Shakespeare fits if I drop the e. Would that be it?"

I don't answer. Two can play at this game.

"Oh come *on*, Allie, we're almost finished here."

Still I'm quiet.

So she shrugs. "Ok, you win. You tell me, I tell you, it's too childish."

Triumphantly, I grin at her. "Wordsworth's who you want there."

She glares at me, scribbles, then puts down the pen. "No, Donald never talked about her. It's like the marriage never even happened. No, that's not right—like a bad investment. I only found out he'd been married earlier from his brother. Inadvertently."

"You're kidding."

"No. It was at a party one night, I guess it was one of our engagement parties. His brother was tight, he was teasing me, and he called me the Second Julia Dalrymple. Like something out of a bad soap opera."

"How mean."

"Not mean, not really. He had no idea Donald hadn't told me. No, not mean, just sloppy. All the Dalrymples get sloppy in their cups. Or haven't you noticed?"

"Well, all Donald ever does is fall asleep."

She stares at me hard. "Precisely," she says exactly the same way Donald will cut short a boring discussion. And she picks up the puzzle again.

Julia's very reticent about sex. All I know is that hers and Donald's sex life is not good. Once a long time ago she said to me almost in wonder, watching how Rick pats me, constantly touches me, "Donald...Donald doesn't know about being tender." More than that she's never been able to articulate. Not to me and I'm her best friend. And I'm positive it's a closed subject with him. Not that Julia and I don't joke about stuff like that. About how Midwesterners are even more uptight than New Englanders when it comes to showing affection in public. No PDA is the Dalrymple family motto. Display what you *feel publicly?* Even holding hands, God forbid!

In Donald's case, I bet there's not even a private display. I bet he's very much of the slam/ bam/thank you /Ma'am school, minus the thank you yet. The rat! This makes me angry for Julia. But she doesn't seem to mind. Julia's not a passionate woman. I think for her it's a happy convenience that Donald's a cold fish. Strange as it seems, I suppose they're actually well-suited. As Rick has said for years, they both have a vested interest in making the marriage work. Julia wanted security. Donald wanted a diplomatic hostess plus a succession of sons. They each kept their side of the bargain. To perfection.

"Still stuck on this nine-letter deal meaning *formerly*," she says.

"*QUONDAM*" I answer.

"Too short. Plus it can't start with a Q. It's the E, the E from seven across, *WEALTHY*."

Donald's very rich. He buys racehorses and hotels and Aegean islands the way the rest of us mortals buy groceries. Not casually exactly. He's much too shrewd to throw his money around. But he buys with a kind of matter of fact, hmnnn, what-do-we-need-this-week attitude. These days he's not as invested in horseflesh as he is in backing hot shot political candidates. The only point of comparison to those satin-skinned thoroughbreds he used to buy down in Virginia or on trips to Ireland is that his candidate has to be a come-from-behind winner in order to excite his checkbook. Also they must have good track records on nuclear disarmament and a solid commitment to the farm lobby. Disarmament is his sop to Julia. The farm question is Donald's way of not forgetting his Midwestern origins and how the Dalrymples made their fortune manufacturing the big tractors that replaced draft animals, those massively lovely Belgians and Clydesdales. Perhaps I'm a romantic, but I like to think their ghosts still haunt Donald—the clip-clopping of those giant feathered hooves.

Now Julia's tapping her front tooth with the ballpoint pen. She squints at the puzzle. "Looks like it's something...*WHILE*," she announces. "Three, no...four blanks *WHILE*."

"*ERSTWHILE*," I tell her.

"Of course." But she winks at me. She knows she can make the quick associations, she's the generalist. But I'm the specialist, the resident egghead, the artist manqué. Rick and I, that's why we came aboard. The Dalrymple Foundation with their corn fed millions—they needed our Ivy League patina, the right contacts with the old boy network, the high gloss of well-bred intellectuals. I mean, Harvard Law School and Radcliffe *Magna Cum Laude*, what do you want? A winning combo from Donald's viewpoint. And the money, the access to power he offered Rick was nothing to sneeze at—which we never have, not in twenty five years.

Gag maybe? Sure. But sneeze? Never.

So all the "literary" subjects are my territory when we do the puzzle. That's why Julia and I are such a good team. We fill in each other's weak spots. Just as when we were raising the children, I was the one who hauled them off to museums, to symphony and the ballet. Julia did the Toll House cookie routine (their cook quit, furious at the mess), Cub Scouts, the private tennis pro. Oh yeah. we're team players for sure, the four of us. A foursome, circling in the deep, me the pilot fish waiting for the scraps. Symbiosis I guess you'd call it. But it's all right. Money can't buy everything, no. But it can buy beauty, beautiful things. They nourish me. They bring me hope. I'm happy...truly!

And Julia?

Julia's happy too, I see. Happy to be reaching the end of the puzzle, so I ask quickly, "You ever meet her?"

"Who?" she mumbles. But she's not really paying attention to me. That's even better. That's when I can slip in the questions so she hardly even notices the prick of the needle. I haven't watched Donald for nothing all these years.

"The first Julia," I answer in a firm voice.

She puts the *Times* down on the coffee table. She glances over at the digital clock on the VCR. "The guys said what time?"

"Not until 6:00. Unless they win, of course." I can feel her attention wandering away, slipping off to the kitchen or the telephone, or any number of distractions by which she manages on a daily basis to evade the truth at various levels.

"Julia," I say sharply. "Did...you...meet?"

"Only once," she answers quietly, but there's a finality to her answer which means I must figure out how to make an end-run around her. Or else this conversation's finished.

So I get up, walk over to the liquor cabinet. "Another cooler?" I ask. And I open two bottles, bring them back to the coffee table.

She has her legs propped up on the table. Julia's legs are nowhere near as beautiful as Donald's. This seems to me a gross inequity. Julia used to be a pretty woman until middle age bloated her figure, and cataracts her clear gray eyes. When you see those swollen eyes behind the glasses, you instantly think of the protruding round eyes of a tarsier—I do anyhow, thanks to Julia and crossword puzzles. You don't even notice her well shaped nose, the delicate curve of the lips. Of course her cheekbones disappeared years ago along with her waistline. This is the fate of the brood mare, I've decided, we Dr. Spock mothers who raised our kids before the era of workouts and personal trainers.

Nevertheless, Julia is still a pleasant looking woman. I wonder again why is it men get even handsomer as they hit their fifties? Maybe it's programmed by Mother Nature. Maybe since women can no longer bear the babies, the men still have to be able to attract egg-bearing females so the race can survive. Biological destiny, so cruel, so inflexible. When the four of us are together, I look at Donald and Rick, tanned from the tennis court—or in winter, the ski slopes—their jaws still firm and strong, their nice coltish long legs. And I suppose that Julia and I might well be taken for their mothers if it weren't for Rick's silver hair, Donald's little bald spot.

"Totally stinketh," I observe, and plop down on the couch again, shoes and all.

"What's that?"

"Getting old."

"We're doing it fairly gracefully, you must admit."

"Not one tenth as gracefully as the men."

"They get to sleepwalk through life, we get to protect them. And it shows." She says this in a half bitter, half joking tone of voice. Scratch the least bit at Julia's lacquer-smooth composure, and you meet a man-hater. Each time this surprises me. She's so gentle on the surface, so accepting and loving. Only with me does she occasionally show the bitterness beneath. And now I know for sure it's safe to go back to my questions.

"The first Julia. Tell me how the two of you met. And why."

She looks down at her own bare legs. She's wearing pale yellow shorts which she should never do. Her ankles are thick. There are networks of lumpy blue veins snaking under the white skin. I'm glad I can still get away with shorts, that my legs are still tanned and slim as the men's. Maybe not my jawline, I'll admit, but the legs still give the guys a run for their money.

I've finally got Julia talking now. She's backtracking, some long boring digression about furnishing the first house. She gazes through the glass doors at the shoreline. Later she and I will take a quick swim, nodding to the young mothers as they gather the kids to trudge back home. A few families linger, but by five o'clock sunburns have started to hurt, the children are cranky, and most of the young daddies would rather unwind at home with a drink and the evening news than come down to the beach. When you live year round by the ocean, you take it for granted after a while—after the children get older and the beach is no longer the world's best babysitter. Fast cars and booze replace sandcastles and playing tag with the waves. The beach becomes simply a place to party; "checking out the action" the kids call it. Children are so fickle. They outgrow their passions so quickly. I guess they learn from us.

"...at the hospital," Julia's saying. It takes Julia a while to get to the nub of a story. With a crossword puzzle she zeroes right in, a hawk to the kill. But when she's telling an anecdote, she circles, she backs and fills, and I tend to tune out until we home in at last on the target.

Which finally she's reached, so I ask her which hospital?

"A state hospital, outside of Topeka. For the criminally insane."

I can't believe I've heard her correctly. "For the *what*?"

But she goes on speaking, ignoring my question. "She sent me a letter. She signed it Julia Dalrymple. That threw me for a moment, I mean *I* was Julia Dalrymple, by then Donald and I had been married for four years. We already had our first baby! She told me she wanted one person to understand. Anyhow, I went to see her, what else could I do?"

I can't think of a rejoinder so I nod encouragingly. For one disloyal split second I wonder if Julia's making this up simply to shut *me* up.

But her face, her hands holding the trembling glass of wine, they show she's telling the truth. They show the backwash of that hospital scene long ago. It seems the First Julia had also married again, and the second husband, like Donald, was also successful and very rich. And also wanted sons. Which she gave him, in quick succession. Two boys in the first three years of marriage. A year's hiatus—and then twins. One afternoon while the husband was away on one of his business trips, she made a batch of brownies for the older boys to have when they came back from school. She also made lemonade which she mixed well with some sort of rat poison. Then she went upstairs to the babies. She drowned them in the bathtub, then lay on the bed and waited for her sleeping pills to take effect. The older kids were dropped off by a neighbor. They came in the kitchen, went directly upstairs to tell their mom they had knocked over and broken the lemonade pitcher—glass all over the kitchen floor—and found their baby brothers. And their mother fast asleep on one of their bunk beds.

Julia stops. She rubs at her eyes. She won't look in my direction.

"But...why? I mean why was she telling you all this?"

Now Julia glances over at me. She picks up the crossword puzzle and fills in the blanks with firm strokes, block capitals as square and dependable as she is. Then she looks up at me again and smiles. She speaks softly.

"She only told me what I already knew."

And now I hear the Mercedes crunching on the gravel outside. The horn gives three happy toots. That means they've won the first round of the tournament, that we're in for a long night of celebrating.

"Go on," I say quickly, although we both have sat bolt upright at the sound of the car, like naughty children getting ready for the teacher's return.

"She said she wanted to...to warn me."

"About what though? About Donald?"

"No. Nothing was said about Donald. They parted amiably enough, you see. There was no big mystery there at all. They were simply incompatible. She just—she couldn't seem to conceive, I guess. So after a year or so, they got the divorce. I can't remember on what grounds specifically, but it was common knowledge back then. She remarried. He remarried."

The men are coming up the veranda steps out back. They're laughing, they're ripe for victory parties—have us call up the Trents next door, the Randalls, cook lobsters, everybody get smashed. We can hear the pantry door swing open. Good, they're going to stop and get some ice.

"Quick!" I say to Julia.

She's looking at the graceful arched doorway of the family room, listening to the crash of ice trays being emptied into the teak ice-bucket. Lots of laughing going on out there. They sound three sheets to the wind before they even get started. Winning does that to people, I've noticed. They seem to get louder, to swell with sound.

Julia puts one finger to her lips. I think she means to shush me, to keep quiet. But then I realize she must be copying that first Julia, her face looks younger, vulnerable, the eyes behind the thick lenses are dreamy, pupils like dark tunnels that never end—dark, so dark. Hush, she's speaking:

"*Be careful!* was all she told me. *Be careful...they hate us.* And then she sort of dozed off, and the attendant said I'd better leave, she was heavily medicated."

I try to see the picture. But the face on the hospital bed is blurred. So I ask my last important question just as the men walk through the archway, slapping their racquets against furry legs and talking a mile a minute about tomorrow's match.

"Was she beautiful?" I whisper anxiously, afraid that Julia's going to leave out the core, the beating heart of this whole damn story.

Julia is beaming at our husbands, and now she's getting up with that gentle rich laugh of hers which she uses like some sort of rare unguent to smooth over the chapped places.

All she says to me curtly is "Yes, she was beautiful. Is that all you care about? Does that make it any better?"

And then she's walking toward the men, moving with the surefooted poise of the professional diplomat negotiating a difficult ceasefire.

Rick's gone over to the bar to fix drinks. But Donald is staring at Julia. He stands very still except for the quick jiggling of the tennis racquet against his calf. He's watching her glide towards him. And now I understand why his face always goes blank when he looks at women. It's the silken mask he wears to preserve that smooth surface the world admires. But the hollowed pockmarks beneath the mask, these are the pitted places known only by the wife. And no one else.

He smiles at Julia. Even from where I'm sitting here on the sofa I can see—yes, I can see it clearly now, the faint tremble of his left eyelid as he watches her move in on him.

"Darling," she's saying in her most loving voice. "So tell us. Did you win?"

PLEASE WAIT

"ELLA?"

No answer; she just twitches again. Then she pushes the sheet away from her face.

"Wake up," I tell her.

Now she's moaning. I put my arm across her, trying to pull her in close. Her whole body's quivering—she pushes away my hand.

"Wait," she says in that sleep-thick voice of hers. "Please wait!" She's still not awake yet.

"You're dreaming, Ella. Roll on over now." I try to ease her over on her side, but she moans again. She's lying on her back, both arms under the sheet, stiff as pokers. She plants her hands deep into the mattress. Her fingers make scrabbling sounds.

I can hear her panting as if she's been running. But I know it's not running she's been doing in her sleep; most likely she's been flying again. Why can't she just have ordinary dreams? Better yet, not dream at all, like me. I hit the sack, turn around, and it's daylight.

"But that's so boring, Wayne," she tells me.

"How can a person get bored sound asleep?" I keep asking her.

But she clams up. She doesn't like it when I go and get logical on her. Women never do, far as I can make out. The way their minds work, it's a mystery to me. And Ella—I don't know what makes her tick any more now than I did four years ago. She's like this gift that just fell into my lap one day out of the blue; I never asked for it. Why me? I wonder. She claims it's because she knew right off I'd make a good daddy. "That's a compliment, sugar," she adds quickly.

"Glad we got *that* straight," I say.

At breakfast she looks up from her coffee. She's already dressed for work. "Wayne," she says. Her eyes look blurred, like she's had herself a good cry, but that's the way they always look after a hard-dreaming night. She tells me she cries inside while she's asleep. "Not real tears," she says.

So in between bites of corn muffin, I say, "Not real crying then."

"Feels like crying all the same," she says.

We go around in circles this way, makes no sense, but we play by her ground rules. She taught me how, starting when we met. Nobody knew her kin, where she came from. She just drifted into town one morning on a cold October day, took a room at Mrs. Barlow's guesthouse over on Elm, got herself a job. She didn't talk like a Midwesterner, or a Yankee either, for that matter. She didn't have any kind of accent, not to my ear.

Fact is, Ella doesn't talk much period, and never about her past. Mike says people at the diner love her. "She got a listening look to her," is the way Joe explains it. Like she's studying folks with her eyes, studying the same way a deaf person reads lips—and all conversation, you might say, is understood by shape, not sound. Her dreams? That's different. Those she talks about. But only with me. That's the way we start off each morning. Sometimes she's scared. Sometimes I am.

"You know, Wayne," she's saying now. "Like the thump a caterpillar makes when it lands?"

I nod, sip my coffee, look first at her then out the window at the drizzle coming down. It's that fine misty rain we all pray for after seeding time.

She's describing the boat dream. She's below deck in a small cabin. The lock jams on the cabin door. She stares out the porthole at the black ocean rising and sinking beyond the little pane of glass. Then the window begins to lift up. The hinges squeak. The ocean's blotted out.

And now moving slow, an inch at a time, something comes lumping through the porthole. It's looking for Ella—not with its eyes though, but with its tongue. She can hear the soft swish as the scales slide across the metal fittings of the porthole. And then that soft loose thump as it lands on the cabin floor and the doorknob's slippery in her hand, but she can't...

"...can't scream," she says quietly. "Or get away."

We sit in silence for a spell. I reach across the table and put my hand over hers; she's trembling.

I start talking in a low voice, tell her it's ok, it's all over, sugar, just a dream. Tell her to think about the baby coming and all those youngsters we're fixing to raise, that new combine we're saving for, our next trip to Padre Island come December. Her hand stops trembling.

She loves it down on Padre Island. Down there she sleeps like an angel. Lies out by the ocean, soaking up sunshine like she can't ever get enough of it. At night, no matter how hot it gets or how sticky it might be lying there on those fancy hotel sheets, she twines around me like she's never going to let me go.

"We got it real good, Ella," I tell her, and hot damn, she's smiling for the first time this morning, her violet eyes all soft-looking, and I'm thinking of all the gals I ever knew, Ella beats them all, hands down. Not just in the sack,

Barbara Leith

either. But the whole package—sweet-tempered, spoils me rotten, helps out with chores, works like a field hand even though she's still waitressing part-time.

We've been married four years now and I've never once looked at another woman. Not that they don't keep trying. Still give me the glad eye when I run into town to the feed store or over to Mel's Hardware. The problem is me having been stud duck around here too long—my buddies damn near dropped dead in their tracks when Ella cut me out from the herd this late in the game.

"More coffee?" she's asking. I shove over my cup, grin. I took a fair amount of ribbing back then. Little wisp of a gal, eighteen years old, blows into Mt. Hope one day, comes to work at the Blue Willow diner and *zingo!* she's got me tied around her little finger first time I slide into the booth and see her standing there in that blue-checkered uniform, violet eyes staring at me so hard, like she's learning me by heart.

Two months later we set the tongues to wagging, "Land sakes, not even a church wedding!" We drove the old red pickup over to Sedgwick County seat and found us a Justice of the Peace. He read out the marriage vows as if he was reeling off grain prices. No fuss, he got the job done lickety-split.

All a matter of timing, this business of loving a woman. The apple's ready to fall when it's ready to fall, not a minute sooner. Why shuffle around wasting time when you know some other guy may beat you to it, may be standing right there under the branch with his hands cupped, just waiting.?

"All things come to him who waits," I say now to Ella, not for the first time. We look out at the rain misting down on the little nubbins of winter wheat. They're sprouting so pretty, those pale green blades of seedlings all nestled down for a long winter's nap—if winterkill or leaf rust don't get them first.

"Ought to be a pretty fair yield this year," I add.

"How much?"

"Any luck, top last year's. Say forty-five bushels per acre's my guess."

She smiles. "It's all this good rain. Those babies are thirsty. "

"Hey, sugar." I grab her wrist, but she wriggles away, laughing.

"Not now," she tells me. "I'm running late." And she fusses with the cuffs of her uniform, primps at her hair. Dark smoke-colored hair, and it fans out from her face in a soft cloud.

"Ella," I say. "You *did* give him notice?"

She puts her hands on her hips. Her waist is just a mite thicker, but otherwise she's not showing one bit. She wiggles her hips. "You trust me or not, buster?" she answers. "Mike's as tickled as we are. Keeps on fussing over me. Says I'm staying on my feet too long."

I get up from the table, carry the cups and breakfast plates over to the sink. "Mike's got good sense," I tell her. This is old ground; we've already worked it pretty thoroughly. Ella gets her patient, humor-him look.

"Wayne, honey, I'll be *back* at two."

"Split shift?"

"Not anymore. Not since I told him about the baby. You two like a couple of broody hens." Then she looks at my face and hers softens. She stands on tiptoe, puts her arms around me, kisses me quickly, feather-light on my lips. She smells clean. I touch her hair, so fine it makes me think of silk tassels on an ear of corn. "You keep busy now, you hear?" she says and pulls away. She glances at the dishes in the sink. "I'll do those later."

"The heck you will," I tell her. "This Kitchen-Aid and me, we got ourselves a fine working arrangement."

"Wayne Gilmore," she says, "you're a good man," and then she grabs her purse, blows a kiss, and is out the door.

I get the kitchen chores done in short order, then phone Mel's Hardware for a couple more heat lamps for the brooder house. Nights turning chilly and those hens go on strike when it's not good and warm out there. I sit at the desk, fiddle with the books for a spell, but it's too much setting for one morning so I put on my John Deere cap and go out to the barn.

Spend the rest of the morning messing with the hydraulic pump on the twelve-row cultivator. Thing's brand new and the fool belt drive keeps slipping. I spend more time dickering with machinery or the loan boys down at the bank than I do straight farming. Sometimes I wish I had a good team of mules like my granddaddy. My, how it's all changed, and how I'd like to be out there in the field, straddling the furrows with my boots sinking deep in that rich Kansas dirt, watching the seedlings lap up the rain. Instead of in here, fooling with this idler pulley. I loosen the bolt on the bracket. "Study the problem, son," my daddy used to tell me. "Don't go rushing in. Don't hurt to wait none. Size things up for a spell."

Got the bolt loose—now let's see what's wrong with the little sucker. I pray it's just loose so I don't have to haul over to Hutchinson for a new belt. Here we go, just need to adjust the tension, easy does it.

Rain's coming down harder now, pelting the galvanized roof—the sort of racket that beats on the eardrums. Can't see a thing in here, it's gotten so dark.

I turn on the light over the workbench. After all the dimness, the bright bulb makes me blink. I wriggle the belt back and forth; she's holding nice and taut now.

I look up. Something skitters behind those hay bales in the corner over there. I listen. Just a couple of barn cats chasing mice behind the semi-retired

John Deere. Ella loves that old tractor. Only ever use it for disk harrowing anymore. Ella learned to plow that first year, sitting up there as if she'd been plowing her whole life.

I tighten up the bracket bolts; pump's going to work just fine now.

I was proud how fast Ella caught the hang of it, farms being new to her and all. Said she'd never set foot on one till she hit Mt. Hope. Wherever she was raised, though, she's got a real feel for mechanical things. She can run anything on this place. She's got a light hand with a piece of machinery, and this—to my way of thinking—is a mighty fine thing in a woman.

One of the barn cats comes hightailing toward me out of the shadows. I straighten up. The cat crouches. She got a wild eye on her. Got herself a new batch of kittens out there and she won't let anybody near them. Half crazy these mama cats, but they get the job done in the mouse department. All they want is a safe place to have their babies. In a few months they take off again, maybe back to whatever wild world they come from, maybe to the tom, who knows?

Cat's staring at me. Her back is arched up. She lifts her top lip and hisses. Her eyes glow a dangerous green. I step forward. With a little snarl, she changes gears, slinks off past the old stall where we used to keep the pony when I was a kid.

I walk on over to the combine. She's jacked up on blocks so I can get at the reel. Ella says the reel reminds her of the old paddle wheels on a Mississippi steamboat. Boats. Planes. Funny how these nightmares of Ella's so many of them set in some sort of vehicle.

Broken tooth on the sickle bar here, got to put in a new one. So I disconnect the drive arm and pull her out endways.

Ella's plane dream is the closest to being a happy one, I guess. After the plane takes off, she describes how she breaks free. "...flying alone, all by myself then," she says slowly. Her eyes get big. The pupils dilate, twin black holes in a sea of violet. They scare me.

Fool rivets all driven out now, so I go back to the workbench and grab a new tooth. The steel's cold in my hand. Thing's got a real heft to it, triangular-shaped like some giant shark's tooth that can slice a man's arm off faster than a knife going through soft butter. I remember when Neil Swenson's kid lost his leg working their combine. You can't be too careful with these babies, what with the old sickle bar slicing back and forth—and I can almost see Ella's hand swooping in front of me, zigzagging like a white arrow. Or a summer hawk over the wheat fields, catching those thermals, lazing up and down with the air currents.

"...beyond the sky we know," she whispers.

I pull out the broken tooth, stick in the new one, and start hammering the rivets back in. Have to stand up straight for a second to get the kink out of my back from too much stooping.

That mama cat's growling back there. She's like to have found herself a meal, teaching those babies what hunting's all about.

When Ella gets to the good part of the dream, her voice always drops and goes husky, as if she's talking love-talk. Which she is in a way, flying in that other place. She says she thinks it's another sky, enormous, shaped like a giant wheel. "And there are these red-and-gold worlds, Wayne," she says. "They're spaced out along the wheel and I float in and out of them. Sometimes I land. Sometimes not. The night's all red, too. And my body makes gold streaks as I fly. When I look back, I can see the gold streams of light following me."

I pick up the sickle bar, fit it back in, reconnect the drive arm. When Ella's finished talking, she folds her hands. She's breathing fast. Her cheeks are bright pink and her eyes—they look purple, they look deep as space itself. Scares me when she looks that way. But she's happy. She's fierce with happiness.

That's the part that scares me the most.

Outside, wheels are spitting up gravel. A car door slams. I go to the doorway of the barn. It's Ella. "I'm home, honey!" she calls, and she sticks out her tongue to taste the rain.

* * *

BY THE TIME WE get back from the square dance, the eleven o'clock news has already started. I wait for the weather report. Good, more rain headed our way tomorrow. Eighty percent chance of thunderstorms tonight. Ella fixes us some hot cocoa. I turn off the TV. We sprawl out on the davenport. "Good caller tonight," she says.

"Not half bad," I agree, and polish off the last dregs of chocolate at the bottom of the cup.

She gets up slowly. "Still get mixed up on that zoom-the-diamond call"

"Not as bad as cross-zooming-the-diamond." We both laugh. I put the cups in the dishwasher and we head on upstairs.

She falls asleep before I do. Used to be the other way around until she got pregnant. Now she's asleep thirty seconds after we hit the sack. I read *Farm Journal* for a spell, calculated to make me follow suit in short order. Then I turn off the light.

Listen to Ella breathing deep and the rain pinging off the drainpipe under the eaves. Between the *ping-ping-ping* and Ella's deep exhaling, I feel myself cradled in this warm bed of ours, rocking real safe and slow, and I figure this baby of ours deserves to have himself an old-fashioned cradle, and I'll find me some hard maple...

In the middle of the night, we get some thunder. It makes a fair amount of racket, but Ella doesn't wake up. The room goes bright as daylight when the lightning flashes. I can see her face clearly. She's smiling, so I know she's having herself a good flying dream tonight. She's tracing gold up there in the sky somewhere, that sky dark as the cloud of hair spread across the pillow, ends still wet from the shower she took just before we went to bed. And then it's morning. I wake up with a jerk. The rain's stopped. I put my hand over to Ella and the bed's warm, but she's not there. The pillow still feels damp.

"Ella?" I call.

No answer. I can see her yellow robe still thrown over the end of the bed; her old scuff slippers are parked neatly on the floor. I call again. The house is quiet. It feels like an empty house.

My stomach starts knotting up even before I go check downstairs, check the driveway. The pickup's still there. I can hear the rooster squawking out back of the barn when I throw open the front door. The front walk's a mess of mud, glossy brown. No footprints.

I go back upstairs and stand there looking at the bed. Then I walk over to the windows, pull aside the curtains. I look across the fields, straight across the long curve to the stand of cottonwood by the creek, careful to keep my eyes level to the ground, afraid to look the whole way across to the horizon. To where the land meets the sky.

Downstairs I rustle up some coffee. When it's seven, I call Mike at the diner. "Hey, good buddy," he says.

I can hear the clatter of dishes in the background.

"No," he says. "Don't expect her till eight o'clock." He stops for a moment, yells, "Pipe down out there!" Then he's saying, voice worried, "Ella ok? Been pushing herself too hard, you ask me. She ok, Wayne?"

I shake my head. "She won't be coming in today, Mike."

"Fine, fine," he says. "Fine by me. But what's wrong?"

I look at the round disk of numbers on the dial—it's an old wall phone, black and shiny. The numbers and letters spill around in a circle the way they're supposed to, none of this push-button stuff. I stare at the wheel of numbers, then simply tell him the truth as I know it. "She's away, Mike," I say slowly. "She hasn't come back."

I hang up the phone. And just start in to waiting. Like she told me to.

IN THE HOUSE OF MY FRIENDS

And one shall say unto him, What are these wounds in thine hands?
Then he shall answer, Those with which I was wounded in the
house of my friends.

—Zechariah 13:6

SATURDAY MORNING LABOR DAY weekend they got off to a reasonably early start, but not as early as she hoped. Zack insisted on working in the garden for an hour while Meg packed, cleaned out the fridge, scrubbed the sink, set up the automatic lamp timers in the living room, and for the last half hour impatiently paced the porch; watching his red-checked shirt flicker beyond the rose bushes, then in and around the trellis of tomato plants.

"Almost 8:30!" she called.

"Give me five more minutes, honey. Got to kill off the rest of these darn slugs." Red shirt disappears.

Handmaiden to slugs. Ridiculous.

But finally he finished. About time. He set the pail of drowning slugs at the bottom of the porch steps and looked up at her.

"Quick shower and we're off!" He ran up the stairs, unbuttoning his work shirt.

"I just *know* we're going to get bogged down in all that weekend traffic," she wailed.

She hated departures. In the old days when the children were little, the beginning of every trip was a nightmare. Infinite delays. Kids not dressed decently according to Zack. Mute and sullen, they marched back downstairs for re-inspection. False starts. Halfway down the street someone, usually Meg, remembered something left behind, back to the house. Zack standing in the driveway, drumming his fingers on the hood of the car. The dog escaping. Then the kids all piling out to corral him. By the time they drove away, everyone in the family was hot and furious before their vacation had even begun, and the collie, stressed by all the tension in the car, vomited three miles from home.

Now with the children gone, their getaways were simpler, less chaotic. And a hell of a lot more efficient. But the old discords still echoed in the ritual of these departures, jarring the present so she had to make a concerted effort to pull down the blinds of memory, erase those pictures yet again.

"Car packed?" Zack called from the bathroom.

"Been packed for an hour. Do hurry, sweetie."

"Relax, babes. It's still early and we don't—" but the sound of the shower muffled his voice.

They left at nine-thirty. Hardly any cars on the road on the first leg of the trip, but once they got closer to the Bourne Bridge, the highway became clotted with traffic, the entire population of the east coast off to an early start to the Cape. Early, ha!

She hated trips. Not humane to be trapped here in the death seat, sealed up in this steel cylinder, sealed off from the real world by tightly closed windows, the hum of the air conditioner, the drone of the engine. But at least now she was a believer. In seat belts anyhow.

Meg shifted her legs. The harness cut tightly across her breasts. Our modern hair shirt, made of webbed nylon and buckles. Are we belted in? Are we safe? Are we saved? You bet.

The backs of her thighs were sticking to the seat. She arched upward and the tender bare skin tore away from the slippery plastic like the sudden ripping of a bandage. That's the problem with plastic. Not textured like leather. No texture at all. No holes, no pores, no interstices. Plastic doesn't welcome us. It rebuffs our touch. No smell either. Slick. Fake. And indestructible. This is the world we've built ourselves, a simulacrum. Synthetic bondage.

"The hell with seat belts!" She unbuckled it, kicked off her sandals and propped her feet up on the dash. Nice deep tan on her legs. She flexed her calf muscles. "You got the long smooth muscles of the born swimmer," a coach once told her. Swimming came easy, running came hard. Better a dolphin than a racehorse, straining and sweating.

The backs of her calves were much lighter, hardly tanned at all. A dirty creamish color, a porch tan. Only the front of her body was brown. Striding towards someone, she was a summer person. Retreating, she looked like winter. Pale. A seasonal Janus.

She shifted again, sighed. Boring. Talk to me, Zack.

He glanced over at her bare feet on the dash and smiled. "I won't let the kids put their feet up there, you realize."

"Papal dispensation for the holy mother?" she asked, savouring her own archness.

"Papal phooey! You just got better legs." Mock leer.

"And you got such good taste, Daddy-o."

"Plus one other thing." He grinned sideways at her.

"Oh?" she asked, enjoying their ritual, relishing the litany.

"Plus they don't get ugly when I say feet on the floor, folks."

"Ugly? I couldn't be sweeter. I haven't said word one for the last twenty miles."

"Try cranky then. Last half hour of any trip you get cranky as hell. I can set my watch by you." Brown eyes twinkling, he measured her reaction.

"Not cranky—restless," she said firmly.

"Yeah, you want to be *there*—an hour ago."

"Two hours is long enough…" She paused and cocked her head. "…for any human being to be trapped in a car," he finished for her. They both laughed.

"We were really and truly…" she began. "…meant for each other," he answered.

She moved closer, nuzzled his neck, then slipped her hand down inside the waist band of his jeans. Cool skin. Silken fur of his belly. Lovely.

"No distracting the pilot, lady. Passenger safety comes first."

"Twenty years ago and you would've pulled the car over by now."

"Yep, but the neat thing today is I can just sit back and wait till tonight at Clara's. No highway patrolmen nosing around. No hurry. And a hell of a lot more comfortable."

"And the whole house just listening for every creak."

"We'll be very, very quiet."

"Not as quiet as they'll be. Hey, you know what? that must be why we always get the double bed."

"We do?"

"Zack, don't you ever notice anything? Five summers in a row now."

"You mean you think it's entrapment?"

"Sure. Clara playing games again. Yep—we're always assigned the same guest-room. She puts the others in the twin beds."

"Then I say," his lips twitching into a broad grin, "Clara's being kind."

"Meaning?"

"Meaning always the thoughtful hostess. She knows we enjoy a little poosh-em-up."

"You're kidding, darling. How could she possibly know?" Was he still teasing?

"And *you*, dearest girl, are fishing."

"But really—how does she?"

"That's the sort of thing Clara was born knowing." He chuckled.

She thought about that one for a minute. "Process of elimination, maybe?"

He looked confused, then understood. "Oh, you mean when she rules out Newells and Glassmans—and of course Bill's a bachelor."

"Exactly…so that leaves us."

"Sure does leave us. By default." He shook his head. "But that's not what I meant. You know our Clara. What's she call herself? Professional people-watcher?"

"Hang on a sec. You know darn well it's impossible to tell a thing about what folks are like in the sack. I mean look at Caroline Newell. You'd never have guessed about her—and she and Paul go at it like rabbits."

"So she claims. To you. Hmmmn." He paused, reflecting. "There *is* a certain steamy miasma old Caroline exudes, I suppose."

"But you still were surprised when I told you. You said so."

"Couldn't figure how Paul ever climbed over her fat belly."

"Don't be mean."

"Mean but accurate. The point I'm trying to make here is this: Clara intuits this stuff. It's no accident she gives us the only double guest bed in the whole house. And it's not a trap. It's a kindness, a simple courtesy. She's the queen mother of hostesses, furthermore she's elevated entertaining guests to a holy art."

"You trust her," she said, trying to make her voice neutral.

"You don't?" He shot back, cocking an eyebrow.

"I really don't know. I've never known." She fidgeted with the radio dial.

"Well, I do trust her. Hell, I enjoy her. More than that—I forgive her."

"She's *so* manipulative, Zack."

"But, honey—she manipulates with such relish! She's magical."

"People get hurt though."

"Wait a sec. Has she ever hurt us?" He paused. "Be fair now."

"I'm not sure. "

"Well, I am. She's a wickedly Clever Clara. But she knows it. And she knows we know it. And by me, it's not only all right, it's actually fun." Enough heavy analysis he was saying to her.

Silence.

The highway was clogging up. The closer to the sea, the more cars. Scrub pine. The water tower, tiny ladders going up the silver sides.

They will never know/ I lie here and dream/
visions of a golden man/ who swims a silver stream.
"Baby's smiling in his sleep"!/ I hear them softly say,
while golden man plunges deep/ through dolphin-dappled bay.

More scrub pine. Thickets of wild blueberries. They were almost there.

"Shit!" he said.

"Now what?"

"Is it the first rotary we bear right?"

"No, the second one. Only a couple more miles."

"Five years we been schlepping down here, and I still get mixed up. How does an out-of-stater ever sort out where the hell they're going?"

"Darling, you know directions aren't your long suit."

"You've been telling me that's the case for twenty five years, dearie."

"Only because it's true."

"That's pure bull shit."

"It's not. You've got navigational dyslexia." She was teasing him, trying for that deep chuckle of his which always bound him to her, made her feel secure. But his face had hardened, gone all stony. And once again it was like tip-toeing in a dark but familiar room, sure of where she was going, touching the comfortable surfaces of this chair and that desk, and suddenly smack! Bumping against the sharp edge of an unknown door. Time to turn on the light.

"Come on, honey, you can't be brilliant at absolutely everything. Give the rest of us a chance. Be mortal once in a while."

"Oh Christ," he groaned. "Here it comes. Resurrected. The little tin god routine."

"I haven't said that to you in eons, Zack, get real."

"You still think it."

"Only when you're being a bear."

"So now *I'm* the bad guy."

"Zack, I did not say that!"

"Minding my own business and out of nowhere all of a sudden I'm the heavy."

"This is pointless. Let's just drop it."

"So why keep at it? When you want to fight, there's nothing I can do or say to stop you, Meg. You just keep hammering away."

"Hang on—here's the turn off."

He jerked the wheel, taking the curve of the rotary so fast she had to brace herself against the door jamb, but still not driving recklessly. In his driving he was always temperate. That she could depend on.

They drove over the crest of the hill. Below them the curve of the bay. Crescent Beach. Well named. The water lay glassy and still. No waves here ever.

"Looks like a mud puddle, doesn't it? Big surf's not everyone's bag. Me and you, babes, we're simply spoiled is all. Give me the Outer Banks anytime!"

She pranced her fingers along his arm. His flesh felt smooth, familiar.

"Friends?" she asked him.

"Friends," he smiled. "Long as you behave yourself, that is."

"I'll behave if you shape up, buster!" she said gaily, her heart lifting as they swung into the driveway. The house—four stories high, perched on a sharp rise overlooking the bay—loomed over them.

"Dead ringer for Tony Perkins' house in *Psycho*," Meg said.

"And about as comfortable," he observed.

Meg giggled. Clara loved the house as much for its Spartan discomforts as its prime location. When she and Spencer bought it six years earlier, they had a new boiler installed, re-shingled the roof, replaced porch timbers, and furnished it in early American attic. But otherwise they left it as they found it. The kitchen where guests would mill round—uncertain where to sit, how to help—was small and primitive. A shallow sink, tiny stove, ancient refrigerator, a deeply scratched linoleum-topped table and two chairs. No counter space.

"Spence and I—we truly adore roughing it," Clara always warned her guests who, undaunted, flocked down each year on their appointed weekend, conscious of the status invoked by casually dropping into a conversation that "We're invited by Baylors to stay at their new place on the Cape."

Zack stopped the car. They climbed out, stretched, peered up at the blank windows.

"Looks deserted," he grimaced, and shook his head. "Identical overture, identical dang symphony every single year."

"And the same dang orchestra arriving in exactly the same order—meaning us getting here first. That said, might as well start unloading." She cranked open the back door of the station wagon.

"We got enough food here, Meggy, for a frigging army."

"Well, she expects it you know. One full meal from each guest. Otherwise, we won't eat."

"Except for breakfast," he pointed out.

"Yep, dear Clara's got a thing about 'hearty breakfasts'. Slow torture watching her burn her way through two pounds of bacon. Drives me nuts."

"Don't sweat the small stuff, babes."

The house towered above them as up the steep porch steps they climbed, Meg muttering, "Oh, the agony and the ecstasy of it all, worse than Annapurna."

Zack set down their duffel bags and knocked on the kitchen door.

"Anybody home?" he called.

"Oh, she's never been here when we arrive, dear. You know that."

"And you figure that's a message?"

"Figure it's a pretty peculiar coincidence five years running."

They staggered into the kitchen. Bleak. Barren. The old floor slanted crazily like the floor of a fun house. Or the deck of a ship. Disorienting. They found a note on the table, scrawled in Clara's spikily elegant writing: *Playing tennis. Back at noon. Make yourselves comfortable.*

Wheels crunched on gravel. Meg ran to the tiny window over the sink.

"Gee, that's not the Newell's car!"

"So...maybe she's invited someone else this weekend."

"But we always are here with the Newells and the Glassmans."

He shrugged. "I'm going upstairs and stow away our gear."

"Ok, and I'll start with this food." But she stayed by the window.

Four people were climbing out a shining silver car. Foreign, low-slung and expensive. They turned and gazed blindly up at the house. She pulled back from the window. Oh, God. Oh, Clara, how could you! You bitch. You *must* have done this deliberately.

She stood holding the frozen lasagne pan in her hands, the cold numbing her fingers. But she couldn't move.

Zack came racketing down from upstairs. "All ship shape. We can unpack later."

"Zack." She felt the numbness creeping up her arms, down into her chest.

"What's up?" He looked at her, staring out the window. "Who in hell's out there—Hamlet's ghost or what?"

"Zack, it's the Glassmans all right. But they've come with someone else."

"Who, honey?"

"Brace yourself—she's invited Alfred and Muffy here this weekend."

A flicker of surprise across his face, which he controlled quickly. He put his arm around her.

"Steady on, Meggy—we're *not* being napalmed. Anyhow, Alfred and I—we're perfectly civil to each other, he outfoxed me for the N.I.H. grant, so he's principal investigator, not me—end of story."

"And now he has the grant money, damn it! Plus he played dirty pool, you said so more than once. Everyone at the hospital feels the same way about him, he's a snake.

"Shhh, honey. What's done is done."

"For god's sake, just don't tell me to suck it up, Zack. I can't. I *won't*! Oh, damn, this is so mean of Clara, she knows full well how upset you were." She paused, adding, "How upset we *both* were." She bit at her knuckle. "Maybe... maybe she figures she can effect some sort of Camp David peace accords deal between you and Alfred. I mean it's the only explanation that comes to mind. Now she's won herself this big deal appointment—you remember, don't you—teaching mediation ethics at the Business School? and we'll all be her guinea pigs, the bitch."

He cupped her chin. "Lissen up, funny face, try to keep front and center what you've always told me. Resentment corrodes—worse than acid." And he hugged her.

They could hear Alfred's high-pitched laughter followed by footsteps clumping up the steps to the back door. Suitcases thumped on the landing. Then footsteps trotting quickly downstairs again.

"Steady on," he told her.

"How *could* Clara pull a stunt like this, drop Newells, shackle us with Carpenters?" she whispered, hissing her s's.

"It's precisely what you just got through saying, Meggy. You know Clara, she simply loves to see the fur flying. Then tah dah! she comes floating in, makes nice, works hard at fixing up the messes, and presto! the white witch scores again. Gratitude and amazement all around."

Another thump on the landing, somebody knocking.

"Relax, honey, all will be fine," one last squeeze of her arm, then he was striding to the back door.

"Alfred! Great to see you! And Muffy—here let me give you a hand. Come on in, you guys. We just got here. Howdy, Glassmans! Welcome aboard. Looks as if we're in loco parentis until Spence and Clara get back. Which should be soon, they said."

They all filed through the narrow pantry leading back into the kitchen. Alfred, small, wiry, his noble head disproportionately large for the rest of him. At his side Muffy, tall and bony, aloof smile, hand extended as she marched toward Meg.

"Dear Meg! Clara told us you would be here. What a delight!"

Delight, smite, fight, BITE! Meg put down the lasagne on the scarred kitchen table. She shook Muffy's hand, fine narrow bones, firm clasp. Not a hand that ever dared to drip wet and clammy as hers was now doing. She murmured greetings, then turned to face Alfred. That high-domed, massive forehead, those deeply hollowed eyes reminded her each time of the head of a gigantic Percheron set on the skittish body of a polo pony.

"Hi, Alfred."

He smiled briefly at her, then turned away and glanced around the room.

"And prithee exactly where hath our bewitching hostess vanished?" The drawl of his light voice had always irritated her. He had the rare talent for the exquisitely timed snub. These rebuffs he half-hid behind a rococo façade of elaborate courtesy.

Then the Glassmans bustled forward—Rebecca, her long kind face lit up with motherly affection, followed by Stan grinning his sleepy-eyed smile. Embraces all around. They all stood there in the kitchen. Everyone was talking at once. Meg showed the women the freezer in the pantry, Clara's one and only concession to a modern kitchen. Rebecca chattered on, surveyed by Alfred and Muffy—all those two needed was a dais, a throne, and two scepters—made of hand-tooled birch, ten to one they were into recyclables.

"Oh, goody, lasagne, Meg! Perfect! And I made my Chicken Divan. We can have that tomorrow. With the fresh corn we just picked from our community garden plot"—here Rebecca rolled her eyes—"along with those scones Zack loves so much, plus bran muffins, my mother's recipe, of course."

"Goodness," Muffy's dry voice broke in. "We're going to get as fat as butterballs with all this delicious food. I'm afraid I brought only hard fruit."

Rebecca laughed nervously. "Well, we can't all be skinny fashion plates like you, Muffy," and kept on talking faster than before. Muffy makes her nervous too, thought Meg, content to hide behind this waterfall of words.

They went back into the kitchen where the men stood awkwardly, piles of luggage blocking every exit. Like being stuck in a drain, Meg decided. Can't go up or down. Or sideways. God, why had they agreed to come? Where in hell were Clara and Spencer?

"Come on, gals," Rebecca clucked. "Let's shoo the boys out so we can make some order out of chaos here. It's almost lunchtime."

Zack laughed. "Just like home. Conditioned reflex of the female animal. Right, Stan?"

"How's that?" Stan was a good internist but slow on the uptake. His sleepy eyes widened with uncertainty. He often tripped when they began playing verbal hopscotch, the quick repartee and word games adored by Clara and the others. But Rebecca was always there beside him, watching protectively.

Alfred answered before she could speak. "Meaning, old chap, that we're persona non grata in the kitchen."

"In short, fellows, scoot!" said Rebecca.

"But Becky, can't we please have a drink first? I could sure use a bloody about now. That's a long hot drive down here."

"Stan the Man, now you're talkin'!" Zack grinned. "We brought all the fixings plus two bottles of Beefeaters plus Schweppes for G and T's. Let's go tend bar."

Stan chuckled, trying to include the Carpenters who stood stiffly, their backs to the sink. "Our annual bash," he explained. "We're duty bound to keep up the tradition of bloodys at high noon."

Alfred smiled politely. "Each to his own. We prefer wine, actually."

"Oh, goodness! I must have left the wine in your car." Rebecca looked flustered. "At least it's in the cooler so it will be nice and chilled. I'll go—.."

Alfred bowed gallantly. "Of course not, Rebecca dear. Allow me. You looked a wee bit winded going up those steep stairs." And exited. Before Rebecca could reply.

"Well!" she said. "That's one way of hearing you're out of shape."

Stan waved his glass at her. "Fat is what he meant, Becky love."

Muffy frowned. "No, no, quite the contrary. Alfred's simply a fitness freak. Simply delights bounding about hither and thither." And then she smiled as Alfred bounced in the door, holding up a huge glass jug of wine.

"What is this remarkable vintage, Rebecca? The house wine special? Gallo, never had the pleasure." He started pouring the wine with a flourish.

"Well, you see it's just that we're so budget-oriented." Rebecca blushed. "And I completely forgot you and Muffy were into serious wines."

"We're extremely eclectic, Rebecca dearest." Alfred lifted his wine glass. "A votre santé, mes amis."

"Bottoms up!" Meg said in a loud voice. Damn it, enough of this phoney baloney's *enough*. Muffy looked over at her, and twitched her bony nose.

Rebecca clinked glasses with Zack and Stanley, then reached awkwardly across towards Alfred, her elbow bumping hard against the jug of wine. It jiggled for a moment, and Meg tried to catch it by the handle. Too slippery. Slid through her fingers, crashed on the floor.

"Oh, my God!" Rebecca shuddered. "What a mess."

They all stood motionless like guilty children, then glanced up as Clara and Spencer entered the room, hand in hand. They were both dressed in tennis whites. Clara studied the shards of green glass, the puddle of wine spreading slowly across the kitchen floor, and crinkled up her fine dark eyes in a mischievous smile.

"You see, my beloved," she turned to Spencer. "While the cat's away, the darling mice all raise holy hell."

Rebecca, cheeks aflame, started in with embarrassed explanations, but Clara gave her low, indulgent laugh. "My dears, in my wildest dreams, I couldn't have thought up a more perfect christening for our weekend! Awash in wine with favorite friends!" And then, tipping back her small, elegant head, she laughed again and wound her thin brown arms around Rebecca's ample waist. "What better beginning to your visit could there possibly be, a veritable benediction, don't you agree?"

She's magical, Meg thought. Our high priestess or goddess of mischief? Talk about Janus! Which face is the real one—fire-setter or fire-quencher? maybe both, whatever. The fact is, she holds us in thrall. Stage manager, white witch, professional mediator—hell, our own professional enchantress!

Because now as if the spell were broken, the guests all surged forward, released from their frozen tableau, once more confident, exuberant—but more to the point, shriven. Stan parceled out the bloodys, each topped with jalapenos plus cocky celery stalks, and Meg was amused to see that Alfred and Muffy did not refuse—get some hard liquor down those two paragons and maybe things would ease up, maybe Clara could actually perform a real miracle and get those two seriously snockered.

Jesus. Three whole days to go.

Meg drank.

Hail Mary—bloody Mary.

A PLATE OF PEAS

SONNY HARPER—EX-FLIGHT ATTENDANT, EX-BELLHOP, you name the uniform, he'd probably worn it—Sonny Harper walked with a limp.

Not a bad limp, no big deal, just a slow drag of the left leg. Women found it attractive, Sonny's limp. He was a big guy, not real tall but well-muscled. Massive chest. Massive shoulders. Even as a shrimpy kid, Sonny knew the limp was a come-on to chicks. At a certain point in the relationship, they always asked the same question, usually while they riffled his hair, "So baby-fine" they'd coo. Then it came, shy and throaty, "Gosh, Sonny, what happened to your...you know...your leg?"

Love me, love my limp; it followed him faithful as any pooch.

So did the girls with their glances always sweeping past his face down to his feet. Then the flick upwards, eyes round with polite concern plus something else...a gleam of plain old curiosity. And then the mouth sliding into a familiar smile. The about-to-embark-on-adventure smile, half sly, half chummy.

That smile. Sonny knew that smile. He saw it lots of places. Saw it at the checkout counter, women peeking down at the gothic romances. Saw it at the flicks, that turned-on look in their eyes as they watched some Hollywood stud bust a few hearts, not to mention cherries by the bucketful.

So Sonny obliged, the point was to score, right? Right. "The limp?" he'd answer, then lay on something totally bogus.

He kept changing the story as he got older. For years it was a sports injury, a different sport with each new move to a different naval base—him and his old man hop-scotching cross-country—and with every new posting, a brand new injury for the hard luck Navy brat.

"Ice hockey, back east," he told the kids at Camp Pendleton. Even the very idea of ice—forget shattered legs—was a big deal in Southern Cal.

"Coming in on a slider, lost my head," he joked when his old man pulled the tour in San Juan, P.R. The Puerto Ricans were nuts about baseball.

So it went. When he hit his twenties, he told them it was football. "Mean and nasty, got sacked in a scrimmage, pre-season." That really got 'em.

"You mean," they wailed, "it wasn't even a *real game?*"

By the time 30 rolled around, all he ever said was, "Old war wound," and let it go at that.

"Oh, my goodness," they said, then looked at his face, changed the subject. Very fast.

The woman who finally landed him was a 36-year-old nursing supervisor at City Hospital. Her name was Kay. She had great tits, level gray eyes, and the kind of cool savvy he admired—just what the doctor ordered, in fact.

All Kay said was, "Congenital hip?" And he proposed three months later.

It was a major relief. She loved him, not the limp. She babied him, sure. In the moonlight she cradled him against her big breasts. She crooned old folk songs, lullabies mostly. "Hush Little Baby" and "Scarlet Ribbons." Or "When Joseph was an o-uhld man." That was his favorite. "Joseph gathered her some cherries." Sonny grinned. Mornings, it was like the nights had never happened. Kay took off at 6:15, she worked the early shift, 7 to 3, and some of the time he got up to make her coffee. But most days he watched her from the bed, watched her first pull on her white stockings, then the truly lame-looking cotton bra that flattened her chest, "A runner's bra," she told Sonny.

"You don't run," he argued.

"It's insurance," she laughed. "So I don't have to any more. I'm an administrator now, no more leching around." Mornings, she talked in a voice as crisp as her no-nonsense uniform, no lacy edges, no frills. He liked the contrast, the chirpy, efficient daylight voice and his private nighttime lady ivory smooth in the moonlight, lulling him to sleep after they made love, singing in that pure soprano that made him think of stars burning cold and bright out in space somewhere, made him forget the damn hip, the ache that never went away. Sometimes she did it the other way around, sang the lullabies as a prelude.

"Foreplay," he told her.

"Whatever turns you on, baby," she chuckled and pushed his head down until he found the nipple.

After Kay left the apartment, he stayed in the sack another couple hours until he heard the thump of the morning paper out in the hallway. Nine-thirty. He hit the deck.

He showered, ate two slices of cold pepperoni pizza, opened a Tab, and began circling his way through CLASSIFIEDS. He circled pretty much everything from SALES MGRS to UNLIMITED CAREER PSBLTIES, which promised the universe but gave no info except a phone number, ask for Lisa. After dinner, Kay checked through each and every ad.

"Narrow it down," she kept telling him. "Focus on something realistic."

"Got to...like, keep my options open," he said.

"How about this, FLIGHT ATTENDANTS; NOW HIRING, Sonny, this is *you*, it's perfect—minimum five years experience, really!"

"Eastern's a sleazeball outfit, I wouldn't fly them again on a bet. Anyhow, they're going down the tubes my buddies tell me."

"Wait, here's something. CHARTER SERVICES INTERNATIONAL." She put on her reading glasses, held the newspaper up to catch the lamplight. "You skipped this one. Why?"

"Sooner shovel shit than fly charter again."

She looked surprised. "But the pay's good. I mean it's scale plus benefits."

He got up, limped over to the fridge. "Brew?"

She nodded. "So tell."

He opened two Buds, handed hers over, then tipped his head way back, drank, chug-a-lugged in fact, let it drain down like rainwater, wash away all the bad stuff. The plugged up toilets. The fat mamas in their black shawls. Aisles blocked with cloth bundles. That lady with bangle bracelets who vomited all over the bulkhead, then started in yelling, "Rotten meat, you feed me rotten meat from X-ray machine, I sue you." They had to call the Senior Purser in on that one. Fly the Friendly Skies, oh *yeah*, man.

He tried to explain how it was, the 16-hour flight time, those incredibly boring layovers in Istanbul...Frankfurt. How the glamorous, glitzy dream went sour. How no self-respecting stewardess ever got caught dead on the charters, no matter how many perks.

"Only dogs on those flights," he ended up.

She stared at him, took off her reading glasses and put them down on the kitchen table. "Only the undesirables, is that what you're saying? By dogs, I mean?"

"You got it. Ugly? I mean we're talking *uggah-lee*." He let his wrist go limp, waggled his fingers back and forth.

She looked at him, put on her glasses again. "That bad?"

"That bad," he laughed, reached down to massage his knee; standing was easier, thing hurt worse when he sat around.

"So logically," she continued with a little shrug and the light winked off her glasses so he couldn't read her eyes, but her voice was still smiling, "the airlines had to hire cripples as well."

"Hey," he said, almost shocked, "cheap shot! Look, like I told you, no way would any carrier block me from being hired once I passed the physical. We took it all the way up to appellate court."

"The same way they did."

"Who did?"

"The dogs, as you call them."

"Give me a break," he said. "You mean job discrimination, all that garbage?"

"Or age," she said with a pleasant smile. "Or gender. And all those other messy handicaps."

"Kay," he said, "don't go fucking feminist on me, ok?"

She stood up, put her arms lightly across his shoulders. She was almost the same height he was, five-eleven in her stocking feet. He liked being on eye level with her, no fun always having to squint down at chicks. But now he felt weird, felt almost shorter than she was. Was he shrinking?

"Listen to yourself," she said slowly. "I just hate—I just wish you wouldn't badmouth everything. You know...the charters, unattractive women, whatever. All this—this negative thinking, honey, know what I mean?"

He winked at her but he still ducked out and away from her arms, then crossed back to the fridge for another Budweiser. "Negative's a no-no, hunh, teach?"

"Sonny, don't *do* this."

He put his hand to his heart. He blinked his eyes fast. "Say whut?"

She took a deep breath. "What I'm trying to tell you is I don't like to hear you whine. Either you're mouthing off jokes or whining. Get a job, dear, get *on* with it. There's bound to be something out there you'll enjoy doing." She looked down at his stomach. "Plus," she added, "you're getting a beer belly."

"Minute I start talking straight, you go totally apeshit."

"We're not communicating, Sonny."

He mimicked her. "Not communicating, not communicating, Polly wanna cracker?" She reached out to touch his hand, but he moved on to the kitchen drawer to get the church key. "Here," she said and handed it to him. It had been right on the countertop. "I'm going to bed," she told him.

"Suit yourself," he answered and limped past her to the living room to watch the Rams play. They had themselves a new wide receiver on board who was really going places.

The next week he picked up the last unemployment check, screwed around for a couple days calling up old pals. The conversations went pretty much nowhere. "Like to help you out, Sonny, but the long and short of it is we're laying off right now." Or, "Hey, let's get together, ok? Couple of beers, couple of laughs, I'll give you a buzz."

The buzz never came. He finally landed a job working security for an industrial park out by the new interstate, mostly high-tech stuff and insurance companies, and what his new partner called these "high-falutin *fink* tanks."

The partner was an old-timer named Izzy. They made a great team, the two of them. They worked the day shift, worked outside making the rounds in a baby-blue GMC pickup with a tow rig bolted on back. Izz referred to the GMC as the Jimmy. The Jimmy was a working member of the team, no question.

No uniforms was the only drawback. They wore standard work duds; despite the job classification SECURITY OFFICER GRADE ONE, it was still your basic maintenance operation, beefed up with a couple of company walkie talkies for checking in with Security Headquarters, big deal.

Izzy handled the repairs when they had to help out some poor jerk stalled in one of the parking lots. Sonny mostly handled the jumper cables and the small talk, mellowing out the drivers, walking back and forth beside the Jimmy, cracking jokes about how "management must have laid down wall-to-wall nails we got so many flats showing up."

"Glad to help," he'd say, rubbing his hands, blowing on his fingers. The men took the longest to thaw. They sat poker-faced in black BMW's or bright yellow Subarus, glancing down at their Seiko watches. They never, but never, climbed out of the car. But the longer Sonny clowned around, the more they relaxed, finally rolling down the car window, even on rainy days. As if the glass shouldn't come between them and Sonny, as if they were on an equal footing. They never asked about the limp, of course. Guys never did, not since grade school.

But the women—the young chicks jumped right out of the cars as a rule. They seemed to know a whole hell of a lot more about distributor caps and blocked fuel lines than Sonny did. They crouched beside old Izzy and peered under the hood, pointing first at this wire, then that one. Eventually their eyes slid over to where Sonny stood, whispering softly into his radio transmitter. They started to smile. Then he walked around to the other side of the Jimmy and he knew they were watching his limp.

Management began getting letters commending the dynamite job he and Izz were doing. The letters were Kay's idea. People asked, "How can we thank you?" And Sonny told them, modest voice, shy foot-shuffle, "Wouldn't hurt to let dah biggadah bosses know." Sure enough, just as Kay predicted, along came a promotion offer: inside security guard, time-and-a-half evening and graveyard shifts, a high-risk position, they were told. Sonny chose day shift in the beginning. Izzy chose to stick with the blue pickup.

"Can't leave the Jimmy," he explained. He grinned. "Been working here five years, never pried so much as a good morning out of those tight-ass Yuppies." He shook his head. "You musta kissed the Blarney stone, Sonny. Ought to go into sales, I mean it."

"Selling sucks. Making people smile, that's my bag, I guess."

Izz scratched at his chin, looked up at Sonny. "Me and the Jimmy," he said, voice sounding rusty, "gonna miss you, no shit."

Sonny punched him on the shoulder. "Give you a buzz, have us a brew, Izz, and that's a promise."

That night he tried on the new uniform. It was pale gray, sharp creases in the trouser legs, big heavy black leather belt with a loop for the holster. And a star-shaped silver badge that clipped on the shirt pocket. Nice. Nicer than anything he ever wore as a Flight Attendant. This had style, nicely cut broadcloth shirt, very roomy, very cool.

Kay ironed the shirt for him. When he put it on, she stepped back to admire. He put on the cap as well, tilting the brim a little to one side. "Not bad, hunhh, teach?"

She saluted. "Your dad would be so proud."

He clicked his heels together, saluted her right back. "He was only a noncom," he reminded her.

"But a big shot, right?"

"Right. Chief Petty Officer. Bossed all the medical corpsmen at Headquarters Battalion. The docs couldn't have run the dispensary without him."

"Quite a guy," she said softly. "Not easy, raising a kid alone, lugging you around the whole country."

"I bet we lived on every base there is, never got to know the townies, we always stayed in base housing and all."

"Lonely," she said. "So hard. For both of you." She was still looking at his reflection in the mirror but he knew what she really saw was that motherless, gimpy little kid, that loser from long ago.

"Hey," he frowned at the mirror, tilted the cap the other way, that was better. "Me and the old man, we did great, a team you know, just him and me, batching it."

She was silent, but she hugged him tight. He could smell the good smell of her hair. *Pert* shampoo she used. He liked that. It fit Kay, big gal but so upbeat, definitely on top of things. Pert Kay, a tiger all right, but sometimes he missed kittens cooing up at him.

He craned his neck, lifted his chin so he could straighten the black tie. "See," he said, jaws clenched as he worked on the knot, "my dad claimed life in the service really made a man out of you. Builds character, he used to say."

And character was what Sonny was short on, to hear his dad tell it. Used the gimpy leg as the perfect alibi for failure, for goldbricking, his dad said. Short on character, short on hip bone. And he could see the shame in his father's eyes, the hope go dead after one more operation at one more naval hospital. "Sorry, Chief," the docs would say, "Boy needs a total hip replacement, we just haven't got the hardware yet." A short silence, his father biting his lip, and the usual suggestions, the docs' voices going brightly upbeat, the bogus cheer as tinny to his own ear as it was to his dad's. "Physical therapy, though, build him up, have him work out. Be good as new."

So Sonny lifted weights, he worked out on the Universal and the rowing machines at the base gyms, his dad pushing him, pushing him.

"Work on those deltoids, just look at those triceps, boy! Stop clowning around, why not try out for wrestling?"

No sports, though; no, he wouldn't budge on that, no matter how disgusted his dad got. Enough to look in the mirror and see the new physique. The swelling lines of the great chest, the powerful throat. Those arms like some massive King Kong hunkering there in the mirror, lurching forward on one leg thick as an oak, the other so skinny, no muscle—truly gross. He was careful never to go swimming but from the beltline up by God, he looked normal. Hell, he looked awesome.

"A hunk," Kay was telling him. And he had to agree.

That night while she cradled him, she stopped singing after only a few bars. She went very still.

"What's up, babe?" he muttered.

She nuzzled her face down into his hair. She was breathing faster, he could feel it. And he could feel his heartbeat race to match hers. "Sonny," she spoke in this low voice. "Sonny, I'm pregnant."

"Jesus."

"is it ok?"

"Ok? Baby, it's great! I mean it's fantastic! I mean just coming out of the blue like that...and you on the pill, I thought you were on the pill."

"I'm 36 years old, Sonny, and time's running out."

He pulled her down beside him, this time he cradled her. She cried a little.

"I'm scared," she said.

And he told her it was wonderful, it was going to be great, and the whole time he was talking, he kept remembering this plate of peas his old man made him finish one time when he was—what? five maybe—even though canned peas made him puke. And how he sat there straight through Huntley-Brinkley...right through I Love Lucy, and finally got the mess down somehow, the peas cold and slimy, green juice pooled on the plate like some gross green dye that stained his insides, he knew it did, and each time he swallowed, it was all he could do not to choke, each pea going down big as a golfball. And with each bite, he thought how if he ate *this* pea, his dad would like him, then the next, his dad would like him. Some things you force down. When there's no options left. No more time for jokes or clowning around. When time simply has run out on you.

Kay was asleep. He listened to the little whistle at the end of each deep breath and prayed to God congenital hip displacement wasn't genetic. They put down dogs who had it, he remembered—no pups.

The next week he told Kay that he was starting a double shift.

"We can use the money. You know, stuff for the baby and all," he told her. She was proud of him, he could tell.

He liked the new job, liked eyeing the secretaries and administrative assistants as they swept through the foyer, their little plastic ID cards perched right over their tits. They brought him donuts sometimes, Valentine cards, once a jelly glass full of daisies. He tacked the cards up over the radio.

When they had to work late, he walked by their offices on his regular rounds. They left the door open, and he'd stand in the doorway, hand on his holster, shoot the shit for a while.

Finally it would come. "And the limp?" they asked softly.

He got off at 10, took them out for a beer now and then. There was a cheap motel across the highway. The Brick Towers it was called. The bar was right next door, and soon, it wasn't even necessary to hit the bar first. He took them straight to the Towers. He brought the six pack along. Cheaper. Quicker, too.

He missed Izzy. They waved at each across the parking lot, but that was about it. He kept meaning to ask old Izz out for a belt now and then, but there wasn't time. Izz was his alibi, though.

"Stopped for a brew with old Izzy," he told Kay. She got bored nights he was working late. She started in some private duty nursing to fill up the long hours until he rolled in at midnight.

He liked patrolling the building after everybody had gone home. Liked stalking down the blue-lit corridors, his heels hitting hard against the polished tiles. He tried marching, despite the limp. He turned the corners in parade drill formation, a column left maneuver, watching his shadow move across frosted glass doors. The flashlight swept over empty desks, Mr. Coffee machines in the corners, the mile-long conference tables in the senior administrator's suites.

He made his check-in calls with Security HQ every hour on the hour. Right after he made the 9 o'clock call, he took out his thermos, drank the hot cocoa Kay insisted he take every day. "Low blood sugar that time of night," she told him. "You need to keep alert."

It was while he was swigging down the last dregs of the cocoa that he heard the noise. He turned down the radio, checked his watch. Noise seemed to be coming from the lower level, down from the maintenance quarters in the subbasement.

He listened.

Nothing.

All he could hear was the hum of the big generators.

And his own breathing; he was panting, he realized. He started to dial HQ, then switched off. What the hell, he hardly needed back-up to swing downstairs again, meant just a couple of minutes, what was he, chicken?

He took the utility staircase back of the freight elevators. He walked softly on his toes so he wouldn't make too much of a racket going down the steel treads.

The humming of the generators was much louder. As he swung open the heavy door to the hall, he heard the noise again.

Creaking—like the creak of wheels—like the wheels of a dolly? He flattened himself against the wall, jammed his flashlight in his hip pocket to keep both hands free.

Like a tomb down here, a mausoleum, strange greenish light quite different from upstairs. Probably reduced circuit load, the bluish white glare sickening down to this sick-o green—jeez, what was *that*? A crash—iron hitting stone.

Then silence.

Three doors down he could see a crack of light. The light went off. He stood still. Sweat was pouring down his armpits, messing up the uniform for sure. The pulse in his throat was hammering so fast he had to swallow twice to get his breathing regular.

He started down the corridor, still tiptoeing, still hugging the wall, going inch by inch, hand on the Smith and Wesson. When he reached the door, he took the gun out of the holster, cocked it, and felt warmed by the cold steel in his palm. He took a deep breath. He listened, his ears ached with listening so hard, but there wasn't a sound coming out of there, quiet as a crypt.

And then, no turning back now, here we go, Daddy-o, he kicked the door open hard, pistol in his right hand, his left hand fumbling then turning on the light switch.

The room was the place they stored the new electronic stuff, off-loaded from the delivery platform out back. The back doors were open, he could see a truck parked there all right, a big delivery van of some kind, except that it was empty, and there was a dolly full of wooden crates parked beside the forklift.

He looked around, saw a big console smashed on the floor, saw a flicker of something moving, moving fast out by the front door of the van.

The light from the room spilled out on the platform, lit up the face of the kid, Christ, he couldn't be more than eighteen or nineteen, narrow face, eyes bugging out, dead-looking eyes, a deadhead, a born loser.

"Hold it right there," he said to the kid.

But the kid turned—what the fuck was he looking for? leaning in toward the seat of the van, reaching over—and Sonny squeezed the trigger, nailed the little bastard right in mid-calf, bull's-eye, bingo, Medal of Honor, so why this feeling like he was going to vomit, vomit right down his pearl gray uniform with the silver badge winking up at him like some misplaced evening star? Nice one, Sonny, nice one; no score, batting zero.

By the time the cops had come, the ambulance, and he got through all the paper work, the reports to HQ, the bull-dickey with the investigating officers, it was past three o'clock in the morning.

She was asleep when he got home, asleep on the sofa, still in her uniform, her shoes kicked over by the television, her reading glasses sliding down her nose. He walked over to the sofa, took them off slow and careful.

But she woke up, came awake with a jerk, gray eyes wide with alarm. First time he ever really saw Kay looking scared.

"What happened?" she said. "Something happened, I know it."

He looked down at her. "Long story, cutie," he said. "No big deal, baby, let's get some shuteye."

"Level with me, Sonny. What's wrong?" She sat up, she tried to smile, she put her knees together carefully, put on her alert yet calm look he loved, the no-nonsense expression he'd married her for.

He stood there, staring at her. She was six months along now, and her face was puffy, her eyes looked smaller in her head, squeezed small by the puffiness. But still so cool, man; so on top of it.

He rubbed his hip, remembered that trapped rat look the kid gave him just before he squeezed the trigger. And he wanted to kneel down in front of Kay, let her hold him, rock him back and forth while he croaked, "It hurts, baby, it never stops hurting."

But that angle wouldn't play anymore, not after tonight. Let that badass kid get some mileage from the limp routine, the kid's turn now—kid stuff, you might say—least his story wouldn't be totally bogus.

"It can keep," he told her gently. "You look totally bushed, let's get you to bed, you sleeping for two now, honey."

He helped her off the sofa. She felt heavy and awkward, and as he led her into the bedroom he pulled her in so close that staring at the mirror, it was hard to tell which was the one that stumbled, which was the one that limped.

LAKE SONGS

EACH HAS HER OWN agenda.

Sally Farnsworth, Vassar, Class of '70, has tried three times to organize this expedition to the island. And three times it's fallen through. She herself has managed to chair the entire Class FUN-Fundraiser in the weeks it's taken Eunice and Jebba to get their act together.

Batman and Robin, she thinks. Some dynamic duo. She puts down the tool box, studies the two of them sitting there on the dock, faces uptilted to the sun. Not the pioneer type, that's for sure. Inept, actually. "Bowline?" Eunice had cried, nearly tipping them over. "Which one's that?"

Poor Eunice, lurching and bawling through life like a newborn calf.

And then there's Jebba. Moody Jeb, brooding about Eunice's recovery, brooding about her German Shepherd. "His toenails!" she'd wailed on the phone.

"Toenails," Sally repeated carefully.

"They're shredding. It could be his liver."

So Sally suggested the dog come too. "He'll be our token male," she told Jebba. "Back to the wilderness for all three of you—him, you and Eunice. Cure what ails you."

Jebba went silent. Sally had to spell it out. "Do it for Eunice *and* the pooch. He can run free. You can paint. And Eunice simply loll. I'll repair the hammock."

"Sally!" Now Jeb was calling from the dock. "Come relax. Enough work-ethic already."

Sally shakes her head. "Almost finished," she answers. "Hold your horses." She might have the gray hair, but those two are the ones that carry on like Granny Grumps. Ditherers, both of them. Really so tiresome. She places the crowbar crossways through the eyebolt, then levers it round and around. She can feel the good ache in her shoulder muscles, she presses harder. Just one last twist. What Jebba—boy—that—is—*tight* and Eunice need is what she's serving up. Plenty of fresh Vermont air, plenty of exercise, and some straight talk. Flush out all the gloom and doom. Like a good enema.

There, that's done. She puts down the crowbar, hooks the hammock securely to the tree, a nice mountain ash. "Sorry, old timer," she whispers, and traces one calloused fingertip along the bark. "All set," she announces. "We're in business."

Eunice glances up. She has huge startled-fawn eyes. When in the world is Eunice going to grow up? Learn to be assertive, dump the apologizing routine? Yes, here she goes, she's in mid-gush, "—just being too much trouble, Sally. I mean, you're spoiling us rotten. Right, Jebby?"

Jebba nods. "Yeah, it's great." She peers over the top of her sunglasses, purple rims, Miami tourist type thing. "You're quite the Miss Fix-it, Sal."

Eunice flaps her hands, as if to soften Jeb's remark, as if to wave it away so it won't bother Sally. "And me, I'm so dumb about fixing stuff. Richard's forbidden me to go near his workbench. Or his computer. Claims I'm a total klutz. And actually," she adds shyly, staring down at the brown spots on the backs of her hands, "he's right, you know."

Jebba cocks an eyebrow in a way Sally finds annoying. "Phooey, he is *not right*, Eunice!" she says. She stands up, glares at Sally. She's got on a ridiculous lavender bathing suit cut way too low in the front, way too high on the thighs, the lavender to match her sunglasses, no doubt. "Dear Richard," she mutters, "could do a whole lot worse. Stuff Richard."

Eunice giggles, stops when she sees Sally's expression.

Jebba walks over to the hammock, flops down, closes her eyes. Her long braid hangs over the side. She starts humming. Sally would like to sing along but can't carry a tune worth a damn. The kids used to pay her not to sing during carpools. She taps her foot, whether in time or frustration she's not sure which. "That's pretty," she tells Jebba.

Jebba nods again, keeps on humming. Eunice starts crooning the words, "Daddy's gonna buy you a mockingbird." Sally remembers how the kids got upset about the cart falling down—but were instantly comforted by the next line, "You'll still be the sweetest little baby in town."

Jeb shifts into a low whistle, Eunice sings harmony. Jebba's dog, Timber, paces nervously around the hammock, whining until they reach the end of the lullaby. Then he sits down on his haunches, triangular ears cocked. This pooch is totally fixated on Jebba, Sally's concluded, a sheep in wolf's clothing. Sean must get jealous. Maybe not, no kids, after all. Typical pet fixation.

To be polite, she tells Jebba, "Truly gorgeous head on that animal. You should have bred him."

"I wish we had," Jebba says slowly. "He's too old now."

Sally scratches the feathered wisps behind Timber's ears. The dog ignores her, eyes steady on the hammock. Aloof bastard. So she adds, "Such a big cry-baby," and picks up the crowbar, jams it in the tool box, starts toward the shed.

When she gets back, Eunice is trying to climb into the hammock. Or maybe out of it? Who can tell? Jebba's doubled over laughing. Eunice is sprawled sideways. One arm is tucked through the white braided ropes. Eunice has lost a good forty-five pounds since she got out of the hospital but still moves like a heavy woman as if her skinny shanks still carry the great mass of big belly, big breasts. Clumsy, she thrashes around, a fish caught in a net. She stares up at Sally. Jebba turns. Their faces change.

"I'm too heavy," Eunice apologizes.

Jebba frowns. "You are not. You're light as a feather."

"Here, try it in stages," suggests Sally and steadies the hammock. The dog begins barking, Jebba and Eunice start laughing again. "See?" Jeb says. "Timber wants to help."

But Eunice is breathing hard. "Give me a hand," she says. So Sally reaches over, takes her firmly by both wrists, gives a good yank. "Have to get you out in the canoe, old girl," she tells Eunice. "Get you limbered up."

"Oh dear. I'm a terrible paddler, Sally."

"Nonsense."

"No, really. I mean at camp like all they ever let me do was bail. Or else sit in the middle."

"Athwart," Sally corrects automatically and takes the cushions, throws them in the canoe. "Jeb? You on?"

"You two go ahead." Jebba's slathering more coconut oil up and down her thighs. She's already stained so brown she looks like a halfbreed, but ok, that's her business. Clearly not an earned tan, not a working tan like Sally's but an expensive poolside brown, all rich oils, glistening smooth skin.

Sally points with her paddle at the opposite shore. Most of the trees have been bulldozed to make a beach area. "See that?" she says to Eunice, and hands her into the canoe.

"That beach?"

"It's all private. Belongs to the new people. The ones with the condos."

"Should I kneel, Sally?"

"No, you sit tight. I'll tell you when to stroke." They glide out into the lake. From the dock, Timber is watching them. He's lying beside Jebba, head on his paws. He twitches one ear, Jeb lifts one glistening long leg. She waggles her foot. "Bon voyage!" she calls. Miss Swimsuit, circa 1979, give or take. Sally turns her head, shrugs. She stares at Eunice's scrawny shoulder blades.

Eunice fumbles with the paddle. "Should I do the J stroke or whatever?"

"No. That's my department. You just pull straight. I'll steer us."

After five minutes, Eunice settles down into a regular stroke, shallow but regular. She looks around the lake. "Where are the condos?"

"You can't see them. Our county Watershed Association played hardball.

We voted they had to build farther inland. Can't trust these new developers. Give them an inch."

"Are you friends with any of the condo people?"

"Oh, we see them out in their Chris Crafts. On weekends. Swamping all the little boats. We nod, that's it. All they do, seems to us, is drink Bloody Marys from dawn to dusk. Or go water-skiing half-tight."

"Good grief. Kinda scary."

"See that little cottage?" Sally points to the inlet past the cove. "That belongs to Reverend Hackberry. He's the retired Unitarian minister. Every single morning, 8:00 sharp, he comes out and takes a bacteria count."

Eunice leans over to peer down at the water. "Is the lake polluted?"

"Not yet, it's not. But we keep a close eye. Too many newfangled bathrooms in those condos. That type person won't hold with outhouses." Sally sniffs, pulls hard and fast. "No," she goes on, "you'll never see that crew chopping firewood. Or boiling water on the stove for dishes. No mice nests in their sofas, thank you very much. Roughing it means washing their dirty hair in our lake," and she thinks of the white lather floes scudding along the surface of the water, God help the phosphate level.

Eunice's shoulders are drooping "Better rest," Sally advises. "Turn around, that's the ticket, easy does it," and as Eunice sits back against the yellow cushion, Sally starts pointing out who lives where, the camps that belong to the old-timers, her married daughter's small cabin at the other end of the island, the famous writer's place, "He just lost his wife, this spring it was. We invite him for cookouts every Saturday now. Take him over the mainland once a week. Marketing. And to the laundromat."

"That's so sweet," Eunice says. "You and Austin are good neighbors."

"Oh, fiddle," Sally says briskly. "You just do what you have to do."

Eunice smiles sleepily, and lets her bony white hand trail among the lily pads as Sally guides the canoe into the lagoon.

* * *

THE LILY PADS FEEL like cool skin, slipping through her fingers as smoothly as Sally's clear voice skimming on and on. Sally's amazing. So energetic. So clever. She's got all the answers, she's like Richard. But mainly Sally's brave. Nothing scares her. That mouse in the sleeping loft last night. The thunderstorm. Timber heard Eunice cry out, "Jebba! Wake up!" and he padded over to Eunice, stuck his cold nose against her cheek, licked her twice.

"Good dog," she told him. The lightning lit up the room. She could see his dark eyes, mournful like her own, staring at her. She felt the warmth of his head, and finally she fell asleep, grateful to this other shepherd God had sent her, He maketh me to lie down in green pastures, I shall not want, wonder how the children are doing?

SLAP! Goes something very near the canoe. She jumps. "A rifle?" she asks Sally.

"Just our resident beaver," Sally smiles. She has very white teeth. "Slapping his tail." She motions with her chin toward the big rock. "See? That's his dam over there. On your right. Past that stand of birches."

Eunice shades her eyes, studies the pile of logs, stones and mud jammed across the narrow mouth of the lagoon. Beyond the dam the water's covered with pale green scum and hundreds of dragonflies darting back and forth. "But where is he?" she asks Sally.

"Long gone. If we crept up and sat there on the rock tonight, sat very still, he'd come out. Start in to working. We could shine our flashlights down there and watch him. For as long as you could stand the mosquitoes. They're fierce back here."

"Oh."

"You get used to them, of course."

"Does he have a family?"

"We haven't spotted any kits yet this year. But I'm sure he does." And then Sally starts explaining about beaver lodges and how beavers breed, what they feed on, "They're crazy about lily pads, you know," and the canoe drifts through brown water, lily pads whispering against the metal sides. Metal? Why not birch bark or whatever? She should ask Sally, but she doesn't really want to know, she wants to dream through this quiet lagoon and let cool water spread her fingers out wide, wide as fluttering wings, or should it be fins? Wings evolved from fins, surely that was right? So why couldn't you say fish fly through water and birds float in the sky, each at home in its very own kind of current...nice...and see how the clouds rock quietly in this lake, Jebba should be paddling here, Jebby who could pass for an Indian brave no problem, long black braid hanging down her brown back, instead of Sally, lecturing, lecturing—a camp counselor grown old in the service of Nature Lore & Crafts for a Rainy Day, maybe tonight they could tell ghost stories, "The Man Who was Digested Alive," and what's that awful one? The one that ends up, "Her hair had turned snow white and she was *chewing on the gangrene arm*"? Jebba would love it. Not Sally though. "Dumb," she'd sniff. But that's not nice to say about a friend, a good friend who's being kind even if the kindness is spooned out like...

"Uh oh," she says to Sally, looking down at her watch.

"What's up?"

"I forgot to take my medicine. At two."

"Then we'll have to go back."

"No," says Eunice, quickly. "The doctor told me, only as needed."

"Good," Sally answers in her clipped voice. She gets impatient whenever doctors are mentioned or any talk about surgery. She always changes the subject. "Hear that?" she's saying now to Eunice. She has lifted up her paddle. Water drips off the tip of the blade. Each drop makes a perfect ripple. The drops fall one after the other, noiselessly kissing the lake. So peaceful.

"Hear what?" Eunice repeats. And then sits up straight. Of course, she thinks. It's so simple. Sally wants me to get well. All this jolly talk. It's all a big bluff. No, it's never thunderstorms Sally will be scared of. Never beavers slapping their tails. What I live with, day in, day out—she can't even bear to think about.

Birds are chirping. A fish splashes nearby. Eunice can hear the drone of an outboard motor in the distance. But that's all. The woods are still. She turns to ask again what to listen for, but Sally cuts her short. "Shhh," Sally commands, resting her paddle across her knees.

The water has gone black. A cloud blankets the sun. Eunice shivers. The pine trees loom much taller along the shoreline, and a swarm of tiny gnats pepper the water. They float straight up in the air and move toward the canoe.

Someone's laughing. Wild shrieks, like a small child having hysterics. Eunice tries to stand up. The canoe rocks to one side.

Sally smiles. "Sit down," she says. "It's only a loon." Her big white teeth gleam. She reminds Eunice of a dappled gray pony getting ready to chomp an apple. Or trample Eunice underfoot? No, Sal will never actually bite, she'll always be the rescuer, the one who takes charge. In a fire, Sally would be the calm one who blindfolds the pony, leads her quietly from the blazing stall, pats her heaving flanks.

"Good grief," Eunice says, "What a weird call it has. I mean, like it's laughing and crying simultaneously. Like it's homesick or something."

Sally shrugs, dips the paddle cleanly into the water. "No kidding," she says. "Simply sounds like a loon to me," and shoots the canoe forward into the main body of the lake.

* * *

"I'LL WASH UP," EUNICE announces. She puts on the flowered apron.

Jebba glances over at Sally. Sally bustles over to the stove. "Kettle's empty. Who wants more coffee?"

Eunice takes the red teakettle, starts to fill it.

"Not *tap* water," Sally scolds. "Get the drinking water from the plastic jugs. Over there on the second shelf. Here, I'll do it."

Eunice doesn't speak for a moment, then her face softens in the same way it does when she looks at Timber. "Honestly," she say, "see what comes of not letting me in the kitchen? I don't know the routine," and she begins washing the breakfast plates, dipping water from the iron pot into the green plastic dishpan. Jebba feels like cheering. Workers of the world unite, she thinks, and holds the napkin up to her mouth to wipe away the smile.

"Easy," Sally's saying. "Not too much water, we have to conserve."

Eunice adds a squirt of *Liquid Ivory*. A bubble big as the Astro-Dome arches over the water, then pops. Nothing to lose but your chains.

"Hold it!" Sally barks. "You'll never get them properly rinsed."

Eunice laughs. "Shoo," she tells Sally. "Give me some credit. Dishwashing I *can* handle, Sal. You scram." Sally steps back. Jebba stares out the window at Timber. He smiles back at her.

"Think I'll go chop some firewood," says Sally.

The screen door slams. Jebba winks at Eunice, Eunice grins. "Comes the revolution," Jeb observes and picks up the dishtowel.

Eunice rinses each plate carefully, running her hand over the surface. The plate squeaks. "She means well, Jebby," she says gently.

"So did Attila the Hun."

"Don't be mean. *Please.* Just another twelve hours to go."

"Anyhow," Jebba looks straight into Eunice's big eyes. "I'm proud of you. Want to go for a walk? We're all done here." She hangs up the dishtowel, waits for Eunice to finish scouring the sink. The porcelain is stained a lovely aqua color around the drain.

"I can't. Sally wants to take me out in the catamaran."

"Captain Bligh."

"You hush."

Jebba grabs her Strathmore No. 2 Drawing Pad, closes the screen door quietly, calls Timber. They start off the path winding through the woods. Between the branches she can see the catamaran, anchored next to the Sailfish. A regular flotilla out there. The catamaran is painted bright yellow with two banana-shaped pontoons. Goofy looking.

Timber forges ahead. She walks past the outhouse, past the shell of a white oak struck three times by lightning, according to Sally. Then up a steep knoll and they're out on the face of the boulder, high above the lake. The boulder juts out of the water like a whale frozen in time, leap never completed, flukes still flattened at the water's edge, as sharply ridged as the pleats of a fan. She likes the way the rough granite of the ledge down there catches light and shade, all bumps and hollows. Tiny chips of mica sparkle in the sun.

For a while Timber sits beside her but then goes off to chase squirrels. She can hear him barking, the hysterical bark which means, "No fair! Come on down!" She whistles twice, the barking stops. She takes out her pencil, fills four pages with quick detail studies of the rock, the lacy ferns growing down the banks, miniature lily pads the shape of squandered hearts floating in the clear lake-water. The stems have long wavy filaments. They undulate slowly, rotating each lily pad just as a kite string hangs high in the air while the kite itself curtseys to the wind. Dragonflies zoom double-deckered over the water—mating flights, Sally's informed them. Mating while they fly. Nice trick. She must tell Sean, "Let's try," he'll suggest, wicked leer.

She puts the pencil down. No use. She'll go back to the studio empty-handed. Five days wasted, unfortunately spoiling Sally's game plan of *constructive vacation*. Too bad.

She can hear a bird warbling somewhere. Do Great Blue herons sing? No, probably just a goldfinch. Sally keeps obsessing about the Great Blue, "a real privilege to sight one," she's told them. Jebba wishes she could wander back to the cabin, announce casually how she's spotted the heron stalking slowly through the shallows.

She picks up the pencil, squints at the long spruce across the cove. All its branches are lopped off except for the one closest to the top. It looks like a ship mast. Or a cross. Dear Eunice. Maybe Sally's got the right idea, maybe the thing *is* to toughen her up.

The pine tree's not a success, perspective's all off. She sticks the pencil behind her ear, closes the pad, whistles again for Timber. She can hear him crashing through the underbrush. "Thunder Dog," she murmurs. The faint drumming of his feet on spongy turf gets louder and then he's there beside her on the rock, all licks and wet kisses. "Let's go for a swim," she says.

He follows her down the rock, whimpering. He feels about the water the way she feels about boats. She dives in, he stands on the rock ledge barking, then lopes along the shore as she swims. She stops, treads water. He trots back to the ledge, leaps in, starts out to her. He swims like a horse cantering, not a dog paddle at all. No splashing. Run silent, run deep. His head veers towards her, a dark wedge with slicked back ears periscoping right at her. She's careful not to let him come too close. His nails are long and can rake skin as he swims by. He circles her. He's breathing hard through his nose. His eyes are glazed.

"I'm fine," she tells him. "Go on back," and she pushes his hind quarters towards shore. When he scrambles up on the rock, he doesn't bark any more. He's checked her out by now. He waits, panting hard. Only his tail looks wet because his coat's so thick the guard hairs keep the pale curls of the undercoat as dry and soft as lamb's wool. The sheep part of my shepherd, she thinks with a grin.

When she gets out of the water, he leads her up the steep face of the rock. She hangs on to his tail, he strains forward, they reach the top. He trots ahead of her. He wants to go home, not back to the cabin but home. Home to Sean. So does she. But even more than that she wants Eunice happy, rested, flushed from the sun. Not a hell of a lot to ask, God, do what you can.

* * *

THAT NIGHT BEFORE THEY leave, they all go skinny-dipping. First they stow the gear in the outboard, sweep the kitchen, close the windows, stack the screens neatly against the wall, gather up all the trash and garbage into a big plastic bag which will return with them to the mainland. Timber jumps into the boat as soon as he sees Jebba's duffel bag stowed in the bow.

Sally's still puttering in the kitchen, laying D CON to kill the rest of the mice. Eunice surprises Jebba. She goes down to the dock, peels off her clothes, dumps them on the canvas chair, drops her beach towel, and slips into the water slick as a seal.

Jebba kneels by the ladder. "Is it freezing?"

Eunice laughs. "It's heaven. Like milk it feels so soft."

"I didn't think you'd actually go in."

"I know you didn't."

Jebba takes off her shift, dives in. Eunice is still laughing. "You look like you're wearing a white suit. I can see where the tan ends. All over!"

They paddle around, keeping close to the dock because Timber's out of the boat now. He paces back and forth, straining to see their white faces in the black water. Sally comes down the path. "You both in already?" she calls.

Gingerly, she steps backward down the ladder, swims out fast to the catamaran and returns just as fast. They float on their backs and look up at the first sprinkling of stars. The sky is still paler than the lake, metallic blue against the notched blackness of the pines. The water is a reflecting pool of stars. Sally tells them a long story about her husband going skinny-dipping with a buddy years ago, both dead drunk, while very important houseguests—corporate big shots from their firm—all waited and watched from the cabin, waiting until the men lumbered up the ladder, "and then the floodlights came on." She giggles. "I'm getting chilly," she says.

Eunice murmurs, "I could stay here forever. I never want to get out."

"Me either," says Jebba.

"But it's so cold," Sally says again.

"Move around," Jeb tells her. Eunice slices some water with the heel of her fist, splashing Sally. Sally jerks her head in surprise, then splashes back. Timber starts barking.

"Hush!" Jebba says.

"Wait till the men hear about this," Sally says. "How I've toughened you two up."

"Credit, credit," drawls Jebba. Sally pretends she hasn't heard.

They finally climb out, dry off, put on their clothes. Timber leads the way to the boat. Jebba climbs in beside him, holds out her hand to Eunice. "I can do it," Eunice says. Sally casts off. The outboard motor coughs, catches. They back away from the dock.

There's a breeze coming off the lake. They all shiver. Timber pulls against his leash. He lifts his muzzle to sniff the night air. He starts whining, a long series of groans from deep in his chest.

"What a crybaby," Sally says. "Mind he doesn't sit on the gas line there."

"He's not going to sit, period," answers Jebba. "He's too wound up."

Eunice strokes Timber on his ruff. "My good protector. He's sad. Sad to leave the island. His vacation's over."

Jebba yanks at the leash. Timber has put his forepaws over the side, as if to lap at the wake. "No," she says between tugs. "He's not a bit sad. He's excited about what's ahead, not what's behind."

Sally leans over, one hand on the tiller, one hand cuffing Timber's rump. "Funny creatures, dogs," she says firmly, summing it all up for them. "See, Eunice, he's thinking about good things. His dinner. His daddy. Seeing his own house again."

Eunice holds out her fingers to catch the spray. "I know, Sally," she murmurs in a patient voice. "It's called being homesick, being happy and sad at the very same time." Then she adds, "You know—like your loon?"

DERANGEMENT OF TIME, DEVIATIONS OF LIGHT

HE WAS NOT A man who complained. Or ever asked for help.

She admired this in him very much, in fact, they both did. He thought of himself as cheerful but resolute, qualities which she realized were valued as virtues in the marketplace. And presumably in a husband as well.

From the newspaper she knew there was trouble at the plant. Layoffs. Takeover threats. Management infighting. He never referred to these troubles, not directly. But he was up-tight. He had insomnia, and in the beginning he tried joking about it.

"Close my eyes," he laughed, "and the old brain starts racing, you know? Round and round, going nowhere fast."

But after a few weeks the jokes stopped. He didn't joke, he hardly spoke to her at all. The chilling silences grew longer and longer. She didn't know how to connect with him any more. When she studied him he looked blurred as if she were watching him from a great distance--an indistinct figure hunched forward, trudging over the pocked landscape of a dying moon. He was carrying his own life-support system. He didn't need hers.

Each afternoon he came home, his mouth set in a grim smile, a false smile, the lips so pale, almost transparent as if the effort of smiling had drained away all the rich red blood. What her mother used to call blue lips when she and her sisters came shivering in from the ocean, hugging their shoulders, waiting for beach towels to be snugged around their matchstick bodies, skin all bumpy with cold.

And that, she told herself, was precisely what she wanted to do for him, enfold him in the softest towelling, rub him warm, see his lips all ruddy and smiling a real smile not this rictus which greeted her at the front door each evening as if to signal all's well, but don't ask. Don't ask. Only their golden retriever still enjoyed these homecomings.

She began working late at the office. There was a major grant proposal due to go off by mid-October. And she was the departmental coordinator. She made the whole operation run like clockwork. She felt like a traffic cop,

"Ok, *move* it!" Four days behind schedule, where are the slides, those time-line sheets, the budget breakdowns? First draft, second draft, the office was drowning in printouts, her desk a yellow patchwork of POST IT messages and interdepartmental memos.

She explained she was staying late to tie up loose ends. But she knew it was really because she wanted to get home after he did. She didn't want to see his face when he came through the front door, pushing past the dog, wincing at the glad barks of welcome.

The grimmer he got, the later she worked. She drew up a master schedule then ran off extra copies to tape on everyone's phone so that at least in the beginning of each workday there would be no confusion. By mid-afternoon, though, things began to fall apart. The printers fast-talking her into another extension. One of the temp workers asking to go home early, sick kid. By 4:00 the perfect symmetry of the morning schedule had become a crosshatched jumble of arrows, big X's, and DO TOMORROWS.

She liked this work. It gave her pleasure. She was happiest when the building went quiet and the phones stopped ringing. She liked stacking the piles of manuscript, the cool Xerox paper as smooth as freshly laundered sheets. It made her heart lift. It made her feel the way she did driving to work in the mornings, crisp September mornings, watching the students as they hurried along the sidewalks to their 8:00 lectures. Fall, the best time of year, with its sharp crackling promise of dead leaves and new books.

She told him that this was the real payoff of working at the university. The annual chance to start over. "Then September," she added, "isn't...you know...isn't the end of everything." She looked over at him.

He was toying with his food pushing the zucchini around on the plate, mashing it with his fork, reducing what had been crisp green into a watery gold mush.

"Remember," she coached him, smiling, "that fresh start feeling? I mean when we were kids?"

He nodded. He smiled back at her. He knew damn well what she was trying to do, how she was trying to buoy him up. But his smile was this thin-lipped lie. It made her nervous and anxious at the same time.

She dropped her eyes, studied the zucchini again. She knew she was going to question him directly. And this was a mistake. But there was a lump of resentment in her throat she couldn't swallow any longer during these death-watch meals, her chitchatting about stuff neither one gave a hoot about. How could he shut her out this way? And not let her help him? He was hurting, hurting.

"Look," she said. "Why don't we simply discuss it."

"Discuss what?"

"Discuss what's wrong. What's eating at you."

He said nothing. He wouldn't even look at her, he was acting the sulky child being reprimanded at supper.

"Honey," she said in a softer voice, "please. Talk to me, I'm worried about you, ok?"

"There's really nothing," he stared straight through her, "to discuss."

"Don't do this!" she cried, and beneath the table, the golden retriever thumped his tail nervously, then nudged against her knee.

"Do what," he said evenly.

"Stop slamming the door in my face."

"Stop climbing all over me, you hear? Show a little consideration."

"Consideration." She paused, trying to pitch her voice very low, *ever soft, an excellent thing in a woman.* "Tell me," she said, why is it you always use that word like a club? A put-down?"

He scraped his chair back and stood up. They were still eating meals out on the porch. They kept the table out there as long as possible, sometimes as late as October even though it meant wearing light jackets while they shivered over morning coffee, hanging on with some discomfort to the illusion of summer.

Without a word he took his plate and carried it into the kitchen. The dog padded after him. She could hear him scraping food into the dog's dish, then a clink as he set the plate on the counter

Silence.

Off to his workshop?.

The dog came back out to the porch, sat beside her chair, waiting for her plate.

She heard the angry whine of the power drill down in the basement. Later tonight he would sleep again alone while she, downstairs, the dog beside her on the sofa, dozed over the long vigil of late night comics, of starry-eyed evangelists praying for both salvation and money in equal measure until finally it was morning. And she heard him tiptoe into the kitchen to turn on the kettle while across the TV screen the Eye-Opener News Team cheerfully ticked off the usual litany of daybreak disasters. A child tumbling around in a washing machine, "First you'd see this little arm go by, then a leg." Mysterious green gases poisoning an entire mountain village. A massacre in a post office, the psychotic mail clerk calmly loading and unloading his rifle without saying a single word.

Like the song said, the days dwindled down. And then it was October, warm October days, shirtsleeve weather. The day they mailed off the grant proposal, the department chairman treated the whole staff to lunch at the Faculty Club. The office had chipped in and bought her a digital watch, very expensive with so much information packed into its memory that glancing down at the numbers blinking and gyrating on its black face she felt disoriented for a moment. As if she weren't gazing down at a watch but rather up at the nighttime sky. A celestial navigator, she thought happily. That's what she was. *Ad astra per aspera.* That should be her motto, her epitaph.

The next day was their seventh wedding anniversary, so he took her out to dinner. He admired the watch, murmured again how proud he was of the great job she was doing at the college.

"Ms. Fixit," he said. "They're damn lucky to have you," and he lifted his wineglass in casual salute.

"They are, aren't they," she agreed, then laughed quickly so he wouldn't know she was waiting for him to say that he was also—lucky to have her. If she asked him, he would simply reply patiently with just the hint of a condescending little smile, "That goes without saying, dear." And she'd feel like a fool, and this whole evening would be ruined. But something of what she was thinking had seeped across the table. He had gone silent again.

The silence was heavy, it was starting to blanket them, a smothering kind of silence which seemed to cut off the air, not just speech, and she wondered if the two of them were turning into one of those couples they both had made fun of all these years. The ones who sat mute, shoveling food into their mouths as if the relationship depended entirely on those shiny fork tines, a desperate feeding which never appeared to satisfy the hunger in eyes that studied everything. The menu. Other diners. Everything but the person sitting across the table—God, this couldn't be happening to him, to her, she wouldn't let it!

"I think..." she began just as he started to speak, so she stopped. "What?" she asked.

"You first," he said.

"Age before beauty," she teased.

He shrugged, glanced down at the wine list. "Oh, just wondering, you want to finish off with a brandy? Would you like that?"

She bit her lip, shook her head. She studied her watch, then said lightly, "It's getting sort of late." It was when her voice got yearningly heavy that he retreated. The more she cared and yearned to help, the faster he disappeared. She thought of how with a high-strung horse you have to coax them by holding your palm out flat, very still, gazing nonchalantly past them at the pasture beyond. And then wait patiently for the soft pressure of a velvety muzzle snuffling wet and warm against your hand. Dispassionate patience is what it took. Kindness once removed, even disguised. She knew this, she *knew* it. Why was it so hard with him? Why did he back away the more she tried to reach out, to heal him, blot away the pain?

"Right," he was saying now in a flat voice. He got out the credit card, slapped it down across the bill.

For a minute she was glad. Glad they kept on getting their signals crossed. At least now he wouldn't go through the charade of waving his wineglass and murmuring "Happy Anniversary, darling."

She couldn't bear to hear him say those words, couldn't bear to hear the travesty spoken aloud—like hearing news of a terminal illness while trying to match it with the bland smile on the doctor's face.

Except, hang on, their relationship was sound. He and she and the relationship. Three separate entities, Yin and Yang forming the circle which enclosed them. The circle was still there, she was still there. He was the patient, *he* was the sick one, not the bond between them. He was sinking. And she couldn't help him.

The next morning they got up early even though it was Saturday. After breakfast she reminded him of chores. The dump. The gutters. And could he sign that birthday card for one of his nieces? The card had sat on his desk since Wednesday. A strategic mistake leaving it there. He never went near his desk any more. When letters came addressed to him, he left them unopened. When the phone rang, he stiffened.

"If it's me they want," he would say curtly, "take a message."

He wouldn't even talk to his folks last night when they called with happy anniversary greetings. At night he lay iron hard beside her, staring into the same darkness she stared into. By midnight she would climb out of bed and go dream in front of the television one more time. The chattering voices, the blinking images from the screen—she couldn't sleep without them—they had become an addiction. Television narcosis? She remembered reading about deep-sea divers going into a trance on a deep dive, losing their bearings and sometimes drowning. Nitrogen narcosis is what they had; but what they called it was raptures of the deep.

"The dump, darling. It closes at noon," she said again.

He was stretched out on the living room couch, his hands folded across his chest. His hobby magazines lay scattered on the rug, his work boots and heavy wool socks as well. On the end table his coffee cup with a plate of half eaten cold toast.

She began to straighten things, picked up all the magazines and stacked them neatly in a pile beside the couch. She took the cup and the plate, then looked down at him.

His eyes were shut. He didn't answer.

"Noon, dear," she repeated. "The garbage? Please, honey, we're having dinner guests tonight, remember? I mean there's a lot to do, gotta get moving here."

His eyelids quivered, but still he kept them shut.

He hadn't shaved. He hadn't even taken his shower this morning. Something sour seemed to waft from him. She couldn't tell whether it was actually him or the mood he was in.

She took two steps backward, away from the couch. She almost tripped over his work boots. "Hey," she whispered, "anybody home in there?" and tried to laugh. But her throat was too dry, it felt as if rubber rings were squeezing down the laughter.

And then she realized that she was afraid *of* him, not for him.

"Get off my case," he said in a voice she didn't recognize. It sounded like it was coming from an ugly pit deep inside, a mucous-thick well of anger.

"I just—" she stammered.

His eyes flew open. He stared at the ceiling.

The dog whined, then turned and went trotting up the stairs, tail tucked between its hind legs.

"You just this, you just that," he mimicked her. "Beat it," he told her. "You can't fix everything. You goddamn well can't make everything better, control the whole fucking *universe!*"

She tried to interrupt him, she even knelt down by the couch and put her hand on his shoulder. "Please…please don't. I only meant…."

But the second she touched him, he jerked away.

And then he was standing up, he was kicking the pile of magazines in all directions. He picked up one of the work boots and heaved it at the sherry decanter, cut crystal, a family heirloom. The decanter shattered on the floor.

He went upstairs. The guestroom door slammed into the silence. The dog shot down the stairwell, whimpering. She cleaned up the shards of glass, then got dry towels to soak up the sherry. The dog kept trying to help, first licking the floor, then her fingers, then her face.

She washed her hands and bathed her eyes, so swollen she looked disfigured. She took a deep breath and went upstairs to the guestroom. The dog stayed down below, watching her from the bottom step.

She opened the door.

The room was empty, the twin beds a mess with blankets on the floor, the bottom sheet half yanked off one mattress.

She stood there listening.

Downstairs the phone started to ring. It gave her the courage to walk past the beds, slowly open the door to the attic.

At first all she could see were old sleeping bags, a couple of suitcases. A fishing rod. Then something moved, and she looked in the corner where the movement came from, and she saw his bare feet—the long white toes pale in the attic shadows—and she listened to the rasping noise of him breathing hard through his mouth.

She went downstairs and called the McPhersons, the Levines, to cancel the dinner party that evening.

"He's sick," she found herself saying and got off the line fast.

The dog came and rested his head on her knee after she hung up. She wished he would go lie down, leave her alone. But automatically she patted the satiny gold head, thinking that this must be a little bit the way he felt upstairs—cornered by compassion.

It was still quiet, too quiet—not a sound from up there. Only the sound of her own heart thudding. And the panting of the dog which reminded her of the panting up under the attic eaves, so she got her purse, took out her dark glasses, and invited the dog for a nice ride.

They rode around for most of the day. They went for a run in the state part beside the reservoir. The dog sniffed at the water's edge, then waded in to where the water came up to his curly gold chest. He stood there drinking deep, such deep gulps he started to choke. "Easy, boy," she told him. "That's a big lake."

Back in the car, the reek of his wet coat made her glad it was warm outside and the windows could be rolled down. He stuck his dripping muzzle out the back window. He was gulping down smells now, smells which served as familiar signposts for where they were headed—he, a veteran suburban shopper, her loyal companion on these weekend errands.

She stopped at the cobbler. She went to the post office just before they closed the doors. She wondered if she should drive over to the main office to make sure these letters got out on time. A new clerk she didn't know stood behind the counter. All she did was ask him the question, but he kept a line of six people waiting while he lectured her on regional pick-ups. "Listen, lady, you don't need to shop around, you follow? We're up to date here, know what I'm saying?"

His eyes glittered at her. The whole time he was talking, he kept his hand flat across her envelopes. She tried to inch her fingers forward to retrieve them. His voice got louder. He leaned towards her, then took the letters and tossed them into the big canvas mail bags. The people in line behind her shuffled their feet.

She turned away from the counter, leaving the guy in mid-sentence.

"Hey, lady!" he called after her. But she went on out the door, walking fast.

She did the marketing. It took twice as long as usual because she kept doubling back, flinching when a cart came rolling around a display case. She kept her eyes down, pretended to study her list. By the time she got back to the car, her blouse was soaked.

She wished they could return to the lake and she and the dog could just go stand in the still water until her feet went as numb as her brain seemed to be this afternoon, numbed from the effort of not thinking about him upstairs. Not remembering those elegant long toes splayed on the attic floor, a strange tropical flower with five pale petals, delicately articulated.

"One more stop," she promised the dog. "Then home." He pricked his ears, barked impatiently when she left the car once more.

The library was cool inside, cool and peaceful. And safe, only a couple of people browsing, nobody she knew. She relaxed, took her usual route from biographies to new fiction to mysteries, piling her books neatly on the big oak table in front of the fireplace.

But when she went to the circulation desk, one of the novels was missing.

"I know I had it," she told the librarian. "It was on top."

The librarian frowned. They both glanced around the reading room. A couple of kids stood giggling next to the water fountain. A man was reading newspapers at the far end of the oak table, next to the bay windows. And an elderly woman sat hunched in the wing chair beside the fireplace.

"I think I know what happened," said the librarian. "Come with me."

They walked over to the fireplace, their footsteps hushed by the soft gray wool carpeting. They stood there, looking down at the old lady. She kept right on reading, her shoulders humped forward.

The librarian spoke to her quietly, explaining the problem.

The old woman turned and began to chuckle, began describing how much she liked this author, wasn't he a fine writer? staring past them at the open windows. She reached down and scrabbled in a white canvas sack next to the wing chair.

"Here you are!" she said with a roguish smile. "I've already read ten pages, you are going to love this, my dear!"

She sounded perfectly normal, perfectly rational, the voice educated, amused, a perfect grandmother's voice.

But as she spoke, a long chain of spittle hung down from her chin exactly like the dog's when he was begging for steak, and through the silver rope of saliva could be seen the books wavering on the shelves behind the chair, their glossy bindings rippling in the same way cottonwood leaves will shiver in a breeze, first a pale olive then back to silver again, quite lovely actually the way light waves bend moving from one density to the next—from air to water—bending the books, the shelves, like crouching behind a waterfall trying to look out, trying to see their faces, the old lady's, the librarian, out of focus and blurred.

And then the silence, a silence not safe any longer, from a question gone too long unanswered. The whole reading room—the women's faces, the shelves shifting and tilting, making her dizzy, making her brace her arm against the solid wood of the fireplace. She couldn't wait to get out of here, to get home.

That night he didn't come down to supper.

She drank two glasses of warm Chablis, put the food back in the refrigerator, fed the dog. Afterwards, she went to the foot of the stairs and called up twice.

No answer.

The hall light had burned out at the top of the stairs so she grabbed the tip of the dog's tail and told him softly, "Go. Go."

The dog climbed slowly. He led her up to the bedroom door and stood beside her, panting hard, as she turned the knob.

They walked in, then stopped for a moment to get their bearings. With a sigh, the dog heaved himself down beside the bureau where there was bare flooring. Too hot to lie on the shag rug. Too hot in here, period.

She opened the window, undressed rapidly, afraid she would lose her nerve and bolt back downstairs, cuddle in front of the television with the new P.D. James. It was still early; the clock on the night table said only 10:15. She rubbed her shoulders and shivered. She had goose bumps even though it felt like July in here, the air thick, almost viscous.

Finally, she stood beside the bed. She could see his face in the moonlight. His eyes were closed, but she knew he wasn't sleeping. She eased down beside him, her arm brushing against his. It felt as cold and rigid as a cocked rifle. She touched his hand. His fist was doubled up, the knuckles a row of cold marbles under her fingertips.

Then she spoke, in a clear voice, very matter of fact. Not questioning him. Not placating. She spoke as if she were answering the phone at work, with absolutely no preconceptions as to who might be on the other end of the line.

"I'm here," she said.

And let the night press down around her. And watched the moonlight coil through open windows in long strands of silver.

Then as he rolled towards her—rolled with something between a groan and an exhalation as if all the air in his lungs were coming out in one final rush—she understood they would lie twined together this way all through the night and maybe even all through the next day and that to give him a hand up was not going to be possible and that she must sink deep, deep down beside him and feel the same hot darkness as he felt crushing her chest wall, feel the pounding in her middle ear which cut off all other noise and signaled something cold was leaking into apertures it was not meant to enter, seeping with chilling pain through intricate canals more delicate than the most fragile crystal.

And now, she thought, the wine of daylight has been tasted. It's all that's poured for us today.

Empty.

And whether they had savored it, or squandered it, that particular wineglass was now washed and put away.

No more. All gone.

Nothing left but the two of them, adrift and drowning in the dark. No escape. No more dreams of rescue. Only him curled here beside her, their bodies interlocked in this complex Yin-Yang configuration, both separate and fused at the same time.

The infinite or the absolute?

Harmony or dissolution?

Did he know? Would they ever know for certain? It made her head pound, these questions. No answers, not tonight.

And so, patiently, she pulled the sheet over both of them, and wide-eyed watched the clock numbers glowing beside the bed, the same luminous green-gold, she realized, that sunlight dancing on water has when seen from far down below, seen from the bottom, gazing up.

TRUE AND TENDER IS THE NORTH

IN THE MOONLIGHT THE chair looks blue. So does the table.

He stands by the open window. It's still hot outside and he can hear the crickets down by the river.

The bottle of beer feels good and cold in his hand, and when he drinks, beads of water glisten like silver along the dark throat of the bottle.

A door creaks. He puts the beer down on the table, wipes his hands on a dishtowel. He waits, taps the shoulder holster lumpy under his shirt, chafing the skin.

Upstairs one of the kids starts coughing. He listens. Somebody's coming.

He waits for the harsh yellow of the kitchen light. Nothing happens except for a floorboard squawking out in the hall. And then a pale shape is standing at the door of the kitchen. It's Anna. His chest tightens.

"Hey, sis," he says. "Los niños ok?"

"Ok, considering."

"Nobody having nightmares or anything?"

"They're fine, Roberto," she answers, stops for a moment. "But exhausted. First funeral they've ever been to."

"Tough losing a grandma," he says. "She loved those boys so much, losing her is going to make a hole in their lives...forever."

"Tough kids," she says proudly. "They'll be brave hombres, they promised." She's walking towards him slowly. She's barefoot and she floats forward, quiet as a ghost.

He turns back to the window, runs his thumb and forefinger carefully along the neck of the bottle, then slides his whole hand down slippery wet glass as it flares voluptuously into the rounded base.

"Cat got your tongue?" she's saying. She's standing beside him now. She's just washed her hair, he can smell Caresse shampoo and Yardley lavender soap. Probably all she gets is a whiff of stale beer and cigarettes. And leftover fear.

"Gracias, chica," he tells her.

"For what?"

326

"For not turning on the lights."

She takes his hand, gives it a squeeze. "I remember," she says to him.

"Remember?"

"How you love the dark."

"Always did, didn't I?" he says, pleased.

She laughs, that same deep, throaty cascade of chuckles she's had since she was a skinny kid. They called it her boom-box laugh. "Remember, Rob?" she says. "That night? The lake house in Gainesville? The night we climbed out and sat on the garage roof. All night long. I was only—what—twelve or thirteen?"

"You were thirteen, chica."

"And the collie followed us out there and almost fell off?"

"And you hung on to his collar the whole damn night, him whimpering every second."

"It was so wild. On the roof at *night*, Robby! So dangerous, I mean we could've fallen—not just the dog—broken our necks."

"Right."

"I always think about that time."

He shrugs. "Except for the dog, nothing much happened." Except my whole God-forsaken life changed, and nothing's been the same since. He tries to relax, takes a deep breath, tries to smile down at her.

She laughs again. "That was the point. Nobody fell off the roof, nobody broke a leg, the collie finally started to snore—whimpered himself right into dreamland. And I was never ever scared of the dark after that. You cured me."

"Verdad?"

"Sure, don't you remember, you told me never to panic in the dark, all I had to do was orient myself by studying the stars."

"Si."

"And you rattled off that poem."

"Tennyson."

"Pretty poem, sorta sad."

"Yeah, *dark and true and tender is the North.*"

"I loved that poem, Roberto."

"I loved it too."

"Papa also loved it, he adored all those guys, Wordsworth, Keats, Shelley. Hey, you remember the one by Lord Byron?"

"Which one, querida?" and he holds very still.

"I think it's called *So We'll Go No More Aroving*, always got a kick outta the way it goes rollicking along—ta dum ta dum *aroving/ So late into the night/Though the heart be still as loving/And the moon be still as bright.*"

"Ahh," he answered. "One of his most beautiful lyrics." And silently he hears the loveliest—and saddest—love song penned by Byron for his sister Augusta but which he never dared publish in his lifetime: *I speak not—I trace not—I breathe not thy name/There is grief in the sound—there were guilt in the fame.*

"Right! And Papa used to say that's how the nuns in Havana teach Latino kids to speak good English, then he'd tell us—" She stops, waits a beat.

"Memorize, niños, memorize!" they both chant simultaneously.

"Roberto." She hesitates.

"Hmmmn."

"I've always wondered, I mean it wasn't something I could ever discuss with Mama, but the thing is I never got a handle on how come our Papa, you know…why Papa ever went to work for…for them?"

"Ah, niña…back in those days, illegal Cuban immigrant washes up in Miami, drug cartel's pretty much the only game in town. Nobody's gonna hire exiled Cuban professors, no matter how well-educated, for God's sake. Everything he ever had was confiscated by Castro, he was lucky to reach the States."

"And you followed right in his tracks."

"You sound like Mama."

She's silent.

"Beer?"

"Why not," she answers. She leans her head back and takes a long gulp. "Bueno," she says and wipes her mouth with the back of her fist which makes him smile. First time he shared a brew with her, she had used that very same gesture. He knew she was copying her brother and dad, she was being one of the tough guys. Bravo, Anna!

Now she tells him apologetically, "I'm really thirsty, it's so hot tonight."

"Anna, you don't need an excuse ," he answers, half annoyed. Mama had despised "the poison drink" as she called it, the endless booze which had stolen the man she married, broken him. But was it booze that killed him? Or a broken heart?

"Not in this fool family, I don't," she says, but she says it in her kid sister voice, half chiding, half loving, and takes another long swig, her head tilted way back, her white throat swelling then contracting as she swallows.

They sit down at the table, side by side, staring out at the spiky black outline of Canadian hemlocks against a dark navy blue sky.

"Mama told me how much she loved it here," he says. He pauses, then adds, "That's the other great line in the Tennyson thing, talking about the south…*bright and fierce and fickle is the South.* You know how glad she was to get away, she used to write me about sitting here, sipping her maté, looking out at the hemlocks. Lonesome-looking tree, she said. Said the trees in Maine are like the people who live here. Survivors. Like her."

"Oh, Robby." Anna leans her head against him. He can feel her shoulders shaking. They remind him of thin branches blown by sharp gusts of wind. He puts one arm around, bracing her hard against the storm.

"Hey, niña. Easy on. She had it really good when she moved north. Talk about healing, Mama had the best ten years of her life up here. With you and the boys."

"I know." She hiccups gently.

He thumps her back. Her skin feels cool and dry even in this heat. "Only woman in this world," he tells her, "who gets the hiccups when she cries."

"The beer doesn't help matters," she says.

"Cures what ails you, chica," he observes and reaches for another. The empty bottle clinks against the other empties in the carton. A good sound. He smiles.

She sits up straight, wiping her cheeks with the heel of her hand. "How many you had?" she asks, voice hard.

He doesn't answer. Outside, the bullfrogs have started in now, deep throbbing bass drowning out the crickets. He can see fireflies twinkling by the bushes.

"A six pack at least," she's saying.

He lights up a cigarette, draws deep. "Who counts?" he says.

"I count. And you ought to."

"Why?"

"You tell me."

"Anna, you sound just like her."

"She worried so about you, Roberto."

"I know she did. The old man all over again. Same old story."

"You hardly ever write."

"I call though. Give me credit, kid."

"Credit, credit! But it's so hard. I mean keeping track of you. Miami one month, Vegas the next. We never know where you are, where you're going."

He stands up, stretches. The holster pulls under his arms and the skin feels raw and very tender, occupational hazard, you might say. "What she tell folks these days?" he asks casually. "You know, about her beloved son's whereabouts?"

She stares up at him. Her face is in shadow and all he can see clearly is the milky roundness of those white shoulders gleaming in the moonlight.

He swivels away sharply, walks over to the fridge. She is speaking with care, picking her way across the river of explanations very slowly, testing each word for solidity, for balance. He half listens, he's heard all this before. It's a familiar river-crossing for both of them. But still dangerous.

"Commercial real estate," she's saying. "Tourist hotels, time-share condos."

He gives a short laugh. "Close enough. Smart like a fox, the old mamacita."

"Rob." She's standing right next to him again, she puts a hand on his arm. He pulls open the refrigerator door, pulls out more beer and some sliced provolone from the deli platter. Nobody ate a damn thing after the funeral. They had laid in enough cold cuts for an army. Only a couple dozen people showed up at the house. He wouldn't let Anna place a death notice in the newspaper.

"Hungry?" he asks her, then closes the door quickly because in the bluish-white light from the fridge, he can see she's only wearing a very thin nightgown, very short, mid-thigh, and it's so sheer he can see right through the filmy gauze to the twin darkness of her nipples and the triangulated shadow below. *Oh! thine be the gladness and mine be the guilt.*

"Here," he says, handing her the cheese. "Slap me some sandwiches together. Lots of the party rye left." And he turns away from her.

"Where you going?" she calls.

"Got to phone someone," he says.

She follows him to the doorway. "It's three in the morning, Roberto."

He stares back at her. "Buddy of mine, expecting the call."

She turns the cheese over and over in her hands, he can hear the rustle of the wax paper. "It never ends," she says, voice gone flat.

He says nothing.

"Even your own madre's funeral," she goes on. She walks over to the counter. Her back is to him. He stands there staring at the soft black mass of her hair haloed by moonlight streaming through the kitchen window. She says something but so softly he misses it.

"What?"

"You're leaving us."

"Have to, querida."

"When?"

"Very shortly."

"You won't even get to say goodbye to the boys!"

"Anna." He tries to make the word sound gentle. But even her name feels raw in his mouth, as raw as the skin rubbed angry red under his arm. "There's a delivery tomorrow. Up near the border. It's a good two-hour run."

She turns back around and faces him, but in the darkness all she seems to be is a series of familiar ovals and the long pale column of her body bent forward in grief.

"…came back up here just for business," she's saying. "Not for Mama."

"You know damn well that's not true," he tells her and walks away. "Make the sandwiches. There's not much time."

He takes his cell phone into the den, switches on the desk lamp. In the orange pool of light, the faces of his nephews smile back at him: three good kids, trusting like their mother. He picks up the silver frame. They have red hair like their dad's, that asshole son of a cockroach! but their dark eyes are Anna's. And their mouths, set firm, strong like their grandmother's, big lopsided smiles, a little cocky. He takes out his wallet, peels off five big ones, places the bills down on the desk and sets the picture face down over the five k.

He dials quickly. The phone's picked up after the first ring. "Yeah," a voice answers.

"Six o'clock?"

"Check."

"Take care of the customs guy?"

"Yeah. Under control."

"No problems, then?"

"We'll be there."

"See ya."

"Check." And the line goes dead. He turns off the lamp, rests his hand for a moment on the desk. He raps hard with his knuckles three times. "Hasta luego, mi sobrinos," he whispers, and shakes his head.

He goes out to the hall. The light's on now in the kitchen. Anna's put on her apron. She's pouring coffee into a big red thermos. She doesn't look up.

"All set?" he asks.

She screws on the lid. "This holds about four cups. I put in the sugar. But no cream. Figured you want it black."

"Bueno," he says. He walks back to the hall, grabs his bag.

She follows him. She's carrying the thermos and a paper sack with the sandwiches. "Careful with the coffee," she whispers. "It's boiling hot."

He laughs. "You know me, sis. Careful to a fault, Papa used to say."

Then she's looking up at him, eyes big. "Robby," she says.

"Not now, Anna. I got to get going."

"Roberto, please!" Her voice slides up and she's his baby sister again, scared of the dark, scared of the night. "What are you running from? It's safe now, it's safe here with me."

"Maybe so, sugar."

"You can come back! They never found us. They never will."

He sets the bag down, puts both hands under her chin, tilts her head up, then gives the chin a gentle nudge. "Long as I don't lead them to you, they won't." He glances down at his watch. "Caramba!" he exclaims. "Almost three-thirty. I gotta split."

She's waiting for him to kiss her goodbye. He brushes his lips quickly over her forehead, an appropriate benediction—all he will ever allow himself.

"I'm coming out with you to the car," she tells him.

But he takes the sandwich bag in one hand, stuffs the thermos in the side pocket of his satchel, opens the door. "No," he says. "You stay here. And make sure not to turn on the porch lights."

"Adios, darling," she says softly. "Tenga cuidado, you hear?"

He smiles down at her. "Hug the boys for me," he murmurs, and then he's out the door, closing it softly behind him.

He doesn't look back. He stows his gear in the back seat, puts the sandwiches and the thermos beside the driver's seat, kicks the tires, climbs in. The driveway curves along the river, then up the hill to the main road.

In the moonlight the highway spools out in a long band of pine-dappled silver. The breeze feels cool on his face. He lets his back muscles go slack for the first time in thirty-six hours. The danger lies behind, not ahead.

The silver road uncoils before him. He steps on the gas. The engine purrs. The road surface is graded fairly smooth for the north country so he cranks her up to eighty-five, perfect cruising speed for an Alfa, and he again shakes his head, shakes it hard, shaking away the booze, shaking himself awake, shaking himself free from the forbidden dreams of a lifetime—from the blurred shimmer of pale young arms pulling him down, down, floating downwards onto wet summer grass speckled with moonbeams in the hot southern night, pale young face lifted up to his while she listens to him murmur that lifelong litany of loss—*Oh best and dearest*—as Byron greets his sister.

"Anna," he groans.

EXIT LINES

MONDAY AGAIN. WHY ARE Mondays so grim? Why can't I ever think of them as the brand new beginning of the week, a fresh start? Hank bounces out of bed like a rubber ball every single morning, Mondays included.

"Come on, honey!" he sings out. "Up and at 'em!"

At 'em? Is this a battle cry, a call to arms? What have we got here?

He tells me I have an attitude problem about waking up in general, Mondays in particular. Hey, he's absolutely correct. "Let me dream," I murmur. "Got to finish this dream." But the dog is whining to go out, so then I know the jig is up.

Mondays I don't have a class scheduled until mid-morning, Freshman Composition, trying to beat into their heads the basics they ought to have learned back in high school. But even at 9 a.m. the traffic is still bumper to bumper on the Expressway, so I always try to leave early. I mean you never know. Better safe than sorry. The early bird gets the worm.

Scratch an English teacher, Hank teases me, and the stale bromides come gurgling out by the bucketful. It's embarrassing. Even more so when I realize I've just said "Early bird" aloud. And our German Shepherd is cocking his head at me. Politely, but slightly quizzical nonetheless.

Poor dog. He doesn't like it when I start rushing in the mornings, walking fast from room to room. He follows me everywhere. I guess you'd have to say he's dogging my footsteps. Why is it, I wonder, so many pejorative terms have the word *dog* in them? Dog tired, dog eared, dog days, dog in the manger, dog's life. Even dogged isn't really complimentary. It's like bullheaded only with a damp doggy earnestness.

"Good *dog,*" I say brightly. But he's not bought off by false reassurances. He knows the morning routine, perhaps even better than I do. That is to say, he will always have hope, but he's also a realist, he knows what's what. He trots beside me. To the basement to throw the last load into the dryer. Upstairs to make the bed, then back down to the study to get my lecture notes. We move in tandem, my heels sound loud on the hardwood floors. His nails click as he leads me (*shepherds* me?) in here to the kitchen. Now he sits down with a heavy sigh, watching me load the dishwasher. I hurry, it's getting late. One more cup of coffee and then I'm off. To the wars, to the races. To the treadmill is more like it, running fast just to stay in place. They turned me down for tenure; I'd like to quit, chuck the whole thing. I do believe in fast exits. Not hanging around when your time's run out, when they don't want you anymore but are too polite to say so. Not wearing out your welcome.

"Always exit fast, Molly," my dad used to tell me. "And always leave them laughing."

My father collected jokes the way some people collect old glass, old bottles colored a strange swamp green or the purest Mediterranean blue. All those years I was away at boarding school, right on through college and beyond, he used to send me clippings once or twice a month. Jokes he clipped from *Reader's Digest*, "Life in these United States" and "Laughter is the Best Medicine". Or two line jokes, fillers I guess they're called, from the *Saturday Evening Post* or maybe *Colliers*, magazines long gone, replaced in the humor department by this mysterious flood of e-mail jokes everyone gets these days from unknown sources, off the wall humor on every conceivable topic. My dad would have been in ecstasy, plus it's so easy now to run off hard copies whereas he made such a big production out of the thing. He didn't simply mail the clippings, he cut them out carefully, then glued them to shirt cardboards he saved from the laundry. (No matter how tight money was, he always insisted on professionally ironed shirts.) At school I was embarrassed to have anyone see this stuff, to have my friends think our family read anything as lowbrow as *Readers Digest*. So I threw the clippings in the wastebasket, usually without even giving them a glance.

"Laugh and the world laughs with you," he always told me. "Cry and you cry alone." I believed him. But this advice seemed strange coming from him, he was not a laughing man, a backslapper. He was in fact quite solemn, a proud man with the automatic yet slightly puzzled courtliness of the displaced Southern aristocrat. I think his fascination with corny jokes came out of an almost wistful need to connect with ordinary folks, the need to be the sort of hail-fellow-well-met kind of individual he admired among his colleagues. Maybe too these jokes shed some light on a world he found both bizarre and dangerous.

No, my father was not a laughing man. But he had crinkles around his eyes so the illusion of laughter was always present, even though the weak lines of the mouth were serious, actually drooping a bit. I'm just the opposite. My eyes look mournful, no laugh lines at all, but I guess my lips just naturally curve up in a happy expression. When I walk down the street, people smile back at me. It's as if we're sharing a joke. Or perhaps an understanding.

Growing up, I thought I understood my father perfectly. And pitied him.

At least I understood what had happened to him, that he was a man broken by life, passed over. That he thought himself a failure long before the world made that same judgement. But understanding *what* happened was not the same as understanding *why*. And how he must have felt inside.

"Don't borrow trouble, Howard," my mother was always telling him.

But borrow he did, even during the years of success, of fantastic promotions in the international firm he joined at age twenty straight out of accounting school and which finally fired him thirty years later. Fired him, his boss, his boss's boss. Simply sheared off a whole line of middle-aged executives as if they were offending appendages no longer useful. Necrosis it's called: "Pathologic death of living tissue." Except that what dies is not the tissue. What dies is the soul, very slowly.

Getting fired is what my dad had been dreading his entire life. Mother used to say, "From his very first promotion, he was totally convinced they were out to get him."

And in the end they did.

He didn't know how to protect himself, I suppose. He wasn't a street fighter, he didn't enjoy political hardball. He was a gentleman. A gentle man with hair that had gone pure white in his late twenties, a tall man with narrow shoulders and a tiny paunch. Very reserved, a sweet sad expression, receding chin. But with the brow, the broad rounded brow of a nobleman. "So distinguished looking, your dad," everyone said.

My mother was the one with the street smarts. While he floundered from one bad investment to the next, she marched off to work. Failure was not a word she allowed herself to use. I don't think it ever occurred to her that she might flinch, or falter. She held us together. She was gallant, she was ruthless. She cashed in his insurance policies first. Then she sold the exquisite jewelry he had bought her during those glamorous years when he was the big CEO in China, in Argentina, and she played to the hilt the role of clever hostess for company dinners and endless cocktail parties.

Finally she sold the furniture, the beautiful antiques her private dealers had found for her in Shanghai. Not all of it got sold. But the big expensive pieces went fast. The teak dining room set: highboy, twelve chairs, the dining room table. I remember that table, playing underneath it when I was small. Those massive legs so intricately carved that the deep black whorls looked ready to engulf a finger or swallow the whole hand of a little child. I can still remember those clawed feet splayed across the Oriental rugs. They scared me. They might easily have been the talons of a restless dragon waiting to spring straight in my direction before taking flight, belching fire and smoke.

I was glad to watch all that teak stuff go. And the huge, loomingly tall screens of inlaid ivory and mother of pearl along with the twin cabinets—

also inlaid with ivory carvings on the doors, pastoral scenes of pagodas and ancient figures kneeling under flowering trees, calmly preparing a meal—where liquor for the big company parties used to be stored. The shelves inside these cabinets were made of rough wood, unfinished and with that musty smell of something very old. Creepy.

A few smaller pieces Mother kept. I can see them from right here in the kitchen.

Three lovely rosewood tables—nesting tables, one fitting inside the other, the latticework scrolls on the sides a delicate black filigree, and the sheen of the wood so lovely to touch, smoother than silk.

I can see the dinnerware from here as well. We keep it locked in the china closet out there in the dining room. Mother commissioned the collection, the Thousand Flower design the pattern is called. It took three Chinese artisans almost two years to paint the flowers. Sometimes I get out the service plates, run my fingers over the bright gold and red of the pattern. The flowers feel bumpy beneath my fingertips. These are not plates to eat on, of course, you serve soup and salad on top of them, then remove them for the entrée. They come by their bumps aesthetically, not practically. The dinner plates are all creamy white, with the bumpy flowers growing only on the rim.

My father loved this china. He set great store by exquisite things. I believe that when the furniture and the jewelry had to be sold, it hurt him more than the day he was fired. All those beautiful treasures he brought back for his beautiful wife. The sable coats he smuggled in from Russia. The cloisonné vases. The ivory madonna. Mother's star sapphire ring with its unwinking blue eye which stared at me with the fixed intensity of something alive. It gave me the shivers, staring out with the same alien intelligence of deep sea creatures trapped behind the glass wall at the Aquarium. Can they see us? Does that murky water blur our faces?

Piece by piece my father's booty disappeared. To pay for tuition costs of my expensive schooling. "She must have the best," he told my mom. To pay bills: rent, car installments, doctor's fees.

And my father clipped jokes, got sick, but still set out each morning to make the rounds of retail stores that might buy his line of "customized" office supplies. The embossed #2 pencils with clever logos advertising this and that. The simulated leather briefcases. Pencil sharpeners made to look like dice or fruit—a slice of watermelon, say. File folders. Any number of desk gadgets. Change purses of the cheapest plastic. They had these triangular mouths you squeezed open to insert nickels and dimes. Desk calendars with cheery aphorisms for each month: "Everyone should believe in something; I believe I'll have another drink." Or "Better to be a coward for a minute than dead for the rest of your life."

Each morning my dad went out to the car to check on his inventory locked in the trunk, carefully covered by an old chenille bedspread. I used to watch him from the window when I was home on vacation. Mother left for work at 7:30 sharp, he never left much before 10. He would close the trunk of the blue Studebaker and then walk around the side, climb in the front seat. Attached behind the windshield visor was one of his own products, a complex accordion holder for credit cards, car registration, plus a small pad of paper with an imitation brass pencil. But the string was too short so the pencil sort of dangled. Totally ridiculous, who could write anything at that angle? But the idea was clever, he told me. "Never can tell when a brainstorm might hit you. Here's the real gimmick," he added, then showed me the hidden pocket for what he called mad money.

He used to sit in the car for a long while, engine running. "Warming it up," he claimed. Even in summer. On the seat next to him he had his mimeographed order blanks, his lists of prospects which he kept in a red and black accounts ledger with all the names painstakingly block-printed in the debits column. He also carried a silver thermos of hot coffee and two packs of Chesterfield cigarettes. Clipped to his crisp white shirt was a plastic penholder, "Executive Shields" they were called. He said they were a very hot item, particularly after ballpoint pens got so popular, and shirts kept getting ruined by the greasy blue ink.

Every morning it was the same routine. First the engine. Then he took the prospects list and his brown map case from the glove compartment to check names against the city map. He studied those names for a long time, at least two cigarettes worth. Then…I don't know what he was doing then. He sat there, his face blurred behind the windshield, hands on the steering wheel, staring straight ahead at the garage door.

This is when I would usually find something else to do. I'd go off in my room, play Edith Piaf records so loud I couldn't hear the car engine running. My heart would start to pound. I wanted to run out to the driveway and yell, "Go, just GO!" I found myself muttering the bitter things my mom said to him when she was cranky, her feet aching from standing at work too long. "You old fool." Or, "Just do it, don't dither!" Or, "Mister, all you need is a little gumption."

These were the only times I was ever really angry with my dad.

But he never knew. Never knew I watched. Never knew my heart was thudding just as hard as his. Or ached like his for what was gone forever, the self-respect along with the servants and the furniture. Or that his stigma was mine as well, the stigma of going door to door with only stale jokes for a motto. The courage it must have taken for him to set out each morning, a

courage nobody credited, certainly not me. Bravery belied by the wounded
look around the weak mouth spelling out for all the world to read: "Loser."

The dog can read my mind. He's whining. And the coffee's stone cold.
Oh, I thought I understood why Mother got so fed up with him. At least she
was only annoyed. My reaction was far more ignoble. I was ashamed of him,
purely ashamed. And later on, ashamed of the shame. Humiliated by his
failure and its corollary result: a mother forced to go to work in a time when
few women did—certainly nobody I knew. I was also bored silly listening to
him brag about terrific commissions and how his prospect list was growing as
fast as the boom in the economy.

Why did he bother? Mother and I—we knew the score. He must have
realized he wasn't fooling us. He'd sit there after supper and spin these pie-
in-the-sky schemes on how to crack this or that new market. How he had a
good shot at becoming the office supply rep for a new discount chain. Maybe
as a sideline, he might set up this fabulous correspondence school deal, get
your diploma by mail.

"That man," Mother would say on the phone to her sisters. "He hasn't
got a practical bone in his entire body."

But in the end the correspondence school was one dream which finally
did come true. When he got too sick to drive. I still have three large cartons
of his official stationery, with its expensive letterhead: *La Salle Extension
University.* Only now, in middle age, can I finally use this paper. By the
same token, I could never throw it away all those years. It bothers me to use
it for scrap paper, it feels disloyal. He was so proud of it and of being the
University's sole New England Director For Marketing. He showed off their
brochures. He valued my opinion, I was a college teacher, I knew what a
syllabus was, knew all about reading lists and matriculation requirements. All
he knew was accounting.

He set up work in the guest room, spent hours typing up query letters
to send out in regional mailings. The sound of the typewriter keys clacking
away in there I found reassuring. He was a crack typist, the best in that little
Southern accounting school he attended. When I came home for quick visits
at Christmas, first alone, then with Hank, the tap-tapping didn't sound
forlorn. It was a busy productive noise, infinitely more bearable than listening
to the Studebaker idling in the driveway.

The last two years he was much too weak even to type. But his files and
what my mother called "all that fool paraphernalia" were still spread out in
the guest room. Neatly lettered files, stacks of brochures, IN & OUT baskets,
another marked PENDING, that one was empty. His mug full of freshly
shaved pencils, #2s naturally, embossed with the Lafayette logo and H.R.
Stafford, MKT. DIR. The tall old Smith Corona with its high humped black

cover prudently keeping dust off the keys. A stack of shirt cardboards; two bottles of Duco cement, unopened. The ornate pen, pencil and letter opener presented to him by his staff when he left the company, his name in gold letters etched across the green marble base.

When I peeked in to say hello, the room looked like the office of a big shot executive, and I know he felt the same way. He liked to sit there in his plaid bathrobe, sit quietly in the swivel chair, peering at the files, the letter opener in his hands, turning it over and over, a lap rug across his bony knees. For my solemn dad, he actually looked cheerful, in fact, he almost looked happy.

"Got some new jokes clipped for you, sugar," he would say quietly.

That last summer my mother had to attend a big sales meeting for a full week, and she tried to find a practical nurse to come stay with my dad. No luck. July, everybody away on vacation. She was afraid to leave him alone so she made arrangements for him to stay in a small boarding house run by a former nurse. He was to stay only on a temporary basis, of course.

When she phoned me in California to tell me about these plans, I asked if he was terribly upset.

"Oh, he got up on his high horse at first," she said. "But I told him it was either that or the hospital, so he came around in the end."

"Don't do it, Mother," I said. "His house is all he has left!"

My mother did not like people disagreeing with her. Her voice got impatient, she had gone through all the other options, she explained. "No other solution, you understand?" she said finally. And reluctantly I said I did. But I didn't. Still don't.

Two nights before she was to fly to New York, I woke up at three in the morning. I thought I heard the phone ring. But the ringing was only in my ears. The darkness of the room pressed all around me, a hot black blanket cutting off the air, the sweet smell of the summer night. I began to cry. Hank held me. He let me cry for the longest time, and then I told him my dad was dead, I knew he was dead.

In a while the phone did ring. Hank turned on the light, but as he crossed the room to answer the telephone, he looked at me. We knew who it was, what the message would be.

Oh, it's been years and years since Daddy died. I think I can honestly say that I understand him now. I understand him most completely in the mornings, getting ready to rush off to work. Or on an errand I dread, having the car repaired, braving the sneers of the body shop guys.

I stand up. So does the dog. Better check my purse. Keys, glasses, cell phone, pocket calculator to work out grade averages—God, Daddy, how you would have loved these electronic gadgets! Extra Flair pens, green for marking exams. A list of stuff to get at the market on my way home. Is that everything? Think.

Let's see. Fresh water for the dog. Note for Hank in case he's the first one home—at least he can activate the microwave. Couple of letters to mail.

That's it. I glance around. Better turn on the radio so the pooch won't get too lonely. He so much wishes I wouldn't leave him.

"Hold the fort," I tell him. But he won't look at me. Nevertheless I give him a love pat on his noble head, dearest companion I so hate abandoning each morning. No, not *hate*—a word along with *fool* Daddy would not permit me to say which is why my using it about <u>him</u> was such an act of treachery—and which even now makes me cringe.

When I climb into the Honda it's so stuffy I roll down all the windows. My briefcase is snug on the seat beside me, my purse on top. I switch on the engine.

My heart starts pounding faster, I light a cigarette, try to relax. Feels as if I'm swimming underwater, clawing through seaweed. I step on the gas just to hear the surge of power in the throttle, then flick on the morning news, stare straight ahead. The windshield's dusty from pollen so I turn on the wipers, clean off the glass. But it's still smeared. The garage doors are flaking, they need paint badly. From here, in fact, the whole house looks shabby, a wavering sickly green, due I suppose to the tinted windshield.

What else? 8:15 already, got to get a move on here. "Roll 'em out!" Hank would say, and I take the market list and the two envelopes from my purse and place them under the little magnetic Scotty-Dog clips on the dashboard. The car radio is full of static. I adjust the dial, searching for a morning talk show so that the angry voices calling in drown out the sound of angry commuter horns on the Expressway.

The dog is standing beside the front window. His nose is pressed against the pane. Even through this blurred windshield, I can see the golden glow of his eyes. His tail wags slowly. He hopes that I've forgotten something, that I will come back inside where it's safe.

What he doesn't understand and I have only understood recently, is not that I have forgotten. But rather that I remember.

ASPHALT

SOME PEOPLE YOU TRUST. Some you don't. It's as simple as that.

Walt would say, "Belaboring the obvious, Page."

Ok, ok, Walt, so it's obvious—I take your point. But it's still true. And no, I can't prove it. Nor can I justify it rationally. Trust—like love or hate— we're talking gut issues here. You can't analyze why you trust one person and not the next. And it's not a question of dislike either although I guess a case could be made (Walt would make it brilliantly) that it's almost impossible to like someone you don't trust. Not for me though—I have—for years.

Take Nora Throckmorton. An old, old friend, Nora. We go way back. She lives down the street, and our lives bisect in a lot of the same places. Like me, Nora's married to a lawyer. Our kids all grew up together, tumbling in and out of the two houses, mostly mine. I loved Nora's children. I practically raised the oldest boy.

Now that the kids are all grown and gone, Nora and I both work full time. She's a draftsman for an engineering firm out on 128. I'm vice principal at the high school and so I'm still around kids, and in a funny way I can pretend they're all still my own. The seniors leave and a new class comes in—and so we never really lose them. There always are more coming along, no matter how fast the semesters slide by.

Yes, we go way back, Nora and I. I've tried hard to be a good friend to her. In the summers we used to go on vacations together, the two families— that all stopped two years ago. But we still go to the same parties, the same church.

Always the church. She's very church-oriented, Nora. That's one place we differ, right there. Church for me is something private, intensely personal. I'm suspicious of organized kindness. Which is exactly why when she asked me to join the Pastoral Committee, I balked. But true to form, Nora kept on hammering away at me, she's like a small bulldozer.

She stood out there in the driveway smiling that chilly smile of hers. In the bright sunlight her hair gleamed flame red, a bit faded with middle age but still that particular shade of red which seems to suck up all color from the skin. Beautiful skin, chalky white except when she's excited—Nora still blushes now and then. I find this endearing, it seems to link her to the young girl she must once have been. Before I knew her. Red hair and blushing— these constitute Nora's only signs of drama—both of them, interestingly, being attributes beyond her control, God-given you might say.

So there she stands, implacable, telling me, "You must, Page. We need the input of a professional administrator, say yes," and finally I let myself be railroaded into accepting. Because I wanted to please her, I suppose. Nora's hard on her friends. She never lets up. So why can't I ever tell her that—to her face? Am I being a hypocrite?

Talk about hypocrisy. The Pastoral Committee's a perfect example. We were supposed to address social responsibilities. Ha! We met once a week on Tuesday night in the tiny hot cubicle off the Sunday School, all of us good doobees sitting in that cramped room, knees rebelling against the child-sized tables, chalk dust clogging the air as well as our minds. The upshot? Totally predictable, every agenda item tabled until the following week. Nothing ever got resolved or solved and after the first couple of meetings, I knew it was a mistake. *Not* my cup of tea.

I quit after six weeks. I told Nora, "It's ridiculous—I mean arguing over pencil sharpeners, who cares! Our mandate explicitly states closer interaction with the entire community, remember?"

Nora just stared at me. So then I added, "It's people I care about, Nora. People helping people. You know, one on one." Even as I was saying the words, I knew she wouldn't understand. Oh, Nora.

"Oh, Page, for pity's sake, the Outreach Committee handles all that," she assured me, poised impatiently with a load of books for the church Flea Market. She was dressed in her usual neat blouse and skirt—Nora, the star of the class, the kind of student who always raises her hand first with the correct answer, precisely worded. The kind I never was. I just blurted things out. It was the cool competent Noras I admired but never, ever could be. They always did what they had to do, no moaning, no floundering. No detours.

And indeed Nora still marches straight ahead in a nice straight line like her nice straight figure, her neat chiseled features composed in the fixed smile of a wooden doll. She has pretty eyes, the color of licorice—sharp eyes that roam nervously when she talks to people. She's always in a hurry. In a hurry to get things *done*. "Just do it, Page, don't wallow so much," she tells me, then laughs quickly. "Just teasing, can't you take a little teasing?" she goes.

The truth is I can't. Maybe as she suggests I'm simply too thin-skinned. I try to talk to Walt about it. I keep telling him that teasing is actually a smokescreen for being mean. "It's a whitewash job," I say. "A way of slipping in the barbs without taking the rap, then cover it all up with a false laugh."

Walt waits for me to wind down. Which always makes me wind *up*, not down, the words tumbling out louder and faster as he…calmly…waits…it…out…with this patient look I find irritating as hell.

"No warmth behind the laugh either," I add. "You ever really listen to Nora laughing?"

He always gives the same answer. "Don't be so hard on her, honey. Nora's ok, she does her best."

"Walt, I disagree. She's cold. She can be judgemental to the point of harshness."

Then he'll smile at me, examining me over his glasses. "You're the one who sounds judgemental, my dear. What's she ever done to hurt you?"

"Forget it," I'll tell him and start banging pots. Or drawers. Whatever's at hand.

It isn't what Nora *has* done. It's what she hasn't. What's left out, sins of omission.

I remember having this long discussion with Walt over which was worse from an ethical standpoint, sins of *o*mission or sins of *c*ommission "Can't evil be," I asked him, "simply the absence of good? The absence of love, for example. You know, like a minus sign?"

But he kept on backing me into corners, saying things such as "Define your terminology" or 'That's totally illogical" or "Ad hominem arguments yet again, Page!"

In the end I got fed up. I so wanted to discuss this, maybe with someone else, someone who could really talk about things, who didn't turn every single discussion into a courtroom debate. Darn him, why couldn't he just *agree* with me? Life would be simpler—and the truth is that life is **not** logical, my dearest Walt.

We have left undone those things which we ought to have done. And we have done those things which we ought not to have done…

…straight from the general confession in our prayer book so how in heaven does Nora kneel there in church, year after year, and recite those words? This is what I wonder each Sunday, watching her small bright head bobbing in front of me, three pews down. Nora and I pray alone. That's another thing we do have in common. Our lawyer husbands won't set foot in church. On general principles—no logic whatsoever in religion.

We have followed too much the devices and desires of our own hearts….

I suppose Nora thinks she deserves the gold medal for good works. She's the very first person in the parish to organize food baskets when someone's sick—she contacts the Outreach Committee—or to call the Bereavement Council when there's a death in the family.

Our church has committees for every known human frailty, every single biblical calamity. In the old days these were the duties of the rabbi, priest or minister. But not any longer. Nowadays we queue up for acts of charity just as once back in 5th grade, we wrote our names up on the big ruled sheet with the gold star for Classroom Clean-Up Duty. Once a week each semester, and then it was over and done with. We felt virtuous, the teacher looked happy and the classrooms looked clean, desks all standing in neat rows, blackboards freshly washed, erasers clapped free of chalk dust. I can just visualize Nora in a state of pure rapture back then.

"So make your point," Walt would say. "What acts of omission? What's all this sin stuff anyhow?"

Oh, Walt. How can I tell you? You're the one Nora adores. You're the one when we go over there for dinner, she flatters you and runs around asking breathlessly, "Can I get you another drink, Walt?" Or "Walt, come out and check my new lettuce." You humor her, and make her laugh. And in turn she does nice things for you, always dropping over here to lend you books on gardening, or have long consultations on what model word processor you should buy. Nora is very mechanically minded. In the best of all worlds, she would be an engineer, not just do their drawings. She thinks in a very methodical way, like you do. The two of you, so rational, sitting together at our kitchen table, poring over assembly manuals for fixing the old ride'em lawnmower, her neat little head beside yours, and I can see her cheeks are flushed.

When she finally goes home, I simply say, "She's got the hots for you, kiddo."

He laughs. "She'd have a fucking coronary if she heard you say that."

"Then maybe I'll tell her. To her face," I mutter thickly. But after a while he kids me out of it. The idea of chilly Nora having a good roll in the hay is too bizarre. She is a woman constricted, laced in a straitjacket of correct behavior, conventional mores: do the right thing, do it efficiently. So totally *bloodless*—which is why her blushing seems such an anomaly. For years Walt and I have tried to figure out her marriage to Scott. Old Scotty's a sarcastic, brittle kind of guy, a hard-headed Highlander, as dried up in his way as she is in hers. Together they look like two middle-aged clerics: both small, wiry, moving with quick gestures, dry little laughs, eyes darting back and forth as they speak. At least Scotty isn't as tightly puckered as Nora. At least he gets angry now and then. Plus he has a marvelous sense of humor—wicked and fun.

When we all get together, Walt cranks Scott up with a couple of starter jokes, and bam! Scott's off and running. Mischievous wit, malicious actually, but his stories about people we know, particularly in the church, are delivered with deadly accuracy. Now he's getting ready with the punch line, takes a gulp of wine, peers over the rim of his glass, eyes dancing, and says,

"Biggest tightwad in town. And they make *him* chairman of the Benevolent Committee!"

He breaks us up. Nora looks on nervously. She turns to me, little smile flickering at the corners of her prim mouth. "You have such a bad influence on Scott," she tells me. "He gets so naughty when he comes over here."

"ME!" I say. "It's Walt, not me. He eggs Scotty on, I—"

"Hold it, children," Scott breaks in. "Page is my best audience, always has been," he chuckles, then adds, "Do behave yourself, Nora." And frowns his clerical frown, his face pinched up and tight.

I smile at her radiantly. Walt starts laughing. Scotty watches the three of us, beady eyes glimmering.

Nora sits there, her mouth still smiling. But not her eyes. Then she says, "Forgot to tell you, Page. Hal's coming home next week."

Ah, Nora, skillful Nora. The only topic she knows that will always soften me. Hal is her oldest son. I love Hal. Always have. I watched Hal grow from an ornery red-haired kid with a hot temper and a brilliant mind into a dazzling man. As a little boy, he used to spend hours, sometimes whole weekends at our house, playing with our kids. Later on he used to come home from college and have these long talks with me and Walt. Or sometimes just with me.

I like to think that over the years we taught Hal how to love people, how to show compassion. How to forgive.

Nora always seemed grateful, not that she ever said thanks, mind you. But she never acted jealous. And it's not that I give a damn about gratitude— that's one of her stuffy words—a smug, buttoned up kind of word, makes me want to do something totally outrageous. It's not labels I care about. It's feelings. I thought Nora and I were united in our love for the boy all those years. And the man the boy became.

Now I'm not so sure. I believe now that Nora is a wind-up doll. She acts as she does not because she loves deeply, but as a matter of duty, that iron sense of duty which propels her at work, at church, around town, in her home so that even the simplest activity becomes a Project. She loves projects, Nora does. Her children used to be her major project, and when the bad times began—those sullen years of adolescence—she chose me as fill-in mother, like enlisting the Hospitality Committee to get the job done. Simple expediency, I suppose. Get the job done at any cost, even if it means running up obligations you have no intention of filling.

"Hal's coming home?" I say to her carefully. "For how long?"

Scott jumps in, frowning. "One whole bloody week. Long enough."

Nora laughs, her cautious laugh she uses when Scotty gets obnoxious. "Hal's bringing Astrid along," she tells me. "They're engaged."

"At last!" I say, and my heart smiles inside. "I'm so glad! Oh, I'm so very happy for him!" Walt's holding up the wine bottle.

"That," he announces, "calls for a toast. Salud!" and he pours the wine carefully in our glasses, mine and Scott's. Nora puts one narrow hand out and covers her glass.

"So when's the wedding?" I ask. Underneath the table I kick off my sandals. The rug feels cool on my toes. I wiggle them luxuriously.

For the rest of the evening Nora and I discuss wedding plans. The two men look bored and wander to down to Walt's shop in the basement to inspect the rebuilt lawnmower. They both love engines as much as Nora does. Ordinarily she'd be down there with them, but tonight I keep her upstairs, peppering her with questions about Astrid, Hal, the wedding reception. Her eyes slide to the basement door, but I keep on talking.

When she and Scott finally leave, Walt and I stand arm in arm on the front porch, waving as they stride briskly down the driveway into the black street. Scotty and Nora never hold hands. All the years we've known them, I've never even seen them touch. And we've spent days and days with the two of them, going off on complicated canoeing trips when the kids were small. Later, sharing the cottage at Siasconset—what we call the Nantucket summers— lots of fun except when Scott took up sailing.

I nudge Walt. "Captain Bligh," I whisper.

He picks right up on it. "And first mate," he answers. We both laugh.

Out back we can hear the staccato chirp of crickets. The darkness feels like black gauze gold-stitched with lightning bugs... LIGHTNING... Scotty's second boat.

Nora is a much better sailor than Scott. He's too fiery. He gets flustered in an emergency—he sees emergencies where none exist—funny, ornery little man. Two summers ago we went for a long sail out past the harbor near the Yacht club. It was a total nightmare. Scott shouted orders, and the boat rocked. That was the day that did me in, the whole experience was hideous. Finally as we were tacking back into the crowded harbor just missing other sailboats by inches, Scotty waving his arms and screaming at the other sailors, I lurched to my feet, bumped my head against the boom while Nora sat beside the tiller looking competent, and announced to the whole crew, "I'm swimming back to shore."

All three faces jerked up when I spoke. Then Scott said with a look of concern, "Mind the tides, lass. They're running out to sea now, they're very strong"

Nora said nothing, just licked her lips, then pursed them in a tight smile.

"Page is a wonderfully strong swimmer, you guys know that," Walt explained, his eyes merry. He understood just why I was abandoning ship, he had no brief for sailing either. We agreed to crew on short trips simply to humor Scott who is like a child with each of his successively larger boats. He loves to sail because he can play captain and boats are his expensive toys. But Nora loves sailing for the sport itself. Talk about projects! Sailing's got to be the apotheosis of task-oriented activities, from trimming the mainsail to the endless year-round chores of painting, checking for dry rot—no end to the upkeep.

Now Walt's shutting the front door, turning off our porch light.

"Remember when I jumped off the boat?" I ask him.

"You goose," he says, and pats me on the shoulder.

The three of them had sailed away from me after I dived off the stern, not one head looking back. Which I found shocking actually—out of sight, out of mind. Steadily the boat drew away from me, sails flapping in the stiff wind. Now I couldn't even see those three heads any longer, and soon I couldn't even see the boat, too much water sloshing in my eyes. I struck out for shore, but as Scott had warned the tide was running heavy and it carried me far, far down from the little beach I was aiming for. It felt as if I were caught in this huge tunnel of water, almost like a water slide at the amusement park shooting me straight out to open ocean, and I could see the channel buoys getting closer and closer. For a few scary minutes I thought good God, I'm not going to make it. I wasn't tired but the water was so cold, the current so strong, and I kept on angling crossways and then little whitecaps slapped at my face, stinging my eyes. I rolled over on my back, peering up at the blank blue sky. The one thing I knew was not to panic which would tire me immediately. I tried to make my mind as blank as the sky, and shutting my eyes I began to backstroke, getting into a good hard rhythm. I backstroked all the way to shore, it must have taken at least fifteen minutes. Then I heard a horn blowing—not from a boat but a car somewhere very close. I stopped swimming, looked around and then stumbled to the shoreline which turned out to be rock shale. And weeds. And tin cans. No sandy beach, not here.

When I climbed up the little hummock, I stood staring at the town parking lot. As far as I could see there was only asphalt between me and the road home.

...done those things we ought not to have done....

I shrugged and started running. A third of the way across I knew that the hot tar was doing a job on my feet. By the time I finally reached the cottage a good half mile away, I was hobbling, trying to put the weight only on my heels, the tender fleshy parts were so badly burned—they felt as if I had dipped my feet in acid. When the pain got close to unbearable, I'd try standing one-legged like a stork for couple of seconds, to give the dangling foot a moment's surcease. For the next two days I was relegated to sitting on a deck chair, a pail of cool water in front of me. Even the water hurt. It took a couple of weeks for the blisters to heal.

Walt and Scotty both joked about it. I mean they were truly kind and all, but their laughter actually made me feel better, less of an ass. Nora, however, averted her eyes and took over the cooking and other chores with resolute good cheer. Little Miss Muffet, go choke on your tuffet. She made me feel like a beached dolphin, pathetic and ridiculous at the same time. She offered me no hand up from my embarrassment but instead pretended as if nothing had happened, leaving me high and dry on hot sand. Mortified is what I was.

In her mind, I'm sure she was being tactful. But tact isn't what I wanted. Nora's version of tact was more lacerating in its silence than the most blurted out remark.

"I wish I could really level with that woman," I say as we load the dishwasher.

Walt goes on stacking cups and bowls. He's got his back to me.

"I do, Walt," I tell him. "She makes me feel inept. Like a turtle lying upside down."

He's starting on the plates now, methodically placing each one in its proper rack. When I load the dishes, they lean all helter-skelter in there. I can cram more in than he can, but symmetrical they're not. Sins of commission all over again—the story of my life. Ho hum. At least committing sin feels good, for an instant anyhow—I was never so exultant, so deliriously free as when I was diving out of that awful sailboat.

I cross back and forth from kitchen to dining room, bringing in the wineglasses, then the two empty bottles of Chablis. I drop them in the recycling carton. They clink against something down in there. Walt glances up.

"You're working yourself up into a snit," he says equably, and shakes in Cascade.

"She treats her friends like agenda items," I tell him, and I stand right in front of him so that he has to look straight at me. "She never thanks anyone. Never has given a solitary damn about our kids. Am I right or am I right?" I stare at him. He looks at me, no expression. So then I say, "She's so...I don't know....so *wooden!*"

He chuckles, reaches down and presses the start button on the dishwasher. It begins its long groaning. Terrific. "Sweetheart, you've been saying that for years," he observes.

"Then why do we keep *doing* stuff with them?" I ask him.

He moves away, begins wiping down the counters. When Walt gets done with a kitchen, it looks like House Beautiful, all shiny and glistening. Walt likes clean bare surfaces. So do I, but there's something in me that can't achieve them. There's always something left out, some cupboard door ajar. I think at some deep unconscious level I'm simply unable to close anything shut, I need to leave things left open...always.

Walt glances over at me. He's not smiling. "Because we have fun with them," he answers. "Because they are old, old friends."

"We have fun with Scott, you mean," I say, and kick the door shut under the sink, but, darn it, the sound's muffled by the drone of the dishwasher.

"Scotty's a package deal, " he replies. "You can't have him without her." He pauses, then adds softly, "Not like you did with her son."

"She pointed Hal at me, told him go talk to good old Page. Remember back then? Back when Hal and Scotty had all those father/son fights?" I glare at Walt, fold my arms.

But he just gives me his patient Clydesdale look, he's not having any. "Nora means well, honey," is all he says.

"Means well! She means well all right, biggest do-gooder in town. But you want to know something?" and I take a deep breath. "Nora's *good* but she's not kind. Kindness is not what she's about. She can't smooth the way for people, stroke them when they need some body contact, or some tenderness. She just tidies UP!"

He puts the sponge back on the sink top. "Ok, babes, let's hit the sack," he says. He's tired, his eyes look heavy behind his glasses.

I walk over to him, take the glasses off very gently. Stroke me is what I want to tell him, but what I actually say is, "Tell me what you see."

"I see a kind person, a loving person. Messy, impetuous. But kind," he says.

I look deep into his eyes. They glow back at me, eyes I trust, eyes I think of practically like my own, they mirror back what I feel...most of the time. "Darling," I murmur.

He doesn't answer. He looks at me steadily.

"Tell me..." but I don't know how to phrase the question. Yet it must be asked, it must not be allowed to go unspoken. "Back then ...in the old days?" I stop.

Now he's smiling again, the patient smile, his fond smile. "Come on, spit it out," he tells me. "Enough sidestepping already."

So I stand there looking at him, and finally I speak. "Back then, were you ever jealous?"

He glances away for a moment, puts on his glasses. He studies the bulletin board next to the refrigerator. An entire wall of family photographs and memorabilia ranging across the corkboard. Pictures of the children grown up, the children as pudgy babies metamorphosing into busy toddlers. High school diplomas, group portraits of the college soccer team, a cousin's wedding. But mostly kids, big and small, running across the wall, mugging at the camera, smiling gravely as they grow older. Hal...at ten, leaping down a sand dune with our two kids, his face triumphant, red hair flashing in the Nantucket sun.

The dishwasher goes silent for a minute, it's shifting into the rinse cycle.

Now Walt is taking my hand, turning off the kitchen lights. In the dark, his voice seems louder, almost stern although I know he's trying to be gentle, trying to reassure me. "Some people you simply trust," he says. "She trusted you too, Page. Still does."

"But not as my *friend*!" I cry. And twist away from him, walk into the living room.

He pads after me in the darkness. "Page, honey," he says. "What is it you want?"

We are standing at the bottom of the staircase. I can hear him breathing beside me. But I reach out fumbling, put my hand on the balustrade for balance. With my other hand I reach down and touch the sole of my foot.

I stand one-legged, listing slightly toward the banister.

INVASIVE PROCEDURES

THE BEEPERS ARE SILENT.

So are we.

They lie on the bedside table, side by side. Mine has that new alpha numerical read-out, but it's turned off now. So is Clarissa's. She's not on call until 6 a.m. tomorrow, and Sheldon would sooner dial God than bother me off duty. He's a competent guy, best chief surgical resident I've had in years, trust Sheldon to handle anything the bastards throw at him. But old habits die hard. I still carry the page around even when I'm not on call. It's my lifeline to the hospital, without it I'm disconnected. Fran said precisely that to me, oh, years ago, before the divorce. She meant it to hurt me. It didn't. I was actually amused—hell, flattered.

I watch Clarissa, she's getting dressed. Her face is calm, lips curved up in that archaic smile of hers. Fran was an art major, she knew all about that stuff. She told me how those prominent cheek-bones and permanent smiles you see in early Greek statues were due to problems in technique.

"Like your house officers, Hartley," she explained. "You know, starting on a new rotation? All thumbs at first? Same thing with those early Hellenic sculptors. They simply didn't have the technical savvy for making the transition from cheek to mouth. Pure ineptness, actually. Nothing magical about archaic smiles."

Nothing magical, but nonetheless charming, Clarissa's smile. And disconcerting. It masks what she's thinking, and frankly, I'm bored with ambiguities and these long pregnant silences. Enough already.

So I say to her bluntly, "Exactly what is it you want from me, Clarissa?" Taken me years, I'll admit, but I've finally learned this is the only way to handle women like Clarissa. You have to call their bluff, make them spell it out in spades. In short, give them plenty of rope to hang themselves.

But she only laughs and pulls up her skirt to fix her stockings. She's wearing a lacy garter belt underneath and not much else. The garter belt's almost the same color as her skin, palest apricot and smooth as satin.

"En garde, Hartley," she growls. "Stand and deliver!" and snaps the garter shut.

"What?"

"What the highwayman says, silly. Your money or your life."

She yanks her skirt back down, puts on her shoes, then jumps up with her left arm flung back, her right leg jutting forward like a fencer lunging. All she needs is a sword. She starts singing: *Stand and deliver became his sounding cry/Stand and deliver, your money or your life!* Her eyes twinkle as she watches my expression, eyes like blue diamonds, flawless and when she's in the O.R., cold. Not cold now, though. I prefer them icy.

"Hey, kiddo," I tell her. "Get serious."

"But Hartley, darling," she answers lightly, "I am." And reaches over to the bedpost, lifts off my stethoscope, she's already wearing hers. Now she's hanging it around my neck, the metal disk—the diaphragm—is cold against my chest. I shiver.

"Definite arrhythmia, Dr. Hobbes," she murmurs, and brushes her lips against the metal. "Nice," she says. "Able to leap tall buildings in a single bound, my lover can, plus warm the coldest steel."

I kiss her. Her lips taste young and soft. The taste of her is what I'm going to have trouble getting out of my system. Obsession, addiction—whatever this is, it's—

"—too much risk," I tell her. "Seeing so much of each other," and I move away from her and start putting on my shirt, the white lab coat. But Clarissa knows what she wants. She's going to make a superb surgeon. She's relentless.

She follows me over to the bed. "Don't forget your page," she murmurs, and hooks it on my belt. "Only thing between us, darling," she whispers. "Just you, me and our beepers," and she laughs, moves her hips against me, the cradle of her pelvic bones rocking slowly.

* * *

AT SURGICAL STAFF MEETING, the team from the Andrews Unit has got the wind up. They're bitching about some liver function studies I've ordered on a patient—first admission of this 64 year old white male bookkeeper for a cholecystectomy—a routine gall bladder to be done Friday. Lou Dahlquist, the attending, is giving me a hard time. Listening to his whiny voice sets my teeth on edge. Beady little eyes on the bastard that never blink.

"What about the research consent form?" he squeaks.

"What about it, Lou?" I answer, and shrug.

Around the table, all the others are carefully not looking at me or Lou. They study their charts, they glance over at the wall clock by the door. So do I, pointedly, but Lou is too upset to notice. I watch the second hand. It's painted a brilliant red and jerks around the clock face in successive flashes of crimson which tire the eyes, as tiresome as Dahlquist, a nervous nelly if I ever saw one, wasting my time, my staff's time. So I interrupt the jerk, patiently walk him through the rationale for the hepatic function tests I want to run—have been running, for god's sake, for months now.

While I'm talking, the staff looks up, except for Sheldon who has gone over to the coffee urn. I insist on freshly brewed coffee for my people. Keeps them sharp, on their toes. No ass-dragging on my service; no fake coffee either.

Sheldon still has his back to me, not a good sign. These sob sisters from the Andrews Unit (the Andrews Sisters, I call them) are upsetting my chief resident, pushing the panic button because they've got nothing better to do. Quickly, I summarize my defense, fold my arms, and sit back.

But Lou Dahlquist isn't having any.

He waves the consent form in my face. "Look here, Hartley!" he says, his voice shrill now, and his lips going paler than an old keloid scar. "*No discernible risks* you claim," he repeats. "Right here in black and white, who you trying to kid?" When Lou is this upset, his voice jumps at least two registers. I try not to smile.

"Lou," I tell him kindly, "May I remind you for the third time, this is a totally safe, routine procedure."

Sheldon has come back to the table. He sets his cup down by the pile of charts, slumps in his chair. He doesn't look up. He's got one more month left in his residency, no way is he going to get caught in this crossfire.

Same with the rest of the house staff. They all sit there like lumps, listening to me and Dahlquist go at it hammer and tongs. Clarissa's face is completely immobile, the little upward curve of her lips like twin commas. She's going to have lines there when she's thirty-five, no question. She has the kind of skin that wrinkles early, not enough subcutaneous fat is the problem. She'll be running back to the plastic guys in no time flat. Buy now, pay later.

Somebody coughs quietly, but nobody says a word. I know the score though. Ho hum, they're thinking, usual dust up—Three Stooges meet Superman, the nervous-nelly gang up against the man of steel—so what else is new? In the end I'll get my way. They know it, I know it. And Lou Dahlquist damn well knows it, so why is he being such a pain in the ass?

I reach over to take the consent form he's waving. I point to the third line. "Can you read, Lou? Or are we talking impaired function here?"

Grinning, I watch his face flame up, beet red against the white line of his mouth. I start quoting from the protocol: "This procedure is theoretically capable of causing complications on a temporary basis," and I glance up. Dahlquist is so pissed I almost want to laugh.

"Theoretically in a pig's eye," he splutters. "Precisely my point, Hartley! Last patient you put through this had an infarct three days later. Made my resident look incompetent, a total klutz."

"So?" I grin at him. We're getting close to the bone now.

"So *'theoretically'* covers your ass but not the poor slob on the table, like this guy, this bookkeeper scheduled for routine gall bladder Friday."

I survey the table again. Sheldon catches my eye, taps his watch.

"Any comments, people?" I ask.

Silence. Clarissa is writing furiously in her notebook, sucking on her bottom lip she's concentrating so hard. She's blocking this discussion completely out, catching up on her charts—shows good judgement on her part, smart cooky, our Clarissa.

I slide the consent form along the table, back to Dahlquist.

"Good of you to bring this up, Lou," I tell him jovially. "I like to think we have ourselves the world's most democratic service here. So important to ventilate these—ahh—these issues. Full and open disclosure, the Golden Rule according to Hobbes."

I chuckle. Sheldon lifts one ironic eyebrow, so I forge ahead, try to strike a more familial note. "As all of you know, we are a team here at Madden Memorial. We share equal responsibility for everything occurring on this service from meds to quadruple by-passes. So, I appreciate and welcome your frankness, Lou," I pause to flash him my warmest smile, "as well as your remarkable concern for diminishing risk. It does not—" and here I lean forward, "pass unnoticed, I can assure you."

I do not look directly at Dahlquist, but from the corner of my eye I observe him squirm in his chair, his shoulders go slack. Good, that last remark struck home, he's deflating fast, a collapsing lung—no more hot air from that quarter, he knows a threat when he hears it. So I clear my throat, nod amiably, and add, "Good! If there's nothing else then..."

And we all stand up, the chairs grating on the floor. Clarissa walks out talking to Dahlquist and a couple of the junior residents, but I can tell from their expressions, it's strictly business. Sheldon comes over to my end of the table. He looks tired, skin gray beneath his horn-rimmed glasses. He's capable and energetic, Sheldon is—superb diagnostician, great technique. My only problem with him centers around his ambivalence regarding research. Only five published papers out of him in all this time despite my warning him again and again that the strength of the department lies in its publications, not to mention it's the only way he'll ever get to be stud duck. "Power, Sheldon," I told him once. "It's the only goddamn thing that's going to keep you afloat when you're swimming in these waters." This is my responsibility to him—it's not that I want clones of myself running around (as Fran screamed at me long ago), no—I owe Sheldon this, teaching him basic survival skills, and more importantly, how to get to the top of the heap fast.

He wants to talk about the promotion meeting tonight, who's going to get the nod for his slot as chief surgical resident come 1 July. He's plumping for his pal, Farnsworth. Lou Dahlquist wants one of the Andrews sisters, the other staff men are split, and me, I'm undecided. So far.

Clarissa's name comes up.

Sheldon shakes his head again. "They'll never buy a woman, Hartley. No matter how good she is."

"You calling us old timers chauvinists?" I kid him.

"Look, Hartley, you throw Clarissa's name in the pot and we'll end up with a compromise candidate *nobody* wants. Don't let her name even get proposed."

I slap him on the back. ""Sheldon, son, you worry too much. Go grab some shut eye." We both grin. He's got a gastrectomy at noon, teaching rounds with the house officers at 4, chart rounds for tomorrow at 6—he'll be lucky if he gets done by midnight.

He turns to go. But I still have one more question to ask him.

"What's your reaction to that dog and pony show Dahlquist put us through?"

He frowns. "Trouble with prima donnas like Dahlquist," he says, "they got too much time to stand around with their thumbs up their asses."

"Good man," I tell him. "You scrubbing on that cholecystectomy he's so worried about? The one scheduled for Friday?"

"Nope," he answers. "The beauteous Clarissa's got that tiger by the tail."

* * *

THE BEAUTEOUS CLARISSA JUST stalked into my office. She shuts the door carefully, stands there with her arms folded. "Look," she says.

"I'm looking and that's all," I answer.

"That cholecystectomy? The one you ran the hepatic function tests on that Dahlquist was screaming about?"

"Yes, I understand you were scrubbing. How did it go anyhow?"

"We just lost him. A routine gall bladder, Hartley! Hour into the procedure and he had an infarct. He croaked right there on the table."

"Very unfortunate. I am sorry, Clarissa."

She glares at me. "Dahlquist's already got wind of it. He's going to squawk to the Human Use people after the Mortality conference on Monday."

The telephone's ringing. "Hang on," I tell her.

Sure enough, it's Dahlquist talking, his voice so high he sounds like a castrato. I hold the receiver a few inches away from my ear, then tell him I'm getting an on-site report, thank you very much, and to stuff it. "I'm satisfied," I add for good measure. "The buck stops here, Lou. And I stand behind my house officers. End of discussion." I put the phone down gently.

"He's right, you know," Clarissa is saying. She walks across the rug slowly, stands in front of my desk. She's still wearing her green scrub suit and her blonde hair looks damp around the temples, darker, stringy like seaweed.

"Who's right?" I repeat evenly, a gratuitous evasion, and we both know it.

"Those tests you're running? I think we may be putting these people through unnecessary risk. I mean it's the third infarct in two months, Hartley!"

"Hang on, we're talking about a high risk population here, sweety pie. Geriatric cases, they don't tolerate major surgery as easily. You know that as well as I do." I smile, but she still looks grim, so I go on. "You remember that story I always tell the first year residents, about the surgeon, very first day on the geriatric ward? He orders some pre-op tests on this old gomer, and damn, the son of a bitch ups and dies on him before he even gets a chance to cut."

"Don't fob me off with jokes, Hartley."

"Look, Clarissa, this is old, old ground. Dahlquist's orientation is toward high clinical-low research. I, on the other hand, am at the other end of the spectrum. And I—"

"—and you are the Big Daddy," she says, smiling.

"I was about to say that the Human Use Committee's my creature. They are not about to listen to Dahlquist. This is an old war, Clarissa. There's really no point your sticking your pretty little nose into it."

She runs her hand through her hair, brushing back the damp curls. "I see," she says softly. She looks down at the beeper hanging from her belt, then back up at me. "Tell me, Hartley," she's leaning forward now, both hands flat down on the desk, she's so close I can smell the cologne she uses, Ma Griffe, expensive, sophisticated, "...is the Committee on Sexual Harassment your creature as well?" Her cheeks are flushed, but her eyes ice cold and lovely.

I stare at her. The phone rings again but I get on the intercom and tell Mrs. Lovejoy to hold all calls. Clarissa is silent, she's watching me.

I pick up the silver letter opener Fran gave me when my appointment as Surgeon-in-Chief came through. Fran had laughed as I opened it, then said with a brittle smile something about my only being happy with things that cut. "Real deep," she added. Poor Fran, we're better buddies now than we ever were during the marriage. I suppose the long and short of it is that women and surgery don't mix. They just damn well refuse to play second fiddle. Even intelligent women like Fran who know from the beginning what a risky business it is to try and compete with the hospital. I find this puzzling, even disheartening. Good god, she knew the sacrifices I made, the nights without sleep, the bone deep exhaustion of eight fucking years training, internship, residency, in debt to my eyeballs, and having to take shit everywhere even from the O.R. nurses, and always, always carrying that time-bomb threat of making a mistake—that a patient's life hangs literally by centimeters and the perfect precision of the scalpel. And here's Clarissa, I mean she's one of us, she's a member of the club, by Christ!

So I clear my throat and say quietly, "Clarissa, dear girl, I will not sit here and listen to even the faintest whiff of blackmail. Not from you, honey, not from anybody. We are just going to forget you ever made that remark. You didn't say it, I didn't hear it."

"You came after me, Hartley. Not the other way around," she answers. She stops for a moment, looks at the silver paper knife twirling in my fingers. She bites her lip. "All S.O.P., right? Except I didn't play by the book, did I? I managed to fall in love—ridiculous, on the face of things."

"Remember my question Sunday? What is it you want, Clarissa?"

"Not this," she answers. Her voice sounds raw and she turns away, walks over to the window. She stands there with her back to me, thin shoulders hunched. The scrub suit floats on her, billowing out over the loose belt, the green cotton creased in a thousand wrinkles.

When she turns to face me, her eyes drill into mine. "Ok, Doctor, here's what I want. Either you put me up for the Chief Resident's appointment, or I go to the Harassment Committee as well as the Human Use folks. You want to play hardball? Fine, so do I. Take your choice." She studies my expression. "All those principles, Hartley," she says slowly. "Minimize risk, build in margins for error. Full and open disclosure, otherwise the whole damn system collapses. Jesus." She's breathing hard and her skin has gone a dusky color, no longer pale apricot but almost splotchy, quite ugly, in fact.

I come right back, making my voice as cold as those blue eyes. "May I remind you the system collapses just as quickly when you violate the pecking order?" and I tap the flat edge of the letter opener hard against the heel of my hand. It makes a slapping noise, she winces twice. But it does not silence her.

"Tell me," she whispers. "Just who are they going to believe is out of line here? You or me? Are you willing to take that gamble, Hartley? I sure as hell am. What have I got to lose? Lots less than you do."

"I think this interview is terminated," I say quietly and stand up.

She doesn't answer. She crosses silently to the door. Then, her hand on the doorknob, she looks over her shoulder, straight at me. "Can you remember the first thing we ever learned back in med school, the bedrock of the whole thing? Hippocrates said it once and forever." She swallows hard, and shivers. "Remember? *Physician...do no harm*," and then she's out the door and gone, the door closing soundlessly behind her.

I sit down again and fish out my yellow legal pad, better write this in longhand than risk saying it into the Dictaphone. One damn thing I will not stand for on my service and that's insubordination, I don't care how cute your fanny is.

Smiling, I start roughing out a memo to the Promotion Committee recommending that Clarissa's appointment not be renewed and that she try a training program less pressured, better suited to her temperament which, despite her obvious technical proficiency, has resulted in numerous personality conflicts here at Madden Memorial with both senior staff members and subordinates, *et cetera, et cetera.*

I shove the memo in my OUT box, then turn to the latest slow charts on Myocardial Infarcts over this past year, excellent batch of statistics from the computer boys on the seventh floor. I am considered somewhat of an authority on the incidence of M I complication following routine surgery on geriatric patients. There's enough data here to be statistically significant and my findings on infarcts are used as standard texts all over the world.

And this is as it should be, I'm thinking, and I pick up the letter opener again.

The steel feels cold and heavy in my palm. I press my index finger against the blunted tip. Ah, Clarissa, Clarissa, and I shake my head. You with your graceful lunges, your Stand and Delivers, your Do No Harms. How could you of all people overlook it—the meaning of infarct, the textbook definition. And I say the words aloud in the silent room: "*Of or pertaining to the death of some or all of the muscle tissues of the heart.*"

I place the letter opener back in its leather case, check to make sure my pager's switched on, then buzz Mrs. Lovejoy to let the calls through now, I'm back in circulation.

TE ABSOLVO

I. LEFT DRAWER

I feel off balance. Strange stuff keeps happening

Guess it started—oh, say six months ago. Once, ok—par for the course, etc. But I see now it's become this pattern, this whole cascade of confusing interactions with people I've never laid eyes on before. Or since.

Unnerving plus not great for morale, for my sense of who I am. Or is it for what I have become?

That initial incident I must admit was purely innocuous. At the market running late, I zoom fast around the corner where the cereals are and bang my shopping cart right smack into somebody else's. Really hard.

A toddler in the front seat jerks up his blonde head in surprise. As does his mother.

"Oh excuse me, I'm really so sorry," I stammer, then bending towards the child, "Did our carts go bumpitty bump?"

The mother smiles. So does her little boy.

"So silly of me, speeding in the super market."

These escalating blunders I've taken to calling the Left Drawer Syndrome. What happens goes like this: say I'm reaching for something I always keep in the same place. No need to look because I'm on automatic pilot. But lately I find myself reaching for the drawer to the left of the one I really want. Quite weird. Happens usually when I feel stressed or worried. As if my brain has shifted over one whole notch in terms of spatial memory.

Used to be confined to the house, this syndrome. But now it's spread beyond home, now it happens when I'm out on errands. Like with this cart collision, the same kind of clumsy misstep as if my body gets disoriented and simply won't do what it's programmed to do. My brakes aren't working right, I can't depend on automatic pilot the way I used to. And being a klutz is no fun.

So I'm standing here by my cart, embarrassed, what next?

But the young mother is still smiling, a sympathetic smile. "No big deal," she tells me.

I shake my head. I know that she's not annoyed, but I am. With myself.

She reaches down, tousles the head of her toddler now happily chomping away on an animal cracker. Then she says in a kind voice, "No kidding, it's really ok." She pauses. " You're fine. You're just fine."

Healing words not heard very often from a total stranger. She's spoken them so gently. And with a kindness pretty rare these days. This touches me deeply—in itself an over-reaction, I mean we've hardly got a newsflash here. What would be the headlines? "**Shopping Carts Collide? Young Mom Nice to Confused Housewife?**" Tabloids: take note!

But to tell the truth, after a half dozen of these brief encounters always ending with that same reassuring coda *you're fine*, I'm thinking so what is this, a brand new shorthand for *chill* or what? Remember when "You're welcome" disappeared almost overnight, replaced by "No problem"? Language constantly evolving, shedding old skins for new.

New, but not necessarily better.

On the other hand, someone could argue these vernacular expressions (that delicious word *patois* springs to mind) do introduce a certain robust vitality, a crucial infusion of new blood. Line breeding is fine but genetic diversity is also necessary: you gotta throw in a wild card now and then. Which reminds me of yesterday at the veterinarian's office. I had left our German Shepherds out in the car while I ran inside to pick up new pills for the older dog's aching bones. His rear legs have taken to collapsing when he goes down stairs. Climbing up, he seems perfectly stable.

While I was paying for the prescription, a young guy strolls in followed by a small pup, mixed breed, stumpy tail wagging furiously in a general hail-fellow well-met greeting. Not leashed, very social—in fact the pup trails me straight out the door. I didn't realize until whoops! he was right in front of me, wriggling his "New friends! my favorite thing!" message.

"Oh, pup!" I go just as the owner opens the door and whistles. The pup scrambled back inside.

"Gosh, my apologies, didn't even realize he was right behind me!"

The man smiles, a nice soft-eyed smile like his dog.

"You're fine," he tells me.

And I was.

I went straight home and tackled Hank. "What have we got here, any ideas? Maybe it's just people finally deciding to be polite again in public. Or is it simply they're feeling sorry for me because I'm acting wing-wong?"

Hank grins. "Hey, babes, I'm not touching that one with a ten foot pole."

"Wimp!" I laugh. "But the thing is when I hear them murmuring *you're fine*—I mean it 's almost like a caress. Ok, I know it sounds goofy but that's how it *feels*. As if no matter what my blunder, it's canceled. Deleted. Say those two magic words and I'm happy-girl. What's going on, Hank? What's it mean?"

Hank chuckles. "Hardly takes a rocket scientist."

"To do what?"

"To see nothing's going on, not the way you mean. Get real, Moll, it's pretty obvious, no hidden sub-texts here. Those strangers of yours, they understand immediately you mean them no harm. Obviously they're going to be nice to you right back, for heaven's sake."

"But listen, that's the whole point! Heaven's precisely the issue. This stuff, it keeps on happening. But why, Hank? that's my question. Makes me wonder if this is some sort of "God, you-talking-to-*me?*" type dialogue. Absolution, sure—but what's the catch?"

"Now you're going overboard. As usual."

"Maybe. But how lovely to be told you're fine!"

"You are, you know."

"I am?"

* * *

II. LONG DOWN

Our youngest Shepherd, Dulcinea, is a sweetheart. She worries about each one of us in her pack. She particularly worries about the older dog, our steadfast Jove. And has done so ever since she was a pup which we thought a fairly unusual role-reversal, a youngster taking care of an old guy. In any event, our noble Jove has always been Dulcie's primary responsibility.

I just love coming home and asking, "Dulcie-darling, where's Hank? where's Jove?" and arrow-straight she leads me to them.

When Jove ambles up the street for his walkabouts, she will wait patiently for him to return, sitting there, ears alert, peering up the driveway, even if it's raining, she waits. She will come fetch us if she thinks that something's gone wrong: he's taking too long to come back; he's wandered up the hill; he's getting sick—at which point she, a non-sniffer, begins checking him out the way a vet does, slowly, thoughtfully, worry frowns etched deep on her forehead. Her batting average is almost perfect; each time it turns out he was truly ill. Dogs *know*, that's all there is to it.

She's Hank's dog. And Hank is such a pushover. She really works Hank, cajoling him, getting away with stuff she knows darn well I won't allow. Hank's never formally trained her, so the commands she knows you might say she's literally picked up on the run. Moving fast and decisively is what Dulcie's all about. Like most females (I'm talking all species now) Dulcie's a supervisor, big time. She rules her world, indoors and out. She bosses Jove, twice her size and age, alternately manages and honeys up to the Alpha pack-leaders, me and Hank.

Actually she would make a superb tracking dog or agility competitor. She's got the nose, she's got the smarts. Her downfall is other dogs. She seems convinced that the entire state park (hundreds of acres of woods and pasture, river and marshes) is under her sole jurisdiction. Same with our neighborhood. Any strange dog encountered anywhere gets barked at. Some are actually confronted, face to face. If they try to run, she bolts after them. Once in a while she downs them, flat on the ground. What we call in obedience training the Long Down, except in this case Dulcie's not obeying commands, she's demonstrating them on her chosen flunky. Triumphant, Ms. Top Gun looks around for applause, giving her great big I'm-the-champ-dog-downer grin, much pink gum showing, white flash of incisors.

Jove, on the other hand, is now a contemplative twelve year old, philosophically accepting of the fact his whole lifetime he's been monitored by bossy females (both two and four-legged). He was six when Dulcinea arrived to fill the emptiness left by her predecessor, Willow, our first girl dog. Right off the bat as if Willow was actually crouched there coaching her, Dulcie gave Jove the official follow-me rules & regs which he accepted without demur, with what Hank calls his imperturbable equanimity. The truth is our mellow fellow is a born aristocrat. He has always followed faithfully wherever his ladies—all of us—may lead him, bless his heart.

Long before Dulcie, Jove had gone through intensive obedience training. Unlike most dogs, he loved it. We knew he was something special the moment we first saw him, this black nine week old puppy, his crate still dry after a twelve hour flight. And him curled up judiciously quiet at the very back until I opened the door and called, "Jove, *come!*" And immediately without hesitation, he came—to a total stranger—brave, perfectly calm, straight into my arms. Ready to learn. Ready to fall in with whatever his pack wanted to do. Back in those early days, our Willow became his senior proctor, and after a short moody period of deep brooding over being displaced, she took up her duties as Jove's caretaker, precisely as Dulcie (minus the sulking) would do years later.

My sense of things was that Jove felt perfectly comfortable indulging both of his girls because essentially he was working very hard on his doctorate while they fooled around being bossy. But now in his rickety senior years (and mine) those endless hours spent in obedience and tracking workouts are mostly sweet memories. When you are perfectly trained, what's to work on?

He can still surprise us, however.

Last week Dulcie had two notably wicked days. The second consecutive day of putting yet another interloper into a Long Down, she absolutely refused to come when I called. Not until I stalked up the driveway did she slink home, ears pinned back, both penitent and ashamed. The woman who had been walking the now patiently recumbent Rottweiler was very tolerant. She told me she hadn't dared unleash him when Dulcie charged up the driveway because he might fight.

"Serve my dog right," I answered. "She needs to be told off by a Rotty."

Back inside the house, I surprised myself at how furious I was. Dulcie cowering over in the corner reminded me of light years ago when my four and five year old kids broke the record player just after I brought home a brand new Joan Baez record. "NOT good children!" I told them, and more.

"NOT a good dog, you come when I call!"

I clipped on a training leash, began running through Come/Sit/Stay/ Heeling exercises. She did beautifully except for the Come to Heel. She was flustered. So was I. Both of us shaking because I had raised my voice and was now actually shouting, a real no-no when you're working with dogs. Or people for that matter.

Neither of us paid a bit of attention to Jove until all of a sudden my great arthritic giant was right next to us, head high, tail aloft, prancing along beside Dulcie then actually taking the lead. Historic first. Dulcie and I stopped and watched as he began circling me in the Go to Heel position we used to practice morning after morning in the kitchen.

Two dogs - stay!

He was teaching her. He was actually doing three things at once, my venerable philosopher: instructing Dulcie; delightedly deflecting my attention away from her; and most important of all, diplomatically changing the subject from punishment to praise. Wise old dog! my noble shepherd shepherding us.

He sat. She sat.

Much heavy panting. They're waiting now, staring at me to see if his magic has worked. "Clever dogs," I say, and laugh.

Jove watches me with the same serenely glowing gaze of that long ago pup in the crate clambering forward to greet his new family. But Dulcie's still off balance. She has upset herself, she's upset me. She droops, her amber eyes flicking back and forth between us. She perfectly embodies that useful phrase "in the dog house". Poor girl.

I pat each head—her fragile bony one, his broad avenue of a forehead inviting the whole palm of one's hand. I kneel down, hug them hard.

"Okey dokey, who wants cookies?" I ask. Rewards for jobs well done. Jove munches his with blissful gusto while as usual she chews hers daintily, meditatively. Then she glances up at me again, still worried.

What else can I possibly say? I have no choice.

"Hey, Dulcie-darling," I tell her.

"You're *fine*."

* * *

III. INDEPENDENCE DAY

Our grandchildren visited us over the 4th of July. Baby Natalie slept and gurgled. Her big sister, precious four year old Francesca, spent five days in non-stop, extremely high-level negotiations with her parents while working equally hard for Junior Terrorist of the Month award. Hank and I judged her Winner hands down.

An enchanting child with this beguiling face of pure innocence framed by long swirling strands of blonde hair, Francesca looks as if she stepped right out of my old copy of *Alice in Wonder-land*. Very serious. Very intense. Extremely determined. Her dad warns me, "Afraid she inherited Nana's genes, Mum." Nana being my mother, Francesca's great grandma, as well as a remarkable reincarnation of Catherine the Great, Empress of all the Russias. The ultimate autocrat. Nobody contradicted Nana, not ever.

Luckily, the dogs were being boarded with a friend. I shudder imagining what Dulcinea and Francesca would have made of each other, each of them being a wild child with a will of iron. On the other hand, who knows? They might very well have been soul mates. And from the imperial court we'd all be cheering this détente of the despot infantas.

Actually Francesca plays most happily when left alone. Supervision from afar, however, *is* crucial. Her daddy spent at least ten minutes bartering back my late mother's French cut class decanter and six glasses which Francesca had smuggled off to the living room sofa. Each item was returned only after a series of complex bargaining negotiations. Her great-grandma must have twirled in her grave at 100 r.p.m. with pure shock and horror. I found the whole scene funny. It reminded me of intense haggling at a Turkish bazaar, and I stood there giggling in the background where father and daughter couldn't see me. Another complex clash of the titans, and not clear who really had the upper hand.

This adventure was followed by another the next morning when Francesca, my son, and I went on a longish shopping expedition for more fireworks—he was short on buzz bombs and sparklers—and then on to K Mart. While her dad searched for Bermuda shorts, our very own Alice-in-K-Martland had fun hiding under the men's clothing racks. Then…poof! she disappeared.

We combed the store from one end to the other. I finally spotted her fleeing towards me and away from her daddy. She looked hot and mutinous. She glared. She practically growled (but obeyed) when I told her: "You put your hands on this bar across the shopping cart and you don't let go until I say so." Not a word, so I decided that the naughty Alice had disappeared figuratively down the rabbit's hole, leaving our good Francesca beside us. But five minutes later as we stood at check-out, she vanished again. This time my son caught her as she tiptoed quickly down the aisle featuring Big Clearance Sale! Choose a Power Wheels Ride on our Barbie VW Bugs only $99.50!

During our private debriefings, Hank and I agreed that Francesca-in-Wonderland was at her wit's end from being posed too many questions all day long, every day. Her folks needed to set limits, speak to her in short declarative sentences, stop the torrent of consultations. Simply too many big decisions for a little kid to handle. I nearly laughed out loud when at breakfast each morning she was asked "Now this morning, Francesca, how many eggs, how much milk would you like mixed up for your French toast?"

One evening after supper, the baby and Francesca finally asleep, we were invited to make suggestions. One tantrum too many had left both parents strung out.

Hank shrugged, "I don't know. Less is more, maybe." He turned to me. "Molly?"

"Seems to me raising kids is pretty much the same as raising dogs. Let them know clearly what is yes, what is no, teach them how to learn new stuff, snow them with lots and lots of praise."

"But Francesca's *not* a dog," countered her mom.

"Right," I said, a truly feeble-greeble response, I admit.

Next day, the long anticipated Fourth of July, we spent with close friends. Their grandson, Quinlan, is almost a year older and a foot taller than Francesca. Quinlan's a boy of few words, a genuine Macho Man like his dad and grandfather. He wore a camouflage fishing vest with a zillion pockets for lures and other exotica. I wasn't at all confident these two kids would get along, but after a brief, silent appraisal—we grown-ups pretending to ignore them—the children immediately bonded. They scampered off to watch *The Lion King* and jump on the bed, shouting so loudly Quinlan's grandmother had to intervene.

"No jumping on beds in this house," she said in her most severe Librarians Rule/Kids Drool voice.And that was the end of that. Maybe Francesca was relieved to get a clear command, not a pulse-taking "How do you *feel* about bed jumping?"

So then the daddies trundled them off for a last minute firecracker replenishment. Hank told me later it was one of the wildest expeditions he ever lucked out on, with the kids sitting bug-eyed in back, taking in some fairly raunchy adult joking and general cutting up.

The rest of the afternoon was spent outside in the front yard. Just about every single house in the neighborhood was putting on a major fireworks display. Hugging the baby, my daughter-in-law leaned over and whispered how Francesca's dad had been waiting feverishly for this visit. "He so loves the 4th of July," she told me. "And to be in this state where fireworks are actually legal—he's in heaven! I've never seen him so happy!"

All that long golden afternoon Francesca stood quietly on the lawn next to the sidewalk, watching. She was all dressed up in her new cowgirl denim skirt I bought for her birthday. As a rule, she prefers to wear long flowing skirts. Her mother told us that this spring Francesca had insisted on wearing her gauzy ballet outfit (down to her ankles, covering her shin protectors) for soccer practice. The coach, bless his heart, never said a word.

Standing guard behind her was her new friend. This whole exciting day she's been what her daddy calls his Francesca Angelica, easy to do when she's finally on her own. Nobody bugging her. No grown-up bargaining. No dumb decisions to make. Just green grass, lots of noise, lots of smoke, and Quinlan at her back.

She felt safe. No questions. No conversation. And a happy, wonderfully silent Daddy busy opening new box of Roman candles, setting fuses, adjusting her safety glasses as stuff started to explode.

Much fun. Much wildness, even the grown-ups seemed to go sort of crazy on Independence Day.

Occasionally Quinlan would give her a quick hug. And in precisely the same reflexive way you keep on petting a sweet pup, the whole time they were standing there Quinlan kept reaching out and stroking her beautiful long hair.

Smooth.

Silky.

And *so fine!*

The deepest red

WHEN I'M UPSET, I vacuum the red rug out here in the family room. It's a tradition by now, and a running joke in this household. Not to me, of course. But to them.

"Time to bail," the boys used to groan, lots of exaggerated eye-rolling here. "She's getting out the Big Guns." Off they'd scatter. Martin too, off to his study, wisecracking the whole way. Leaving me alone with the collie. The collie always looks resigned; he curls up on the couch. He watches me, his tail thumps in sympathy.

Running the vacuum is great camouflage. I feel insulated, just me, the machine, and the noise. Plus nobody dares come right out and accuse me of being in a bad mood. Vacuuming is socially acceptable.

My friends disagree. "For heavens sake, Shelby!" they fuss. "Join the millennium, get yourself a decent cleaning woman!"

"Don't want a cleaning woman," I keep telling them. And I don't, too expensive. We can't afford that sort of luxury, not on a faculty salary, not with two sons in college and one in grad school. What a laugh.

Martin teases, "Who do you love more, darling? Us or the floors?"

Martin's wrong. It's the rug I'm focused on, not the floors. The red rug and I are in deep communion, we share secrets that go way back.

People kid me. "Nasty neat," they claim. "Compulsive." I know where they're coming from. Nobody except Martha Stewart is house proud these days, and look what's happened to her. The reality is simply this: what's defined as virtue in one generation becomes sinful in the next. Disconcerting when you think about it. So when the kidding starts I shrug, offer my standard reply. "Spring fever is all. This too will pass."

But, it hasn't, it's getting worse. Even Agnes has gotten the wind up. Agnes is my dearest friend, we both detest e-mail so instead we talk on the phone just about every day. We share sad stories, symphony tickets, and an addiction to slapstick comedy.

Agnes lives all alone with her cat out on the beach past the Coast Guard Station. She gets lonely. Like I do. It's not geography, it's the condition of our lives. Not where we live, but how. When I hang up the phone after talking with Agnes, for just a little while I think that I know who I am again.

Yesterday she called at ten as usual. "What's up?" she asks. I love her voice, there are always smiles layered beneath the words.

So I smile back. "I'm just washing the clock face," I answer. "And vacuuming the dog."

Short pause, then Agnes laughs. "You going off the deep end?" she asks gently. But there's humor bubbling around in all that gentleness, and hearing it buoys me up. "No," say I, "*He* is. He's shedding everywhere. We're drowning in hair clumps over here." I ease down in the old rocker. The dog wags his tail, a good quarter pound of fur on that collie tail alone.

"You mean tufts," Agnes suggests.

"No, I mean clumps. Like something uprooted. All over the red rug. It's raining dog fur in this house, visibility zero."

Agnes chuckles. "Summer's coming early. Samantha's shedding too."

"She is?" I ask, relieved. Samantha is a calico cat. She looks like a child's drawing, bright orange and pure black splotches neatly colored in with Crayolas, their waxy points all nice and sharp. I still keep a couple of Crayola Crayon boxes around, the kind with 64 Brilliant Colors and a Built-In Sharpener. Nobody uses them now, of course. But it pleases me knowing they're here, a link.

"Right into my poached egg," Agnes is saying.

"How can she shed into your egg?" I ask, always a good straight man. Have to be in this household.

"Easy," says Agnes. "She likes watching me eat. She's crouching right here beside my plate." This newsflash I find mildly shocking, but I don't say word one. Sooner criticize someone's kids than I would their pets. And anyhow, what are pets but surrogate children?

I clear my throat. We discuss next week's concert, chat about the new Jane Austen biography we're doing for Book Club, hang up.

The collie ambles over and puts his long nose in my lap. He's heard me talking about him. He knows the crucial word. *Dog.* Also the pronoun *he.* When Martin and I discuss him, we have to tiptoe around his name which is Dusky. And if we cleverly substitute *he* a lot, *he* will cock his head and glance over at us, ears alerted. He likes to lie at the far end of the sofa, a perfect place to monitor what's going on indoors with his family, but also strategically stationed right next to the window beside the front door where he can check out the general lay of the land—dogs strolling by, UPS trucks, postmen, and any other potential invaders of this quiet neighborhood of mostly empty homes (until six o'clock) what with everyone working these days, and the kids all grown up and gone.

Martin claims this sofa has become the "world's fanciest dog bed."

I tell him Dusky loves the couch because he's sensitive to color and texture. Also being a tri-color, he's perfectly camouflaged, exactly matching the fabric: black and gold cut-velvet. I used to think that velvet was reserved for royalty and formal Victorian parlors, but I found out it wears forever, one of the world's toughest fabrics. Barring accidents, it takes decades for velvet to give up the ghost. This couch must be at least fifteen years old now. Martin chose it for me as a surprise for my birthday. But we didn't get it in time, they had to build it to order way down in South Carolina somewhere. Actually it took nine months. I tease Martin. "A literal accouchement," I told him. He groaned. Groaning is the way this family acknowledges a fairly witty pun, or even a half-baked one.

I stand up, motion Dusky towards the sofa. "Go lie down," I tell him in a firm, mildly irritated tone of voice. He looks puzzled as if to say, "What have I done?" so I pat his silken head, murmur "Good dog, it's ok." And I make the *all done* signal with my hands flat out, moving back and forth. This he does understand. He sighs, meanders back to his command post next to the window.

The drone of the Hoover when I turn it on goes up a register, from a low bass to a higher-pitched whine as I put on the attachment to pick up crumbs beneath and between the sofa cushions.

Once when the boys were very small, Martin and I went off to the Caribbean for a week. My mother, the big time career woman, took care of the kids for the first and last time ever. She left a cigarette burning and it fell behind the cushion, and the whole sofa began smoking. The fire department came and dragged it out into the garage. When we returned home, the room looked strange. No sofa, just a pile of velvet cushions lying there on the floor, their gold and black vivid against the bright red rug. Only one cushion was badly scorched. It's covered now with solid black velvet. And dog hairs, I might add. We couldn't match the original fabric.

I didn't get angry that time. It frightened me too much. Accidents will happen and all that. But when the boys were young teenagers, one of their buddies got drunk and vomited all over the sofa. I wouldn't allow them to invite him back for almost a month. He didn't even offer to clean up. I still don't like that kid. He's grown and married now, let his wife clean up his messes.

That was the time I finally got smart, unzipped the covers off all the pillows and threw them into the washing machine, then air-dried them in the dryer so the nub of the velvet was all shaken out and fluffy, soft as baby's hair or Dusky's coat.

These are the practical tips like squeezing lemon juice on your hands to take away the smell of garlic, or persuading Sears we have a mutual problem in the billing department—the insights that come to a person slowly through careful observation, trial and error. The unadorned wisdom I have accumulated through the years.

I can't announce these truths to anyone. My friends look at me strangely. "Velvet? Nobody *washes* velvet, Shelby, it's too delicate."

Phooey on rigid mind sets. I've learned to keep my truths to myself. I think about them as I vacuum the rug. I think of the willowy daughter Martin and I always wanted but never had, how I could pass all this wisdom on to her, and how much she'd relish it. I can see her just as clearly as I can see Dusky over there spooled up on the sofa. He's watching me watch her. And now his eyes shift beyond me, to the kitchen where she leans against the counter, curly dark hair like mine, long golden legs.

She's chopping vegetables for a Thai dinner. Skinny as she is, she's always dieting. She tells me about this med student she's been dating. We discuss what she will wear to his graduation next month. Any clothes discussion, or for that matter practical advice of any description, the boys go, "Oh chill out, Mom," their deep voices sliding down the scale with exasperation as they fade off to their rooms, calling back over their shoulders, "When's chow time?"

My daughter shakes her head, grins at me. "Pigs," is all she says. We understand each other, us against the guys. We are in communion, you might say.

She likes to walk along the beach with me. We search for shells, listen to the gulls shrieking, watch Dusky playing tag with the waves, and dream together about her career in the theater. Yale Drama School has already sent her an acceptance letter for next fall. She loves what I love, we laugh at the same silly stuff. No sullen camping out in her bedroom, no, she talks with me. Hardly teases me at all. Listens to me analyze the new play at the Wilbur, joins me in drooling over Victorian novelists—we both loathe Trollope, however. Review our favorite movie, we both cried over *Atonement*. At college she starred in *Camelot*—she can sing as beautifully as she acts. In so many ways, we connect—she fulfills my dreams.

But hey, reality check here. Having a daughter, it wouldn't work, I know that. A child is the last person on earth who wants maternal confidences. Or wisdom for that matter. But still I wish I had her around. Then I could pretend I was leaving a legacy that mattered. To somebody anyhow. I'm here to tell you it's tough living in an all male household. Even Dusky's a boy. But at least he's tuned in to the way I feel, my moods. He suffers when I suffer. He doesn't think it's hormones. Or plain funny.

Sometimes cleaning house, I figure things out. Like when you come across a magical sentence in a great book and you realize the writer's saying something that exactly matches what you are thinking. Or feeling.

"Yes!" I say aloud. "That's true!" True because it matches. True because it's my very own discovery which I've stumbled on by myself, and right there in print the author's luminous words are actually voicing my thoughts, more fluently, of course, but a validation nonetheless. And now what was knotted, breaks free, and for one quick moment I'm happy. And I wonder, "Can I hang on to this? Can it comfort me tomorrow?"

I switch off the Hoover. In the silence, Dusky pants in time with the radio, and I stand here staring down at the embossed pattern of the rug swept almost free now of dog hair and lint and shiny bits of sand and pine needles. The deep crimson color pleases me as much as the truth I've found at my feet.

I love colors. I'm in tune with them the same way Agnes and my youngest son are sensitive to music. I can retain different color values in my head for weeks at a time just as they can remember complex chords and intricate melodies. The year after we bought this house, we spent two whole months steaming off hideous mustard-flowered wallpaper so we could paint the walls in the dining and living rooms. Martin and I drove all over town trying to find this particular shade of red to echo the rug here in the family room. No luck. But then as the car stopped at an intersection, I glanced over at a window display in a hardware store. And there was this tiny circle of our red. I grabbed his arm. "Wait!" I told him. "I see it!"

We marched into the store and bought gallons and gallons of red paint. The clerk kept shaking his head. "Never sold much of this shade before," he said. I nudged Martin, and whispered while the guy was tumbling the paint cans in the machine, "He thinks we're opening a bordello." Martin laughed his easy light baritone laugh. Our boys sound just like him these days. On the phone I get confused as to whether it's Martin speaking or one of them. They look like him too, tall and blonde and rangy with his round blue bullet eyes. They have none of my darkness, lucky for them.

A couple of years ago when the youngest left for college, we had the house repainted, the inside. I sent the painters back to the same store. The man claimed he didn't stock the identical brand but he could mix it to order. The color is almost a match, but not quite. There's still a patch of the original paint inside the cabinet where I keep the good china, the red there is richer and deeply saturated. Whenever I look at it, I realize you can never exactly duplicate anything with colors. But in my mind I carry that first deep red as pure and clear as the patch that still remains in the corner cupboard. The color is still true.

It's hard matching things. My own childhood with our children's, the way I felt when I was young, the way I was raised. And then when our sons got to be twelve or thirteen, trying to match gawky adolescents against those first sweet toddler years when they ran gladhanded into the living room shrieking, "Can we open now? Please, please, is it time?"

No, that time is gone. And it's too hard, the long letting go of those sleepy mornings when gaudy packages blazed as bright as their pink faces. I don't understand—they run to play outside, and the next minute they're trudging back, small boys transformed to men, as taciturn as they are tall.

Now when we open presents, they pretend to be excited. "Hey, Dad, totally!" Or "Excellent, Mom. Can't wait to read this." Or listen to it, wear it, lose it.

Is it time? Yes. Time to pay the bills, make out lists, go to the dentist, take Dusky for his heartworm shot, listen to Martin talk about his lectures, shop for birthdays making a careful detour around the toy department where catcher's mitts and shiny blue trikes announce another spring.

And now Dusky's announcing he's spotted his golden retriever pal outside. I let him out the door and watch him tear up the pale green fuzz of April grass, hurdle over the crocus plants budding along the edge of the driveway, and soon he's disappearing down the road, him and the golden loping neck and neck.

The air smells fresh. The sun slants through the window, and as I close the door I notice the panes are streaked from the long winter. Time for a good windexing after I finish the rug.

I switch on the vacuum again. The drone sounds good to me, dulls the silence of empty rooms. It even manages to drown out the ringing of the telephone—Agnes checking up on me—and the blunted sweetness of a Brahms Trio playing on NPR while I stare down into the red rug and watch the detritus of the past twenty four hours get sucked up inside the darkness of a bright yellow bag.

A magic bag, I've decided. When I empty it, I'm always amazed at the way it's able to transform each golden particle of sand and dog hair into a uniformly gray mass.

I poke at the dirt. It's feather soft. Puffs of dust float upward, and I can feel the grit layering my finger, my wrist. A nice dove gray color this dirt, as muted as fog floating in across the waves, first a few wisps and then a solid blanket so that soon all that's left of the ocean is the memory of curling blue and turquoise. And bright sunlight quivering across pure white foam.

My eyes are watering, from all that dust.

I blink them a couple of times, smile. She smiles back at me.

"Chill," she tells me. "No big deal."

BON APPETIT

"...SO THEN HE SAYS—BEAR in mind it's *my* home we're discussing—he says I should not have bought that new patio furniture at Bloomingdale's, I should shop the sales, he tells me, quelle merde!"

Luisa stops for a long guzzle of wine, she's thirsty. So are Jill and I. We have each ordered a carafe apiece, three carafes of Riesling for three friends. The bar's only a dozen steps away from our table but it's so noisy in here, the TV blaring, and the backs of the men hunched on their stools—they form a wall, quite impenetrable, quite impossible to catch the eye of Fred, the bartender. As for our waitress, she's vanished, of course. She goes into hiding the moment she serves us. It's an old war, we're used to it.

"This to me is fascinating," continues Luisa.

She perches like a tiny jungle bird in the booth opposite me and Jill. She's wearing a man's Guatemalan shirt tonight, thin orange stripes against a fuchsia background which exactly matches her brilliant lipstick.

Fuchsia's not a shade I'm crazy about as a rule, but on Luisa with her short white hair, elegantly cropped ("Sixty-five dollars they're charging now," she tells us) and those great hollowed dark eyes, the color is perfect, like the flamboyant plumage of a toucan. Luisa's a poet—her third collection comes out next fall—and she dresses very much the way she writes, in a style both richly textured and disconcertingly bizarre. Her word for it is "earthy"—mine would be exotic.

"Why is it?" she asks us (but I feel sure this is a rhetorical question), "the minute you give a man a key to the house he comes on like, comment s'appele-t-il—Alan Greenspan?"

A guy at the far end of the bar is staring at Luisa, checking out first her shirt, then her white hair.

Now his eye catches mine. He's a regular here, nice looking man with a nice slow smile. I glance away but not before I've smiled back. Three weeks running he's tried to buy me a drink; three times I've said no.

Beside me Jill shifts her legs and slides over to the corner of the booth. We do not look at each other, we don't need to. These discussions—so frank, so intimate—about Luisa's lovers make Jill nervous. For a professional social worker (she runs a Rape Crisis unit over in Yonkers), Jill's pretty prudish on the subject of sex. Still, like me, she's intrigued when Luisa talks, reluctantly intrigued. Jill and I, we have foregone lovers for safety, for permanence. That's what we tell ourselves. And to some extent out of a sense of loyalty; I mean you can't rule out loyalty, of course. But at bottom I think we both know it has been for lack of courage, nothing more, nothing less.

Luisa's describing now how scared Joe looked when she blew up at him about the patio furniture. "Joe, I say to him, you have the narrow soul of a peasant. My money, I go, is *my* money. To a penny-pincher like you, money seulement has meaning. But my life, I say, is larger than that. And so..." and here Luisa waves her hand, a small hand but beautifully shaped, the pale olive skin as smooth as baby skin, "he backed off, bien sûr, he backed off immediately. We went to the Army store then. To try on shoes, the kind a busman must wear. You know, big and black." She rolls her eyes at us.

We three are here tonight celebrating the fact that the busman lover has finally moved out. It's taken six months of after-work consultations with Jill and me every Friday night plus many phone calls and at least four visits to the fortune teller who is now in semi-retirement over in Newark but makes exceptions for Luisa.

She stares down into her wine glass, raises it to her lips, but she doesn't drink. She's still smiling, a lopsided smile. Once years ago during our matinee play period before I started teaching again, we went into the rococo restroom of some theater, the Barrymore, I think. Luisa sat down in front of the gilt mirror and fussed with her hair, still black in those days and worn long—this would have been in Luisa's pre-widowhood era before she lost all the weight. She touched her lips, her crooked smile, and told me she had no true idea of how "this strange mouth of mine really looks."

We both stared at her reflection. "You see me as I truly am," she had murmured then. "I see myself only in reverse. Very appropriate, I can assure you." And she laughed. It's a wonderful laugh, Luisa's. It starts with a deep chuckle, climbs up in steps of three and then skids back halfway to a long-held middle note. A lopsided laugh to match the mouth which smiles now at me and Jill, smiles ironically, affectionately, with rueful wisdom.

"Alors," she sighs and folds her napkin in her lap once more. "The thing about those shoes was they squeaked. The squeak never went away—that is to say, not until he did, che porcheria!"

When Luisa swears, she automatically slides into another language. She speaks fluent Italian, of course, she was born in Trieste. And also French because it was to France she was sent during the war. Plus German because of her Austrian mother whom she never saw except for brief holidays. It seems Luisa's mother too had lovers. (Is this, I wonder, a genetic predisposition?)

A professional golfer, she abandoned Luisa first to the father and then to an uncle in Paris. She swept in for quick visits between golf tours, hugged Luisa and disappeared onto the links. When war broke out, she married a Brazilian meatpacker and disappeared very conveniently to Rio. Luisa never saw her again. Needless to say, Luisa does not golf.

Frowning, our waitress doles out three Chef salads. Jill has just lit a cigarette. She pushes the wooden salad bowl aside, then leans forward to ask Luisa a question. Jill is ten years younger and reminds me of a small blonde cocker spaniel, high-strung and droll and wriggling with impatience. She has a great sense of humor when she finally relaxes.

"What about Joe's junk?" she says. "He all moved out?"

Dear Jill. There are times when she comes on like a housemother. Maybe it's because she still has kids at home and we don't. But to be honest, I must admit all three of us take turns mothering, hectoring, advising, forgiving. It's important, and I have to remind myself of this when Jill starts up. She does have this tendency to bore in, what Luisa calls "Jill's bulldog instinct, not knowing when to let go." Luisa doesn't mind it, Jill's bulldogging. In fact it amuses her. She becomes more and more ironic, her roguish laugh punctuating the end of Jill's earnest questions.

"Only five more cartons left," Luisa answers between rapid mouthfuls of lettuce. She eats fast, she's always hungry, Luisa. She has strong appetites. And they do not shame her, not a bit.

Jill, on the other hand, pokes at her food, toys with it long after we have finished. Then she will look down at our plates, surprised, "How can you two be finished so soon?"

"You make damn sure he comes and gets them," she says firmly to Luisa. She frowns, stubs out her cigarette. Now, finally, she picks up her fork.

"Don't worry, he wants to stay on the good side of me," Luisa smiles. "You must remember this is a very lonely man. That, in a nutshell, was the whole problem. I felt this…comment ça dire…this black hole of loneliness in this man. In other words, I felt sorry for him. Not a sensible way to start a relationship. And almost a guarantee of how it will end, n'est-ce pas? exactly the way it began, full of pity—not much else."

"He's a jerk," says Jill, and pokes at a chunk of tuna fish, then turns it over and begins to dissect it, shredding the pink flesh with delicate jabs of her fork.

I look away, glance at Luisa as I speak. "Come on, Jill. He's not such a bad guy is what she's saying. Simply your typical L H B."

Beside me, Jill begins to giggle. She has the giggle of a young girl, it's quite delightful. Her eyes crinkle, she wrinkles her snub nose. Getting Jill to laugh makes me feel lighthearted in a sort of clownish way. Whereas when I make Luisa laugh, I feel witty, sophisticated—in a word, cosmopolitan.

L H B is our shorthand for Limited Human Being. Of which we seem to meet an increasing number, particularly these days as we grow old. Or could it be that our tolerance for human limitation decreases proportionate to age? Luisa believes it's not a question of tolerance but rather of finally understanding with some degree of clarity what we like and dislike. "Before then we were trying them on for size, our opinions, our attitudes," she says. "We didn't know which salons suited us, much less which styles. We thought as we dressed. For the trends, for the men—not for ourselves. Incroyable, to come of age so slowly."

Our waitress, sauntering by, has stopped at our booth.

"You ladies ok?" she asks, giving this big grin, totally fake, a make-sure-of-the-tip grin. We hate this waitress. She's very moody and has managed to offend Jill at least once a month. Usually we don't meet for our weekly confabs until well after 7 p.m. so we're sure to miss her shift. I get very nervous as she stands beside me, tapping first one foot, then another. I am afraid Jill will ask for hot tea. This never goes down well as it takes too much time to go out back for the little pewter teapots, then wait for the hot water to boil. The waitress told us this once, grinning the whole time. But her eyes were angry. Jill's got even angrier. At which point I knocked over my coffee cup and open warfare was avoided in the rush to mop up the table, blotting up the coffee with soggy paper napkins. A few drops rolled off the edge of the table and scalded my knee. But I chalked it up to getting wounded in the line of duty.

"Everything's fine, just fine," I say quickly. The waitress tosses her long black pony tail and swishes off. She's left us the bill.

Jill mutters, "I hate that bitch, she's so hostile!"

As if she hasn't heard, Luisa lunches into a long description of the junk Joe brought to the house when he moved in a year ago. By now she's finished her salad. She takes little pellets of French bread and rolls them in the leftover garlic and raspberry vinaigrette dressing pooled at the bottom of the salad bowl. This she does with stylish precision and great speed. She reminds me of the efficient gray rabbit who each spring munches his way through the lettuce patch in my husband's garden, oblivious that what he's doing is neither socially nor horticulturally acceptable. Neither the rabbit nor Luisa gives a damn about propriety. For this I applaud them both.

"…his collection of brass buddhas," she's saying now. "At least a dozen meerschaum pipes, although to my knowledge he smokes only those dreadful menthol cigarettes, pardonne, dearest Jill," and she glances at the ashtray, goes on. "Ah yes, a ten pound jar of Kennedy quarters, no, I do not exaggerate, I assure you! Not to mention a winter's supply of Geritol, that is when my heart started sinking. Let me consider—porcelain teacups, rather exquisite, they belonged to his wife, poor soul, evidently *she* had taste. He brought me coffee in these cups each morning, brought it to my bed every morning before he left for work. In other words..." and cocking an eyebrow, she gives me a sharp look, "I trained him as I trained dear Alexander." Luisa's husband Alexander died seven years ago, a dear person as Luisa says. But quite impossible to live with. A fussbudget of a man, fifteen years older than Luisa, he made her middle-aged before her time. Now she's making up for it and with such high spirits that I know Alexander looking down from his high-backed family pew up there somewhere, must approve. He adored Luisa so—despite his limitations.

"Alack and alas, the Busman Brew..." she adds and washes down the last oily bit of French bread with the last of the Riesling, "it was always bitter. The coffee pot Joe used was not big enough for sufficient water." She swallows. "A reasonable metaphor for the man, n'est-ce pas?"

On the butter plate, Jill has made a collection of green olives which she now transfers to Luisa's salad bowl. They disappear one by one as Luisa continues listing the dowry Joe brought to her house.

Jill nudges me.

I hear the faintest giggle begin, and I too am smiling because when Luisa soars into one of her monologues, it's like being carried along a current of wild water, riding first up and then over a waterfall, not a high waterfall but the words rush you along and downwards and you fall knowing there are no sharp rocks beneath only more water foaming and churning, spinning you around but still carrying you, carrying you swiftly and I think this is what good friends mean to me, a source I go to be refreshed, cooled off and buoyed along swift currents which I absolutely trust not to sink or smash me. Or even worse, side-stream me into weed-tangled shallows choked by marsh grasses and a muddy bottom. Luisa and I prefer the risks of rocks any day to the mud. I'm not entirely sure about Jill, but we are working on her. Jill's frightened of fast moving water, she won't swim in the ocean on principle. "Treacherous," she claims, "the undertow." I picture Jill as a dammed up pond. Luisa of course is a cataract—one of those great pongos plummeting from the headwaters of the Amazon. And myself? Oh, simply an ordinary sort of river, the kind where you can do some sedate whitewater canoeing, nothing expert, mind you.

We sit quietly for a moment. Quiet is not the right word in such a noisy place. We simply do not speak. The men at the bar are watching the New York Knicks on TV. Every so often a tremor seems to run along their hunched shoulders.

"*Go* for it!"

"Atta boy!"

"*AwwwRIGHT!*"

These are the words that erupt periodically from their throats. Not their mouths, their throats. I wonder about this. About these atavistic shouts men produce. And how curiously and inextricably such bellowing is linked with both sports and sex.

"Stalking their prey," I observe, nodding at the bar. But the bartender turns on the blender so I can't hear what Luisa answers, still the gleam in her eyes indicates she's caught my meaning.

And indeed after the high pitched whine of the blender stops, she's saying, "Men at play, mais c'est impossible! They gave Joe a party, the guys at his local Carmen's union. A birthday party—what is the word—an elk dinner?"

"Stag," offers Jill. Her mouth twitches.

"Short for stagger," I tease.

Luisa pretends to look stern, fixing me with a headmistressy glare but indulgent behind the mock frown.

"Tais-toi, mon lapin," she tells me. She never calls Jill this even though twitchy-nosed Jill looks like a lapin, and she herself eats like one. But not me—me with what Ken calls fondly my "beak—married you for your beak," he goes. As good a reason as any.

"At midnight, voilà!" continues Luisa. "Home is the warrior mit loot. They have made him gifts, these men, obscene objects of every description, my eyes do not believe what he shows me, there was this cordless—"

Jill clears her throat significantly. Luisa stops short, then nods and pours a bit more wine from my carafe into her wineglass. "Alors," she murmurs, "I just don't know. He was a man who…he just had a lot of stuff. You might say I'm convalescing. Convalescing from the weight of his possessions."

"I'll drink to that!" cries Jill and pours us both more wine. We all clink glasses, "Salud!" we tell each other.

"Now here is the good news. Tomorrow Gordon comes for dinner," announces Luisa and cocks her head, runs her fingers through the short white hair.

Jill's smile falters, fades away. "Oh no, Luisa! Is that wise?"

Luisa shrugs. "The fortune teller clearly predicted this three months ago."

Jill is frowning. She glances over at me. But I keep my expression bland as vanilla pudding. Jill will have to stir this particular pot alone.

"Now listen," she says to Luisa. She's using her let's-be-reasonable coaxing voice which she uses with her clients. But I know full well it will make no mark on the diamond hardness of Luisa's mind. "You can't convince me you believe in this stuff, Luisa, I mean you're too smart, ok?"

Luisa answers calmly, "The simple truth is I believe in psychic forces."

"Like clairvoyance, you mean. Precognition, the experiments at Duke."

"But of course. And ghosts as well."

Jill swallows hard. I am careful not to look at her any longer, this is low profile time.

Now Luisa adds, "So, in fact, does she." She jerks her head in my direction.

"You *can't* believe in ghosts, Luisa, this is the 21st century we're in!"

Luisa begins ticking off invisible presences, one gracefully tapered finger at a time. "Ghosts, ESP, psychics, mediums, and last but not least, tarot cards. Which is precisely how Madame Merle was able to foretell that Gordon would come back to me. Come back the moment that other one left the premises, the very same week, in fact."

"It's crazy, Luisa! I mean your poems side by side with all this mumbo jumbo. Darn it, I mean I can't accept the fact you literally buy into such childishness, honestly, it really bothers me."

"But the truth is, ma chère, I do. There are forces—"

"There are *not*, Luisa!"

"Very well, there are not." Luisa leans back, gazes at Jill's face. At the hot eyes, the pink cheeks, the clouds of smoke from the cigarette.

"Alors, dearest Jill," she says in her low voice, "you seem much more excited by the fact of my believing in ghosts than I am over your non-belief. Something is cuckoo here." And Luisa laughs, but the third high note is cut off by Jill breaking in, "I find that a very hostile remark, Luisa."

"This hostility, it is not from me, dearest Jill, vraiment. Be reasonable now."

"I am being reasonable, for God's sake!"

I poke Jill, "Want me to whistle up our waitress, make it a free-for-all?"

"Ok, sorry. I apologize, I'm making a scene." This from stiff lips, but she's trying hard to smile again.

Whew, past that particular whirlpool so I turn back to Luisa. "How is Gordon, you've talked with him?"

"Many times." She gets that Renoir tilt of her head, a way of moving that American women don't have, the head tilts down, from under half-closed lids the eye glances up and sideways. The smile is something between frank flirtation and tolerant amusement. I can't think of another way to characterize it except as a species of sophisticated worldliness that has little to do with the hard, high fashion veneer we Americans associate with the word. Sophistication for us means glossy surfaces, a kind of pseudo savoir faire totally devoid of wisdom. Or wit. Or, for that matter, genuine charm.

"And Gordon's wife?" I ask Luisa.

"She's going to law school these days, perhaps she can work up to divorce law as her specialité, we can only hope." Luisa sighs, begins whisking up bread crumbs with the flat side of the matchbook. She dumps them in the ashtray. "C'est à dire, it's quite different now, with me and Gordon. He's no longer trying to romanticize me. I now represent simply a woman to him, not a fantasy."

"How can you tell?" asks Jill, but she asks this in a neutral voice.

Luisa shrugs again. "For better or worse, I don't believe we can do any more harm to each other. He doesn't deny this. He was deeply wounded in the beginning, L'Affaire Omnibus."

"So what did he expect?" Jill bursts out. "Going away like that, off to London every six months. Never calling you, it was *rotten*."

"He's a painter, he has commissions, obligations. When it comes to men, dear Jill, au fond it is yourself you must learn to trust. All must flow from that beginning. Ah," she says in a low voice, "quelle misère! Mais non..." and she straightens up and looks around the restaurant, the guys at the bar, then back at us. "I think now he's hooked on me. Permanently, in other words. But this time I suspect we shall be a couple of old fogies, sort of—how does one put it—nebbishing around."

"We're never going to get to meet him," I say with regret. I've seen pictures, many pictures of Gordon, but it's not enough. He could be any well-preserved, wind-tanned man of sixty or so.

Luisa stares at me. "You would so love his eyes, mon lapin. Opaque gray. A gray that looks more like wet sand than water. Quite unusual."

"I just don't want him to hurt you again," mumbles Jill.

I pick up the check. There are grease marks splattered by salad oil across the paper.

"All I know," I say slowly, "like I was telling Jill yesterday..." and I grin at Jill who is smiling now, this is the kind of supportive quasi-professional talk she believes in, "whatever Luisa wants to do, I told Jill—I'm for it, one hundred per cent."

Luisa beams. The mouth is a fuchsia diagonal lopsided with pleasure. "Écoute, you will both relish this story. You know Grace, my new friend in the poetry workshop? The Southern aristocrat?"

Jill and I both nod.

"I gather that her lover, the latest one, is much younger. She feels much guilt over this. And the fact that she still sees the other man. She told me: Where one is, the other is, I shall always be stuck like this. Each one spoils the other for me. So I talked to her, nothing to feel guilty about, I go, it's simply the concept of monogamy is so deeply inculcated here in the States." She laughs and a couple of heads turn at the bar in our direction. "The whole situation is delicious, outrageously delicious, I mean here we are, Grace and I, we both appear to be the sort of women who sit at home reading Henry James. Nobody could imagine us as having these slightly irregular—what should we call them? These torrid liaisons dangereuses."

Jill giggles, "You know what? Somebody ought to tape these conversations we have here, sell them to Senior Citizen Clubs."

"My point exactly." Luisa folds her napkin, then slips on pale violet gloves. "So there is Grace. In a bind, two men, the usual problem. So I told her: Mais alors, ma soeur, the solution is simple, *ENJOY THEM BOTH!*" She says this with such relish and such a comical leer that Jill and I both burst out laughing. The man at the far end of the bar salutes us with his glass.

We stand up and start putting on our coats. But Luisa is not finished yet. "Grace also predicted Gordon's return. She said she felt strongly something was going to happen to me. Good or bad? I ask. I don't know, she said. Quite an honest answer. And that, mind you, was a week to the day before Joe left." Luisa is smiling now at Jill.

"Hey," quips Jill, "least she didn't charge you a fee."

Luisa reaches over and pats Jill on her sleeve. "Grace feels these things intuitively. But she feels storms in her knees as well, which is, I suppose, a little less uncommon."

"Psychic rheumatism," grins Jill.

"Ok, loves," says Luisa. "Home to our lonely beds."

We hug each other. Luisa and Jill start walking to the cashier's desk out in the entrance hall by the front door. I hang back to put down money for the tip which we have forgotten. Luisa turns to look for me, Jill has gone on ahead and disappeared.

"You coming?" asks Luisa

I wink at her, then hunch my shoulder in the direction of the bar where the nice slow-smiling stranger is watching us both.

"Tell Jill—tell her I had to make a phone call…uhh…call home."

Luisa's eyes widen. "But I thought Ken was away."

"He is," I answer. "As usual. For a whole 'nother week yet."

Luisa glances down the bar at the stranger, then back at me. And then she says, "I see. I will take care of Jill. And you, mon lapin" she smiles at me with shrewd tenderness, "you take care of yourself, bien entendu?"

And then she is gone. I stand there beside our booth, I don't know how to do this, how to approach the bar, breach the long line of backs, breach the impenetrable wall, and just as I fumble with the clasp of my shoulder bag, a kind voice says in my ear…

"Buy you that drink?"

I swallow hard, then turn to look into his eyes, wry smiling eyes they remind me of Luisa's, so with a quick nod I hop on the bar stool.

"You ready now?" is all he asks.

CHARTING THE COURSE

AT THE LAST MINUTE the 5:00 cancelled, so Scott Farlow told his nurse she might as well go home early.

"But Doctor," she said, round eyes blinking behind the thick glasses, "what about all these records? I've got at least two days worth of filing here. And those Blue Cross claims must go out this week, no later."

"Fine, fine, Doreen," he told her. "We'll just let the whole batch ripen till tomorrow."

"Thursday, you mean, Dr. Farlow," she said. That was pure Doreen. Dot your i's, cross your t's—a necessary astringent to his casual way of running the office, the paperwork anyhow.

"Right." he said. "Wednesday, my day of grace." And smiled at her.

"'Well, goodness knows you deserve it," she replied, briskly loyal. She started to walk toward her cubicle facing the reception room, then paused, hand on the doorknob, turned and looked at him.

"Doctor," she said, her fingers flicking up to the nurse's pin on her collar, nervously rubbing the small blue and gold caduceus, the snake coiled lovingly? ominously? around the staff. "Pardon me for asking but are you feeling ok?"

He shrugged, spoke tersely. "I'm just fine, Doreen," he said, then hearing the replay of his voice, he softened it. "Why do you ask?"

She cleared her throat. "It's just that you've seemed kind of peaked these past few weeks," she told him. He laughed, the practiced, reassuring laugh which he knew damn well made his patients feel good as any prescription he'd ever written, occasionally even better.

"Doreen, my dear," he chuckled, "you worry too much."

Doreen pursed her lips and started in with the starchy apologizing routine, but he interrupted her, holding up his hand, "And that's what makes you so special as a nurse. You really care. I know it, and most importantly, the patients all know it."

Then she smiled, round face relieved, prim mouth curved in pleasure. "Thank you, Doctor Farlow. It's good of you to say so." She walked toward the door, adding, all crisp again, "Don't you stay too late now, and don't

385

forget Mrs. Aldrich said she'd call Thursday, she needs the referral for that breast biopsy, remember." Efficient to the end. And concerned. Bless the prickly Doreens of this world, they keep us afloat—try their damndest, at any rate.

She shut the door behind her quietly. He could hear her closing file drawers, her steps crossing and re-crossing the small prison where every day (except Wednesday, Doctor!) with calm efficiency she greeted their steady stream of bratty kids and brassy mothers and the occasional old gomer usually retired and on Medicaid. The rich ones were all in Sarasota or Phoenix or wherever the hell old elephants wander off to croak these days.

Now he could hear Doreen crashing the coat hangers in the coat closet out in back beyond the waiting room, getting her pale pink angora sweater which she wore to work all summer long, no matter how hot it was. "Better safe than sorry, Doctor," she had said when once he asked her mildly why tote a sweater along in 90 degree heat. The toilet flushed—Doreen battening down the hatches in the tiny lav they'd finally had to install after the Zoning Board raised so much hell—when was it? five, six years ago. The practice was booming, back then ah, yes and he'd been on the verge of remodeling the second floor upstairs. Big expansion plans. The big bang. Gotcha!

The telephone shrilled. He switched the lever to the answering service. Ok, Walker, old buddy, it's your show till Thursday. This turkey's gone, folks. Flown the old coop, too bad.

He stood up, stretched, stared outside at the patchy hedge separating the strip of lawn from the parking lot. Five-twenty and counting. Not too many cars parked out there—just the usual collection of last minute shoppers schlepping home from work, darting in to the market for chicken tenders and frozen vegetables—whatever they could buy and cook quick. He knew that routine pretty well. He looked down at the phone. Better call Stephanie. She'd be back at the apartment by now. When she answered, he asked right off how her mother was doing.

"Pretty good today," Steph said, voice cautious, in neutral. "Actually she got up and walked twice this afternoon."

"You get to see the attending?" he asked, doodling on the pad. COMPLIMENTS OF SCHERING PHARMACEUTICAL, he read; CHOOSE DRYXORAL...CLEAR TODAY...CLEAR TONIGHT...CLEAR TOMORROW. He smiled. "Just for a few minutes," Stephanie was saying. "He seems real pleased with her progress."

"Fine...fine. He—what's his name again?"

"Dr. Carruthers," she said.

"Yes, well—my guess is Carruthers will want to keep an eye on her over the weekend, probably release her, let's see, say either Monday or Tuesday."

"He wouldn't commit himself," Steph said dryly. "Mother asked him pointblank."

"Ah," he laughed. "We never do, do we."

"You mean commit yourselves?" she asked. She sounded a little less tense, starting to play back to his deliberately easy rhythm.

"Sho 'nuf, petunia, not til we're pretty dang sure we-all's home free."

"Called Scott-free, I believe," she said. "Also called hedging your bets, from the patients' point of view that is."

He frowned at the phone. "One way of putting it," he answered evenly. Not now, Steph. Not now.

Small pause.

"Well, dear, how you been?" she asked, sliding into her sprightly women's-college cadences, what he called her "Gold Slush" voice. "How about meals?"

"Getting by, getting by," he answered.

"Scotty!" she scolded. "Have you really cooked *anything* while I've been gone? Damn it, I just wish there'd been time to freeze some casseroles for you, it all happened so fast."

And he saw her looking back at him from beyond the barrier at the terminal, pausing for a short moment. PASSENGERS ONLY the sign ordered, and she had waved at him, soft eyes worried about what lay both ahead and behind, blonde hair clipped back with the silver barrette he'd given her years ago—one long tendril straggling free—and she brushed at it impatiently as she turned towards the boarding gate. NO VISITORS BEYOND THIS POINT. No, indeed.

He glanced down at the pad, at his fingers moving independently, automatic writing? Drawing a repeated series of rectangles, beginning out at the perimeter and tunneling, maze-like, into the center. He counted the rectangles ranked across the page, then began to number them neatly.

"...from the kids?" she was saying.

"What?" he asked. He laid down the pencil, began twirling it between his thumb and first two fingers, watching the inter-phalangeal joints cross nimbly back and forth like a cantering horse smoothly changing leads—but different because no one was signaling with legs and reins, no one calling the shots. From the instant he touched the pencil, his hand had moved with intricate autonomy, quite detached from the rest of him. Fascinating. Left brain, right brain stuff, lot of good work—provocative actually—from that Stanford study on profound epilepsy.

"Scotty!" Her voice broke through again. "Are you listening or what?"

"Yeah...the kids...no, they haven't called," he told her.

"I *know* that, dear. I just got through telling you they called the hospital last night."

"Both of them?" he asked, surprised. "On the same night? Are they doing ok? What gives?"

"Yes, same night," she laughed. "Two-for-two. But it was Grandma's birthday. That's why. And they're fine, college is awesome, Paula says. Sent their love to you, of course. And so does their Grandma."

"Shoot," he said. "I clean forgot it was her birthday, honey. Give her a hug for me tomorrow. God, I am sorry."

"Darling, she knows you move in a complete fog about this stuff, birthdays, whatever, just like Daddy used to. You seen one doctor—" She stopped, waiting.

"You seen 'em all," he finished it for her.

"Old fuddy-duddys, the pack of you, right?" she asked. She was building a bridge for him, as always, to carry him across, but these days the bridge swayed and lurched in a high wind, and he was afraid to look down at the water churning below.

"Listen, Scotty," she sounded shy now. "I guess what I'll probably do is book a flight home in a couple weeks, after getting Mummy all squared away in the apartment. I really must hire someone reliable to clean house for her, line up meals on wheels, stuff like that."

"Good plan," he said, then added, "and just *insist* to your ma she stay off that leg as much as possible, definitely prop it up when she's sitting down. She can't afford to throw another clot, one femoral by-pass a year is her quota, tell her."

"Okey dokey, but I'll probably have to hog-tie her. You know how she is about sitting still." Stephanie laughed, rich and throaty. It was her laugh which he loved first.

"Just tell her I said so...official word from the Big Doctor," he said.

"I will, honey." Her voice went all soft. "You're the only person she listens to anyhow...ever since Daddy."

"Nice lady, your mom," he said with a goodbye inflection, trying to wind up this dialogue she wanted to spin out as long as she could hold him.

"So, I'll give you a call Sunday?" She was talking fast. "When I know a little bit more, ok?"

He answered her with his brisk professional voice. "Fine, fine," he said.

"Well," she murmured, "you take it easy, dear heart."

"You too," he hesitated, then took a deep breath. "You never have believed me, have you?" he said.

"Believed what?" she echoed, pretending not to understand.

"Believed I...loved...you," he told her, even now stuttering over the word.

Steph spoke so low he could barely hear her. "Oh yes, Scotty. I believe. I finally believe all right. But..." and she added something else unintelligible.

"What? I couldn't hear you," he asked.

"I said," she replied—her bottom lip would be quivering now—"I just wish it were enough."

"Stephanie, darling, it's *not* you...it's me." He ached for her hurting like this.

"Bigger than both of us, hunh?" She tried to giggle.

"Right," he said. But she said nothing. All he could hear was the sound of her breathing, shallow and irregular. "Do good work, darling," he told her, their coda of farewell.

"Goodbye, my dearest," she answered but again he couldn't say it so he just muttered a quick "Take care!" and very gently placed the receiver down in its cradle.

He tore the sheet of paper off the pad, crumpled it up, lobbed it into the wastebasket under the window. When the children were small, they all had a standing bet about going three-for-three, tossing balled-up paper napkins twenty feet down the narrow kitchen towards that old beat-up wicker basket bought so many summers ago at some tourist stand on the Cape. And the expression on Troy's face—what was he? five maybe, a jock even then—that first time he scored three in a row, looping the wad of paper with a long graceful arching toss with his skinny arm, then looking up at his father, eyes blazing with triumph, as he shouted, "BEAT you, Daddy! I WON!"

Forged there and then, the boy's determination to shine in the one arena his super-dad couldn't compete: the world of sports. Why hadn't he ever been able to let the kid win at anything else? Why always squelching him when something was being discussed at dinner, when some question came up and Troy would argue, matching wits, playing the word games as best he could, until trapped in a corner once again by the indisputable logic and the battering sarcasm of his father's voice, that square-jawed little face would turn beet red, the thick carotid in his scrawny throat pulsing visibly, and then he'd go mute, sullenly refusing to answer, finally stalking up to his bedroom.

Paula usually kept quiet, the advantage of being the younger sibling. Not Stephanie though; she would start in, trying to explain the damage away, explain what Troy meant, on and on, and finally, he, the "Pig-Daddy", would lash back at her: "Stop trying to come between me and the boy. Stop playing mediator!" and she would keep it up until at last, disgusted, he too went mute and stalked out of the house, pausing for one last shot before he slammed out the door, "Leave me alone, will you. Stop beating on me."

And so, eventually, she had. Stopped acting as interpreter, stopped defending her son and mediating between the boy and the man who had over the years grown so far apart that now when they were in the same room, it was like making polite conversation with a neighbor, casual pleasantries, carefully impersonal. "How's college?" "Fine. How's work going, Dad?"

"The boy's shut me out," he used to tell Steph.

And sometimes, not very often, she had answered, "You wrote him off a long time ago and he knows it."

"You were the one who taught him to believe all that garbage."

And she would look up like he'd slapped her: "Scott, you've got it all twisted. You never talked *with* him, just *at* him every single time he challenged you."

"And now we're strangers," he'd answer.

"But that's what I was trying to stop from happening all those years, Scotty, can't you see!" and her voice would swoop up and hold on a high note of pain.

"I see all right. I see a momma robin still bent on feeding her little chicks, and pecking the hell out of anybody who dares come near them."

"You're twisted," she'd choke out finally, eyes swollen and red, and he would just slam the door and leave again.

Leaving. He was real good at leaving. Leaving the lab before the tenure committee would take the final vote. Leaving all that beautiful research—the manuscripts dog-eared with age—unpublished because he was too over-committed (read: lazy) to take the little bit of time for the final polishing, the final diagrams.

Leaving Steph night after night: "Experiment to finish" and later, "Patient to see in ICU." Leaving her behind with the kids year after year.

"Just spend a couple of hours with them on the weekends," she used to beg him. "Give them a bath. Read them a story. Take them canoeing. Whatever." And he usually answered something like, "Get off my back. I'm having a hard enough time playing catch-up ball at work. Don't start in on me the minute I get home."

Leaving the teaching hospital. "Too much pressure," he had told them. "Want to be my own boss, small clinical practice out in the suburbs. Primary care stuff. With real patients, not guinea pigs. God knows they need good medicine out there."

What in Christ's name had he been smoking back then? The kindly GP myth was dead as Stephanie's dad. Gone forever the Norman Rockwell doctors of early childhood, replaced by jazzy clinics, the big HMO's so much more convenient, and most importantly, less expensive for the average patient.

So now here he sat, isolated professionally and starved intellectually, wiping noses and making referrals, merely a medical switchboard which come to think of it was pretty damn funny, exactly what Steph used to call herself. No use kidding anymore, this practice boiled down to the most primitive kind of triage, keeping only the routine cases for himself. His patients were sophisticated and suspicious of generalists yet, at another level, many of them still nostalgic for the simpler medicine of long ago. So they came to him for their flu shots, the routine annual check-ups, the physicals for summer camp, boring scut-work which—let's get real here—Doreen could handle with one arm tied behind her. And handle a hell of a lot better than he could because Doreen really *liked* people. She suffered with them over the most trivial of presenting symptoms.

Sure, he could fake it. Do the jolly-laugh routine, pat their shoulders, but ideas were where he really lived, probing for the weak point in the hypothesis. Asking *why not?* and *can you prove it?*

"Elegant experiment," the big guns had told him. "Write it up! Write it up!"

But something had made him keep sailing onto the next study and the next, always impatient with the nitpicky grind of rewrites, and bitter, so bitter at the publish-or-perish sword they held over his head.

"It's the quality, not the number that counts," he had argued.

"Brilliant!" went the chorus.

Brilliant all right. A brilliant failure, all washed up at 50, mewling like a baby not ready to be weaned. And so, here he sat in this suffocating hellhole serenely overlooking a suburban shopping mall, serenely overlooked by his colleagues.

Leaving. Leaving so often that finally he was left with nothing.

He stood up, checked the drug cabinet to make sure Doreen had locked it, propped the two envelopes against the phone, then pulled down the Venetian blinds. It was almost dusk now. He switched on the outside lights, then looked back at his office. The door to the examining room was closed and locked. What else? the autoclave Doreen had turned off. Her cubicle looked as uncluttered at the end of each day as it did at the beginning. Only the charts stacked neatly on top of the filing cabinets betrayed the volume of work the two of them had put in today. He turned off the office lights, checked the burglar alarm, and went outside.

Getting a bit cooler. Hottest October in five years the paper said, new records yah-tee-dah. He crossed the street, edged around his car parked beside the small brook which ran past the old elementary school. In the grassy oval in front of the school where the kids used to play kick ball during recess crouched the weird grasshopper statue about eight feet high, made of twisted bronze which looked to him pretty much like baked papier-mâché. A grotesque piece of work, the huge mandibular head, the rippled planes of the carapace, hell of a thing for a school playground. But then, of course, this wasn't a place for kids any longer. The town had bought the building and leased it to artists for studio space. He stared at the weather-beaten doors of the classrooms, at the cheery red paint flaking off along the window sills. Many of the windows had been refitted with cheap plastic panes all scarred with scratches. The pinkish colored bricks still looked solid enough though. *Blow, blow, blow my house down.*

He walked past the building to the wooden forts over by the far end of the playground beside the brook. The lawn had just been mowed; he looked down at his shoes. The wet blades of grass were layered across the shiny black leather, crisscrossing each other like jackstraws. He stamped his feet several times. Grass, go lie back down where you sprang from. School is over and he refused to hear those recess screams, to see again that old snapshot of Troy standing proudly by the bus stop, TROY FARLOW, FIRST GRADE, BROOKSIDE SCHOOL, printed neatly on a white card pinned to his bright red shirt, clutching his Batman lunch box, nothing but conquering that new world on the kid's mind or if the fear were there, hiding it carefully, brazening it out, bluffing his parents, his teachers, himself—his eyes shining, cheeks so pink and gold in that long ago dappled September sunlight. Ah yes, little Troy, stay back there where it all lay before you, the golden days. And Scott stamped his shoes again, and walked across to where his car was parked across from the office.

He drove fast. Long past rush hour now so the traffic was thinned out even on 128. The radio was set on WBUR—classical all day long, but he switched the dial to the mood-music station, bland, mellow, impersonal. No more memories. No more pain. Concentrate on the damn traffic. Ignore the landmarks, the tall oblong building sheathed in smoked glass in which the kids had always tried to see their car reflected back at them as they rolled by. "I *see* us!" "You do not, does he, Daddy? We're already past it!" "No, I *see* us! Right, Dad?" Ah, God….

And past the exit to the Howard Johnson's where once he used to meet Penny. Christmas shopping had been their alibi at first, then what? He couldn't remember, the lies had come so smoothly, uncoiling out of his mouth. And past the road leading to the Polynesian restaurant where the children had always wanted to order a Pu Pu Platter, but each time he'd told them brusquely, "No, guys, too expensive," until that night it was somebody's 16th birthday and when he made the suggestion, the boy turned to look at him, eyes bored and cold, and drawled, "That's kid stuff, let's get the Mandarin chicken." Too late, too late.

The highway rolled on. To his right the haze of the city hung in a yellowish penumbra across the horizon. Almost dark now; he glanced at the clock. Seven-thirty, and all's well. The violins wailed on the radio, too damn syrupy-sweet. He reached down and switched them off.

Ahead the exit to the Maine Turnpike. He eased the car onto the ramp. Lots of cars now, lots of action along this honky-tonk patch before the actual state highway began. Neon signs flashed by: bars, massage parlors—finger-lickin' good all right—McDonalds, Burger King, Video Palace, more bars, discount sweater factories. He was getting close, only a quarter mile or so past that old-fashioned diner and right beside the miniature golf course which now swept towards him. He could see the motel sign just beyond, the blinking orange bulbs spelling out SHANGRI LA-LA, which he and Penny used to giggle about, so seedy as to be perfect, no one they knew would ever stay in such a dump.

The place was rigged up like an imitation Moorish palace: lattice-worked balconies, wooden minarets, geometric tiles, the works. He drove by the Sultan's Fountain, a scummy-looking swimming pool, the citron-yellow underwater lights gleaming out unblinkingly through the green murk. He swung the car into the parking space in front of the office, jumped out and walked inside.

The desk clerk glanced up from the miniature Sony T.V. on the counter, pushed over the register, droned between yawns, "Singles 45 bucks, Doubles 55, pay in advance, no credit cards, no personal checks."

He signed the register, handed over the 90 dollars, then asked the guy when check-out time was.

"Eleven a.m.," the clerk said, yawning again.

"I'll be staying here the two nights," Scott told him. "Need some shut-eye, been a long haul today."

The clerk winked. "Sure, sure," he said, grinning. "Nobody'll bother ya, mister, except the chambermaid. You wanna sack out, you hang up the DON'T DISTURB SIGN. No problem."

"Right. Thanks very much." Scott turned to go.

"Hey, mister!" The clerk spoke sharply. "Not so fast!"

Scott wheeled around. The guy was glued to the T.V. again, but pointing at Scott with one long hairy arm.

"Yes?"

"You need a key to get in, buddy," the clerk snickered. And then, swallowing hard, Scott saw the stretched-out arm wasn't pointing at him at all, just handing him the paddle-shaped room key.

"Room 24," the clerk said. "Building A, over to your right past the pool."

"Thanks," Scott answered and took the key.

When he got inside the car, his hands were shaking and so sweaty they slipped off the steering wheel. He wiped them on his pants, backed the car out slowly, then drove past the pool.

Building A looked just the same. And when he unlocked the door, it still smelled the same. Strong disinfectant, musty sheets not aired too often, and the faint stench of old plumbing. He closed the door, pulled the curtains shut with a quick jerk.

Christ, better lock the car up. And bring in his black bag. He went out quickly, ducking his head down as he crossed the lighted passageway. He opened up the trunk, took out the bag, then locked all the doors. Better safe than sorry, right, Doreen? As he turned back to the room he ran his hand over the fender. Good car. Dependable.

Then he went inside. The walls were thin, and he could hear a woman laughing, toilets flushing upstairs, the thump of country music far away. He opened the bathroom door, switching on the light. The fluorescent glare hurt his eyes, white on white on white. He ripped the tissue paper cover off the toilet, then swung open the frosted glass panel to the shower. Not too gross; the tiles were only a little splotched with mildew.

He undressed very slowly, tie first, then his shoes, placed his change and wallet and keys on the bureau. His suit he hung up carefully in the closet, fussing with the creases of the trousers until they were perfectly aligned. His tie, shirt, and jockey shorts he folded neatly in the bureau drawer. Last, his watch, the 25th wedding anniversary present she'd given him last spring, with his initials on the back. This he placed gently on the bedside table, face down.

He went back into the bathroom, took off his socks, stepped into the shower stall and turned the taps on full blast, enjoying the sting of the hot water pelting his shoulders, prickling his face. He stood there for as long as the hot water lasted, then got out and rubbed himself dry, rubbing so hard his skin felt raw. The mirror was completely steamed up, thank God.

Towel twirled around his middle like a primitive loin cloth, he padded back into the room, picked up his black bag from the chair, carried it to the bed. Then he took the DO NOT DISTURB SIGN from the table by the window and pushed the door out just wide enough to snake his arm through the opening and hang up the sign on the doorknob. The metal clanked against the jamb as he closed the damn thing and slid home the bolt. Home to port.

The room was hot but his feet felt like icy stumps, toenails snagging in the fuzzy loops of the shag rug. "I'm mowing the lawn!" she used to laugh when she vacuumed the old green rug in that first tiny apartment.

He crossed over to the bed, pulled back the fake satin bedspread, then sat down on the edge of the mattress, and placing the black bag beside him, slowly and very systematically began the ritual preparations for healing his final patient.

THINGS TOO FIERCE TO MENTION

MOLLY WAS THINKING ABOUT hard things.

About times of hope, times of despair. About betrayal. Particularly about loss, and how her best friend had reacted when Molly told her, voice lowered so Jove couldn't hear, "The thing is, Janet, I've come to a rather major conclusion."

"I'm listening. "

"It's just that—oh, I don't know—just that somehow every decade that goes by seems more and more defined by the death of dogs."

She'd been so very sure Janet would immediately connect with this. But what Jan actually wanted was an immediate *dis*connect.

"Really! How totally depressing."

This "Really!" Molly understood to mean "Don't rub our noses in this particular truth, puhleeze."

Her right calf was cramping. She stretched her leg out, slowly massaged the muscle. Night after night for an endless six months, she and Jove had spent the long hours side by side in front of the flickering television, his rump solidly against hers, his paws twitching as he dream-loped, panting hard, through tawny clumps of tallgrass, racing after Willow, chasing after Dulcie.

Their new floor-sleeping arrangement she labeled "safe on the flat." Going downstairs panicked Jove now. He simply couldn't make it to the bedrooms below on the ground floor. Halfway down his hindquarters collapsed. Splayed out, they looked like flippers on a sea lion, all floppy. He tried to leap the bottom six stairs but she grabbed his collar just in time. He kept whining louder and louder. His poor hind feet dragged over the lip of each step. Then the left hind leg got twisted under his right so she had to lean over and straighten them out. Horrible. No wonder he was scared silly.

So was she. She remembered the veterinarian telling her, "If these dogs were people—perfectly healthy in every other way—we'd simply pop them into a wheel chair. But with dogs, big German Shepherds like Jove, once they can't walk..." He shook his head.

Hank was being wonderfully sympathetic. He agreed about keeping Jove "safe on the flat." He told Molly, "Hey, we should be so stoic! Jove's a trooper."

So here they were, she and Jove, upstairs, safe on the flat and *very* hard floor while her remark to Janet kept scrolling by—she simply could not get it out of her head. Or Jan's reaction which was, she supposed, understandable. "Don't wallow in it" was what Hank would advise. Put it aside, bury it—these hard truths, the death of dogs too soon, too often. The fear of abandonment. How loss fuels love. How the pain of first love never fades, nor the pain of letting go—lovers and friends, children and animals. A whole army of large and small betrayals of trust. Bury them quickly, bury them deep.

Jove was snoring which made her smile. His chase ended, officially permissible now for exhaustion to set in. How lovely for him to still run in his dreams! In this way he stayed young. Forever.

Then the scroll began rolling past her again, and she punched her pillow. Damn it! She had to make this stop, punch the delete key. The rest, all that other secondary stuff—humiliating incidents, upsetting revelations—slowly gets blurred over time like vaseline smeared on glass. Welcomed smudges. Sometimes we don't want to see too sharply.

Perhaps, she wondered, this is a good thing? And when memory fumbles, we start making up stories to fill in the gaps. Stories that don't hurt, that shape reality the way we *want* it to have been, turn failures into successes, dark into light. And soon it's almost impossible to tell what's real, what pretend. This blurring of fact into fiction—everyone does it! Which strongly suggests, she told herself, we are all liars. Perhaps more palatably, she grinned, we're all storytellers.

Then she flicked off the television, stared into the darkness. She touched Jove's leg where the great artery beat steadily on, good and regular.

She remembers.

She begins telling herself a story.

And indeed her very first dog *was* a story, living and panting only on the page. Her beloved Sara gave it to her that last day when Molly and her parents left Argentina never to return.

She has no clear picture of Sara presenting her with the book. Wrapped in brown paper, it appeared mysteriously in her school satchel she carried on to the plane. She tore open the brown wrapping, touched the cover with the beautiful sable collie gazing up at her. Her very own copy of *Lassie Come Home!* Inside, inscribed on the flyleaf: *Para querida Molly, con todo carino, Sara.*

Sara, pretty, tart-tongued Sara knew Molly so well, knew that opening her farewell gift when they said goodbye back at the house would have surely ended in tears.

Sara had no patience with tears.

"Señoritas of good breeding, they are not cry-babies, Miss Molly." And with thin-lipped intensity she would jerk Molly's hair.

"Ow!"

"Be still, por favor."

"No ribbons, Sara?"

"No ribbons for babies. Only for grown-up muchachas. Basta! We are done. Vamos, you'll be late for school. Antonio, he waits with the car. Hurry, before he makes those bad noises with the horn and wakes up the Señora, dios mio!"

She could almost hear their conversation. Still see Sara's serious face watching her in the mirror where every morning Molly practiced multiplication tables taped to the glass while Sara braided her hair. Her hands worked fast separating each strand so neatly, it was like watching fingers curtsying in a dance. Her knuckles were stained from orange peel she rubbed on them every night. "Orange peel softens the skin," she told Molly. And Molly had answered that Sara always smelled deliciosa, smelled like this beautiful grove of blossoming orange trees which even though Sara didn't reply, just rolled her eyes, meant that she understood she was being given a big compliment.

Oh, Sara understood. Everything. She saw through everyone in that household. Animal-crazy Molly; her mild, worried daddy trying to calm down the dragon mother; their ill-tempered cook, Consuelo; Antonio with his shiny jet black boots nicely matching his trim moustache. Each Friday when he picked up Molly from school, they enjoyed a weekly treat. Antonio would park their big Packard limousine in front of the little newspaper store that sold ice cream and candies but most importantly carried American magazines. First they would order ice cream sodas, and sit at the counter while Antonio placed bets on Saturday's horse race, a secret shared between them, not even telling Sara, in fact, particularly not telling Sara. Sodas finished, he would then buy *Jumbo Comics* for Molly, *Sheena Queen of the Jungle* was always featured on the cover, but what Molly really loved were the grisly horror stories, the best being *The Man Who Was Digested Alive*. On the drive home, she would translate them aloud for Antonio, who listened carefully, his eyes expressing pure terror in all the right places.

"Oh, Sara! He's so handsome, Antonio, muy guapo! He looks exactly like Rhett Butler."

"Muy guapo and so foolish," muttered Sara while Molly practiced fluttering her eyes in the mirror. "This is an hombre who gambles, then dares to try and borrow money from us in the kitchen, caramba!"

Time to change the subject. Quickly. "Guess what, Sara?"

"What, little one?"

"Antonio told me he knows where he can get me a puppy."

"Where?"

"His cousin José."

"Miss Molly, do not get your hopes up."

"But Sara, he wasn't joking, he really meant it."

"It is not Antonio who is the problem, querida."

Silence. They stared at each other. Sara had backed up very close to the unmentionable. Nothing more could be said.

For over two long years Sara had been listening to Molly's pleas for a dog.

First, Molly had approached her father. He hugged her, looked at her with sad pouchy eyes.

He said slowly as if he didn't enjoy the taste of these words in his mouth, "You best talk to your mummy, sugar. Mummy's the one who makes executive decisions in this household." He paused. "She's the boss, Moll."

Molly could not figure out how a poor little puppy fit into this executive stuff. But she knew only too well that her father spent most of his time trying not to do anything that might set off her mother's temper. Which could flare up so quickly, burn so hot. She was scary when angry. Even Sara tiptoed around La Señora.

Molly waited until ten o'clock on a Saturday morning when her mother liked to lie in bed, read her mail, drink coffee—iced in the hot summers—talk forever on her glamorous white telephone, and labor over complex invitation lists for the next cocktail party.

She was sitting very straight, propped against silk pillows, smoking and jotting notes on her monogrammed paper. She glanced at Molly, frowned.

"Darling child, don't slump, you need to stand up straight and tall. Being tall is something to be proud of. Not hide by slumping."

Molly straightened her shoulders. "Mother," she croaked.

"Yes?"

"The thing is…." she faltered.

"Darling, I'm way behind schedule, the caterers are screaming, spit it out, for God's sake."

"Mother, the thing is I would like to have a puppy, a collie puppy." She gulped. "Like Lassie." Her mother looked blank. "You know, that movie Sara took me to see last month?" Every Saturday Molly and Sara rode the train into the city to see the Saturday matinees. Molly had chewed through the thumbs of all her white cotton gloves after a weekly diet of Frankenstein, Dracula, and the Wolf Man. Luckily, Sara loved movies as much as Molly. She was the perfect movie companion. She had adored *Gone with the Wind* and when they reached the lobby afterward, she bought Molly the official program from the movie, with nice color photographs of all the actors and Atlanta burning, and beautiful Tara—which never burned down and this for Molly was deeply important.

Her mother arched one beautifully plucked eyebrow, inhaled deeply, then ground out her cigarette. She tapped her pen impatiently as she spoke.

"You know, darling Molly, a dog simply does not fit into our lives here in Buenos Aires. We do far too much entertaining for your father's company. We can't have collie fur flying everywhere, not to mention dog turds."

Molly swallowed hard. When her mother started using what Sarah called vulgar language—lengua grosera—watch out. She spoke carefully, "But I promise to keep him outside in the garden. Or upstairs in my room, Mummy, please, oh please let me!"

The telephone rang. Her mother blew her a kiss. "Run along, honey, Mummy's terribly busy this morning."

What else did she expect? Molly asked herself. When wasn't her mother always busy, always in a hurry? And always impatient?

Months went by. Some very important men from her father's company came to visit. One big fat guy with rimless glasses and a slobbery smile brought Molly a huge, terribly ugly stuffed dog with black spots and a goofy expression. He told her in this strong German accent, "Your father tells me that you haff a great luff for dogs, fraulein."

She hid the stupid thing away in a closet, covering it with a blanket. Cartoon dogs were just plain silly looking. She was quite embarrassed to own him. Not long afterwards the fat man asked if they could board *his* dog while he and family traveled to Brazil for several weeks.

At first Molly was thrilled. Until her father came home with a creature the shape of a swollen frankfurter. Didn't even look like a dog. It was named Schnitzel, and the first thing it did was to nip Molly when she tried to pet it. Growling deep in his tiny chest, the frankfurter spent most of its traumatic visit out in the kitchen, beside the pantry door not far from the stove. He was always shivering.

The staff hated him

"He has no manners!" sniffed Sara.

"Perro diabolico!" swore the cook, jerking her chin at the long black snout poking around the pantry door. Actually Molly had assumed Consuelo and Schnitzel might get along because they were both so cranky. But they kept snarling at each other from either end of the kitchen, she in Spanish, he presumably in German.

Every afternoon, Molly joined the servants for teatime. They were all sitting around the kitchen table sipping maté and nibbling Consuelo's scrumptious scones drenched in butter. Molly had her very own sipping straw made of real silver which fit right down into the tortoise shell gourd, a present from her father when he visited Peru. She always drank maté with heaps of sugar just like Antonio. Quite often Schnitzel was the chief topic of conversation.

"It's not fair!" she tugged at her braid. "Mummy won't let *me* have a dog, but she and Daddy get to have one."

Sara shook her head. "It's business, Miss Molly."

"Business?"

Antonio leaned back in his chair. He smiled. "You understand, niña, nuestro perrito caliente, his owner es muy importante." He winked at the women. "I listen to them talking in the car. He is big stockholder in Señor's company." Then turning back to Molly, he said in a kind voice, "Your father...he could not refuse."

"Still not fair," Molly mumbled, finishing off the scone with a vicious bite.

Sara patted her shoulder. "Venga, cara mia. Now we go play my little radio." During siesta time Molly was often invited to Sara's room where they listened to Spanish music while Sara did the ironing. Molly's favorite song was *Arroz con Leche*, a lullaby, Sara told her, crooned by all Spanish madrecitas to their babies.

The house would have been very lonely without servants, Molly often thought—still another important reason for a puppy! She ate all her meals in the kitchen except once in a while as a special treat she was permitted to have breakfast with Daddy in the formal dining room. Not a room she felt comfortable in. The table and chairs and sideboard were made of carved teak, black and gnarled like the spiky-armed trees in *Snow White*, looking as if they could bend down and snatch you any minute. This furniture her mother was very proud of. She had it specially made in China where they had lived until Molly was five, when they moved to Argentina.

Their years in Shanghai were a big blank. Molly recalled nothing except the gentle touch of her amah's hands. She would examine closely the pictures of Amah holding her in the rickshaw, or in the garden with other amahs, or tying a bow in Molly's hair for her second birthday party. A lovely oval face, so serene—how could her very own beloved Amah have vanished? She strained to remember. But no use, it was all black emptiness, and made her feel as if she were sitting in a dark movie theatre without a screen. She sat there, always peering forward...at nothing.

When she was five years old, Molly and her mother had been evacuated during the Japanese bombing of Shanghai. The mothers and children, crowded into small motor launches, were steaming out of the harbor, waving to the fathers on the quay when the planes appeared out of nowhere, strafing the shoreline. All the men fell flat down on the wharf. Molly remembered none of this. Hearing the planes, seeing Daddy fall—that's when the delete button got pushed and all of China, all of her first five years disappeared as if the bombing, the evacuation, Amah, had never happened. Six weeks later the family were safely reunited in Hawaii. Throwing her lei overboard as their ocean liner left the port was the very first thing in her life she could recall. Her lei sank. This meant according to the crew, that you would not see the islands again. Ever.

Confirming what Molly believed then and afterward: she could never go back. Never return, it was too dangerous. She could not go home because she had no home. From then on she didn't think of home as a place on a map she could find again. No, home was a place located only in your heart. Those whom Molly longed for, deeply cared for became substitutes for home, a complicated intertwining of hello and goodbye, of permanence and loss. She confirmed this by looking up the definition of home in the big dictionary in her father's study:

The definition that fit was the third one: *Home, the abiding place of the affections.*

That second week of Schnitzel's visit, a very bad thing happened. Even though she disliked the animal, Molly was horrified. So were the servants. One day while Molly was at school, her mother, fuming because she was running very late for her Red Cross Auxiliary meeting, jumped into her car, not the company Packard Antonio drove but her very own small coupe. And promptly backed over Schnitzel, sleeping underneath. Molly wasn't told until that night. Sara was ordered to be the one to tell her. Molly wanted to know if Schnitzel had suffered.

"No, niña. He died instantly. He was only a small sausage, verdad?" And she chucked Molly under the chin, both of them knowing this was an invitation to smile. And both perfectly aware that Molly could not.

"The tires must have gone up and over him, Mummy must have felt the bump, she must have known it wasn't right. Wouldn't she?" she asked Sara.

Sara nodded, then told her that even though he was a difficult perro, Schnitzel was probably already nipping the angels in heaven. Finally she murmured, "Bueno, querida," in her very sweetest voice. She began humming *Arroz Con Leche*. And hugged Molly who was terribly surprised to find herself sobbing.

That was the end of any further discussion of dogs. A now forbidden subject, her mother being both ashamed and angry at her own carelessness. Schnitzel was never mentioned again.

Sara knew all this. About angry mothers. About dead dogs. About dogs everywhere denied the chance of meeting Molly. About the hot need inside Molly's heart to love, to hold something warm close to her heart, to find that reciprocal love she needed, fixed and steady. And which she had tried to find in the tender care of servants. But servants kept coming and going, they kept on disappearing forever from her life over and over again, like the places she had lived.

And so when at last it was time to say goodbye, Sara saw to it that Molly was finally given a dog, who would never grow old, whom she could visit and re-visit decade after decade. In Lassie Molly found not only her first dog. She found her first home.

Neither of which has ever disappeared. The cover is tattered. Periodically Molly mends it with scotch tape. Sara's inscription inside makes her smile. She has always in her mind added to Sara's formal message three words she was sure Sara had wanted to include, certainly what she felt, but was much too proper to write down: *Querida, come home.*

In the darkness, she listens to Jove's deep regular breathing. One decade plus two years he has lived with them. "Good dog," she tells him. "Stay. Please stay."

IN THE SHALLOWS

I WATCH HIM.

Not for long. Just now and then.

I watch him cleaning the stock tank down in the lower garden. Made of galvanized steel, it's ten feet in diameter and was given to us years ago by good friends who were selling their ranch. They used to run Longhorns on 300 acres; they also bred Arabians. Our stock tank was off in the pasture where the horses hung out. I liked to watch them at the tank, exquisitely delicate heads bent down, muzzles pushed deep in the water, silently, solemnly drinking for long minutes at a time. A scene of almost sacramental beauty, I thought. And now we have their tank, and the connection pleases me. Arabians were bred for the desert by Bedouins who cherished water second only to their horses. Drinkers of the Wind, they called them.

I like to imagine the presence of those Wind Drinkers still lingers around our stock tank whose water, I now observe, is adrift in leaves fallen from the cottonwood tree which shades and shelters this oasis. These past four years a brown decoy duck floats in the tank next to the elegant fountain Jake's rigged up. I love this fountain! The spray arches high in a sparkling fleur-delis pattern three abreast, then splashes down like glittering diamonds into the water.

To remove the algae from the sides and bottom of the tank, Jake uses a long-handled scrub brush, then pours in chlorine. Now he begins skimming up the leaves. While these complex ablutions are taking place, the duck has been removed, chucked over onto the grass where it lies like some sort of beached sea creature. At least it doesn't quack.

The thing is I can't watch this cleaning ritual for more than a few minutes at a time. It's too painful—I feel pierced by sorrow. I stop, make some coffee. Jake has to work on the tank every couple of days in the hot summer. His long arms wielding the skimmer reach back and forth in a lazy rhythm. He's wearing cut-offs and a brick-colored T. His skin's almost as dark as the shirt, his lanky legs stained the same color as the legs on our maple dining room table. But this is *not* a wooden man, far from it.

I watch him through our kitchen window. From up here as well as from the street you can clearly hear the fountain—a lovely running-river sound. Or the quicksilver chatter of raindrops on a still lake.

Some days we see walkers up on the road stop, cock their heads, listening, even venture a few steps along our driveway. Enchanted, they peer down through the cottonwood branches at the stock tank, the fountain, the duck. They smile, sometimes even nod in approval.

Here on the High Plains, the sound of running water reassures pretty much everyone—ranchers, wheat farmers, fishermen, Corps of Engineers, the Chamber of Commerce. No wonder fountains and pools were treasured so highly in desert cultures. They fit equally well here in the baking heat of Kansas summer days. In the desert they called them Gardens of Paradise. We simply call ours Eden.

This whimsical mélange of Moorish fountains and midwestern stock tanks amuses us, even makes Jake grin once in a while as he works on the darn thing year in, year out. Dismantling it in the fall. Lugging it up the hillside before deep winter, then sliding it back down come early spring. Heaving it onto its summer dais of railroad ties. Setting up the filter system and the complex fountain apparatus. After he fills the tank with the garden hose, he launches the duck decoy with a quick flourish of satisfaction. The duck usually gravitates toward the fountain, gliding in serene eddies closer and closer to the triple cascade of bubbling water pinging into the tank drop by drop.

The fiction we tell ourselves is that we're keeping the stock tank operational for purely aesthetic reasons. It's both soothing and beautiful. Staring at that circle of blue water cools and calms a person. Pleasing to our senses, this music of the fountain, the sedate circling of the decoy duck. These two, however, are both newcomers—ornamental additions arriving late in the game after we stopped swimming in the tank.

The truth is we will never get rid of it. We can't. We've kept it all this while as a sort of talisman, like a lantern shining at night for somebody lost. Of course we've never articulated this to each other. We don't need to. And whenever we glance down the hill, what we see in our mind's eye, recall in our heart's memory, is the polar opposite of serenity.

EARSPLITTING screams!

Shrill voices arguing, followed by mini-explosions of laughter.

Seemingly violent thrashing games. Gallons and gallons of water swooshing over the sides of the tank as three kids try to duck each other.

They yell cheerful threats.

"I'M GONNA DROWN YOU IF YOU DON'T CHILL OUT!"

"STOP SPITTING AT ME OR I'LL PULL DOWN YOUR TRUNKS!"

In quieter moments, they have told us they adore swimming in the stock tank because it's their chance "To go like totally BALLISTIC!"

Usually the younger two climb out first because now they're truly chilled out, almost blue from the cold. And tired. They leave behind the oldest, Madison. Dearest Madison, our lovely laughing girl—kind, at ease with herself and others. Her teacher said long ago that she wished she could have a daughter like Madison. Warmhearted and so funny, she tickles us. I mean she makes us laugh right out loud like that time she and her sister were squabbling.

Jake asks her, "Why are you complaining about Cassie?"

Madison: "I'm doing more than complaining."

Jake: "What else are you doing?"

Madison: "I'm calling her names."

Jake: "That's sweet."

Madison: "Grandpapa, I'm not *always* nice."

Or the time when pressed by us as to what she was going to be when she grew up, she answered patiently, "I can't know the future, Papa."

Now she floats on her back in the stock tank. She stares up at the sky. She is chanting what we have named the Madison Water-Chant Songs. We first heard them at the beach at Nantucket when she was about four years old. She'd stand in the shallow water well beyond the shorebreak, encircled in her granddaddy's arms. Wave after wave rolled past them to crash on the beach. And Madison began to sing a complex aria about how she loved the ocean and the dolphins and Granny C and Papa, Mummy and Daddy, on and on, endless verses that curled around and went back to the beginning.

She sang almost fifteen minutes. Then goosebumps determined it was time to go warm up on the hot sand.

This afternoon, fifteen hundred miles from the ocean, the tank finally emptied of noisy siblings, she floats, gently flutter-kicking round and round in a circle, mirroring the circles of her songs. Her hair fans out behind her like pale brown sea grasses waving in the water. She stares blissfully upward. At the cottonwood leaves trembling above her. At the sun playing hide and go seek with three pillow-shaped clouds. She sees the immense shadow of a zopilote slope-soaring past over the house, soon joined by a buddy as they head across the lake.

I have told the children that the zopilotes are the most beautiful of all the flyers which is why we call them by their Spanish name instead of ugly words such as buzzards or turkey vultures. They always travel in pairs. Like nuns. This information having been duly absorbed, extremely heated discussions take place whenever the Smalls spot a group. Much counting a-LOUD. Much swiveling of small heads as they try to locate the missing partner perhaps swooped too low behind the treeline to be visible now. The Saga of the Zopilote Nuns I'm fairly certain Madison will some day stitch into her songs.

On very hot afternoons the grandfather may climb into the pool with the kids. The screaming gets louder. Water gushes over the sides in great cataracts. All three Smalls compete for his attention—Niles by pummeling, his twin sister Cassie by diving between Jake's legs. And Madison by hanging on to his back in a strangle hold. He chokes and sputters and laughs almost simultaneously. The dogs bark. What *must* the neighbors think?

I smile down at the colander I'm holding, then stare out the window.

Jake is fastening the long-handled brush and the skimmer on their hooks in the trunk of the cottonwood. He fiddles with the filter one more time, picks up one last leaf out of the water. He whistles for the dogs, who leap up gladly, cavorting in circles, happy for some action at last. He starts his slow climb back up to the house.

Where I stand washing pounds and pounds of tomatoes in the sink.

And wait. And remember.

Another day. Niles has just been given a model of a lobster boat made by his grandfather. "You're the BEST!" Niles tells him.

We all decide to skip breakfast until later and instead go drive to the park and try out the new boat. All the way over there three evil children make up naughty songs, the naughtiest words being "squid pack".

"What's squid pack mean?"

"Don't ask, Granny C. You don't wanna know."

Just as we near the parking lot, Niles launches into their favorite song, joined instantly by the girls, of course.

"All I wanted was some chick-en wings,
From the nearest Bur-ger King,
And all I got was…
Di-ahhhhh-rheeee-ahhhh!"

"Oi vey," I moan.

Their last ditty has been shouted so brazenly that a red-faced woman in the parking lot whips around to stare at our van.

It's early enough in the morning that a few wisps of fog still float across the pond. I start telling the children how spooky it is watching fog creep from the lake up the hill towards our house.

I'm groping for the right words. "Creeping like…." and I pause.

Cassie promptly finishes for me. "Creeping like evil spirits searching for rest?"

Now it's my turn to scream. "Exactly, clever girl!"

The car has come to a stop. Niles takes off his new glasses, places them carefully in their case, hands them to me for safekeeping. Family legend (factual, actually) has it that when the twins walked out of the optician's office, one twin's crying because she *can't* have glasses, the other because he *must*. Between sobs, Niles announces, "I'd rather…I'd rather have a whole pig stuffed down my throat than have to wear glasses!"

We all tumble out of the car, the dogs barking, immensely pleased to see their favorite swimming hole. They plunge in the water still barking loud *let's play* barks. Niles and Jake walk to the far side of the pond. They steer the lobster boat using a remote control device. The girls and I throw *stick in the water* fetch games with the dogs, Then we all pile back in the car, go home for a late breakfast.

Because it's turned so hot, Jake has set up the giant wading pool on the driveway to help the dogs stay cool. The female German Shepherd leans over the side of the pool, waggles her dainty nose in the water, snuffling back and forth; she's washing her face. But the big male slowly eases himself down like a giant hippo. The water hardly reaches his back, but he seems gravely contented. He gets up, shakes, exits.

Niles decides it would be great fun to take this huge running leap into the wading pool. He's immediately followed by Cassie. I caution them not to slip on the concrete, but I might as well be cautioning hummingbirds. They dart back and forth, hovering for a moment, then zooming off again. I'm sitting beside the pool, brushing the girl dog. As most females do, she enjoys someone fiddling with her hair.

Madison waves from the corner of the house, announces she and Papa are going to tape record some of her Water Chant Songs downstairs in the study.

Niles comes over and sits beside me. He's panting hard, his rib cage fluttering. He's subject to asthma attacks but this, I'm sure, is simply hard exercise breathing.

"Did you know my daddy's going on a trip next month?"

"Where's he going?"

"He's flying to Michigan for a whole week."

"Wow. That's a long time. Will you miss Daddy?"

"I will miss him. But he lies close to my heart."

He glances up at me. His eyes are not the incandescent blue of his twin, but he studies people as if he's taking careful notes, writing them down in his memory. And I am reminded so much of his father at the same age. The sharp intelligence. Their intensity. The terrific energy. That candid way he cuts straight to the bone about his feelings. He is without guile.

I stroke his hair. Papa has just given him a crew cut, and the short hair sticking up above his temple feels like the softest velvet stubble.

"You still love me, Meister Boy?"

He answers gravely. "I have always loved you, C."

This exchange reminds me of when he was only three years old and called me up on the telephone, a long distance call, rather a big deal at that age. But he had already memorized our number. We talked about how he had finally relinquished his pacifier.

"I threw Passy in the garbage. Passies are for babies. Niles is a big boy now. Yay, Niles!"

I compliment him. We discuss the nine planets, how very cute tiny Pluto is, the entire Solar System, and peanut butter. Then it's time to sign off. I tell him goodbye and that I love him big as the ocean.

He says breathlessly, "I love you, C. I love you *tomorrow!*"

Cassie zooms over to where we're sitting. "Let's go bug Madison, she's down in the stock tank again. And you must promise us to come in the water, Granny C!"

We walk—that is to say, I walk, they gallop down the hill, followed by the two dogs who find this stock tank fixation a big bore. They are not allowed in the tank so they fling themselves on the lawn, and shoot us deeply profound German Shepherd looks.

Madison's floating. She peers up at the twins and groans.

Niles asks, " Hey, aren't you glad we're here, Maddie?"

She sighs. "I am glad, Niles," she says kindly. She looks over at me. "Hi, C. We finished taping. For now. We can do more later, Papa said."

We clamber in. The water feels like cool satin sliding over my legs, quite marvelous. We sink down.

Niles suggests, "Maddie, tell us about Boringville. And I get to help Cassie."

Madison begins. "Our neighbor next door kept dying and coming alive again."

On cue I say, "Ooh, how awful!"

"It was boring. Do you know why?"

"No. Why?"

"She'd done it before."

I start in giggling. Cassie pipes up. "Let me do the slave girl."

Niles reminds her, "Remember I get to help the slave."

Madison speaks imperiously. "Bring me---a soufflé!"

Cassie blinks.

"Slaves! Give me what I want. *Now!*"

Niles jumps out, comes back carrying Madison's sandal carefully overhead like a platter. On top of the sandal he's placed a rock. He hands it off to Cassie who bows her head, and says, "Here is your soufflé, your Royalness."

Madison glances down, instantly rejects it. "This is *stone* cold!"

Again I have to smile as I rub my hands hard with the towel, my fingers ache from the cold water. Now I will cook and puree fifteen pounds of homegrown tomatoes. I hope I have enough containers for the freezer. I hope he won't plant so many tomatoes next year.

Jake opens the door from the deck, clumps over to the fridge, swigs down a tall glass of grapefruit juice. "Hot out there."

I agree.

"Guess I'll go think lying down."

"Good idea," I answer and swat his retreating backside with the towel.

I remember when the Smalls were truly small—infants in fact—how we stood in the shallow end of the little condominium pool and dandled them up and down like rinsing out tea towels in the sink. Their sopping diapers kept ballooning out with rich squishy sounds.

But then I see them years later, at nine and eleven—in this huge Olympic size pool swimming past me like flashes of silver—minnows in the deep end, sharks in the shallows. Their matchstick arms cleave the water so smoothly there's hardly a splash. They leave only quiet ripples behind them.

Cassie invites me to dive down for stones. Diving for quarters proved too difficult in the bright sunlight. Too difficult for me, that is. The silver coin disappeared in the dazzling white bottom of the pool, brightness camouflaged by brightness, light that blinds us. Sometimes I think there's a need for darkness.

"This is my favorite stone," Cassie tells me. "It has this wicked striped thing down the middle, see? And feel how smooth, Granny C."

She is named after me, Cassandra, but she goes by her nickname just as I go by my initial. We both agree that being stuck with a name like ours is totally the pits but, as I always remind her, "Nobody consulted either of us, so what are you gonna do?"

She repeats her favorite quip, the one she's been saying since she was three. "I had *nuh-thing* to do with it!"

"Me either, kiddo, " quoth I.

"You may hold this."

"May I throw it?" She nods.

"You ready?"

"Granny C, " she says sternly. "Remember now, first you gotta say On Your Marks, *then* Ready Set Go." My lips twitch with a grin that must be held back, I love how Cassie always pluralizes On Your Mark. I never correct her, these minor misquotes are too quaint. The stone arcs high into the deeper blue water thirty feet away. We both launch ourselves forward. Cassie's wearing goggles and homes in on the stone like a hunting dog—straight to it, swimming so fast underwater she might as well be wearing fins. First beside then behind her, I erupt in a fizzing cloud of bubbles I'm laughing so hard.

Cassie's treading water, holding up the stone. "I heard you laughing underwater," she says.

"I was laughing so hard I lost the race."

She thinks this over, chewing on her lower lip, then in a diplomatic but firm voice, she tells me, "I think maybe you lost because I got there first."

"Plus," I add, "you're wearing goggles and can see better."

She frowns. "Is that *really* why?"

"No, darling girl, absolutely not! You won, I lost because you're so wicked fast, faster than a dolphin or a baby shark, that's exactly what you look like underneath, you absolutely streak across the bottom, it's unreal!"

"Want to see my gills?" she gurgles in a throaty voice, puffing out her cheeks.

"Sure do. Where are they? Oh right here, beneath your ears. Does anybody else know?

She giggles, rolls her eyes—eyes of such a pure, deeply saturated azure I'm reminded of the Aegean. Or the robes of the Virgin Mary in a Quattrocento painting. Or maybe just plain blue dye staining small fingers as they fumble with the wire holder for dipping Easter eggs.

I hug her hard. I can still stand up easily but she can't in this deeper end so she winds her long legs tight around me, and slowly I walk us back to the shallows.

Cassie nudges closer, lays her head next to mine. We sway back and forth.

"I wish I were a dog."

"Why's that, honey?"

"So then I could come and live with you."

We stand there together. Then, a very strange thing happens. Bubbles appear, coming closer and closer towards my feet, then up pops her twin, right in front of me, Madison directly behind him. They've been underwater so long their eyes are red, their lips almost bone white.

Nobody says a word. But they move in close, then they hang on to me, Niles on my left side, Madison on my right, and Cassie clinging like a limpet in front. We all hug each other. Silently for what seems many minutes. Kids up at the deep end are cannonballing off the low dive. The shallow water slaps against us gently. The children shift a bit, hug me tighter. This has never happened before. Not since they were very, very small.

And, I think, it will never ever happen again.

This was the last. This was the last.

Empty days with sunshine.

Down under the cottonwood, the stock tank is waiting. The fountain waits. The duck waits. They wait for children.

Who will never come.

After the Ceremony

"Nice wedding," I tell him.

He nods. I nod back.

What next? What do you say to a thirty-five-year-old bachelor?

My mind's gone blank, and Hank's gone off somewhere. My shoes hurt. We both study my shoes. His name is Wynne Gallagher. He's one of Hank's fair-haired boys. Hank is Department Chairman so I guess that makes me the boss's wife. The jolly den mother full of chit chat, "How's the research going, Wynne dear? Did you get the grant?"

"Did you get the grant?" I ask, and glance around the hall. At the far end, French doors are open to the veranda where small tables have been set up for the wedding banquet. The drapes stir in the breeze which is nice because it's hot in here, crowded and hot.

Wynne throws me a grateful look. "The grant..." he starts in.

Good. That's a bone he can gnaw on for a while. I keep making the right head motions as he talks. I can barely follow what he's telling me, what we have here is total brain death, Hank, come back to me, damn it! I can't pole my way through this logjam of guests, tracking you down. So what else is new, it's always the same at these departmental parties. Hank thinks of these people as family, and by extrapolation that I'm part of the tribe as well. It's not that he leaves me to fend for myself exactly. That he abandons me, leaving me to sink or swim alone. No, it's simply that he's so happy, so buoyant in these waters that the possibility of sinking never occurs to him.

"...that first site visit," Wynne's saying. "Hank made me Principal Investigator, damn nice of him. So I told him, Hank, I said, why not put in for a second lab technician, so then he says..."

He says yes, I bet. Hank always says yes to his lab boys, his cubs. He puts up with stuff from them, behavior he's never tolerated in his own sons, all this living together, smoking grass, you name it. The way Hank feels about Wynne and company, I guess I'm jealous. Not that I want him to love them less, but that I don't understand why he can't love ours the same way. Uncritically. Totally accepting. It hurts me.

"You follow me?" Wynne is asking. He jerks his chin down. It's a very nice chin. When he jerks it down this way, his eyes stern, he reminds me of Hank making sure I haven't gotten lost in the thicket of abstractions he tries so hard to lead me through. From Hank's point of view it's a bouquet he's presenting me, a beautiful nosegay of thorny ideas carefully plucked, delicately wired together. For me, it's still a thicket, wild, overgrown, and the thorns prick if you're not careful.

"I'm following,'" I tell Wynne. "Every word." I throw back a brilliant smile. There, that should dazzle him.

He's sketching diagrams in the air now. His fingers are long, the fingertips stained a pale orange color. The nails are trimmed very short. "My *Wild Men*" Hank calls Wynne and the others. His brilliant but flaky wild men.

"Wynne's totally screwed up," he said once, shaking his head. When I asked what he meant, he went vague on me, said Wynne ought to get his personal life together, get over his case of terminal adolescence. But then he added, smiling, "He's not heavy, suh. He's muh brother." He's said this so many times it makes me want to gag. But on the other hand, I know he loves them, his wild men, although love is not a word he would ever use. He thinks he's the total rationalist.

I know different.

I've watched them. Men at play. Men at work. Men as cubs. They can't afford to show tenderness explicitly. Not with other males, they can't, whether they're sons or fathers, brothers or simply competitors. I guess men seek in rituals—things like sports or hobbies—camouflage for their passions. I mean like it's ok to be enthusiastic, not ok to be tender. They disguise their affection with neutral words of approval, words like respect. I can hear Hank right now: "Yes, I really respect the way he thinks. Conducts himself." Whatever. Or coming closer to home with his own kids, a small sigh, a frown, and then: "They behave in ways I can't respect. You can't reason with them! Rational behavior's all I ask."

These to me are foreign words. Respect? Rational? Who ever loved anybody because they were rational? Would he have been the same with daughters?

"...totally unreasonable," Wynne concludes. I nod again. He's standing here like a guard dog until Hank returns. Lambs may safely graze; not wives though. Not safely. A restless guard dog, this one, his eyes on the prowl. He's telling me who's who; he knows just about everyone.

This is a very collegial wedding. I glance around, nod to the Whitsons, some of the other junior faculty. All younger staff people; nobody our age. Flattering in a way, I've decided. The groom, Tony Stavros, told Hank he only wanted his best friends here, the people he's close to. It pleased Hank. Tony is making what we used to call years ago a "late marriage." I smile. He's thirty-three, so is the bride. She's also a biologist. During the ceremony, she looked so laid back, wearing glasses and this relieved grin. She and Tony have lived together for years.

Wynne's listing the names of the bridal party. I keep nodding, keep my eyes fixed downwards again, still checking out my shoes. They're new, open-toed slingbacks. My toenails are a pretty red. Three coats of nail polish I put on for this affair. A new shade, Rambling Rose.

He's asking me something. I'd still rather keep on staring at my feet. He makes me nervous, he looks so much like Hank did when we first started dating, or even one of our boys although they're much younger, of course. The thing is this character here's too handsome. He knows it, too, that cocky smile, a double for Harrison Ford. The scene in the barn, that slow jitterbug. I shake my head, try to focus.

"Who?" I murmur.

"That guy there," he says. "Standing next to the band."

The five musicians are squeaking away in the alcove over there. So far it's been only chamber music. I sure hope we don't have to dance at this reception.

The groom is Greek, second generation his father told us proudly. Maybe we'll all have to form a circle, do the *Chamiko*, the Sailors Dance, Anthony Quinn stomping like a wild thing in *Zorba*. I can see Hank getting into it. Hank likes ethnic everything—jokes, foods, especially dancing.

Not my cocky friend here. He's the kind who holds you too close, pelvis to pelvis stuff so that all movement becomes a fusion of hipbone and thigh. What these days I will do only with Hank in the privacy of the kitchen. He grabs me and we just sort of melt into a slow tango type deal. Or fling into a polka. No ethnic romps for this character, though. I'll bet money on it.

His elbow touches mine. I blink but I don't flinch.

"...hate weddings," he's saying. He waves his glass at the crowd, takes a final gulp.

We've been plied with champagne since we left the parking lot down there in the meadow by the old barn. Four waiters on each side of the steps leading up to this historic inn. Their silver trays gleamed in the sunshine. "You seem to be doing just fine at this one," I observe, staring at his empty glass.

"Thirsty," he says. He holds his glass upside down, twirls it by the stem. A drop falls on my left foot, it feels cool. I try to remember the name of the movie star who used to bathe in champagne. Or was it milk?

"This is the pay-off," Wynne goes on. "The reception. The booze. All that good chow, baklava the climax."

"Nice ceremony though," I suggest. "The bride got the giggles," and I wriggle my big toe. It looks exactly like a maraschino cherry. It matches my dress.

"So did Tony." He smiles. "Thought maybe he'd lost it there for a sec."

We both laugh. I fan my cheeks. A little champagne sloshes out, cooling my toes again. My cheeks are flaming. Why, though? He's the one wearing a jacket. It's tweed. I've never run into a tweed jacket at a July wedding before. Poor guy, it's probably his only good coat. I'd like to see him with his sleeves rolled up. He has skin the color of fresh honey.

"Want a beer?" he asks. He doesn't call me by name, interesting. But then neither have I, as if we're both here incognito. No name, no label.

"Beer? Will they serve plain old beer at a do like this?"

He grins down at me. "Listen, all the comforts of home at this bash. Tony promised. Plenty of Coors, he said. Plenty of Molson's. Retsina for the old folks." He has a raffish grin, very familiar to me. His eyes slide sideways, the mouth goes all crooked. It's a good smile, the kind that makes you want to smile right back because you're both in on the same private joke.

But I shake my head, take another sip of champagne.

"You'll be ok?" he asks, but he's looking past me, peering over at the bar in the dining room, poised forward like a pointer flushing a pheasant.

"I think I can manage," I say dryly.

"Back in a flash," he says into my ear and disappears in the crowd.

He won't be back. I'm over the hill. He's still climbing up, he's nearing the steepest part, the escarpment before you reach the top.

I shift onto my other foot, I'm getting tired huddled here in the vestibule, smiling at this sea of faces. Where's Hank anyhow?

I'd love to go out on the veranda, walk barefoot on that cool green grass. The photographer's out there now, taking pictures of the wedding party under the big copper beech.

The bride takes off her glasses. A breeze whips her veil across her face. Tony bends forward and adjusts the veil with a proprietary yank. The photographer's waving his hands. He's the expedition leader here, even the two priests had to restage the exchange of vows so he could get good close-ups. If they're going to fake it, why not take posed shots at the rehearsal the night before. "Dumb!" I say aloud.

"What is?" Wynne's back. So quickly. I nod in the direction of the garden. He glances out there, then back at me.

"Cinema verité," he says.

"Exactly."

"One of the reasons," he sighs. "I hate weddings."

"Eloping. That's the only way to go."

"Did you and Hank elope?"

I wave my hand at the sweating musicians, the white carnations wilting on the marble topped table. "No," I answer. "But I wish we had. So much simpler."

"Cheaper too," he adds. He tugs at his collar.

"The whole thing's ridiculous." I say crisply. "Hank thinks it's very important. Important to preserve ceremonial traditions. Tribal events, he calls them. Hank's very caught up in tribal events." I sniff; my nose, my whole head feels fizzy, bubbles everywhere, inside and out.

Wynne is smiling but not the raffish smile of before, this is one is slow and gentle and surprisingly tender. I prefer the earlier version.

"One of the reasons," Wynne says slowly, "that the department loves Hank so."

I look sympathetic and tap my foot.

"Yeah." He shrugs. "1 mean it's cornball, I know. But we're all like family. And it's because of him. He's kind, none of this cutthroat stuff. He's always there for us."

"I know," I say quietly.

"One of a dying breed."

"A dying breed?"

"You know, the old-fashioned kind of scientist. Who's curious about the world, what makes it tick. The man of principle. But unselfish, invested in *us* not just grinding out papers, not just getting published."

"Yes," I say very softly. "You guys—I guess all of you—you're the sons he really wanted."

Wynne studies me, something flickers in his eyes. "So tell me," he says. "How are your kids?"

"All grown now. All gone."

He leans forward. "You know the damndest thing—"

But I don't want to talk about children so I interrupt him, surprised at the loudness of my voice, sharp, almost angry. "So bloody **hot** in here!" and I put down the champagne glass on the marble table. Two silver ashtrays have been placed in front of the vase, but instead of cigarette butts they hold grayish olive pits—quite ugly. Olive pits and wooden toothpicks. Fallen on the field of battle, their frilled tops make bright flashes of red and yellow among the olive drab.

"Outside," Wynne says in a firm voice and guides me through the crowd.

Outside on the veranda it's a little cooler. I put my clutch bag down on the snowy white tablecloth. Wynne tilts two chairs forward.

"Stake these out," he tells me. "We'll go find Hank and some of the gang."

"No," I say. "I've got to sit down a minute. My feet…" I add, collapsing into the chair, "…are killing me." This is my signal he should go on without me, leave the older generation to rest up, enough fun and games.

But he doesn't take the hint. "Great," he says. "And my collar's too damn tight."

We sit in silence for a while.

Out by the beech tree, the photographer's smoking a cigarette. Tony gestures to his best man. The bride has disappeared.

I bet her feet hurt, too. She's probably hiding from the photographer. He'll be tracking her down pretty soon, changing his lens, stalking the quarry for the candid shots. Cutting the cake. The toasts. Catching the bouquet. These are the tribal rites Hank adores, but perhaps, I'm thinking, best left unrecorded, best left to an oral tradition, "Remember at our wedding, dear? When your dad got drunk, Monica got the flu? When…"

Wynne's saying something. He has a fresh bottle of Coors in front of him, and I, another glass of champagne. "Think I'll go scrounge us some eats," he tells me.

"Wonderful," I tell the back of his tweed coat. He's off like a shot, probably doesn't want to hand me over to Hank half-looped.

I spot Hank down on the lawn. He looks up, grins and waves at me. He's having a ball, I can tell. Somebody's stuck a carnation in his button hole. At least it's not behind his ear. No, Hank wouldn't do that, would he? But he should be wearing some kind of native costume, a loincloth maybe. In the old days we used to dream about sailing to Tahiti. Too many tourists now. Hilton's built a hotel about twenty feet from where Gaugin's thatched hut used to stand.

Tahiti. The High Sierras.

We camped once by a river, the Lochsa River. In the morning our sleeping bags were soaked from the dew, and the fog was lifting off the water like a dream just beginning. Those dreams fade so fast. Now we've heard you have to make reservations for a campsite months in advance. And the bears are a big problem. They've switched diets, from wild berries to junk food. Doritos, canned beans, you name it. People say the bears are addicted now, their whole metabolism as messed up as their habitats, littered inside as well as out.

Bears make me sad: their clumsy beauty. Homesick like us, still mourning Eden.

Wynne's back. He puts down two plates, heaped with calamari, chicken wings, and stuffed grape leaves. "Let's chow down," he says. "Stave off starvation. At least till the main attraction—three huge lambs on a spit."

"Looks delicious," I say weakly. The grape leaves glisten, moist green fingers pointing straight at me. I turn my head, listen to the violins. They've switched from chamber music to Broadway show tunes.

"*They Call the Wind Maria*," comments Wynne. "Her name's Maria, the bride."

"Cute," say I.

He chews and chews. He eats neatly, stacking the chicken bones picked clean in a little mound on his butter plate. He bites into a grape leaf. I know I'm staring but I can't help it, this is the kind of messy food I cannot eat when other people are around, it's too intimate. I get self-conscious and everything begins oozing out, dribbling down my chin. Subs, spaghetti—forget it. The best I can manage in public is hard fruit. Eating, like dancing, strikes me as something you do in private.

But Wynne here, he's like Hank. He's perfectly relaxed. The grape leaves disappear into his mouth, one by one. His lips are clean.

He wipes his mouth, cocks his head in my direction. "What's so funny?" he asks.

I giggle. "How's your love life these days?" I hear myself saying; where this question comes from I don't know. It pops out unbidden.

Wynne lived with a strange woman for years. They used to come together to all the departmental parties. She had feral eyes, hot and anxious. He always stood with his arm draped around her. She never spoke; Hank says she finally gave up, went back home, out west somewhere, maybe Ohio.

"A mess," Wynne answers. His mouth curves down, a bitter curve. "Practically everyone my age is like already starting on their first kid, ya know?"

"There's time," I tell him. This is easy, same as talking to my boys. So I say gently, "Believe me, she'll turn up one of these days."

"Listen," he says, and hunches closer. "I wanted to tell you before." He's smiling, the secret-sharer smile. I shift in my chair. Our knees knock for a moment. I hook my feet safely over the chair rung and silently admonish them: *Behave, feet!*

"Anyways, like I had this dream last night," Wynne's saying. He takes a long swallow of beer. His throat muscles work so smoothly I can hardly bear not to reach over, touch that tanned neck, feel those strong muscles swell up huge, then relax.

But I sip at the champagne instead, stare resolutely across the lawn.

"This dream, ok?" he says. "About you and Hank."

Hank has moved on to another group of guests. He's talking to a little woman, very old. She's wearing an old-fashioned print dress with a white lace collar. A couple of the bridesmaids stand beside her, and I wish Wynne would go chat them up, ogle their chiffon dresses cut so low in front, young goddesses, vestal virgins, nobody's a virgin any more, who cares?

"...then finally," Wynne's saying, "I met your daughter."

"But we don 't have—" I say, but he cuts in.

"I know you don't, but in this dream you do. She's about twenty-five. She looks exactly like you. And you and Hank tell me..." He stops and his mouth goes into its one-sided upward twist. But this time I look straight into his eyes. They're the palest blue and the expression in them does not match the cocky grin, not at all, what's the right word here, wistful?

"Hank and I tell you..." I say, trying to help him out, he's obviously stuck.

"You give me permission to fall in love with her. And I do, it's ok. It's all ok. I guess that was it. Fadeout. Weird, right?" He stops. He squints down at the beer bottle. His ears are bright red.

"That's a lovely dream," I say quickly.

But he doesn't look up. "I don 't know. I mean at the time, sure. At the time I was dreaming it, I was so...so happy. Sounds lame now."

"Listen, Wynne," I tell him and now I do touch him, put my hand over his. "We had a daughter like that, we'd save her. Just for you. And I'm glad you gave us one. I mean in your dream."

He doesn't say anything, but he's still smiling. A private smile, him and Coors Lite. "Hey." I tap his arm. "Know what I want to do?"

"What?"

"I want to walk barefoot on the lawn, go down there and give my poor sore feet a new lease on life."

"That..." he grins at me now, "...that's definitely the kind of high quality grass that can do it." He stands up, tilts the chair against the table. I pick up my shoes in one hand, purse in the other.

"I hear you're the grass expert, correct?" I say as he takes me by the arm and steadies me under the elbow as we walk down the old stone steps.

"No tokes, Tony said. His family, you know. They're very orthodox. Tony claimed they'd stroke out."

I laugh. "So would Hank," I say and then add lightly, "You'd be surprised how orthodox Hank can be." And I'm surprised I can say this without a trace a bitterness.

We've reached the lawn, the grass feels so lush. I wiggle my liberated toes. "Heaven," I tell him.

"There's Hank." He points.

Hank's standing a foot away in a cluster of people, none of whom I recognize except Mr. Stavros, Tony's dad, a courtly man with silver hair and a huge cigar. Hank reaches out and draws me into the circle. Wynne stands a few feet away, drinking his beer, pulling at his collar.

"Ah, the lovely wife," exclaims Mr. Stavros, bowing. "We have missed you." And he makes the round of introductions, all relatives, ending with the grandmother in the print dress. She's so tiny, with shrewd black eyes and white hair looped into a bun.

Her hands grip mine. "Your husband does my grandson great honor by coming to his wedding," she tells me. "Antony is so proud to be the student of such a fine teacher."

I smile into her eyes; not old eyes, they glow back at me. Eyes that have seen much, I suspect, forgiven much, still watching the world with sharp interest.

"Molly," She says my name with pleasure. "With your hair, your coloring, my dear, you could be one of the family," and she pats my cheek.

For a second I think I may start to cry right in front of her, her fingers feel so soft on my cheeks. But then Hank puts his arm around my shoulders, and hugs me hard. And I'm restored again, able to laugh at the jokes that Hank and Mr. Stavros are taking turns telling us. They both use the same clumsy gesture when they get to the punch line, they too might be from the same family, and again I feel tears sting behind my eyes—homesick for sons who have gone—for the family we used to be before the long, long letting go.

I turn away, wave to Wynne to come over and join us.

He's taken off his jacket, slung it over his right shoulder. He has not, however, rolled up the sleeves of his white shirt—that particular temptation I've been spared—which strikes me as funny. He smiles back at me, lifts his empty bottle and sketches a quick salute—he's given me a gift, we both know it. Then he turns and goes up the veranda steps.

From the drawing room the violins have launched into the *Tennessee Waltz*. "Jesus wept," I say to Hank.

He gives me a mock stern look, shakes his head...like Wynne. "Do behave yourself," he whispers and pulls me in close to him.

Over the laughter of the guests, the melody waxes and wanes with sentimental trills and flourishes. Mr. Stavros bows to his mother. The old lady holds out one white hand, crooked with arthritis but still slender, fine-boned, and now being kissed by Mr. Stavros, bending low at the waist. She curtseys, then they begin to move across the grass. Step...swoop...glide. The little hesitation after their first step exactly matches the hesitant lilt of the music, ONE two three, ONE two three. Solemnly, they spin and twirl on the lawn.

People around us are clapping. Up on the veranda, Tony Stavros raises both arms over his head in a victory salute. "GO for it, Dad!" he shouts.

Beside me, Hank is singing slightly off key. His face is pink from the sun. His glasses have slipped halfway down the bridge of his nose. He's got to get bifocals, he keeps telling me.

We watch the grandmother. She holds her head erect, her back still strong and graceful. I decide I want to look exactly like that when I'm old. I want to be smiling at my own son exactly like she's smiling at hers. And my son, too, shall be the very proud father of our talented grandson whose wedding we'll celebrate—all of us together again—to the stately measures of a dance once enjoyed only by Viennese aristocrats. Hank will beam, eyes shining, a tribal event in his very own tribe. And I see now that he's going to be an indulgent grandfather in a way he's never been free to indulge his own sons. This thought makes me shiver with a sort of pure sweet hope.

I shut my eyes, lean against the warmth of Hank's shoulder, and listen to the waltz, keeping time with one bare foot tapping the cool blades of grass. I can picture the hall of mirrors, the fuzzy halo from the guttering candelabras, the brocade curtains billowing at the open French doors, the intimate rustle of taffeta. I want to tell Hank about Wynne, but now is not the time.

"You ok, babes?" asks Hank.

I blink, throw him a quick smile. "Happy," I tell him, "it's like coming home," but he doesn't hear this last part, he's cheering the dancers.

It doesn't matter. We're together here and I'm thinking that no Viennese ballroom could be more beautiful than this scene before us, than our hot July sun slanting through those copper beeches over there, backlighting Mr. Stavros waltzing with his mother.

I look at the beech trees, trying not to squint. Squinting makes wrinkles.

The branches of the trees are massive. They cast long dappled shadows across this machine-clipped American lawn, a wavy pattern of light and dark which—like some sumptuous bolt of watered green silk—has been unrolled for bears to prance upon.